The Privileged Few

Richard DeBenedictis

authorHOUSE®

AuthorHouse™
1663 Liberty Drive
Bloomington, IN 47403
www.authorhouse.com
Phone: 1-800-839-8640

Published by AuthorHouse 11/10/2015

ISBN: 978-1-4969-5473-2 (sc)
ISBN: 978-1-4969-5474-9 (hc)
ISBN: 978-1-4969-5475-6 (e)

Library of Congress Control Number: 2014920803

Print information available on the last page.

This book is printed on acid-free paper.

Acknowledgements

There are literally as many stories to be told as there are people on this earth. Those of us who choose to tell a story, whether its fact, fiction or a combination of both, don't do so in a vacuum. We are often stimulated by events we experience; by those who are close to us and situations we read or hear about. When I first started on this venture of telling the story of an America becoming a nation governed by the privileged few, I asked several friends and family members to read my initial manuscript. Although of various political and religious beliefs they were all enthusiastic about reviewing my work. As a tribute to them, I hereby acknowledge the efforts of this "beta group" and their important contributions to this work.

I start with Bob Hunt of Tewksbury, MA, a friend since the 5th grade; and then there's Bob Cummings, a friend and colleague for more than 35 years, a compassionate man and business partner, formerly of Rochester, MA now of California; Deb Cullen of Florida, the former manager of my engineering business in the 1990s and a woman who is always upbeat, speaks her mind and cares about people; Ralph Moore, a neighbor, friend, commercial editor and short-film maker from Plymouth, MA who gave me my introduction to the art of editing a manuscript; my cousin Rene Welch of Florida whose sincerity, enthusiasm and compassion is unmatched, and most important John Temple of Barnstable, MA, a friend, former neighbor and a professional commercial writer who took it upon himself to formally edit my original work and provide advice that energized this project.

Their enthusiastic response; intelligent insight and constructive criticisms made writing this story a most enjoyable task. But, without the extraordinary support of my family and their encouragement enabling my recent victory over cancer, it would never have been completed. My twenty-something college graduate daughters, Nicole, Danielle and Michelle gave of their exceptional talents and efforts, supporting me in my attempt to tell a story that I believed needed to be told. My twin sons, Adam and Eric, recent high school graduates, gave of their creative talents and advice from the view of teenagers viewing 50 years of history from a different perspective. Eric created the back page and Adam used his editing talents to complete that work. And most important, my wife Betty, an avid reader and the most sincere and candid critic one can have gave critiques that, although I resisted at first, were validated by professionals, resulting in a significant improvements to the work and a humbling of my ego that was well deserved.

Book Cover Concept by Nicole DeBenedictis
Back Cover Concept by Eric DeBenedictis

Please Note: *The first chapter is in tribute to my late parents, Richard and Claudia, who are portrayed as I remember them, sincere, compassionate and loving. The character of Anthony Benedetto in the first chapter, although reflective of my early years growing up in South Boston, becomes a fictional character in the remainder of the story. All of the other characters, other than the known public figures, are fictional or composites of people I have known and do not represent any particular individual. Any resemblance to any individual or any incident other than known historical events is purely coincidental.*

Prologue

I began this novel in 2009 when I realized the strong correlation between the happenings of the last 40 plus years and the historic rise and fall of unique and ancient civilizations. The Egyptian and Chinese Dynasties; the Roman Empire and even the Aztec and Mayan nations, had something in common. Although separated by time and geography, these civilizations, which were advanced for their era, succumbed to the greed and the self-interest of a very few! In ancient times they were the royalty, those families of immense wealth and power who controlled the masses while draining the resources of their respective societies. In our enlightened and sophisticated America they are often referred to as the "One Percenters," Are they *the Privileged Few*, a term used in the film "Fair Game" to describe the wealthiest of the wealthy? They are obsessive in their belief that *they* are the entitled, the privileged class who have the means and the desire to subdue those who oppose their rule!

This fact-based fictional story begins in 1959. The facts are historically undeniable. The fiction is the manner by which the stories of millions are depicted by the lives of four families of diverse means and ambitions. The families in this story are characteristic of those who lived within the socio-economic spectrum of those days. The main characters' lives are followed from their formative years and as they emerge into their adult worlds.

The story is about the challenges that Americans have had to overcome in their pursuit of their personal "American Dream," a term coined by James Truslow Adams in 1933 at the height of the Great Depression. The American Dream is described in his book, *The Epic of America,* as being, *"that dream of a land in which life should be better and richer and fuller for everyone, with opportunity for each according to ability and achievement."*

For many Americans wealth is part of their American Dream. Many of us, who lived our childhood during the fifties remember it as "the good old days." A time when finding a good job, having a family and providing them with a decent home was more than just a dream, it was what we strive for as Americans and what the bravest of the brave fought for.

It's not the riches that are gained that are the problem with society; some would say that is part of the American dream, but at whose expense and at what price were they gained? Will the very wealthy eventually control all aspects of our lives with their purchased power? John Dean, former White House Counsel to President Richard Nixon called them *Conservatives Without Conscience,* in his New York times bestseller of that title. Will the fears that were debated by Franklin, Madison and Jefferrson during the creation of our Constitution be realized? Will America become a nation ruled by ***The Privileged Few?***

Introduction

Their story begins in the late 1950s, the era of hope, dreams and, some believe, innocence. This fact-based fiction story follows the lives of four individuals as they pursue their American Dream. They are impacted by the actions of those who use their wealth and influence to manipulate the American system of capitalism. Their lives have been affected by those who have successfully "gamed" the system to create an ever-widening inequality of income and the diminishment of the standard of living for the average American.

Tony Benedetto, a young Italian-American living in South Boston, believed in the promise of the American Dream. His grandparents came to this country in the early nineteen hundreds seeking a better life and found both opportunity for success and hardship. An optimist, he believes in the American Dream and is the first in his family to go to college.

Diego Martinez, the son of illegal immigrants from Mexico who worked the California vineyards and farms, was born an American citizen. His mother died of a treatable illness not having the means or the legitimacy to receive the benefit of health care. His desperate father was deported for illegal activities while trying to support his son in a hostile environment. Young Diego sees no way out of the poverty. He lives with his paternal grandmother, also an American citizen, in the volatile Los Angeles ghetto known as Watts.

Sharon Polowski, is the daughter of a traditionally conservative politician who is the Mayor of a Michigan City. Sam Polowski provided for his family and achieved his American Dream, gaining middle class status. Along the way he took advantage of available government programs, union membership and a well-paying job, benefits that he would now deny others. He's considered to be an honest man, sincerely believing that the solution to all of society's issues is smaller government. Sharon sees the poverty and the hopelessness of people in their city being exacerbated by that ideology.

And then there's James Buckman III, the son of a wealthy financial entrepreneur. His father is a behind-the-scenes political manipulator who is determined to protect the financial gains to which he believes his family is entitled. As the eldest of two sons, James III is considered the heir apparent to the family dynasty. He's groomed and educated for that role despite the objections of his brother Jonathan. To his dad, capitalism is a game played to win by those who understand how best to manipulate it.

This is their story of how the effects of greed and political self-interest in American society have affected their lives. That ideology is represented by six men, corporate heads whose goal is to control the country's economy and the politics for their unique benefits. Their objective is to assure that American democracy is the best that money can buy. The elected politicians whom they support have done a better job of representing them as constituents than those who claim to represent the interest of the average American. In the last fifty years poor representation and apathy have put those Americans on a path towards reaching a critical mass of desperation! To survive they must now overcome the power of those Privileged Few!

February 6, 2009

The flames spiked more than a hundred feet into the frigid February night sky. Firemen coated with crystallized ice tried to control the uncontrollable. The heat countered the effect of the icy winds as they advanced towards the blaze. Their heavy rubber boots provided little protection or stability on the slick sheen formed on the road by their intense dousing efforts. It took all night to quell the blaze so that the evacuated neighbors could come back to their homes. The smoke was eventually dissipated by the same frigid winds that encouraged the flames.

It was a five alarmer. The old brick building had been abandoned for more than 20 years. The last owners tried to rent it out as a flea market to local antique dealers and craftsmen. They lost it to the bank during the 1990 Recession. Now the two-story, 85 year old brick building housed only memories of the days when Pittsburgh was America's center of the steel industry.

Since the structure was totally engulfed when they arrived, Dave Ferguson, the city's Fire Chief was concerned about whether anyone was in the building. "Lieutenant Bronski did you inspect the building for victims?"

"No sir, we need the engineers here to check out what's left of the structure before we can enter. I doubt anyone would be in there. Its five degrees below zero and it's been abandoned for years."

"Don't take any chances, but check it out when it's safe and let me know what you find."

"Will do Chief! I'll call you when we complete our inspection."

The news from Lieutenant Bronski later that day wasn't good. "Chief, we found the remains of two bodies in a room on the second floor. They were in pretty bad shape, burned beyond recognition, but it appears to be a man and a woman. Another thing, the State Fire Marshall says that the fire started in that room. They probably set it in a steel barrel to keep warm. Sparks must have set off the dry wood and cardboard boxes that were strewn around the room."

"Damn homeless, why didn't they go to the shelter? What's wrong with these people? They kill themselves and almost take a whole neighborhood with them. It's 2009 and this problem seems to be getting worse. Did they have any identification on them?"

"No sir, there wasn't much left but charred bones," answered the Lieutenant.

"How do you know it's a man and a woman?"

"Well we found a women's wedding ring on the female's finger and a man's wedding band on the left hand of the male. One other thing, the male might have been a veteran, there was a medal lying beside him."

"What kind of a medal, Bronski?"

"A Purple Heart!"

Part One

The Early Years

Chapter 1

The year was 1959. General Dwight D. Eisenhower, a true American hero, was completing his second term as President of the United States. His presidency presided over the ending of the "Korean Conflict" and the building of the country's interstate highway system. Americans were inspired by his leadership and believed in the American Dream as a reality that could be theirs. He was a Republican and he was admired for creating jobs and ending unnecessary wars. He was the last of a breed!

Anthony Benedetto was a third generation Italian American whose parents knew the benefits of hard work and the emotional drain of the Great Depression. To Anthony the values of his proud and caring parents could not explain the actions of the three boys who yelled to him as he walked home from his neighborhood school in South Boston. "There he is, that guinea that beat up my little brother. Let's get him!" At 11 years old Anthony had no idea what the boy was yelling about. He didn't know his accuser, never mind his "little brother," but he knew that he had to run as they crossed the street in pursuit. He had heard words like 'guinea' and 'wop' to describe his Italian heritage before, but he didn't understand why they would want to hurt him.

Although smaller than his seemingly barbaric pursuers, screaming out profanities as they chased after him, Tony was very fast. He bolted through the streets stretching the four blocks to his triple-decker home. As he turned the corner of the final block at Douglas Street, Tony felt a swift and jarring yank backwards bringing his mad dash to a sudden and painful halt. The tall lanky boy who had been leading the charge grasped him with brutal force, glaring at Tony with a mischievous smile and fire in his eyes.

"You little guinea bastard... thought you could outrun us."

The first blow came to his stomach as the tall one held back his arms. He gasped as the air in his lungs escaped and the pain of the next punch from the third angry pursuer crushed his nose, the warm blood gushing from his face. Another blow to his head and he was on the ground feeling the boots of his aggressors. "How's that feel meatball?"

He heard someone, a woman, screaming at them, "Leave him alone, or I'll call the cops."

"Let's get out of here," ordered their 'brave' leader, as they ran laughing like wild hyenas.

Tony's grandparents came to America during the first decade of the 20th Century seeking to better their lives and escape the poverty of their respective villages and cities. They soon realized that their dreams were shared by many, each bringing their strange and intimidating languages and customs to their newly adopted country. For many the opportunities would be a test of the survival of the fittest bringing Darwin's evolutionary theory to a very personal level.

Competition for jobs would pit ethnically diverse people in a struggle to better their lot and improve the lives of their families. The challenge was not fully realized when they first boarded the ships that were to take them to the "promised land."

Tony's father, Richie Benedetto, was born in the America in 1915. He left school during the Great Depression finding work in the government's CCC camps, planting trees on Cape Cod. He wanted to help his mother support her nine children after her husband had abandoned his family to pursue his own dreams of wealth in the mid-west.

Richie Benedetto, was a hard working guy who thought of working overtime as a bonus. He, like many of his generation, wanted only to provide a good life for his family. His wife Claudia believed that her three children were the purpose of her life and anyone in need was worthy of her efforts.

"Are you ok, Tony?" the familiar voice was Mrs. Hurley, a neighbor and friend of his mother's. She was armed with a broom handle. "Come inside and let me clean you up, your mother will have a conniption if she sees you like this." He didn't know what a "conniption" was but he didn't want his mom to see him like that. Mrs. Hurley washed his face, put a bag of ice on his nose and let him catch his breath.

"I think you need to go to the hospital. It looks like your nose is broken. Is your father home?"

"I don't think so," Tony said in a voice that was more nasal than vocal.

"Well we had better get you home. Your mother will be worried."

His mother was visibly upset and couldn't understand why he would be beaten up by three older kids that Tony didn't know. She put a fresh bag of ice on his nose and told him not to lie down. "The blood will rush to your head and it won't stop bleeding!"

"They're those fresh Irish kids from H Street, they like to beat up smaller kids especially Italians and Lithuanians," explained Mrs. Hurley.

"Richie won't be home until after midnight. He's working the three to eleven shift this week. I told him that we shouldn't move here. The Irish and Italians don't get along. We were better off in East Boston where there are mostly Italians."

"Well that's not true of all Irish. John and I are Irish and we are all friends in this neighborhood, aren't we?" said Mrs. Hurley.

"Yes, but why did they do this? Richie is going to be upset and he'll want to go see their parents and tell them off. You know that he has a hot temper," worried his mom.

Tony's mother knew her husband had his own troubles in Southie. He grew up in this part of the City. He knew the perils and the benefits when he decided to live back here. He loved the area, and wanted to raise his kids here. It was near one of the city's few beaches. It had parks and open spaces that made it feel like a suburb and it was closer to his work, a chocolate factory in Dorchester.

He recently experienced first-hand that not much had changed since his childhood. He had an encounter with the Irish tenant that he inherited when he bought this three-decker the previous year. The guy was a drunk and like so many alcoholics he took out his rage on his family. You could hear his loud, angry voice through the ceiling and the furniture crashing as he chased his wife in a drunken rage, beating her and sometimes his children.

One night the abused wife came to the Benedetto's door, bruised and crying trying to get away from her liquored up husband. Tony's father had her come into the sanctuary of their small four-room apartment and blocked the pursuing husband, hand on his chest. Tony's mom tended to her bruises and tried to console her as his father attempted to restrain the tall grizzly and highly intoxicated Irishman.

Tony stood behind his dad as the big red-haired, ruddy-nosed tormenter smacked his father's hand down and took a swing at him. He missed, but his dad didn't, knocking him down the stairs from their second floor apartment with a perfect uppercut to the jaw. His mom called the cops, who were quite familiar with the abusive guy. They took him to Police Station # 6 on West Broadway for a night of peace and tranquility.

The next night the big jerk lay in wait for Richie in an alley up the street from their home. He jumped him, only to find the previous night's result repeated. This time Richie broke his jaw. Although Tony's father had a hot temper, he had a sense of justice that guided his life. Once his antagonist was down he wouldn't continue his punishment.

Tony's father had only an eighth grade education, but was well-read and intelligent beyond his limited academic credentials. He was tough but he was also very creative. He was an excellent illustrative artist as evidenced by his elaborate battle-scene drawings of the World Wars that Tony discovered in an old chest in the basement. Although he only served briefly in the Coast Guard at the end of World War II, the letters that his younger brother Albert wrote to him while on the frontlines at the Battle of the Bulge inspired his art work.

He was so talented that when he decided to quit school to help his mother support him and his siblings that were still living at home, his teacher, Mr. Mahoney, a brawny Irishman, offered to pay his tuition to art school. Tony's father had too much pride and dedication to his family to accept the offer and now, 20 years later, he was working in a factory to support his own family.

Richie's father, who had gone to Detroit to gain his own wealth, wanted him to go with him. He recognized his seventh child's ambitious, hardworking attitude and wanted him and his older sons to join him. He declined the offer and had bitterness in his heart that lasted his entire life.

Tony didn't sleep for most of that night anticipating his father's reaction to his defeat at the hands of those Irish punks. He laid awake planning his revenge and imagining their brutal demise at his hands. He would put thorns facing out under his jacket so that the next time they hit him in the stomach they would be cut and bleed. He would hold a small metal rod in his hand to return a punishing blow if they attacked him. His dreams of revenge continued through the night.

At 7:00 AM his dad woke him for school and asked what happened. Tony told him and he asked, "What did you say to them?" Tony was shocked to hear those words. Did he think I started it?

"Dad, I don't know them, they're big kids, like 13 or 14!" Tony exclaimed, disheartened by his question and seeming lack of sympathy.

"Well, stay away from them!" He was stunned by his father's lack of understanding, not realizing that he had gone through similar experiences growing up. He left Tony's room saying, "Get up and get ready for school," without a hint of compassion in his voice.

At breakfast, after his dad had gone out to get the morning paper, Tony's mom tried to explain his father's seemingly unsympathetic behavior to her son, "Your father had to deal with prejudice and violence when he was growing up. He sometimes acts like he doesn't care, but he does. He loves you and he wants you to be able to survive in this world."

"But why does he always think I did something wrong? It isn't fair!" cried Tony.

"He doesn't! He acts tough with you because he knows he can't be with you every day to protect you from hurt," answered his mom, her soft hand on his cheek gently wiping away his tears. "Someday you'll understand."

Tony learned later that year, after the attacks continued from the same antagonist, that his dad found out his name. He paid a visit to the punk's father, a big Irishman of considerable reputation as a hater of "guineas." His mom said his father told the man if there was another attack on his son, he would answer to him. Although it didn't improve Irish-Italian relations in the neighborhood, it worked. His father had a reputation for being a no nonsense guy and for keeping his promises.

Over the years, Tony would learn the lesson his father tried to convey with his shorthand response to his whining. He needed to learn to protect himself. The anti "WOP" sentiment was not just the work of the bullies that found safety in numbers. It was the fabric of a bigoted society, borne of fear and a response of the primitive need for survival. It was the 1950s and the class system was in full effect. In America, "the land of the free," the ethnic English hated the Irish, who despised the Italians, who feared the blacks, who had no use for the Hispanics. To Tony it seemed that each group had this need to look down on another in order to feel good about themselves. It didn't make sense and he would have no part of it.

At age 11, he was one of the smallest in his class and considered somewhat of a nerd, but like his father, he was also an artist and was favored by teachers for the school's creative projects. He befriended the toughest guy in his class who assisted him in holiday art-work for the various classrooms. It was his first experience in "it's not what you know, but who you know that counts." It also helped that the school's Principal, Mr. Mahoney, had been his dad's eighth grade teacher.

Johnny Mackney was from an alcoholic, dysfunctional family. Looking at his scarred face, earned from beatings from his father, and his muscular physique, one would think that he was a bully. Tony never saw Johnny start a fight, but he did see that he would not hesitate to finish one when a wannabe bully challenged him. Tony knew that Mackney had a respect for art. He liked to draw to escape his tumultuous world but didn't think that he was good enough. He would look over Tony's shoulder when he was drawing a cartoon in class and smile. Johnny would attempt to do the same and show his work to Tony with pride.

Mackney was the obvious choice to be Tony's assistant when his teacher asked him to use his art to decorate the school's class rooms for the holidays. There were few that would risk challenging Tony, when they were doing their thing as the school artists.

Tony taught himself defensive techniques based on the martial art of jiu jitsu. He used his lack of height and good speed as advantages over bigger kids with less control over their balance. If chased, he would go full speed and, if their bigger strides gained on him, he would suddenly drop to the ground causing them to trip and fly over his curled-up body, often landing head first.

One of his friends said that he often over-did his retaliation, giving back three or four-fold what he got. Tony smiled at the thought that his pay-back tactic was becoming his reputation, as he hoped.

In his junior year of high school he decided not to work after school as he had since he was 11 years old. He and his friends sold newspapers during the afternoon rush hours at South Station in downtown Boston. He wanted to try out for the football team with a number of his friends. At 17 years old he was only 5 foot 5 Inches tall and weighed just 135 pounds. But he played sandlot sports with reckless abandon and wanted to be on the school team.

The School was Boston Technical High, a city school that was preparatory for college in the engineering fields. Although, well before the forced busing fiasco that was Boston's lowest point, Tech was a racially mixed school and it required the passing of an exam for entrance.

The Boston district and city schools played their games at White Stadium in the predominantly black area of the city known as Roxbury. Boston Tech wasn't playing on this brisk fall day, but some of the team came to watch Boston English High

School play South Boston High. Midway through the game a riot broke out in the stands.

Tony was sitting next to a black teammate when both white and black students began battling in the stands, knives were flashing and fists were flying. They stayed out of this historic battle and used each other's presence to deflect violence from either of them. "He's with me," worked for both of them until the cops arrived. The Stadium was shut down for the rest of the year. One boy from Southie was stabbed near the heart but lived after a long recuperation. He became the poster boy for the anti-violence. Ironically, he was one of antagonists in the early days of Tony's "physical education."

Although, they were considered bigots in the national news scene, the people of Southie were very conservative in their lifestyle, but Democrats in their politics. Living in Southie was about being in the right Catholic Parish, ethnically, and if possible the right elementary school, of which there were several. Families wanted their kids to go to the school that they attended as a child. The church, whether Irish, Lithuanian or Polish was the center of social life in this blue collar community.

There was no Italian Parish but the Gate of Heaven Church was as ecumenical relative to ethnicity, as it could be. It was the childhood Parish of the sitting Bishop of Boston, Cardinal Richard Cushing. The Benedetto's considered it their Parish and made sure that, although their children went to public school, they followed the dogma of the church to a "T." Church, Sunday school and Religious classes on the first Thursday of the month were a routine that could not be varied.

For many, prejudice was indistinguishable from pride. It was enhanced by the competition for ethnic survival and for favored living areas. People had only their territory to make them feel special. The black element of society was excluded in what Judge Arthur Garretty called "de facto segregation" a term that served to exacerbate, rather than resolve, the problem of social injustice.

Families took pride in sending their children to the school a few blocks from their home, often to have teachers that they had. Both black and white families were pitted against each other in a simplistic political solution to a complex problem. Good intentions, but very poor intelligence prevailed to nearly destroy a city. The people of Southie formed the elements of the next generation of middle class America. They worked hard so that their children would live a better life.

Chapter 2

Westport Connecticut, known for its beautiful seashore, is a bedroom community for the wealthy Wall Street financiers and corporate leaders. It also has one the highest income per capita ratios in the country. The population consists of both "old money" and new. Many of the nouveau rich, as they were labeled, made their fortunes in the markets trading in petroleum stocks and high interest credit sources. A number of them were CEO's or presidents of prosperous companies.

Westport is sometimes compared as the modern day Newport, Rhode Island, the playground of the very wealthy and privileged in the pre-depression, pre-income tax and lavish excesses of the 1920s.

James R. Buckman III, a handsome young man with dark hair, hazel eyes and an athletic build, was the oldest in the family He would have a portion of his daddy's fortune to play with when he turned 24. The plan was that he would preside over a part of the family portfolio, which included blue chip stocks such as General Motors, Boeing and Texaco as well as the family owned bank. In advance of his taking over for his father in many of his business dealings, he would have to start at the "bottom" as an assistant to the Chief Financial Officer (CFO) when he had completed college.

His younger brother Jonathan was slight of build and less athletic, although he tried to compete with big brother, he always fell short. He was considered the brains in the family. He could not overcome the tradition that mandated that James III was the heir-apparent and would preside over the family-owned businesses and its wealth. Jonathan could only hope to be its Corporate Financial Officer. As CFO he would eventually answer to his older brother, a fate that he did not appreciate.

James III's childhood enjoyed the benefits of private schools and high paid tutors from the early years, through college. He learned at an early age that there's safety in numbers and power in leadership - a lesson that far too many poor kids learn in their embrace of the street gang mentality. The private elite schools of the more fortunate call them clubs, rather than gangs, they consist of societies and fraternities or sororities, designed to protect their turf and secure advantage over their classmates.

It was the summer of 1959 and Dwight D. Eisenhower, the former General of the Armies and Commander of the European forces that defeated the German War Machine in WW II, was completing his second term as President. Ike, as he was called, was considered to be a moderate Republican. He ended the "Korean Conflict," initiated the Interstate Highway system in the name of national defense and embraced the idea of civil rights having seen tens of thousands of minorities die for their country under his command in World War II.

The talk of the social and political scenes was of this young upstart Senator from Massachusetts who was challenging Richard M. Nixon, Eisenhower's Vice President, to become Ike's successor. James' father was concerned about the potential of a liberal Democrat becoming the leader of the free world. John F. Kennedy was a Catholic and a member of a very wealthy family but was considered by conservatives to be a threat to their political philosophy.

James had heard all of the rhetoric from his father about the Kennedys and the Roosevelts and how he believed that FDR sold America out to the commies by allowing Stalin and the Soviets to join the Allies in the final days of World War II and divide the spoils of war by taking East Berlin. Now the son of Joe Kennedy was trying to become the next President of the United States. But James was only 17 and really didn't care. It didn't compare with his goal of becoming the leader of his prep-school's "Society of the Bear Claw," a group of the wealthiest of the wealthy and the most righteous of the righteous.

The name itself was to strike fear in the hearts of the less powerful and servitude to those who opposed them. Their code of honor required complete obedience to the group and secrecy as to its goals. The "good guys" were those who did their bidding and any who resisted were labeled the "bad apples," and dealt with accordingly. They didn't get to share the cheat sheets that they bought from corruptible school staff or be invited to secret parties at the Lake.

The uninitiated would suffer the consequences of a grade system that used the so-called "Bell Curve" that adjusted the grades according to the number attaining the highest percentage of A's and those with the lowest as Ds or Es. Those falling within the middle of the "Bell" would be considered average or at the "C" level. The grade of C was considered to be passing, but wasn't acceptable to their parents who were paying the exorbitant tuition and fees to keep them out of their hair. The grades skewed by the "cheaters" would assure their academic superiority and add obstacles to the fringe students, some of whom had parents who sacrificed in an attempt to have their child achieve their version of the American Dream.

Although the practice of advantage in the form of cheating by the wealthy was well known within the school, its benefits were thought to far outweigh its negatives. The families of the chosen ones would reward their academic accomplishments with endowments to mitigate any inconvenience the caring and guidance of their future champions would incur.

Young James knew instinctively that his father would always reward accomplishments, no matter how they were gained. The "Buckman Doctrine" was often expressed by the family patriarch after consumption of a third stress-reducing martini. "It's a tough world out there my sons and you have to outsmart those who would want what you have, and you have to make them regret even wanting it!" To James it was understood to be a mandate for his future role of carrying the family banner.

The hypothesis of the wealthy was that those who weren't successful and wealthy were lazy and not deserving. It wasn't until his first year of law school that he began to question his father's wisdom.

Chapter 3

As the Mayor of a small mid-western city, Sam Polowski thought he'd achieved all that he wanted and needed, but there was the feeling that there was something else out there calling to him. He was urged to run for higher office, "You'd make a great Governor and the state needs you," was the exuberant advice of his friends and political associates. He had balanced the budget during trying times and kept the largest employer in the city by helping them resist and overcome the unions. He hadn't raised taxes, but cut what he considered non-essentials to the point of pain.

His family was not as enthusiastic of his potential rise in the political hierarchy. Sam, a former auto worker, had been in politics for more than twenty five years, initially as a City Counselor and after the corruption of the previous administration tore the fabric of the city apart, as Mayor. He was elected to his first of three terms as Mayor of a city in crisis. Sam was a veteran of the Navy serving in the Pacific. He was educated on the G.I. Bill and received benefits from the Veterans Administration.

His wife Laura, his two daughters, Sharon and Cindy and his son Josh, felt that he'd done enough. Despite his accomplishments there were those who didn't appreciate losing their city jobs and there was the antagonism from the less than scrupulous contractors who could not buy business from the city any longer. He had enemies who did their best to let him and his family know that they were there.

Sharon, the oldest of the siblings at seventeen and a red-haired, green eyed beauty, was about to enter college. Although she loved her dad and cherished his honesty, she had empathy for those whom she believed to be less fortunate – the ones who were falling through the cracks of the socially indifferent system. There wasn't money to assist them in their respective plights. Fiscal responsibility had a price and it was paid by those who were the least capable of that burden. Education funds were reduced by 25%; police, fire and social services bore similar impacts.

Her fear of future office for her dad was not only compassion for her hard working, no nonsense father, but for his strict and dogmatic reluctance to spend money or raise the revenue needed to properly run the city. Taxes were the only means to gain the funds needed to improve the lot of those who didn't otherwise have the means to "pull themselves up by their bootstraps," a phrase her father often used as the solution to social inequities in defense of his fiscal frugality. As Sharon saw it, most of those struggling to survive his frugality could not afford boots with or without the straps.

The current poor in their city didn't have the benefit of the good paying jobs that her father and his generation secured after returning from "the War." They didn't have the advantage of President Franklin D. Roosevelt's (FDR) New Deal programs that lifted them from poverty or the construction of the American Interstate Highway system under President Eisenhower that served to overcome the recession brought on by the Korean Conflict or a well-funded school systems that recognized the impact of knowledge and its socioeconomic benefit.

Her father had responsibility for a crumbling city infrastructure that hadn't seen proper servicing in more than thirty years and unions that were unable to secure the kind of benefits that he was assured of as an auto worker and a veteran. His affection for the poor of the city that earned $1 an hour doing menial task, lacking the skills and education to better themselves, was best displayed at election time in photo opportunities that showed him serving at soup kitchens and visiting nursing homes and, of course, kissing babies.

Then there were the programs that the wealthy, who didn't need them, love to hate, but that many rely on for survival in their later years. Social Security was initiated under the FDR's New Deal without Republican support but with antagonistic analogies to a socialism and communism. The Medicare program, without which many elderly would not have health care, was passed under the Johnson administration bearing the same Republican criticisms of being an example of socialism. Fortunately, there were enough politicians with a social conscience to pass it.

The wealthy right-wing element of the Republican Party rationalized that if they could reduce the benefits paid to the retirees or eliminate it completely, they would pay less taxes and that would mean they could afford another vacation home, a newer Rolls or a Lear jet to make their hectic and deserving lives more livable.

Sharon believed, if her father could read her thoughts he would most assuredly strike her from his will. Not that he had much to leave his family in his will. His integrity did not allow for illicit gain.

She loved her father and admired his honesty, but feared his leadership as being too narrow and potentially destructive. As Governor, she believed he would oversee the demise of his State under his fiscally responsible and socially indifferent policies.

She also felt that he was an unsuspecting pawn of the elite, but she knew he truly believed that he was doing the right thing for his constituents. He didn't realize, nor did he want to realize, that only the 'Haves' were truly benefitting from his fiscal frugality. His honesty was needed, but his blind eye to the realities of life and the plight of the poor and working class, were negating the benefits of his integrity.

Sharon hoped to someday make a positive difference, if she was given the chance and the means to do so. She liked what she heard from the Senator from Massachusetts, the candidate for President, but was it just political rhetoric? After all isn't he the son of an obscenely wealthy, powerful and some say, unscrupulous father?

Chapter 4

Diego Martinez was only 13 years old when his father was deported to Mexico in 1959 as an illegal immigrant. His mother had been very sick with pneumonia, they had no insurance. His father had a doctor come to his home, fearing discovery of their illegal status if they went to the hospital. He was unable to pay the full cost of his visit and the good doctor dropped a dime to the authorities.

His mother was taken to the hospital but didn't survive and Diego, an only child, was alone in the country of his birth. His grandmother, on his father's side, took him in. Her status was legal and she was only 52, working as a waitress. She was still young enough to raise a child in need. Grandma Martinez gave him a sense of home and he gave her all she could handle as a teen searching for his place in a tough Los Angeles neighborhood known as 'Watts.'

She hoped her son Manny would find his way back to the States to share in the duties of raising his son. He did two years later, but as a courier for a drug cartel. Her son had always been an honest man who worked hard to earn enough money to take care of his family. He struggled with his forced absence and rationalized he had been treated unfairly, given the number of illegal's being welcomed through the "back door" by the farmers, factory and business owners. The country was eager to take advantage of their willingness to take low wages, pay unreasonable fees for room and board in cramped unsanitary housing, accept having no benefits and, of course, tolerate their abuse. This modern version of slavery was not just the practice in the Border States; it was the economic underbelly wherever "the law" looked the other way.

Manny knew that the men and women of Mexico played an important role in the economy of the country. They provided cheap labor and were afraid to complain about working conditions. The farmers needed them! They were controlled, and often victimized by long hours, poor food and the high costs back-charged to them for those "benefits" by the wealthy and powerful. Consumers of these products enjoyed their relatively inexpensive cost and abundant availability, unconcerned that serious profits were made on the backs of the migrant workers.

The capture and incarceration of his father in the spring of 1961 for drug dealing as a cartel courier sealed the deal for Diego; he needed to make money to help his grandma. He was told that if he joined the local gang he could make more money than he could spend. He was being recruited by his neighbor Joey Consalvo, a high ranking member of "The Street Devils." At 17, Joey was 3 years older, tough and always smiling as if he was cool and in control. Joey told him that he had to do for himself! No one was going to help him survive.

"Hey, you owe this country nothing man, they took your momma and your papa and left you to die in the streets," was Joey's mantra. "You're a smart kid. You don't need no school; you need money. You want a car and girlfriends, be with us or.... or we will see you as against us and that ain't good!"

The eviction notice to his grandmother was the last straw; he went to Joey and said, "I'm in! What do I have to do to make some money?"

Joey smiled and embraced him in a bear hug to show his strength and his macho superiority. "You meet me at the liquor store parking lot at 1 o'clock tonight and I'll show you how it's done amigo. Sanchez will be there with me in a red Chevy Impala convertible."

"I didn't know Sanchez had such a fine car," Diego said surprised at his good fortune.

"He doesn't yet, we're delivering it to a chop-shop downtown, but first we got some business to do. You be there at I o'clock tonight if you want to make some money."

The night passed slowly as Diego pondered his new job and Joey's words. Are they going to share the money they make on the car or are they going to rob the store? Keisha Johnson's mom works in that store. Keisha's my only friend in that boring math class. I hope her mom isn't there tonight. She might recognize me?

At 12:45 am Diego opened the window in his closet-like room, being careful not to drop it to the ground in its rotted state. As he let go of the window sill and felt the ground below his feet, he could hear his grandmother coughing in her room. He stopped to be sure that she didn't hear him, then slithered off to his new job.

Joey and Sanchez were there as promised, the new red 1960 Impala convertible, an awesome sight. "You ready to earn some pesos amigo?" Joey said smiling and glancing towards Sanchez who reflected a half-hearted smile back to him through teeth long wanting the effective use of a tooth brush.

"I guess so man. What do I do?"

"You just sit here in the back seat and Sanchez will park at the door. I'll already be in the store. I'll knock over the coke display at the back of the store and the clerk will come to see what happened, Sanchez will break open the cash register with this crow bar and take the money. I'll push the old lady to the floor so she can't sound an alarm and run out the door behind Sanchez. We jump in the car and take off. You get a third of what we get."

"You're not going to hurt anyone?" asked Diego worried about Mrs. Johnson, if she was there working in the store.

"No, amigo! We don't have no guns. We're just going to get in and get out. No one's going to get hurt."

"But what do I do?" puzzled Diego.

"You watch for the cops or anyone else and signal us by beeping the horn twice, keep the car running and stay in the back seat so I can get in and drive," explained Diego's new mentor.

The plan seemed to work as Joey described until he tried to push Mrs. Johnson to the floor. She used her forty pound advantage to throw Joey against the beer coolers and whacked him on the side of the head with a can of beans from the grocery shelf. Joey screamed in pain, holding his swelling head. Sanchez ran to his aid still holding the crow bar. Diego screamed "No!" as he saw the attack and the bar slam into Mrs.

Johnson's head. She turned, and as if looking at Diego through the store window with pleading eyes, slumped to the floor.

Joey picked himself up and grabbed Sanchez before he could strike another blow and ran out the door. The car was still running, as was Diego, as fast as he could crying and screaming "no, no," like he had been the victim. All he could see was Keisha's mother's eyes as she reeled from the blow of the iron bar.

Naomi Johnson was unconscious when she was rushed to the hospital. A week later she was still in a coma and on life support. Diego couldn't face Keisha, making excuses to not have lunch with her. She missed a week of school in her sorrow and confused state. Diego worried that if her mom survived she would remember his face in the window, but he wanted her to survive and for Keisha to be happy again.

It was a month before he had the courage to see her face to face when he met her for lunch. He had run out of excuses such as using his lunch period to study for tests or for playing basketball with friends on the school's outdoor court.

"How are you doing?" asked Diego with a sincere concern.

"I'm ok... I guess. Momma's still in a coma and Papa is very sad and angry," Keisha said with a tear in her eye. "He wants to find whoever did this to her and beat them until they are in a coma too."

Diego believed that if he ratted on Joey and Sanchez they would get his grandmother and him. He didn't care about his fate; he deserved it for being so stupid, but he couldn't let them hurt his grandmother. He realized if her mother survived, he may eventually pay the price for his actions. But he knew he had to be there for Keisha.

Chapter 5

It was the day of the Presidential election. The polls were closed for an hour but the election was too close to call at 9:00 pm Pacific Time on election eve. Nixon and Kennedy had battled for several months, using television debates to appeal to the American electorate via the latest technology. As the sitting Vice President under the popular Eisenhower Presidency Nixon was thought by the media to be a sure thing until the Kennedy charisma took hold. His handsome presence and sense of humor was enhanced by the television screen's unforgiving depiction of the sweating, defensive and obviously uncomfortable persona of Richard M. Nixon.

In contrast, the 43-year old Kennedy belied his youth with intelligent and witty retorts to Nixon's antagonisms. His smiling eyes and wide boyish grin made him a "rock star" of the new generation of politicians to this first-of-a-kind television audience. After the debates Nixon was obviously on the ropes and Kennedy was readying the knockout punch. The punch, however, was thrown using the old style City-Boss tactics of Mayor Daley of Chicago, who at the urging and, no doubt, encouragement of the Kennedy patriarch, Joe Kennedy, delivered the swing state of Illinois.

The election of Kennedy shocked the conservative elements of society. The Kennedys were a wealthy family, but they were the nouveau riche, an Irish clan with many children and grandchildren. Some believed they earned their money the "old fashioned way" from questionable practices! Although, they may not have stooped to the level of the land stealing and brutality of the railroad barons or the unhealthy practices of the mining and steel industry nor did they use slaves and eventually cheap migrant labor to grow cotton, tobacco and various other staples of the agricultural economy, they were not accepted as part of the American hierarchy. Theirs was not old money sanctioned by the conservative guard of the elite.

Actually, Joe Kennedy used the era of the prohibition of alcohol, the result of the 18th Amendment to the U.S. Constitution in 1919, to make his first millions by securing the import rights to Schenley, Gordon's Gin and Dewar's Scotch, all alcoholic beverages, from their foreign manufacturers. Once the ban on alcohol was lifted by ratification of the 21st Amendment in 1933, he had accumulated a large inventory and a strong presence in that very lucrative market. He then invested into the efforts of those "old money" scoundrels who built America on the backs and lives of the immigrants and minorities who laid the track and dug the ditches for pennies an hour with hopes of obtaining their piece of the "American Dream."

He befriended Franklin Delano Roosevelt, known as "FDR," while Assistant General Manager of General Dynamics, a major ship American builder during World War II. Joe Kennedy played several roles in his administration, including Ambassador to Great Britain, a role that was tainted by his isolationist response to a potential conflict with Germany. His poor choices of rhetoric while in the limelight of the FDR administration eventually caused a chasm in their relationship.

Jack or "JFK," as John Fitzgerald Kennedy was later known, was the second oldest son in a family of nine children. Joe Jr., the eldest son, had been the patriarch's choice to carry the family banner to the White House. He was also the first to bear the burden of the curse that followed the Kennedys. Joe Jr. a navy pilot in World War II, volunteered to fly a secret mission over Germany in a plane loaded with explosives. He was to bail out and allow his plane to act as a powerful bomb on a military target that manufactured the German's V-2 rocket that was causing havoc in Britain. He never made it. He took his place in the tragic history of the cursed clan as his lethal weapon exploded prematurely in flight on August 12, 1944. His sister Kathleen, the fourth child of Joseph and Rose Kennedy, also died in a plane crash in Europe in May 1948. She was the second casualty of what many came to believe was "the Kennedy Curse."

The Kennedys claim to patriotic calling became legendary with Jack's heroism as a PT boat commander in the Pacific.

After his boat was rammed by a Japanese destroyer, Kennedy managed to rescue his remaining crew, having lost two members in the collision. He took his badly burned engineer, Patrick McMahon, in tow swimming to an island more than three miles away. Joe senior's dream of having a son in the White House became Jack's burden. His heroics on PT 109, and his best-selling book, *Profiles in Courage* distinguished him from the crowded field of political "wannabes."

The Kennedy success in Boston politics, the playground of the old-money Boston Brahmins, gave them credibility as contenders. But most important, Jack and his younger brothers Bobby and Teddy embraced a political realm of compassion for the poor and less fortunate that brought fear to the established rich who wanted it all and believed that they deserved it.

Kennedy took office in January 1961 declaring in his memorable inaugural address, "Ask not what your country can do for you; ask what you can do for your country." In the nearly three years he served, he proved to be a fiscal conservative, but a social liberal striving to provide opportunity to those left out of the prosperity picture.

The Peace Corps and volunteer programs he embraced were designed to bring the haves and have-nots together in a joint purpose for the benefit of all. It had the effect of healing wounds inflicted during years of war and strife. Civil rights, which were first recognized by Eisenhower as an issue to be reckoned with, became JFK's emotional base for domestic policy. The severity of racism remained a blight on the American landscape as the 100th anniversary of Lincoln's Emancipation Proclamation approached.

His announced goal of the United States being the first to reach the moon in a manned flight was to inspire the competitive spirit of an America that was becoming docile and apathetic about its role in the world, seeing only war as a means to express its interest and belay its fears in foreign lands. The American people had watched as its cold war enemy, the Soviet Union, successfully launched "Sputnik," the first satellite into space in October 1957, leaving them behind in the technology race. He believed that reaching the moon first would compensate for that loss in prestige. His words brought hope to those who needed it, and his efforts, which included balancing the budget, and staring down the Soviets in their most dangerous threat of nuclear war during the Cuban Missile Crisis, made him a credible leader of the free world. He allayed the fears of those working class citizens who did not vote for him, many of whom began to recognize his talents and abilities.

This only caused more trepidation and anxiety to those who were threatened by his successes. They answered with hateful rhetoric in the media and scare tactics hoping to defeat him in the next political round...and possibly before.

His Vice President, Lyndon Johnson, a former leader in Congress, disliked him for the way he overcame his own bid for the Oval Office. He thought of JFK as an arrogant upstart who hadn't paid his political dues to be rewarded with the most coveted position in the world of power and wealth. He resented the Kennedy family wealth, although he had compassion for the poor having been a school teacher in Cotulla, Texas with Mexican immigrants as students, before he attained his own wealth by marrying "Lady Bird," a Texas woman of means.

Detractors would say that the Kennedy politics of social sensitivity was just another way to satisfy the voting masses. His supporters believed it to be a sincere effort to share a bigger piece of the pie with those who also lacked the opportunity to access the benefits of the American dream.

Chapter 6

The trip to Dallas, Texas was to be a social and political event to show the colors of the American Presidency to Vice President Johnson's statewide constituents. In less than three years in office the Kennedy charisma was winning over many of those who were skeptical about his abilities, and he needed to keep the momentum building for the next election, but most importantly for his social and economic programs, which were before Congress. The heat of hateful rhetoric was being turned up by a panicky right-wing sector of the Republican Party.

It was Friday morning, November 22, 1963 when President Kennedy's convertible limousine turned the corner towards Dealey Plaza in downtown Dallas. Seated next to his wife Jacqueline and behind the Governor of Texas, John Connolly, JFK took the full force of a bullet, fired from behind the motorcade, in his neck. The shot was said to have been fired from the sixth floor of the Texas Book Depository building. It was relatively quickly determined that the assassin was Lee Harvey Oswald; a man of unstable character and an unquenched need for notoriety as recorded in the official government files of the subsequent investigation.

JFK died of his wounds soon after arriving at Parkland Hospital. His death was announced on television at 1:00 PM CST by a tearful Walter Cronkite to a nation in incredulous shock.

Most Americans mourned the loss of the young man from Boston who purveyed hope and a determination to make the world a better place, although as a result of this barbaric act America was looked upon by some in foreign lands as being no different than third-world countries that change their leaders by permanent elimination. The sadness for the loss of this man of vision, with the young and beautiful family, was contagious throughout the world.

For those who were relieved by the events of the day, they would rejoice in quiet celebration and if asked, would express their sorrow as if genuine and sincere. The act of a madman was not their doing, but it did solve what they perceived to be a serious problem.

The day before Kennedy's visit to Dallas a handbill was distributed throughout the city by a disturbed eccentric. It pictured JFK in both profile and front view, as if it was a "Wanted" poster for a criminal. The caption said that he was "Wanted for Treason." Among the treasonous activities cited was betraying our friends in Cuba, Katanga and Portugal. The desired relationship of the accused assassin Lee Harvey Oswald with Fidel Castro's Cuba was well documented in the media. Was it a coincidence or a conspiracy? Conspiracy theorists would ponder that question for generations to come.

CHAPTER 7

It had been four years since Diego Martinez learned a life-lesson about making easy money the hard way. He had separated himself from "smiling Joey" realizing that he had to work hard to get what he wanted out of life. The trauma of that night stayed with him, even as he found love in his friendship with Keisha Johnson.

Keisha's mother, Naomi, survived, but was still in her beating-induced coma. Her doctor told Keisha she could recover at any time; a possibility that struck both fear and hope in Diego's heart, but the prospects for that to occur were very low.

Joey and Sanchez were never suspects and they warned Diego that they would "do in" his grandmother if he ever squealed and implicate him in the attack. They told Diego that if Mrs. Johnson fingered them, they would both say that he was the attacker. The liquor store didn't have a working surveillance camera. It had malfunctioned months ago and the owner didn't have the money to replace it. It would be their word against his.

Diego felt somewhat relieved when Joey and Sanchez were arrested after advancing to bank robbery and sentenced to ten years of "rest and recreation" at San Quentin.

Diego was having lunch with Keisha at school when the public address system announced that President Kennedy had been assassinated. JFK had given the Hispanic/black community hope that things would be different. Many felt that his expressed compassion for the plight of the poor and the inequalities faced by minorities were the reasons for his demise. There were tears, anger and shock mixed in the surreal moment.

This kind of stuff doesn't happen in America, thought Diego.

Tony Benedetto was on his way home when he passed the Broadway Appliance Store in South Boston. There were people, men, women and children weeping outside as they watched the television sets displayed in the window.

"What's going on?" he asked no one in particular.

"They shot the President! He's dead!" came the words from an unknown source in the crowd."

"They killed Jack!" exclaimed a woman's trembling voice. The people of South Boston knew Jack intimately. He was a familiar site every St. Patrick's day walking in the big parade, or at Dorgan's Restaurant on Carson Beach, where the politicians hung out on election eves and before the big parade. The loss of JFK was not just the tragic loss of a sitting President but of a son of the Irish and a patron of Southie.

Tony ran home, a confused and sad young man knowing that his family, although Italian and having had their share of torment from some of the haters who happened to be of Irish descent, voted for and respected JFK.

How could this happen in this country? He asked himself. He shared the grief of his Irish neighbors amongst whom he had lived for more than a decade.

Sharon Polowski, a college senior at Michigan State University, wept openly in her off-campus apartment. She knew her father was not a fan of the young President and was often outspoken and critical of his social policies. Her mother was not openly political and avoided confrontations with her husband on issues of social injustice. Her views and compassion for people were similar to that of her oldest daughter. Sharon's siblings marched in lock step with their conservative dad, not wanting to alienate their meal ticket as their ambitions didn't involve the well-being of others.

She wondered if she was the one that was out of step with reality. Maybe her father was right in his thinking that less government was the solution to the woes of society. Less taxes means less government and more money in the pockets of the some people. Her concern was always for the people who have no hope of having money in their pockets and without the help of government, little opportunity to benefit from this "land of opportunity." She called home not expecting empathy for her sad and confused state of mind.

The financially secure world of James R. Buckman III viewed JFK as a threat to its wealth, power and security. Although respectful, collectively they were somewhat relieved by the day's events. James, however, was shocked that his America was not as secure a democracy as he had believed it to be. There had been presidential assassinations in the past, and several unsuccessful attempts in history, but this was reality at its worst.

He didn't like the disruption of structure or the chaos that it fostered. Having repeated his sophomore year, he was only three months into his junior year at Yale's School of Business. His life to date had been one of controlled and predictable experiences. This insane act changed that. What would the future bring? He called his father seeking to make some sense of the incongruity of it all, but knowing that there would be little sympathy for the plight of JFK and, more than likely, relief for the plight of the nation, as he envisioned it.

Chapter 8

Lyndon Johnson, thought by conservatives to be the lesser of two evils, proved to be their movement's worse nightmare. He had gained their support by expanding involvement in the Vietnam War and in defense spending, but he also used his formidable influence with Congress to pass JFK's major initiatives. Civil Rights, Medicare and the NASA space program legislation would be his most important efforts and notable accomplishments.

NASA's potential was enhanced as it became a significant asset of Johnson's home state of Texas. Houston would be the headquarter location for the most ambitious and expensive project on American soil. JFK's goal of having an American presence on the moon within a decade was embraced by the pragmatic Johnson as an opportunity to swell the financial coffers of his great state of Texas, while providing much needed employment for his constituents.

As the sitting President, he easily won re-election over Senator Barry Goldwater, the Republican candidate from Arizona. Goldwater was a straight talking conservative who left the electorate with a fear that he was trigger happy in an era of nuclear paranoia. The Democrats did what they believed was necessary to keep that message alive.

Vietnam was initially a place where JFK sent military advisors to train the pro-American South Vietnamese, in anticipation of North Vietnam's ambitions for its territory. However, Vietnam was becoming a war that seemed to expand both unilaterally and rapidly by political considerations that few understood.

Many of the dissidents believed that it was a civil war that couldn't be won by massive bombings and interventions by third party powers. Kennedy, according to his then Secretary of Defense, Robert McNamara, was considering withdrawal from the quagmire that Vietnam was becoming. There were only 16,300 military advisors in South Vietnam when JFK was assassinated.

Before Americans believed that they were the solution to the turmoil within third world civilizations, the French had attempted to control Vietnam. The French sought to colonize Asian territories until they felt the wrath of a desperate people, as did the British colonists before them. The French found that the costs far outweighed the benefits of controlling the lives of those they considered to be the *unenlightened.*

When the French left, the void was filled by philosophically diverse governments. The North had chosen communism as a means to better their society. They depended on China for direct support and the Soviets for more discreet aid. The South tied their hopes to the western culture and the United States, anticipating the potentials and wealth of democracy.

To the many military minded in the United States., this was a chance to prove the superiority of a democratic government over communism. It represented a microcosm of what was believed to be a worldwide problem that needed a solution. To those who believed that the Korean conflict left doubt about American military might, it was an opportunity to show our strength and resolve to the world, in particular, to the Soviet and Chinese communist governments.

Johnson rolled the dice. "We will fight them in their own backyard so that we don't have to fight them in ours;" was the gist of the rallying cry. We soon found that people fight fiercely and are willing to die to defend their backyards and their families; a lesson that is all too often lost or soon forgotten.

Chapter 9

At 19, Diego thought that he had seen and experienced poverty at its worst in the Watts section of Los Angeles, his "hood." He didn't realize that there were people in this world of supermarkets, televisions and jet planes that lived in one room huts with dirt floors, lacking running water, toilets and the basic means of life. He was in Vietnam as an American soldier. The Army told him that he was there to save and protect the Vietnamese from the evils of communism, but he soon learned that the Vietnamese just wanted to live their lives without the threat of being killed for a "greater cause." He also learned that he could not tell who "they" were.

Diego had been drafted to serve as an infantryman by his all-white draft board, being told that it was an honor to serve his country. He had dropped out of the local community college to earn some money as a mechanic's helper. His grandmother could no longer support herself and him as her diabetes diminished her energy and mobility. No longer deferred as a student he was vulnerable to conscription into the Armed Forces of the United States.

Diego had seen television reports of protesting young men burning their draft cards and of some moving to Canada to escape the draft. He was not a coward, as they were called by some, he would serve *his* country honorably and bravely. He was an American!

He was now in a strange country and following the whims and orders of others. However, he was comfortable with his squad. They, like him, were from the inner cities of the United States and like the people in his hood, they were mostly black and Hispanic. They were, for the most part, the tough guys, at least on the outside. Being tough was their first line of defense against their fears. Diego just wanted to do his time and go home, alive and whole, a universal wish that for some of the 4th Squad, 2nd Platoon of Able Company, was not to be.

Their squad leader was a white guy named Tony Benedetto, he was a sergeant in his first tour of duty. He was a year from finishing college for his engineering degree. He had to repeat his senior year after falling below graduation standards, while working two jobs to pay for his education. Losing his student deferment was the prelude to being on the short list for conscription into the armed forces. The draft board informed him of his good fortune and invited him to join the other lucky men selected for service to their country.

Diego was point man for the search, and possible destruction, of a suspected Viet Cong controlled village. He had only been in "Nam" for four months and had done several of these clean-up operations. This was the first time as the point man. Only three had resulted in fire-fights, all of which they succeeded in their mission, but at the expense of losing four men and having 50% wounded casualties.

Benedetto had replaced one of those lost; an end-of-tour sergeant that smothered a grenade thrown by a young woman hiding in her hut, protecting her children. He had saved a dozen soldiers who were at his side and received the Silver Star posthumously, for his heroism.

Sergeant Leroy Stevens was a black man from New Jersey; a former police officer respected for his courage and his empathy for the lives of his "men." He didn't wait to be drafted, but joined with a sense that they needed him, and to the men of the 4th Squad, 2nd Platoon of Able Company, he was right. Benedetto did not share his predecessor's convictions on the rightfulness of the war, but did have compassion for his men.

The village seemed quiet, too quiet, as they approached from a well-worn pathway through this jungle-like, bug infested land. Diego could see the thatched roof tops from his point position halfway up a tree. He climbed higher to get a better visual and signaled the Sergeant that there was no one visible, a determination that usually meant trouble.

Sergeant Benedetto decided to wait and watch, spreading his men out in a perimeter arc about 100 meters from the edge of the village. Diego stayed in his observation perch, binoculars scanning the village for any activity.

Benedetto pondered the situation. It would be dark within an hour, should they wait that long or move in at dusk? His decision could mean lives lost. He wished he were back on Carson Beach in Southie, checking out the chicks.

His decision was made for him with the firing of a weapon from the village. He looked around and then to Diego's position. He wasn't there! Yelling "fire at will" to his men, he ran full speed, head down, through the bush reaching Diego as he squirmed in pain at the base of the tree. His wound was at shoulder level but he had also broken both his legs in the fall. He was bleeding badly and without medical attention he would die.

The fire-fight intensified. Benedetto had to decide whether to use his mortar and rocket capabilities to counter or to call in air support. Either action could obliterate the village and possibly kill innocent villagers. His medic was at their side attending to Diego. "Stop that bleeding." ordered Tony, "and stay low."

He rejoined his squad and ordered the full force of their firepower onto the village. Rockets and mortar rounds hit the huts and village grounds setting off fires and screams of pain and terror, which pervaded the thunderous and rapid sounds of fire.

His radioman Billy Perkins yelled, "No air support available for more than an hour. The base commander says good luck!"

Fire power was returned from a distant source by the enemy's own heavy artillery. Three of his men were down and it looked like they were all entrapped in a position that was doomed. "Pull back" he repeatedly yelled and signaled over the deafening sounds of battle. Carrying their wounded as they fired towards the village they moved rapidly away into the forest. Benedetto carried Diego so that his medic could attend to the other wounded. It was nearly dusk and the night might favor their escape.

Perkins again called for support and rescue. He was told to go 800 meters east to an open field position that would allow for a helicopter rescue.

Tony saw his squad being cut down by the lethal rounds of the distant artillery. There was no chance to counter. He didn't have the weaponry. There was no indication of a ground pursuit by the enemy, but he was sure that there would be. He knew that their only chance for survival was to reach the rescue point. His medic took Diego.

It had been an unusually dry period; the forest was a tinderbox and there was a significant wind blowing to the north, towards the enemy's positions. Benedetto noticed that the enemy's heavy artillery had set off some isolated fires. He decided to enhance them with the use of the squad's flame thrower, a weapon that he personally despised as being cruel and vicious, but they needed to cutoff any ground attack by the VC. His flame-thrower infantryman had been hit on the retreat and was being carried to the rescue site.

Tony picked up the weapon, strapping its heavy fuel tank on his back and started to move eastward. Moving parallel to the enemy's position, Tony sprayed the forest with his weapon of flaming death as his squad stumbled through the forest, many laden with the burden of their wounded comrades.

The fuel ignited the parched vegetation in a deadly line of flaming fury that quickly spread northward carried by the late-day wind, as he had hoped. A shift of that wind would surely wipe out his squad. He had to get them out of here. The heat was blasting back towards the running squad leader. His foot became entangled in a vine, sending him down into the bush, the weapon fell forward and stopped operating, but the fuel tank split. He had to get the tank off his back and get out of the threatened area.

Freeing his entangled foot and dropping the slowly leaking tank, he got to his feet and started running away from the raging fire, not knowing for sure if he was following his men or going into enemy territory. The tank that he left behind exploded, showering the surrounding vegetation. He didn't look back remembering how he had to run for his life as a kid, but this was not some punk chasing him, this was real death. He would not stop until he reached his men, his feet barely touching the ground.

The squad made it to the departure point just as the incoming rescue helicopter cleared the forest canopy. They could see the hell-fires of Benedetto's work in the distance, but their squad leader was not behind them. They looked back again as they heard the explosion of the abandoned tank knowing that it was not the sound of an artillery shell. "What was that?" asked Diego, still conscious, but now on a stretcher being loaded on the copter.

"Damn, it's the flame-throwers fuel tank," came the answer. "Benny's bought it!" a voice proclaimed, using the nickname for their new squad leader when he wasn't around.

"Let's get out of here!" yelled the medic from the copter.

"What about Sarge?" came the unidentified response!

"He couldn't have survived that blast, let's go," repeated the medic.

Tony reached the edge of the clearing in time to see the rescue helicopter, a HU-1E, better known as a Huey, as it exited clearing the trees at the far-end of the open field more than 200 meters away. His heart sank as he dropped to the ground sobbing despairingly. He heard and then saw some streaks of rounds fired from the forest at the copter at the eastern end of the field. They made it out, but he was left behind to his fate.

He looked around despondent and confused and decided to go back into the forest, climbing a tall tree that would afford him some camouflage until morning. Maybe the rescue copter would be back to look for him. As he sat in his high perch he realized that he was trembling with fear and that this might be his end. He could hear voices in the distance. They were not friendly. It would be a long night!

Chapter 10

Of the sixteen members of the 4th squad, 2nd platoon of Able Company only eleven returned, four of whom, including Diego Martinez, were badly wounded and would have a ticket home. None of the five missing soldiers were accounted for and were assumed to be dead, although their capture was a possibility.

The squad Leader, Sergeant Anthony Benedetto, was thought to have been the victim of an enemy round hitting the flame-thrower's tank that he was last seen carrying. His survival was deemed to be highly unlikely. Weather permitting, the Army would send out a reconnaissance team in the morning to do a body count and bring home their dead.

Diego Martinez lay in a field hospital; his wound was treated and his loss of blood would mean that he needed to gain his strength back before being released. His legs, broken in several places, would take time to heal. He would be going back to the States in a few weeks.

He wondered about the Sarge, were they right about him. Did he die in the blast that they heard as they boarded the copter? He knew that he wouldn't have made it if it weren't for his action. The pain in his body was not as bad as that which he had in his heart for his buddies that he only knew for a short while, but thought of as lost family. The loss of people he cared about was something, he thought, he should be used to.

The night passed slowly and Tony held tightly to his tree-haven as the Viet Cong patrol passed under in their quest for American soldiers. He held his breath as they slashed the bushes with their machetes, occasionally looking up at the canopy for any sign of their prey. They stopped beneath him talking very fast, seemingly confused about where they were. The leader looked around and then pointed in directions that split the squad into three parts; each moved out at his command.

As dawn approached he climbed down, intent on following the path of the previous night's helicopter to what he hoped would be a U.S. base. He could still smell the smoke emanating from his protective firewall, now more than 1000 meters north of his position. His journey was slowed by the thick underbrush which ripped at his clothing as he tried to stay within its camouflage. He listened intently for any sound that was not natural to the forest and tried to step lightly so as not to add to those sounds.

More than two hours into his travels he heard a rustling ahead. Startled, he lay quietly in the bush awaiting the source of his distress. As they approached from his right he could see that it was two armed men in the traditional black pajama-style of the Viet Cong. He had one hand on his Smith & Wesson Revolver and the other on his M-6 Bayonet; his M-14 rifle lost when he dropped it to secure the flame thrower gear.

The one closest to him caught movement out of the corner of his eye and turned suddenly towards him, less than five-feet away. Before he could respond or his VC partner could react Tony was on them, first with his bayonet to his enemy's gut and then his revolver, blunt end to the other's head, attempting to be quiet in his kill and to not alarm any others that may be in their patrol.

The head blow didn't stop the bigger of the two antagonists who had dropped his rifle when hit. He came at Tony with his knife drawn. Tony used his childhood defensive skills, grabbing his extended arm and falling back, he pressed his feet to his enemy's chest so as to continue his perpetrator's momentum into a flight over him. The startled combatant landed, crashing his already bruised head into a sturdy tree. Tony finished the task as quickly and efficiently as he was taught in boot camp, and stopped to listen and watch for any additional company. There was none!

He continued his deliberate trek to what he hoped would be his safe haven. After several hours of tedious advance, he approached a sound that he thought might be a river. He had no water, having lost most of his gear during the battle. The river was where he thought it would be, but so were a group of peasants drawing water. In this country peasants could be VC. He waited quietly until they left. It was near sunset and he needed to find a safe place to hide, or should he continue in the cover of night?

He wondered where this river would bring him if he followed it until morning. From the position of the setting sun he figured it was flowing south, but he knew that rivers can wind in ways that one may be turned 180 degrees from their assumed destination. He decided that if the night sky was clear he would use the stars to "stay on course." He silently thanked his South Boston Boy Scout Troop 16 training for that option.

The reconnaissance patrol assigned to survey the battle site of the night before found only four bodies from the 4th Squad. Sergeant Benedetto was not among them, but they assumed that the explosion and fierce fire had incinerated him instantly.

The Commander of the Able Company was thinking about his letter to Tony's family when he was told that a Marine platoon in pursuit of the enemy fleeing from their successful mission came across two Viet Cong killed in the forest about five miles south of the 4th squad's rescue point. They reported that a U.S. Army bayonet, which was found in one of the Cong, was marked with Sergeant Benedetto's name. At dawn two helicopters were in the air; their assignment to find Benedetto.

Tony had walked within sight of the river for most of the night, as the sun rose to his left he felt relief that he was still on a southerly path. Hopefully, if he stayed on course he would reach an American force moving up from the south.

Suddenly he heard the distinctive 'whomp, whomp' sound of a Huey as it came upriver from the south. Excited, he ran to the banks of the river waving in their direction, throwing all caution to the wind. The pilot saw him as shots rang out towards the chopper... and towards Tony. Tony took one in the chest and fell into the slow moving river.

"Let's get him!" commanded the Huey's captain as the doorway machine gunner took out the squad of Viet Cong on the other side of the river. Hovering over the point of Tony's fall into the water, Sergeant Mackney, tethered to the copter, dove in and pulled him out of the river, securing him to his own body as the Huey turned, lifting them simultaneously and rising rapidly into the morning sky as if it was a movement in a choreographed ballet.

Tony was bleeding from a bullet that may have pierced his heart, but he was breathing and conscious, "Thanks for the ride guys," were his only words before he passed out. Mackney thought he knew the name assigned to them for rescue, now he knew the face of his little artist buddy from the 5th grade. He pressed against his wound to slow the flow of blood, hoping that it would be enough.

"Base 101 we have Sergeant Benedetto, prepare for a serious chest wound. We will be there at 0730," radioed the Captain.

The bullet missed the right ventricle by less than an inch but pierced his right lung. The M.A.S.H. unit was able to save his life, but he needed more attention. They weren't equipped for long-term care. He was transported to the hospital in Saigon.

Three days later Tony awoke to the faces of two of his Squad: Diego Martinez, sitting in a wheel chair, casts on his legs and Billy Perkins his radioman, head bandaged and face scarred.

"Hey you had us worried. We thought that you took the easy way out," joked Diego. "Thanks man for saving my ass."

As Tony told them of his unwanted adventure, a third person walked up to his bedside. "Hey little buddy, how did you get into this mess!" exclaimed a face that he knew but couldn't place. "I thought that you would be the next Picasso not some dirt-dog infantryman?"

Tony blinked in disbelief, "Johnny Mackney? No it can't be? I thought that you'd be in jail by now," laughed Tony painfully.

"This guy saved your ass, you know each other?" asked a confused Diego. "He fished you out of the river after you were hit by fire from a VC patrol."

"Well we Southie guys stick together, right Tony?" Johnny said with a wink. "I hear you did some good work out there. You take care. I may not be around the next time to 'fish' you out," Johnny smiled, "I gotta go, just wanted to say hello. You may be heading home soon. Say hello to the guys for me."

Tony grabbed his hand and pulled him to him in a man-hug. "Thank you man. I probably wouldn't have survived childhood if it weren't for you," Mackney smiled broadly at the compliment and left the ward.

When he had left for his next rescue assignment Tony told his visitors about Johnny Mackney from Southie. "He's as tough as they come!"

Perkins and Diego each came from black and Hispanic ghettos and didn't realize that there were places where white guys hated other white guys. They had renewed respect for this "little guinea" from Southie.

During their stay in the Saigon Hospital Tony and Diego spent hours telling stories about their respective "hoods" and of their hopes for a better future when they're home.

"I heard from Keisha, her mother recovered from the coma."

"Did she say anything about the robbery or you?" asked Tony knowing the story.

"I don't think so, but that was last week and she was just coming out of a four-year sleep, she was very weak and Keisha said that they weren't sure if she had brain damage."

"Well, don't worry, you didn't do anything but be a dumb kid, and I doubt that she would remember even if she did see you in the backseat of the car."

"Don't think that I'm not happy that she recovered. If she fingers me I'll have to answer for my stupidity, but I'll lose Keisha. That would hurt me more than doing time."

"Does she know how you feel about her?" asked Tony.

"I don't know. I've been afraid to let her know how much I care. I won't know until we get home. Do you think we'll get more respect at home because we fought in this war?" asked Diego his eyes fixed on Tony's hoping for an encouraging response.

"I don't think that this war will get us any respect. Most people want to know why we're even here when we can't solve our problems at home. We're spending billions of dollars to destroy a country when we have people living in slums at home because we can't afford to give them a chance at a decent life? I don't know. It makes no sense to me," pondered Tony.

Chapter 11

The 1960's, after JFKs untimely death, was a decade of frustration and anguish, and yet there were profound accomplishments. President Johnson, driven by his insecurities and desire to be a popular President tried to be all things to all people. In his first *elected* term in office, he managed the passage of some of the most important legislation since the days of FDR, but was entangled in the macho philosophy of those who believed that the United States had to be dominant and protect its "interest" throughout the world, particularly the financial interest of the wealthy. In time, he found the turmoil of an unwinnable war too much to overcome.

The Buckmans wore their patriotism on their sleeves. Young Jim's grandfather rode with Teddy Roosevelt's Rough Riders in the Spanish-American War; his son James Jr., Jim's father, was an intelligence officer under Ike in Europe. James III would serve his time as a Patriot with the Connecticut National Guard, under the watchful eye and influence of his father, Reserve Officer Colonel James Buckman Jr.

James III lost his student deferment to the pleasures of partying, which led to the repeat of his sophomore year. At the suggestion of his father's advisers, he became a part-time soldier in the Guard. Young James still had to worry about being deployed, but only if his father wasn't paying attention.

His dad thought that Vietnam was a dirty war not to be fought by society's elite. "There are plenty of poor and unemployed kids to send over there to serve their country. It keeps them off the streets, and they can earn a living legally," was his rational.

In reality, it was becoming clear to many that they were the pawns in the chess game of war. Their role is to protect the elite at all cost, including giving their lives. If they do their job they'll be honored for their sacrifice with a medal. And if they return they will continue in their role as the pawns of society.

James hoped to graduate from the university and continue at Yale Law School, anticipating his future role in the family business. Except for the two weeks of summer camp and one weekend a month when he had to play military games, James Buckman III was not troubled by the war but most important, he was not a "Conscientious Objector." His father was proud!

Young James didn't begin to develop a social conscience until he was a law school student at Yale where he met someone who was independent minded, beautiful and who cared about others. Her name was Sharon Polowski, a graduate of Michigan State in Political Science. It was mid-July and they were taking summer courses. Sharon was a second year law student and James was taking courses to complete his first year in law, having graduated from the Business School in December, he would enter Yale Law School in January 1965.

At first she had no interest in his pompous attitude or his politics of self-interest.

"What's important to you?" she asked on their first date, one that took three weeks of diligent pursuit by James to secure.

He wasn't used to being evaluated or the subject of an inquisition, "Being successful, I guess?"

"Hmmm, and what is being successful mean to you?" inquired Sharon in a cynical tone.

"Well we have a three-generation family business and, as the oldest, I'm expected to take over when dad retires."

"And how do you feel about that? To me it sounds like a sentence rather than a goal that would make you feel successful."

Jim, as she insisted on calling him, was taken aback at her response, "What do you mean? You don't think running a multi-million dollar business is achieving success?

Her answer was very succinct, "No, do you?"

"Why do you say that? Not every guy gets to be at the top of the pyramid."

"No, but it's not your pyramid; it's your dad's!" retorted Sharon without reservation and with a smirk that was cute but, at the same time a serious put-down.

Jim took a deep breath. He had never met a girl who wasn't impressed by his status, good looks and wealth, or who was as tough as she was pretty. He knew that his next words would determine their future together. He paused, "I see your point, I'm a product of my environment, but I'm open to your opinions and views, in fact I'm very interested in hearing them."

"I'll bet that you say that to all the girls that you're trying to score," Sharon responded at a heightened level of sarcasm with a broad and sparkling smile.

Jim knew he was in trouble, and noticed that neither had even sipped their beer since they were served 10-minutes ago. "To diverse opinions and open minds!" Jim toasted as he raised his beer mug and clinked with hers. She reluctantly followed his gesture of conciliation. Her smiling eyes gave him a sense of relief that he found difficult to hide.

He wasn't sure there would be a second date and was surprised that she didn't make any excuses but agreed to dinner on Saturday night.

It took several weeks of lunch and dinner "meetings" before he was feeling the sway of Sharon's social philosophy. He was more surprised than she that he began to see her point of view. Her arguments weren't complex or esoteric, they, for the most part, were based on fact and common sense. He was finding it difficult to support a position that was based on selfish goals and the subjugation of others. He thought that Sharon was an excellent debater and she would make an excellent litigator.

Even when he spoke of his family's philanthropic activities, he was countered by Sharon's terse rebuttal, "Isn't it nice that they choose to give the poor some crumbs off their table instead of paying the government taxes to support programs that would provide them with opportunity. But then being in control of the money is power and it serves to allay the guilt of the wealthy... if they have a conscience that allows guilt. And best of all they look good when they get that public service award and they have further subjugated the Have-nots."

"So you think we should have a socialistic society and cater to those who feel entitled?" he countered.

"Listen sweetheart, that is what we have now, only the wealthy believe that they are the entitled ones!" The rest, for the most part, work their asses off to survive! She smiled with tightly closed lips showing her disdain for the question. "I need to study for an exam, so I think I should say goodnight."

Jim knew he had struck a nerve, which seemed to be an unwelcome habit in their fragile relationship, but then she did call him "sweetheart." He couldn't understand, she wasn't one of the disadvantaged and her father was a well-known right-of-center politician. He had lost his bid for the governorship when Kennedy's victory swept a number of Democrats into office, but he was now contemplating a race for a Senate seat. Isn't she supporting his efforts? He wondered what made her tick and why she would embrace philosophies that were so far left of her family's and, of course, his.

His life to date was a series of preparations for his future as head of the family business and caretaker of its fortune. He wondered, was this just a physical attraction and a challenge to his manhood? At first he thought that Sharon was playing hard to get. Sharon had the looks and intelligence to pull it off, but he was now realizing that this was much deeper than any game for romantic conquest and that it was becoming a serious concern to his self-worth. He also realized, reluctantly, that she was making sense.

That evening James responded to a terse telephone message from his father. "How are things going son? I hope that you're not out partying? Give me a call when you get in."

Anxious to find out what was on his father's mind he called back, "Hello Dad. Is everything okay? You sounded ominous in your message!"

"Well, it isn't good news son," he responded. "You have a notice to appear for a physical prior to deployment with your Guard unit."

"Deployment, I thought we had that all figured out. Where's the battalion going?"

"Where do you think? There's only one war going on," was his dad's sarcastic response.

Young James was in a cold sweat, "Can't you do something about it?"

"I'm trying to get you assigned to a unit in Germany, but it's tricky."

"Germany, what about law school and the business?" asked a panicky James.

"Listen, we'll be lucky to keep you out of Nam! Our plans for your future will have to wait!" reprimanded the patriarch. "I'll call you tomorrow."

The next day he came across Sharon in the Law Library. At first he thought to avoid her, but that option was negated by her glance in his direction.

"What's up rich boy?" was her whispered attempt at being funny, but her smile disappeared when he didn't respond. The blank look on his face gave her concern. "Are you okay?" she asked in a voice just above a whisper.

"Yeah, I was just worried about a paper that's due Friday," he answered as he sat across from her.

Not convinced, she intuitively knew it was a lot more serious than that. "Since when do you worry about your work?"

"Do you have time for coffee?" he asked in a voice that was more pleading than social.

"Sure, I have an hour until my next class," she answered with a feeling of compassion that she had never had before for this self-proclaimed man-of-the-world.

Jim told her of his father's call, leaving out the part about a possible fix to go to Germany. He would be leaving Yale and his unit was being deployed to Vietnam.

Her eyes widened at the news, she knew that he was a sergeant in Connecticut National Guard, but she assumed that his service was contrived by his family to keep him out of the war.

"And your daddy can't pull strings to get you sent to D.C or the Bahamas?" she said unable to resist the opportunity to knock the family. "I'm sorry, that was out of line."

He looked up from his downward stare into the cafeteria table, thinking, Damn she's right on!

"So you would be happy to see me go?" he said in a voice that was less than manly.

"No, I don't think anyone should be there, but there are tens of thousands of young men who had no choice and no rich family to keep them out of there, and many of them are coming back in body bags or with fewer limbs than they left with."

His hesitation and avoidance at looking into her eyes to respond, told her intuitively what she suspected was true.

"I have to get to class, I hope daddy is able to take care of it for you," she gathered up her books and left wondering why she couldn't give him the empathy that he sought, but angry that the system of social hierarchy would be at work again.

James now knew her well enough that he began to understand her attitude, but was disheartened that she didn't care if he went to war and became a candidate for a "body bag."

The next morning he got the word from his father that his unit would join a support group in Saigon. It was the better of two evils. It would be in South Vietnam, not in the war zone of the North. His group was in logistics support. They would be concerned with supplying the ground troops with whatever they needed to fight on the front. He had 30-days to take care of business and prepare for deployment. Law school was to be put on hold.

Unlike those who protested the unfairness of the draft by burning their draft cards or others who sought asylum in Canada, James was already in the service and he couldn't go AWOL. He would be prosecuted, thereby ending his law career and possibly his potential role as head of the family business.

His options for avoiding Nam were limited to the power of his father's influence, which was further limited by his Republican Party affiliation in a Democratic Party controlled government.

"Sorry son, I guess the draft boards are running out of the indigent elements of our society, I couldn't get a reassignment for you. I'm afraid that you'll have to deploy with your unit," he said with a sincerely sad tone in contrast to his usually strong demanding voice.

Young James had a light go off in his confused head prior to this call. Sharon is right, we are the privileged class in all our arrogance and self-serving rhetoric. We want to live off the bodies and labor of the poor and disadvantaged who can fight for us, but not share in the prosperity.

"Thanks for your efforts, Dad! It'll be all right. I'll do my duty and pick up where I left off in a couple of years." He wasn't sure whether he really meant what he heard himself say, but he wasn't sure that he didn't.

His father was shocked, but deep down he was proud. He didn't think that his hard-partying, self-centered first born had it in him. "Well I'm relieved that you're taking this so well, you'll be fine, just stay out of the fray." He was also feeling impotent as the head of a powerful family who could no longer fix things, but he wasn't going to let his son know that.

Jim didn't see Sharon for a while due to their conflicting class schedules and their reluctance to initiate unnecessary contact.

After two weeks he had a message on his phone from her, "I just heard, and I'm sorry for my lack of compassion for your plight. Please call me." Her voice was without the usual sassy attitude that she wore like armor when in his company.

He dialed her number but got her answering machine. He left her his best effort at a goodbye message, "Thanks for the call, but you were not totally wrong. Dad couldn't fix it, but you know, I'm all right with it, and I owe that to you. I have to go home tomorrow so we may not be seeing each other for a while. Good luck with your studies and keep up the good work, you may yet save the world!"

Sharon had heard goodbyes before, ending her hopes for a meaningful relationship. They usually had reasons, from "I'm not ready for a long term commitment" to "I've decided to become a monk."

This was different, she wasn't interested in a relationship with a wealthy self-centered, narrow minded pretty boy, so why did she have this hurt in the pit of her stomach and why was there a tear in her eye?

It was 11:30 pm, but she needed to call home.

Chapter 12

Tony decided to stop in California on his way home to Boston from Saigon. Diego had been discharged three weeks before and had invited him to visit. Diego's injuries resulted in a struggle to walk without crutches. Both legs had multiple fractures from his fall. His shattered knees proved to be the deciding factor in his discharge. His bullet wound healed without incident, but his blood loss in the field caused some temporary brain damage, not noticeable unless he was engaged in a long conversation or required to remember an experience, both good and bad. This was obviously a mixed blessing. The legs were still sore but healing. He would be on crutches for a while.

The flight, with a layover in Tokyo, was long and tedious, but that was fine since it was going in the right direction. He had his Purple Heart and a recommendation for a Silver Star for heroism, but he would not be discharged.

He was told by his Commanding Officer that he might not have to re-deploy to Nam. He was being recommended for duty at Fort Devens in Massachusetts as a "Boot Camp Drill Instructor." He wasn't sure that he was cut-out for that kind of drama, but considering the alternative, he might find it attractive.

The Martinez family, Diego and his grandmother, stood at the bottom of the crowded escalator at the Los Angeles airport, not waiting until he got to the baggage claim area to greet him. Mrs. Martinez was a stately woman, not what he expected, at 58 years old she was an attractive middle aged woman. Diego had said that, although a diabetic, she was taking her medication and had become a health nut. She walked five miles every day and had lost 30 pounds. Diego's wide grin at seeing Tony was overcome by her expansive, sparkling white, bright eyed smile.

Before he could step off the moving escalator step Diego dropped his crutches and, falling into his arms, bear-hugged his heroic rescuer. Tony responded by lifting him to the side before they initiated a domino effect pileup of anxious travelers behind him. Mrs. Martinez picked up his crutches before they also caused the travelers to go on an unwanted trip.

"Sergeant Benedetto, it is a pleasure to finally meet you. I'm Diego's grandmother, Carmella Martinez," she extended her hand in a dignified manner, greeting Tony as she handed Diego his means of mobility.

"The pleasure is all mine, Mrs. Martinez," he said with as much dignity as he could muster in the chaos of the mob of scurrying travelers.

"Let's get your bags and take you to our home. You've had a very long flight and I'm sure that you want to freshen up. Hopefully you are hungry for a real Mexican feast," grinned a proud Mrs. Martinez.

"Yes, let's get you home. We'll make you forget lasagna and Chianti, at least for tonight," boasted Diego as he winked his affirmation.

They wanted to take a cab to their home in the Watts section of Los Angeles. They didn't own a car and had taken public transportation to the airport, but didn't want to show their poverty to the man who saved Diego's life. Watts had a reputation for being a tough place to live, and for cab drivers to drive to. They had to ask several before they found a black Army veteran who, seeing Tony's uniform, had empathy for their plight.

As they drove into Diego's neighborhood Tony had a sense of déjà vu having heard it vividly described during those long days of recovery. He even recognized the liquor store that Diego tearfully recounted in his story of the second worst day of his life, being replaced by the impact of the bullet and the fall from his observation perch in that tree in Nam.

Knowing that Mrs. Martinez was not privy to Diego's involvement in the liquor store events of that night, Tony carefully asked, "How is Keisha doing?"

"She's fine. She got a scholarship to Southern Cal. She's studying pre-med hoping to become a doctor," said Diego with some noticeable sadness in his tone.

"Her mother was in a coma from a robbery almost four years ago. They were thinking about taking her off a respirator to allow her to die in peace when she came to," offered his grandmother not realizing that Tony knew the whole story.

"Keisha wouldn't allow that, she had hope," added Diego.

They reached the Martinez home continuing the discussion about Mrs. Johnson. It was as Diego described, a small one story stucco structure, freshly white washed with a garden of flowers on both sides of the narrow brick walkway to the front door. The picket fence, gate and well-kept exterior distinguished it from its neighbors' homes that showed the wear and tear of life in the ghetto.

The interior was sparsely furnished, but very neat and clean. It was a very hot and humid day and Mrs. Martinez had two large fans on at full force in an attempt to make the room more comfortable. Tony knew that this wasn't normal procedure. The cost of electricity to run these fans made keeping cool a luxury they couldn't afford.

Tony and Diego retreated to the small living room, sitting on a well-worn, overstuffed sofa, which shared the room with a wooden rocking chair, built by his dad, and an old black and white console TV. Mrs. Martinez put on her apron and began preparation of their feast.

"How are you doing Diego, are the legs better?" asked Tony.

"They're better than they were, but I don't know how much it's going to improve. I have trouble sleeping with the pain, I can't get comfortable in bed, so I sometimes sleep in that old rocker," lamented Diego. "Hey I'm lucky to be here to complain amigo," said Diego with a sheepish grin, "Thanks to you!"

"Well, I'd like to take the credit, but it was the work of the medic, Bobby Ramos that saved your butt. If he didn't stop the bleeding and carry you to the copter I would be here consoling your poor grandmother, lying to her about what a great soldier you were," smirked Tony.

Diego laughed, "She wouldn't believe you. She knows me too well."

"What happened, did Mrs. Johnson remember you from that night?" whispered Tony concerned that Diego was in trouble.

"No, but the doctors say that her memory could come back at any time. They say that it's probably a good thing that she doesn't remember, I agree," Diego said realizing that he was smiling inappropriately.

"Hmm, that's like sitting on a time-bomb. Are you and Keisha seeing each other?"

"Yes, but I try to avoid going to her house. I don't want to trigger her mother's memory. Hey, how long can you stay in LA? You're welcome here as long as you want to be," offered Diego, changing the subject.

"I have a flight out on Saturday night, that red eye, but I can stay at the base."

"No way man, barracks cots can't beat the comfort of sleeping on this sofa and grandma's home cooking will keep you fattened up so your mama will recognize you when you get home."

"Ok, I was hoping to spend some time with you, if it's ok with Carmella."

"If what's ok?" responded Mrs. Martinez, as she peaked into the room to announce dinner was on the table.

"I invited Tony to stay with us until his flight home on Saturday," said Diego.

"Of course you're staying with us, I have all the meals planned and you're not going to eat at some McDonald's while you're here."

"OK, I'm in," laughed Tony.

They hadn't finished the cheese and onion enchiladas when the phone rang. She knew it could not be good news at 8:30 on a Wednesday night. She answered with a look of concern that was apparent to both Diego and Tony.

"Oola! Rosa what's wrong? Where did this happen? But why did they arrest Mrs. Frye and her sons? Marquette did what? Oh no, how many people were there? Throwing rocks?

Diego and Tony looked at each other confused and anxious at her responses.

"What is it grandma? Is someone hurt? Who is that?"

"Oh my God, what should we do?" Terror started to flow onto her face.

She hung up and slumped into her chair, her lip trembling as she looked up into Diego's eyes. "A policeman arrested Marquette Frye for drunk driving, but he resisted arrest and a crowd of over a hundred people gathered and started throwing rocks at the cop. They also arrested his mother and brother, making the people angrier. There is talk of showing the city how angry we are at the way we are treated," explained Carmella. "I think there will be riots and people will die. They have had enough!" She went to her room, tears flowed from her eyes.

"What is this all about Diego?"

"LA has been ready to explode since the State of California passed Proposition 14, which 'Whitey' devised to weaken the civil rights law in California that the Congress passed last year. The Proposition overturned the 'Rumford Fair Housing Act' and really pissed off the community. It took away their hope of being able to get loans and buy homes and get out from under Whitey's hammer. They're fed up with being beaten and treated like dirt by the city's politicians, and especially by the cops. The people here in Watts don't need any excuses to stick it to 'the Man.' She's right! This is a very bad situation Tony!"

Tony listened intently realizing that prejudice and bigotry still controlled many levels of government and people's lives. The Civil Rights Law, passed as the legacy of JFK, with the force of his surviving brothers Ted and Bobby, and the President, Lyndon Johnson, was just a bunch of words and not a reality for them.

It took over 100 years since Lincoln issued his 'Emancipation Proclamation' ending legalized slavery in 1863, to pass a law in 1964 giving the oppressed black race the same rights as other American citizens. He wondered when the rhetoric and actions of the ignorant haters and their insecurities would stop controlling this "Land of the Free!"

"What do you think will happen?" asked Tony.

"I don't know, but it won't be good. There's a lot of anger out there!"

They could hear the distant sirens of police cars blaring, a warning of the seriousness of this day's events, as they entered their troubled neighborhood.

Chapter 13

The arrest of Marquette Frye; his mother and brother set off a series of events that culminated in one of the most serious riots in California history. Thirty four people were killed and hundreds were injured in the response to looting and damage by those who had lost their hope and their composure and chose to react in unlawful acts.

Diego asked, "Is the value of a television, a sofa, or a chair worth the life of anyone?" To those firing into the crowds of the protesting and angry people of Watts who were looting stores the answer was clear! They were just doing their job; protecting property!

Stores owned by white people were set afire, rocks and bottles were thrown at police, guardsmen and white people driving through the area. By Friday the 13th of August, 1965 much of what was Watts was charred and the streets bloodied. Homes were not attacked, only businesses owned by "Whitey." The rioting, borne out of frustration and reactions to the abuse of authority, could not be sanctioned and neither could the actions that exacerbated it.

"What will we do? This is an angry place. Our wounds can't be healed with words," cried Carmella Martinez, "They'll continue to punish all of us. We've given them the excuses to do that."

"They didn't need any excuses. We're just inconveniences to them and they want us to stay in line and out of their sight!" declared Diego. "You saw it Tony. Why is there so much hate?"

"People hate because they're afraid of those who are competing for survival with them. I learned this growing up in a place that seemed not to tolerate their non-Irish neighbors, but that was not the whole story. Those who hate are the loudest and the most aggressive, but they are a very small part of the community, the rest are, for the most part, apathetic as long as they are not drawn into the situation."

"That's bullshit, there are many people who are haters, and we suffer for it!" responded Diego.

"I thought that every person of Irish heritage hated me and other non-Irish people, but I learned that there were many who just wanted to live peacefully, but would not challenge the haters. I had to challenge the haters and prove to others that I was a good person and not a threat to them. By the time I was in high school most of my friends were Irish, but some were Lithuanian, Polish and a few, Italian.

"It is too late for that, the explosion has already occurred. It can't be put back to normal. Once people hate, they hate forever."

"Diego, I don't believe that, and you don't want the normal of the past. Sometimes change requires dramatic events to shake people into positive action. This black preacher, Martin Luther King, talks of non-violent protest...like Gandhi in India, he's saying don't give 'the Man' an excuse to use his hate. This guy King has the right message. He should be listened to by both sides."

"No, you think that we should just turn our cheek and get hit again and again! All you get is pain and death from not defending yourself and allowing them to abuse and kill at their will. Look at the history of black people in this country. They have listened to promises for more than a hundred years when Lincoln freed them from slavery, and many have given up hope that real change will come and some have died for protesting."

"I can't argue that, but it'll never come if we feed their hate with violent retaliations and we encourage those who are on the fence to join them. We need to be better than the haters, not like them," pleaded Tony. "Look at those who overcame the actions of the haters, like U.S. Supreme Court Justice Thurgood Marshall; baseball Player Jackie Robinson and Scientist George Washington Carver. They found a way to open doors for themselves and for others."

"That's easy for you to say, you're Italian and you're white, and you can pass as one of them, besides Italians hate us as much as the Blacks."

"Yes, there are Italians who are bigots, just like there are Hispanics who hate Blacks and Blacks who hate Hispanic people. Why do you think that is Diego?"

"I don't know, but we just want jobs! We want to live in dignity and be respected by our families. I know that we compete for the same jobs, even the low paying jobs, and that 'the Man' puts us down and keeps us poor so we'll work for nothing."

"So you're going to give up and let those sick, hateful people control your life," retorted Tony, "You need to get to know a person eye to eye, as another human being. We need to show them that we're not to be feared and that you share their need for love and understanding. Yes, there are those whose minds can't be changed and who are infected with hate so deep that it is a disease that consumes them and needs to be isolated."

"You sound like a priest, but I know you too well," laughed Diego. "It would be great if what you say really worked, but life isn't like that. It's cruel and filled with selfishness and hate. Those people who have it all don't want to give up any of it and they will do anything to keep us down."

"And what are you willing to do to change that?"

Diego looked deep into Tony's eyes and said with sadness in his own eyes, "I don't know, I thought that fighting *their* war was going to do it!"

Chapter 14

Sharon called home not knowing how to deal with her emotions over this elitist, James Buckman III that was causing her such discomfort. It was 11:30 pm, but she needed her mother's comforting words. She was relieved when her mother answered her call. "Hello honey, are you okay?" obviously concerned at this late night call.

"Hi, Mom, I'm fine, I just needed to talk to somebody. Did I wake you?"

"No dear, I was watching the late news. Dad's in Washington trying to get support for his campaign and I thought he may have had a photo opportunity with one of his friends in the Senate. Is there anything wrong?"

"No, well I need a mother's advice. Was he on TV?"

"Well I didn't see anything, but I'm sure that he tried... okay, so who is he?" said her mother smugly.

Sharon laughed, she could picture her mother's dimpled smile as she spoke, "You know me too well, but I'm not sure about my feelings. He's just not my type and he has a self-centered attitude that just sets me off!"

"That would set you off! So what's the problem?"

Sharon went into a long story about their reluctant relationship and the possibility that she may be wrong about his convictions, or lack of them. "He's a wealthy Republican, his dad's a banker. I accused him of being for a war that he would not fight in having enlisted in the National Guard to avoid going. Now he is being deployed to Vietnam."

"And you feel guilty about your assumptions?"

"No, not really, he admitted to me in his last voice message that his father was trying to keep him from the war zone, and that I was right in thinking that it was supposed to be fixed. He said that he's "all right with it and that he owes that to me."

"Hmmm, so that's where the guilt comes in? You can't blame yourself for him making the right decision. Obviously, you affected his thinking and his moral character, poor guy," her smile and wit coming through.

"Thanks for the support, Mom," she said with loving sarcasm. "So what should I do? I think I care about the jerk."

"Dad's right when he says that you're your mother's daughter."

"I guess we're both bleeding heart liberals attracted to right wing conservatives," laughed Sharon.

"Maybe it's that womanly instinct that makes us believe we can change a man. It's an instinct that only leads to a life of frustration. What are you going to do?"

"I don't know that answer...yet."

"Well, it sounds like you may have the answer to part of your question. The only part remaining is, whether your instincts will overcome your intellect?"

"Thanks, that's encouraging, Mom!"

"Well good luck, keep me up to date, and remember you can never change a man's politics or his devotion to his sports team!" quipped her mother.

"Bye, Mother, as usual I am overwhelmed by your infinite wisdom!"

"Anytime honey, I'm known in the sewing circles as the poor woman's Dear Abby."

Chapter 15

The Buckman family was disheartened by the prospect of young James being deployed to Vietnam. Their significant power had been limited by their lack of political clout with the Democratic administration in Washington. They were not going to make exceptions for wealthy Republican families attempting to have their sons avoid their patriotic duty. After all, weren't they the flag waiving conservatives who criticized the Democrats for being soft on Communism and reluctant to fight wars?

Mrs. Buckman was particularly anguished by the inability of her husband to keep their eldest son out of harm's way. "Where are all your friends now? You know, those who have the utmost respect for you and would do anything you asked? Are their sons going to war too? I am so disappointed in you!"

"I did everything I could, short of paying off the Secretary of Defense. This is war and I supported it as necessary for the security of our country. What else can I do? The Democrats love the idea that I attempted to use our wealth and position to keep Jim out of there. If I pushed any harder the media would have a feast on my bones."

"So it's all about you and your ambitions. You don't care that our son may never come home alive or in one piece? What kind of a father are you?" her voice trailing and quivering as she left the room.

"Well, Dad what are you going to do?" Jonathan's voice came from the doorway.

"How long have you been standing there?" asked Mr. Buckman, surprised to hear his younger son's voice in such an antagonistic tone!

"Long enough to know that I'll also be in trouble when I graduate in June. I'm prime draft bait, but I'm not going! I didn't get a degree in business to shoot at some slant-eyed bastards in Nam. I'll go to Canada!" he turned and stomped out the room as he did when a child and he didn't get his own way.

Buckman felt both impotent as a father and disgusted at his son's attitude. He had served his country in the World War II under General Eisenhower and although he wouldn't want his sons to be in a war as seemingly hopeless or dangerous as Vietnam, they needed to show some courage. It seemed that his oldest son found that elusive characteristic in his acceptance of his duty and possibly, his fate.

He wasn't a politician; he was a "behind the scenes guy" who supported all of the right-of -center actions as protecting the values that he believed in, particularly those related to his family's status. The Democrats wanted to tax the rich to support programs that only served the poor and disadvantaged, as they called them.

Whenever the subject came up he would go into a lengthy diatribe about the cost of supporting the so called entitled. He called them the lazy, indigents of society who had no ambition and wanted the government to take care of them. He would cite cases like the widowed mother of five from New Jersey who cheated the welfare program out of $2,000, she claimed so she could feed her kids.

And he would tell the story of the guy in Texas to whomever would listen, who committed suicide when he lost his job in the oil fields and couldn't support his family of six. "That bastard cheated the insurance company out of $200,000, a policy he had in his company, by paying the premium for three more months until he knew he couldn't find a job and then he did himself in. The coward knew that the two-year restriction on suicide coverage had expired. He knew what he was doing! Okay, it was legal but it wasn't right and the company had to pay an increase in premiums to keep the plan for the rest of its employees. The investors take a hit every time some scumbag takes advantage of their goodwill, and we are investors," he told his unsympathetic wife.

"And what about their families? Wouldn't you do the same if we had nothing and our children would starve otherwise?" was her response.

"The government has to protect the rights of the productive members of society, people like us. In order for the country to prosper, we need to prosper." He believed that government must protect his wealth and his way of doing business, after all this is a capitalistic society. He believed that the more taxes the government took from him to support Medicare, Social Security, Peace Corps, Vista, welfare, job programs, and of course wars, which are everybody's responsibility, the less he and his peers had to invest in speculative money making schemes that, he believed, kept the country strong!

Jim Buckman was a smart businessman who knew how to take advantage of every loophole in the law and of the incompetence and greed of regulators. He would tell his colleagues, "That's what capitalism is all about, isn't it? You need to be smart enough to work the system to your advantage. That's why we put those subsidies and deductibles in the law. We amend bills with compromises that work for us and they work for our businesses too!"

He lectured his children on the subject of war when they were about to enter college. "We need to show the world that we have the power and that we will not tolerate any behavior that attempts to overcome that premise. Our best interest is only served by assuring the subservience of others in a manner that is both definitive and prosperous to us. History has shown that only the strong survive!"

He told them that only the naïve believe that we can be the kind patriarchs of the world. There's not enough oil or vital resources for every one of the more than five billion people in the world to share or to support a quality of life that we Americans enjoy.

When asked by a right-wing publication about the rational for war he said, "We have to protect our vital resources. We need to try to control those that we don't own, but that we rely on. We need to be sure that wealth and power remain in the hands of those who are intelligent enough to manage them and who have *earned* the right to enjoy them!" He was sure he was right and he concluded, "If we need to fight a war to protect our God-given status, we will do that willingly!"

In the same article he rationalized his anti-social ideology of not spending tax payer dollars on the poor and indigent, but providing unlimited dollars for wars by stating that, "Of course, the American people have to pay for those wars to protect their freedom and show their patriotism to their country. That's where our tax dollars should go, for national defense. It would be un-American to think otherwise. The ambitious will find a way to make it. They'll get educated. They'll learn what it takes to gain wealth and power in this land of opportunity. It's a world of survival of the fittest." He declared, although, as a good Christian he didn't buy Darwin's theory of evolution, but he did adopt its premise.

It was early evening and time for a martini. Young James would be home in a couple of days to get ready for his deployment to Nam. "Sometimes life isn't fair, but it's still life!" he thought out loud.

Chapter 16

It was a short drive from Yale in New Haven, Connecticut to the Buckman family home in Westport, but James decided to spend time alone to contemplate his future. He drove to Vermont, to the family vacation compound in Stowe. James had spent many a winter vacation skiing the mountains of Vermont. He found the brisk winter air refreshing to his spirit and the beauty of the falling crystal-like snow exhilarating as it played across his face in his swift descent along well-worn paths, through the pines.

This late-summer retreat was not without precedent. He had sought out the serenity of this rural Green Mountain sanctuary whenever he had to do some serious soul searching. His life until now was relatively structured, but he questioned whether it was really his life or a continuation of his father's ambitions. He had yet to realize that the answer to that question was to be found in a woman who seemed to have no use for his attitude or his family's basic values.

As he drove along the mile-long gravel road leading to the secluded Buckman log cabin, he remembered his youthful exuberance at the expectation of being here, away from the demands of his often frustrating life as the heir apparent to the family throne. He now realized that he was not cut of the same cloth as his father. He could do without much of what his father believed to be important, but he also realized that his dad had done his best to give him and the family a good life, and that was his choice.

The cabin was made to appear rustic but it was architecturally designed and had all of the conveniences of their Westport home. The walls displayed art of wilderness scenes that were expensive and indigenous to this special place. The five bedrooms had fine New England furnishings. The living room was centered with a gas log fireplace, hardly the amenity of a primitive country cottage.

A three-car garage housed a four-wheel drive Land Rover and four snowmobiles used frequently to explore the deep forest of this undeveloped land, a venture that brought one back to another century when, we believe, life was simpler.

The phone and electric services were left on for any of the family that happened to visit, but James was here to get away from the stresses and diversions of daily life. He was not about to let anyone know that he was here.

He checked out the kitchen and except for two six packs of Heineken and three bottles of white wine, it was devoid of food, but it did have a pound of coffee. Anticipating that he would need nourishment he had stopped at the village market and bought a two-day supply of steak, hamburger, potatoes, corn, bagels and cream cheese, knowing there would be a supply of cold beverages.

Needing some refreshment he popped open a beer and went to the back porch to sit on the white wicker sofa to contemplate his future. The view of the Green Mountain range was highlighted by the glowing red-orange sunset that was a source of his mother's joy whenever it appeared at the dusk of the day. She would say that no matter how the day went, that special view would lift her spirits and make her grateful for the chance to enjoy Vermont's offerings. He now knew that feeling and it made the trip worthwhile.

Jim wondered if he would survive the war. Would he be able to see that sunset a year or so from now? He also wondered if he would act with courage or would he fail to live up to the Buckman name as a courageous soldier in battle. He was never one to stand up for anyone. He avoided conflict and had no desire to be a hero, and didn't want to think about the possibility of pain or death.

He knew of the protest and the draft card burning and, at the time, thought that they should be quiet and do their duty. He had a completely different perspective now. He asked himself many questions trying to make sense of what lay ahead of him.

Why are we fighting a hopeless war? What do we gain from the blood of our men and women, some not old enough to take a legal drink of beer, but are forced into such painful and useless duty? And why are we killing people who have the misfortune of living in the way of our prideful conquest? What if he were one of them, wouldn't he fight to the death to stop such cruel and vicious actions against his loved ones? Aren't we making more enemies than friends?

He was getting more confused with every thought ... and with every sip of his brew. He fell asleep on the porch, exhausted from the long drive and the lack of sleep from the previous night's anxieties.

He was startled to wakefulness by a flash of lightning and the clap of thunder that followed closely behind. He looked around in the darkness, confused as to where he was. Breaking into a cold sweat as a second thunderous lightning strike brought the fear of battle into his heart. He looked around again in time to see an old and stately pine tree split in half by the pinpoint accuracy of the ancient god Thor's bolt of light. Gaining his composure he quickly got to his feet and stumbled inside as the torrents of a cooling summer rain deluged his mountain sanctuary.

Safely within the haven of the sturdy log cabin, he looked to the west where the jagged threads of lightning flashed across the sky, illuminating the canopy of the pine forest and silhouetting the distant mountains. The thunderous sounds of the multiple burst permeated the air. "Is this what war will look and sound like?"

The three-foot diameter pine tree that bore the brunt of Thor's attack missed the cabin but lay across the driveway, blocking the exit of his BMW.

Damn it! How the hell am I going to get out of here? I wonder if Triple A has chain saws.

The storm intensified and James decided to just relax and enjoy the solitude and the sounds and lights of nature's symphony. He'll deal with reality tomorrow. He opened another cold brew and thought about Sharon, I wonder if she'll miss me?

Placing his beer on the hand carved coffee table, he lay his head on the throw pillows that decorated the arm of the imported sofa and fell again into a well-needed sleep, as the last chords of nature's serenade drifted into the distant mountains.

Chapter 17

The red-eye flight to Boston was uneventful, but Tony couldn't sleep. His mind raced with thoughts of Diego and the rebellion of his neighbors in Watts. The national news called it a riot, and it had all of the frustrations and anguish associated with riots. But riots happen in prisons. Was Watts a prison in that its inhabitants couldn't escape its poverty and oppression? Were they there serving the sentence imposed by those who believed in their own God-given superiority?

He could not forget the image of a young woman being attacked by a police officer as she tried to run to safety while being beaten by this "brave" man with his nightstick until she could not, and would not move again, or of the Guardsman who took careful aim at a man running down the street carrying bags of stolen food with his young son trailing, and then pulling the trigger taking him down like an animal in a hunt. Tony thought that the Guardsman would have shot the kid too if he didn't grab his rifle screaming at him that he was a disgrace to his uniform.

The young citizen soldier, startled at the presence of an Army sergeant in full uniform, stood frozen until Diego, who caught up to them, dropped his crutches and slammed him to the ground with the full force of his weight and started beating him about the face. Tony pulled him off before the rest of his squad turned the corner.

Tony ran to the wounded man and his son in the street with Diego close behind using his crutches as best he could to catch up. The young son was holding onto his wounded father crying and screaming "Papa, Papa, don't die Papa."

Ambulances and fire fighters couldn't enter the area without being stoned by angry mobs, a tactic that could cost the wounded man and others their lives. Tony picked him up and carried him to a neighbor's home with terrified people staring out their window at the approaching trio. A heavy-set black woman took the Hispanic man and his son into her home and told Tony and Diego that she would take care of them.

Fires raged everywhere on 103rd Street, burning down buildings that housed white-owned businesses. The mobs didn't discriminate between the good whites and the unscrupulous ones, just as they were not given the benefit of a doubt if they were good people, black or Hispanic, all "the Man" needed to know was that they weren't white.

Tony couldn't stop thinking about the stench of burning buildings; the ungodly screams of victims, and the sounds of indiscriminate gunfire. He had already seen war and innocent victims die too many times for one lifetime.

By Saturday morning there was calm in the streets. The preachers and respected people of Watts prevailed upon the frightened and angry mass of residents to go home. Carmella and Diego visited the homes of victims that they knew needed help.

When they saw him off at the airport, she hugged Tony like she was saying a last goodbye to a son and with tears in her eyes, she asked that he pray for them. Diego, grasped his hand and asked with a deep sadness in his expression of lost hope, "Do you still believe in Gandhi and Martin Luther King Jr.?"

Tony was met by his father at Boston's Logan International Airport. As they hugged he noted a tear in his tough, normally emotionless eyes, "Where's mom?"

"She's busy cooking up your favorite lasagna, and she was afraid that she would break down and embarrass you in public. How are you? Are you all right? We were afraid we lost you!"

"I'm okay, they tried to do me in but you can't beat a tough guinea from Southie," he laughed and his father smiled broadly.

"They say that you're a hero, and that Johnny Mackney saved you? Wasn't he that tough kid from the projects that was always in trouble?" he asked as they waited for his bags.

"Yes, that was him, but he's getting others out of trouble now. He's with the rescue copters, and obviously he's doing a great job," Tony said with a smile and open arms as if to say, just look at me.

"So what are you going to do now, go back to school?" asked his father as he packed his bags in the trunk of his 1955 Plymouth Savoy.

"No, I'm not discharged. They've assigned me to Fort Devens as a drill sergeant. It's close to home and safe."

"I thought they'd let you go, you were badly wounded?"

"Well, I guess they feel I've fully recovered and have something to offer new recruits. The Army says they probably won't send me back to Nam."

"Probably? I don't like probably! Let's get home and see your mother, she'll need some time to stop crying before we can have lunch," quipped his dad with a smile that Tony had never noticed as a boy, maybe because it was reserved for the "man" that is now accepted. It was infectious! Tony responded in kind.

Chapter 18

James managed to get the Land Rover running. He found an old chain hanging in the garage and fixed it to the fallen tree. With the rear wheels of the Rover digging into the gravel driveway he managed to pull the heavy pine enough to allow for his exit, but first he wanted to drive the back road to the pond on the northern border of their land. It would be almost a mile of narrow, barely drivable trail, with deep ruts from erosion, steep hills, small stream crossings, and most likely fallen trees.

The snowplow, which was still connected to the Rover, would move most of the fallen debris. He strapped the old wooden canoe onto the roof racks, grabbed a paddle and started his journey to revisit his youthful innocence.

After more than an hour of recreating the passage to the pond he arrived to see several deer quenching their thirst on its shore. The blue waters reflected the late summer sky, cleared by the previous night's storm.

Startled, the deer bolted into the security of the forest. James smiled at their astute senses and shut off the engine, sitting in the quiet solitude of the isolated, picture postcard spot, taking in the calmness of the crystal waters and the palette of colors and sounds of this special place. He needed this!

The canoe was in better shape than it first appeared, at least it was pond worthy. Gliding across the glass-like waters he had a sense of calmness that fulfilled his expectations. He noticed a black bear with her cubs on the eastern shore. She had few enemies but was still alert for the protection of her family. She would fight to the death to protect her cubs and her territory and no one should attempt to test that resolve. Mountain lions would occasionally try to separate a mother from her cubs but few prevailed to overcome those instincts to protect the next generation.

As he reached the northern shore he noticed an overhanging tree branch that he and his friends used with a rope swing to fly into the pond's cooling waters in the hot days of summer. A worn-out, frayed rope still hung from the sturdy branch, swaying in the breeze, inviting him for one more try at that double back-flip off the far-end of the swing's arc.

"I wonder if it will still hold me?" he thought out loud as he pulled the canoe to shore.

He stripped to his boxer shorts and climbed the rocks to the usual point of departure. He caught the rope on the northerly breeze and tugged on it to test its integrity, then tied the frayed end into a knot to minimize its degradation and give him something to hold onto.

It's been more than 10 years since I tried this dive, he thought, should I be so foolish?

He took the traditional four steps back along the smooth, table-top-like boulder that served as the launching pad, then with an energy that he had thought was lost in his youth he ran to the edge and lifting his legs high in the air at the height of the arc of his trajectory, he let go of the rope. With his feet pointing to the cloudless sky he grabbed hold of his knees to complete his fete, but only did a half a turn before he cannon-balled into water, head first.

Recovering from his less than perfect attempt at regaining his youthful diving prowess, he swam to the shore spitting out the unexpected drink of mountain chilled water.

I guess I was a little short on that one, he thought to himself, and climbed back up onto the boulder.

As he reached for the rope he was distracted by rustling sounds behind him. Looking over his shoulder he saw a flash of the eyes and teeth of a mountain cat moving in his direction. Without hesitation he tightened his grip and ran to the edge, and with renewed exuberance became airborne just as the mountain lion reached the rock. Fortunately his new wilderness friend was water-shy and stopped short, reaching out to claw him back.

James decided there was not going to be a second attempt at immortality and threw his body forward to put the greatest distance between him and the snarling, growling and obviously hungry cat. When he surfaced, after many underwater strokes to gain additional distance, he looked back to see his nemesis taking up a comfortable position beside his canoe.

He's a wise old guy, he thought. "Well, enjoy the canoe, buddy. I'll be back for it, someday," he mused. As he looked at the far shore he hoped that his swimming ability hadn't diminished as much as that of his diving.

Judging from the position of the sun, directly overhead, he assumed that it was about noon. Although, he was hungry he decided not to go to lunch with his new feline friend and began the long swim toward his Land Rover. No hurry, he had all day to make it with long, slow strokes. He rationalized that he needed the exercise if he was to endure deployment to Nam.

By the time he got back to the cabin it was mid-afternoon. The long swim and ride through the forest gave him time to contemplate his future. He decided he would call Sharon.

Chapter 19

Claudia Benedetto was putting the final layer of lasagna on her culinary masterpiece when Richie and Tony walked in. She looked up from her work and gave a broad smile, her eyes moistened with emotion as she opened her arms to give her middle child a loving hug. She was an attractive women just five feet tall with black hair that was fighting off the inevitable grey, and hazel green eyes that showed her love to those she cared about, which was most of her world.

Born in East Boston in 1918 she was the oldest of four children. She had taken care of her three younger brothers since she was 11 years old, her mother having to work in a clothing factory as a stitcher since her husband died of tuberculosis in 1938. Her parents had migrated from Naples, Italy in 1910 hoping to find a better life in America. They found disease and hard work, but were grateful to be Americans.

Tony's hug lifted her off the floor as his father laughed at her embarrassment.

"Put me down you'll hurt yourself." she said in a concerned motherly voice. "Are you okay? Did they hurt you badly?

"I'm fine Mama, just tired and hungry for your world famous lasagna, unless you've already committed it to the entire neighborhood?" He smiled thinking of all the times she had sent pans of lasagna or pots of homemade ravioli to her friends in the neighborhood when she knew that they were dealing with stressful situations.

His best friend growing up was a Lithuanian/American boy who, when he returned from a tour of duty on a ship off Vietnam asked if she would make him a pan of lasagna. He told her that it was one of the things he missed most while overseas. The other things he missed most he was not about to share with Tony's mom. She was thrilled at his request. She was very proud of her Italian dishes.

"So what are you going to do now that you're out of the Army?" asked his mom. "Are you going back to school?"

"He's not out. They want him to be one of those nasty drill sergeants at Fort Devens," offered his dad before he could answer.

"What do you mean, they almost killed you and they won't let you go?"

"Whoa, it's not that bad. They want me to stay here in Massachusetts, at Fort Devens in Ayer, to train new recruits. That's good duty Ma."

"Where's *air*, I never heard of it?" puzzled his mom.

"It's out past Worcester, only about seventy miles from here," explained Tony. "I can come home on some weekends, and I'll get a promotion to Sergeant First Class, it means a higher pay rate."

"But can they send you back to that awful place?" she asked concerned that the Army will take advantage of her son.

"I doubt it, but for now this is the best that I can hope for, other than getting discharged, which isn't going to happen."

"I hope that it's good for you! You always work so hard."

"Go get cleaned up Tony, your mother will have dinner ready in an hour. Your brother will be getting home from band practice soon and your sister is looking forward to seeing you."

"Do you still have to light the boiler in the kitchen to get hot water for the shower? That will take an hour just to warm up," chided Tony. He hated that inconvenience as a teenager getting ready for a date.

"No, we got central heat and hot water, see the baseboards, Tony's dad pointed with pride at the latest improvement to the Benedetto household.

Tony remembered his father taking down or putting up a wall at 9 Douglas Street since he bought the three decker home in 1949 for $4,900. He was always redoing the bathroom or kitchen or wallpapering a room. It was never anything fancy, they didn't have money for fancy. It was just to make things more functional. He was very proud of his home with the view of Carson Beach in South Boston.

When he was very young Tony slept in the remodeled pantry, off the kitchen. It had a high open, glassless window on the wall shared with the living room for ventilation, in this small four-room, second-floor apartment. His sister slept on the sofa-bed in the living room when his, then baby brother had the second bedroom as a nursery. Eventually, when he was in college, they took over the third floor adding the four rooms and two bedrooms to their living quarters.

Chapter 20

The phone rang at Sharon's apartment. Jim was anxious to hear her voice even with its sarcastic tones. He was about to hang up when it was picked up.

"Hello?" It was a man's voice!

"Sorry, I must have the wrong number," Jim said in a weak voice that he was not accustomed to hearing. *"I guess that she's not thinking about me?"* He hung up bewildered at what just happened.

"Who was that Josh?" asked Sharon as she was drying her hair after her shower.

"I don't know some guy calling a wrong number. So you're sure you don't mind if I stay here tonight? I don't want to drive home after the party, I already have one DUI offense."

"Of course you're welcome anytime. Dad will disown you if you get arrested again for drunk driving," advised Sharon.

"Well thanks, I appreciate it and I'll be good," he said with a smirk and a smile.

James was sad and disappointed that he wouldn't see Sharon before he left for Nam. She obviously has other interest, so what's the point, he thought. He would be leaving for combat training next week. It was time to move on.

"I'd better call dad and let him know I'll be home late tonight. He hates surprises. He'll want to give me the benefit of his military wisdom, so I'd better get it over with."

"Hello, Jonathan?"

"Hi brother, what's up? Are you okay?"

"I'm fine, is dad there?"

"Yes, he's in the Library, sorry that he let you down bro, I guess he's not as influential as he thought he was. He's lost his fastball!"

"It's ok Jonathan, I can deal with it, don't worry. Would you tell him that I'll be home later tonight? I'm at the cabin in Vermont."

"Okay, I'll let him know. I'll see you later, drive carefully!"

The drive home to Westport, Connecticut down Route I-91, would take more than four hours. He would stop for lunch along the way and arrive in time for dinner with the family. The long drive would give him time to think about his future, which he seemed to be doing a lot more of lately.

Young Jim arrived at his family's home at 7:45 pm entering through the kitchen door. As he walked through the living room he could hear a voice coming from the Library, which served as his father's office when he was at home. He approached the double 10-foot high African mahogany doors, which were often locked when the old man was working at home.

He heard his father's commanding voice through the doors. "Listen to me, Johnson was supposed to be playing ball with us. Who does he think he is? We got him in office and now he's pushing all this liberal bullshit," the senior James spoke loudly into the speaker phone.

"Jim he's in a tough spot, he's keeping the pressure on in Vietnam, and he's trying to keep his Democratic colleagues happy in Congress. Don't forget he's one of them," came the barely audible reply.

"I know all that and I realize that damn Bobby Kennedy is pushing his buttons. We've got to neutralize that kid. And that King guy is stirring things up with his marches and talk of equal rights. Why they get all kinds of rights without working for them, and we pay for it. You need to get to Johnson, and let him know that we will be supporting Nixon in '68' if he doesn't get on board, even though Nixon is a bit of a nitwit with the personality of a stone."

Young Jim had stopped before testing the door. He was listening to his father's ranting, but was it ranting or something more serious?

"Well Jim, we have all the right wing whacko media talkers out there scaring the hell out of people about these 'traitorous' demonstrators. You know if you tell a story enough times it replaces the truth and inspires the wing-nuts out there to act as patriots and vote for our people."

"Yes, we know how that it works, thank God there are people who'll believe anything to protect what we convince them is their self-interest, but we have a lot at stake here and I'm not sure that Nixon can deliver. He turns off even the conservatives."

Jim was shocked that he was hearing his father talk such nonsense, or was it nonsense, maybe it was the reality of life?

"We're meeting in Washington next Wednesday Jim, I think you should be there. We know that Humphrey is thinking of challenging Johnson in '68' and we wouldn't be surprised if Bobby throws his hat in the ring. Either one would be a worse choice for our purposes than Lyndon. They're both too liberal to be gotten to. We need a plan to head that situation off."

"Okay, I'll be there, is it at the usual place?"

"Yes, but you had better plan to stay for a couple of days it could take some time to get a consensus."

"Okay, and by the way, did we let Johnson know I'm unhappy about my son's deployment to Vietnam?" queried the senior Buckman.

Young Jim's ear pressed to the door.

"Yes, he knows but he said he couldn't do anything without McNamara hearing about it and that would mean that Bobby would be told, but don't worry, he has assured me that your son will stay in the background and not be assigned to a fighting unit."

Before he could respond, the senior Buckman heard the door creak as if someone was trying to come in, or was listening. He immediately took the phone off speaker as he said, "I'll see you next week" and he hung up.

The brass door handle jiggled as Jim tried to enter. "Hello, Dad, its Jim."

The door lock was released from a button under the senior Buckman's desk. His eldest son walked in, a solemn look on his face.

"Hey Jim, it's great to see you son. How are you doing? Mother will be home about eight o'clock. She's at her book club meeting. Maria's making a special dinner for the occasion." he said, in a nervous, uncomfortable voice, as he rose from his fine Corinthian leather chair to greet his protégé.

"I'm fine Dad, but we need to talk!"

Startled at the seriousness in his tone he asked, "Why? What's the problem? Are you worried about this tour of duty? Well don't be I just got off the phone and..."

Young Jim interrupted, "I know. I heard. What was that all about?"

"What do you mean? That was a friend in Washington he assured me..."

"That I would stay in the background, safe and sound!"

"And what's wrong with that? Do you want to be a hero? Maybe you should go to the front and be a hero then you can run for President like JFK. You have no idea what it takes to make things work in this country!" he snarled at his ungrateful son.

"You're right, Dad I have no idea how corrupt you're thinking is and how manipulative your friends are. What's this about neutralizing people with lies?"

"I don't want to talk about it while you're in one of your righteous moods. You don't understand. You're too young. You've had it too easy. It's that liberal bitch from Yale that has you turning on your family's values. You think that everything is like what's portrayed in those television shows, simple and black and white, like *Leave it to Beaver*."

"You're right and you think that everything is 'white.' I suggest that we don't bring this up in front of mom, but you and I need to have a talk and an understanding. I'm going to get ready for dinner," Jim said as he turned to leave.

"It would break your mother's heart if anything happened to you!"

Jim turned and pierced into his father's pleading eyes. "She would be able to join the tens of thousands of mother's who have had *their* hearts broken because of *your* war."

"My war? We need to protect our country from those commies who want to take us over. Don't you care about our country? What are you, a damn liberal?"

"Sure Dad we need to fear those commies in Vietnam living on what they can produce from rice paddies and trying to defend their homes and families from a country that thinks of them as animals. They might get in their long boats and attack us. You know that we instigated this war when we faked the Gulf of Tonkin incident to give us an excuse to invade their country, and once they started shooting back and killing our guys it was easy to hate and kill them too," he continued.

"So you're an *isolationist*, like old man Kennedy who wanted to let Hitler run all over Europe?"

"That was different. The Germans had a powerful military that was subduing all of the countries around them and they *were* an obvious threat to the world, that's why it was called a World War!"

"What do you know about war? I was there during the blitzkrieg that almost obliterated Britain and much of Europe!"

"Yes Dad, and the world appreciated your diligent efforts as an intelligence officer from Eisenhower's deep underground war-room bunker."

"You incorrigible, ungrateful bastard, I've given you everything and all I get is your arrogance. How many times have I bailed you out of trouble and you talk to me like that? Who do you think you are?" his voice trembling and enraged, his face red with anger.

"I don't know, but I hope I find out before I wind up like you, valuing power and money over people!" Jim turned and walked out slamming the library door behind him, as he turned the corner he came face to face with his mother.

Her unconditional love was shown by the tear in her eye and the warm hug she gave him saying, without words, I'm with you son.

"I'm sorry, Mother. Did you hear all of that?" Jim asked in a soft and caring voice.

"Yes dear, but your father isn't a bad person he just has some not so nice ideas about people. You know that he loves you very much and would do anything for you, don't you?" she questioned with a forced smile.

"Yes, and I love him too, but I'm concerned about what else he loves, and what he would do anything for!"

"What do you mean? Does he have a mistress?" responded his mother with an anguish look that anticipated his answer.

"Yes, he has two, money and power!" he said looking into her tearing eyes. "You're the only one who means more to him."

"I wish that were true, son. You're right though, he's consumed by his self-righteous attitude of importance. He wasn't always that way. I remember when he actually cared about people. I believe that he's afraid that someone is going to take all that he is, and all that he has, away from him."

"I'm afraid that he may lose it all because of his attitude," suggested Jim as they entered the dining room.

Nancy Buckman turned to him with a startled look as if he may know something that she wasn't aware of. "What do you mean?"

"I'm not sure. Ask him why he's going to Washington next week."

Chapter 21

Fort Devens, which was located in the north-central part of Massachusetts, encompassed parts of the Towns of Ayer, Shirley, and Harvard. Established in 1917 as Camp Devens and named after a Civil War General, Charles Devens, it played a significant role in conflicts from the World Wars to Vietnam. During the Vietnam era it was home to the 196th Light Infantry Brigade.

Tony Benedetto had the previous unwanted pleasure of training here before he was deployed, in late 1964, to Nam. The "war" was a result of the attack on U.S. destroyers in the Gulf of Tonkin by what was said to be three North Vietnamese torpedo boats. The "incident" led to President Johnson ordering attacks on the North Vietnamese under what was known as The Gulf of Tonkin Resolution. The Incident was eventually proven to be a fabrication to create an excuse to retaliate and invade the country to quell the spread of Communism.

Vietnam had been recovering from the First Indochina War with the French and was seeking its independence in 1954. By 1961, North Vietnam had become governed by a Communist regime while South Vietnam's government was supported by the United States. The stage was set for the classic conflict of ideologies and a war that was as unnecessary as it was bloody.

The military hierarchy uses the expression "lessons learned" to appear they are actually aware of their mistakes and have learned from them. What it often means instead is that they have learned how to do a better job of covering up those mistakes.

The United States government believed that the conditions were right to thwart the spread of Communism by confronting it in this tiny area of Southeast Asia before a "domino effect" resulted in all of Asia becoming Communist. Although this was also the premise of the "Korean Conflict" that resulted in a stalemate at the 49th parallel, the U.S. saw Vietnam as another opportunity to prove a point. The irony was that most of Asia was already Communist and their leaders were doing poorly practicing the self-destructive doctrine of the totalitarian control of people.

Tony had no fixed ideology he just wanted to complete his tour of duty and begin real life as an engineer. While a freshman at Northeastern University in Boston, he had been "gung ho" referring to a Japanese expression for courage and fierceness. Boys who grew up in Southie learned the words to an old standard, "Southie is My Home Town," which told of the heroics of the "Yankee Division" made up of South Boston and Dorchester kids who went to Europe to "win the war against Germany."

Tony joined the Army's Reserve Officers Training Corp, better known as ROTC, during his first year of college at Northeastern University in Boston. He decided against committing to the Advanced Program in his junior year since it was taking up too much of his time, time that he needed for studying since he had to work every night in a supermarket to pay for his tuition.

He was interviewed, or debriefed as they say in the military, about his reasons for not signing up for the Advanced Program, a decision that would have assured a tour of duty in Nam as a first lieutenant. He told the Army captain conducting the debriefing his reason for opting out of the program assuring him that he would go to Officers Candidate School when he graduated. The stern and war-toughened soldier leaned forward and said, "We won't allow you to do that if you don't go forward with this program. We'll make sure that you are assigned to an infantry company."

Somewhat startled at his ridiculous response, Tony retorted in his best Southie wise guy mode, "Well sir, you just gave me another reason not to continue with the Army program."

Unfortunately, when the Army-green bus pulled through the gates of Devens almost a year ago, packed with naïve and scared kids, he realized that the Army had the last laugh. Thanks to the draft he was a foot soldier and his "almost completed" education meant nothing. A year had passed and he was now going through those same gates with an even greater conviction that the Army was not going to be his career path.

He was now a battle toughened soldier as he reported to the commanding officer to get briefed on his duties. It was there that he met Master Sergeant Bobby Franklin. Franklin was a two-tour Vietnam Vet, a head taller and without a warm and friendly demeanor. A southern white boy with blonde hair and a mean looking grin, he spoke in an intimidating low-octave voice. He was the picture-perfect drill sergeant and Tony knew that *he* was not!

"I hear you got out of Nam in just six months? You must know somebody," he drawled as he walked him to his quarters.

"Actually two months of it was in a hospital in Saigon, I forgot to duck," smiled Tony nervously attempting to break the ice with his new mentor.

"Yeah, I know the place well. Is that pretty little nurse Betty Lou still there? She made the stay a lot more pleasant."

Ah thought Tony, a crack in the armor, he almost sounds human!

"Yup, she was there; about five, five, blonde hair, blue eyes, from Tennessee?"

"That's her, did she mention missing her handsome master sergeant?"

"Nope and she didn't mention you either," Tony quipped in an attempt at humor, with a side glance to Franklin, holding his breath until big Bobby slapped him on the back and roared like it was the funniest thing he had ever heard.

"Well here's your luxury hotel suite. I hope you like the special accommodations? Get cleaned up and I'll introduce you to your trainees. They're at mess right now. They arrived three days ago and I've had them crying for their mommies," he said with a satisfied grin.

Tony looked at the rows of bunks, twenty on each side of this long barren room. To his right was the community bathroom/shower, to the left was a ten by ten barely furnished room with a metal desk, a bureau, and a single cot. This would be home for the next 12 months.

"You will shadow me for the next two weeks; you will learn by observation, but you will not comment or speak to me or anyone else unless I ask you to. My quarters are at the far end of this palace. We'll communicate by intercom. Be ready to meet these monkeys in 15!"

With no further ado Master Sergeant Franklin strutted down the length of the barracks to his quarters, more than likely thinking about Betty Lou.

He stopped suddenly and turned, "Oh and did they tell you that these monkeys are citizen soldiers out of Connecticut? You will have your hands full trying to get them in shape, they're a bunch of rich kids and momma's boys!"

"Really, I thought those guys joined the Guard to avoid fighting?"

"They did, but Uncle Sam had other ideas and they are not too happy about it!" His broad grin lit up the otherwise dark barracks. His mean spirited laugh echoed through the room as he turned and proceeded to his quarters.

Well I guess there is some justice in this world, thought Tony as he started to unpack, smiling at the thoughts of his assigned task.

Tony lay on his bunk and closed his eyes hoping to clear his mind of the distractions in his life and concentrate on his assignment as a drill sergeant to a bunch of whiners and misfits. Hmm, he thought, he hasn't been here a full day yet and he is already thinking like Master Sergeant Franklin. The Army does that to you, he thought, no, I'm not going to become anyone's nightmare. I'll do my best to train them so they'll have a chance to survive the hell that they're about to become part of.

The sound of forty men double-timing across the wide plank floors, chanting some incoherent army song, awoke him from his five minute nap. "Time to meet the troops," he said to the empty room, as he transformed himself into some respectable looking level of authority.

Master Sergeant Franklin had them standing at attention and "yes sergeanting him" to a series of loud and intimidating questions designed to humiliate them by the time he entered the barracks room.

"Ok, you low level, ignorant excuses for soldiers, you are privileged to have Sergeant Anthony Benedetto here to teach you to be men and hopefully, soldiers in this man's Army! For the next six weeks Sergeant Benedetto will take the place of your momma and, if you mess up, I will be there for you as your daddy..., and believe me, you don't want to mess up!"

"Sergeant Benedetto joins us from his recent tour of Vietnam where he enjoyed all the comforts that the Vietnamese could offer including a restful stay in a Saigon hospital after he took a couple of rounds of their hospitality. He is being recommended for a Silver Star for his actions in saving his squad from annihilation at the hands of a company-strength force of enemy combatants. He personally took down two armed VC in hand to hand, held off the full complement of enemy while his wounded and well were evacuated, and managed to escape the enemy's aggressive search after his squad left him behind believing him to be dead.

Sergeant Benedetto will attempt to teach you 'citizen soldiers' how to be a good combat soldiers and, most important to your loved ones, how to survive. He will do this in spite of your basic inability to comprehend the seriousness of this endeavor. So, at ease men and let's hear a warm welcome for First Sergeant Benedetto."

Standing at ease, but being far from it, Tony was emotionally overcome by the introduction by this no-nonsense Master Sergeant, who obviously knew more about him than he did of his superior and who showed him a respect that he did not anticipate.

In unison, which belied their inexperience, and on command the men turned their eyes sharply to him and in a loud and unified voice they bellowed, "Welcome First Sergeant Benedetto!"

"For the next week I will be working with the First Sergeant to orient him to the training procedures. During that time, when I am present, you will continue to follow my commands until we reach the point that the First Sergeant is comfortable with the routine. Are there any questions?" asked Franklin.

"It is now 1300, you will be ready in 20 minutes, in full combat gear, to join First Sergeant and me in front of these barracks, for our afternoon jog around the base," With that announcement the Master Sergeant turned and stepped in military fashion to his quarters.

Tony followed his lead and left the open barracks, going to his quarters, to get into his gear for his first training regimen.

The week was long and hot for late September. Tony was impressed at the level of effort and their individual accomplishments that gave credence to their training in the Guard. However, as firmly expressed by the Master Sergeant, "never let them know that they are doing well or they won't have the incentive to improve."

Although Tony believed that only positive motivation will get positive results, he respected Franklin's advice and realized that in combat there is no time for praise, only total obedience to commands and immediate, and decisive response to the situation at hand. Their lives and the success of their mission depended on it.

The highest ranking guardsman was Sergeant James Buckman. Tony noticed that he made an extra effort to lead by example even when dressed down by Franklin. The Master Sergeant used the opportunity to lean on Buckman as a way to show the guardsmen that they are all subject to his wrath if they don't perform. But more importantly he wanted to show them that their leader was buying into the rigors of training without complaint and to an extent it was a challenge to their individual pride.

Tony had heard that Buckman came from a very wealthy family and was 'the heir apparent' to that fortune. He respected him for his effort and questioned his own stereotype of people who had it all. He decided that he would give him some respect when he took over the full training regimen so that his men would not question his authority in battle.

Master Sergeant Franklin had cautioned Tony that his job was to prepare these men for war, even though they are support troops and are not expected to meet the enemy face to face. "We can't be sure of anything over there. It's not a conventional war. Your interpreter may be the enemy; the local policeman may do you in. There is no safe ground and there is no front. These citizen soldiers have to be trained to react without hesitation to any potentially offensive act and to be aware of where they are at all times. They cannot question authority or themselves. Do you understand what you need to do to get them to that point? Do you, Sergeant Benedetto?"

After several days of intense training Franklin recognized Tony's compassion for his charges and knew that, although he had been in battle, he didn't have the assertiveness that he needed to do the job of training men for battle the way it needed to be done...yet. He decided to have an off-duty beer with him at the local tavern in town to discuss his concerns.

"You know that I'm worried about you and those guardsmen. Next week you'll be on your own. I have a new group of recruits coming in that will take up all of my time."

"Yes, I know that and I assure you that I will do whatever I have to do to prepare them, but I don't believe degrading a man makes him a better soldier. I know the military's theory that you need to break a man then rebuild him in character and instill him with a level of courage, but I believe that you can do that with encouragement and support just as well."

"We don't have the time or the training to be their psychiatrist. We have only six weeks to get them ready to fight and possibly die for their country."

Tony countered, "When you break a man you need to spend time to repair his self-esteem. I believe you need to know the mentality of your men and improve their strengths while helping them overcome their weaknesses, and we all have weaknesses."

"That may work in theory, but we don't have the time for all that bullshit. What we can't improve upon they will take into battle as a weakness that may get them and their fellow soldiers killed. When the firefight starts you need to know that your men are all doing their jobs," lectured Franklin.

"But all that breaking of a man's will does is instill fear in them of their superiors so that, hopefully, they will be more afraid to disobey than they are of the enemy, but that doesn't work. They don't fight any harder, some go AWOL or commit suicide because there's no way out," retorted Tony.

"There is no other way to get them ready Sergeant. This method has been used for over a thousand years. It works!" responded Franklin.

"Does it work? How many men actually fire their weapons in a battle? It's something like less than 50%. Those who show courage and act on it do it because it's in their upbringing and their character. The military may seem to make them stronger, but except for teaching them the basics of fighting it does nothing for those who haven't got it in them," Tony continued.

"We don't have time to figure all that out. Those who get it will fight to protect those who don't. For some it will be their downfall," lamented Franklin.

"How was it growing up in your town, were you called insulting names and treated like dirt? Do you think that would have helped you to mature into what you are today? It didn't do anything for me except get my nose broken five times and relocate a couple of ribs."

"I wasn't treated like that, I was respected. You've got to earn respect. I was the High School quarterback and my dad was the county sheriff. He was a World War II hero and he kept that county tight. Look, what you did in Nam, what was that all about? Survival, it was survival, and you learned it on the streets, not from some head doctor," Franklin countered.

"And where did you learn it, not from the streets, but from the encouragement and respect of your peers and your community, who probably feared your dad," responded Tony, breaking a smile to offset any retaliation.

"So what do you do with those weaker guys, let them out of the service; coddle them at the expense of those willing to fight?" Franklin asked.

"Well, when you put them in harm's way they only add to the problem. Maybe being tough in training can weed out those who can't take the heat, but it can never make them capable of fighting effectively. They just become cannon fodder to throw at the enemy's firepower. You can keep them in the service, but not as fighters. Everyone has something to offer. Don't give the behind-the-scenes jobs to the kids of the wealthy and send some poor sap to his death who isn't capable of doing the job or buying his way out."

"So you think the Army should be like those liberal social service organizations? We're here to protect our country and its citizens against those who would like to take us over, not babysit the weak!" chided the Master Sergeant.

"If you believe that then nothing I can say can change your mind. We both know what it's like to be scared and to be in a fight for your life. All the training in the world didn't prepare us for that fear. Our life's experiences and our survival instincts prepared us, and Sarge you need to realize that we're not fighting to protect our turf, it is to protect the wealth and power of those who control our lives! When we were in battle we were just trying to survive and that's what those who devise and encourage wars are counting on, that our instincts for survival will overcome those of the enemy."

"I hope you're right or there are forty-men in that barracks that will suffer for it!" concluded Franklin.

Chapter 22

Christmas was only two weeks away as Sharon was completing her semester's work so that she could spend the holidays at home in Michigan. Her father's campaign for the United States Senate was heating up and she knew that he wanted her help.

Although they had differing political philosophies Sam Polowski knew that his daughter was a very intelligent young woman with keen instincts and good management skills. He also knew that these were capabilities that his campaign was lacking.

Sharon was sure that there would be little rest and relaxation during her month at home but she was willing to do her part, if asked. She also didn't believe that he had a chance to be elected given the Democratic majority in the Senate and a Democrat in the White House.

She still had thoughts of that man-of-the-world "James the third," and wondered how he was doing in the military. She had called his home to get his contact information from his mother, who was surprised to hear from a young lady friend of Jim's that she did not know.

"Hello Mrs. Buckman, my name is Sharon Polowski. Jim and I met at Yale last year, and I thought I would just say hello. Is he still in training?"

"Yes dear, he's at Fort Devens in Massachusetts. I spoke with him yesterday. He says he's doing fine but the food is awful. He'll be home for Christmas but he's being sent to Vietnam on the December 30th. Are you a close friend? I'm afraid I don't recognize the name."

"Not really just a study partner of sorts. We had some interesting discussions on the American political system. We were not always in agreement."

"Oh, are you the one who Father refers to in unkind terms," she said with a subtle laugh.

"I don't know what you mean, Mrs. Buckman?" Sharon asked, dismayed by her question.

"Well, excuse the expression, but Jim took on his dad on the rights of the poor and the middle class and caused him to refer to you as that socialist bitch. I believe you have had a profound effect on my son. Yes, I remember now. He said that your father is a Mayor in Michigan and a Republican, like dad, but that you're a Kennedy liberal."

"I hope that doesn't make you want to hang up on me? I don't consider myself a liberal, I'm more of a progressive." said Sharon somewhat shocked at Mrs. Buckman's bluntness.

"Well, whatever you are you have certainly caused my son to think and act like the man I hoped he would be!"

Stunned by her complimentary words Sharon said, "I didn't think he was listening, but I haven't spoken to him for weeks. I thought that he was angry at my sassiness about politics."

"Not at all, in fact he said that he tried to call you, but a man answered and he hung up. He said 'she's moved on.' It sounded like he was serious. I'm sorry I didn't remember your name. It's just old age, I guess."

Sharon couldn't speak, she had no idea that Jim even thought about her in kind terms. Thinking back she remembered the mystery phone call that her brother had answered. "So it was Jim saying goodbye?" She felt awful and exhilarated at the same time.

"I'm sure that he'll be happy to hear from you, my dear. Let me find his address. Please hold on Sharon."

Her enthusiasm was diminished realizing that he would be home in Connecticut when she was in Michigan for the holidays. She thought that she would at least keep in touch and maybe talk to him when he was at home.

Chapter 23

Mail call in the service is greeted with varied enthusiasm depending on a serviceman's expectations. For many it was a connection to loved ones they hungered to hear from in their isolated environment.

For others, especially during deployment, it might mean a 'Dear John' letter from their girlfriend or, if married, from their wife who had found someone new to share her love and wanted to be free of their relationship. And yet others learned of the death of a loved one or a need for their presence that couldn't adequately be fulfilled.

For Tony Benedetto it was a letter from Carmella Martinez that Diego had been arrested for the robbery of the liquor store that happened when he was very young, and for the attack on Naomi Johnson. She said that Diego told her of the incident. Tony was surprised to learn that it wasn't due to the recovered memory of Mrs. Johnson. It was the result of a deal made by Joey Consalvo that gave up Diego as the leader and mastermind of the crime and as the one that struck Mrs. Johnson down. Tony was shocked and disheartened at the news of his good friend's trouble. According to Carmella, Joey would be eligible for parole next year because of his cooperation with the prosecutor's office.

Tony,

"I don't know what to do, Diego's dad is still in prison. Diego will go to trial in January for this crime. He told me what happened and he admits that he was there, but the prosecutor, who is running for re-election, isn't interested in the truth. Diego says that you are very smart and I should listen to your advice. Can you help us?"

Yours truly,
Carmella

Tony sat back in his chair behind his metal, army-green desk, chilled by the thought of his buddy being in jail and looking forward to facing the white-man's justice in a place that has shown contempt for Blacks and Latinos. The fire and smoke from the Watts 'riots' was still smoldering in the minds of many of the prosecutor's constituents. The exaggerated charges were not what Diego had expected when he said that he was ready to do time for *his* part in the robbery, if he were identified by Keisha's mother.

Jim Buckman anxiously opened his mail, the return address was that of Sharon Polowski. He was nearing the end of his training and had not received much mail except from his family, usually his mother, and an occasional 'glad I'm not there' note from one of his fraternity brothers.

Dear Jim,

I hope that you don't mind me writing to you but I thought you might need some encouragement from your old nemesis. I am very proud of you and your commitment to doing your part in this so called war, even though I believe that we shouldn't be there.

As you probably know I, unlike many, do not blame the men and women who are there believing in a cause, for their participation. Most of them had little or no choice. You probably had a choice and decided to do what you believed was your duty and not rest on the privileges of wealth and power. Having said that, I am very concerned and I pray that you will be safe and return a better man having learned the perils that poor decisions put our young people, their families and our country through.

Oh, and another thing, I spoke to your mother and learned that it was you who called me when my brother was visiting that weekend two months ago. Josh said that whoever it was hung up without leaving a message.

Well I have a message for you Jimbo, there is no other guy in my life, except my dad and my brother. The vacancy sign is still out there! I will be home in Michigan for the holidays, but I hope to hear from you, you have the number. Shape up and good luck!

Your devoted sparring partner,
Sharon

The smile on Jim's usually stoic face caught the eye of Sergeant Benedetto as he walked the path between his charges bunks. "Good news Sergeant Buckman?" he asked.

"Yes Sergeant. A young lady from Yale, who I thought had moved on to better things, just wrote me for the first time since I've been here."

"Yale, oh yeah you were in law school before you got activated with your Guard unit," remembered Benedetto.

"Yes that's right, but I had a ways to go. This woman was my antagonist on every social justice issue, but she had a way of making sense that made me want to challenge her, just to hear her rebuffs. That sounds masochistic, but I realized it was why I was originally so enamored by her, aside from her obvious beauty."

"Yeah, the 'obvious beauty thing' makes up for a lot of other faults," joked Tony as he sat down opposite Buckman's bunk.

"Well, I wouldn't call them faults. She grew up in a conservative Republican household. Her dad was the Mayor of the City and he's now running for the U.S. Senate from Michigan. My dad is also into politics, but he's more aggressive and much wealthier. He doesn't run for office. He just 'runs' those who need his help to get into office."

"I know the type, they're on both ends of the political spectrum," added Tony. "Sergeant Buckman, you're going into your last week of training, can I ask you what you thought of my methods and do you think the men are ready for war?"

"Do you want to know what I really think?"

"Yes I do, there'll be no repercussions Sergeant, but it may help me to improve my training methods."

"Well, I think that all of the men appreciate the respect you showed them, even though you were demanding and relentless on those who slacked or gave you a hard time."

"You mean Privates Berger and Ramirez?" asked Tony remembering having to restrain them, with the help of Buckman, when they lost it and attacked him during the rigors of training.

"You gained the men's respect for handling it decisively and without retaliation, except for that unscheduled flight, after you took one on the chin from Berger. It didn't go unnoticed that you allowed me to deal with their punishment rather than make it a Commander's affair," acknowledged Buckman.

"I'm glad you appreciated that. I thought it'd be more effective and give you the status when you're fully in charge of your squad," explained Tony.

"But to be honest Sarge, I don't believe that anyone can be prepared for war. You did a good Job, and I believe that the men have a greater respect for command when it's delivered fairly and without ego or malice," concluded Buckman.

Tony found it difficult to hide his grin as he thought of his debate with the Master Sergeant.

"The truth is that you were probably much harder on Berger and Ramirez than I would have been," laughed Tony, "Shining every man's boots each day and cleaning toilets for the week was a bit harsh. After all I did make them airborne with a crash landing before you intervened."

They shared a laugh and then, after some hesitation, Tony asked, "By the way, do you know any criminal lawyers on the west coast?"

"Why, are you in trouble out there?" Buckman asked wondering where that question came from. "Actually I do, my college roommate's father has a law firm in Los Angeles. He's supposed to be one of the top in his field. Why do you ask?"

Tony suggested they take a walk over to the weapons qualifying range so they could talk in private. He told Jim the story of Diego's teenage indiscretion and showed him the letter from Mrs. Martinez. "What do you think, is he cooked?" asked Tony, trying to judge the look on Buckman's face as he read the letter.

"I don't know, but Brown, Kellerman & Jones is an expensive law firm and I doubt that they would take a case pro-bono. They represent big time politicians, film companies, and actors. He may have to rely on the local legal aid or the ACLU for a defense."

"What's the ACLU?" asked Tony

"Well my father would have a heart attack if he even thought I was advising someone to use the *American Civil*

Liberties Union for legal intervention. They are considered to be very liberal, but they do work within the Constitution, often to protect Americans from their own government. They were founded about 1920 by a guy named Roger Baldwin, with the intent to preserve the Constitutional rights of people, many of whom cannot afford their own defense. They're funded by members' donations. Sharon is a member. She tried to get me to join."

"Are they any good and will they take on a case like this?" asked Tony.

"They're good, but they deal with people's civil rights and especially free speech under the Constitution. I doubt they'd intervene in a criminal case unless it was related to those issues," advised Buckman.

"How can we find out? This guy is a veteran who served with me and he's a pretty special friend and needs a break," pleaded Tony.

"I'll ask Sharon. Can I use the phone in your office?" Noticing the smirk on the First Sergeant's face he said, "I know what you're thinking and you're half right," he said returning a slight smile.

"Okay, but let's wait until the men are at mess. I don't want to create a problem with their phone privileges. Get back to me at 1700."

Buckman arrived on time. Tony sat on his cot while Jim dialed Sharon's number. Four rings and her answering machine came on. "Hello, this is Sharon, leave a message and I'll get back to you, have a nice day."

"Hello, Sharon this is your favorite right-wing Republican..." The phone was picked up.

"Jim, sorry. I just got in and I heard the phone. How are you?"

"I'm fine and how are you? I got your letter. It was great to hear from you."

"I didn't think you could use the phone while in training or I would have called you."

"Well actually you're right, but I'm in the drill sergeant's office and..."

"Are you in trouble?" interrupted Sharon with concern in her voice.

"No, nothing like that, he's right here and by the way you'd like him, he shares your political philosophy," joked Buckman. Tony grinned in the background.

"He asked me to call you because he has a close friend who may need assistance from the ACLU."

"Really, a drill sergeant who is left-of-center and who has a friend who needs ACLU help? Wait I need to write this down," she responded with her usual sassiness.

"Yes, but before I get into that, I missed you. I'll be back home by December 14th, will you still be in Connecticut? Let's have dinner?"

"You're on Jim. That would be nice, but your drill sergeant must be getting anxious. What can I do to help?"

Jim explained the situation in detail, not hesitating to extol the virtues of Benedetto and his reasons to help his Army buddy, Diego Martinez.

"Jim, I don't know. This doesn't sound like an ACLU type case. It pits two minorities against each other and it's not a civil rights or free speech case. Is there any possibility that Mrs. Johnson will remember that Diego was outside the store when she was attacked? That would lessen the charge to accessory and his age of 14 at the time of the incident, might help to minimize the sentence?"

"Yes, I thought of that, but so far the victim hasn't shown any indication that she is going to regain her memory and she has had a mild stroke that complicates things. And to add to the issues, her daughter and Diego were engaged before his arrest."

"Oh no, did they break up?"

"Well, according to Sergeant Benedetto, the daughter, Keisha, believes Diego's story but is angry that he was involved and that he didn't tell her or name the two perpetrators who almost killed her mother and put her in a coma?"

"Hmmm, I can see that being a problem. Is this guy a jerk or just dumb?"

"I don't think either just that he was young and confused, according to the Sarge."

"Obviously, he needs counsel or he's going to spend some time as a guest of the state of California," advised Sharon. "I'll see what I can do. I'm looking forward to seeing you in 10 days," she said softly and with a sensitivity that was not familiar to Jim.

"I'm looking forward to seeing you too Sharon. You can call this number and speak to First Sergeant Benedetto when you have any information."

"Benedetto? Is he from the Bronx?" asked Sharon curiously.

Jim laughed, "No, he's from South Boston, one of the few Italian survivors of an Irish dominated community."

"Oh, okay, he must be pretty tough. Did he kick your butt?" chided Sharon.

"Well, he's tough, but not in that way. I wouldn't be calling you for a favor if I didn't consider him to be a friend," answered Jim with a seriousness to his voice that caught Sharon off-guard.

"In that case, I'll do my very best. Tell him that I'll be back to him in a couple of days."

"Thank you, I do appreciate it, and of course you," responded Jim in a quiet voice.

When he looked around he saw a wide grin on Tony's face. "What? You must have a girlfriend back home," remarked a somewhat embarrassed Buckman.

Tony's face grew solemn, "Not anymore!" as he got up from his cot and opened the door for Jim. "You can still make mess, I hear they're serving yesterday's chicken," he said, cracking a half smile.

Buckman left, knowing that he had struck a nerve, something that he was becoming adept at. Except for the problem that his west coast friend was having, they had never discussed their personal love lives with each other. Jim felt badly about his intrusion into the Sarge's personal domain, but soon overcame that feeling with thoughts of seeing Sharon.

Tony turned on his radio in time to hear the final verse of the Beatles song "Michelle," he thought, sometimes you can't get away from reality!

Chapter 24

Mrs. Martinez was happy to hear Tony's voice when he called, but she soon became solemn when told that the situation wasn't going to be easily resolved. He told her that he wouldn't give up and that there's always a possibility that Diego would be acquitted of the more serious charges.

"Acquitted, Diego's a good boy. He didn't do these things that they say. I'm very angry that he was even with those drug-heads, but he was young and he thought that I needed his help. What am I going to do?" she cried.

"I don't know, but he needs you to be strong. I'll do whatever I can to help him. What's his bail?"

"It is too much for me to get. It's $25,000 cash bail. I don't own this house or I would borrow against it...or even sell it if I could," despaired Carmella.

"I have some money, but not that much. It may be better to use it to pay a good lawyer," offered Tony.

"No, you can't do that, I will not allow it and Diego would not allow it. We will find a way...we will," Carmella's voice tapered off as she finished her thoughts, "Just be there as his friend. He needs a friend."

"I will! Don't worry, he has a friend, and I'll be out there in two weeks. I'll be on leave for thirty days. I'll come out as soon as I can."

"Aren't you going home for Christmas? We don't want to interfere with your life. Your family will be disappointed if you're not home for Christmas. We will be fine."

"Don't worry, I'll be home for Christmas, but I'll come to see you and Diego first. My mom would be angry with me if I didn't take care of a good friend in need. That's what Christmas is all about! Isn't it?"

"You're a good boy Tony. Thank you! I will tell Diego. He needs some good news."

"Now you take care of yourself. We do have some options. I have friends working to see what we can do. I'm looking forward to your cooking," he said with a smile in his voice.

Tony hung up feeling that their options were minimal and not likely to work without Naomi Johnson's memory returning.

Chapter 25

"Since our last meeting in August, Johnson has been told that he wouldn't get the support of our organization in the '68' election," reported Jim Buckman Jr. to the six prominent businessmen seated around the ornate mahogany conference table in the Washington, D.C. law office of Harold, Larkin & Watkins.

"Is he aware that we'll put our efforts and financial power toward the election of Dick Nixon?" asked John P. Carlton, CEO of American Defense Industries, Inc. His declared war on poverty made people think that he has a heart. Thank God Vietnam has derailed that effort. The more money we spend on social programs, the less profits there are to be made!"

"He *is* aware and he knows that if he succumbs to the pressure of ending the Vietnam operation before the election we will air his dirty laundry and destroy his reputation. One suggestion is to stir the public into thinking that Kennedy's assassination in Johnson's home state may not have been a coincidence," answered Dale Watkins, his eyebrows raised at the thought of such a devastating tactic.

"Yes, he would be destroyed by the innuendo alone. Johnson is paranoid about the Kennedys and the legacy of JFK. He wants to be remembered for civil rights and social programs. He disliked Kennedy. He wants that popularity for his own, but he isn't young and handsome with a beautiful wife and a young family. He can't overcome the image that the American people admired," offered Donald T. Peters III, CEO of Continental Trust Corporation. I think Johnson is vulnerable."

"What do our intelligence people think he'll do under this kind of pressure? He has it coming from all sides. I almost feel sorry for the poor bastard," smirked Dale P. Watkins, counsel and host for the group.

"Well, he's a fighter and he has a number of allies in Congress who want him to win another term, but they also rely on our financial support and that of our colleagues. We'll get the message out that they'll go down with him if they resist our efforts," responded retired Air Force General Bertram Obersham, now on the board of directors of Consolidated Aeronautics Corporation.

"Gentlemen, do we have a plan or is this a discussion of personalities and of the games that we are going to play and hope for the best results?" All eyes turned to the opposite end of the table where, Thomas 'Bulldog' Masters sat puffing on his Cuban cigar. Masters was the chairman and major stockholder of the International Petroleum Conglomerate.

Although not a Georgia bulldog, he wore the "Bulldog" tag proudly since his college days at Texas A & M when he was known to hold-tight a tackle until his man was slammed to the ground. What he lacked in finesse and style he made up for with his 6-foot 6-inch, 320 pound frame and the viciousness with which he applied it.

Masters was an impatient man. He wasn't interested in details, just results. He considered his colleagues obsessed with the intellectual aspects of the situation and not focused on the required action. "How are we going to get Nixon elected? He's about as popular as the plague. I'm pretty sure that he'll play ball, he wants that office more than he wants love or money."

"I doubt that he can beat Johnson, even with the demonstrations. Johnson can turn that around by ending the war just before the election. We need to scare Lyndon into not running," offered Buckman.

"Yes, but Humphrey or Bobby Kennedy will probably run on the same platform, they're already taking the side of the anti-war demonstrators. Nixon has to take up that cause as the outsider who will end the war, if he's to be elected he needs to steal their thunder. Once he's in he'll adopt our policy of victory at all costs, or suffer the consequences," suggested Peters.

"I think that if Johnson were out of the race there would be so many liberal Democrats running before the convention that the party will be split four ways to Sunday. Whoever emerges will have to put it back together, and we have to make sure that they can't easily do that."

"I like it gentlemen! Now you're talking a game plan that can work. Let's get on it!" commanded Masters, but right now let's go to dinner!?

Buckman chaired the group but much to his chagrin, it was obvious that Masters was its leader.

As they gathered their respective notes and brief cases to leave for dinner at an exclusive Washington club, General Obersham approached Buckman. "How is your boy doing? I understand that he'll be deployed to Nam next month?"

"Thanks for asking Bert. He's doing well. He'll be home next week to begin a short leave before he's deployed. It will be good to have him home for Christmas," Buckman answered, his eyes on the papers he was stuffing into his briefcase.

The lack of eye contact from his friend concerned the General, "Is there something wrong Jim?"

"No, everything's fine. I'm just a little tired. I'll have to miss dinner with you and the boys, Nancy asked that I be home tonight, if possible."

"Of course, you need to spend some time with your family, and when a wife asks it's as good as a command," smiled the General. "I'll see you next month. I guess we're meeting here?"

"Yes, that's the plan, and thank you Bert for your concern. Can I ask you one favor?"

"Anything Jim, we go back to the Eisenhower War Command days. I remember you having my back on more than one occasion. What can I do for you?"

"I'm worried about my son. Do you know his Commander in Saigon? He's with the logistics support group."

"I think that General David Albertson is in that position. He's a great guy, West Point, highly decorated and a personal friend. I'll give him the word to keep an eye on young Jim."

"Thank you again Bert. He doesn't want any special privileges, so it needs to be discreet, but I would appreciate it if he stays in Saigon until his term of duty is up. His mother thinks that I failed him, him being deployed and all."

"I understand, it will be a 'clandestine operation,' he won't know that his dad is watching over him from afar," winked Bert.

"I better catch up with our friends, Masters might give me KP duty for being late."

"He is a bit of a character, but a good ally to have in this kind of project," offered Buckman as he shook Bert's hand. "Let me know if anything develops during dinner."

"I will Jim, but you'd better get moving if you want to make your flight to Hartford tonight."

Chapter 26

The call from Sharon didn't come until the end of the week. She did some serious research and had spoken to the California ACLU chapter about representing Diego.

"They're really trying to find a premise to get involved, Sergeant," reported Sharon with regret in her voice. "But it doesn't look good. The case needs to fall within their purview of protecting the Constitutional rights of the individual."

"I appreciate your efforts, Ms. Polowski. What do you think he needs to do?"

"Please call me Sharon, Sergeant."

"...Only if you call me Tony, Ms. Polowski."

"Okay, Tony! My opinion, for whatever it's worth, is that he needs to get a good criminal lawyer and he needs to get out of jail, or at least be put into protective custody, immediately! My contact in Los Angeles cautioned me that Diego is in serious danger in prison as a Hispanic accused of nearly killing a Black woman in Watts. He said that Watts may explode again!"

"Damn, that can't happen! Are there any alternatives?"

"Well, the feedback I get is that the politicians are only focused on the prosecution of your friend to get the black vote. They figure that they have a good share of the Hispanic and that a cut and dry case, as they see this one, will not alienate too many of them."

"I think they're wrong, I was in Watts during the riots and the hate for the white establishment is the only thing that binds these two cultures together," answered Tony.

"Well, the one thing that we might be able to work with is that Diego is being accused by another Hispanic, a man who has little credibility and is a convicted criminal. The prosecutor wants this to be a quick and easy conviction before the election next April. Diego's best bet is to have this process slow down. In time, it could lose its political value and time also allows for a better opportunity for Mrs. Johnson to remember, but your friend shouldn't be left in that environment."

"I understand, I've contacted a bail bondsman in L.A. I have $10,000 saved that I can put up for his bail with the bondsman. I was hoping to use it to hire a lawyer, but if he doesn't get out of there soon, it will be a problem. I'll be out there on Monday."

"Please don't hesitate to call if there is anything I can do to help. I'll continue to pursue the ACLU angle."

"Thank you for all you've done already. I can see why Jim is so attracted to you."

"Really, did he say that? I can't be sure what he thinks. He isn't there, is he?" she asked hopefully.

"He's at his bunk packing up his gear, hold on."

Tony called Buckman to his office, "You have a phone call, Sergeant," he said with a smile that was reflected by Jim as he stumbled over his Army issue duffle bag to get to the phone.

"I have to go catch Master Sergeant Franklin before he leaves. I won't be back for 45 minutes, or more, if anyone's looking for me," Tony said with a parting wink and a smile.

"Thanks Sarge, what did Sharon find out?"

"She'll explain, but it wasn't good," lamented Tony as he closed the door behind him.

Tony wanted to catch Franklin before he left for his 30-day leave and thank him for his advice and support. He was not unhappy with his performance in his first assignment as a drill sergeant. He had learned something about people, and more important, about himself.

He spotted his mentor going towards the Devens bus for a ride to the Hanscom Airbase and went into a jog to catch up, "Hey Sarge," he yelled as he ran.

Franklin turned and spotted Tony sprinting towards him from across the Parade Grounds. "Hey what's up, Tony, are the troops after you?" he laughed as Tony reached him.

"No, didn't you hear? They all love me," he smiled, "but the CO told me that you're volunteering for another tour in Nam. Are you okay? Did you get hit in the head?"

"No, I'm fine, but I need to do this. There's unfinished business there and I'm totally bored with this 'potty training'

Job. I know what you think, but we're on different wavelengths when it comes to this war."

"I know that. I respect your position and what you're doing. I want you to know that although we disagree on certain issues, I'm grateful for your friendship and mentoring. It made me think, and realize, that there are many ways to achieve a goal and my way might work for me, but it isn't the only way," Tony explained as they continued walking towards the bus.

"You take-care Bobby, and take heart in that you may have to rely on soldiers that I trained to protect your ass!" cautioned Tony with a broad smile and an extended hand.

"That's very comforting. I'll sleep much better knowing that," Franklin said as he shook his hand and boarded the bus, turning to give him an informal salute, not required by their respective ranks.

As he returned the gesture, Tony thought, These southern boys are still fighting the Civil War! They don't realize they're just pawns in a game of chess. Bobby Franklin's a good guy and a very good soldier. I hope he survives this third tour into that hell hole!

Jim Buckman was sitting in Tony's office when he returned.

"What time are you leaving for home, Jim?"

"I'm taking the five o'clock bus into South Station, and the eight o'clock train to Westport. I have a couple of hours to kill. Have you had lunch?" Jim asked. "I'll fill you in on a strategy Sharon and I discussed to help your buddy out of his troubles."

"Sounds good! I don't think the mess hall is serving lunch at 2:30 p.m. Let's go downtown. There are a couple of good restaurants in Ayer. I'll commandeer a Jeep. The base is almost deserted," offered Tony.

On the ride into Town Jim reiterated his conversation with Sharon, some of which Tony had already heard. Jim re-emphasized the concern for Diego's safety while in the County Jail and the need for adequate counsel.

"Sharon confirmed that the $25,000 cash bail does not have a 10 % fee to the county." Jim said as they drove.

"What does that mean?" asked Tony," and why do we care?"

"Well, when you post bail you either put up the cash amount or you engage the services of a bail bondsman who you pay 10% of the bail amount to, and they guarantee the balance to the court, or you can deal directly with the court and put up the full cash amount, but in some court jurisdictions they also will charge 10% for that service." instructed Jim.

"And LA doesn't charge that 10%?" responded Tony.

"That's right, but if Diego didn't show for any of the court required appearances he would be arrested and the bail would be forfeited," continued Jim.

"So how does that help Diego? He doesn't have $25 never mind $25,000?" quizzed Tony as they arrived at the restaurant.

"How strong do you feel about Diego's integrity? Do you believe his story?"

"I'm 100% sure, not only of his story but of his integrity, but I'm not going to be on his jury."

"No, but we want to make sure he gets that far," answered Jim in a very serious tone."

"You're serious about that being an issue?" responded Tony, "I know Sharon was concerned, but do you think the racial issue may do him in?"

"Yes, I've spoken to Jake Kellerman's dad, the attorney in LA?" I didn't think you'd mind me using your phone for that call. He verified that this trial could spark another riot and, that given the racial population of the County Jail, Diego is in serious trouble.

"But wouldn't the District Attorney isolate him under protective custody?"

"Normally yes, but Kellerman's feeling is that unless he has a strong attorney representing him, the DA will only do the minimum necessary and not spend any of his budget on security."

"So what do you suggest? I told Sharon I have a little over $10,000 in savings. How far can we get on that?"

"As I said earlier, Sharon and I discussed a strategy that could work. We get Diego out on bail and delay the trial as much as possible, hoping to bring Mrs. Johnson's memory back about that night, or find a way to discredit Joey Consalvo's story. It's also wise to have the trial after the elections so that it's no longer important to the prosecuting DA's career."

"That sounds good, but isn't Diego in more danger being out on the street than in jail?"

"Yes, unless he can be hidden away in a secure place. The court would have to approve, of course, but it would be confidential and any documents would be sealed as to his location."

"I still don't understand how these things can be done," puzzled Tony.

"Well here's the deal. When I'm home, I'll go to my bank in Westport and draw a bank check for $25,000 for the cash bail. It will be made out to the Los Angeles County Court."

Tony looked Jim in the eye, startled at what he was saying, "Are you crazy? You don't know this guy. Twenty five thousand dollars is a lot of money. Most people don't make that much in a year!"

"Well I'm not qualified to testify as to my mental health, but one thing I do have is money and it's not going to do me much good for the next year or so. This is a loan, unless your buddy skips town, then I will have him pursued by some big burly bounty hunter and returned to jail."

"Why would you do that?"

"That is only part of the strategy, I will do this loan if you will engage Kellerman's firm to represent him. They're very good at what they do and their presence will sober up the DA as to his actions. They don't expect Diego to have the money for a decent defense and are counting on this case being highly visible."

"But I don't have that kind of money, Jim? You're being more than generous and very trusting to even offer your financial help, but I hope that you're not doing it to impress your girlfriend," advised Tony.

"She doesn't know about that part of the plan. She'll think that you and his grandmother raised the bail money."

"Then what's your motive, Jim, I know you're a nice guy and I know you're wealthy, but it's not your battle."

"I'm not sure Tony, but I've learned a lot about myself in the last few months and I need to do this for me."

"Is this some kind of attempt to make up for the sins of your father?" Tony said without thinking, and regretted it immediately. "Sorry that was rude and insensitive."

"It's okay, it's the drill sergeant in you!" smiled Jim making light of it. Stop trying to figure it out and go with it or you'll regret not doing what you can for your friend."

"How much money are we talking about for the lawyer?"

"Well, they don't do pro-bono, as I told you before, but I'm very close to his son Jake and as a favor to me he will start action immediately for a retainer of $5,000."

"But this could cost more than that, especially if the case goes on for months, right?"

"No, not necessarily, the $ 5,000 will go far if he succeeds in getting the trial delayed for a year or so."

"What is the chance that he can do that, and where can Diego hide that won't be too expensive?"

"The chances are excellent! All of the County Judges respect Kellerman and several went to law school with him. They'll honor a valid argument for a delay. As for the hideaway, Jake Kellerman has a place in the Santa Anna's that is remote, that he's offering, but we won't have security for a while. His dad will try to get someone assigned to that task by the court, but that isn't a sure thing."

"Okay, I'm in, but I still think that you're nuts!" joked Tony as he extended his hand across the table. "I'm wondering what you have on your roommate Jake and his dad for them to do this?"

"Let's just say that Jake owes me big time!"

"Okay, but maybe you should keep that favor banked until you need it personally."

"Don't worry there's still a significant balance left in that bank," laughed Jim.

"I think that I don't want to know any more!" smiled Tony. "I just hope that you never need him to defend you. Payback is a bitch!"

Chapter 27

Jim Buckman senior's flight home wasn't until 10:30 pm. He had scheduled a 6:00 pm meeting that he wanted to keep private from his fellow corporate "conspirators." He took a cab to a small church on the south side of D.C. He was invited to a meeting by a former Army buddy he had worked with in the Intelligence service.

Retired Colonel Jeffrey Barnet was a well-known politician in his Alabama County. He was also suspected of being a high ranking Ku Klux Klan official. Buckman was not, by his own assessment, a prejudiced man, but he didn't like the idea of the Civil Rights Law or giving "coloreds," or anyone else special treatment, as he saw it. Jim rationalized his politics and his actions as doing what needed to be done to preserve the rights of the *capitalistic system* of government in the United States.

The democracy part of the Constitution was just a means to an end, the end being to reward those who take advantage of the opportunity that freedom gives them. The fact that the wealthy control the power to govern was an obvious benefit to be had by those tough enough and rich enough to do what had to be done to get their people into power, and that took money!

Buckman was greeted at the door by his old friend. "Glad you could make it Jim. There are a few people I want you to meet in the office. How are Nancy and the kids? How's young Jim doing?" he said in his slow southern drawl that didn't allow for interruption.

"They're all fine, Jeff, and how about your family, is your boy still in the ministry?" asked Jim politely.

"Yes, in fact he's here, this is his church. You haven't seen him since he was in high school," answered the Colonel as he led Jim to the rear of the church.

As he opened the door to the meeting place, Jim looked into four stoic faces barely visible in the subdued light, as they responded to his entrance.

"Boys I want you to meet my good friend and former Army buddy, Jim Buckman. He's the only Yankee I ever trusted," said the Colonel, qualifying their friendship and his presence.

Jim smiled as he looked around the room trying to assess their facial expressions for acceptance. "Nice to meet you gentlemen," was his only response until his friend began the personal introductions of those sitting around the table.

"This here is Bailey Goodwin. You two have something in common. Bailey's the owner and President of our local bank back home," Goodwin nodded, not bothering to get up or reach for Jim's hand. He was not impressed by big city bankers, especially from the northeast.

A little concerned about the relatively cool reception Jim's host went on to introduce his son Jeff Jr. who had the smile and personality that distinguish a true man of God.

"Hello, Mr. Buckman, it's been a long time since we last met," as he took his hand in a friendly gesture.

"Yes, it has Jeff, I see that you're doing well in your calling," responded Jim with a sweep of his hand as if to say, *a*ll this being yours.

Jeff senior encouraged by his son's learned diplomacy continued, "Next to young Jeff is Hank White. Hank's the Sheriff of our county and a solid citizen!"

Hank smiled and shook Jim's hand. "Thank you for taking the time to meet with us, sir," he said as he glanced at banker Goodwin.

"Jeff and I go back a long way. At one time we had only each other to rely on in some very serious situations," offered Jim referring to their covert operations during the "Great War."

"And finally, I want you to meet one of the finest Southern gentlemen you will ever meet, George Wallace, the governor of our fine State of Alabama," emerging from the dark shadows of the far end of the table was a face familiar to Buckman, but he was shocked to see him here. Yes, he was told by his friend, the Colonel, that this meeting would be about getting support for Wallace's presidential campaign, but he didn't expect him to actually be here.

The Governor rose from his seat and walked around the table to greet Buckman face to face. "The Colonel has told me a lot about you. Thank you for making time for our little group," Wallace held Jim's right hand between both of his, in a warm gesture of a friendship that he hoped would develop.

Still somewhat off-balance from this unexpected scenario, Jim responded. "It's a pleasure to meet you Governor. The Colonel has also told me a lot about you."

"I hope that most of it was good!" he said with a wide grin.

"It was all good, Governor. What can I do for you gentlemen?" asked Buckman as he looked around the room, still trying to compose himself.

"Jim, we are all here to seek your help in getting George elected president in 1968. After telling Governor Wallace about your ability to make things happen, while you stay out of the limelight, of course, he insisted on meeting you," explained the Colonel.

"Yes, Jim," interrupted the Governor. "Jeff here tells me that you're not very happy with Johnson's liberal leanings, I believe I can offer the American people an alternative to him as a Democratic opponent from the South. I'm sure that you realize that this Civil Rights Law is going to tear up our beloved South. The people of the region didn't realize that Johnson, a man from the Deep South, was going to act like those carpet-bagging bastards that ruined our country after the war. State's rights are an important part of the Constitution, we're not going to stand for any more intrusion on our rights to govern as we see fit."

"I empathize with your cause, but what can I do to help?" responded Jim, remembering the television image of the Governor Wallace standing in the doorway of a southern white-only school, surrounded by Alabama state troopers blocking the entrance to a little black girl. Jim Buckman was a lot of things, but he didn't think that he was a bigot and he was disgusted by his host's past actions.

But he also saw an opportunity here. If Wallace was a viable candidate for the Democratic nomination, he would split the party during the primaries and affect the southern vote against the emerging Democratic candidate nominated by the Convention in Chicago in 1968. This was a tactic that could prove favorable for Nixon. He knew that Wallace had a better chance at becoming Pope than being elected President of the United States, but why not use him to help get Nixon elected?

"Well Jim," added Colonel Barnet, "what do you think, can you help us restore the Republic?"

"Let me think on it Jeff, but I would like to know the Governor's positions on some issues."

"Of course Jim, ask me anything that you want to know," offered Wallace.

"Well Governor, what is your position on the war in Vietnam?"

"That's an easy one, I believe that we need to stop the communists from expanding their tyranny to the free world. We can fight them there now or fight them here in the future," lectured Wallace.

"That's a good answer, we're on the same page Governor," agreed Buckman. "But I'm concerned about your traditionally Democratic leanings for increased taxation of corporations and the regulation of banks. What do you think of capital gains taxes and new regulations on banking practice?"

"The boys in this room can tell you that I am conservative on those issues. The government needs to stay out of the lives of fine upstanding people and their businesses, like Mr. Goodwin here. He runs a bank that is an important benefit to his community and he should be able to run it as he sees fit to serve that community. As for capital gains, it's the incentive for a business to grow and prosper and that means more jobs for people and I'm for the people."

Buckman listened and started to believe that George was no more a Democrat than he was a shoe salesman. "I like what you're saying, Governor. Let me think on this for a few days, but I may be able to help." Buckman didn't really care how Wallace answered his questions, but he wanted to seem that he was serious about his involvement.

"That would be good, Jim. We would appreciate any help you can give us to turn this country around."

"We believe that we have strong support in the *Bible-Belt* churches, right Jeff?" the Colonel said deferring to his son to validate his statement."

"Yes, there is a movement that is gaining momentum in the South, in many of the white Christian churches. They are united against the interference of government into their religious lives. Christianity is a white man's religion. The blacks have their voodoo cults and witchcraft. There is a large constituency out there in God's houses throughout the South," young Jeff preached as if addressing his congregation.

Buckman couldn't help thinking how his wife would be outraged at this sick rhetoric, but business is business and his participation would be for a purpose that she wouldn't understand.

"If I decide to help the Governor, it would have to be behind the scenes, a good distance behind the scenes," emphasized Buckman. "I can raise money and help you with your strategy, if you wish, but if my name ever came up I will have to deny any involvement. My business requires that I remain visibly neutral on political issues."

"We understand! Right boys?" assured Colonel Barnet.

"I don't know, are you ashamed to back the Governor Wallace, Mr. Buckman?" the words came from the formerly silent banker, Bailey Goodwin.

Buckman was taken aback by this blunt statement but responded. "No, Mr. Goodwin but I have a lot of commitments that require my public objectivity on these matters."

"I know that Jim is trying to catch a flight home tonight, thank you again for meeting with us," interrupted his old Army buddy, attempting to cut short the rude local banker before he killed any chance of Buckman's assistance.

"Yes Jim, any help you can give us will be greatly appreciated," chimed in Wallace. "We understand the sensitivity of your situation."

Jim left the meeting with his friend by his side, but before he reached the front door of the church he heard the Governor blasting Goodwin as a "dumb Ku Klux Klan Wizard who could screw up a free lunch."

"Sorry about that Jim, he won't be involved in any more of our meetings. We do appreciate your involvement, if you choose to be part of our team," said Colonel Barnet apologetically.

"Don't worry Jeff, there's one in every crowd, but it would be wise to keep him under cover, and I don't mean under a white hood!" winked Buckman.

As Buckman rode to the airport in his waiting cab, he thought that he would indeed help strategize and financially support the governor's primary campaign, but would not involve the men from this day's earlier meeting. He smiled to himself when he thought of that old cliché, "Keep your friends close and your enemies closer!"

Chapter 28

Attorney Kellerman performed as predicted. Diego was out of jail by the end of the week and on his way to young Kellerman's hide-away in the mountains. Mrs. Martinez would follow, if it was determined that she was in any danger.

Joey Consalvo was up for parole, and was given immunity from prosecution on the liquor store robbery, if he proved to be a reliable witness.

Tony was getting anxious. He felt that the pot was boiling in Watts and although delay was a good tactic for the reasons expressed by Jim and Sharon, he wanted to speed up the process. He thought it was good time to pay a visit to Joey.

Tony's research found that Joey and Sanchez failed to register for the draft. He thought he would give him some friendly advice about the consequences of being released from prison only to be drafted. He was taking a chance, but he didn't have faith that the legal process would work and he had to at least give his plan a try.

Tony, in full uniform, and after much discussion with prison security about needing to interview Joey about his draft status, managed to enter San Quentin prison on "official government business."

Joey didn't want to meet with him. "Hey kid, it's the government. You gotta talk to him." The guard took him by the arm and led him to the visitor's room.

When he entered the secure visiting room he looked at Tony sitting on the other side of the room-wide counter behind a stainless steel screen. "Who are you? I ain't talking to no soldier boy," Joey said arrogantly.

"I'm Sergeant Benedetto, I'm here to inform you about the draft. Do you know what the Selective Service system is, Mr. Consalvo?"

"I'm in prison! What do I care about the draft?" asked Joey confused about Tony's presence.

"We understand that you're up for parole next month. I just want to inform you that you may have to answer to the federal government for not registering for the draft or you may face another stay as a guest of the United States government," explained Tony in his most serious tone. "If you're paroled there's a good chance that you'll be drafted within a few months. Your draft board is in need of some good men to send to Vietnam," Tony tried to sound convincing realizing that he could be court-martialed for this act.

"What do yeah mean? They can't draft me, I'm a con. Who are you trying to kid? Are you a cop?" responded Joey, his face grimaced in his best tough guy look.

"Okay, we'll see you on the outside, if you make parole. Good luck!" said Tony, smiling as he placed some official looking papers back into a file folder that he brought with him for effect.

"What do yeah mean, if I make parole, it's the deal. I get out and they get Diego," responded Joey as he looked curiously at the papers being shuffled.

"I'm sorry, who's Diego? Did he register for the draft?" asked Tony, without looking up, playing with Joey's head.

"No he's the chump I gave up to the DA to get out of this hole," smiled Joey, caught up in his own brilliance.

Tony tried to hide his surprise at Joey's stupidity, "Oh, so you gave up an accomplice to get out of here. You're a pretty clever guy, you would probably make sergeant the first year. The army needs guys like you!" continued Tony, sensing a crack in Joey's defensive armor.

"No, Diego's a momma's boy, he was there but he hid in the car and ran home screaming like a baby when Sanchez whacked this old lady and...wait a minute; who are you?" Joey panicked and got up from the counter. "Guard, get me out of here, I want to go to my cell!" he exclaimed, glancing back at Tony behind the heavy metal screen.

Tony gasped and then smiled broadly as he lifted the battery powered recorder, which he brought to tape the interview, from under the counter. Waving the recorder at Joey he said, "Thanks for the chat, Joey, I don't think that you have to worry about being drafted or being paroled."

Joey's jaw dropped and his eyes widened as he realized that the game was over and that he might have committed both himself and Sanchez to another prison term.

Tony's feet hardly touched the ground as he left the prison and hurried to a waiting cab for the ride to the San Francisco airport for the flight back to LA and the Martinez home. He was almost embarrassed by the smile on his face.

He decided to bring the tape directly to Attorney Kellerman for use in his negotiations with the DA, making a copy for Diego to hear. Tony would have to leave LA in a few days, but he was hoping to see the end of this legal fiasco before he left.

Attorney Kellerman, impressed by Tony's efforts, smiled as he listened to the recorded parting words of Joey and Tony. However, he was anxious over the way the confession was obtained. "I don't know if I can use it in court, but it would be a real embarrassment for the DA and not help him in his campaign for re-election. I'll pay him a visit tomorrow," he shook Tony's hand and made a comment about a possible career in police work.

Tony called Jim Buckman at his home in Westport and told the story of his visit with Joey Consalvo. Jim couldn't believe that Tony had it in him to be so ingenious and laughed at the thought of him conning the con.

"You almost convinced him that he was going to Nam. You are something Sarge. Poor Joey, he shot himself in both feet. You know I believe you are devious enough to be a lawyer," he laughed. "I need to tell Sharon, she will enjoy your ingenuity and scorn your abuse of the legal process."

"Thanks, but we haven't won yet. It's now up to your guy Kellerman to close the deal," cautioned Tony.

"Let's hope he's as good as his reputation," offered Jim.

"By the way, how is your relationship with Sharon going?" inquired Tony.

"Ask me tomorrow, we have a real date tonight," advised Jim. "We only have a few days since she's going home at the end of the week. She has final exams this week."

"Well, I have a date with a beautiful Hispanic woman. Mrs. Martinez and I are going up to the mountains to visit Diego. I rented a car for the occasion. She's preparing one of her world famous Mexican feasts to celebrate."

"Sounds exciting, give them my best regards and call me when you hear anything from Kellerman."

Chapter 29

It was a pleasant drive to Jake Kellerman's cabin in the Santa Anna's. The city traffic was left behind and Mrs. Martinez was pleasant company. She found Tony's story of how he outwitted Joey Consalvo to be hilarious, repeating "you didn't...oh my God and he didn't say that, did he?" several times before he came to the final scene in which Tony displayed the tape recorder shocking the smart-ass Joey like he had stuck his finger in a live socket. Tony thought that she was going to have a heart attack, she laughed so hard that she was turning red, which was not easy given her dark Mexican complexion.

"Tony, where did you get the idea to do this? You are a very bad boy!" she waved her finger at him to emphasis her point, and then laughed in a giggly way unable to contain herself.

"The truth is I ad-libbed it all the way. I only knew that I wanted to scare him, but I think I just confused him. He was on to me, but he lost his concentration when I praised him for his strategy in making the deal with the DA. Then his pride took over and he forget who he was talking to," explained Tony.

"Did you call Diego and let him know that we are coming to visit?" he asked.

"I tried but his phone was busy. I don't know who he could be talking to?" puzzled Carmella.

"Probably Kellerman. If not, then he doesn't know about today's events," surmised Tony.

The last mile and a half to the cabin was on a winding gravel mountain road.

"Does he have a body guard?" inquired Tony.

"He didn't this morning, he said that he was told he would have one by next Monday. Do you think he's in any danger up here? How would they find him?" worried Carmella.

Not wanting to alarm her Tony said, "I'm sure that he's fine, don't worry, we'll spend the night with him."

As he made the last turn on this mountain road he could see the cabin on his right. There were no lights on at the front porch, but there was a dim flickering light from a window in one of the downstairs rooms of the two story cabin.

"There's a car over there, Diego doesn't have a car!" exclaimed Carmella. "They drove him here and told him that they would be back in two days."

Tony shut off his headlights as he stopped the car about 100 feet from the Kellerman cabin.

"Wait here until I check it out!" directed Tony as he reached for his duffle bag in the back seat.

"What are you doing? Is that a gun?" she asked, concerned and frightened.

Tony tried to hide his Army issue Smith and Wesson, but Carmella spotted it as he slipped it into his pocket.

"Don't worry it's just a precaution. Hold this hat over the dome light when I open the door," instructed Tony. "Stay here until I come back for you," he said as he started towards the cabin then stepped back to the car. "Do you drive?"

"No, Tony, I'm scared, can I come with you? I'm afraid here!" she pleaded. "It's so dark!"

"That wouldn't be wise! Just lock the doors when I leave, okay?" directed Tony as he slipped off into the moonless night.

Tony stayed low as if he was approaching an enemy bunker, being particularly careful as he climbed the front steps to the porch, lit only by the faint light glowing from the window.

Keeping low until he reached the window, he peaked into the room and noted that the source of the light was a fire roaring in a large stone-faced fireplace on the far side of the room.

Beyond that room, through a doorway, he could see another room, possibly the kitchen, which was well lit. He could detect shadows on the wall opposite the doorway. It was of two people, but he could only hear the muffled sounds of what he believed was Diego's voice.

Tony inched back down the front steps to make his way to the rear of the cabin. As he slipped around the perimeter of the building he heard a dog bark.

Suddenly the light in the rear room went out. He stayed still, trying to evaluate the situation. The barking came from within the cabin. He knew that Diego didn't have a dog. He must have a visitor!

The barking continued, turning into a growl, he had to act quickly, moving in full stride up the rear steps with gun drawn he kicked open the door to what was, as he thought, the kitchen.

As he got both feet into the room he felt the force of what turned out to be a wooden stool, across his back. As he landed flat-faced on the pine planked floor his gun went off and he heard, a woman's voice exclaim, "Oh my God, it's a soldier!"

Then Diego's voice, "Tony, what are you doing here?"

Tony rolled over, nose bloodied from its impact with the unforgiving floor, gun still in hand he looked up at the fog-framed familiar face of his buddy Diego and the frightened face of a pretty black woman as she looked down at Diego for an explanation, a cast iron frying pan in her hands.

"Keisha, I'd like you to meet my good friend Sergeant Tony Benedetto," as he broke into a reluctant smile.

"Are you okay, Sergeant?" Keisha asked, dropping the frying pan, just missing her cocker spaniel with the big voice.

"I'm fine except for my nose, but it should be used to this kind of abuse," Tony said finding some humor and relief that Diego was fine too.

"Sorry about the nose amigo," Diego said, as he helped him up, still unable to hide his smile.

Keisha, was filling a face cloth with ice to treat his injury when Mrs. Martinez appeared in the doorway wielding a three-foot tree limb as if it was a lethal weapon.

"What happened, are you okay Diego?" ignoring the bleeding Tony, who was sitting on the stool that had so profoundly impacted his arrival.

"I heard the shot and I didn't know what to do. Oh, Tony are you all right?" noticing his bloodied face as Keisha applied the improvised ice pack.

"Abuelita, Tony, what are you doing here and why didn't you call?"

"I tried, but your phone was busy all day!" exclaimed Carmella as she hugged her nieto.

"Oh, I guess it was. Well, I got a call from Attorney Kellerman about Tony's dumb, but I guess, successful visit to Joey Consalvo at San Quentin. You are not all there amigo, what if he didn't say what you wanted him to say? You could be court-martialed for doing such a crazy thing, but thank you," He said still unable to wipe the smile from his face as Tony looked at him, his puppy-dog eyes just above the bloody facecloth.

"Then I called Keisha and, we had a lot to talk about," he said with a sheepish grin. She wanted to come up to see me."

"Wanted, I insisted, and thank you Sergeant Benedetto. We owe you a lot, I'm so sorry that you got such a rough reception tonight," she said as she kissed him on the forehead.

"You're both welcome," he said with a nasal voice induced by his seven-time broken nose, "But judging from that frying pan that was in your hand, the worst was yet to come!"

They laughed, "We thought it was Joey's friends, and that they may have followed Keisha here. Sorry, but you would make a lousy point man," joked Diego.

"We should take you to the hospital Tony," suggested Keisha.

"No, I'll be fine, hopefully it heals straight. I'll check it out tomorrow on the way back to LA."

"Great, you're staying tonight! We have some hamburgers that we can grill and..."

"No hamburgers! We have a five-course Mexican feast. You two help me bring it in, the car is at the front door, let Tony rest," interrupted Mrs. Martinez.

Tony looked up at her. "I thought you didn't drive?"

"I don't, where do you think I got this tree branch?" her eyes widened, eyebrows raised as she left Tony with something to think about. She led Diego and Keisha to the front door and the rental car, the front bumper of which was over the first step.

"I knew I should have gotten the insurance," declared Tony.

Chapter 30

At first, Patrick Nordstrom, District Attorney for Orange County, was not impressed by Attorney Kellerman's taped Consalvo confession. "You won't get that admitted as evidence in court and you know it, Kellerman."

"You may be right, Patrick, but I think our young man has a friend in the media and they may be interested in how their DA trumps up cases for political benefit. Here I made this copy for you," he said as he took the tape from the recorder and covertly replaced it with another.

"Are you trying to blackmail me, you son of a bitch?"

"Quite to the contrary Mr. Prosecutor, I have no control over where the original of this tape goes, but I wouldn't antagonize this young man if I were you! People might wonder why you're so quick to prosecute someone who was a lookout when he was only 14 and let a couple of dangerous thugs out of prison, who assaulted and almost killed a black woman in Watts?"

"Well, maybe it would be wise to prosecute your guy and those thugs? How would that be Mr. Big-shot Attorney? I don't care what Consalvo said. I'm going to get your guy just to teach you and that smart-assed guinea soldier boy a lesson."

"We can work with that, go for it!" challenged Kellerman as he gathered up his brief case and said goodbye to his least favorite DA. "Oh, by the way I hear that the county dog catcher is retiring, you can give that a shot after we finish with you on this case!" Kellerman smiled on his way to the door.

"Damn it how do you turn this recorder off?" winked Kellerman as he opened the door to the reception area.

"You can't do that! I'll get you for that," he threatened before he noticed the State's attorney general, Dave Wilder waiting in the outside office for his friend Bob Kellerman to join him for lunch.

"He can't do what, Patrick?" asked a bewildered AG. "Aren't you joining us for lunch Patrick?"

Nordstrom's jaw dropped as he realized that the jig was soon going to be up. No, sorry Dave, I've got a case to prepare." He closed the door slowly, taking his handkerchief to his sweaty brow knowing that Kellerman got him good recording his self-incriminating words.

"What was that all about?" asked Wilder. "I thought he was going to lunch with us, didn't you say to meet you at his office, that he wanted to discuss something with us?"

"Yes, I did, but he forgot about some work he had to do. Running for office can be very stressful," grinned Kellerman.

"He did seem a little stressed. What was he yelling at you about? Are you still pulling his chain like you did at Stanford Law School 25 years ago?"

"Well he has such a long and pull-able chain!" cracked Kellerman. "Let's go to the Brown Derby. I hear Bobby Kennedy might be there today."

"That sounds good to me. I understand he might announce his candidacy for the presidency even if Johnson runs for a second term," noted the AG.

"Yes, but I think he's crazy to run given the potential for his demise at the hands of some nut case," observed Kellerman. "Let's take my car, it's here in the garage."

"Tell me about this case against that army hero from Watts that you're defending?"

"I'd love to, Dave. It has some unusual elements you may find interesting."

The next day Nordstrom announced that he was dropping the charges against Diego Martinez due to the lack of evidence. He said nothing about charging Consalvo and Sanchez with the crime against Mrs. Johnson, thinking that would cause more problems for his campaign than it was worth to him. If I'm re-elected, he thought, I may reconsider that decision.

Chapter 31

The trip to Washington had given the senior Buckman some interesting cards to play and he was anxious to play them. In spite of what his son thought he was not liberal or conservative. His party affiliation was best defined as "the party of the opportunist."

He was swayed towards the right–wing Republicans who were aggressively taking over the party since they had no conscience when it came to righteously deceiving the masses for the benefit of the few, and he was one of those few. The Democrats gained their political strength by promising the masses everything, and once in a great while they were able to deliver on those promises.

The right-wingers would pull some insidious scare tactic and divert attention to some non-funding issue. They were expert at convincing the poor and the hard-working-class of Americans that they were respected by their elitist masters.

They convinced President Johnson to spend $66 million per day on the Vietnam War instead of on his declared "War on Poverty." Their solution to poverty was to draft the poor and the disadvantaged, giving them the job of defending the wealth of the powerful.

He knew that the vast majority of Americans respect wealth and power and those that have it. "Isn't that the card the Kennedys have played for more than 30 years?" he reasoned.

He also knew that the only candidate for the presidency who could be controlled by the "powers-that-be" would be Nixon. Although he had little respect for him, he was ready to do what was necessary to get him in the White House.

Johnson proved to be too liberal and too effective in getting his agenda for social programs through the Congress. He had to go! Obviously the first step was to make sure that Johnson didn't run again. He realized that it would be very difficult to defeat a sitting president, even with the war as an issue. He also knew that the Democrats, in their frenzy to fill that office, would split their party's loyalty into many factions. He would help them self-destruct.

He decided to bring General Bert Obersham into his confidence to discuss a strategy that involved supporting Alabama Governor George Wallace in his bid for the Democratic nomination.

"Hello Bert, this is Jim Buckman. How's the family?"

"They're fine Jim! My daughter just completed medical school and is going to do her residency at Johns Hopkins. The wife insists that I retire so we can have a less hectic life, but I know she wouldn't want me around the house all day. How is young Jim doing in Nam?"

"He's doing fine. He was promoted to 2nd Lieutenant and General Albertson has kept him out of harm's way for the past five months, but I spoke to the General last week and he says that Jim is getting upset about being held back from certain missions. He's almost halfway through this deployment. I hope that he can restrain him for that time."

"Albertson will do what we asked. Jim has no choice but to obey his commanding officer."

"I hope that you're right Bert. He's a very stubborn young man."

"Don't worry, he won't be leaving Saigon until he's ready to come home," assured Bert.

"Well, I hope so, but I called you to tell you about an initiative that I'm involved in that should help get Nixon elected." Buckman told Obersham of his meeting with the Wallace people and how he believed he could use the situation to derail the Democrats.

"You're kidding? You met with George Wallace there in Washington that night we met with our friends?" remarked Obersham surprised at Buckman's audacity.

"Yes, and I was more shocked than you are now. I was tongue-tied for a moment, but he's desperate for any help and I intend to give the bastard what he deserves.

"How do you intend to do that, or is that information on a need-to-know basis?"

"Well Bert, you're the only one I've told, but you'll need to know a lot more if you're willing to be involved. Basically, my theory is that a political party that has a southern bigot; an anti-war/civil rights liberal named Kennedy, and a sitting liberal Vice President as potential candidates for the Presidency of the United States is vulnerable. They may seem like a party with a diversity of interest, but with some encouragement, we can exploit those differences and get Nixon elected," continued Buckman.

"It's an interesting theory, but how does it play out as a strategy?" questioned Obersham. "It would seem that Humphrey, who is highly respected and more liberal than not, would rise to the top of the pile."

"Keep in mind that the natives are getting restless about the war. They blame the current Democratic administration for perpetuating it and Humphrey is part of that administration. We need to encourage their discontent!"

"Confusing the German officers in the WW II may be easier than using the misguided southern bigots and know-it-all college students to dupe Wallace and the other Democrats into doing your dirty deeds Jim," laughed Obersham. "You were good at covert deception. Do you think that you still have your fastball?

"No, but I do have a wicked curve ball!" laughed Buckman.

"Okay, I'm in. What's the plan?

"Do you remember how we infiltrated the Nazi brain trust?" asked Buckman.

"Yes, you made friends with the Vichy French government, the Nazi sympathizers, and got into the social circle of their leader, Marshall Philippe Pétain. Where did you learn to speak French that proficiently? There were times when I wondered if we were on the same side."

"My mother was French. She insisted that I speak to her in her native language whenever possible. Her family was living in Burgoyne when you and I were subverting their conquerors."

"You never told me that?" Why would you keep it a secret from me?"

"Because if we were captured you would not have information that could get them killed."

"You didn't trust me? We spent more than three months behind enemy lines and you didn't trust me?"

"I trusted you as much as anyone, but I'm not a trusting person. In war trust gets people killed."

"I understand! I relied on your cold-hearted discipline to complete the mission, and to keep us alive. I was just a young Captain looking for excitement. Are you as cold-hearted about this plan to destroy the Democratic Party?"

There was no direct answer, just a silence that said it all. The general knew the answer. This was survival and no one could match the retired Colonel Buckman's determination or his ruthless will to survive.

The first step is to feed the Wallace campaign with sufficient funds to make him a legitimate candidate. He will pull the southern vote from his liberal antagonists. When he loses the primaries they will look to the more conservative, Nixon to carry their banner.

The next step is to encourage the anti-war demonstrations. The fuel is there, we just need to light the fire. The liberal public is disgusted with their Democratic Party regulars for not ending the conflict. They're short-sighted enough to lose the Presidency to a Republican who will stay-the-course until we have a decisive victory and stop Communist expansion.

"Do you really think that they are collectively that naïve?" asked Obersham.

"I'm counting on it! Let's get together this weekend for a strategy session. Come up to Westport. We can meet at my club."

"Sounds good! I'll be there by noon Saturday."

"Bring your wife. Nancy would love to see her. They can play tennis, Jill still plays doesn't she?"

"Good enough to beat me," laughed Bert. "Bye, Jim."

Chapter 32

The Senate race in Michigan was heating up and Sam Polowski was losing ground. His daughter Sharon attempted to assist his campaign staff during her brief Christmas vacation from Yale Law School, but it was not enough. The end of the semester in late May allowed her to take on more duties to help his beleaguered organization. Although reluctant to help a person with a diametrically opposed ideology get elected to the United States Senate, since that person was her dad, she owed him her help.

"Dad, if you're hoping to beat out your Republican opponent in the Primary you need to spend money to advertise. He's outspending you 5 to 1!" advised Sharon.

"How do I do that if we don't have the funds? We have less than $100,000 in the Committee's coffers and that won't buy much television time?" lamented Sam Polowski.

"Well, you have two choices. Either you continue to hold back your advertising, and try to raise money behind the scenes from friends and known supporters, and give it the big push late in the campaign with whatever money you have - *or* you spend money now, to appear more real to the voters and hope that they will respond with their financial support."

"And if I don't get the financial support from the voters I will be out of money by the end of the summer and have no chance in November 1968," retorted Sam.

"But won't that be true as well, If you hold back?"

"I don't know how to predict the future. If I did I'd be Governor now. I have an idea though, one in which you can really help. Are you still on good terms with Jim Buckman?"

"I guess so, but he's in Nam. We write at least once a week. How does that help you?" puzzled Sharon.

"His father is one of the top conservative supporters in the Republican Party and one of the richest men in the country..."

"Whoa dad, I see where you're going and you should know that his dad thinks of me as 'that liberal bitch' and a contaminant to his son's ideology," Sharon said, shaking her head rejecting the idea of her contact with the Buckman family being helpful to her father's campaign.

"Well the liberal part I agree with," smiled Sam, showing his rarely displayed sense of humor. "But he could provide the resources to turn my campaign around."

"And you would use my relationship with his son to achieve that goal?"

"I know that it sounds selfish and arrogant of me, but the United States Senate is where I want to be and I think that the country needs me to be there. All I want you to do is open the door for me to meet with him. I'll do the best I can to convince him to support my candidacy," pleaded Sam.

"I don't know. I need to think about it, but what if he doesn't see the benefits of supporting you? He's a very powerful man in political circles and he has his own agenda."

"Then we'll go to your 'all or nothing' plan and give it our *all* immediately and hope for the best in the long run."

"Let me think it over tonight. If I can figure out a way to arrange a meeting I'll do it, but you need to realize that it may not get you what you want."

"I know it's a long-shot but it may be my only shot. Thank you honey, I realize it won't be easy for you to overcome your liberal instincts," smiled Sam as he hugged her and kissed her on the cheek.

Sharon went to her room, picking up her mail on the way, from the kitchen. "There's one here from Jim," her mother said as she handed her the envelope with the stamp from Vietnam.

"How is he doing? He's been there for five months and you get a letter every week. It seems serious," inquired her curious mom with wide eyed anticipation of her daughter's answer.

"We're just *serious* friends. That's all, Mom. I just want to keep his spirits up. I owe him that."

"Okay, if you say so. I'm sure that he understands that," smiled a knowing Mrs. Polowski.

"I'm going to get ready for dinner. Do you need any help?" answered Sharon, attempting to change the subject.

"No dear, dinner will be ready in about an hour. You can help with the dishes."

Sharon was anxious to read Jim's latest letter, which was sent more than a week ago. Her mind was also on her commitment to her father to arrange a meeting with Jim's dad, hoping that it would lead to his support of her father's candidacy. How would she do that without risking her relationship with Jim?

Dear Sharon,

I hope that this letter finds you well and happy. I know from your last letter that you're struggling with the idea of helping your father in his campaign for the Senate. I don't envy your situation, but as you have said many times, he is a good and honest man and we know that we need more of his kind in government. You have a very strong ideology that will have a voice whether he is elected or not. Having said that, I'm glad that I am not in your shoes.

On the other front, we are not having any fun here either. The brass spends much of its time trying to make excuses for bad decisions. They act as if they are fighting Caesar's Gallic Wars, a mistake the British made when they marched their red coats into the musket fire of the colonial militias. The enemy is, for the most part, invisible until they can confront you on their terms. Our troops, which as you would say, are those who couldn't go to Canada or avoid the draft, are in the position of trying to make the idiots at the top look good. I am starting to sound like you!

Speaking of sounding like you, you were right about the role of minorities and the poor in war. They represent the vast majority of the so-called fighting force, yet they are a small minority of our society. It's ironic that they are fighting for a system that tends to exclude them, although I'm not sure that it's on purpose or that it's just a convenience.

In any case, I have made a decision to overcome that convenience. My squad is scheduled to go to Khe Sanh as support for a Regular Army company and my Commanding Officer is assigning me to a

Saigon based company. He has done this several times before. I know that my father's hand is pulling some strings.

This time it isn't going to happen. There's a young black lieutenant who is being sent in my place. He is 35 days from completing his second tour of duty. His wife just had their third child and they are sending him into harm's way, without regard for his life. I have gone to the CO and told him that I will go public with the AP reporters here if that happens and if I am not with my company when they leave tomorrow morning. He has reluctantly agreed, saying it is at my risk.

Since we will be in somewhat precarious situations I will not be able to write you each week and I will miss your letters. They have given me a sense of caring and grounding that I realize was lacking in my life.

I ask that you continue to write as I will return in about a month and will be in need of your wisdom, wit and encouragement.

Thinking of you,
Jimbo

Sharon's eyes teared at the thought of her influence on Jim's life and possibly his survival. He's now in a very dangerous area although he had the option to play a safer game. How could she go forward with the promise to her dad knowing that she might have caused serious harm to the Buckman family? And she realized that, in spite of what she said to her mother, her feelings for this guy were going beyond friendship.

As she thought about it she realized that Jim's advice about her political predicament seemed to be an affirmation of her support of her father's campaign. She rationalized that he would not oppose her plan to arrange a meeting with his dad to enhance his chances. She would call his mother first to ask her advice. She seemed to have some rapport with her and, according to Jim, his mother was the only one who could influence his father.

Chapter 33

"Bert and Jill will meet us at the Club for lunch. Can you keep Jill entertained for the afternoon? She likes to play tennis," asked Buckman.

"It looks like rain. We may just go into Manhattan shopping. We can take the train and avoid the traffic and enjoy a cocktail or two. Nieman Marcus is having a sale on furs."

"Of course they are! Its mid-June!" remarked Mr. Buckman with a smile. "Well, whatever you ladies decide is fine. Bert and I will have dinner at the club if you want to stay in the city for dinner."

"Oh, I got a call from Sharon Polowski this morning. You remember her, Jim's friend from Yale?"

"Yes I do. She's that left-winger that was influencing our son's logic," he responded finding it difficult to hide his resentment.

"Well I think that she's a very intelligent woman who was encouraging him to think for himself, and I think she's very fond of him... and that it's mutual. Besides, didn't you call me a damn liberal when we were dating?" reminded Nancy.

"Well at least I've gotten you to the level of independent," responded Jim with smiling eyes and wide grin.

"She got a letter from Jim. They write each other every week. Jim's company is being sent to Khe Sanh, to where the fighting is."

"Don't worry he won't be going. He'll stay in Saigon where he's needed."

"I'm afraid not, he volunteered to go with his men. He's already there. I'm scared."

"What do you mean? He can't be there. I was promised by Bert that it had been arranged."

"They were going to send someone in his place. A colored boy who had already served two tours of duty and was supposed to be going home soon to a new baby. Jim wouldn't allow that."

"What do you mean he wouldn't allow that? It was all arranged. Damn it, what is he doing? Does he want to be some kind of hero?"

"Maybe he's more like his dad than he thinks. What would you have done? Would you want another man to do your duty? That wasn't you in the big War. You risked everything, even our life together when you volunteered to go to France to subvert the Germans."

Jim stopped and looked into Nancy's eyes. "Is that what I did? I guess I didn't see it that way when I was a young idealistic soldier. I only thought of what I needed to do. It was my job and my responsibility. I guess you suffered more than I did not knowing where I was for months at a time. I'm sorry!" he exclaimed as he held her tight.

"You did what you thought was right and that's what Jim is doing. I knew that he wouldn't avoid his duty if he was there. That's why I was so angry with you for not protecting him, but I was wrong. He needs to be his own man and I'm proud of him."

"And that girl encouraged him..."

"To be a man, Jim...to think for himself. Isn't that what you really want of your son? Do you think he can step into your shoes if he's protected from the real world? If she motivated him to be that kind of man we owe her."

"Okay, I get the point. Where is she, so I can give her a big hug?" Jim said with sarcastic humor.

"Actually she and her family would like to visit. They're driving out to Cape Cod next month and will be passing through Westport. You remember that her father was the Republican mayor of a city in Michigan. Sharon is helping him with his campaign for a Senate seat."

"She's helping him? Did she have a revelation and come to her senses? Maybe Jim influenced her too?" quizzed Buckman.

"I don't think so, I think that she just loves her father," remarked Nancy. "And I think that she loves our son too. She was very upset when she was telling me about Jim's decision and she blamed herself, but I told her it was his decision."

"Okay, so when will they be visiting?" asked Jim without enthusiasm as he stood still for Nancy as she tied his tie.

"They'll be going to Chatham on Cape Cod for the Fourth of July. They should be here on the second. I would like them to stay with us that night."

"Why don't we throw them a party too and introduce them to the neighbors?" continued Jim with added sarcasm.

"Great idea! I'll call the caterer and..."

"I was kidding. No party, please!"

"I was kidding too, don't get stressed over this. Let's just be good host. You have a lot in common with Mr. Polowski, you're both right-wing radicals!" smiled Nancy as she left the room.

The Obersham's arrived at the Club as anticipated and were joined by the Buckman's for lunch. The ladies went to the powder room to freshen their makeup and discuss their shopping trip to the city.

"Bert, I understand Jim is in Khe Sanh. Did you know about this?"

"I found out yesterday. I got a note from General Albertson. I thought I would tell you today. How did you find out?"

Jim told him about Sharon's call last night, letting him know that he was disappointed in his friend's performance.

"Listen Jim! He's not a child, it was his decision. He threatened to expose the protective circumstances that we created for him. If the press got hold of that story it would have been devastating to our cause and inhibit the viability of continuing the war effort."

"I don't give a damn about the war effort. My son had better survive and be whole or Albertson will wish he were in a firefight."

Bert knew Jim well enough not to continue the argument. "I'll see what I can do to get him back to Saigon."

"You do that, but don't say anything to anyone, even your wife. I don't want Nancy to know that we are intervening," whispered Jim as the ladies returned to the table.

"What are you boys being so serious about? It can't be that bad," declared Jill with a humorous pout.

"Nothing, my dear, we were just discussing the Red Sox chances this year. I think 1967 will be their year," answered Bert, an avid baseball fan.

"The Yankees will make them wish they were playing basketball," offered Jim.

"Okay boys, don't fight. They frown on brawls here!" joked Nancy.

After lunch Nancy and Jill drove to the train station in Westport to catch the two o'clock express to Manhattan. Jim and Bert retreated to a private conference room to discuss the coming elections.

"Bert, where are we with the background investigations on the opposition candidates?"

"Where should I start? At least three of the people you met at the invitation of your friend, Colonel Barnet, are either former or active Ku Klux Klan leaders, including the colonel."

"Why am I not surprised? Now tell me something that I don't know."

"Your friend the colonel has a kind of militia group that 'takes care of business' when called upon."

"What do you mean, 'takes care of business?" How??"

"It ranges from dirty tricks to eliminating any interfering opposition. I would be very careful dealing with these nuts!" cautioned Obersham.

"Are you saying that my good friend Colonel Barnet is capable of being involved with assassinations?"

"It hasn't been proven, but it is highly suspected. All we know for sure is that they are dangerous and irrational. If you're going to deal with them you'll need to be very careful...It's Vichy France all over again."

"Do you think it's worth it, Bert?" asked Buckman solemnly.

"I guess that depends on what the needs and the goals are of our plan. Are we trying to get Nixon elected by aggressively eliminating the competition or are we just trying to confuse the issues and the electorate? The more aggressive and deceptive we are with these guys, the more you expose yourself to dangerous consequences, given their paranoia and violent disposition."

"I think we can be helpful to their cause enough to create the dissent we need in the Democratic Party and not put ourselves in their cross-hairs for revenge. They need money and some political support to be credible and we need them to be credible!"

"Okay, so how do we do that, and do we include Masters and the Group in our plans?"

"I think it's best to keep this operation on a 'need to know' basis and at this point they don't need to know," responded Buckman.

"I just hope that Masters doesn't find out on his own. He can be dangerous if he thinks that he's being deceived! We'll be walking a tightrope between the two groups and without a safety net!" warned Obersham.

"Well Bert, let's take the next step. I'll contribute to Wallace's campaign from one of my off shore resources. That will go far in gaining me credibility with these characters and I'm sure that they'll understand why my participation has to remain confidential."

"What's the budget for this action Jim? You don't want to go broke supporting these idiots."

"We'll cap it at a million dollars and see how that goes."

"That's your call! It's your money," advised Bert.

"Yes but it's a small price to pay to keep those socialistic Democrats from taxing me poor to save their lazy, low-life constituents!"

"That's true, but don't forget we need those same people to vote for our Republican candidate. The party doesn't have enough members to carry a country-wide election."

"Yes, I realize that. I'm working on a national strategy that will appeal to those dead-beats and that won't give them a dime of *our* money!" smiled Buckman.

"What kind of strategy?"

"Religion! We need religion my friend! The southern electorate is, for the most part, under the control of its churches and they represent a significant majority of the Democratic Party's membership. They've been unhappy with the Democratic Party of their fathers since the Civil Rights Act in '64.' If our

Wallace tactic works the bigoted ones will be disgruntled with his defeat in the primaries and look to the Republican Party for their salvation. We may even appeal to the holy-rolling coloreds with our position on moral values."

"That sounds like a strategy that will take some time and a significant effort to be successful."

"You're right, but it's a strategy that has a strong potential in the long run. The southern ministers will jump on the band wagon, especially when they find their coffers becoming fuller."

"I'm impressed with the idea, but I don't know if it can overcome the growing resistance to the war!"

"Only time will tell, my friend. The weather's clearing up. How about a round of golf?" suggested Buckman.

"That sounds like a plan devoid of controversy," Bert responded, grinning at the prospect of beating Buckman once more, this time on his friend's home course. "The usual $100 per hole?"

"Why not? I need to win my money back. You've taken me for $3,600 in the past month," responded Buckman with a reflective smile.

Before they reached the locker room Jim Buckman was paged by the club's concierge. As he approached the front desk he noticed that there were two uniformed Army officers standing there. He looked at Bert and noted the pale look on his friend's face, as Bert exclaimed, "Oh my God!" Buckman looked back to the officers, his stomach churning, his chest tightening and a cold sweat flushing from his face.

"Colonel Buckman we were told by your house staff that you were here. This is Captain Myers and I'm Major McMahon."

"It's my son, Jim. Is he dead? Did they kill my boy?" Tears began to well in his eyes.

"We don't know sir. His convoy was ambushed 20 kilometers south of Khe Sanh and he was not found among the casualties, we believe he may have been captured. General Albertson wanted to inform you immediately and to express his deep regret and ...."

"You tell that bastard that he'll have plenty to regret if my son has been harmed."

Bert grabbed his arm and suggested that they go the Club's conference room as heads turned to the direction of Buckman's outrage. "Come, Jim, let's talk to these gentlemen in private."

General Obersham had never seen Jim Buckman show his vulnerability. He remembered his stoic and ruthless demeanor as they ran through the fields from that Mansion in France. The grand old house was filled with Vichy officials and German officers, as well as the host family. Colonel Buckman hadn't even looked back as it exploded into a ball of fire...the result of their final covert task of the war. It was the day before the Allied invasion of Normandy.

As the tall oak doors closed on the Colonel and his guest, he pulled his arm from General Obersham's grasp and attempted to bring himself into a military demeanor, embarrassed by his outburst. "What do we know?" he asked as he took command.

"Sir, at this point we only know that Lieutenant Buckman and his company were transporting supplies to a battalion located on the perimeter of Khe Sanh. They were accompanied by an infantry company from that battalion when they were ambushed on the road by a North Vietnamese Army force estimated at more than 200. By the time our gunships arrived there were only sixteen men holding off the company strength force."

"Where was my son?"

"Lieutenant Buckman was in the first of eight vehicles. One of the survivors observed that he was firing his weapon from a ditch at the side of the road during the first 15 to 20 minutes of the attack, but his position was eventually overrun. We suspect a capture since he and two of his men were not found after the air support drove the enemy into the forest."

"Didn't they try to find him? They didn't just give up, did they? Damn it!"

"No sir, the troops transported by the Hueys searched and fought their way into the jungle until nightfall. We lost four men during that pursuit. The initial attack resulted in 24 killed and over 100 wounded."

"I'm sorry Major. I know they did their best, but what do we do now?"

"General Albertson has a company of Rangers searching the area with orders to bring back our men. We will keep you informed Colonel Buckman. The General said that he will personally call you at 2200 this evening."

The officers left Bert and Jim to ponder the situation. They knew that they didn't have the power to bring young Jim back and that they had to trust in General Albertson's perseverance and ingenuity to complete the task.

"Our wives will be home in a few hours. What can I say? Nancy blames me for Jim's deployment. This will break her!" lamented Buckman.

"I think that Nancy's a lot tougher than that Jim, and your son is a smart young man. He'll find a way to survive."

"Why would they take him? Isn't that unusual?" wondered Buckman.

"Maybe they'll want to trade for prisoners being held by our side?" offered Bert.

"I hope you're right. We need to talk to Albertson about that prospect."

Jim knew that Nancy would blame him for young Jim's situation, but that didn't really matter since he blamed himself. He didn't like not being in control and he feared for his oldest son knowing the consequences of war and the terror of being a prisoner of those who hate you. He even thought Jim might be better off dead than captured, but he couldn't bear losing his son. He could only hope that he would be found soon.

Nancy would be home by about 9:00 pm and he needed to prepare himself for her emotions.

The call from General Albertson did little to enlighten the Buckmans. "We're searching more than a 200 square mile area and we'll keep going until we find him, Jim. We suspect he's being held in one of the tunnels that hide their forces. Our Rangers will find and search all of them," informed Albertson.

"We know you'll do your best, but we're very worried, Dave. Why would they want to capture a 2nd Lieutenant and his logistics support company? Do you think that they are looking to trade? Do we have someone important to them in our custody?"

"I don't know that as yet, but the possibility has crossed my mind. I'll check it out Jim."

"Thank you, Dave. I'll check with Washington to see if we have any diplomatic avenues we can access to find out more about their motives."

"Good luck breaking through that bureaucracy!" chided the General. Half of them think Vietnam is in China."

"Speaking of China, they're supporting Ho Chi Minh and his North Vietnamese efforts to overthrow the Saigon government. I know a government official in China that was educated at Yale, I will try to contact him and...."

"Hold it Colonel. I don't want to hear any more. They're a Communist country and as such, our enemy. You do what you have to do, but you will have to do it on your own."

"You're right, Dave. I'm sorry for mentioning it. You know where I stand on fighting Communism!"

"I do and I know how much you love your son. Let's leave it there! Don't give up on us yet Jim. My Rangers are very good at what they do."

Jim hung up the phone and began to look for his old college yearbook for the name of that Chinese law student that he couldn't beat at table tennis when they were young law students at Yale University Class of 1946. After the war, Jim decided to add a law degree to his Masters' Degree in Business and finance.

He met Choi, last name forgotten, in their political science class. They spent hours, when not playing table tennis, discussing the pros and cons of each other's political philosophies. The anti-communist sentiment of the right-wing of the Republican Party had not yet surfaced, although it was festering after the Soviet takeover of East Berlin as Stalin laid claim to their "spoils of war."

Chapter 34

The news of Jim Buckman's suspected capture by the North Vietnamese Army reached Sharon Polowski through a newspaper account of the battle. The words, "2nd Lieutenant James Buckman III of Westport, Connecticut is missing in action..." caused her to catch her breath as tears began to flow. He refused to take the safe road when it was offered and he credited her with changing his attitude and his values. Thanks to her he was either dead or captured. What did she do?

She needed to know more, but thought it wouldn't be wise to contact the Buckmans. His mother would be emotionally distraught, and possibly as angry as his dad, for Sharon's perceived interference in their son's life.

She was living at home for the summer to help her father with his senatorial campaign. She had heard from Jim just the week before when his letter informed her of his decision not to allow a fellow soldier take his assignment a month before he was to go home. Her worst fears could now have been realized and her heart was hurting! She would call Tony Benedetto at Fort Devens. He might know something that wasn't yet public.

"Hello Tony, this is Sharon Polowski. Have you heard about Jim?"

"Yes, I'm sorry, Sharon, Jim's a really cool guy and I know how much you care about him. I got a call from Sergeant Bobby Franklin about an hour ago. He's in Nam now, but he was my supervisor at Devens when Jim was there."

"Does he know anything about what happened to him?"

"Yes, he was with the ranger company that counterattacked the NVA force. He also spent two days searching for Jim and his missing company members."

"What did he say? Do they know where he is?"

"They know where he was, but they lost track of him and his captors about three kilometers from the original point of encounter."

"I don't understand. How could they lose a whole company of enemy soldiers?"

"Tunnels! They're everywhere and some are said to run for miles. The enemy uses them to appear from nowhere, attack and disappear just as quickly."

"Oh God, you mean that Jim may be held underground where no one will find him?"

"Don't give up, Sharon, they'll find him. Have faith!"

"I don't know, Tony. It doesn't seem possible. He could be anywhere and with all the bombing that we do over there, how would he survive if he is alive. What if he's wounded?"

"I doubt they would have taken them if they were wounded, and Jim is a very bright guy. He'll find a way to survive. May I suggest something that may help? Continue to write Jim letters. He will appreciate them when he gets back and you will feel that you have maintained some contact with him."

"He asked me to do that in his last letter, but I don't know if I can. I'm not as tough as some might think."

"He needs you to be tough, Sharon. I promise I'll keep you informed of anything I hear from Franklin."

"Thank you, Tony, I appreciate that. I'll be staying here at my parents until Labor Day."

The visit to the Buckmans, which was planned for the following weekend to introduce her dad to Jim's dad, seemed unwise given the current circumstances. She felt that she was letting her father down, but there was no way that the Buckmans would welcome them now.

It was early Tuesday evening when her mother called her to the phone. "It's Nancy Buckman. She wants us to visit this weekend as planned," Mrs. Polowski knew that Jim Buckman was missing and of her daughter's sadness, but her conversation with Mrs. Buckman convinced her that she was not upset with Sharon and that she appreciated her influence on her son.

"Jim is a man who made up his own mind during a difficult time for him, and I'm proud that he chose not to allow another man take on his responsibility," she told Mrs. Polowski. "His father would have done the same thing under the circumstances. We still have hope and we are praying for some word of his well-being."

Sharon held the phone in a trembling hand as she greeted Jim's mother. "Hello, Mrs. Buckman. I'm so sorry and I wish that I had never tried to convince Jim of my thinking."

"Stop it dear. He had to learn about life from someone who cared about people and you happened to be that one. His father can't protect him his whole life. I'm sorry that it took me this long to contact you, but I've been crying and questioning myself for three days now."

"I am so sorry. What can I do to make it...?"

"I was not crying about your relationship with Jim. I was crying about ours as his parents. Did we give him enough for him to survive the ruthless horror of war? What will he be like if he survives? At first I blamed his dad for trying to protect him from the realities of life, but then I realized that I too participated in that charade."

"You gave him the means to think the way he does today. He told me many times about your compassion and kindness. That's what influenced him more than anything. I just nurtured the seeds of caring that you planted in him as he grew into manhood. He respects his dad but questions his views just as I do with my conservative, self-absorbed father. They think they have the answers for everyone, when they haven't found the answers to their own lives," Sharon paused. "I'm sorry, I guess I have that affliction too."

"No, Sharon, I know what you mean. This war is not the means to a positive end. Allowing hard working people to despair while others prosper is not fair! Giving up our youth to fight the youth of another country so that old men can claim victory for an ideology, as if it's a college football game, is too surrealistic to rationalize."

Sharon could detect a sob in her voice as she finished her words.

"I'm calling because I thought you might feel some responsibility for Jim's plight, but he joined the National Guard and he made the decision to be with his men when they needed him. Please come this weekend. I need to see you and you need to help your father seek his dream, even if it isn't yours. Jim senior will behave himself. I promise!"

"Are you sure? I don't want to add to your family's sorrow. I do have some information I can share. I spoke with his former drill sergeant, Tony Benedetto, who had contact with another former Fort Devens' drill sergeant, Bobby Franklin, who's now with the Ranger unit that's searching for Jim and his men."

Sharon relayed Tony's information and his promise to keep her informed. "He was told that there are orders from the high command to find Jim and his men. They believe they know the area where they're being held." Not wanting to stress her out any more, she left out the part about the tunnels and the "underground prisons."

"I'll tell his father the news but I'm sure that he already knows since my son's CO, General Albertson, is a friend. He's reluctant to tell me anything other than he's missing and they're searching for him. Thank you for telling me. You will be coming this weekend, won't you, please?"

"I'll speak to the family but I'd like to very much! May I call you tomorrow?"

"Call me anytime, dear."

The visit to Westport was important to the futures of both Sam and Sharon Polowski. For Sam it was a chance to become a serious candidate for the Senate seat from Michigan. For Sharon it could determine the direction of her life. She needed Jim to be part of it. She wasn't going to give up on him.

The gate opened to a long tree-lined driveway that wound through manicured grounds to the multi-columned façade of the Buckman mansion. Sam looked at his wife with eyes wide and mouth agape. "Isn't this something?" was all he could say. Sharon shared his wonder, but reserved her comments as she noticed Mrs. Buckman at the front door, a gracious smile inviting them to her home.

She came down the marble steps to greet her guests and to meet Sharon for the first time. They hugged as if they were close friends and looked at each other with tears in their eyes, as they shared their sadness.

"I'm so happy that you could make it!" she exclaimed as she gave both Mr. and Mrs. Polowski a salutary kiss on the cheek and a warm hug.

"You all must be tired after that long drive. Come in and relax, Jim is making welcoming martinis in the study. Where are your daughter Cindy and your son Josh?"

"They're flying into Hyannis Monday. We'll pick them up at the airport," offered Sharon. "They each had plans with their friends for the Fourth."

As they entered the study Jim looked up from his assigned task of preparing the perfect martini to welcome the Polowski family to his home. He kissed Sharon on her cheek, noting her beauty, and held her hand in his as he expressed his gratitude for her friendship with his son.

"He's a very special man and I have been privileged to know him, Mr. Buckman," she responded with a sense of confidence that impressed Buckman.

He gave Mrs. Polowski a hug and a kiss on the cheek. "I know you must be a special woman to put up with a politician in your family," he said, smiling to assure that he was being complimentary.

"And Mr. Polowski, I understand that you're in a tough Senate race. I hope we can help you take that seat for the Party. We need your votes in Congress."

Sam was startled at his immediate offer and could only say "I would appreciate any assistance you can offer Mr. Buckman."

"Call me Jim. We can talk about that, if you would like, after dinner. Right now let's toast to the man who brought us here, as he handed them each a glass of perfect martini. To our son Jim and his safe return."

They all raised their glass towards Buckman. Sharon was not sure if the toast was meant to embarrass her or to allow them to be part of their hope for their son. She looked to Mrs. Buckman, whose smile encouraged her to assume the positive, if for no other reason but to diminish the tension that would be aroused otherwise.

Dinner was like a movie production complete with a butler and servants, seven courses and intelligent conversation. There was none of the negative political talk that Sharon expected. There was some talk of Jim's childhood and of their most recent word of the search. There were some laughs and an occasional tear as they reflected on Jim's possible capture and hope for his release.

After dinner Buckman invited Sam Polowski to walk with him in the garden to discuss his campaign.

"What do you think are your chances, Sam?"

"The incumbent is a moderate Republican with rapidly diminishing support. He's considered to be a taxing liberal and the independent vote is leaning to the right."

"Who will you support for President? There are several good candidates out there already."

"Well you probably know that I'm a conservative. I'll support Nixon during the primaries, but I wouldn't be averse to supporting any Republican candidate against that field of liberal spenders."

"We're on the same page there, Sam. We need to be able to defend ourselves against Communist advances and we need to reduce taxes so that hard working people like you and me can invest in our country and prosper as was the intent of our forefathers. We can't afford all these social programs and still pay for our defense. We need to reward those who take the risk of investment," lectured Buckman.

"I'm with you, Jim. This country has been going in the wrong direction since Roosevelt and his so-called New Deal." It took away the American incentive to work hard and take care of your own."

"It's only gotten worse with Johnson. Medicare will kill the spirit of entrepreneurship and capitalism. This civil rights, minimum wage and union shop bullshit are just ways to get the labor force to control the country. If they control the money they will eventually sit on their asses collecting welfare and nothing will get done," continued Buckman.

"That's the problem, Jim. If the wrong people make the rules, the rules will work against the interest of the hard working American businessman. I believe I can bring some common sense as a conservative to the Senate, but I need your help."

"I'll see what I can do, but first I need to understand your race and especially your opponents, both of the Republicans. And if you survive the primary I'll need information on the Democrat selected to carry their banner," declared Buckman. "If I do help you, Sam, it has to be confidential. If not I'll not be able to continue to support you. Do you understand? It's important that I seem objective in these matters!"

"I understand perfectly, Jim, and as I said before, I'll appreciate any assistance that you're able to provide. You'll have a devoted friend in the Senate, I assure you," Sam concluded with a handshake and a smile.

Jim senior returned the gesture and the smile. "We had better get back to the women before they accuse us of neglect. I'll discuss your candidacy with my colleagues and we'll see what we can do to help get you elected."

Chapter 35

The summer went by without word of 2nd Lieutenant Buckman's whereabouts or his condition. The strain on the Buckman family was matched by Sharon Polowski's despair as she tried to be optimistic that Jim was still alive. The weeks turned into months and she could no longer watch the news without tears and the thought of her influence becoming a death sentence for James Buckman III.

The New Year brought focus to the Presidential campaign in mid-March as Robert Kennedy officially decided to take up the family banner and pursue the highest office in the land. The hope for the year 1968 was that it would be a turning point for getting the country back on course and out of the quagmire of an indeterminate war.

The field of challengers addressed a full spectrum of voter sentiments from Eugene McCarthy, the original choice of the war-protesting college students to the segregationist last hope, George Wallace, the Governor of Alabama and a Democrat turned American Independent.

Robert Kennedy's candidacy and his surge to the top of the polls was supported by the ethnic element of the Democratic Party, but was also gaining with the anti-war supporters of McCarthy. By late Spring Hubert Humphrey, the sitting Vice President was still favored, but beginning to lose ground to the array of party hopefuls.

On the other side of the political ideology a battle was brewing with a challenge to Richard Nixon as the Republican nominee. The opposition was led by George Romney, Nelson Rockefeller and Ronald Reagan, the GOP was experiencing its own level of dissent as each candidate attempted to wrestle the nomination from the inevitability of a Nixon selection.

The country was in a state of confusion and anger over the war. People who would normally share philosophical positions on labor, education and civil rights under the banner of the

Democratic Party were divided by their perspectives on the war and civil rights. The hard-hat labor class rejected the anti-war demonstrations of college students and supported the government's position.

Some believed that the hate and vitriol purveyed by those who profit by such actions resulted in the assassinations of Martin Luther King on April 4, 1968 and of Robert Kennedy just two months later. Kennedy had just won an important primary victory in Los Angeles, California. The win would have given his campaign much needed momentum.

The 1968 Democratic National Convention in Illinois became the setting for one of the worst examples of democracy in action in a century. Public opinion was reaching its volatile limit. The scene was highlighted by police attacking rock throwing students; violence replacing reasonable debate and subversive tactics leaving little to chance.

A fragmented and totally unfocused Democratic Party lost its way, as well as the election, to Richard M. Nixon. Some wondered was the chaos a result of a master plan of covert and effective actions or chance happenings involving three successive assassinations; hundreds of riots and numerous disruptive political efforts.

In California the tension from neglect was still building in the ghettos of Los Angeles and other ethnic and minority cities. Diego Martinez did not get the hero's welcome that he had hoped for while he was in rehabilitation in the Tokyo hospital. He, like thousands of veterans of the war were not received with the respect and honor normally afforded a returning soldier. He was grateful to his Army buddies Tony Benedetto and Jim Buckman, without whose help he would be taking his three square meals in a prison. It had been more than a year since his return from war and the only job he could find was that of a dishwasher in a diner.

Carmella Martinez' health began to decline as she tried to work two jobs as a hotel maid and house cleaner to pay her bills. Diego was engaged to marry Keisha, but knew he couldn't support her, his grandmother and her mother. His check wouldn't be enough to pay even the rent if his grandmother wasn't able to work. His dad was up for parole, but would be deported if released.

Keisha had to quit school, being unable to pay even the relatively inexpensive state college tuition. Her job at a McDonald's barely supported her and her disabled mother. Her hopes and dreams for the future disintegrated into the daily routine of life.

Every day seemed to be another step down the ladder of desperation and each day Diego would ask himself, "What did he fight for?" Neither his service nor his wounds had gained him the respect or equality as an American citizen that he sought.

Like many of the disenfranchised, he had hoped that Robert Kennedy would be the compassionate leader who would help his America realize its promise of equality and provide the opportunity for prosperity. That ended that evening in June when a hater decided not to give him that chance.

The temptations of the streets were calling to him again.

Chapter 36

Jim Buckman had never known such horror or despair. The stench of decay and filth surrounded him in this dank, dark endless hole in the ground that he was forced to be in by his captors. He was tied foot to hand within a line of crawling like-souls. A dim light, about twenty yards ahead, was all that he had to distinguish a path.

Threatening voices to the rear prodded him and his men forward. Just as he wondered if this would be their grave the mole-hole opened to a full height passageway, a tunnel room constructed of wood pillars and beams. A number of enemy soldiers in the full combat fatigues of the North Vietnamese Army and with bayonets at-the-ready were waiting to greet them in a room carved out of the soils beneath the seething, damp, insect infested jungle. As his eyes acclimated to the lantern-lit cavern he could distinguish the soiled, blood stained faces of his fellow prisoners. Counting him, there were seven in all. Three were from his company.

All he remembered of his capture weeks before was the flash of light and the sound of the blast as they were turning onto a narrow road towards Khe Sanh. Then they were ambushed, overwhelmed by the numbers of screaming enemy soldiers charging towards them. He remembered the loud blasts and heat that consumed his position as he continuously fired rounds towards the ominous wave from his automatic weapon, and then he went blank. How did he survive that onslaught and where in hell was he? He soon realized that he had not yet reached hell!

Private First Class Hiller asked where they were and was answered with the butt-end of an AK-47 to his jaw. "No talking!" commanded the NVA officer in charge, a young steely eyed Asian man with obviously little patience. Buckman surmised that since he whispered the command through gritted teeth that they must not be far from the surface and that his action was to demand silence to avoid detection, rather than just assert his authority.

He figured that they had crawled twice the distance of a football field before reaching this wood-structured "room," which he assumed to be about 20-feet square. The ceiling was about 8-feet high and there was a full-height, 4-foot wide dimly-lit passageway out the other end. This room appeared to be a staging chamber in which the NVA prepared for an attack.

Lieutenant Buckman and his sergeant, a young Native American Indian named Joe Eagle, took care of Private Hiller, being careful to keep him quiet. There were 21 enemy soldiers sharing the room. A number of others had passed through before them and there were many more entering from the crawl space as they sat against the carved out dirt walls.

The disciplined soldiers didn't even glance in their direction; their focus was on moving through as quickly as possible to the next point of encounter. The prisoners would wait in this area so as not to delay them in their imminent task.

So this is how they do it. Surprise attack from a hole in the ground, like an army of ants and then disappear into nothingness, as we search the jungle and villages for them, thought Buckman. But what do they want with us? Why didn't they kill us out there?

As the last soldier passed through, the young commander ordered the Americans to their feet with a gesture of his bayonet. The assigned guards took their places to the front and rear of the select group of captives. Recognizing Buckman as the ranking officer, the group's commander, whom Buckman assumed to be a captain in the regular North Vietnamese Army, whispered to him in distressed English, to "keep your men under control and moving or they will die here."

Jim nodded and waved the men on, now tied wrist to wrist, one to the front and one to the rear. Travel through the full-height passageway was fast, even as they were tethered together. There were lanterns every fifty feet or so casting eerie shadows and promises of doom. Most of the tunnel was in a straight line, the only turns being by design to reach their destination as swiftly as possible.

The tunnel shook and the deafening sounds of war filtered through the earth as they moved at a fast but stumbling pace. Jim felt that it was only a matter of time before they would be buried in this rat hole. He thought of his parents...and of Sharon. He knew that if he didn't make it she would blame herself.

As he was pulled through the dark oblivion, his arms acting as the links in this chain of humanity, he tried to count his steps knowing that every two would be about 5-feet in length. He noted the distances to turns and began his count again, hoping that if he survived, he would remember enough to prepare a rough map of this underground menace to his fellow soldiers.

They walked for what seemed like hours, occasionally passing an intersecting way leading in a perpendicular direction from their path. Jim noted the locations, but soon realized the immensity and impossibility of his task.

They came upon another room of similar dimensions to their first resting place. A narrow crawl tunnel led out one side. They were directed into it after adjustments were made to their ties. This would be their "home" for the next few weeks. They were put into bamboo cages like animals in the zoo. The cages were tied together side by side and each prisoner was bound hands to feet to limit his mobility.

Jim thought the crawl tunnel at the end of the room was probably of similar length as the entrance tunnel. He assumed there must be a standard design to this troop-transport system of tunnels. He also assumed that they turned about 45 degrees at the halfway point, as did the original entrance. The design was to prevent the easy entrance of an attack force and a direct view and rocket launch into the main tunnel system. They've figured out how to fight a war without matching their enemy's technology, but by using their instincts and ingenuity to counter it.

During the next few weeks their captors fed them once a day, some kind of mushy rice, which appeared to be half rice and half maggot-like filler. The enemy commander would taunt each of them with threats of leaving them behind to die in this hole. They didn't attempt torture since they were in such confined spaces, but promised them that they would not enjoy their accommodations at the Hanoi Hilton, the name given the North Vietnamese prison that housed the "invaders."

There was little conversation with their captors. An occasional backhand would accompany their daily lunch or if they asked for anything, like water, which was rationed from a canteen every two days.

Their confinement was torture in itself. Jim's wrist and ankles were raw from his ties. He knew that fighting the ropes would only lead to bleeding and infection that could kill him out here without medical attention. He cautioned his men to not cause such wounds. If they were to survive they needed to stay as healthy as possible. They lost track of time. They could hear the sounds of war above them and feared that their forces success would turn their trembling cave into their grave.

The long days and nights ran together so as not to matter anymore. They were ready to give up all hope of leaving this dung hole when the commanding officer, the NVA captain, yelled for them to get ready to move. They were going to the surface and to their "permanent home." The guards opened their bamboo cages that had become more latrines than cells. They had dug holes in the dirt floor to minimize the effect of such unsanitary conditions, but in time there was no more floor to dig up.

The prisoners were tied foot to hand, as before, to allow for crawling and then they were led to the tunnel opening at the far side of the "room." The Captain led the way with six guards behind him and three behind the prisoners.

As they came closer to the exit point and fresh air, they could hear the familiar sound of truck engines idling above. Buckman knew that it was their waiting mode of transportation to their prison camp and possibly their only chance to escape.

The lead, after the captain and five soldiers who preceded Buckman and his fellow captives, reached the tunnel's exit as the familiar roar of jet bombers overwhelmed the sound of the truck engines. The screaming voices of his captors could be heard as they ran for cover. The soldier lying prone at the mouth of the tunnel turned, the look of horror on his face erased without warning as he burst into flame, the smell of Napalm sucking the welcomed fresh air out of the mouth of the tunnel.

The barrier of incinerated enemy bodies that lay in front of them in the pipe-like exit tunnel, saved the captives from certain death. They turned and once they reached the full height tunnel they moved as fast as they could, still bound hand to foot, stumbling through the full-height passage behind their retreating captors, seeking refuge in an intersecting tunnel that they had passed a few minutes earlier.

Buckman could feel his lungs burning, almost dragging Sergeant Eagle behind him, he came upon an enemy soldier's bayoneted weapon, dropped in his panic to escape certain death. Buckman stopped and holding the weapon with his unbound hand used the bayonet to free the captives from their bonds.

The deafening sounds of war were amplified through the tunnel, but the heat of the Napalm bomb had subsided.

"They may be back," referring to the enemy captors. "Follow me, we need to find another way out," ordered Buckman.

"Lieutenant, it may be better to go back to the entrance. They must be in full-flight or incinerated. I don't hear any return fire," offered Sergeant Eagle.

"You might be right, but let's be ready for the worst. Let's see if the weapons of any of those poor bastards' that were in the lead survived," advised Buckman.

Cautiously, the group of seven American soldiers led by Buckman, walked and then crawled back to the tunnel's entrance, the smell of burnt flesh caused Private Hiller to vomit. Sergeant Eagle protected the rear with a found AK-47. Two SKS weapons out of five remained after their carriers were nearly fully cremated alive. They also found several grenades and bayonets that were intact, but in order to get out they had to remove the bodies of those charred human barriers that saved them from certain death. The lead soldier, whose facial expression anticipated his macabre demise, was only ash and no longer a barrier to passage.

Buckman was not prepared for the site before him as he emerged from his near-grave. The idling trucks were but smoldering chassis, surrounded by charred and near ashen bodies. As he walked through the debris and burning tree limbs, he estimated that there were more than a hundred sons of Vietnam that met their hell here in this hostile jungle.

The bombers were clear of the area and there was no sign of the NVA but he knew they wouldn't be far. Dark rain-clouds were gathering from what he guessed was the south, bringing relief to this fire-ravaged land and, most likely, enemy patrols to gather the dead and wounded.

They searched the area and collected as many weapons and ammunition as they could carry and headed in the direction of the still green jungle about a mile to the south.

"Lieutenant, this man is alive. What should I do?" cried Sergeant Eagle as he stood over an enemy soldier, his body still smoldering and writhing in agonizing pain from his burns, and screaming in an incoherent language that seemed to be pleading for death.

Before Buckman could respond a single shot fired from their right flank found its target putting the agonizing wounded enemy soldier to rest.

Buckman reeled to the sound, sighting the young enemy officer that had silenced Private Hiller with the heavy end of his weapon in the tunnel. He was on his knees, his Russian made pistol still pointed towards his victim. Looking towards Buckman, he collapsed forward into the still smoldering forest debris.

Buckman ran to him with his newly formed squad following close behind.

"Is he alive?" yelled Hiller his weapon ready to finish the task.

"Yes, bring me that canteen," ordered Buckman.

"We need to get out of here, Lieutenant. They'll be back for their wounded. Let's go!" pleaded Sergeant Eagle. "Besides he shot his own man. What kind of a guy does that?"

"One who knows how much he was suffering and answered his plea? He could have easily picked off one of us instead! Help me with him," ordered Buckman as he lifted him to his feet. "Do you know where we are? He may be our only way out of here."

"This sucks! He almost killed me in that tunnel. If you're too soft, I'll take care of him," offered a bitter Hiller.

Eagle grabbed his enemy's arm and, confused but trusting in his lieutenant's judgment, helped drag the semiconscious NVA officer towards the cover of the forest. "Stand down Hiller or I'll take care of you!" retorted the Sergeant, his eyes piercing into those of Hiller's, to emphasis his resolve.

The seven American soldiers, burdened by their wounded captive, found cover in the depth of the forest underbrush on a densely vegetated rise that gave them a view of the area. They could see enemy forces regrouping back to the point of encounter. Their former captor was unconscious, making it more difficult to transport him without a stretcher.

"Listen, Lieutenant I don't see how we can make it dragging this guy with us. I know you respect his compassion for his men but we've got to get moving tonight to have any chance at all," advised his loyal Sergeant quietly so as not to alert the men to his dissidence. "If we leave him here his troops will find him."

"And if they do, he can alert them to our survival and we'll be tracked down before we ever see another friendly face. If we can take him with us we might find our way back, but first we've got to get him walking."

"Lieutenant why don't we just take care of him right here? I know I sound like Hiller, but I'm not saying this out of hate. It's our only chance."

Buckman knew that Eagle was a good soldier. His Native American background imbued him with skills and wisdom that were invaluable in this warzone. His advice was sound.

"Let me think it over Joe. I will have an answer by nightfall," answered Buckman.

It was at least four hours until dusk. He had secured the Viet officer's hands and feet and gagged his mouth lightly to prevent him from yelling for help. He was conscious as Buckman departed. His eyes caught Jim's as he turned to check his captive. Somewhat startled by the intensity of his look, Jim returned to his side and put his hand on his chest as if to hold him down; in his other hand he held the captives bayonet with the blade to his neck, and assured him that if he made a sound it would be his last. The fear in his eyes told Buckman that the bound officer understood the situation.

"You understand English! I heard you give my men commands in the tunnel!" asserted Buckman.

The officer looked into Jim's eyes, but did not answer. "Why did you kill your man out there?" asked Buckman.

His eyes dropped in a look of lament and then closed. Jim recognized it as a sign of his understanding and pulled his gag from his mouth, hoping that he would not yell. If he did he might have to silence him.

"He was from my village, a friend, I could not let him suffer anymore. He asked to die."

The words came as if they were having a casual discussion about a mutual friend. Jim was somewhat startled and relieved at the same time. "Here drink!' He said as he held the canteen to his lips. "Where are you wounded?" What is your name and rank?

"I am Pham Van Binh, a Captain in the NVA.

"Binh, it is the word for peace and peacefulness isn't it?" responded Buckman, having heard that name in Saigon.

"Yes, you are correct and I am a man of peace, but I must defend my country, my family and the honor of my ancestors"

"Can you walk? I don't want to leave you here, because if I do, it will not be alive. Do you understand?" the sharpness of his own bayonet in Jim's hand, just touching his throat. "If you lead us out of here I promise that I will release you when we sight our battalion. If you don't, I promise you will die here," Jim said in his best low-toned Bogart impression. He looked down at his captive's scorched legs, exposed as the uniform pants had burnt away from his the body.

"I can no longer feel my legs," Captain Binh stared at him, his eyes becoming more intense, his facial expression one of anger and pain. "You will kill me anyway. Why should I help you escape? You are in *my* country. We didn't invite you here. We didn't invade your country. You kill our people with bombs, not even caring who we are. You burn us like we were just trees of the forest. You have no compassion for our people only the desire to occupy our land as a base to destroy other countries."

"Listen, I don't have time to discuss our political and social philosophies, but I assure you that we aren't going to solve them here, or between you and me. You know the deal. You have one hour to decide your fate." With that, Jim tied his gag and checked his bindings. A rope secured his neck to the closest tree. The slightest attempt at escape would throttle him.

"Think about it my friend. I know you have a family. I saw the pictures of your wife and two children in your pocket. Think of them before you make your decision!" advised Buckman with some compassion in his voice.

Jim turned away too soon to notice the tear in his captive's eye and his expression turn from anger to sadness.

"Sergeant, prepare to move out in one hour. Set up a perimeter at about a 30-foot radius from our captive and within sight of each other, and tell them to be alert, stay low and camouflage with vegetation. It will be dark soon. I'll take the northern post. No firing without my command, unless the enemy is upon us.

"Yes sir. Is he willing and able to go with us?" questioned Sergeant Eagle.

"I hope so Sarge. I hope so!"

Dusk came sooner than expected, with the sun disappearing behind the mountains to the west, a sight reminiscent of the spectacular sunset views from the family retreat in Vermont. He thought of that night of beauty and of the fearful storm that shook him into reality. Was that a premonition of this time and place?

Having seen no movement from below, in the valley to the north, Buckman slipped back to the bound captain's position. "Sergeant, come here!" he said in a low and careful voice.

"Yes Lieutenant, is he ready to go?" whispered Eagle.

"He's not going anywhere! He's dead, strangled by the restraining rope around his neck."

"Did he try to escape?" You didn't...?" Eagle's question was cut short.

"We need to bury him before we leave. We don't want his NVA friends to find him and figure out that there were Americans up here."

"That may take time that we don't have Lieutenant."

"You're right! Unbind him and take every tie with us," Jim said as he put the captain's pistol back in his hand. "Leave him in the open as if he died escaping the bombing attack. They won't suspect that he was captured if he still has his weapon. Sanitize the area so they won't see signs of us when they get here."

"Okay, but there are all kinds of animals out here, including tigers, he won't be recognizable for long," offered Eagle.

"Just get it done and done fast Sarge! We'll move out in 20 minutes. It looks like there will be some moonlight tonight. That could be a blessing or a curse!" advised Buckman. "I think that we should go south and then east, towards our troops. The northern route towards Khe Sanh will surely be defended by the enemy. We can expect to encounter them in any direction, but we need to rely on the advance of our forces from the South. Although it is a much longer route than continuing to Khe Sanh. If we can make it to the river and secure a boat from one of the villages, we may be able to move faster towards the delta. What do you think?"

"Yes sir, I concur as far as not going to Khe Sanh, but we'll have to contend with their gunboats if we use the river. I think we have a better chance going east towards our base at Da Nang. There's a full battalion there on the coast and we may encounter their patrols heading west towards Khe Sanh."

Sergeant Eagle slipped away into the darkness to pass along Buckman's orders to the five men on the perimeter. He couldn't help noting their collective sense of relief, especially the expression on Hiller's face on learning that the NVA captain was dead.

Buckman stayed to the rear to watch for any enemy advances in their direction. He could still see the glow of the smoldering forest in the valley that was laid to waste by the napalm bombing. The smoke flowed away from them in a northward direction and was about three kilometers from their position. It was not far enough for comfort. He was hoping to be at least 12 kilometers farther south by dawn, and then head east towards Da Nang, as Eagle advised. It was going to be a long night.

The moon began to show itself over the ridge of hills to the east as the rustle of under-bush alerted them to, hopefully, Eagle's arrival. Camouflaged and laying low in the bush with weapons trained towards the direction of the sounds, the anxious soldiers awaited sight of their visitor, prepared for an enemy patrol or a hungry tiger.

Chapter 37

It had been more than three months since they heard of their son's possible capture by the North Vietnamese Army. The Special Forces Ranger unit under General Albertson had given up the formal search, but the General assured Jim that they would pursue any leads that came their way. To Buckman senior that was just to appease him and keep him off their backs. It only made him more intent on getting personally involved in the search.

Buckman answered the phone in his library, expecting a call from General Obersham.

"Hello Jim, this is Bert."

"Yes Bert, any news from the boys in Washington?

"Yes, I checked with the Intelligence community and found the name and whereabouts of your old college friend. His name is Choi Yang. He is, as you thought, a Chinese diplomat, but he's stationed in Hong Kong. That's a break for us since it's still under British rule."

"What else do we know about him? Does anyone in the State Department have contact with Choi? Can I contact him?

"They know of him, but very little about him, other than his American experience as a student. He does have family back in China and is well-thought-of in the Communist Party. My contact in Intelligence suggest that you go to Hong Kong and visit your old college buddy."

"Can we arrange that Bert? I don't want this to get out to the press. They would seriously damage our political potentials, but I need to know what happened to my son."

"You may have to bring the Washington Action Group in on your plans. They'll worry about your commitment to the cause if they hear of your actions from others. You know how Masters thinks. Everything is a conspiracy to keep him from getting what he wants," remarked Obersham.

"I know, Bert. I'll need to think on that."

"Well, let me know. I'll see if I can make it into some kind of diplomatic trade mission."

"Thank you, Bert. That will help ease the suspicions and potential for controversy."

It only took a week for Obersham to arrange a "trade mission" to Hong Kong. But first they decided that it would be wise to meet with their political allies in Washington to soften the story in anticipation of their true intentions eventually being exposed. The Group, which was as anti-communism as Senator Joe McCarthy, the black-listing demagogue of the 1950s, were also driven by their beliefs in the benefits of a pure capitalistic market. They had achieved their riches and power by thwarting the opposition in business and gaining whatever advantage there was to gain from their version of manipulated capitalism.

The success of their business model depended on limited regulatory actions to allow their free-wheeling actions in their pursuit of more wealth and power. Jim Buckman and General Obersham shared their enthusiasm for minimal oversight and maximum flexibility in business dealings and they would use their philosophy to their advantage.

They would emphasis the potential for developing a market in Asia through Jim's Hong Kong based diplomat. They would sell them on the theory that once Communism was defeated, there would be more than a billion Asian customers for American products and services and cheap manufacturing labor.

Their candidate, Richard Nixon, was as much a Commie hater as they were, having served loyally with Senator McCarthy destroying the reputations of so many socially minded Americans, particularly those in the media and entertainment industry.

Nixon would need to be convinced that his ego would be best served by being part of the team that got him to the White House or he would find himself following the path, and the demise, of his predecessor, Lyndon B. Johnson.

"I like it!" was Masters' succinct remark at hearing Buckman's plans to get a head start on the anticipated boom market of the far-east.

"After all, we have those Commies on the run in Vietnam and next we'll get a foothold in Cambodia. China will be surrounded with our allies and our bases. They'll want to do business with whoever is the strongest both militarily and financially. Yes, I think that you're onto something here, Jim. Good luck, and keep us informed."

The Group agreed enthusiastically, backing both their real and virtual leaders.

Breathing a sigh of relief, Bert and Jim left the meeting with a sense of accomplishment. "You know, Bert, we may have inadvertently stumbled onto a feasible game plan to further enhance our prosperity."

"Jim, you could stumble into prosperity in the middle of a deserted island!" laughed Obersham. "Let's go to dinner. I'll explain the arrangements and describe your contacts in Hong Kong."

Chapter 38

Tony Benedetto had heard from his former mentor, Ranger Master Sergeant Bobby Franklin, that their search for Lieutenant Jim Buckman and his men was unsuccessful. His company was being re-assigned to the Cambodian border to stop Viet Cong forces from seeking refuge in that country.

The enemies' hit and run tactics were gaining strength and success. The American military believed the enemy needed to suffer a significant defeat to discourage morale. They also believed that a strong enemy body count would help advance their own morale in a war that was not scored by the number of successful battles or by the acres of ground being held.

"What do you think Bobby, is there a chance that they're alive?" asked Tony almost afraid of the answer.

"It's tough to say. They could be held prisoners next door and we wouldn't know it. This is a very strange theatre of war and an even stranger country. It doesn't follow any of the rules of engagement. It is very frustrating! Last week our Vietnamese interpreter blew up our field headquarters tent, killing three officers and wounding twelve others. The week before a kid about 12-years old walked up to a guard at an outpost and took out three soldiers with a grenade." They are a vicious people, Tony."

"Wouldn't you be if someone invaded your country and you didn't have the conventional weapons that they had to fight back?" responded Tony.

"Okay, you haven't changed. You're still the bleeding heart liberal caught up in the real world. I thought that you would harden after your experiences and especially after your contacts at Devens with guys before and after their combat experiences," chided Franklin.

"I have hardened, Bobby. I'm convinced that we're being exploited for the sake of the few, the wealthy, and the powerful. They depend on guys like you, the true heroes, who are unassuming in their dedication to their country and to their duties. They need people like you to fight for their wealth and power. I'm willing to fight to protect others who are drawn into the horror of war without a voice, but I don't believe in blind devotion to the few greedy egomaniacs that control our country and our lives!"

"Whoa, I'm sorry I asked, but we obviously don't agree on that issue. If we don't have a strong defense we'll be over-run by those who want what we have."

"I'm sure that's the same story the enemy is telling its people. The only difference is that we're the ones who are running over *their* country!"

"Tony, we'll never agree on the value of war and national defense, but we do agree that Jim Buckman needs to be found, even if he's one of those few! I have a contact within the Marine battalion that is deployed in that area. I'll keep you informed of any progress. I know that the fly-boys burned-out a large North Vietnamese army battalion just north of where Buckman's convoy was ambushed, but they found no sign of them there."

"Thanks Bobby, and stay safe! I don't want to have to come over there and search for you," responded Tony with a smile in his voice.

"Hey, I didn't know you cared. Don't worry about me, only the good, the dumb and the careless die young."

"That's why I'm worried about you old buddy!

Tony's call to Sharon would be heart rending. He knew that hope was fading fast and she needed hope to get through her days. He needed time to think about what he would say. He decided to check in with his west coast friend, Diego Martinez.

"Hello Carmella, how are you?"

"Not so good Tony, how are you doing?" How is your family?"

"They're doing fine, but what's the problem? Is Diego there? Is he all right?"

"He's not here right now. I'm afraid for him Tony, he's running with some bad hombres."

"What do you mean by running? Is he in trouble? Didn't he learn from his experience with the law last time?"

"I don't know, Tony. He's all mixed up. He can't get a good job. He got fired from his last job because he asked for a raise. He was only making $4.00 an hour with no benefits and he had to work all kinds of hours. He asked the Veterans Administration for help and they put him on a list. He's trying to make up for me not being able to work. My diabetes is getting very bad and I can't pay for the medicines I need."

"I'm sorry to hear that, Carmella, but about these bad hombres? What do they do?"

"Anything they want to, at least that's what Diego says. They know how to beat the Man. They make big money, drive big cars, you know the kind with the wings on the back, and they always have women around them."

"Well Diego wouldn't care about the women, he's in love with Keisha."

"Keisha told him to straighten out or they were through. He didn't take her seriously, but she was very serious. After she broke up with him he got in deeper with these guys. It is not good, Tony!"

"Where is he now? Will he be home later tonight?"

"I don't know, sometimes he doesn't come home for days. What can I do, Tony?"

"I don't know Carmella. You've done everything you could for him. You've been his mother and father for many years. He has to do this himself. Maybe I can help. I have some time coming to me and I'm in between training sessions. I'll be out there next week. Just tell him I'm visiting friends in San Diego. Don't say anything about this conversation, except that I asked for him."

"Thank you Tony. I'll prepare a feast for you," a lightness came to her voice.

"That will be worth the trip alone. I'll see you soon."

The call to Sharon Polowski was as trying as Tony thought it would be. She had already heard from Jim's mother that the search was fruitless. Tony could hear the tears in her voice as she told him what she knew as of the previous day. He had little to say to enlighten her or give her hope. All he could say was,

"Don't give up, Jim's a resourceful guy and if he's a prisoner he is safer than he would be in the jungle war."

"That's rationalizing, Tony. You know that he may be dead or wounded and in poor health, and if he is captured, we know what happens to prisoners of war in third world countries."

"Don't think that way it won't help you to cope."

"I don't need to cope! I need to know what happened to Jim Buckman."

"If I find out anything Sharon, you will be the first to know."

"Thank you Tony, you take care of yourself."

Tony hung up the phone and sat at his desk trying to make sense of a world where people prey on other people and where killing is thought of as the solution to political and social problems. He wondered if the apathy of the masses would always allow the greedy and devious to control their lives.

Chapter 39

The flight to Hong Kong would take the senior Buckman through San Francisco. Thanks to Bert Obersham, he would not be traveling alone. Michael Wong was to join the flight in San Francisco. Wong, a Chinese born American Citizen who served with Obersham in the Korean Conflict, would now serve Jim Buckman as both interpreter and bodyguard. He was a former Army Ranger Captain and CIA operative who was fluent in a number of Chinese dialects and at 34, a master in several forms of combat martial arts.

Jim appreciated the company and the concern of his good friend Bert. At six foot four inches tall and with an athletically maintained body, Mike Wong provided an excellent physical buffer for Buckman and as a graduate of Stanford University, a person of intellect to engage in interesting conversation. They were not strangers, having met socially a number of times in Washington.

The stopover in San Francisco was only long enough to refuel and take on new passengers. Wong joined Jim in first class, addressing him in rank.

"It's a pleasure to accompany you, Colonel Buckman. I hope that I can be of assistance to you."

"It's good to see you again, Michael. Did the General brief you on this assignment?"

"Yes, he did, but I have some questions on what role you would like me to play to best help you achieve success. How was the flight from New York, sir?"

"You can drop the 'sir' and the Colonel, Mike. Just call me Jim. We'll have time to go over the plan when we are in a better place. Right now I need a drink. Are you still a Scotch-on-the-rocks man?"

"You have a good memory, Jim, Chivas, if they have it."

"That's my drink too, when I drink scotch. If they don't have it, I'll send out for it," laughed Jim.

Mike could tell that he had a head start on him with the Scotch.

After two more rounds of Scotch and a dinner of filet mignon accompanied by bottle of a dry Cabernet Sauvignon, Buckman suggested that they try to get some sleep. We should arrive in Hong Kong at 0800. "I believe the General has set-up a lunch meeting for us with a U.S. embassy contact that will lead to an arranged dinner meeting with Mr. Yang. This will be our best time to catch up on some sleep."

"You go ahead. I have some reading to do before I'll be able to rest. Don't forget you're three hours ahead of me," Jim was asleep before Wong finished his sentence.

Chapter 40

It had been a more than a week since Buckman's squad had escaped into the forest. They survived on Army rations and the killing of small animals with their knives. No shots had been fired and, so far, they had stayed off the paths and avoided contact with the enemy. They had sighted several American helicopters and fighters but weren't able to get their attention, fearing too much of a display might alert nearby enemy forces. Jim guessed they had traveled more than 100 kilometers, but he couldn't be sure.

They knew there was a company of NVA in the area and moved cautiously through the dense underbrush in the forest of bamboo and pine. Sergeant Eagle was the point man. He was the only man Buckman trusted to detect the enemy's presence before *they* were detected. The moon would occasionally peek through the high thin clouds and the forest canopy, shedding some light onto their surroundings.

Hiller, the high-strung member of this group, was in the middle of the single file formation, behind two members of the infantry company assigned to protect them in their original mission to Khe Sanh. Most of the group suspected that Hiller was responsible for the NVA Captain's death, but were quietly relieved, knowing they would no longer have a wounded man in tow. They kept their suspicions to themselves but were growing weary of Private Hiller's whining.

Corporal Sanders and private Rogers, young black soldiers from the Bronx, were captured with Buckman together with privates Harper and Ortiz, both from Brooklyn and trainees at Devens with Buckman. The seven men had survived an enemy ambush, their capture, imprisonment in underground cages, a bombing attack and their escape. So far they were riding a lucky streak!

A map that Jim took off of the NVA captain, indicated a village at a location about 45 kilometers farther to the south.

Buckman worried it might be infiltrated by Viet Cong. He was hoping that it was one of the few friendly villages in the area. If not they would have to take it by force in order to get supplies for the long trek to the nearest friendly base. He believed their best chance was to find the river and a usable boat.

The rise turned into a series of hills as they made an irregular path, in a generally southerly direction. The next hill led to a valley with a small stream flowing west to east. Buckman knew that crocodiles and venomous snakes inhabited some of these waters and cautioned his men to create a crossing of tree limbs over the narrowest expanse, which proved to be about six meters wide. The clearance over the water was less than two feet. Vines were used to strap two fallen tree trunks together.

Once their makeshift 'bridge' was in place they moved at a quick, but cautious pace to the opposite bank. Buckman started across, just past the halfway point he heard the water breaking behind him. Instinctively he leaped the last four feet of the man-made bridge and turned to see an eight foot crock leap at his heels. His thoughts ran to his Vermont encounter with the hungry mountain lion, bringing a nervous smile to his otherwise fear-stricken face.

"Let's keep moving, we need to climb that hill over there." He pointed to a shadowy rise more than kilometer away across a field of tall willowy grass.

"That was close Lieutenant. Are you okay?" asked Eagle as he came back from his point position to see what the commotion was all about.

"Yes, I'm fine, but there's something about waterways that just doesn't agree with me."

The sergeant just looked at Buckman and smiled knowing there must be an interesting story there somewhere.

"We'll stop to rest within that tree cover near the top of that hill," instructed Buckman. "Tell the men to stay close together. I don't know what we'll find in this tall grass."

"Yes sir! I have a bad feeling about this place too!"

As they moved slowly through the grass they could hear the rustling of movement to their west. Eagle held up his hand to stop them, and gave a sign to stay low and quiet. Buckman, still protecting the rear of the small column listened to detect the exact direction of the approach. Eagle signaled to the men to draw their sheathed bayonets.

The pace of the approaching sound picked up and then there was a leaping mass of animal upon them. A tiger looking for an early breakfast found Private Rogers, a 220 lb. former high school wrestler who was not going down without a fight. Eagle and Buckman, simultaneously jumped onto the big cat, both slashing it with their blades until he whimpered and fell to the ground beside the gasping Rogers, his right arm a mass of mangled bleeding flesh.

Eagle cut away what was left of his shirt sleeve and used it as a tourniquet to stop the bleeding. Buckman put the handle of his bayonet in Rogers' mouth for him to bite down so as not to scream in his obvious pain. The rest of the men circled them at the ready to greet any more uninvited guests.

"We need to get out of here, Lieutenant. This blood is going to attract some nasty characters," said Eagle.

"Okay, we'll need two men at a time to carry Rogers until we can reach better cover in those trees." Buckman used the last of his water to wash away some of the blood on Rogers' arm as he grimaced in pain, biting down hard on the blade handle.

Ortiz and Hiller made a sling seat with their ammunition belts and began the trek to the hill rising from this unfriendly valley. The makeshift patrol made it about 300 meters when the sound of animals and rustling grass made them aware that the feast that was left behind was being appreciated.

His arm in the tourniquet and secured by a sling made of his other sleeve, Rogers told his bearers to let him down. "I can walk, you guys are slower than mules in molasses."

Buckman smiled, he knew that Rogers was a tough dude and agreed to let him try. "Stay with him, guys. It's only about another 500 meters to cover," he whispered.

Ortiz and Hiller nodded, relieved to shed their heavy burden. Ortiz linked his right arm under Rogers' good left arm to give him some support as he walked. "Good job, brother, you're doing fine."

They reached the top of the hill and waited for Sergeant Eagle's return. The men were able to fabricate a primitive stretcher using bamboo and vines from the forest. Rogers, weak and exhausted was tied to the makeshift device as they prepared for the next phase of their journey.

"What do you think Sarge, will they come after us when they finish?" asked Buckman thinking that his American Indian instincts would provide the answer.

"I don't know, Lieutenant. That was a pretty big cat. They should be well fed after that meal. Hopefully they'll take a nice long nap and leave us be."

"This trail of blood may lead them to their lunch. We'd better make this a quick rest stop. We need to get to the river as quickly as possible," advised Buckman in a soft whisper.

"I hear you, but the sun will be rising in a couple of hours. It'll be difficult to travel undetected in the light of day," remarked Eagle."

"That depends on what kind of cover is on the other side of that hill. You'd better scout ahead. I'll take the point."

"Good idea sir, I'll be back before dawn."

"We'll meet at that tall pine that's rising above the others at the top of that hill," instructed Buckman as he pointed to the silhouette of a tree that rose at least fifty feet above the others.

"Okay, I see it." Eagle went ahead at a fast pace. Buckman got the men together and told them of the next phase of their ad hoc plan.

"This is crazy Lieutenant. We'll either be shot or eaten by wild animals. Maybe we're better off surrendering?" whined Hiller.

"Cool it, Hiller, we don't have a choice. Do you think the enemy is going to treat us with kindness and compassion? They'll see these NVA weapons and figure out where we got them, and they may not be willing to drag us along especially with a wounded man," retorted Buckman. "Are you ready to die here Private?"

Hiller looked down in despair and slowly walked away to join his fellow soldiers.

"The Lieutenant's right, especially if they're Viet Cong. They would rather have your head than capture you live," added the two-tour-of-duty Ortiz to anyone who was listening.

Rogers' bleeding had stopped but he had a fever that indicated infection and he was in partial shock. Buckman worried that he wouldn't survive the rest of the journey.

Chapter 41

The luncheon with the U.S. Embassy contact, John Taylor, was fruitful. He had a personal relationship with diplomat Yang and had been successful in his contact with him yesterday.

"He was excited to hear that you were coming here Colonel Buckman. He said something about kicking your, ahem, butt in table tennis," reported Taylor with a smile.

"He hasn't changed; always the competitor," said the Colonel with a reflective smile. "Does he play golf?" he asked hopefully.

"Yes, but not very well," responded Taylor, smiling at the thought of such a two-pronged tournament. "Wouldn't it be great if we could solve international differences by competitive sporting events?"

"Yes, that would be the ultimate Olympics, but I doubt that Mr. Yang or I would be participants," laughed Buckman.

"Well, he's anxious to meet with you, but it'll have to be for dinner. He has commitments for lunch. He suggests the Paradise Room at the Hong Kong Hilton at 7:00 pm."

"That will be fine John, you can confirm our attendance."

"Great! I'll send a car for you this evening at 6:30. I need to get back to the Embassy. The ambassador thinks I'm having too much fun here already."

After Taylor left, Buckman took the opportunity to explain the game plan to Mike Wong. He brought up the issue of finding information on his son as a secondary reason for their meeting, emphasizing the potential for a trade agreement with China.

"I'm sorry to hear about your son, Jim. You don't know yet if he's a prisoner of war?"

"No it's a very frustrating situation. He was last seen at the ambush site, south of Khe Sanh, but there was no sign of him after the battle."

"Do you think that Yang can find out where he is? I know that China supports Ho Chi Minh but they are not exactly in control of that war. The Soviets also have a stake there," offered Wong.

"I'm hoping that they have enough clout to get an answer from them. If not, then there'll have to be a Plan B," reflected Buckman his eyes and voice telling of his deep sadness.

"Whatever I can do to help, Jim, just ask."

"Thank you, Michael. I appreciate your service!"

The dinner meeting with Choi Yang was more productive than anticipated. After the traditional greetings the group sat down at a special table in a quiet corner of the elaborately decorated Paradise Room. The low lights lent a feeling of antiquity to the Ming Dynasty décor. Carvings on the columns that separated the area from the main restaurant added to the ambience, which was further enhanced by the hypnotic sounds of ancient instruments.

"Jim, I was very happy to hear that you were coming to visit this beautiful city."

"I am delighted to have the opportunity to be here and, of course, to meet with my good friend. It has been a long time since we challenged each other in the classroom and in the Yale Student Union."

"Yes, I think I had the edge at the tennis or ping pong table as you call it, and you were always a point or two ahead of me in the classroom," smiled Yang. But before we begin I know that you're concerned about your son Jim's situation. I did some investigation before you arrived."

"You did, I'm very grateful. What did you learn?" asked Buckman surprised and anxious.

"Not enough to put your mind at ease, my friend. I know that he was taken prisoner south of Khe Sanh."

"And where are they holding him? Is he all right?"

Taylor and Wong were caught up in the anticipation of Mr. Yang's next words.

"He was taken through their complex of tunnels to a staging point for transport to Hanoi, but the site was attacked by American bombers and destroyed. You're aware of that battle."

"Yes, that was a major victory for the American forces," responded Buckman. "Was my boy killed? Didn't they 'napalm' the forest for miles?"

"That's where the story is not clear, Jim. Neither he nor any of the Americans captured with him were found, not even a dog tag. My contact believes that they escaped in the confusion. They did find the officer that was in charge of their transport some two kilometers south of the battle area. He had been strangled by a rope. He was also badly burned giving credence to the belief that he was in at the napalmed site when it was attacked. They're not happy about his 'execution,' as they call it, and they have several patrols in pursuit. Please keep in mind that this is all highly confidential. The information did not come through channels."

Jim Buckman was stunned by what he was hearing, could his son be on the run and who was in charge of their escape?

The answer both worried him and gave him pride.

"Your son was the ranking officer, Jim. He has five or six combat veterans with him including an American Indian by the name of Joseph Eagle. I found out that Eagle is well known for his courage and that he's in his third tour of duty in Vietnam."

Dinner was served as Yang concluded his unexpected report.

"I know this is very emotional for you Jim. I suggest we meet again tomorrow evening to discuss your trade mission. You need time to reflect on what I've told you."

"Choi, I am very grateful for your efforts. You are certainly a good friend. It is much more than I expected, but I feel helpless and you know me well enough to know that I'm not happy with that feeling."

"I'm sorry if I shocked you my friend, but I just received this information two hours ago and I could not do trade talk without letting you know what I know. I wish that I could do more, but I must rely on you, Taylor and Wong to keep this confidential or I will be called back to China to grow rice or worse."

"We'll keep your confidence. Do you both agree?" Colonel Buckman gave them his stern command look.

"Yes, it is better that the Embassy doesn't officially know anything about this. They would just make things worse," offered Taylor.

"You know my answer, Colonel! My loyalty is to you alone on this mission!" answered Wong.

"Thank you, men. I appreciate your silence on this matter. I'm afraid that I've lost my appetite. I appreciate your suggestion to meet again tomorrow evening. If you will excuse me, I need to regroup and think things out."

"I understand, Jim. We'll meet here tomorrow for dinner, same time," answered Yang, extending his hand in an American style handshake adding his other hand to emphasis the true compassion that was reflected in his eyes.

Buckman and Wong departed leaving the rival diplomats to enjoy their dinner.

"Knowing Jim Buckman, he will be dressed in military, armed and hire a helicopter to go find his son by the end of the week," remarked Yang.

"Well, we better not know about it!" added Taylor.

"You won't!" smiled Yang as he took a sip of his wine.

On the way back to the hotel Buckman's thoughts were of his son's plight, "What do you think, Michael? Does he have a chance to make it out of that hell?

"Truthfully, not without help. He has to travel almost 1000 kilometers to reach Saigon. His best chance is to access the rivers, or head southeast towards Da Nang, on the Coast."

"How far is Da Nang from Khe Sanh?"

"That depends on how you travel, but it is about 300 kilometers. There are roads and rivers that could make it faster, although more dangerous if they are exposed to enemy forces. They would need to avoid the roadways"

"I would think that the NVA will assume that they will take the fastest route to the nearest American base," added Buckman. "Are you trained to fly those helicopters?" asked the Colonel with a mischievous look in his eye.

"Yes sir, but that would be suicidal and not very practical without guidance from the American command. We could be shot down by friendly fire as well as by the enemy. And where would we start to look?"

"Do you have a better plan Captain?" asked Jim using Wong's military rank to emphasis his command position.

"With all due respect, I think that we need to get the Special Forces involved. They have the training and the knowledge to optimize the chances of finding your son."

"But we can't disclose that information. It would spell doom for my good friend Choi Yang and end any chance to negotiate a trade treaty."

"Not if we stay covert sir. The Special Forces don't publish their assignments or disclose their intelligence to any other entity. I know. I was part of that operation for four years."

"Can we work directly with them without going through General Albertson?"

"We can, if I can convince my former Commander that it's important to do so."

"I understand, Captain and thank you for your help."

"My pleasure sir, I'll do what I can. It sounds like your son's a tough soldier, like his father!"

"I just want him to be a live soldier Michael!" A look of sadness crept across his face.

Chapter 42

Tony found Diego at the local corner bar holding court with his "bad hombres," as Carmella called them. His entourage looked like a reunion of the San Quentin class of 1966. Five guys with one thing in common, desperation! Diego had his back to Tony as he walked into the dark, dingy smoke-filled room.

The uniform got the attention of Miguel Rodriguez, the neighborhood pusher, sitting opposite Diego at the booth in the far corner. At 10 am they were the only patrons in the bar.

"What does this boy scout want?" Miguel said, his eyes raised to acknowledge Tony's entrance.

Diego turned towards the door. His eyes unaccustomed to the morning light filtering through the filthy window at the front of the room, he could only see the silhouette of the subject of Miguel's attention.

His eyes adapted as Tony's voice broke the silence. "Hey Diego, how's my old buddy doing?" He asked with his arms opened ready to man-hug his former point man.

"Tony, is that you? What are you doing here?" he responded as he stood and turned to greet him. "You slumming or you need a drink to start the day?"

His friends looked at each other wondering who this character was to Diego.

"Hey amigos, this is my friend Sergeant Tony Benedetto. He's the guy that saved my ass in Nam."

"Have a seat Sarge and tell us why you would risk your life for this useless bastard?" laughed Miguel, setting off a like response from his entourage.

"Well that's a long story guys, but I just need to see Diego about some unfinished business, if you can spare him for a couple of hours?

"Well, I don't know soldier boy. We also have some unfinished business with your old Army buddy and we have a very busy schedule today!"

Tony was told by Carmella that Diego was in trouble with these characters and that he owed them money for gambling losses. They wanted him to sell drugs for them to pay his debt.

"Yeah, Tony, I have some business with these guys. Where are you staying? I'll meet you for lunch amigo."

Tony could see that his eyes were glazed and that they showed fear. He was not comfortable leaving him there.

"I'm only passing through and I need your help to solve a problem I have out here in California. Let's go and I'll explain."

"He don't want to go, didn't you hear him?" said the big guy on Miguel's left.

"Yeah, you deaf or somethin'. He said that he'll have lunch with you later, gringo!" added the gruff looking little guy with the oversized mustache, at the end of the table.

"Tony, I'll see you later buddy," Diego said trying to calm the situation down.

Knowing that he would have to leave in a couple of days, Tony decided to back off. "Okay, I'll wait for you outside amigo. Nice meeting you boys." As he reached the door he heard the big guy say to Diego, "Who's he, your mothah?" bringing a laugh to the table.

Tony sighed and took a deep breath as he opened the door to the fresh air outside. He went across the street to wait in the Ford Falcon that he had rented at the airport.

How did Diego get himself into this mess? He wondered.

Tony had been sitting in his sweltering rental for nearly an hour when he noticed the door to the bar open and the tough looking, mustached little guy come out. The guy looked around and saw Tony in the Falcon across the street. He smiled as he swaggered over to his car. Tony rolled down his window.

"Your little boyfriend is going to be awhile; he says he'd call yuh lada."

"That's okay. I'll wait for him here," responded Tony.

"I said that he'd call yuh lada gringo. You'd better move out of here while you still can," growled the little enforcer.

"Well, since you put it that way, I guess I'd better get going. I do have to meet someone. Tell Diego I'll call him tonight."

"Good boy, you're not as dumb as yuh look, meatball," he responded, through a smile that displayed an array of missing teeth.

Tony rolled up his window, waved goodbye with a smile and took off down the street."

He drove to a Salvation Army store that he had passed on his way to the bar. He found some street clothes that were hardly flattering, making him look like a derelict in search of his daily refreshment. He added a 50 cent pair of dark glasses and an LA Dodger's cap. He was now ready to revisit his new friends.

He parked two blocks from the bar and began his imitation of a drunken street person to get into character before he reached his destination. His soiled LA Dodgers' cap was pulled down over his brow as he stumbled in the door. He peeked from under his cap and saw that his "friends" were no longer in the room. There were several patrons at three different tables, who looked up to see who was coming in as he continued his act, nearly falling over a bar stool. Slurring his words he asked for Rodriguez.

The burly bartender responded, "What do you want with the boss?"

"I got a message for him, it's ...important."

"Yeah, well give it to me and get the hell out of here."

"I don't know. My boss will be pissed if I don't give it to him pursonnnelly," continuing his slurred speech.

"Oh yeah, well, I guess he's going to be pissed," the bartender said as he lifted the bar's counter to get to his pesty uninvited guest.

Tony waited until he reached for him then stuck his non-issued .357 Magnum revolver into his gut, grabbing his arm with a twist to complete the surprise encounter.

The bartender, in pain and thinking that this guy must be nuts said, "Are you crazy, Rodriguez will kill you."

"Hey it will be the last thing you see buddy. Let's go!" his weapon prodding him on.

Tony heard a scream from behind a closed door that looked like an entrance to the office.

"Let's go see Mr. Rodriguez," said Tony as he twisted his arm harder, now behind his back, and cocked his weapon, pushing it hard against his ribs. The patrons bolted from the room knowing that no good was going to come from this confrontation.

"Open the door!" Tony commanded.

The bartender opened the door and Tony, shielded by the big guy entered.

"Hands in the air, boys!"

Rodriguez went for his gun. Tony's well-aimed round blew out his shoulder. He yelled in pain as he spun around from the impact and went to the floor, his gun flung into the air. The little guy to his left tried for his shot and Tony put a .357 hollow-nosed round into his hip that threw him over his chair screaming in pain.

Tony looked at Diego, tied to a chair, his face bloodied and his head down. He was a defeated man. He grabbed their weapons and had the bartender untie Diego and tie Rodriguez and the little guy neck to neck with his belt; and then hog tie their hands behind them and ankles together, as they squirmed and moaned in pain and bleeding from their wounds.

After securing the startled bartender to a chair, Tony used the office phone to call the LA police figuring that they may be interested in the cache of drugs on the boss's desk, but not until he was sure that the raid would be well covered by the media. He called the LA Times and the local TV news station and told them that they had better get to Rodriguez's place if they wanted to assure that the evidence wasn't destroyed. He noticed that there was a syringe full of a liquid, which he assumed to be heroin. He figured that Diego was about to be given his final high by these bad hombres.

By the time Tony and Diego reached the Falcon sirens were coming from all directions followed by TV and newspaper logoed vehicles.

"We need to talk, old buddy," he said as he laid him out in the back seat. "Stay down! We've got to get out of here."

The evening news considered the event to be the result of rival gangs' drug war. The presence of the press and TV kept the often suspect police honest. It was now up to the courts.

Rodriguez and his boys didn't want it to be known that they were taken down by a little gringo. They went quietly to the hospital under police escort but obsessed with the idea of revenge.

Tony, realizing that someone could have been killed, was in a cold sweat, his hands trembling, as he drove to Diego's home, but grateful that he didn't have to tell Carmella that her grandson was dead. He was counting on the pride and arrogance of the bad guys to keep his name out of it, but he knew that bad guys like them had ways of getting revenge. He was barely aware of Diego's repeated mumblings that he was sorry. What do I do now? was Tony's only thought.

Chapter 43

The Michigan press had Sam Polowski trailing his primary opponent by less than five percentage points. The influx of monies from Buckman's resources had allowed for an aggressive media blitz that took him from virtual oblivion to within striking distance of the leading Republican candidate, a moderate who had often voted with liberal Democrats on such issues as civil rights and Medicare. The Polowski campaign's message was that Sam was a fiscal conservative and his opponent was a free spending bureaucrat. Sharon was not happy with the image but knew it was the only way he had a chance.

That message was being pounded into the subconscious of the voting public who believed that less social spending meant less taxes and smaller government. The costs of precariously declared wars, such as the Vietnam "conflict" and so-called national security was never considered as the real reason for high taxes and expensive government programs that valued $2,000 toilets financed by the Pentagon over feeding and educating the poor.

To many conservatives in government, like Sam Polowski, dollars spent on military actions were an investment in the future. Of course for many of the war advocates, that investment was also one in their own future as it was tied to the military/industrial complex that was the source of their political funding. And for others it was often their retirement income "earned" while sitting on a defense contractor's board of directors.

Sharon Polowski did everything she could physically do for her father's campaign, but she could not give fully of her spirit and her profound intellect. Her only hope, if he won, was that he would see the real picture and moderate his philosophical positions on the truly important issues facing the country. She realized, however, that she had helped him make a pact with the "devil" when she introduced him to Jim Buckman.

The primaries were less than two months away and she had to return to Yale to complete law school. She had done her best, improving the efficiency and effort of her father's election committee and staff, and would return the week before the primaries to help in the last minute effort to get him to Congress. She also took some solace in knowing that if her father won the primary to become the Republican candidate for the U.S. Senate, that he would face a very popular Democrat in the 1968 election.

Sam, grateful for his ascent in the polls, called Buckman to let him know that he was definitely committed to his conservative program. His commitment would play an important role for his financial backers if he won the Senate seat from Michigan.

Chapter 44

Tony and Diego arrived at the Martinez home to find Carmella on the phone with her son, Diego's father, Manuel. He had been released from prison and was now back in his home town in Mexico. Her smile and joy at this news was broken as she saw the battered and bloodied face of her grandson Diego.

"Oh my God!" she declared, dropping the phone's receiver. "What did they do to you?"

Manny Martinez yelled into his phone, "What is it, mama, what happened?"

Mrs. Martinez ran to Diego, being held up by Tony. "What did those pigs do to you?"

"He'll be okay Carmella, but you both need to get out of here!"

"Get out of here? Where would we go? Tony, I am very scared....what happened?"

"Who's on the phone?" asked Tony, concerned about someone overhearing his explanation of the day's events.

"My son, Manuel, Diego's Papa," answered Carmella.

"Isn't he in prison?" asked Tony.

"He was paroled and deported to Mexico. He's calling to ask me and Diego to visit."

"Great idea! Let's get Diego cleaned up. Tell your son you'll be there tomorrow. Get his address and telephone number. We'll be in touch with him in about two hours."

Carmella explained to her son what little she knew and told him that she would call later to explain more.

As they worked to clean and bandage Diego, Tony explained the craziness that he and Diego had just experienced. "These guys are killers and they have many people working for them who will seek revenge. I'm sure they'll be out on bail by his time tomorrow, and you and Diego are in serious danger." explained Tony as calmly as he could.

"Tony, why did you do that? You put everyone in danger," cried Carmella.

"I know, and I'm scared, but they were going to kill your grandson. I couldn't let them do that. I just couldn't. You and Diego have to go to Mexico and be invisible for a while. You're both American citizens, so you'll be able to come back. Where is your son?"

"He is in Guadalajara, it is in Jalisco, a Mexican State in the central part of Mexico. It's so far away Tony. How will we get there? How will we live? We have no money. I can no longer work, and I don't know if Diego's papa has a job," wept Mrs. Martinez.

I don't know, but I have twenty five hundred dollars that I got back from that law firm. It was what was left of the $5000 retainer that I gave them to represent Diego. It's yours. It will go farther in Mexico than here," Tony said as he handed her the cash.

"We can't take this, you've already done too much, and even if we did take it how will we live after this is gone?" Carmella asked as she put up her hands refusing the money.

"Carmella there's no choice. If you stay here, Diego and probably you, will die. Diego is smart, he'll find work. I'll help as much as I can, you know that! You can come back to this country when the government has sent these guys to prison and broken up their gang."

"You know that might not happen. They have a lot of money and can pay lawyers and judges to get them off!"

"This is a big country. If that happens I'll help you find a safe place to live, but we need time to figure all that out. You need to leave, now!" declared Tony.

Carmella broke down in tears as Tony continued to repair the damage inflicted on his friend.

Tony called the LA airport and found that there was a flight to Mexico City at 11:20 PM that evening. They could then catch a flight to Guadalajara in the morning. He booked the flights on his credit card and began helping his friends pack.

Carmella called her son and explained what had happened to Diego and how Tony was helping.

"He's right mama. I know these people. They'll kill you both and not even think about it. You need to come here. I'll find a way to take care of you. Diego can find work. Don't worry!" Carmella could sense the tears in his voice. "I'm so sorry that I failed you," cried Manny.

The drive to the airport was quiet. The emotions of the day had consumed their energy and their thoughts. Diego bandaged and solemn, sat in the back seat, his head down in shame and regret.

They didn't need passports or visas to travel to Mexico or to return. They just needed proof of their American citizenship. Tony made sure they had the proper papers and cautioned Carmella to keep them safe.

Tony waited at the airport with his friends until he was sure of the flight's scheduled departure.

Diego looked at his loyal Army buddy and said, "Tony, I'm sorry that I've caused you such pain. I'm no good." His hand went to cover his face as he wept. "What will you do? They will be after you too. Where will you go?"

"I am flying out of here in an hour. I'll be back to Boston by morning. Don't worry about me; take care of your grandmother."

"I can never do enough to thank you!"

"Yes you can! Straighten out your life and don't be a victim. I know you couldn't get a job in LA, but you can't let the haters win. You're a smart guy. You can beat the system and you can do it legally."

The airport's public address system announced the boarding of the flight to Mexico City.

"I'll be in touch. I have your father's telephone number and address. Just stay low and don't contact anyone but me back here in the States," Tony advised as he hugged them and they said their goodbyes.

The flight to Boston was uneventful and Tony managed to sleep for most of it. He hadn't told his parents of his precarious adventure or of his return that morning. He needed time to sort things out. His life was in a state of chaos and he had no answers.

He decided to stay at his parents' home in South Boston for the rest of the week. He needed to think and he did that best during his long walks on Carson Beach. The moonlight played its reflection on the glass-like bay and the gentle breeze calmed his spirit.

He would walk to Kelly's Landing for its famous French Fries, which he would consume on his trek on the causeway to Castle Island. By the time he reached the ancient fortress that once protected Washington's militia from an attack from the sea he would be ready for a soft-serve chocolate ice cream cone, double-high and covered with chocolate jimmies from Sullivan's. It reminded him of the kind of chocolate topping his father made at the Walter Baker's chocolate factory in Dorchester.

The long walk was a nostalgic relief from the trauma of the last few days. He thought how ironic it is that when he was young almost every day seemed to be an act in a long playing drama. Now as he looked back he realized that those were the good old days, and although they seemed to be tough times they didn't adequately prepare him for the real world of surreal conflicts and irrational behavior. As he crossed over from the beach-way to his parents' house, he saw his mom and dad sitting on their front steps with their neighbors enjoying the cool breeze off of the bay on a warm September evening. This brought back memories of his childhood when neighbors would gather on each other's front steps to exchange stories, news and jokes. He enjoyed listening to their tales and relished their laughter as their day's stress and tension were released into the night air.

"Tony, how are you?" asked Mrs. Hurley as she got up from her comfortable seat to give him a big hug. "It's so good to see you home again."

"I'm fine Mrs. Hurley. How are you?" Tony greeted the neighbors who treated him as if he was a war hero. He didn't feel like a hero and he wasn't proud of his actions of late. After giving his regards he went up to his parents' second floor apartment to catch the evening news.

The evening news didn't break his mood of despair. The Vietnam conflict was the main story. It was about body counts and destruction. There was no significant progress towards the promised victory, only more death.

The news report shifted to Los Angeles. A local CBS Affiliate reporter was standing in front of a burned out home in Watts.

> "Los Angeles Fire Chief Donovan believes this home was fire-bombed early this morning as the result of a mistaken identity gang retaliation. He said that the residents of this home were peaceful people; that Mrs. Carmella Martinez was a community activist who was known as a kind and caring person. Her adult grandson, Diego Martinez, was a wounded war hero who returned from Vietnam last year. The chief said that it was highly unlikely that they were the target of this horrible act. The LA police are investigating. There is no trace of the Martinez family and it is feared that they may have been incinerated by the intense fire that prevailed. Back to you Peter at the news desk."

Tony was stunned as he sat staring at the television. His jaw dropped and he was in a state of disbelief at what he just heard. He realized that they had just escaped a horrendous death. He was torn between feeling relief and an overwhelming feeling of inadequacy.

He thought he might go back to Fort Devens after dinner tomorrow. He needed to prepare for the next group of recruits scheduled to arrive the following week, and he was also afraid that his parents would pick up on his down mood. He didn't want them to worry or, worse, become a target.

The drive back to the base, after a home-made ravioli dinner, made him feel somewhat lethargic, but the dinner was worth the wait. He thought about whether he should call Diego tomorrow and let him know about the reports of his death.

By the time he reached the base and checked in with the Commanding Officer he was ready for a hot shower and bed. It seemed like he had just fallen asleep when his phone rang startling him to awaken. It was dark outside but that was not unusual since he often rose before dawn.

"Hello, who is this?" he asked still not sure if he was dreaming.

There was a pause that is often a prelude to a long distance call and then, "Hey little buddy, where you been?"

Tony recognized the distinct southern drawl of Master Sergeant Bobby Franklin, "Hey Sarge what's up with you? I've been on the west coast. Where are you?"

"I'm still in Nam. I've been trying to reach you for a couple of days. What's on the west coast? You got some California babe interested in that ugly face?"

"No, nothing that good, just visiting friends. So what's going on, old man?"

"Well, speaking of friends, I've got some news about your friend Lieutenant Buckman."

"Did they find him? Is he alive?" asked Tony anxiously.

"It's a long sorry, but the short version is that he and six others escaped from an NVA underground holding facility near Khe Sanh about three weeks ago. The word is that they're heading towards Da Nang hoping to meet up with our forces before they are recaptured and sent to Hanoi."

"How do you know this? Did one of them make it already?"

"Nope, and I don't know the details, only that your rich friend is in charge and that they are kicking ass along the way. I thought you might appreciate the fact that your kind and compassionate training methods worked, at least on one soldier."

"Well, I'm sure it worked on all of them to some extent, but the truth is you either have it or you don't and Buckman has it."

"Well it's good to see that you've gained some humility since we last met, but the real reason I'm calling is that I'm with the Special Forces unit that's seeking to rescue your protégé. We have good reason to believe that he's within 40 kilometers of our base at Da Nang. It's reported that his makeshift squad took out a Viet Cong patrol waiting in ambush for our guys in that area."

"Why didn't they rescue them?"

"There was no trace of them when they arrived probably about an hour after the firefight. The Company Commander had to move fast to support an attack more than five miles north. They did find one soldier, a private Rogers. He had died of wounds from what appeared to be an animal attack. He was one of the men captured near Khe Sanh and is believed to have been with Buckman's squad."

"So they surmised from that information that Buckman must have been there?" asked Tony.

"I guess so. It makes sense, doesn't it?"

"Yes, it does. It's too bad about Rogers. He was one of our guys. He was a good man! What kind of animal was it?"

"They think that it was one of those tigers that roam the hills near Khe Sanh. He had been carried to the location of the firefight and was still strapped to a makeshift stretcher when they found him. I'll call you when we return later today. I've got to get packing. We move out in ten minutes."

"Hey good luck, buddy and remember to keep that big head down. It's an easy target," Tony's laugh was joined by Franklin's.

As he lay back, his hands behind his head, Tony felt some relief from his despair, he felt a smile break on his otherwise solemn face. He wondered if he should call Sharon as he had promised to do if he heard anything. After much thought, he decided to wait to hear more from Franklin. He didn't want to get her hopes up, only to be dashed if Jim didn't make it.

Chapter 45

Lieutenant Buckman's journey had encountered several enemy patrols and one Viet Cong Company in the weeks since they escaped from their NVA captors. They stayed close to the rivers and streams for water and food, since forest animals were also more plentiful near the waterways. Losing Private Rogers was hard on their morale. They had struggled for miles, taking turns at carrying the wounded soldier and considered it a defeat that they weren't able to save him. Even Private Hiller sobbed at his passing.

They had stumbled on an enemy force at dawn that was obviously lying in wait along an east-west path to ambush any American infantry force that ventured into their trap. Sergeant Eagle could see the enemy from his perch in a pine tree, forty feet above the ground, on a hill that overlooked the enemy's position. Up to now they had tried to avoid any unnecessary contact with the enemy. They were not always successful, but they usually had the element of surprise on their side.

"What should we do? We can avoid them by heading south for about two kilometers and then east along that ridge," reported Eagle pointing towards the south.

"How's our ammunition holding up? Do we still have grenades?" asked Buckman.

"Yeah, we have ammunition. Each man has four NVA grenades and their AK-47s are fully loaded. We also have the reloads and rations that we secured from the dead VC in that last encounter. What are your orders, Lieutenant?"

"I think that we wait until we identify an American force. We don't want to engage too soon and lose the benefit of alerting our guys and getting rescued," advised Buckman.

"I'll deploy the men in the bush."

"Take the right flank and I'll take the left. Don't fire until I do, unless fired upon," ordered a weary Buckman.

An hour passed before a VC soldier spotted a flash from the hill behind him. It was the rising sun reflected off Hiller's glasses. The VC leveled his binoculars towards the flash and distinguished a number of figures in the underbrush staring down on them from about 300 meters, high up on the hill. Alerting his company, he opened fire. A round hit Hiller in the throat. Buckman's men returned the fire with as much fury as five men with AK-47s could muster.

Eagle spotted a rocket mortar being set up and carefully aimed and fired, taking that team out. He then looked up, trying to find the source of what sounded like the roar of a jet fighter. He could see the distinctive silhouette of an American Phantom Jet coming over the horizon and heading straight towards their position. The VC saw it too and held their fire so as not to present a target to this lethal weaponry. The pilot knew that Buckman's squad didn't have a radio and he pulled the nose up before he reached the potential target.

"This is Hawkeye One to Charlie Brown One. I have identified a firefight at North 16 degrees 8 minutes and 14 seconds and East 108 degrees 16 minutes and 5 seconds."

"We read you, Hawkeye One. Can you distinguish the combatants?"

"Negative, Captain. Both parties ceased firing when they spotted me."

"We'll be there in seven minutes. Circle the area at a safe altitude. Keep them in sight, but don't fire."

Buckman realized that the VC were trying to outsmart the Phantom jet by not firing, but he also realized that they were slowly advancing up the hill towards his position. The enemy correctly figured that the closer they were to the Americans the less chance of being fired upon by the American fighter.

Buckman ordered his men to fire at will, to pin down the VC advance.

"Charlie Brown One, the group to the south has opened fire on the northern troops. I estimate that it's a patrol sized force. The northerly force is much larger. What are your orders, Captain?"

"We're in sight of them Lieutenant. I'm going down 'Main Street' to confirm identities. Be ready to make an east-west run on whichever side opens fire on us. For now assume it will be the northerly force that you have identified."

"Roger, I'll get into position for that run Charlie Brown One."

The Huey set a course to fly at a 500-foot altitude between the two, yet to be identified combatants, "Door gunners at the ready," ordered the Captain.

Buckman and his men weren't sure what was happening, but welcomed the site of the advancing helicopter followed by the Phantom Fighter.

"Cease fire and stay down men." Buckman gestured to stop firing and go down as he yelled to be heard over the roar of the oncoming aircraft to their position at top speed. As he rose to signal the Huey he felt a sting in his shoulder as an enemy round hit his collar bone. He went down bleeding from the wound.

The VC, nervous and scared started firing. The Captain radioed the fighter, "We have a visual confirming your report. Start your run but keep it tight to the northerly force. Our guys, are at the top of the hill," ordered Captain Lisa Marshall as she swooped her Huey out of harm's way and prepared for the rescue. "Sergeant Franklin, prepare the winch and the basket. We won't be able to land in this thick forest."

"Yes, Captain, we're ready for the rescue. I'm dropping in to assess their condition."

The Phantom Jet, guns blazing and rockets deployed, came down like the hawk that was its pilot's reputation, lighting up the enemy as they fled down the hill to their nearest safe-haven tunnel.

Buckman and his men jumped to their feet at the sight and waved frantically at the Huey that would be their ride home. Eagle, his head cocked back looking to the sky, raised his arms in an Indian tribute to honor his ancestors' spirits.

"We'll hold at one hundred feet Sergeant, make it quick," urged Captain Marshall. "Hawkeye is leaving us and the VC will be back if we hang around here too long."

Sergeant Franklin was lowered with a basket stretcher for any wounded. "What's your men's condition, Lieutenant?"

Buckman stared in disbelief at his former boot camp nemesis. "Damn, I never thought there'd be a day that I would be happy to see you, Sarge," as he wrapped his good arm around the big guy, his eyes tearing with joy and relief.

"We have a wounded man, shot in the neck. Private Hiller, he's over there. Private Ortiz is trying to stop the bleeding. The rest of us are just beat up and exhausted. I just took a hit in the shoulder, damn that was dumb, but I'll be okay."

"Let's get Hiller into the copter, Lieutenant, and get you and your men out of here."

The rescue was quick and efficient. "Welcome aboard men. Next stop Da Nang. Time of arrival 28 minutes." greeted Captain Marshall. "Charlie Brown One to Base, mission accomplished! We have our six heroes aboard and we're coming home. Two men are wounded. Be prepared for a serious throat wound and a shoulder wound."

The rhythmic sound of the whirling blades was like a symphony to Jim Buckman's ears.

"How are yeah doin', Lieutenant?" asked Franklin in a loud southern drawl.

"I'm doing fine, Sarge, just fine, thank you!" as he allowed the stress of the last month to leave his body.

He closed his eyes, refusing the ear protection so as to absorb the rhythmic music of the blades as the helicopter rose into the sky and headed towards the now blazing morning sun. As he started to give in to his need for a deep sleep he wondered, "Did I hear a woman's voice?"

CHAPTER 46

"Captain Wong, there's a telephone call for you in the lobby." The interruption of dinner by the head waiter was expected having heard that there was a chance that the Special Force team might find young Jim today. It was a private dinner, just the two of them. They had concluded their introductory trade talks with Choi Yang earlier in the day and had planned to stay a few more days to see if there was any progress in the search for his son.

"I can bring you a phone if you want to take it here sir."

Wong noticed the anxious look in Buckman's eyes and said, "We'd appreciate it."

The head waiter brought the phone and plugged into a jack near the table.

"Hello, this is Captain Wong. Yes, Major, how are you? That's great and they're in Da Nang? He looked up at the Senior Buckman, the broad smile on his face the only message he needed.

Buckman broke the stern look with a reflective smile. "They did it! They got Jim?"

Wong answered with a 'thumbs up' and an even broader smile. "Yes, we'll meet them in Saigon, Major. Thank you and your men for a great job."

He hung up and sat back in his chair. "Unbelievable," was all he could say.

"What happened? Is Jim all right?'

"He's a little banged up and exhausted but they rescued him and five of his men this morning 32 kilometers west of Da Nang. They were in the middle of a firefight with a VC company that was lying in ambush for our troops. A Phantom Fighter, which was escorting a Huey, took the enemy out while the Huey rescued Jim and his men.

Major Stratford said there's a C-119 leaving Hong Kong for Saigon in the morning and we're invited to join that flight."

"Wonderful! Great job Captain, I need to call Nancy."

"Well its early morning there, but hey, go for it Colonel," encouraged Captain Wong as he handed him the phone. "I've got a report to write, so I'll see you in the morning, sir."

"Goodnight my friend, and it is a very good night!" Colonel Buckman responded exuberantly.

The Colonel's call to his wife awakened her at 5:10 am on Sunday morning. "Hello Jim, is that you, is there anything wrong?"

"No, honey, everything is right. They found Jim and he's fine!" he blurted out. "He made it and he's fine!"

There was silence then, "Oh my God Jim, where is he? How did they find him?"

"It's a long story honey, but he's become the man that you spoke of. I'm very proud of our son!" Buckman responded, with emotion seeping into his voice, emotion that Nancy had not sensed since her husband was a young man. He relayed what he had learned of his son's leadership and courage.

"I'll see him tomorrow in Saigon. I'll try to get a call through to you from there."

"Oh, Jim this is such a gift. I don't know if we deserve it. Please be careful. I love you!"

"I love you too, Nancy."

Sharon got a message from Tony when she returned from class at 2:25 p.m. She was to call him as soon as possible. He had good news about Jim.

"Tony, this is Sharon, do they know where he is?"

"Hello, Sharon. Yes they do. He's in Da Nang. He was rescued during a firefight with the Viet Cong west of Da Nang and the report is that he's fine given the circumstances."

"Tony, that's fabulous. Are you sure?" How did they find him?"

Tony told her the story as he knew it. "Do you remember Jim talking about Master Sergeant Bobby Franklin who was his first Drill Instructor here at Fort Devens?"

"Yes, he wasn't very fond of him. You were such relief to him when you took over. He called him a frustrated southern redneck."

"Well, he's his new best friend. Bobby Franklin led the Ranger squad that rescued him!"

"Wow! That is unbelievable. When will he be home?" tears of joy welled up in her eyes.

"They're transporting him and his five men to Saigon later today and I assume that he'll be back in the States within the month."

"Do his parents know?" asked Sharon, thinking that she should call his mother.

"I'm sure they've learned the good news through official channels. Although it just happened within the last 24 hours. I heard it from Franklin, but that should be kept confidential. I'm not sure that he was authorized to tell me," cautioned Tony.

"I'll keep the source confidential, Tony. Thank you for calling. If you manage to talk to Jim tell him I send my love."

"I will, but hopefully you'll be able to tell him yourself within a few days. They'll debrief him before they let him out into the public, but that shouldn't take long."

Sharon was going to wait a couple of days before she contacted Jim's mother. She was surprised when she got a called from her that evening.

"Hello, Nancy?"

"Sharon, I have great news! Jim's been found and he's okay! Can you believe it?" Nancy Buckman declared exuberantly.

Sharon was not going to take away her moment of joy. She acted surprised and, of course, happy. "When did they find him, and where? When will he be coming home?"

Nancy told her all she knew including the part her husband played. Sharon was stunned for a minute, then realized that it was a good thing that he had the power to set a plan in motion that saved six men.

"Where is your husband now?"

"He'll be in Saigon tomorrow to see young Jim. The Army is allowing him and his interpreter, Mike Wong, to fly into there on one of their cargo planes. He said that he'll call me from there. I hope that I can talk to my son. Isn't it wonderful?"

"It is and I'm so happy! I've been praying for this for weeks. Jim's a good man!" Sharon's voice cracked with emotion.

"Yes he is, and I thank you for helping him to recognize that. You brought out the sensitivity in my son and he's a better man for it. They say he and his men fought their way through the jungle and that he was a good leader. His father is very proud of him!"

"You give me too much credit. Jim would have figured it out eventually."

"Eventually might have been too late! He needed that push from someone he respected and cared for."

Sharon caught her breath at the thought that Jim actually "cared" for her in spite of her attitude towards his beliefs. "Please let me know if you talk to him and tell him there are letters waiting for him."

"I will dear, but I'm sure he'll want to talk to you as soon as he can."

Sharon wondered if the war had changed him. What happened while he was a captive of the North Vietnamese Army? She had heard horror stories of American military men being tortured. And what was it like trying to live in the jungle with the enemy all around and having to fight their way out of there. She thought of him as a gentle person who was shielded from the real world by a protective father. He wasn't a fighter. Would he still have compassion for his fellowman or would he be paranoid and hateful? She wanted to know, but was afraid that the answers might be heartbreaking.

Chapter 47

The flight to Saigon was not exactly what the senior Buckman was used to. No first class service just uncomfortable canvas jump seats, lined along the fuselage walls. A large tracked front-end loader was chained down within a meter of his feet. The loader was followed by various pieces of heavy construction equipment similarly secured. The smell of grease and oil pervaded the air.

"Sorry about the accommodations, sir." offered Wong, "but it was the quickest way to get to Saigon and I know you're anxious to see your son."

"No apology needed, Mike. It's good to rough it once in a while. It brings back memories of my service years. I had to jump out of a plane like this once. It was over France. General Obersham, who was a Captain then, and I had to infiltrate the Vichy French government a few months before the invasion of Normandy. Parachuting at 5,000 feet in the fog over enemy territory is not one of my favorite memories."

"Well, I have had to do many jumps in my career and none were much fun. So I know what you mean, Colonel. We should be there within the hour, if the weather holds. I noted before we left that it was clear for the entire route."

Mike Wong's words had barely reached Buckman's ears when the pilot announced that there were three enemy fighters at 2 o'clock. "We will be taking evasive maneuvers, please stay secured in your places gentlemen. Our escort Phantoms will engage the MiG fighters, but it may get rough."

With that announcement the massive, heavily loaded plane banked hard left to put the fast approaching enemy planes behind them and allow for a better approach for the escort fighters. The C-119 was now flying due south as the Phantoms swooped down from their high altitude positions, aligning themselves in a confrontation path towards the challenging MiG-21 fighters.

The two American Phantom F-4s had the advantage of altitude as they made their run at the three aggressive MiGs. They simultaneously released their Wasp Missiles as their M61 Vulcan Cannons laid down a deadly screen of firepower into the MiGs' oncoming path. Two of the enemy attackers were unable to avoid the missiles, but they had fired their own air to air missiles before being destroyed.

The Phantoms split right and left leaving an array of hot decoy fragments within the flight path of the enemy missiles. Each enemy missile sought the decoys to their respective destruction. The third MiG dropped to a lower altitude, passing under the Phantoms on its way to its target, the C-119.

The cargo plane banked hard right at the suggestion of the pursuing Phantom squadron commander, Captain Berkowitz, returning to its original flight path, but gaining altitude in a maneuver to force the enemy jet to come back into the Phantom's kill zone. The MiG-21, with its delta-wing design, was slow in responding to the C-119's banking maneuver.

The heavy equipment cargo shifted precariously towards the passengers. Buckman and Wong pushed their bodies hard against the plane's fuselage wall, staring incredulously at the Army- green multi-ton loader, expecting it to roll onto them. Fortunately the cables held firm. The plane leveled off, returning the threatening cargo to its original berth.

The lead Phantom launched its remaining missile at the pursuing MiG as it simultaneously fired its own towards the big lumbering cargo plane. The American pilot knew that he couldn't decoy the enemy missile since it was to cross perpendicular to its own flight path. His last missile destroyed the renegade MiG, but the enemy's rocket was in flight and fixed on the tail of the C-119, he knew that he couldn't shoot it down.

Without hesitation, Lieutenant Commander Mulcahey aimed his jet at a point calculated to intercept the deadly enemy missile, ejecting from his cockpit seconds before impact. The last ditch effort worked as the Phantom was sacrificed for the benefit of the cargo plane.

Captain Berkowitz circled his Phantom Jet over his wingman's parachute observing his descent until he hit the water, making sure that there were no other enemy aircraft in the area. Not hearing a 'May Day' from Mulcahey before he ejected, he radioed his position to their base carrier. A helicopter was on its way for the rescue. He would stay as long as his fuel allowed.

A cheer went up in the C-119 upon Captain Berkowitz's report of the success of their mission. The communication between the Phantom escorts and the C-119 had been broadcast on the plane's speakers during the encounter. Another escort was on its way to complete their flight to Saigon.

"Damn, that was something!" declared Buckman commenting on the pilots' real-time communications during the engagement. The Navy flyboys know how to handle those MiGs!"

"Yes sir, we were like a fat cow being chased by a pack of hungry wolves. They did a hell of a job, but remind me not to book any more flights with a 10-ton loader as a fellow passenger." Wong's nervous smile was reflected by Buckman, as was his burst of laughter.

Buckman wiped the sweat from his brow and relaxed his tense body. "I hope that we'll be able to see Jim tomorrow. Did your contact say whether he was wounded?"

"They said that he was banged-up, and had a shoulder wound, but no serious injuries. I'm sure that they'll check him out thoroughly and debrief him just as thoroughly," Wong responded.

Chapter 48

Manny Martinez had not seen his son Diego or his mother Carmella much during the years he was incarcerated. The prison was too far for them to travel and visit often. He was very happy that they were able to come to Guadalajara, although he was concerned about the reason for the good fortune.

"Diego my son, how did you get involved with Rodriguez. You're very lucky to be alive my son!"

"I don't know. I thought I could make enough money so grandmother wouldn't have to work. She hasn't been well. But then I started using, and everything went wrong. I'm so sorry papa."

"I'm sorry too, sorry that you didn't learn from my mistakes. I have failed you my son." Manny's eyes dropped to avoid contact with Diego's. He didn't want him to see the tears. "Our people go to America to work and to make more money than they can make in Mexico. The illegals are afraid to complain about their working or living conditions, so they can be used. They live two or three families together in shacks that their bosses wouldn't let their dogs live in. They get charged for food and a room and are threatened with jail if they complain. I hoped to give your madre a better life, but I failed!"

Diego responded, "They don't believe they can make enough profit unless they make it on our wetbacks," added Diego using the derogatory slang for illegal aliens from Mexico. "But even if you live there as a citizen you can't get a job that pays you enough to live."

"They don't want us to be legal. They don't want to pay us like we are Americans. They use us and they know we're desperate for what little money we earn. And when they are through with us they throw us away like garbage. But I've had enough of their abuse. I must stay here in Mexico and live as best I can, but you are an American citizen. You have rights that I do not. Don't let them deny you. You must return. My mother will stay with me and my brother. I have a job at the hotel that pays enough to take care of mi madre."

"But Papa, if I return I could be killed by those thugs. If it wasn't for my friend I would be dead already. We are in serious danger!

"You know why I was arrested. I was a mule, bringing drugs into the United States to make enough money to take care of you and mama. But that was a stupid thing to do. I'm not a bad man. When I was doing that I was working for your uncle, my brother Juan Carlos. He's a big man in the drug markets. He has people in Los Angeles."

"No. Papa! I don't want anyone else hurt. Please don't ask him to do anything."

"He knows already and he is very upset that Rodriguez tried to kill you and his mother. He knows that they bombed your home thinking you were both there. My brother cannot be stopped, but he told me that he will not have him killed. He will make sure that he stays in prison for a long time and that he does nothing more to anger his jefe."

"His jefe? You mean his boss? Rodriguez works for Uncle Juan Carlos?" Diego said in disbelief. "And what about my friend Tony, is he in danger?"

"I'm told that Rodriguez doesn't know who your friend is, but he has gotten the message that if anyone even gets a scratch, he and his men are done! He is very scared and has pleaded for his life. He knows that he is not safe anywhere, even in prison, if he does not do as Juan Carlos demands."

"Where is Uncle Juan? Should I thank him?"

"Your uncle is a wanted man. He is in the mountains hiding from the Policia. I suggest you go back to the States next month, but go to another place, far from Los Angeles. It is still be too dangerous for you there, in case there is someone who hasn't gotten the message," suggested Manny."

"Where would I go? I have no money and no job?"

"We'll figure that out my son, but for now we are together, and it has been a very long time."

Carmella appeared in the doorway, "What are you two talking about? Dinner is on the table and its getting cold."

"We're talking about the future mama. Diego's future!" responded Manny."

Chapter 49

It was two days before Buckman Senior and Captain Wong could see young Jim. His encounters along his path to freedom provided valuable information on enemy movements and locations. The debriefing was thorough as was his medical checkup and the attention to his wound.

On the third day Colonel Buckman and Captain Wong waited in General Albertson's office until Jim was free from his duties. Buckman didn't know what to expect. He had visions of a battle-worn man, not of his well-groomed, athletically built, handsome and usually upbeat son.

"I know that you're upset with me Colonel, but I had no choice. We have enough morale problems here without adding preferential treatment exposed by the press," explained the General.

"Obviously, I was upset, but I understand David, but it has turned out positive. At least he survived!"

"I'm told he showed strong leadership ability and led his men like a professional. That has to count for something in his life's experience. He was challenged and he responded in a way that would make any father proud," continued Albertson. "He's a lot like his old man!"

"Thanks, Dave! What's going to happen now? Does he get some time off? Will he need to be re-deployed? His mother would like to have him home, but I realize that he may not be able to go all the way to Connecticut."

"Well, he did take a hit just before he was rescued, a round to his shoulder, but he's fine. The good news is that he'll be re-assigned to the States for a few months. We're sending him to the Pentagon to work with some of our strategist. He has some very interesting information about the enemy's tactics and the use of their underground network. The bad news is that he might eventually be re-deployed."

"But he's all right? Have you talked to him about a reassignment?" asked the senior Buckman, thinking that the new assignment in the U.S., although temporary, would boost his spirits.

"Yes, and I informed him that he is being considered for a combat promotion to Captain and, of course, a Purple Heart. I believe that he will get the promotion and take command of a company. He'll have a 30-day leave before his Pentagon assignment begins."

"That's good news, but I wish he didn't have to go back to the front," lamented Jim.

"The fact is that there is no real front in Vietnam. The enemy is everywhere in this theatre. But here is something that he might want to consider. I know he was studying law at Yale. He may be able to continue his studies in D.C. He would be wise to ask for a transfer to a Judge Advocate General's Corps. I'll recommend him for JAG, if that's what he wants. I owe you that much Colonel."

"You don't owe me General, and I'm sorry I put you through this. Jim will have to decide his future for himself. I realize that he may take my place in business some day and that he will have to make some very tough decisions in the future. He's already shown me that he has sound judgment. I trust that he'll make the right decisions when given the choice."

The intercom on the General's desk buzzed. "General, Lieutenant Buckman is here."

"Show him in, Marie."

The door opened and Jim Buckman appeared, his face scarred from battle; his body at least 30 pounds lighter, his eyes deep and dark, without expression, and his arm in a sling, as he looked upon his visitors. He forced a smile to his father, but wondered why he was here. "Hello, Dad."

"Jim...son, are you all right? This is Captain Michael Wong, He accompanied me on this mission."

"I'm fine, just a few bruises and a wounded shoulder, but mostly I'm just very tired and happy to be here alive. What mission are you talking about? How's mother?"

"She's much better now that you're back. She was very upset. We thought we lost you!"

"I had my doubts too. We were, well, some of us were very lucky," His eyes looked down and his face grew solemn as he thought about those who didn't make it out of the ambush and of Private Rogers, who died in the forest.

"General Albertson tells me you'll be coming home for a 30-day leave. That will be all your mother needs to get her spirits back."

"I'm grateful for that General, but how did you get here, Father? I didn't think that commercial airlines flew into Saigon."

"Well, that's a long story, but the Army provided transportation. We were in Hong Kong on a trade mission when we got the good news."

Young Jim knew that there was more to the story and that somehow his father was involved in his rescue. If he was, it was the one time he was thankful for his interference in his life.

Jim spent the evening reading the many letters written as promised by Sharon while he was in captivity. She tried to keep her messages at a social level, informing him of her life's "news of the day" but he noted her concern, as he detected her sadness and regret between the lines.

She wrote, "I know that you will be fine. You're a persistent man, as you have shown me in our relationship. Don't lose your ability to love and laugh. Life will be good again!"

She knew that if he survived that he would have suffered damage to his spirit and possibly to his ability to trust and love. She hoped it wouldn't be permanent.

Chapter 50

Sam Polowski's bid for the Republican nomination for the Michigan Senate seat gained significant momentum with the financial and behind the scenes backing of Jim Buckman. Sharon worked tirelessly to do the best job she could for her father. She recruited hundreds of sign holders and managed to get his name in the media.

Buckman's efforts included his starting rumors of possible improprieties of the leading Republican challenger. The tactic was to insinuate that the sitting State legislator was a puppet for free spenders, even though he was a Republican. He had voted with liberals on several bills to help the poor and needy of his State and would continue to spend taxpayers money if elected, was the mantra.

Moderate Republicans were losing favor, with the advantage going to the far right toward, Sam Polowski. Sharon didn't like the tactic, but she knew it was out of her control. It was the price one paid for the support of the wealthy and powerful.

The primary was held on the same day as the State's Presidential primary. Michigan's favorite son, Republican George Romney, was considered a moderate and an anti-war candidate for the office, a situation that had little support outside of his home state. Without the support of the national electorate in the various state primaries, he decide to drop out of the race in February 1968.

Sam Polowski found the political battle overwhelming, but he managed to survive and looked forward to the possibility of challenging the Democratic incumbent. Sharon was proud of her father's accomplishment, and her efforts, but was not enthused at the possibility of his success. The country was being torn apart by assassinations, riots and brutal police retaliations that left hundreds of protesters dead and wounded. She didn't see Nixon as the compassionate leader that the country needed.

Jim Buckman's return from war was the only thing in her personal life that was positive. She would complete her Law degree in the spring and be able to spend more time with him. He had opted to take General Albertson's advice and accept the transfer to the Army's JAG unit in Washington D.C. He would complete his work towards a law degree at George Washington University.

He had survived the anxieties of war, but as she feared, Jim was not the same man that left to serve his country. He was burdened by the effects of war and was no longer the light-hearted guy with a sense of humor or open to new ideas.

They would talk about the men that he served with and the desperation, which was a major part of their lives. He was military now, but he was haunted by the realities of a war fought without provocation by men and women whose courage was being used with little compassion for their lives. Eventually, as a defense attorney in the JAG he would be able to help those who were used as scapegoats for the failures of their political and military leaders. He had become, in many ways, a political moderate, but he was hardened in his resolve to rectify the injustices that he was exposed to by the very system that encouraged them and brought his family wealth.

Sharon worried that he was becoming obsessed with society's major problems at the expense of his emotional well-being. He was frustrated and angry at the system. He talked about how a man like Sergeant Joe Eagle served a country that deprived him; his family and his ancestors of the dignity they deserved, yet he gave it everything he had. He was now honorably discharged with medals of appreciation, but unable to find a decent job. He was living on the Indian reservation in the stark desert of Arizona, which was given to his tribe a hundred years ago as compensation for the government taking everything they had of value. Eagle thought of rejoining the military.

He held back tears as he spoke of the death of Private Rogers, a young black man whose family lived in a ghetto in the Bronx. He was raised by his mother. His father had left them, unable to find work that could support his family. His father knew that they wouldn't qualify for government assistance unless he left. Only as an abandoned family would his wife and children meet the standards of the righteous purveyors of benefits.

When he was eighteen Rogers decided that he wouldn't allow his mom, brother and sister to live that way any longer. At first reluctant to respond to the draft, he joined the Army, accepting his fate. It was a paying job. He sent his checks home to help his mother. He would say that he was one less mouth to feed at home and when you're living a level below the poverty line, one less is important.

For Rogers, his service, and only reward, would be to have his casket draped by an American flag that would be handed to his mother in a triangular fold, at his funeral. Jim often thought that the cost of his own family's dinner at the country club would feed Rogers' family for a week. They weren't looking for advantages, they were trying to survive!

He told Sharon about Private Hiller's life in a dysfunctional white family. He was the product of a chronically ill mother and a drunken father who worked the coal mines until his lungs would not allow him to continue. Hiller was outspoken and bitter. But he was not outspoken anymore, his voice box having been destroyed by an enemy round, just minutes before the rescue.

The stories were slow in coming. It had been days before he could even talk about Vietnam, but Sharon knew that he had to tell them and encouraged him to trust her love. He needed the catharsis of closure of those experiences that were eating at his heart, and at his well-being.

She was most touched by his story about the North Vietnamese Army captain who declared that he was defending his family and his homeland from an invasion. He told her of his tough and seemingly ruthless demeanor having had them beaten while in his charge as prisoners of war. Yet he cared enough about his friend to end his pain from the napalm bombing that racked his burned body. Jim knew that he could have chosen to kill them, his enemies, instead.

"I don't know if one of my men tightened the rope around his neck that was restraining him from escaping, but I do know that, at the time, I felt relief at his death. Not having him as a burden gave us a better chance of reaching our troops. But Sharon, he had a family, a wife and kids who were waiting for him. Maybe they were victims of the war. What would we do if we were invaded for some quasi-political reason? I convinced myself that he did it to himself rather than help us find our way back, but I have my doubts and I am ashamed of my thoughts."

Jim's ability to give his love fully depended on freeing himself of the guilt and self-doubt by the war. It was a conflict that eventually cost the lives of more than 50,000 Americans and the quality of life of tens of thousands more, on both sides.

Chapter 51

Diego took his father's advice and returned to the States. His call to Tony Benedetto caught his good friend by surprise. It had been several months since they spoke.

"Where are you? Are you and Carmella alright?" asked Tony with some anxiety.

"Tony, I'm in New York City. My father told me I needed to get back into the U.S. since I was a citizen and I didn't belong in Mexico. He still sees the U.S. as a place of hope and prosperity. I hate to burden you, but I don't know where to start. I can't go back to LA and I can't rejoin the military with my bad legs. I need your wise counsel, my friend."

Diego went on to tell him the story of his time with his father and of the new respect he had for the man whom he only knew from a distance as an imprisoned criminal.

"I thank you for having us go to Mexico. I was not in a good mental state to make such decisions. I owe you, amigo! Carmella is fine. She's with her sons and even though my uncle is a drug lord, she's safe and not wanting for anything in her home village. She sends her love and appreciation."

"I'm happy to hear that it worked out for both of you. Have you straightened out your life, my friend? I've worried about you since we said goodbye at the airport."

"My padre warned me about fast money and the consequences, as he has experienced them. He kept telling me that there is no easy way. He says that I need to accept the burdens life has given me and overcome them with dignity."

"Your dad has become a very wise man, but he took the hard road to get there. I hope he's convinced you to do otherwise and it isn't a burden if you're serious about doing the right thing.

"He has and I am trying to do the right thing! And how are you? Has anyone given you trouble since our adventure in LA? My uncle, Juan Carlos, assured us that they would not," Diego had explained the connection his uncle had with Rodriguez in a previous call.

"Do you have a job in New York?" asked Tony.

"Just temporary work as a laborer on construction jobs, but it's not steady. I live in the ghetto in the Bronx with five others and it is not where I want to be. Two of them are druggies. The others are alcoholics."

"It sounds like a nice family atmosphere, Thanksgiving will be fun!" joked Tony.

"Yeah, it should be a warm and loving experience," added Diego. "I need to get out of here!"

"Well, what can I do for you? Do you want to come to Massachusetts? I can ask dad if there are any jobs available at the factory where he works. He's no longer working for the chocolate factory. He was there for 28 years. They were bought by General Foods and moved to Delaware where they could pay a third of what they were paying workers here, without the union. He works for a non-union candy company in Cambridge. They don't pay well, but its work. There are other opportunities, especially if you can get into a skilled union, such as an apprentice carpenter or plumber. You're better off working in a union shop."

"I don't know. I've been a burden to you since Nam. I just need your advice right now. I was thinking of going to a place where there are a lot of Hispanics, like Florida or South Texas."

"Well, why don't you come to Boston for the weekend? I'm living at my parents' home since I got out of the service. I'm working part-time in an engineering firm and finishing my degree at night. They own a three-family and kept an apartment open for me while I get my life together. In fact, if you haven't got any commitments you can stay until you figure things out."

"I can do that, really? But only for couple of weeks. I would like to meet your family. Hey, and what about you, do you have a girl friend?"

"Not really. I date, but I'm not ready for a commitment. Like you, I'm not certain where life will take me."

"Have you ever heard from Michelle? Did she marry that jock that she left you for while you were in Nam?"

"The last I heard she was living in Tennessee. I'm over that relationship. I realized in Nam that there are more important things in life and too many opportunities to dwell on the negatives. Besides, if you really love someone you want them to have a happy life, even if it's not with you."

"Well Tony, I see you are still the optimistic philosopher. If you're hit in the face you would think that it proves how well you can take a punch," laughed Diego. "I'll be there on Saturday, if you're serious about your invitation, amigo."

"I'm serious, and you're very welcome buddy. It will be good to have some time together. By the way, speaking of love lives, what happened to Keisha?"

"She got a scholarship to go to Kent State in Ohio. She's studying for a degree in Biology. She's still hoping to be a doctor someday. That would mean a few more years of college. I've written, but haven't received anything from her. I think she's moved on."

"How are you with that?"

"I'm not sure yet, but you're right, I do love her and I want her to be happy. I just wish that her happiness included me."

"Well, it may someday, but if it doesn't, you'll find love again, if you're open to it!" advised Tony. "First, you need to get your life in order, before you can have a serious relationship with anyone, including Keisha."

"Yes, I know and I'm ready to do that Tony!" declared Diego.

Although Tony was happy to hear from Diego and looked forward to seeing him, he was worried that he wouldn't be able to overcome his demons. He wondered, was he really sincere in his resolve or was he to become another "emissary" of his drug lord uncle? He would know soon enough.

Chapter 52

Jim and Nancy Buckman's lives returned to normal with the return of their eldest son. Jim was home long enough for his mother to detect the change in his personality, although he attempted to be the fun-loving guy that they had raised to manhood. His dad relished the change to a more serious young man. Maybe the war had hardened him to the level needed to make the difficult decisions he would have to make if he was to have success in the dog-eat-dog world of business and politics.

"Mike Wong told me what you did in China and how you learned of our escape and figured out where we might be. I want you to know that I'm very grateful for your actions and for your love. I know that we don't often see eye to eye, but I do know that you care!" exclaimed young Jim.

"Jim, I'm your father and I've always cared and I will always love you. When we thought we lost you, it was devastating to me and your mother. The things that we disagree on are not important. I hope that someday you'll realize that. I do what I do because my family is the only important part of my life. I know some people think I'm ruthless, but I'm only working to make sure that those I love survive in this world of self-serving bastards. And I need to teach my children that lesson of survival or they will be part of the disadvantaged that you and your liberal girlfriend care so much about."

"Dad, I've learned the lesson of survival the hard way, but I've also learned that it doesn't have to be all or nothing. We don't need to destroy innocent people to survive. Most of those who die or are maimed by war are not militants or politicians. They are fathers, mothers, sisters, brothers, sons and daughters who are forced to submit, to fight or to die. And far too many never have the chance to do anything but die. It's primitive and barbaric to believe that collateral damage is an acceptable element of selfish goals. We can be better than that. We need to be better than that!"

"Well, that's what the liberals want you to believe. They think that everyone should be equal, that "the weak shall inherit the earth." Well son, if the weak inherit the earth it will not last very long because it's the strong and determined that have kept our civilization from perishing."

"I'm afraid that history is against that conclusion, father. All great civilizations succumbed to the whims and excesses of the very wealthy and powerful as they became wealthier and more powerful. Those ancient civilizations were destroyed by the greed of their rulers that eventually caused the demise of their middle class. It's the middle class that's the backbone and intellect of their societies. But the monarchs took the bread from their subject's tables and the political ideologues used their entrusted power to protect the obscene wealth of their friends at the expense of the masses.

"I don't buy that nonsense. It was the Caesars, Pharaohs and Kings that made this world what it is today!" responded the senior Buckman

"You're right about that. The world is a mess. Every society from the Roman Empire to the Chinese dynasties squeezed the life out of their citizenry until they would take no more. The greedy took from their people until they were so poor that there were few consumers and fewer entrepreneurs. The power became embedded in the wealthiest of families while others struggle just to have the very basic essentials of life like food and shelter, until they had enough!"

"Jim, you fought the enemy, you know that they want what you have. If we don't fight to protect our wealth it will be taken from us by those who are willing to destroy us. That's what patriotism is all about, son. The United States constitution was written by men who were landowners and businessmen. It was written and adopted to protect *their* rights and *their* property, not to protect the rights of those who are weak and indigent."

"The Constitution was drafted by men like Jefferson and Madison who worried that this country would become a monarchy. Franklin feared that the Republic, which was to be a government for and by the people, would become a government of a privileged few who would care only for their own well-being at the expense of the masses. They rejected the idea of government like the British monarchy that they fought to gain their freedom!"

"I doubt that we'll ever agree on such issues. We need to be stronger and more intelligent than our enemies to survive, as you did in Vietnam"

"But Dad, we're products of a world that is mired in wars and not reason. We believe that everyone must think as we do or suffer the consequences. I realize that our participation in some wars is unavoidable like the big one that you served in. General Albertson told me of your war efforts. I'm sorry that I accused you of sitting behind a desk in Eisenhower's headquarters. You fought an enemy that was a real threat to our way of life, an enemy that had no respect for the lives of others. But so did many of those who were poor or struggling, or as you call them, the *indigents*. Could we have beaten that threat to our way of life or the Japanese in the Pacific, without the millions of so called *indigents* who gave their lives for the promise of what was America? Were they just cannon fodder?"

"Son, you're tired and recovering from a terrible experience, but you're an example of what this country needs, strong leaders. You'll feel differently after you're home for a while. You need, as they say a taste of home cooking and you'll see things differently."

"I don't think so, Dad. This country is supposed to be a place of hope and dreams for all its people, not for a select small class of wealthy landowners. Instead it has become a place of greed and opulence of the very few, at the expense of most of its people and its future. Like you, I saw men die, but this time it was for no well-defined reason other than greed. I'm convinced that we're on a dangerous track, one that will end with little warning and will lead to a chaos that will benefit no one. The vast majority of American people, the masses, may be struggling to survive and many are very poor, but they are not dumb. You can't always fool them with righteous rhetoric and religious nonsense or rally them with hate to get what you want. History has shown that eventually the subdued will react.

Although believing his efforts would be futile, Jim went on to tell his father the stories of his squad of brave young men. He tried to bring Joe Eagle; Rogers, Ortiz, Hiller, Sanders and Harper into the narrow view of his father. He was amazed that he actually listened to him without interruption. He realized that his plight, as terrifying and debilitating as it was, had gained him his respect, and that was worth something.

Part Two

The Nixon Years

Chapter 53

By the late 1960s the American people had tired of war and its empty rhetoric. Their desire for peace and an end to the hopeless fighting made millions begin to see the rational of the protestors. But many also wanted peace from protests and considered demonstrations to be a provocation to both the police and to the law abiding society.

The country was being torn apart by the war after having survived the "civil disobedience" of the civil rights movement in the same decade as the assassinations of three socially conscious men. In his bid for the Presidency, Nixon promised the American people "domestic peace." He also promised that if elected, he would end the war.

The enemy was not going to wait. In February 1968 the Viet Cong launched the Tet Offensive, on the religious holiday of their New Year. The surprise attack succeeded in overrunning the American Embassy in Saigon. Although it was eventually repelled, it sent a profound message to those who had believed their optimistic leaders in Washington. It became obvious that we were not winning the war.

A month later President Johnson surprised the nation announcing that he would devote the remainder of his term in office to seeking peace in Vietnam and that he would not be a candidate for re-election. Some say that it was the declaration of Walter Cronkite, a highly respected television news anchor that caused Johnson to decide not to run for another term as President.

On February 27, 1968, after covering and reporting on the Tet Offensive for CBS News, Cronkite spoke solemnly to the American people stating in his deep fatherly tone:

"It seems now more than ever that the bloody experience of Vietnam is to end in a stalemate. But it is increasingly clear to this reporter that the only rational way out then will be to negotiate, not as victors, but as honorable people who lived up to their pledge to defend Democracy, and did the best they could."

Cronkite's words were considered by some to border on treason and by others to exude a wisdom that was already obvious to many. Lyndon Johnson considered them to be the words of a man whose opinions were well respected, influential and indicative of the people's passion.

In the months ahead the Democrats made a frenzied attempt to fill the void left by Johnson's non-candidacy and be all things to all people. Demonstrations and riots became the norm of the political process. Americans were being beaten and killed by other Americans in uniform, who responded to what was perceived to be civil disobedience. They were beginning to realize that their lives were being controlled by the very few who cared only for wealth and power. It was a behavior by our own government that would be declared a violation of human rights if it occurred in another country.

Chapter 54

It was April 10, 1968. The senior Buckman flew to Washington for his monthly meeting with the "boys." Bert Obersham met him at the airport and drove to the usual meeting place.

"Well, Jim it looks like our strategy to get Nixon elected is working," commented Obersham. "Johnson's dropped out of the race and Wallace is far behind in the polls. The Democrats are divided and totally disorganized. Without Bobby Kennedy they have no center. They should self-destruct by their convention."

"We shouldn't get too cocky about this election. Humphrey and Muskie are still running strong. Either one of them will be tough for Nixon to beat," cautioned Buckman as they entered the offices of Harold, Larkin & Watkins.

"Good afternoon Jim, Bert, thanks for making this meeting on short notice," greeted Bulldog Masters. "We have some serious business to discuss."

"What do you mean? We thought that the strategy was working well for Nixon?" asked Buckman, puzzled by Masters' words.

"The problem *is* Nixon! As we feared, he's getting arrogant and pompous. He thinks that he's going to be the people's choice and that he's doing it all by himself. The word is that he's going to support the creation of a super environmental enforcement agency and that he's against dealing with China. He's got to be reeled in!" demanded Masters'. "He's even thinking of ending the war."

"Do you know what would happen to our defense industries if the war was suddenly stopped? There would be more than a million people out of work directly, which would start a domino effect. If he became President, Nixon would face a very serious unemployment problem. Our troops would be thought of as losers, after all they sacrificed," declared John Carlton, CEO of ADI, one of the United States' largest defense contracting companies.

"The economy would collapse if we had high unemployment and a federal agency harassing businesses for environmental violations. The banking industry would have unemployed customers. People out of work can't pay their mortgages and credit card bills. If businesses close down facing lost revenues, they lay off more people," commented Donald Peters III of Continental Trust Corporation.

"So what do we do about it? Can we change his mind or is he too caught up in his perceived popularity?" asked Dale Watkins, counsel for the group.

"We need to be sure that there's someone in the White House who is tough enough to control him or take over if he doesn't play ball," stated Masters. "We've put too much into this to allow him to go off the program. The Clean Waters Act passed by Congress under Johnson will severely damage the petroleum industry's exploration efforts. A new federal agency overseeing environmental laws will cost us millions in profits and add to an already oversized government bureaucracy. We need to get the price of oil up and we have to do it soon."

"The convention might nominate a moderate Republican or that actor Reagan for the vice presidency. They're both trouble for us and they'll interfere with our objectives," offered Obersham, a former general and a director of an aeronautics company.

"What about this guy in Maryland, the Governor, Spiro Agnew. I understand that he can be trusted to be a tough and loyal guy," added Buckman. "He seems to be a rising star in the party and he's favored by the conservatives."

"Do you know him, Jim? Maybe we should find out if he's interested in the position of vice president?" suggested Masters.

"I do know him, but I'm probably not the right person for the job. I'm already out there in too many places right now. Bert, you know Spiro. What do you think?" asked Buckman of his close friend.

"Let me check it out gentlemen. I can meet with him and feel him out on his ambitions. He is another big ego guy, but then what politician isn't?" answered Bert.

"See if you can meet with him soon, Bert. We need to do a lot of work to get him to the front of the pack. Do you think he's strong enough to handle Nixon, if he goes off-track?" asked Masters, noticing a piercing look from Jim Buckman as he spoke.

"The Republican National Convention follows the Democrats convention. There's not much time to put a plan in motion that would result in securing the Vice President candidate's position for a relative unknown," added Watkins.

"What about that Democratic convention in Chicago, do we have the moles in place with these groups to assure that there are enough protestors outside the convention hall to maximize the turmoil? They want to self-destruct and we should take advantage of their lack of loyalty to their liberal party," smiled Masters. Our people will need to be aggressive to fire up these idiots and make the authorities act to control them. We want to embarrass them with their own dysfunctional supporters."

"We're ready with more than a hundred ringers who will suck in the protesters and cause a small riot for the police to handle," offered Carlton.

"Do you think it's wise to have our people involved? What would happen if someone were caught and they disclosed who they were working for? What if someone gets hurt? I'm not sure it's necessary to add to the chaos that seems inevitable," suggested Buckman.

"They don't know who they're working for Jim. They have been recruited as advocates for a cause, but without knowledge of their benefactors. They know they're to be disruptive, but they don't know why they're doing it," explained Carlton.

"Well, I have a bad feeling about it, John. I hope I'm wrong!" added Buckman.

"Okay, gentlemen we'll meet here in two weeks to evaluate the strategies we discussed today. Bert, try to make that initial contact with Agnew before that meeting," instructed Masters expressing his authority over the group much to the chagrin of Jim Buckman.

"Let's make that meeting in three weeks to give Bert enough time to fulfill his task and so that we can monitor the

Democrats as they start their convention," declared Buckman, regaining his position as the group's leader, a tactic that did not go unnoticed by the "boys," including Masters, who knew that Buckman, a major shareholder in his company, could make his life miserable.

"Good point, Jim, we'll see you all in three weeks," affirmed Masters, attempting to rescue some semblance of authority in light of Buckman's counter assertion.

Jim Buckman and Bert Obersham left the meeting with diminished enthusiasm. "Nixon isn't the only one needing to be reeled in," declared Buckman.

"Masters does seem to be getting a little too aggressive with this campaign against the Democrats. It's personal with him and that could get us in trouble," offered Bert.

"We need to watch him a little closer, Bert. We have a lot riding on this election. This isn't about ideology. It's about protecting *our* American way of life, which is based on capitalism and profits, not egos and arrogance!"

Chapter 55

Diego found living in Massachusetts to be a rewarding experience. He had heard that it was traditionally a liberal State in its politics and that meant that they were progressive rather than regressive in their attitudes.

"I've only been here a couple of months, but I'm liking this place, Tony!" exclaimed Diego as they walked along the broad sidewalk that spanned Carson Beach in South Boston.

"Does that mean that I'm stuck with you?" quipped Tony with a smile.

"All I know is that I like what I see so far, and don't worry, amigo, I need to find my own place. But I'm thinking that it may be in Boston. What do you think?"

"Well, this isn't exactly Malibu Beach, California, but we have some special qualities here, but not unlike LA, we have haters here too. I told you how I had to deal with it growing up. I think the difference here is that there is less apathy and more activists when it comes to caring for others."

"I think I'll survive better here with a good friend than in LA where everyone is trying to do me in! At least I have a job. It's only painting houses for $2 an hour, but its work."

"Well, I'll be moving out of my parents' home soon. They won't say it, but I know they'd like to rent the apartment we're living in. I don't think it's good for me to be there much longer. They won't let me pay much rent. What do you say? We could continue to be roommates, if you don't mind my snoring?"

"It's annoying, but it isn't as bad as the gunfire and sirens in Watts," Diego responded with a wide grin. Massachusetts does seem to be a place where people care."

As they continued their walk to Kelly's Landing for their popular French fries Tony tried to explain the anomaly that was Massachusetts politics, "Massachusetts is one of only four states in this country referred to as a commonwealth. Supposedly it was called that so that it would be governed for the common good. But the premise for the common good hasn't always resulted in fair and just governing."

Tony continued to explain that it was an unspoken policy of Massachusetts voters to split the ticket between the two parties. "In Massachusetts Republicans are often elected to the governorship while the legislature has always been overwhelmingly ruled by a large Democratic majority.

"Was Kennedy in your legislature?" asked Diego. "They called him a liberal and a socialist because he believed in civil rights and helping poor people but he was a rich guy, right?"

"Yeah, he came from a wealthy family. He never served in our legislature. He went right for Congress. His father pushed his sons into politics. His grandfather, on his mother's side, was the Mayor of Boston in the early 1900s," answered Tony, "People here think Republicans are the party that protects the rich so they must be able to handle money better. But they know they need the Democrats to assure that the workers and shop owners, are taken care of too.

"Tony, you're giving me a headache! All I know is that people think that California is the place for opportunity. I've found living here that Massachusetts is a better place for me. I saw this ad posted when I arrived at Logan Airport. I'm thinking of becoming an air traffic controller, they make good money and are respected. Do you think I can do it?"

"Of course you can do it, if you want it bad enough, but Diego, that's a federal Job! You can do it anywhere there is an FAA controlled airport, but you probably need a degree of some sort."

"I know that, but I like it here and there are a lot of good schools. I can become a resident and go to a state college on that GI Bill, but even if I work hard, like you did, will they hire a poor Hispanic guy to control their planes? Don't just the Irish get the good jobs in this town?"

"Who told you that? That may have been true at one time, but also at one time, not too long ago, there were Help Wanted signs that said "No Irish Need Apply!"

"I know you had a tough time with some of the Irish kids in this Town, but you got by that. And look at you now, man.

You're an engineer and you're going to make the big money. You always say that unless I do something to make me more valuable in society, I can only hope to be "the Man's gardener," Diego said with a half-smile. "I don't know Tony, are the cards stacked against me because of being from Mexico?"

"If that's where your head's at, then that's where you'll stay, my friend. Yeah "the Man" wants to use you to make money for himself, but it's up to you to make his greed work for you."

Diego stopped walking and turned to Tony, "How do I do that, amigo. I'm a poor Hispanic guy from the ghettos of LA. I just barely got through high school and I'm lucky to be alive and not be in jail. You're the brains man, and I can't be you. You think things out and you're not afraid of screwing up."

"You should be happy you're not me. You're better looking!" responded Tony with a broad smile, to lighten the moment. "Hey, Tommy O'Neil, a good friend of mine, is having a party up on Broadway. He lives near the movie theatre, you know, where we saw that re-run of that James Bond movie. Let's go by there. You can meet some of the fine people of Southie, including some pretty ladies."

"I would like that, but I would like those fries first! I'm getting hungry from this long walk and talk." declared Diego.

The walk from Kelly's Landing, up Farragut Road, past the namesake Admiral's statue in the park, to Broadway seemed to go by quickly as the two friends ate their hot salty fries and talked about the future.

Tommy O'Neil lived on the third floor of a three-decker. The first floor was an insurance broker's office and the second was the apartment of a retired fireman. Tony explained that he met Tommy in the seventh grade and they've been friends since. Tommy was a musician and he and Tony would do their version of a "jam" whenever possible, depending on whose parents weren't home. If they were lucky they would be able to go to Danny O'Malley's house where he would join them with his drums. They were in the Patrick F. Gavin Junior High School band; Tommy on saxophone and Tony doing his best to imitate Herb Alpert on his trumpet.

"I know you're an artist, but you're a musician too? asked Diego incredulously.

"Well, I wouldn't actually say that I'm a musician. I try, but some people have it and some don't. It's like real life!" quipped Tony. "Let's just say I did my best with my limited talent!"

As they crossed L Street on Broadway approaching Tommy O'Neil's place, they could hear the loud music from the party. The Rolling Stones "I Can't Get No Satisfaction," sounded through the otherwise quiet night, broadcast through O'Neil's open windows, which was the only cooling to his apartment on this hot summer night that Tommy could afford.

Tony and Diego climbed the steep stairway, and knocked on the door hard enough to be heard over the party's din. A pretty young woman whom Tony recognized as Tommy's girlfriend Kathleen answered.

"Tony, how are you? She greeted him with a big hug and a kiss on his cheek. "Where you been? Tommy was hoping you'd make it up here, where the other half lives. And who's your friend?"

"Kathleen, I'd like you to meet Diego Martinez. Diego was with me in Nam. You remember my war stories. He's from LA. He's staying with me and my family while he's out here. Where's the old man?"

"He's in the kitchen. Glad to meet you Diego," Kathleen's hand extended to welcome him. "Follow me guys. It's a little crowded in here."

The small four-room flat was wall to wall with people. Some Tony knew, but many he didn't.

Tommy spotted them through the kitchen doorway and weaved his way through the crowd.

"Hey, where you been Mr. Engineer? Is this the guy you talk about as your west coast buddy?"

"Yes, Tommy! Diego Martinez meet Tommy O'Neil."

"Hi Diego, welcome to Southie, the home of the Yankee Division. You've heard the song *Southie's My Home Town*? Tony must have sung it for you. Make yourself at home, if you can find a piece of floor to stand on. The beer is in the cooler on the back porch."

Tommy led them to the outside porch overlooking a small fenced yard and the service station garage next door.

"Did you hear about Mackney?" Tommy asked once the door to the porch had diminished the noise so that yelling was no longer necessary.

"No what about him?" Tony asked fearing the answer.

"He bought it trying to reach a squad trapped in an ambush outside Da Nang," Tommy looked up from his downward stare to see the sadness on his buddy's face.

Diego looked at Tony. "Hey man that sucks. He was a good soldier! Sorry Tony."

"When did it happen? Is he already back here?"

"No, it was two days ago. His body will be back home next week."

"I'm sorry to be the one to tell you. I know that he saved your life back there, but he was doing what he wanted to do and what he was appreciated for. He was a career soldier on his fourth tour of duty in Nam. This was the only way he was leaving there. And you know that he had a rough time with his family growing up. He came back home after his service time was up, but he couldn't handle the attitudes of the protesters and he couldn't find a decent job. He was working in that gas station down there, pumping gas. He re-enlisted last winter and asked for combat duty," explained Tommy.

"He only wanted to be needed... and he was needed over there. Johnny had no fear and there's no appreciation like that of those you save from certain death."

"Well, I know that dampens your party spirit, but I knew you'd want to know. Let's have a beer in tribute to the guy."

After a reflective pause Tony opened a Bud and said, with a tear in his eye and beer cans raised to the night sky, "To Johnny Mackney, may he finally be rewarded in whatever after-life there is, for his caring and courage."

The solemn scene was interrupted by the squeaking of the porch door opening and Kathleen's voice chastising them, "Hey you guys, the party's in here. You can talk war and peace inside with your friends. "

"We'd better go in and make sure they don't wreck the place," Tommy said, a hand on Tony's shoulder guiding him to the door.

Tony eyed some old friends sitting at the far end of the living room and brought Diego over to meet them. "Diego these are people that were in a Southie drum and bugle corps that I joined when I was sixteen. Mary, Jack, Don, Karen and Molly I'd like you to meet Diego Martinez from LA. Diego was in my squad in NAM during the bad old days."

"Nice to meet you, Diego, they all said, somewhat simultaneously," politely extending their hands.

"Is it true that Tony was a hero over there or are those just stories he tells to get us to buy him rounds?" asked Jack, tongue in cheek.

"Well, he saved my life and ten others, so I would say he deserves a free drink for that, but then I'm biased," answered Diego. "So Tony you said that you weren't a good musician but you were in a drum and bugle corps?"

"He was telling the truth Diego. We had to play really loud to drown him out," laughed Don, joined by the group.

"Yeah, you know how they say that a certain player makes everyone on a team better, well compared to Tony we all sounded great," added Mary, the former captain of the color guard, not able to resist the opportunity to chide her teen-age crush.

The beer, loud music and conversation temporarily overcame the sad thoughts of the news of his friend's death. He would find out the arrangements and be there to honor him.

As the night got later Tony found himself reminiscing with Tommy and a few friends in the Kitchen leaving Diego with Mary, Jack and Karen in the living room. Karen seemed particular interested in Diego's charm, broad smile and accent. Neither noticed the attention their compatibility was getting from Butch Mulligan who was standing in the doorway to the Kitchen observing the group, while he downed his sixth brew.

Butch was a former Marine who washed-out because of his drinking and resultant rages. Without warning Butch yelled across the room, "Hey spic, who do you think you are? Get away from my girl."

The loud burst of his voice caused the people in the room to stop talking and look in his direction as he began to walk towards the Diego. Only the music of the Beatles, "Keep Your Hands off My Baby" was heard in the background.

Karen looked his way, "I'm not your girl and you're drunk. Go home Butch."

"So you want to go home with that grease-ball, huh? Well he ain't going home. He's going to the hospital, if he's lucky," threatened Butch as he advanced towards them.

Butch was not without allies, he had several friends with him who were also not impressed by Tony's new buddy. They looked his way for a signal that "it was about to start" and moved from where they were sitting, leaning or just standing, to join their leader.

"Oh shit, I was afraid that this might happen!" exclaimed Tommy as he started on a beeline to intercept Butch.

Diego, shocked at the outburst and the derogatory words, stood to face his foes. The first blow sent him against the wall, his head hitting the picture of JFK, as Tommy and Tony reached Butch to restrain him. Two of his "gang" grabbed Tommy and threw him to the floor. The girls ran screaming to the front door and down the stairs. Tony tackled one of the gang, but was pummeled by two others.

Tommy rose with an uppercut to Butch's jaw sending him towards the door. Tony managed to flip one, then another over the sofa as Diego dropped an attacker with a right hook. Jack used his bottle of Bud to advantage on Butch's brother Kenny.

The battle went full blown with everyone choosing sides. Tommy and his followers tried to get them out of the front door and down the stairs to the street. Don, a former Southie High football lineman, rammed his body into the oncoming charge of two aggressors.

The fight continued into the hallway and onto the stairway with one the instigators falling over the rail to the next landing. Tony threw one guy over another, to the stairway below, as

Tommy and his friends' fists and feet responded to the tough guys' attacks.

The old gentleman on the second floor, who had put up with the party's mayhem, peeked out his door, yelled something indistinguishable and then shut the door quickly as one of the combatants was slammed against it.

The brawl went out onto Broadway as the movie theatre next door was letting out. Surprised movie goers were drawn into the fray as the fists were flying, not knowing why or who they were fighting. To Tony it was reminiscent of hand to hand combat in the jungle. Within minutes, sirens blasted from the distance over the screams of the combatants. The men in blue would be there in seconds.

Tony ducked a wild punch and grabbed Diego by the arm and yelled to Tommy, "We're out of here!" as they slipped away from the ill-conceived battle. The trio ducked into the mob of exiting movie patrons and into the theatre, to avoid the impending police rout.

"Hey, Tony tell me about the 'commonwealth' thing again," Diego said, following close behind, one eye half closed from his introduction to Butch, and a belated smile on his bruised face.

Chapter 56

Buckman invited Sam Polowski, the freshman Senator from Michigan, to dinner to meet some of his team of advisors just before an important vote on regulating the price of oil came to the floor of the Senate. As a true conservative, Polowski was anxious about allowing the availability and cost of such a vital resource to become an impediment to America's growth.

He realized that the price of energy was a determining factor in the economic health of the country. Energy was needed to manufacture and ship its gross production. People needed oil to commute to and from their jobs, to heat their homes and to generate electricity. Sam believed that the bill would effectively keep the oil companies from price gouging the American people into a serious recession. Sam was a conservative, but he did care about people. High oil prices could hurt the automobile industry and that was his constituency, the people who worked for the manufacturers.

"Sam, I want you to meet Thomas Masters, the Chairman of International Petroleum Conglomerate's Board of Directors; John Carlton, CEO of American Defense Industries and Bert Obersham, a Director of Consolidated Aeronautics Corporation. These are the people that backed you in your election."

The group welcomed Sam with outstretched hands and congratulatory remarks about his triumph in a tough campaign.

"Jim told us you would be a good man to have in the Senate, Sam. He said that, unlike your primary opponent, you're a team player and you could be counted on when we needed you," stated Masters in his usual blunt manner.

"Well, I certainly appreciated your support. I know that without Mr. Buckman's assistance I wouldn't have won the election. You have my undying gratitude.

"Sam, as much as we appreciate your gratitude, what we need is your vote!" asserted Masters in his characteristic crude style.

"My vote? On what issue? What can I do for you gentlemen?" asked Polowski. "I'm not sure that I know what your interests are, but tell me about your concerns."

Buckman interrupted Masters' presentation, thinking that it was going in the wrong direction. He knew Polowski well enough to know that he could be persuaded, but not intimidated.

"Sam, as you know, the price of oil has remained relatively stable for many years, but the costs of exploration; drilling and refining have escalated rapidly. If this Senate bill succeeds in limiting the price of domestic fuel, it would make it impossible for Americans to meet their demands for energy. This would give the Arabs and the South Americans an advantage in oil production that could hold our country hostage to their profiteering. We can't control their prices and they can put a strangle hold on us that would be a serious blow to our national defense. We can't let that happen!"

"I understand, Jim, but the passage of that bill would keep the oil companies, all due respect to you, Mr. Masters, from having a free hand to price us into economic chaos. Now, I'm sure your company wouldn't take undue advantage of that freedom, but there are those who would."

"Sam, my company imports more than 50% of its oil from the Mideast because we can't afford to produce our own. The environmental restrictions and the cost of labor here are serious impediments to domestic production. Why, it cost more for a glass of wine here than for a gallon of gas in this country. There is no incentive to explore and drill new areas, given the prices at the pump," lectured Masters.

"If we need to rely on foreigners for oil we're jeopardizing our ability to fight our enemies. They could shut us off and we would be like the German tanks that drove into Russia and went dry in World War II, our vehicles would not survive the battle," added Carlton.

"I realize there's the potential for such impacts, but have you studied the impact such legislation would have on the average Joe? And since we're still fighting a war that consumes a lot of energy and dollars, what will happen if prices doubled? I believe that it would seriously affect our national defense. We would have to retreat or go bankrupt fighting this war. We couldn't afford a defense, or an offense," retorted Polowski. "In fact, we would probably have to borrow from a foreign country to pay for our defense. That would put us into a very poor negotiating position internationally."

Masters glared at Buckman as Sam gave his honest opinion of the bill. Buckman knew what "Bulldog" was thinking, but he wasn't going to buy into his attitude.

"Sam, your concerns are well noted, but this is an issue that is very important to our country. We must increase our domestic oil production and free ourselves from the foreign influence. Yes, it'll hurt for a while, but if we continue the way it is now we'll certainly lose our competitive edge in the world. Do you trust me, Sam? Didn't I do what I said I would do for you?" argued Buckman.

"Yes, you did, Jim, and I guess you're right, gratitude isn't enough to repay you. I'll take another look at the bill and see if there's any way that I can oppose, or maybe amend it."

"That's good enough for me. You're a good and honest man, and I trust in your judgment!"

Buckman glanced at Masters. The piercing look in Bulldog's eyes didn't indicate a similar trust. After dinner Buckman thought it was best to change the subject. Masters, Carlton and Obersham left to go to a Georgetown basketball game. Jim and Sam stayed to have a drink and discuss family.

"How's that brilliant daughter of yours doing, Sam? Isn't she in practice in Michigan?"

"Yes, she's in a law firm that specializes in civil liberties cases, you know ACLU litigations. She's definitely her mother's daughter. Mother tells me that she still has contact with your son Jim here in Washington. How is he doing with the JAG?"

"He's doing fine, but he's obviously been influenced by the women in his life and is often crusading for the poor excuses for soldiers. Usually he's defending ghetto kids who can't take orders or punks who have caused trouble. I'm afraid we both raised bleeding heart liberals, Sam," declared Buckman with a smile.

"That must put a damper on your hopes for him to take over your businesses."

"Yes, but I have great respect for Jim and his accomplishments. I still want him to work with me, but my son Jonathan is also very bright and more in tune with my philosophy of life. He's running one of my banks and is determined to be my successor. I haven't heard much from Jim about his relationship with Sharon. Do you know what's going on with them?" asked Buckman.

"Well Jim, all I know is what they tell me, but Laura says that they are trying to work on their careers right now. But she thinks that they're serious and that they'll eventually be together. Sharon's coming to visit me this weekend in Washington. At least that's her excuse for coming to see your son."

"You're probably right. Nancy hints that their relationship is going strong, but I think she's hesitant to tell me too much. She loves Sharon though and often taunts me with the liberal views they share. I think that she enjoys the taunting," Buckman responded, a wide grin on his usually stoic looking face.

"I guess that with respect to their politics we created a couple of monsters, Jim." They both laughed and raised their glasses to toast their renegade offspring. To their eventual conversion to the real world," offered Sam.

CHAPTER 57

It was 7:00 p.m. and Captain James Buckman III was nervous about his date with Sharon as he pulled up to the apartment building that Sharon's father called home while in Washington, D.C. He had written and phoned her at least twice a week trying to keep the spark from going out as they pursued their busy careers as young attorneys, nearly 1500 miles from each other. His tour of duty would end in eight months and he had decisions to make about his future. They had a lot to talk about.

Sharon seemed enthusiastic about their date, but he also detected a guarded tone in her voice. She made it plain that she was there to visit her father and would only be available Saturday evening and possibly Sunday afternoon. Jim had cleared the weekend, hoping that they would share some quality time, not having been together for several months.

As he approached the guard at the front desk in the lobby of the Watergate apartments, he wondered if she had grown tired of their distant relationship and had found someone new to share her ideologies. He smiled at the thought of her opinionated attitude realizing that it was one of the elements of her personality that he was attracted to from the beginning.

"Good evening. Could you contact Senator Polowski's apartment and let his daughter Sharon know that I'm here?" asked Jim.

"Yes sir! And your name?" The young black uniformed guard asked politely as he eyed his decorations admiring the Silver Star, Purple Heart and battle ribbons displayed on his uniform. Nam, sir?" he asked.

"Captain Buckman. She's expecting me. And yes, are you a veteran?"

"82nd Airborne, sir. I was there in '68," he responded proudly, as he pushed back his chair to reveal a prosthetic left leg.

Jim's thoughts went to his men who didn't make it back. "That's a tough outfit. I'm sure that you did yourself proud, and I thank you for your service soldier."

"Thank you Captain. This note was left for you by Ms. Polowski. She left about 30 minutes ago with the Senator."

Jim could not hide the startled look on his face as he took the envelope from the young man. Jim turned and strode to his BMW parked in front of the building, ripping open the sealed envelope as he went. A hand written note inside attempted to explain away his disappointment. He pulled out the note and read it.

Jim,

I am sorry to have to leave you this note, but my father asked that I accompany him to a White House dinner. Mother was feeling poorly and didn't come to Washington. He felt strange going alone. He still feels out of his element here, but he loves being a Senator.

I tried to call you but you had already left your apartment. If you're not totally angry with me can we meet up at 10:00 PM, sorry, I mean 2200 hours, at Dominic's on Connecticut Avenue. I promise to make it up to you. I am very sorry. If you are not there I will understand.

Love,
Sharon

Jim put his head against the headrest and closed his eyes. I guess this tells me where I stand! He thought. For someone who disagrees with her father on almost every issue she is his best ally when he needs someone to stand with him.

After a few minutes of wallowing in self-pity he decided that if she intended to stand him up she would have left a different kind of note, or no note at all. He knew she was as close as any daughter could be to her father. If he's in need, she would be there for her dad. She had said earlier that her mother wasn't feeling well and didn't accompany him to Washington. Sharon said that her mother was excited about meeting the President, but she wasn't going to do that looking like she felt. Women, it's always about looking perfect.

It was only 7:15 pm, too early to go to the restaurant. He would go to his office at the Pentagon and catch up on some work. His superior in the Criminal Investigation Division asked him to look over some material on a case that was coming before the military court.

It was an unusual situation for the military, a civilian, a former soldier by the name of Ronald Ridenhour from Phoenix, Arizona, had written a letter to President Nixon, the Pentagon and a number of others. He alleged that on March 16, 1968, there was a massacre of Vietnamese civilians perpetrated by American soldiers in a village in Quang Ngai Province. He claimed that, although he was not there, he had evidence that hundreds of unarmed men, women and children were slaughtered. The village's name was My Lai. Jim remembered it being called Pinkville and that it was a known habitat of the Pro-Communist Viet Cong.

The word was that Nixon wanted to downplay the incident since it could hurt the war effort. He called it an "unfortunate aberration" and "an isolated incident." Congressman Morris Udall, a Democrat from Ridenhour's home state of Arizona, was pushing the Pentagon to investigate. Congressman Mendel Rivers, a southern Democrat and Chairman of the House Armed Services Committee, said it never happened. Rivers was not a fan of the progressive wing of his party, having fought against Johnson's Civil Rights bill.

Captain Buckman had not been involved in any serious cases before. Most of the court proceedings he had investigated were disciplinary actions involved the potential for dishonorable discharges or a relatively short incarceration.

The walk down the hall to his closet-like office at 1940 military time was eerie in its solitude. These halls were usually busy with the clickety-clack of military shoes from 0600 to 1800. The business of dealing with war was not a 9 to 5 job. There were many parts of this massive building that operated three shifts every day. The old cliché that was part of a Jimmy Buffet song and was heard at bars to justify that early drink, *"its 5 o'clock somewhere,"* was true for attending to wars and other military actions around the world. There's always a military action somewhere to manage.

Buckman had a feeling that My Lai would add the Criminal Investigation Division to that around-the-clock scenario. He had less than a year left to his active duty assignment and he was anxious to get back to the civilian world. The JAG had served him well. He finished his law degree at George Washington University and would be taking the bar exam in D.C. in the spring. But this would be an interesting case to go out on!

I'll check out the package that the Colonel sent down to me this afternoon and be out of here by 2130! Sharon said that she would be at Dominic's by 2200. Maybe I'll be a little late to worry her, he thought with a smile.

Dominic's was one of the restaurants that survived the April 1968 riots after Martin Luther King was assassinated. A dozen people were killed and over a thousand wounded in a four day riot in D.C. that rivaled Watts. It was the end of the Johnson era that saw his presidency go from outstanding accomplishments in social program legislation, such as civil rights and Medicare, to conclude on the slippery slope that was the Vietnam War. Johnson had to send federal troops into his adopted city of D.C. to help quell the turmoil, adding to his already low popularity and one of the reasons he did not run for office again!

It was now the freshman year of the Nixon presidency and cover-up was the program that would be his legacy. The military-industrial complex, as it was called, was his constituency. He promised to end the war, but he didn't say when.

The envelope marked *Top Secret* and titled *My Lai Investigation* had been placed in the middle of Jim's desk, an indication of the project's priority status. Jim sank back into his leather chair and lifted the bulky envelope off his desk, holding it as if he was weighing its importance. He thought for a moment that maybe it could wait until the morning. His curiosity overcame his hesitation and he slit open the package with his replica bayonet letter opener, a gift from his fellow escapees that came with a note saying that it would be the only "weapon" he would need from behind his Pentagon desk.

The cover page from within the package was a handwritten note from his superior officer, Colonel Hoffman. "Jim, this is a very sensitive case. At this point, consider it for your eyes only! See me when you complete your review."

He noted some photographs in the middle of the report and before he read a word of the field investigator's report he pulled the photos out of order. The first was of Lieutenant Robert Calley, the accused. He had heard talk of some horrendous action that Lieutenant Calley was alleged to have perpetrated in Nam.

The next six photographs showed, in explicit detail, the carnage that was My Lai. There were bodies of old men, women and children, some as young as infants, blood soaked, fly infested, laying in random piles of death.

Jim thought, this can't be, no American soldier would kill so many people in this manner. This is like those scenes in the World War II movies where the German SS eliminated their captives rather than waste time taking them back to their lines for imprisonment. It must have been the act of the Viet Cong who controlled that village.

As he read the report it was clear that it was the unthinkable. One eyewitness, a soldier who refused to fire his weapon at the pleading villagers said that Lieutenant Calley ordered them to "clean out the village" and that he saw a soldier take aim at a fleeing woman with her infant in her arms and fire, killing them both. Others started firing into the crying, pleading mob of villagers. A little boy about two years old, who ran crying towards his mother in the crowd, arms outstretched, was alleged to have been gunned down by Calley as if he was a rabbit in a hunt.

Buckman could feel his stomach tightening and the sweat on his brow as he pictured the events of that day. Why didn't someone stop this maniac? He had been in situations where you could not tell the enemy from the friendlies, but he could not imagine killing them all as a solution to the problem.

He thought, yes, the VC would use women and children, strapped with a grenade, to kill their unwary enemies. He knew that young men and women, who feared Americans after losing family to indiscriminate bombing attacks, could be persuaded to give their lives in a suicide attack on the 'invaders.' But we don't fight that way, or do we? Buckman thought of the North Vietnamese Army captain who had died as a prisoner on his watch. Had he done the expedient thing by leaving him tied to a tree with a noose around his neck?

Buckman continued reading the field report. An Army helicopter pilot, Warrant Officer Hugh Thompson, came upon the scene and landed his Huey copter between Calley's company and the victims, threatening to shoot any soldier who fired upon the villagers. For most it was too late, more than 500 villagers had been massacred.

Thompson's act of moral courage was cited by one Congressman as a despicable act of a traitor against American soldiers doing their job. Mendel Rivers, the Representative from Louisiana and Chairman of the House Armed Services Committee, wanted Thompson court marshaled.

Buckman was not only disgusted, but he was embarrassed for his country; the country that had given him and his family tremendous wealth and power.

As he turned the page to read the reports of other eye witnesses he glanced at the clock on the wall. It was 2145 or 9:45 pm civilian time. Oh, damn it, Sharon will think I stood her up. Well she deserves to be worried, he thought. He closed the file and hurried down the hall to the garage. He was at least twenty minutes away from the restaurant. He was looking forward to seeing her.

As he got into his car his thoughts went back to the investigative report. What does the Colonel want me to do? The report seems comprehensive. What else is needed for a conviction?

Chapter 58

Jonathan Buckman was supposed to play the role of the "Prince-in-waiting" behind his older brother James III, who was considered the heir apparent to the family business. Jonathan didn't expect the sassy, "I'm special attitude," of his brother to change as the result of an epiphany, especially one which had a woman as its catalyst. His handsome looks, devilish wit and carefree personality was tamed by a woman whose beauty was matched by her toughness. It was a challenge that Jim couldn't win.

Although Jonathan was not prepared for his sudden rise in stature within the family hierarchy, he welcomed the recognition and accepted the role that his father described as being the future "Captain of the ship." His father told him that there was a lot to learn, and much of it had little to do with what he was taught in business school.

The world was a tough arena to have success and prosperity within. It was a coliseum in which the gladiators wore suits and ties but were just as vicious. "Winning was the only thing," as Green Bay Coach Vince Lombardi, extorted to his championship football teams in the 1950s.

"There's no place for compassion in business!" He knew that his father had some serious reservations about his intestinal fortitude. He would prove that he was capable of doing whatever was necessary to keep his family on top. Jim was a war hero, but he became soft when he started to care about people and fell in love.

Jonathan was given goals to meet for the family banking businesses. Buckman Bank and Trust had sixteen branches in Connecticut and New York. The objective was to add seven more operations within the next two years; three in Rhode Island and four in Massachusetts. In spite of the war and the chaos in the streets, the economy was still strong. He knew that he must pass this test.

Expanding a banking business was not an easy task. The State and Federal laws and regulations were a maze of paperwork and politics. Consumer protection Laws, made popular during the Democratic Administrations, added to the complexity. "Caveat Emptor" or buyer beware, the basis of many successful, and numerous unscrupulous businesses, was being challenged at every level of the economy.

Jonathan was also aware that banking was not the only business that his family was successful in achieving immense wealth. They had numerous investments, some of which would not survive the light of close regulatory scrutiny. Banks were not allowed to invest in their client's or their own ventures. Their role was to *lend* money to those businesses that had balance sheets that showed that they could pay it back with the appropriate interest. After all it was the people's money that they were entrusted with and not really their own.

He knew that many of the Buckman investments would not survive the smell test, but they all needed to be nourished and protected. But he would not be allowed to play in that game until he proved himself to qualify in his father's eyes. He knew that his father wanted his brother to join the family business as its in-house counsel. Jonathan didn't want that to happen. Jim had found a sense of morality and there was no place in their operation for a do-gooder. He feared that if he was the family's business counsel it would only be a matter of time before he attempted to re-direct the operation towards a more consumer oriented culture. He wasn't going to let that happen.

The family fortune was not acquired by timid actions or by succumbing to moral conscience! As the Chief Financial Officer of Buckman Bank and Trust, Jonathan was in a position to show that he was the one to lead their family to the next level and beyond. His brother was not going to stand in his way!

Chapter 59

Jim pulled up to the valet standing at the curb and flipped him the keys as he headed into Dominic's. It was 20 minutes past 10 o'clock. He was sure it was too late to order dinner, but he hoped that Sharon hadn't left.

"I'm looking for a pretty woman with red hair and an amazing smile," he told the maître d'.

"Ah yes, you and half of the men in Washington," he responded with a dry wit as he gestured for Jim to follow him. "My name is Joseph."

There were several elaborately decorated rooms of a Tuscan nature. All were intimate in size and romantically lit. The maître d' led him to a corner table, where he stopped suddenly. "She was here waiting for you Captain. I spoke with her just 10 minutes ago." The table was not occupied and a glass of what appeared to be Cabernet was half full, set aside of an empty salad plate.

Jim's heart sank. She was leaving tomorrow night and he had missed his opportunity to see her.

"I'm sorry sir, I didn't see her leave, but then I was in the kitchen before you arrived."

"It's all right. It's my fault for being so late."

"You can say that again, Jimbo!" Sharon's voice was upon him as he turned to see her approaching with her gracious smile and sparkling green eyes in the candle lit room. "A lady needs to powder her nose at least once a night."

Jim broke into a broad smile as they hugged and politely kissed, in front of an embarrassed, but pleased maître d'.

"I'm truly sorry dear for being so late, but then I guess we're even, for tonight anyway. I believe it's too late to order dinner, so how about a drink or are you up for Chinese?

"Sir, please stay, the kitchen can stay open for your order," offered Joseph. "Dominic's is here to serve you and the beautiful lady."

"How can we refuse that eloquent offer?" responded Sharon, flattered to a blush by Joseph's comment.

"Your wish is my command, if it gets me off the hook," laughed Jim. "Joseph, I'll have what she's having for wine."

"Yes sir, I'll have the waiter take your order."

"So how was the President this evening? You must have already had dinner?"

"Actually, I only had the appetizers. I was looking forward to our dinner date. I left before dinner was served and *your* President Nixon was fine, a real gentleman. He's much shorter than I imagined. I think he has that Napoleonic complex. You know, trying to be respected as a real man."

"I see that you're still the relentless persecutor of the rich and famous. And for the record, he grew up poor and I didn't vote for him, but that's top secret information!" grinned Jim as he raised his glass to hers.

"Bravo, my dear. You have made progress! You may be ready to burn your country club ID card!

"Sorry, I still play golf with dad when I'm home. Speaking of dads, how's the Senator doing?"

"He's fine. Actually he's doing very well. He's in his glory at the attention he's getting."

"A freshman Senator and he's attracting attention? That's unusual in this town."

"Well, he has the key vote on a bill that's coming to the floor next week. Something about regulating oil prices. I think that's the reason he was invited to the White House for dinner this evening."

"Really, well I hope he makes the most of his popularity, it will be short-lived until someone else needs a favor."

"Well, this favor is for someone near and dear to you," Sharon smirked.

"Hmm, well payback's a bitch when it comes to having my father as a benefactor. I hope that he doesn't have to do too much damage!" grinned Jim.

"He's a strong minded man. I'm sure he won't do anything that he believes wouldn't be for the better good. Although we might differ as to what that means, he's an honest and good man!"

"Hey, that's enough talk about our fathers. How's the business of defending the guilty going?"

"Now be kind. Not all of those arrested are guilty of the crime, especially the poor that can't afford a lawyer. But I've had some interesting cases and what about you? Are you still defending kid soldiers for running from the big bad enemies who want to kill them?"

Before Jim could answer, the waiter approached their table. "Good evening, my name is Michael. I will serve you this evening."

Sharon ordered an exotic pasta dish while Jim went for the filet mignon, medium rare.

"You are a daredevil. Why not eat it raw?" chuckled Sharon.

"Believe me I have eaten raw meat when I had to. Have you ever had raw Sikkim?" asked Jim in a soft voice just in case there were any patrons who knew Vietnamese.

"No, what is it? Does it taste like chicken?" responded Sharon, knowing he was going to try to shock her.

"No, actually it taste like rat, but Vietnamese rat. It's a real delicacy when you're starving in the jungle and can't light a fire. My Native American Sergeant was good at trapping all kinds of four legged creatures."

"Oh Yuk! Well, that takes care of my appetite!" laughed Sharon. "Okay, let's change the subject. You made your point jungle boy. What are you working on in that big building that generates most of the conspiracies and chaos in the world?"

"Well, I'm afraid it's Top Secret my dear," he said in his best 'Gone with the Wind' Clark Gable voice. "But I have a feeling that it will take me back to Nam to investigate."

"No, you're kidding. Why would you do that?" Sharon asked becoming serious in her concern.

"Well, I won't do it because I want to vacation in a tropical climate, but it is a very complicated case. There's a lot at stake in finding out the truth."

"You're not involved in that massacre case, are you? The one about the soldier who killed hundreds of innocent people? Where was it ... My Lai?"

"What do you know about My Lai?" asked a surprised Buckman.

"It's on the news Jim. Don't you read newspapers; have a television or even a radio?" The TV Journal '60 Minutes' had an exposé on it last Sunday night.

"I'm too busy to listen to news propaganda. What did they say about it?" asked Jim concerned that the case may become a media circus.

"I think you already know more than I do, and you're going to be drawn into it. I can tell," responded Sharon. "It's going to tear the heart out this country when it is finally realized what war does to people, under the shadow of Old Glory and that we don't always wear the white hats, like in those TV westerns."

"Yes, I believe you're right, but I can't talk about it yet. I may ask for your advice as I get into it, but let's not spoil our night together."

"And you're also right! We don't get to see each other very often and I did miss you."

"The feeling is mutual. Let's set the world aside for a while and enjoy this rare occasion," Jim spoke in a soft loving tone reaching across the table to hold her hand.

Sharon raised her glass of Cabernet in a toast, in a gesture that had become an intimate part of their infrequent dates since Jim's successful attempt at salvaging their first encounter at Yale, "Here's to a better future and a smarter electorate."

"And to the prosecutors who have the misfortune to have you as the loyal opposition," remarked Jim with a broad and loving smile, as they clicked glasses, eyes locked in an embrace.

Dinner was served and they concentrated on enjoying their evening.

"When are you flying back to Michigan?" Jim asked as they finished their dinner, hoping that they could spend time together on Sunday.

"My flight is at 9 am on Monday morning. Why do you ask?" quizzed Sharon.

"Do you have plans for tomorrow?"

"Yes, I do!" answered Sharon smugly.

Jim's heart sank, "Oh, is your dad invited to a White House barbecue?" he reacted sarcastically.

"I don't know. I won't be seeing him until I leave. I told him the deal was that I would go to the dinner with him, but that I have plans to spend the rest of the weekend with a handsome soldier that I have been neglecting for some time. I have some making up to do."

Jim's expression went from a frown to a broad smile, "Well, what are we waiting for? You do have some serious 'making up' to do."

"Well, I have to get my things at dad's apartment. Are you ready to go or do you want dessert?"

"Can't I have both?"

"Maybe, if you're a good boy!" responded Sharon with a smile. "I make a terrific tiramisu."

Jim, laughed at her witty response, but hoped that she wasn't serious. He was not a tiramisu kind of guy.

Jim signaled to their waiter, "Michael, may we have our check please?"

"Let's walk the Mall, Jim. It's a beautiful night, with a full moon and a starry sky. Your apartment isn't far from here, is it?"

"It's only about two miles. Are those heels comfortable? I don't know if I can carry you."

"I'll take them off. We can walk on the grass. Come on, where's that adventurous spirit that got you through the jungle."

"I think I left it in a swamp back there, but okay, we can walk off that delicious meal."

"Great! I've never walked it all before. Whenever I'm here it's been too hot or too crowded to deal with."

As they reached the Mall, the two mile long grassy park stretching from the United States Capitol Building to the Lincoln Memorial, the full moon was lying at the far end, shedding its light on the reflecting pool leading up to the statue of Abraham Lincoln, sitting majestically in his chair.

"Did I tell you that I'm going to be a maid of honor in my sister Cindy's wedding?" informed Sharon as they walked hand in hand on the grassy mall.

"No, isn't she younger than you?" asked Jim.

"Yes, she's 21 but says she's in love. She's been going with this guy for two years and they say it's time."

"Marriage is a major commitment. Is she ready for that?" queried Jim.

"How would one know when they're ready? I think that when you want to be with that person every minute that's available, it's a good sign," answered Sharon. "There are people that you date for companionship and maybe even sex, but then there's that one who you want to spend your life with because you love them and it feels right. Don't you agree?"

"Yes, but you need to be ready to give of yourself fully in that relationship. She's kind of young for that kind of commitment. I don't think we know ourselves until we're in our thirties, if we're lucky," cautioned Jim, not realizing that there was more to this conversation than the announcement of Sharon's Maid of Honor status.

"So a person at 25 or 26 is too young to commit to a lifelong relationship?"

"I think so. There's so much in life to experience before one can commit to one person."

"Do you really believe that, Jim, or are you just being philosophical?"

"I believe that. But it depends on the person. If you're only into getting married and having two kids and a dog, then might as well do it sooner than later. But if you want more out of life you need to have time to experience it. Don't get me wrong, but I believe marriage is forever and when you haven't experienced life you have no real framework as to what you really want from it."

"Oh, really?" With that Sharon grabbed him by the lapels of his uniform and pulled him down to her lips. The kiss was long and passionate as Jim got into it, lifting her off her feet, feeling her body against his.

"How's that for your life's experience!" quipped Sharon, eyebrows raised, eyes widened and an innocent questioning smile on her face.

Chapter 60

"Mr. Buckman, there's a call for you on line one. It's General Obersham," announced his secretary on the intercom.

"Hello Bert, any news on the Senate vote?"

"Yes Jim, the Senate blocked the Petroleum Price Restriction Act. Masters will be pleased," reported Obersham. "Your man cast the deciding vote, as you predicted. He proposed an amendment to the bill saying that it needed more study. His vote sent it back to the Joint Committee, where it will probably die a slow death."

"That's good news, but I'm not sure what it will mean when Masters has his way. If he manages to double the price of oil it could have real repercussions on the economy and our investments," worried Buckman. "It will affect every aspect of our profit-base from production to transportation, to distribution. In fact, although, I hate to admit it, Polowski was right in his argument to us for favoring the Restriction Bill."

"Maybe Jim, but we don't need, or want any government regulation limiting our actions or our profit potential," offered Obersham.

"I agree Bert, but the real problem may be that consumers will have less money to spend on products and real estate if they're hit with high energy costs to heat their homes and run their cars. Then they'll want more money to spend, and higher wages would have the biggest impact on our bottom line. The unions would kill us financially," advised Buckman. "We need to keep a close watch on Masters!"

"So you think that he'll take advantage of the lack of oversight on oil pricing and stick it to his friends as well as to the public?" asked Bert.

"What do you think? Can he be trusted to go easy on this opportunity? Although he says that he imports 50% of his oil from the mid-east, what he didn't tell Sam was that he is a major investor in OPEC controlled oil production. I know that my investment in his company will profit, but the overall effect would be devastating to all of our other involvements."

"I don't think he'll hurt Nixon's potential for re-election by causing a recession in the middle of his term. As long as Nixon's in office, or some surrogate of his, I think that the 'Bulldog' will not attack."

"I hope you're right, Bert. We need to find out more about his intentions at our next meeting. I believe our colleagues would also have concern if he decides to take full advantage of the situation. But he'll be worried about the bill resurfacing if Nixon loses his re-election bid to the Democrats."

"It would take a major crisis and mismanagement by Nixon to have that happen. The Democrats pretty much imploded in the last election."

"I wouldn't assume too much based on that fiasco. History is replete with comeback stories in politics!"

"If he's intent on making a killing it would be difficult to stop him, Jim."

"I realize that, but the sooner we know those intentions the better our chances to mitigate them. We need some intelligence from your cohorts in the middle east."

"I'll contact Hassad in Kuwait, he's a reliable source of information. I'll ask him to find out what OPEC thinks of the Senate vote. I don't think we should disclose our true concerns at this point."

"Good thought, Bert. Keep it simple and business like. Let me know when you hear something pertinent and we'll meet in Washington to discuss a counter plan, if we need one."

Buckman wondered if he had been manipulated by Masters. If it wasn't for his influence on Polowski the price restriction bill would probably have passed. A significant increase in the cost of energy was not in his game plan for continued prosperity.

Chapter 61

Diego decided to pursue his goal to become an air traffic controller. His first step was to take flying lessons. He had moved to Plymouth, in southeastern Massachusetts, taking a job with a cranberry grower. He knew that his ethnic background as a Mexican was qualification enough for a menial job in the agricultural field. He had a second job at night washing dishes in a waterfront restaurant. He only needed a place to sleep. He lived with ten other workers in a converted airplane hangar at the airport. He thought the accommodations appropriate given his ambition. His lessons in a Cessna 175 trainer were all he could afford. He took his meals at his night job and usually managed to save leftovers for the next day's breakfast and lunch.

The feeling that he got when he took the controls of the plane and brought it to 5,000 feet over Cape Cod Bay was as exhilarating as he had ever experienced. "Tony, I was like an eagle with nothing but beautiful ocean, bright blue sky and fields of green below. The world looks so nice and peaceful when you're mile above the chaos," he blurted to Tony from the pay phone in the lobby of the restaurant. "I hope it was okay to call you collect?"

"It's okay my friend. I was hoping to hear from you, but isn't this only your third lesson? Does the instructor know that you have a reputation of falling from heights?" kidded Tony.

"Hey, I was shot out of that tree and if it wasn't for that, you wouldn't be a hero," countered Diego with a smile in his voice.

"So you've been bitten by the bug. Are you going to be a pilot now or are you still planning to confuse pilots who try to find your airport?" continued Tony.

"I still want to be a controller, but I think I should know something about flying to do a good job, don't you?"

"Yes, I agree, when do you start that air traffic class?

"In the fall, it's called the Air Traffic Collegiate Training Initiative. I took a test to qualify. I wish I had taken flight training in the Army. As you know, it's a federal job. You work for the Federal Aviation Administration. Tony, the benefits and pay seem to be really good. They have a union that keeps the FAA honest. Guys I met tell me that the hours can be very long and that there's a lot of stress, but hey, there's a lot of stress being poor and living with a bunch of gringo strangers."

"You're a hard working guy Diego. You'll do fine!"

"You think so? I do worry if I'm good enough, but it's an important job and it will get me respect. I would be a professional, like you Tony, you're an engineer and people respect you because you're a professional person."

"You're doing the right thing. People like you and me always need to prove themselves in order to be treated equal to our white Anglo peers. But we can't just be equal, we need to be better. I'm proud of you Diego!"

"Thank you Sarge, and I do appreciate you as my friend."

"How is your family doing? They must be proud that you're working towards a goal."

"Well, that's the second reason I am calling you."

"What is it? Did something happen to Carmella or your dad?"

"No it's my uncle Juan Carlos. The military police ambushed him and seven of his men yesterday on a mountain road. Juan Carlos thought that they were meeting people who wanted to buy guns. It was a setup."

"Is he in jail? What happened?"

"They killed him, Tony. My father called this morning. He says that we may be in danger. I'm sorry Tony, I'm always bringing you bad news and trouble."

"Why would we be in trouble? No one knows about what we did except those goons that I shot up, and they're still in jail... aren't they?"

"Rodriguez escaped last month. My father thinks he made a deal and led the American FBI and the Mexican police to my uncle."

"And you think he knows about us and that we're here in the east? Doesn't he think that you're dead? He had your house blown up."

"The city did a good job of finding out that we were not in the house when it blew up. If he doesn't know where we are, he'll probably find out, but maybe not. I don't know, but we need to be careful. He probably knows I'm not in Mexico."

"Well, amigo, we need to find him before he finds us. We can't wait for him to show up."

"How do we do that? He's on the run. He could be anywhere."

"I don't know yet, but I'll figure it out. I'll be down there to see you this weekend."

"I work every day, but I don't go into the restaurant job until eleven on Saturday and Sunday mornings. I usually have flying lessons on Saturday morning too, but they're over by nine. Can you meet me at the Plymouth Airport? There's a coffee shop there."

"I'll see you at the coffee shop at 9 o'clock Saturday. Don't worry. There's always a way, we just have to find it!"

"Yeah, before 'it' finds us! Be careful amigo!"

Chapter 62

Juan Carlos Martinez, was the benefactor to his own people at the expense of many thousands of drug addicts, their families and anyone who tried to stop him. He was revered as a saint by those in the cities and villages of the state of Jalisco, Mexico. He used a small portion of his profits, reaped from the pain and blood of many, to put food on the tables of the poor and pay for medical care for many who were ignored by their government and had no chance to survive otherwise. They were his base because they needed him and they protected him and his gang from the law, when the law could no longer be bought.

But to Carmella he was a son. She had given birth to him forty two years earlier in a one room adobe hut with a dirt floor, no doctor and no husband. Her husband had died of tuberculosis four months earlier. All she had was her two year old son Manuel, crying for his momma's attention, as she delivered her second son.

By the time he was twelve, Juan Carlos had learned that money meant power and that power meant more money. He led a gang of preteen hoodlums stealing from tourists and local shops. He would be the cute little boy with pleading eyes begging for money for food. Any kind tourist who stopped to give them money would be a target for his thugs to bludgeon and steal from. An older couple from New York City were their first victims. They got $243.45 and a taste for blood.

By the time he was 17 he had to leave his home or face prison. He took to the mountains where he created a ruthless organization that rewarded those whom he needed and destroyed those that got in his way.

Before he was killed he had established a fund for his brother and his mother so that they would never know poverty again. Only Manny knew how to access the money. It was not in a bank. They knew that their mother would never accept the money if she knew that Manny didn't work for it. He used it wisely, and in moderation, so as not to gain the attention of the authorities. No fancy cars, homes or jewelry, just basic subsidence for himself and his mother. Had she known, her wrath would have been worse than that of the law.

"I need to find Rodriguez. I will not lose my son to that madman." declared Manny as he and Carmella left the cemetery after burying his brother. The funeral was attended only by those close to Carmella and Manny, his many friends afraid to show themselves to the authorities. "They took his money and kindness, but denied him in his death," lamented Manny.

"Your brother was not a good man. He was my son, and I loved him as a mother would, but he hurt many people and now he is facing his reward. I hope that God is merciful to him!" Carmella said with tears of remorse for her son's reckless life and cruelty.

"There will be no more untimely deaths in our family!" promised Manny.

The next day Manny took their 1960 black Ford pickup and started on his journey to Nuevo Laredo, a border town on the Rio Grande more than 1000 km northeast of Guadalajara and the sister city of Laredo, Texas. He had heard from one of his brother's surviving gang members, his former lieutenant Pedro Valdez that Ramon Rodriguez, Miguel's cousin lived there. Valdez had been on a business trip to Mexico City when Juan Carlos and his entourage were gunned down. He suspected that Ramon would know where Miguel was hiding and he was told that he had taken the wrap for Miguel in LA and was deported for his cousin's crime. Miguel had promised him a substantial reward for his loyalty but never paid the debt. Manny believed he could be persuaded to tell what he knew, for a price. He made a substantial withdrawal from his deceased brother's secret joint account for the effort.

He left a letter in his bureau drawer, addressed to Diego, telling him of the location of his brother's money with instructions on how to use it to support his grandmother. He told Carmella that it contained information about Miguel

Rodriguez and that she was not to open it but to send it Diego if anything happened to him.

The roads from Guadalajara to Nuevo Laredo were very poor. The trip would take several days. He would sleep in the truck and stop at predetermined towns and villages where he knew he could find food and water. He had a .357 Magnum that he accepted, reluctantly, from his brother's former lieutenant. He had no intention of using it, but he knew the reputation of Nuevo Laredo as a very dangerous city. It was only about 100 meters from the American city of Laredo. It was accessible by two bridges over the Rio Grande, and was a major gateway for smugglers of people, guns and drugs.

His plan was to capture Miguel and leave him bound for the police to take back to prison. His prison escape should be good for ten or more years added to his sentence. Ramon, he was told, was a bouncer in a club in the Boys Town area of the city. Boys Town was a seedy, walled compound of strip clubs, brothels and gambling bars frequented by American men looking for a good time. In Boy's Town almost everything was allowed for a price, and nothing was illegal except for actions by an unruly American or cheating the establishment out of their due. Bad behavior was not tolerated and was severely punished, that was Ramon's main job and he was good at it.

Ramon was a bruising 300 pounds. He was 6 feet 2 inches tall, with hair everywhere but on his head. Although he went to jail for five years for his cousin Miguel's crime, he could have gotten a much longer sentence if he had been tried and convicted of his real crimes, as a hit man for the cartel. Manny knew he would have a tough task getting the information he needed from Ramon, but he was on a mission that would not be denied. He had money, and he believed that money could loosen the tongue of a man like Ramon. He would hide the money before he met with Ramon so as not to tempt him into an easy score. He also knew that he would probably have to cross the border to complete his task. He had doubts that this would be a round trip.

Chapter 63

Captain James Buckman III didn't welcome the trip back to Vietnam, but there were too many loose ends in the case labeled by the media as the 'My Lai Massacre.' He tried to surmise what had happened. Were the victims part of the VC support caught in a cross fire? Was Lieutenant Calley following orders or did he totally lose it, unable to endure the stress of war? Did Captain Medina, his superior officer, order him to "clean out the village?" Did Medina mean to kill every man, woman and child? Was the helicopter pilot, Hugh Thompson, acting out of compassion or was he betraying his own military when he aimed his weapons threatening Calley's company? He had rescued a number of potential victims from their certain fate by flying them out from under the guns of Calley's troops.

The answers had to be found. He would find the truth in spite of his orders to..."find an explanation that will calm things down, the President wants this buried!" which were the last words spoken to him by his Commanding Officer at the Pentagon.

He would meet with his former Commander, General Albertson in Saigon, to brief him on his orders and to be briefed on what the General knew about "the incident." As he reviewed the reports the night before his fight from California, he noted a familiar name in one of the helicopter crews; Master Sergeant Bobby Franklin, his original drill instructor at Fort Devens, and as a Ranger, his rescuer from the jungle near Da Nang. He hoped to catch up with Franklin, get his story on My Lai, and thank him again for his heroic action in saving his ass.

As his flight touched down in Saigon, Buckman felt a twinge in his stomach and began to sweat, a cold sweat that started at his forehead. He had thought that he could handle this assignment without the emotion of flashbacks and the painful thoughts of those he left behind, but it was obvious as he viewed the jungle and its terrain that he would have to deal with the trauma inflicted by the fear, stress and sorrow of his Vietnam experience.

He had led his men through the jungle and overcame many obstacles but he believed that it was his instinct for survival and not any leadership ability that drove him on. For most of that adventure he was emotionally numb and believed they were not going to make it. He had little hope that they would see their families again.

The sight of that Huey piloted by a young woman from a farm in Arkansas; of the Phantom Jet coming over the horizon like the cavalry in a John Wayne movie, and the courageous act of Bobby Franklin, weaving himself through the forest canopy to rescue them were all surreal. He had gained enormous respect for the Bobby Franklins' of the world and for all of the men and women who did their job in the military. He was proud to be one of them but lost respect for those politicians who callously sent them into harm's way for selfish and ill-defined reasons.

General Albertson greeted him like he was his own son. "I'm so happy to see you again Jim. I hear you're doing good things back there in D.C."

"Thank you, sir. I'm still learning about the complexities of military law, but it's been interesting. Thank you for the recommendation to serve in the JAG. It has been an enlightening experience."

"Yes, I'm sure, and there isn't any case that will be more complex or disheartening than this My Lai incident. They gave you a bear to wrestle with, but you must be very tired after your long journey. Why don't you go to your accommodations? Your driver, Sergeant Barker, will take you there. Take some time to rest and clean up. We can have dinner at 1800 and discuss that whole mess."

"I would like that sir. It will give me an opportunity to put my thoughts together."

"Great, I'll have Sergeant Barker pick you up at 1730."

The ride to the base housing went through the marketplace. Jim noticed the faces of the people who filled the streets with their carts and bikes. They were more somber than he remembered. He was always impressed by their resilience and smiles while they dealt with the tremendous burden and fears of war. His driver told him that things were different since the Tet offensive. The people felt vulnerable. Having their enemy over-running the American embassy and fighting in their streets brought them a reality they hadn't anticipated. They no longer believed that the Americans were capable of protecting them, or of winning the war.

"How do they feel about My Lai, Sergeant?"

"I'm sorry sir, I'm not at a liberty to talk about My Lai," responded Barker in a military tone that signaled Buckman that this was not going to be an easy assignment.

Chapter 64

The Plymouth Airport, on the west side of "America's Home Town," was a typical small town airport. It was not designed to accommodate jet engine aircraft and was most comfortable with recreational twin and single engine props. It was perfect for Diego's purposes. He lived at the airport in a converted hangar. He was close enough to where he tended cranberry bogs in the adjoining town of Carver and only a few miles from where he worked in the seafood restaurant on the Plymouth waterfront. He traveled between sites on his 10-speed Schwinn bike that he bought at a goodwill store for $20.

Tony made the trip down Route 3 from Southie in less than an hour and was able to watch Diego approach and land his Cessna from his table in the coffee shop just off the runway. He knew it was Diego having heard one of the patrons, an older man wearing a well-worn Boston Red Sox cap, tell another about the Hispanic kid from LA that scared the hell out of his instructors.

"The last time he landed the plane he wound up off the runway, across that open field," he said nodding his head in the direction of the tall grass on the far side of the runway, "and into the woods way over there. He's got a new guy with him today. His instructor, Billy Johnson, called in sick when he saw the flight schedule. I don't blame him."

Tony smiled, knowing that Diego was probably having a blast of a time not realizing that he was gaining a reputation for his flying skills. Tony watched as the small plane's overhead wings flapped like a drunken bird as it approached the landing strip. It was at about 300 feet above the ground and not more than 200 feet from the far edge of the landing strip when the nose dipped and then pulled up. "Oh my God he's going to crash," he said to himself as the plane's nose rose, the wheels touched the paved strip, then lifted off the ground and down again, bouncing, like a skipping rock on a calm sea. The plane veered to the left, towards the coffee shop and his vantage point. He looked back through the picture window, just in time to see the shops customers run for the front door. He ran to his right figuring to stay out of the runaway plane's path.

He could see Diego, his terrified face and his even more terrified instructor as he grappled the controls away from Diego. The plane stopped less than 10 feet from the coffee shop's rear door, its prop still spinning. Tony, his back against the wall when the plane finally came to a stop, ran to the pilot's door and opened it.

"Hey Tony, what do you think, not bad for a kid from the ghetto, hey?" Diego said with a wide grin and a deaf ear to the words of the screaming instructor, as he shut down the engine.

"I think you should keep your feet on the ground. You and heights don't seem to go well together!"

"I'm doing better than I did the last time I landed. Look, I'm only about 50 feet from the landing strip," he said pointing over his left shoulder.

"I heard you tried to turn the plane into a lawn mower the last time out. I think you better have your instructor take the plane back to the hangar. We've got a lot to talk about. Let's go to my car. I think the coffee shop is closed, or at least it's abandoned."

"Okay, I heard from Carmella late last night. My father has gone to find Miguel. He took his truck and left early yesterday morning," Diego said as they rounded the building and headed towards the parking lot.

"Where's he going? How does he expect to find him, and what will he do if he does?"

"She said he knows Miguel's cousin and she heard him on the phone say something about Nuevo Laredo, it's a tough town on the border with Texas. She also saw that he had a gun in his bag."

"If Miguel's hiding in Mexico he isn't any threat to us. Maybe he's just hiding out? He wouldn't risk getting caught just to settle with us."

"Well, we don't know if he's in Mexico. We only know that his cousin is supposed to be there. I think my father believes that his cousin will tell him where he is, but I don't know why he would do that. She did hear him say that the cousin, a guy named Ramon, didn't like Miguel for some reason. She heard him say something about Boys Town, and that Ramon worked there.

"Boys Town, isn't that the place where they take in troubled boys. I thought it was in Nebraska. A Catholic Priest, Father Flanagan, started it back in the thirties. Maybe this guy Ramon isn't a bad guy, if he helps kids?" questioned Tony.

"I don't think so. I remember my father and his brother talking about this place in Nuevo Laredo that it was a place for 'boys,' actually men, to have fun with booze and women."

"Really, that's too weird. So if your dad finds out from Ramon that Rodriguez is in the United States what good will it do? Your dad can't cross the border and travel here. Immigration would catch him and send him back."

"I don't know, but I do know that he's a very determined man and he'll do what he has to do to protect his family. What should I do? I can't let him get killed."

As they approached Tony's Chevy pickup he said, "Get in. We'll discuss it on the way to your restaurant job."

"Okay! My bike is over at the hangar, we can put it in the back."

"I'm going to stay at the Governor Bradford Hotel on the waterfront tonight. There's a little café down the street. Have you had breakfast?"

"No, I haven't and I'm really hungry after that flight."

"Well, from what I saw it was a good thing you had an empty stomach when you made that landing!" Tony looked at his friend, eyebrows raised, and they both laughed.

"I've been awake all night thinking about this situation and I've an idea I want to discuss with you. Your father's involvement complicates things, but I think we can deal with it."

"Hey, Tony you always have ideas ... some even work. You're the problem solver, that's why you're an engineer."

"Yeah, you know what I always say...*a problem by definition, has a solution, otherwise it's a condition that you have to learn to live with*!" they recited simultaneously as Diego mimicked Tony.

"So, Tony is this a problem or a condition?"

"I hope that it's just a problem, but we'll soon find out."

The café on the waterfront was a stone's throw from Plymouth Rock, the main tourist attraction in the coastal town of Plymouth, Massachusetts. Legend has it that the Pilgrims came to the Americas in 1620 in search of religious freedom. The "Rock" is said to be the first land they set foot on in their quest for that freedom. In truth, they actually landed on the outer coast of Cape Cod in an area that is now part of Provincetown, before their feet touched down in Plymouth.

Tony and Diego each ordered the biggest breakfast on the menu and began to consume their first cup of coffee before they got into Tony's plan. My family brought me here when my dad first got his driver's license. He was 42 years old and I was only 12. He got stopped by a state trooper for crossing over a double solid line on Route 3A, it was before the highway, Route 3, was built. He was really embarrassed. He was always lecturing me about obeying the law," recited Tony.

"Well, my dad lost respect for the law when it turned on him in LA. He and thousands of others were brought into this country by the farmers and sweat shops to work for pennies so they could make big profits. When he needed help for my mom, because she was very sick, they turned on him, not wanting to admit that they brought him here, and they did, what you say, 'threw him under the bus.' My mother died. We had no insurance and no money for medical care. He was deported to Mexico with no compassion for his loss."

"He's just one of thousands of so called illegals that have been victimized by American businesses while they wave the flag and declare themselves patriots. They're discarded like useless, obsolete equipment when they're no longer able to be used for profit. Some have turned to crime to survive, as you know. But there is hope with this man from Arizona, Cesar Chavez. He's organizing a union of migrant workers to fight for their rights as human beings and not to be treated as slaves by those who take advantage of their desperate poverty and need for work."

"Yes, Chavez is our Martin Luther King, but there's talk that he will wind up the same way as King if he doesn't back off. People are scared for him and for themselves. 'The Man' isn't going to do the right thing as long as he can pay-off some political hack to look the other way."

"I hope you're wrong, Diego, but I'm afraid history is on their side. They're trying to make people believe that they're the benevolent ones and that these families are lucky that they give them work, housing them in crowded shacks and giving them food enough to keep them working. It's pretty much the same thing that the southern plantation owners did for the slaves that they kidnapped from Africa, only they did it with less formality and no token pay."

As they finished their pancakes, eggs, sausage and third cups of coffee, Diego brought Tony back to the subject of survival, in particular to his plan to counter the threat that Miguel Rodriguez presented to both of them, and to Diego's dad.

"We need to find your father before he gets hurt, but we also need to lure Miguel into a trap. Obviously, if he's to do the deed himself he will have to enter this country and he is an escaped convict who, if caught, will spend some serious time back in his cell."

"Yeah, I know all that, but what's your plan?" asked Diego.

"Well, we can't go to the law and tell them the real reason Rodriguez wants to kill us. What I did in that bar would also be considered a crime, especially since we left the scene."

"So far I'm not getting excited about your plan, Tony."

"Be patient, the good part is coming. You're going to send a message to Miguel, through his old friends in LA, that you will set me up if he promises to leave you and your family out of it. You're going to tell him that I cheated you out of money from some deal and that we're not friends any more. You're going to let him believe that I rescued you out of that bar because I needed you to pull off this deal and I wanted to take advantage of your relationship with your uncle Juan Carlos."

"Are you crazy, Tony? He will kill you and then go after me."

"I won't be where he thinks I am, but the cops will be, I hope. We need to come up with a credible story of why he is after us, one that will not lead to my arrest, and we need to find a place that is far from here to keep him away from my family, but also on this side of the border so that he can't easily escape back to Mexico."

"I don't know, Tony. Your plan doesn't thrill me, and what about my papa?"

"He may be able to help us with the plan, if we can get in touch with him before he makes contact with Miguel's cousin, Ramon."

"And how do we do that? I have no Idea where he is until he reaches Nuevo Laredo, and he could be anywhere in that hell hole. He might be there now!"

"We'll work that out, but you need to contact Carmella and tell her to have your dad call me immediately if he contacts her, or to get his number and I'll call him, and you need to do that now. Let's go to the hotel and use the phone. We don't have much time to set this up."

When they got to Tony's hotel the desk clerk checking him in told him he had a message from a Mr. Benedetto, to call him. Tony had told his dad where he would be staying if he needed him since his mother wasn't well.

"Hello, Dad. What's the problem? Is mom okay?"

"Yes, she's fine, but I got a call from some guy with an accent, like your friend Diego's. He wanted to know where you were. He didn't ask if you were here, just if you were my son and where you lived. I thought it was strange. Are you in trouble, Tony? I didn't like his tone."

"What did you tell him?"

"I told him I hadn't seen you for a while and asked who he was and why he wanted to find you. He hung up on me. If he was a friend he wouldn't have hung up, would he?"

"No, Dad and you did the right thing."

"Oh, there's something else. I could hear the announcement of a flight arriving. I think he was at an airport, probably Logan."

"Thanks Dad, is mom all right to travel?"

"Yes, why is it that bad? What is this all about?"

"It's a long story. I'll have to explain later, but this guy's a very bad character. He escaped from prison in California and I helped put him there. You, mom, Marie and Joey have to get out of that house. He may try to go there to convince you to tell him where I am."

"You know me Tony, I don't run from anyone. I'll take care of him if he shows up. He'll wish he were back in prison."

"I know you're tough, Dad, but he'll be armed and he's very dangerous. He tried to kill Diego out there in California. You need to leave now. Go to your sister Mary's in East Boston, for the family's sake."

"Okay, but what are you going to do?" his father agreed reluctantly.

"I'm going to call my old friend Sergeant Danny O'Malley at Station 6. This is now police business. Call me from Aunt Mary's house. Leave a message here at the hotel if I'm not here."

Diego looked at Tony startled at what he was hearing.

"Jeez, did I hear right? Rodriguez is here? What are we going to do, amigo?"

"Well, he doesn't know that I live on the other end of Southie from my parents so he called them. My phone is unlisted so it will take him time to find my apartment. We still need to get in touch with your father. He may get himself in trouble with Miguel's cousin down there. Call Carmella while I figure this out."

"Aren't you going to call your cop friend, like you told your dad?"

"I don't know. I told him that so he would leave the house and not worry as much. I don't have my story down yet. If it comes out that I shot the bastards I could be indicted for assault or even attempted murder."

"But Tony, you did it to save my ass, that isn't assault."

"No, but I would have to prove that to a judge and jury. Listen Diego, right now we have one problem to solve, let's not make it more complicated."

"Yeah, I know or it will be a *condition*, but one that we won't be able to live with! I think you should call this cop O'Malley. How well do you know him? Can he be trusted with the truth?"

"Well, he was one of the leaders of kids that used to chase me home and beat the crap out of me. But we were kind of friends when I played baseball. We were on the same team. He's not a bad guy. I'm just not sure that it's the right way to go."

"Tony you must have been a very popular kid with all the bullies. Did they practice on you or something?" chided Diego.

"Very funny coming from a guy who had such great friends as Joey Consalvo and Miguel Rodriguez," responded Tony with a smirk.

The call to Carmella was not enlightening. "She said that she hasn't heard from my father since he left Monterey late last night. She thought that he would be in Nuevo Laredo later today," Diego relayed to Tony.

"I'm going back to Southie. You need to go to work. I'll call you there later."

Chapter 65

The flight to Da Nang on a HE-1E troop transport helicopter, similar to the one that rescued him, was stressful for Captain James Buckman III. He was being flown to the base from which Bobby Franklin's Rangers operate, less than 30 miles from his rescue site. Franklin had seen a lot of war. He didn't envy him.

The sound of ground-fire as they approached the base from the southwest was too much of a nostalgic moment for Jim. The Huey returned the fire quieting the action of the VC unit. He was surprised that they were so close to the base of operations.

He was told that Franklin was on a mission that would take him until early morning. Buckman would be leaving the base the next day at 1400. He hoped to interview several other soldiers who were in Franklin's company at My Lai. The base commander, Colonel Stratford, agreed to have the requested interview subjects available in his office in the morning beginning at 0800.

Jim Buckman couldn't sleep as the record file of My Lai with its photographic evidence stirred in his mind. What do they expect me to do here? The evidence is there in black and white. I know they don't want this to go where I believe its going. So why am I here; to validate the reports?

The next morning he was picked up by Colonel Stratford's driver. The Colonel was a cordial host, but it was apparent to Buckman that he had an agenda. "I'm happy to see you Captain. I see that stateside duty has helped you gain back the weight you lost on your jungle diet. You looked pretty beat the last time I saw you. How's your dad doing?" queried the Colonel, attempting to put Jim at ease with small talk.

"He's doing well. Thank you for asking. He's going about his usual business of trying to solve, what he perceives to be, the world's problems."

"Well, I'm sure you know he's well thought of in military circles. Colonel James Buckman's exploits during World War II are legendary, although not well known outside those circles. That's a price paid for working within the shadows."

"Actually, it was not well known to me until I met dad here in Vietnam, after I was rescued. We had a long heart-to-heart talk, which was an unusual occurrence between us. I guess my military venture qualified me to be in 'the circle.' Which brings me to my reason for being here; do you know if Master Sergeant Franklin has returned from his mission?"

"His unit is on their way back. They should be on the base by 1200. You probably know that there's been a lot of action going on in this sector since you left," Colonel Stratford sat back in his high back leather chair; his hands locked over his chest, his eyes on Buckman's, attempting to detect his attitude about his assignment.

"Yes, I understand things have changed around here since my departure. The population seems to be less enthusiastic about our presence and our Huey was attacked by ground-fire less than 5 kilometers south of the Base. That was a fairly secure area when I was here last."

"I'm afraid you're right Captain. The NV Army is moving down from the north and the VC have surfaced in areas where we had confidence in our security. I wouldn't admit this publicly, but the troops are feeling the pressure. Many of them are on their third and fourth tours of duty. After Tet the landscape changed dramatically, but we're resilient and we'll recover and push these bastards back into their holes." The Colonel's fist gently tapped the desk emphasizing his determination and displaying his frustration.

Buckman took the opportunity to ask the question he had been hoping to ask since he walked into the Colonel's office. "What do you think happened at My Lai, Colonel? Was that a result of the frustration or of a renegade soldier losing it?"

Colonel Stratford sat up in his chair presenting his best military posture, his eyes again locked onto to those of Buckman. "I don't know that anything happened at My Lai except for soldiers doing their duty to clear a Viet Cong village. A village that has directly supported the VC in their cowardly killing of far too many of our men and women, some of them in field hospitals and many that were wounded only to be executed by those black pajama-clad gooks, before we could rescue them."

Buckman was taken aback, but was not totally surprised at the defensive and passionate response of the hard-nosed Colonel. "You don't believe reports that innocent people, women, children and old men, were massacred there?"

"Captain, I don't believe there are any innocent people in war, especially not those who are assisting our enemies!"

Buckman accepted his answer without retort, not wanting to create a chasm between them since he needed the Colonel's cooperation if he was to get through this investigative process in the time allotted by his Commander. He also realized that the time allotted was limited to ensure that his inquiries would also be limited. It was important to Washington that the investigation be perceived to be thorough in its interviewing of eyewitnesses.

"I have arranged for several of the men who were present at My Lai to talk to you this morning. Franklin is scheduled to meet with you this afternoon at 1200. Captain Thomas Moriarty, our base JAG officer, will sit in on those interviews. He'll be here shortly. I have business to attend to, so please make yourself comfortable at my conference table and good luck. I'll have coffee brought in for you."

Before Moriarty arrived Buckman did a quick surveillance of the Colonel's office and found a bugging device taped to the underside of the table. They're leaving nothing to chance! He thought as he opened his brief case and placed it on the chair beside him. He stacked the reports neatly in front of him with the gruesome photographs on top. He placed a recording device next to the reports and began reading his notes from his original review of the record.

The office door opened and Captain Moriarty entered without fanfare. "Good morning Captain Buckman, I'm Captain Thomas Moriarty. I'll be assisting you in this part of your investigation," extending his hand as he sat across the table. "I hear you had some excitement on your trip up from Saigon."

"It wasn't too bad the Huey crew handled it well. It does seem the VC are getting more comfortable at closer range than they were when I was here last."

"Well, I would say more brazen than comfortable, but we're doing our best to make them pay for their aggressive behavior," Moriarty declared.

"I guess that they thought that this was their home!" responded Buckman with some regret, realizing that he was revealing an attitude that might not be looked upon favorably by his JAG colleague.

Moriarty squinted a look of disdain on his face. He knew that he was in for long day.

The day went as expected. There were five men of rank from Private First Class to Sergeant paraded in and out of the interrogation room. They were all scripted and well-rehearsed.

Their testimonies were similar. "They didn't see much. They were firing into the village and there was some collateral damage. Yes, some were women and children, but then they have lost friends to the actions of women and children throwing grenades and shooting automatic weapons. No one noticed Lieutenant Calley, they were in a fire fight!"

When asked about the bodies in the ditch as they were shown the photographs, some would look to Captain Moriarty, who would say something to the effect that, "Isn't that where your company placed the bodies of those killed in the attack on the village by the VC?" which would get the positive nod and response from the witness. Others would deny seeing the depicted carnage. "I'm sorry sir but I was at the rear, I didn't see anything like that," was a usual response.

It seemed that most of the company was at the rear of the 'fire fight' and otherwise unaware of what was obviously displayed by the photographic evidence.

As each witness left the room he looked to Captain Moriarty for whatever sign he could muster to indicate that he had done a good job. He would give them a standard, "Thank you soldier. We appreciate your time," but was careful not to show too much enthusiasm for their choreographed performances.

It was obvious to Buckman that they were scared, not only of the enemy but of those who had complete control over their lives. It was also obvious that he wasn't going to get a straight story as long as Moriarty was present. He looked forward to meeting with Franklin.

Master Sergeant Franklin appeared on time and after the traditional salute reached out to Buckman in a long, warm and friendly handshake exchanging smiles and small talk bringing on a look of disdain from Moriarty. Buckman felt a piece of paper within the clench of Franklin's handshake and managed to lower his hand, which had, what was obviously a note from Franklin, He put it into his pocket while distracting his counterpart with the story of his rescue.

Franklin's responses to Buckman's questions paralleled those of the previous witnesses, putting Moriarty at ease. It was 1240 and Buckman was anxious to read the note discretely passed to him by the former drill Sergeant and heroic rescuer. He was to leave the base at 1400.

"The Colonel has lunch being brought into here for you, Captain. He regrets that he won't be able to attend, but we can talk about your conclusions," announced Moriarty.

"That's great, but I need to use your rest room first."

Buckman went down the hallway of the makeshift military complex, to the rest room, anxious to read Franklin's note.

Hidden within a stall he pulled out the piece of paper. "Meet me behind Hangar #5 at 1300." The words were brief and not identifiable as to its author. He needed to eat quickly and minimize the conversation with Moriarty. He ripped up the note and flushed it.

Chapter 66

On the road back to Boston Tony decided that it was too risky for him to meet Rodriguez, if he showed up, alone. He pulled off the highway in Braintree and drove to a service station to get gas and to call O'Malley. He explained the situation as he had to his father, leaving out the part about the gun play in the bar in LA.

"Okay, Tony I'll meet you at your father's house. I had the wanted notice pulled on your guy as we speak. He's a bad actor. Tell me again how you got involved with him?"

Tony repeated the part of the story about Diego and left it there, as a mystery to be solved later, if necessary.

"If you think that he may be in the neighborhood I'll go with detective Burns in his unmarked vehicle. We don't want to alert him. We'll meet you on the corner of G Street and Columbia Road."

"I'll be there in about 25 minutes, unless I get stopped by a Statey," kidded Tony.

"Yeah right, well just don't, a few minutes shouldn't bust this deal. I'll have a plain clothes cop across the street watching the house."

"Thanks Danny, I owe you one!"

"Let's hope you're around to pay off."

Tony, got into his truck and went screeching up the on-ramp to the highway. Damn, I should have called Aunt Mary to make sure they got there okay, he thought, Maybe Rodriguez got there before they left! Worried that he put them in real danger he picked up speed, but kept within ten miles of the posted limit, not wanting to attract the attention of a state trooper.

Unlike downtown Boston with its meandering roadways, South Boston Streets were laid out in a grid pattern. Streets running north and south were designated by letters of the alphabet A through P, and those running east and west were given numbers beginning with the lowest number at the north section of Southie to the highest number, Eighth Street being on the southern perimeter, closer to Columbia Road and Day Boulevard, which runs along Carson Beach. The numbers were further designated as to whether they were on the east or west side of town. So East Eighth Street was on the east side of Southie. The main drag was Broadway, a commercially developed east-west running avenue, which split the northerly neighborhoods and industrial properties from those residences on the south side, nearer the Beach.

Tony took Morrissey Boulevard through Dorchester to Day Boulevard into Southie, driving along Carson Beach. As he turned onto Columbia Road at G Street he noticed several Boston police vehicles at the bottom of Douglas Street, lights blaring. Sergeant O'Malley was on the corner of G Street standing alone, waiting for Tony. "What's going on, Danny? Is my family ok?" Tony asked, unable to mask the panic in his voice.

"I'm afraid we missed the action but, yes they're okay. There's a guy up there hog-tied with a large egg-shaped lump on the back of his head and your dad's standing over him with a Ted Williams special. The guy's out of it, but he'll heal enough to make the trip back to prison. Let's go ID him. I hope he's not the mailman," joked O'Malley.

Tony and O'Malley climbed the stairs to the second floor landing, passing an entourage of Boston Police personnel, to where Tony's dad was still standing over the fully bound body of someone that was not Rodriguez.

"Dad, are you all right? What happened? Where's mom and the others?"

"I'm okay. They're at Aunt Mary's. You didn't think I was going to leave you to meet this thug alone. He tried to push his way in through the kitchen door from the hallway. I came out of the living room door into the hall behind him and whacked him with your favorite bat. He was very surprised!" Richie smiled, he was still shaking from the trauma, his hands gripping the bat as if he might use it again.

"Dad, he could have killed you."

O'Malley showed Tony and his father the perpetrator's Glock, a very lethal weapon. "It looks like that was his intent Mr. Benedetto."

"Well, I tied him up good with clothesline and stuffed an old sock in his mouth so he couldn't even burp."

"Who is he, Tony? He doesn't match the description of Rodriguez," questioned the sergeant.

"He's Rodriguez's henchman. I don't know his name. I thought he was also in prison. I didn't know he escaped too. This means that Miguel is still out there."

"Well, maybe we can find out from this guy where he is. Take him to the station, Dave. He may need to see a doctor, but keep him secured."

"Thank you, Danny, I'll be down there in about twenty minutes. I have to make a couple of phone calls."

"Mr. Benedetto, we'll need you to file a complaint so we can keep this guy wrapped up until we check the warrants. There must be an APB out for him if he escaped prison. I'll leave an officer outside to make sure you're not surprised again. He'll take you to the Station to file the report when you're ready."

When the police left with their alleged criminal, Tony got on his dad for taking such a chance. "Dad, you're 55 years old. What were you thinking? You could be going out of here on a stretcher, or to the morgue! And your heart! Don't forget you were in the hospital only a couple of years ago with a massive heart attack."

"Don't worry about me. Anyone tries to invade my home will suffer for it, son. You knew I'd be prepared."

"And what if there were two of them?"

"Then there would be two guys lying hog-tied on the floor! The bat swings both ways!" his father smiled at his own wit.

"I don't know, but the other thug might be nearby. I need to call Diego."

The call to Diego at his job was fruitless. "I'm sorry, sir, but he's busy right now!" was the assertive response of the day manager. "He'll be on a break in two hours, please call him then."

"Please tell him that Tony called and that it's very important that he call me back ASAP."

"Yes sir, I'll do that, when he goes on his break," responded the voice in a condescending and sarcastic tone.

Tony wished he were there to teach him some people skills.

"Let's go to the station, Dad and get this over with. Officer, we won't need you to drive us, but could you hang out here for a while, just in case?"

"Yes sir, I'll keep watch until you return. The Captain will probably want an all-night stakeout here. It sounds like we have a really bad boy out there."

"That's an understatement! Don't take chances officer. He'll kill for the thrill of it."

The ride to the station was filled with silence. Tony's dad had a way of saying what was on his mind without speaking and right now he was not happy with the situation that his son had put himself and the family in.

As they pulled up to the police station on West Broadway, his father broke his silence, "I don't know what's going on, Tony, but you better tell me the whole story before we go in there." The look in his eye was reminiscent of a look that Tony got as a warning before the roof fell in on him. He decided that he had a right to know why he had to defend his home and family against a vicious prison escapee intent on killing his son. He gave him the full story, in short bursts as he watched his father's jaw drop, his eyes widen and finally his exclamation, "You did what? Are you crazy?"

"What would you have done? Your best friend is about to die and you have the possibility to save him? I remember, as a little boy, listening to your stories as I lay in bed and you and Mom would be sitting at the kitchen table talking to the neighbors about the fights you had to survive and the friends that you cared about. You never backed down or left them to face their fate alone. What would you have done, huh?"

"I would have killed them both, let's go in!"

Tony followed his father up the steps of Station 6, shaking his head, a grin creeping across his face. "Okay, so I made a mistake!" A thought crossed his mind: his father always said that the job wasn't finished until you cleaned up! But he knew that his father couldn't kill anyone. The only time he even held a gun was in his brief stint in the Coast Guard at the end of World War II.

The walk down the hall of the station to Sergeant Danny O'Malley's desk was not pleasant. It was like passing through a herd of rambling sheep and it smelled as bad. Officers and alleged criminals attached at the wrist weaving in and out, bumping, and otherwise making the trip quite uncomfortable on this very busy crime-stopping day. Danny sat in a large room at one of a half-dozen grey metal desks on an equally aesthetic grey metal chair. Two army-green metal chairs were placed on the opposite side to accommodate his guests. Municipal budgets and protocol required the look of austerity.

"Hey, Tony and Mr. Benedetto, have a seat," his hand extended in a welcoming gesture. "It's a little chaotic in here today, but then it's always chaotic."

"How's your prisoner doing?" asked Tony.

"Oh he's recovering nicely. His name is Chico Juarez, at least that's the name he had on his ID card and he isn't talking. He also had a piece of paper with the name 'Miguel' and 'McGrath's, Plymouth waterfront at 4,' written on it. Does that mean anything to you?"

Tony, startled, stood up, "Call the Plymouth police. That's the restaurant where Diego, the other guy they're after, works. Diego's there now."

"Diego? Is that the guy from LA that you told me about? Tony It's almost 3:30. "O'Malley dialed the Plymouth Police Department and quickly explained the situation to the desk sergeant who answered. "They're sending a car out there to get your friend," O'Malley told them to pick him up gently, but to say that Tony needed to see him at the station.

Twenty minutes later the Plymouth police called back. "He's not there?' asked Danny, "Yeah, his name is Diego Martinez. Yes, he's an American citizen and not wanted, but he may become a victim. Did they say where he went? Okay, please stay on it, there's a hit man looking for him. The assassin is an escaped con from LA, name of Miguel Rodriguez, you'll find his photo on the wire," O'Malley continued his explanation to the desk sergeant in Plymouth. "He has an APB out on him. This guy Diego helped send him to San Quentin. We believe that Rodriguez is armed and obviously, very dangerous. Thank you Sergeant Benson."

"Well, the Plymouth Police were told by the manager that Diego left in a hurry. He threw off his apron and ran out of the rear door. They said that a waitress saw him get on a bike that he kept near the dumpster and head towards the boat docks. She didn't see anyone else near him."

"He must have spotted Rodriguez and decided to run for it," surmised Tony.

"Where would he go? Does he live nearby there?" asked his father.

"No, he doesn't. He would have a long ride on his bike, to the west side of town, towards the Plymouth airport."

"Let's go to my apartment. He might call there. I'm the only one he knows well enough to call for help. Here's my number Danny. Please call me if you hear anything."

"I will, Tony. Here, take Sergeant Benson's number. Call him in Plymouth, and tell Diego, if he calls you, to stay put until they can pick him up."

Diego had his Schwinn Special at top speed as he crossed Main Street onto Leyden Street and then turned down Market to Summer Street heading west. The sight of Rodriguez leaning against a parking lot light pole, lighting up a stogie, was enough to give him an adrenalin rush that would maximize the old bike's potential. Dark clouds formed overhead and rain started to fall as he passed the cemetery where many of the original Pilgrims were resting in peace. He didn't want to join them.

He picked up speed on the far side of the hill, the rain washing against his face, the road slippery, causing difficulty in maneuvering his old bike with its worn tire treads. The passing cars, their drivers oblivious to his presence, splashed muddy waters onto him as he pedaled for his life, adding to the treacherous conditions as he attempted his escape from a determined assassin. The biking to work every day proved to be good therapy for his legs. He could make that old Schwinn fly.

Drenched, cold and distraught Diego turned into a gas station near the Plymouth airport. He needed to use the payphone and hoped he had enough money to call long distance to Tony in South Boston. He realized that since Miguel knew where he worked, he must know where he lives, and feared that he would be waiting for him.

The phone in Tony's apartment was ringing as he took the stairs, to the third floor flat, two steps at a time. "Hello, Diego?" he answered, hoping he was not too late.

"Tony, he was there, at my work. He's going to kill me, Tony," sobbed Diego as he tried to get the words out, breathless and scared for his life.

"Calm down, amigo. Where are you? The Plymouth police will pick you up and take you to their station. Are you in a safe place?"

Diego tried to catch his breath and explain what happened. "I saw him, Tony, and I ran. I'm at that gas station that you stopped at near the airport. I can't go home. I know he'll be there."

Tony's dad came in as he hung up from Diego and dialed the Plymouth police. "Sergeant Benson, this is Tony Benedetto, yes, Sergeant O'Malley from the South Boston police called you about an hour ago. I know where my friend Diego is, can you send a car for him? ...an accident on Route 3? What do you mean? All of your vehicles are tied up at the scene? This guy's life is at stake! No he's not some illegal immigrant, the guy whose after him is though and he's also an escaped con."

"Damn it! There's a storm and a major accident on Route 3 in Plymouth and all of their squad cars are tied up at the scene.

"You'd better call Diego and tell him to sit tight!" suggested his dad.

"Can't call him, he said the payphone didn't accept calls. I'll see what O'Malley can do."

"Okay, call O'Malley, but let's go down there, Tony. We can make it in an hour," ordered his dad, taking charge.

"That may be too late!

Chapter 67

The call from Bert Obersham was not good news to Buckman senior. "Jim, I've heard from Hassad. I'm afraid you were right about Masters."

"What do you mean, that he's an egotistical, self-centered bastard? Tell me something that I don't know," answered Buckman anticipating the worst, but trying to add humor to the discourse.

"Well that's obvious, Jim. Hassad told me that the Organization of Petroleum Exporting Countries, which we know as OPEC, has taken Congresses negative vote on the Petroleum Price Regulation bill as a signal to dramatically limit supply and let the demand boost the price."

"So they're going to go for the gold? How does Masters figure into this?"

"He is a cosponsor and conspirator. He has assured OPEC that he and his colleagues will not increase American petroleum production to fill the void. He'll let the 'water', or in this case, the price of oil rise to its maximum level and then agree to pay a discounted, behind the scenes, per barrel cost to be negotiated with the Arabs. That price will give the American oil producing companies some advantage over their world competitors."

"It's ironic, Bert. Teddy Roosevelt, a Republican, will turn over in his grave. He always feared that, if allowed, monopolies and conspirators would ruin the balance afforded by capitalism's supply and demand interactions by manipulating the supply. I guess his anti-trust laws would be hard to implement in this case and Masters knows it. We can't regulate the actions of foreign countries without going to war, and we can't force our American companies to increase production. Where do you think he'll go with this? How high will the price of energy have to rise before it's enough for him?"

"I don't know that there is an answer to that question, Jim. My opinion is that the sky's the limit. He and his foreign friends will see how much pain the American public will take before they'll open the spigots and allow the process of supply and demand to become natural again."

"When will this fiasco go into effect, Bert?"

"I'm told that they're preparing their internal agreements and that they'll need to implement their plan while Nixon is in office, probably closer to the middle of his term."

"That doesn't give us much time to either offset or stop his actions. If he does this without concern for its effect on inflation and the economy he could do significant damage. There'll be long lines at service stations, production at manufacturing facilities will be held hostage to the cost of fuel, and trucking will be curtailed and become more costly. I'm all for making money and lots of it, but this is just plain stupid. Masters' greed could backfire and send us into a depression!"

"You're right, Jim, but I think the train has left the station and I don't know how we can derail it, even if we were to persuade our good friend not to go through with this stupidity. Hassad said there is much enthusiasm among the rulers of the Arab countries for this plan. They would love to stick it to us, believing that we've been stealing their only resource at prices and production levels that will someday leave them without the cards that they now hold in their hands."

"Yes, but the fact that they're the richest countries in the world, at least at the ruling class level, is of no consequence. In fact they encourage their subjects to believe that they could be doing better if it weren't for the Americans, obviously disregarding their own greed and opulence. Bert, we need to know if any of our fellow 'Group' members are involved in this mess. But we have to be careful not to expose too much of our knowledge or it'll get back to that slobbering Bulldog!"

"I'll work on it, Jim. We have a meeting in two weeks. I'll see what I can find out."

"Okay, keep in touch."

Chapter 68

Lunch with Captain Moriarty was like being on a blind date with someone your sister fixed you up with. Jim could only think of his other date, his pending meeting with Franklin. He wolfed down the roast beef sandwich, drank his warm soda pop and agreed with everything that Captain Moriarty said in order to avoid time consuming controversy.

"Well, Tom, it was nice meeting with you and thank the Colonel for the lunch, but I have to get ready for my flight back to Saigon," explained Buckman clumsily, as the clock reached 1245.

The walk to the helicopter hangars took about 10 minutes at Jim's inconspicuous pace. He was not surprised that Franklin's integrity would not allow him to be part of the charade that he was exposed to on this fact-finding mission. He was anxious to hear the truth about My Lai.

Franklin was waiting as promised. The look on his face was solemn and his body language was telling of his anxiety. "It's good to see you, Captain. You look a lot healthier than you did at our last encounter," a smile cracked his otherwise stern face.

"Yes, Sergeant and as much as I appreciate seeing you again, it's not as much as I appreciated seeing you sliding down that tethered cable through the forest canopy. I also appreciate your message to meet you here. What do you have for me, Bobby?"

"Well, Jim, I don't know how much I can help you, but if you're looking for the truth about what happened out there at My Lai you won't find it here. The so-called eyewitnesses have been intimidated to keep silent on the facts."

"That's obvious. So far I've been stonewalled by both the officers and the troops that I've interviewed, but then you knew that I would be, or you wouldn't have slipped me that note."

"Remember Sergeant Benedetto? He and I used to argue about what was the best way to motivate the troops in training.

He believed that positive motivation would get the best results. I believed that you need to tear a man down in order to rebuild him into a soldier. But there's no stronger motivation than fear. The word is that too much talk will only serve the enemy. There is a not-so-subtle threat that a talker will see a lot more action and will see it for a long time. These men have had all they can take. They have only their fear left."

"Then why are you coming forward. Aren't you worried about a reprisal?"

"I'm not worried about seeing more action. That's why I re-upped, but I'm not really coming forward, Jim. I'm just here to give you my best advice. The truth is the soldiers at My Lai were angry, scared and tired of war. They had taken a high level of casualties for months and they focused their anger on that village. All they needed was someone in command to sanction and direct that anger and their actions of revenge. They got it from men who were poorly trained and hardly qualified to be officers in this complex war. The officers behind this fiasco were simple minded men who were entrusted with responsibilities they were not capable of fulfilling. They too were angry and fearful of the enemy, but they lacked the sophistication and intellect to keep those emotions under control."

"I understand your reluctance to testify, Sergeant, but you may be called, if I can convince Washington to seek the truth. I promise that I will not call you or disclose this meeting to anyone. I owe you that much. There's enough on record already to bring this atrocity to light."

"Thank you Jim, but if I'm called to testify you know that I will not lie. I do appreciate that call not coming as a result of this conversation, Captain. You've been here. You must realize that the troops that followed the orders of their commanders were good men, mostly kids from the ghettos and poor families. They'll suffer their whole lives for their actions in those moments of poor judgment and emotional breakdown. The pictures you have in your briefcase are the images that are imprinted in their heads. The screams of those poor villagers as they were massacred will ring in their ears forever. As the Bible says, Lord have mercy on their souls!"

"And what about those innocent people who died as the result of the actions of emotional and broken soldiers and their incompetent commanders? There were hundreds of lives, generations of villagers destroyed, caught between the ambitions of madmen and the hell of a war they never asked for and would have never benefited from. What about them, Bobby?"

"I have no answer, because there is no answer. It is done and we can't change that. I hope that justice will be served and that there will never be another My Lai, but I know that those who are truly responsible will not be tried or even be accused."

"I'm reluctant to agree, but you're probably right. The walls of self-defense are being constructed as we speak and they'll be fortified by those who are at the top of the structure."

"Well Jim, I can only wish you good luck and Godspeed. My mother always said that the truth will survive all lies and liars."

"Thank you, Bobby. You've given me a perspective that I was reluctant to accept and I'm grateful for that. By the way Benedetto was right!" offered Buckman as he gave Bobby Franklin a man-hug and a smile. "You take care Sergeant. This man's army needs you."

Buckman had less than five minutes to make his flight as he went into a full run to the waiting Huey on the opposite side of the field, but he was satisfied that the trip was worthwhile.

Chapter 69

Tony tried to push his old Chevy pickup at its top speed down the Southeast Expressway coming out of Boston to Route 3 South. He figured that if he was stopped by the State Police he would try to enlist their help. It wasn't a well-thought-out plan, but it was all he had. His weaving and passing soon slowed to a crawl. "Damn it! It'll take forever to get there in this mess."

As he contemplated his plight he noted flashing blue lights coming up fast from the rear, the cars parting to allow its passage.

"You better pull over son. He probably saw you driving crazy through the traffic back there," suggested his dad.

"Oh Christ, what now?" he pulled over to the right side of the road as the police car pulled alongside. He looked over to the smiling face of Sergeant Danny O'Malley who used his PA system to say, "Follow me, cowboy."

The cars parted like the waters of the proverbial Red Sea with "Moses" O'Malley leading the way. "Now I know him! Isn't he the kid who used to beat you up?" asked his confused dad.

"I don't know. There were so many," Tony grinned in response.

By the time they reached Exit 12 in Pembroke, the traffic had cleared and O'Malley turned off at the ramp with a wave that was returned in kind.

"I guess he's not going to go all the way," concluded Tony's dad.

"No, he lives in Pembroke. I guess he was late for dinner."

Tony put his foot to the gas pedal. They would be there in less than twenty minutes. He learned later that O'Malley had called ahead to the state troopers to allow him to pass. He was relieved to see that the accident had been cleared and that he could take Exit 6 onto Route 44 West, to the Plymouth airport, and the service station that Diego was last heard from.

As he made the turn into the gas station he looked to see if there was any sign of Diego. He pulled to the side of the lone building and caught the attention of the attendant.

"Can I help you sir? Do you need gas?" the young attendant asked as he wiped the grease off his hands.

"Is there a young man here? He was riding a bike and...?"

"No sir, the Plymouth police picked him up about 15 minutes ago. What did he do, kill someone?"

"No, he didn't do anything. They were here to protect him."

"Hey, he left his bike, can you throw it in the back of your truck?"

"Sure, where is it?" Tony got out and got the bike into his truck.

Relieved, the Benedetto's drove to the station, downtown behind the Plymouth Court house.

Sergeant Benson was all business. "Sir we will need identification from both of you. Mr. Martinez is in protective custody."

"Yes Sergeant. I appreciate your diligence."

"Just doing my job. Your identification please gentlemen!"

After completing the formalities they followed another officer down the hall to a stairway that led to the basement and the detention cells. Surprised and offended for Diego, Tony asked, "What is he doing locked up down here in this hole. He's not a criminal!"

"It's procedure sir, at this point we don't know who he is and whether there's a warrant out for him. If he's clean he'll be released in due time. This guy might be after him as the result of a drug deal gone badly. These dagos are into that sort of thing."

"Would he be detained if he weren't Hispanic?" responded Tony indignantly.

"What are you, a wise guy? You want to keep him company?"

Diego's head was hung low in his hands as he sat alone on a cot in the stark cell. He looked up at the clanking sound of the iron cell doors opening. There were tears in his eyes and despair on his face as he greeted his friends.

"I'm sorry, Tony. I always bring you trouble."

"I don't know if you bring it, Diego. I think that it seeks you out. Come on we're getting you out of here."

"I don't know? They think that I'm involved in some drug deal with Rodriguez."

"Did they find him?"

"No, but they found his car, he stole it in Boston, from the airport parking lot, and there's a car missing from the parking lot at McGraths. I heard them say they think he's headed back to Boston. I don't think he'll leave until he's done what he came for."

"Are you okay? Maybe you're safer here until we figure this thing out."

"And what about you? How will you be safe? He must know where you live. He's going to wait and he's going to kill us Tony."

"The police will catch him. They have one of those APBs out on the wire for him. They want him, he's an escaped convict and they want him badly," reassured Tony.

"The cops said that they've got Chico up in Boston."

"Yes, thanks to my dad. He took him out with a home run swing of my Ted Williams autographed bat!" Tony slapped his old man on the back in a congratulatory gesture that brought a smile to his face.

"Oh, Mr. Benedetto, I see where Tony gets his craziness," his words brought a smile to his lips. They all laughed, a nervous, but badly needed laugh.

After much haggling with the station commander and threats of suing for false arrest, Tony managed to get Diego released.

"I need to bring dad back to his car. He still has to drive to my aunt's house in East Boston, but first we should get something to eat. There's a Howard Johnson's restaurant on Morrissey Boulevard in Dorchester. It's on the way. Dad, you should call mom from there and let her know that we're all okay."

"I need to call Carmella and find out about my Papa, he was supposed to be in Nuevo Laredo today. I wonder if Ramon knows that Rodriguez is here?" commented Diego. "I hope that Grandma will take my call collect."

Knowing that he was no longer sanctioned under the protection of Sergeant O'Malley for reckless driving, Tony drove the speed limit back to Boston. They used the time to discuss the dilemma fate handed them. They needed a Plan B!

The Howard Johnson's restaurant on Morrissey Boulevard was said to be one of the originals of a national company that began in Massachusetts. It was getting old and tired unlike the newer editions that were a welcome sight for weary travelers along the major highways from New England to Florida.

After ordering, Diego and Richie made their respective phone calls. Tony could see Diego at the wall phone on the far side of the restaurant. He was animated and he could hear his voice, but not understand what he was saying. He was attracting the attention of the patrons as he got louder. He came back to the table still hyper and talking to himself.

"What's going on Diego? Did Carmella hear from your father?"

"No, she heard from Miguel's cousin, Ramon. They've got him. They kidnapped my papa. It was all a setup. They want me to meet with them in Nuevo Laredo within 48 hours or they say they will kill him. She thinks they want to take over Juan Carlos' cartel and they want to make sure we don't interfere. Miguel must be behind it. I've got to go down there."

"They'll kill you both, why would they allow you to live?" asked Tony.

"I think because Juan Carlos was a very popular man, and he had over a hundred followers. They don't want a war with them, they want to lead them. I think they want to make a deal," surmised Diego.

"I don't know, amigo. I wouldn't trust that theory, and what kind of a deal could assure you and Manny's life for very long?"

"I don't know, but what choice do I have?"

Tony's dad returned from his phone call after a stop at the men's room. "What's going on? You two look like death warmed over!"

"We were just discussing the weather in Mexico," responded Tony. Not wanting to alarm him. He was dealing with enough of his son's life dramas already.

"Why, what happened? Was there a hurricane?"

"No we were just thinking we should go down there to visit with Diego's grandmother."

Diego shot a look of disbelief to Tony, but hesitated to react in front of his Dad.

"Why would you do that? Won't this Rodriguez character be waiting for you? Let the law handle this, son," pleaded his father.

"Dad, there is no law in Mexico, except the law that is bought and paid for by scum like Rodriguez," explained Tony.

"Well that makes me feel much better. Stay here! At least if he shows up we have our law looking for him," suggested his dad.

"Let's finish up and get on the road. Mother will be worried," said Tony, cutting short the debate.

Tony brought his father back to Southie to pick up his car so he could drive to East Boston and his sister Mary's house. They decided not to cause him any more anxiety and kept the plight of Diego's dad to themselves. They drove to Tony's apartment where they discussed the next move in this chess game they were being forced to play.

After much discussion it was decided that they would go as far as Laredo, Texas, which was on the Rio Grande River, the sister city to the neighboring Mexican city of Nuevo Laredo. The plan was to draw Miguel across the border and entrap him, but they would also need to find Diego's father. The plan was a work in progress!

"Tony, I fear for my padre. They are vicious animals. They don't care about life, except their own, but you have done enough I will take care of this!"

"Hey, what are friends for!" countered Tony with a smile and a grip on Diego's shoulder. "I need to get a report out tomorrow, but we can leave sometime after 7 pm. Can you check on the flight? There's a travel agent on Broadway near that theatre. Talk to Hank, he'll make the arrangements. Tell him to call me for payment."

"Okay amigo, I'll take care of things, don't worry."

"Good, let's get some sleep. We're going to have a busy week."

Chapter 70

Captain Buckman planned his trip back to Washington D.C. to include a stopover in Detroit, Michigan to visit with Sharon. She worked the busy public defender's office in one of the highest crime areas in the country. She believed it to be her calling.

His visit to Nam only affirmed his suspicions that a serious cover-up, from the top down, was in the making. In a strange way, he was encouraged by his discussion with Bobby Franklin. Here was a man who bled Army green, but he still had his moral character and he was not buying into the official cover-up games. Franklin realized that lies were destined to poison the military's integrity and diminish the proud service of those who served their country with dignity and courage.

Buckman wanted Sharon's validation of his position on My Lai in order to do what he believed he had to do. He also missed her and needed to see the smile in those beautiful green eyes telling him of her love. It was seven o'clock, Saturday morning and she would probably still be asleep. He hadn't expected to be in Detroit until the following evening, but had found an earlier connection in Tokyo that avoided the layover in San Francisco.

He was anxious to see the look on her face when he announced his intentions for the future. The last time they were together he wasn't sure what he wanted. Was he ready to commit to a life with that one special person? Was she ready to commit to him? She was a strong minded person and was unlikely to do something that was not right for her, but then that was one of the reasons that he fell in love with her. It was almost five years since she encouraged his epiphany on life and what was truly important. He was different from the man he thought he would become and he was grateful for her intervention.

He thought about her last words when she had seen him off at the airport when he left D.C. for Vietnam. She said maybe they should see other people if he was not in the relationship for the long haul. He had responded badly, saying that it was up to her. He regretted that insensitive remark and had a lot of flight time to think about what it would be like to not have her in his life. He bought the ring in Tokyo.

The one-hour drive to her apartment gave him time to rehearse his presentation. He wanted it to be profound and yet loving. She isn't the mushy type, but she did appreciate romantic moments. He wanted this one to be special. He thought he might wait until the evening when he could take her to dinner at her favorite restaurant. It would be nice to have candlelight and music in the background. Yes, he would wait until evening.

The apartment building was a low-rise on the outskirts of Detroit. The area had a touch of suburbia but was in view of the city skyline. He had tried to convince her to live in a building that had security but she would have none of it. She said it would be like living in a college dorm. He wasn't able to reach her when he left Tokyo so he decided to just play it cool and surprise her. What if she said no? He pushed that thought back into his subconscious.

He knocked on her door, Apartment 310. There was no answer. He listened, his ear closer to the door, he thought he could hear a shower running. He knocked harder and heard footsteps coming to the door. A smile came across his face, anticipating her surprised look.

As the door cracked open he saw the face of a handsome young man. "Can I help you?" Jim's smile disappeared as his jaw dropped and his heart sank.

"Are you Josh?" Jim asked remembering the name of Sharon's younger brother.

"No, I'm Darren, are you looking for Sharon?" he said as he opened the door wider revealing his towel wrapped muscular body. "She's in the shower. Would you like to come in?"

"No thanks, I just stopped by to say hello. I'll call her later." He turned and not wanting to wait for the elevator, headed towards the stairway. He felt like a fool. "How could he have been so wrong?"

"Okay, who should I say came by? The words trailed off as Jim strutted down the hall towards the Exit sign.

Darren closed the door, somewhat confused. Sharon came into the room also wrapped in a towel, drying her hair with another towel. "What are you doing at the door, Darren? Did we make too much noise? These walls are paper thin."

"No it was someone looking for you, an Army Captain. He said he would call you later."

"Oh my God, no it couldn't be. He's in Vietnam until tomorrow night."

"Why the concern, who is he?"

Sharon ran to the window and saw Jim getting into his car, then driving off with tires screeching. Tears welled up in her eyes as she thought was it worth losing Jim to have one last evening with her high school sweetheart? The answer was clear, but it came too late.

Darren Nowak was in Detroit for a tryout with the Lions. He had been a star quarterback and her first love in high school. He played at Kentucky during his college years but didn't get drafted by the pros. She was surprised when he called to say he was in town. They went out to dinner and the wine and the reminiscing about their past love was too much to overcome. She thought about what Jim had said at the airport, about their dating others. It happened, and now she regretted it. She caught herself thinking of Jim while she was with Darren, but she didn't mention his name thinking it would have been rude to Darren. Or was it that she wondered if there was still something in her heart for her first love?

CHAPTER 71

It was almost 4 pm and Tony hadn't heard from Hank or Diego. Diego was supposed to make travel arrangements to Texas with Tony's travel agent friend Hank Walsh. Diego was to go see Hank and have him call him for payment. They were supposed to leave sometime after 7 pm. Tony had to work today to meet a report deadline. He had completed his work and sent his report to the client and was now free to go. He decided to call the travel agency to see if there was a problem.

"Hello Hank, this is Tony Benedetto. Was my friend Diego in to see you today?"

"Yes Tony, thanks for the referral. He should be boarding his flight to Texas as we speak."

"Boarding? I was supposed to be going with him?"

"He didn't say anything about that, Tony. He said that he had to catch the next flight to Texas for a family matter. I booked him through to Laredo Texas on American Airlines. He has a layover in Dallas."

"Did you book his hotel in Laredo?"

"Yes, he's staying at the La Posada Hotel. It's right on the Rio Grande River. It's a fine old hotel. You can look across the river and see the city of Nuevo Laredo."

"Hank book me on the next available flight tonight and at the same hotel."

"Okay, Tony. Did I do something wrong?"

"No, he must have misunderstood me. I'll be by before you close to pick up the tickets." Now he knew what Diego meant when he said he would take care of it. He intended to go it alone. Tony had not yet figured out a feasible plan that wouldn't get them all killed. He knew Diego was too emotional to act rationally. He needed to find his father, and wouldn't be constrained by logic.

Tony was able to make a two-stop flight through New York and Houston. He would take a nine-seat "puddle jumper" to

Laredo. He wouldn't get to the hotel until late morning. He had taken the week off from his job but hadn't told his parents he would be leaving. He used the two hour layover in New York to call his father. He didn't want them to read about their adventure in the newspaper if it went wrong. It was going to be a rough night as a prelude to a rougher week. He needed to think.

Tony arrived at the La Posada just before noon, his flight from Houston delayed by a fierce thunderstorm. The Hotel was pure old Mexican. This part of Texas had been governed under six different flags. A small building next door to the hotel was the headquarters of the "Republic of the Rio Grande," the least known of six flags and the shortest lived independent government, lasting less than a year in 1840, before being overrun by the Mexican government.

Tony waited behind an elderly couple to check in. He looked around at the hacienda décor. For a small hotel it had atmosphere. The city itself was somewhat rundown. The streets of Laredo lacked romance, but this hotel seemed to try to make up for it with its ambience. Tony reached the check-in desk after the clerk managed to settle the couple's issue with their room location.

"I believe you have a reservation for Anthony Benedetto?" he asked the clerk.

"Yes sir, we were expecting you. How was your flight from Boston?"

"Much too long, but I'm here. Can you tell me what room my friend Diego Martinez is in?"

"Yes, he's off the courtyard in Room 121, but he left the hotel about an hour ago with two men. Was he expecting you this morning?"

"Probably not, but do you know where they went?"

"No sir, but I recognized one of the men. His name is Ramon Rodriguez. He is from Nuevo Laredo. It is just over the border."

Tony's heart skipped a beat. He took a deep breath. Was he too late? Did Diego get kidnapped? How did they know he was here? Damn it! What should he do?" his face went pale.

"Sir, are you all right? Do you need some water? Is there something wrong?"

"No, I'm fine. I guess the long flight just got to me. Do you know where I can find this Ramon?"

"I only know that he works in Boys Town across the bridge. Any taxi can take you there, but it can be a very dangerous place, especially if you are alone."

"Why is that? Aren't there any police in Nuevo?"

"Yes, there are police and they are well paid...by the criminals. It's a place that is legal for gambling and prostitution, but you are most likely going to have your pockets picked or worse there."

Tony took his key and the words of the desk clerk to his room on the second floor overlooking the Rio Grande with a view of the City of Nuevo Laredo. It was not a pretty sight. As he looked to the left he saw hundreds of trucks waiting in lines to go through customs at the easterly bridge; to the right, on the west side of the hotel, was a much smaller bridge that seemed to have a steady stream of pedestrians and taxis flowing in both directions.

He needed to think of a plan. Diego's plight gave an added urgency to that task. He thought he had it figured out, but the current circumstances negated that plan. He was going to have Diego contact his father's captors and tell them that Tony had cut him out of a deal for a lot of money and that he was angry enough to turn him over for the release of his father. He would tell them they were here to make a drug deal. Tony needed time to enlist the help of the Laredo police or possibly the FBI, but that would take a few days. He had also hoped that the Laredo Police would be able to convince the Nuevo Laredo police to assist them in finding Manny, if the perpetrators didn't cooperate. It wasn't a very sound plan, but it was all he had, before he learned of Diego's obvious capture. He needed a Plan B!

Chapter 72

Jim Buckman decided to drive straight through to Washington D.C. He needed time to think. Could I have been that wrong about Sharon? I was only gone a week. Who was this guy Darren? Where did she meet him? He was very confused and depressed.

By the time he reached Philadelphia he started to question his reaction. He hadn't indicated he was serious enough to commit to her. He remembered his words the night before he left for Vietnam. He practically told her they should date others and experience life. Well, I guess she took me literally, he thought.

He would be in D.C. by early morning. His mind would be occupied by this My Lai mess for some time. He began to think, I can get through this. And Sharon deserves to be happy. If I really love her I would want her to be happy, even if it's with someone else. But it sucks!

He would go to his apartment and try to get some sleep before checking in with his CO. He wasn't in any shape to write his report today. He'd promise to complete it by the end of the week knowing it wouldn't be well received given his views on the subject. But then the army wasn't going to be his career.

The distraction of My Lai passed as he entered his apartment and the memory of his last night there with Sharon hit him hard. The red light on his phone was blinking. He had a message. In his heart he wanted it to be from Sharon. Maybe Darren was her cousin?

The first message was from his father;

"Hello, Son,

I'm going to be in Washington on Tuesday and would like to meet you for dinner, if you're not tied up with your liberal lady friend. We need to discuss your intentions when you complete your active duty. You know I want you in the family business. I hope I can convince you to be part of our team. Call me and let me know if the date is okay with you."

There was a pause, a beep and then;

"Hello, Jim.

I know you're very upset with me and I don't blame you. I wish you had stayed so I could explain." Sharon's voice was cracking and her emotions were obvious. "I made a mistake, but I thought you really didn't care about our future together. Remember our conversation about relationships and commitments the night before you left for Vietnam. You said that people are not ready for commitments at our age; that they need to experience life. Well, Darren was part of my past life. He was my first love in high school. He had called me the night before saying that he would be in town and we went out to dinner. I didn't expect it to be any more than that, but obviously the wine and the confusion of our relationship led me to make a very foolish mistake. I'm so sorry, but I know that it may be too late for that..." a pause and then, "I do love you. Please call me!"

Jim replayed the message several times. He started to feel badly for her, but he believed that there must have been something there between her and her ex-boyfriend for her to spend the night with him. Sharon didn't do stupid things. In the end he concluded that he was right. They were not ready for a serious commitment. They both had to experience life before they could hope to realize that kind of relationship. He would write her tomorrow and let her know that he's not angry and that he understood why she did what she did, but that maybe this was a good time for a break. He decided to sleep on it, and after fifteen hours on the road, he desperately needed that sleep.

Chapter 73

Tony showered and went to the La Posada's Tack Room, a sports bar in the hotel. It had a racing theme decor, with saddles and various memorabilia of the *Sport of Kings*. The desk clerk recommended the room for a late lunch. The main dining room was not as comfortable for a single person. He could eat at the bar.

He engaged a local rancher in conversation at the bar, hoping to find out more about the area, especially about Boys Town. The white cowboy hat and leather vest was so stereo typical that Tony thought of the early Tom Mix westerns he had watched on his neighbor Vinnie's 10-inch diameter television set when they were only five years old. He introduced himself, attempting to hide his South Boston accent, and managed to segue into asking about Boys Town.

"It's a very seedy place, son. They prey on businessmen from the cities. You're from Boston, right? It's supposed to be a place to go to have the kind of fun that you can't have in the U.S., but for some the only fun they have is getting robbed, beaten up or diseased."

"Have you ever been there?" asked Tony, realizing that he must have missed some 'Rs' that gave away his Boston hometown affiliation.

"Well, not that I would admit it in public and I would never go there without at least a dozen friends. You know, like a bachelor party," he said with a wink, a smile and an elbow to Tony's side.

Tony started to laugh but his eyes were drawn to the figure walking into the bar, the sun causing their form to be silhouetted in the doorway. He was shocked when he realized that it was Diego walking through the door, and he was alone.

"The desk clerk said that you were here. You're a stubborn gringo my friend." Diego put his hand on Tony's shoulder and said, "We need to talk."

The cowboy just looked on, confused but not really interested in their camaraderie. "Well boys, I'd better get back to the ranch. Now you be careful if you go to Boys Town."

Diego looked at Tony and wondered what he had said to this stranger.

"Thanks for the advice. I think we'll stay on this side of the border," answered Tony.

"What was that all about? You didn't tell him why we're here."

"No, I was just getting some local information before I rushed in to save you with my guns blazing," joked Tony. "Oh yeah, we already did that scene, didn't we?"

"Very funny, amigo, but I'm afraid this is not a funny situation."

"What happened? The desk clerk said you left the hotel with Ramon and another thug. How did you escape?"

"I didn't escape. They took me blindfolded to see my father. He's being held in the city over there, but I don't know where. They drove me around for a while and then led me into this building. The shades were all pulled down so I couldn't see the street or anything that I would remember to be able to find it again."

"Is he ok? Did they hurt him?"

"No, he was fine. He wasn't even tied up or anything. They wanted me to see that he was being treated well, but they said that it would be temporary unless I cooperated and played ball with them."

"Cooperated how? Do they want me? What do you mean play ball with them? What do they want of you?"

"They want to take over Juan Carlos' drug Cartel. They thought they could do it by having him killed, although they didn't admit that. They realize that the people that worked for my uncle were devoted to him and they're very angry about how he died. I believe his lieutenant, Pedro Valdez is behind it, but they need me and my padré to be, what you call figureheads, to keep the cartel members calm and loyal. My Papa heard Pedro's voice through the walls, but he could not hear his words. They told me if we agree they will not harm me or my family. I know that it's for fear of revenge from the members, and I believe that they will not harm you, if I cooperate with them."

"But what kind of cooperation do they want from you and your dad?"

"Because I am a United States citizen they want me to run an operation in San Diego and my father to be, what you say, their liaison, with the people who are still loyal to Juan Carlos' memory."

"Are you crazy? They're asking you to be a criminal. They'll use you until they believe they don't need you and throw you and your family away in the garbage. You'll be their fall guy. It won't work!"

"I have 24 hours to think it over before they make my father disappear, they said. What can I do Tony? What would you do if it were your father and your grandma? You need to go home. They don't know you're here."

"Why did you leave without telling me?"

"When you went to your office I called my grandma. She was crying. She had instructions to tell me to come down here alone and to call a number in Nuevo Laredo and ask for Ramon or I would never see my father again. I got here last night and called. Ramon and his friend showed up at 10 o'clock this morning to take me for a ride, and you know the rest."

"Let's go to my room. We need to figure this out," declared Tony.

"There's nothing to figure out. I have no choice and if they know that you're here they'll take you too. It's such a mess, Tony." Diego's hand went to his sweating forehead as tears of despair ran down his cheeks.

Once in the room Tony had an epiphany. "Diego, why would they kill your father if the purpose of having you and he involved is to win over your uncle's loyal gang members? Wouldn't that negate any chance of that happening? If they wanted you both out of the way they could have done that easily today, right?"

"I guess so, but how does that help us?"

"Diego, what was the first thing you learned when you trained for war"

"I didn't learn much, or I wouldn't have been shot out of the tree."

"You learn to use your enemy's weakness, or vulnerability, to your advantage and they exposed their vulnerability to you today. They can't kill you or your dad and still expect to complete this coup. But we can't take any chances. You'll call them tomorrow and agree to the deal."

"Agree? I thought you were going to have a plan so that I wouldn't have to become a member of the FBI's Most Wanted List?"

"You're only agreeing in order to buy us some time. Are you familiar with the members of your uncle's Cartel? Do you know any of them well?"

"Yes, some of them are my cousins. Juan Carlos' son and daughter are members."

"Is the son strong enough to take over the cartel?"

"Well no, Gonzalo is strong, but not in his mind. His older sister Karime has the brains and she is also a fighter. I met them when we first went to live with my Papa, but I didn't know that they were part of my uncle's cartel until recently. Karime is well respected and she has become close to Carmella. She lives among the people and is not suspected of being in the organization. Her father wanted it to be that way. She's an attractive and bright woman and very tough. My Papa told me that she used to beat up her brother, who is bigger than her. She is a black belt in karate and won't back down from any man."

"Okay, then she's the one we need to contact. We'll need Carmella's help. She must have credibility with Karime. I'll go to Guadalajara, to Carmella's. Your new friends don't know I'm here so they won't miss me, but you need to stay here and keep them occupied with your story of cooperation."

"I don't understand the plan, amigo?"

"The plan is to make these guys comfortable. We want to make them think that you'll work with them to get the support of the cartel members. We will then draw them into a trap set by those members of the cartel who can be trusted and who want revenge. They will insist on the release of your father for the acceptance of Valdez and his friends into the control of the organization and then we will, hopefully, snare them."

"And then what do we do with them?"

"Good question, I'm working on it. Be patient, but it may not be our choice my friend."

"I don't want any more shootings, Tony. I just want them to go to prison for a long time."

Tony managed to get a puddle jumper flight to Guadalajara and arrived at Carmella's home before dusk. The house was more impressive than their American home in Watts. He wondered why they would ever want to return to that life of poverty in America. Juan Carlos had taken care of his mother before the law took care of him. The home was what Tony thought of as a hacienda from the old Zorro movies. It was surrounded by ten-foot high white-washed walls and had a black ornate iron gate.

Carmella came to the gate as one of the servants opened it for his entrance. "I don't believe it. You are here!" as she embraced him and kissed his cheek. "Why do you do these things, Tony? It is not your fight. You have done enough!"

"Everyone needs a little excitement in their life. Do you know how boring engineering is?" he said in jest. "Is Karime here?" he asked as they made their way to the house.

"No, but she will be here soon. We are both very, how you say, curious about why you are here. Have you found my son Manuel? Is he all right? Where is Diego? I'm so worried," Carmella declared as she brought a handkerchief to her eyes.

"Manny's fine for now. Diego has seen him, but we must do some things to make sure that they both stay fine. We need Karime's help. Do you think we can trust her?"

"I don't know what you mean, 'trust her.' She is very upset about her father's death. Juan Carlos was not a good man, but he was good to his children. We have talked and she does not know what she should do."

"What do you mean by 'what she should do?" asked Tony.

"She did not like the life of drugs and killings. She tried to get her father to give it up but he loved the money too much, and see what it got him. He only loved her and her brother more than money, but would say that he was doing what he did for them. His Rosetta died when their son was born. He trusted Karime more than anyone and she tried to protect him."

"Has she dissolved the cartel or has someone else taken it over?"

"No, it is still operating, but she is thinking she will just give it over to Pedro Valdez, her father's lieutenant, and try to get Gonzalo out of it too. She's hoping that Pedro will pay them something for it."

"Does Valdez know this?"

"No, not yet, she is still thinking about it and he is not around to talk to."

"Yes, and for good reason Carmella."

"What do you mean, have they killed him too?"

"No, but you and Karime might want to!" Tony told her the whole story as he and Diego had pieced it together.

"Oh Madre Maria, Tony you are telling me that Pedro Valdez, Juan Carlos' closest friend had him killed. He killed my son, the man who took him out of the filth of the pigs and gave him a home. How could he do that? You must be wrong!"

"Diego believes it, and your son Manny believes it, he whispered to Diego 'beware of Valdez,' when they were together for a few minutes early today, he heard his voice through the walls of where they are holding him."

"No, it can't be!"

"What can't be Granma?" the soft but firm voice came from the far end of the hall as the shadowed figure of a woman entered the home, her riding boots rhythmic on the tile floor.

Tony looked in the direction of the voice as its owner came out of the shadows. His eyes caught hers, dark brown framed by long flowing auburn hair and a glistening smile that caused him to catch his breath. He didn't expect the daughter of a drug lord to be so stunning.

"Tony, this is my granddaughter Karime. Tony, are you ok?"

His senses restored, he looked at Carmella whose smile at his reaction made him realize that he had been mesmerized by the beauty of this woman.

Extending her hand Karime said, "I am pleased to meet you, Tony. I have heard a lot about you and your exploits with my cousin Diego."

Tony reached out to her hand, not expecting the firm grasp that was his introduction to her strength, which was as startling as her physical beauty.

"And I have heard many good things about you from Diego and Carmella, but I think they fell short of reality," responded Tony

"You are very kind, but as you Americans say, do not judge the book by its cover." Her smile broadened as she released her grip on Tony's hand. Grandma told me that you have news of my uncle Manuel's kidnapping."

"Please, let's go to the dining room so that we can discuss this," suggested Carmella.

Tony explained the circumstances that brought him and Diego to Mexico, beginning with Rodriguez and his thug hit-man's attempt to find him and her cousin in the U.S. He continued describing the situation that he encountered in Laredo, Texas when he reunited with Diego at the La Posada Hotel.

"Diego met with Manny's kidnappers and visited him, but he was blindfolded, so he doesn't know where he is being held. His father told him that he heard the voice of your father's lieutenant, Pedro Valdez, through the walls of his room, but could not understand the words that were spoken. Manny believes that Valdez is in with them. Manny's captors want Diego and your uncle to front their takeover of your father's cartel."

"Tony, may I interrupt you?" responded Karime. We know where my uncle is being held, and I assure you that Pedro is loyal to our family."

Startled, Tony's eyes widened, "What are you saying, are you part of some plot against Manny and his family?"

Carmella, equally concerned, looked deeply into Karime's eyes, obviously confused and holding back anger.

"No, we are aware of their actions because they contacted Pedro with an offer to support him as head of the cartel here in Mexico if he would work with them to be in charge of the operation in the U.S. As I said before, 'do not judge a book by its cover.' Pedro is loyal to me and to my Papa's memory. He wanted to meet with them and take several of our young angry men with him to respond to their arrogance. I convinced him that it might result in the death of another Martinez. Diego and your presence have complicated things."

"Why did you not tell me of your plan?" interjected Carmella.

"We knew that you would involve Diego and we needed to be free to work our plan."

"What is your plan, Karime?" Carmella asked the question before Tony could respond. "Are you going to continue the killings my son Juan Carlos used as his response to anyone that opposed him?"

"We will do what we have to do grandma. I wish there would be no more killings!"

Tony saw the look of a woman who was not to be dissuaded from her mission. "Is there something I can do to help you? I agree with Carmella that more violence will not solve the problem. They have many people in the U.S. who will follow their lead. May I ask you a personal question?"

"Yes, of course, you have earned the right."

"Do you intend to continue the operations of the cartel? I understand that you're the natural successor and the only one that can keep it together. I'm told that the people respect you, but you must realize, based on the assassination of your father, that the government is no longer your ally."

"The government is for sale, my friend! My father refused to pay them 50% of his profits to continue the cartel. The Rodriguez people offered to pay that, if the government helped them take it over."

"Why do you want to keep it going? You must realize that it will always be a target from both sides. Diego tells me you were educated in America, at Stanford, and that you have a graduate degree in business. Why do you need this?"

"I am Mexican, not American, and because of my father's chosen profession, I will never be an American citizen. My education was encouraged by my father who hoped that it would be my way of becoming an American citizen, but we know it is not possible."

"How do you know that? Have you tried?" asked Tony.

"Yes, when I completed my graduate studies at Stanford I was picked up by your FBI and told that the only way I could become an American citizen was to disclose the names of the key people in the cartel and, in effect, give up my father. I learned that they had been watching me for years and wanted me to have a reason to want to become an American. I found out my roommate was an informant whose tuition was paid by the FBI. Until that time my father kept me isolated from the cartel."

"Why not use your intelligence and education to peacefully try to change the conditions here in your Mexico?"

"I was told that you grew up in a neighborhood that was not very friendly to you and that you were often beaten by those who did not want you there. That is, what you would call a microcosm of Mexico. The government is the bully and they want to protect their status by keeping the people down and subservient to them. They don't want us to share in their prosperity or their quality of life. They know there is only so much wealth in our country and they want most of it for themselves and their families."

"But it was different. My antagonists also wanted a better life. They weren't wealthy or government people. The Irish and the Italians came to America about the same time and they were looking for the same jobs. They both struggled against the oppression of those who came before them. Both survived and got their piece of the American dream by being represented in government. Yes, they still had their differences, but they knew that together, with other ethnic Americans, they could overcome those in power by participating in the democratic process."

"I'm afraid, Tony that you are not aware of two things; one, Mexico is not a true democracy and two; your government is no longer working in the interest of its people. It's only a matter of time before the haves overcome the have-nots. They have convinced many to use their vote to help them gain incredible wealth and then they say they are against the redistribution of wealth. It's a joke and it's being played on those who are easily played. Those who don't want to think, and are easily swayed by hate and innuendo."

"I can't argue that logic. I realize we have lost good people, but I can't buy into the conspiracy theories, although I do believe that the hateful rhetoric of the last decade has contributed to that situation. I believe that if a delusional person who's obsessed with gaining fame, is given encouragement, they will do the deed that gets them recognition and believe they have been heroic in a cause."

"And I agree with your logic, Tony, but keep in mind that Mexico was once made up of an enlightened people. They were exploited by the greed of their Mayan and Aztec leaders who secured their wealth and power by making the people believe that they were gods. And they were eventually exploited by the even greater greed of their Spanish conquerors who brought them a new God to worship and gave them disease and death in return. Wealth, in the form of gold, led to our demise, and it is no different today. Those who control the wealth, have the power to keep the masses poor and subject to their whims. They gain their wealth by working them to their death in poverty. But I believe that once the numbers, within those masses, reach the lowest point of despair and are without hope, they will take back what is rightfully theirs."

"I hope there's a better way to attain that, but isn't what your father did just another way of gaining wealth and power at the expense of the poor and oppressed?"

"Yes, you're correct! His goal was a purely selfish one. He did what he did so that he and his family could live the 'good life.' He did share his wealth with the poor in this region, but he demanded their loyalty. He also paid a corrupt government in order to survive. I am not saying that he was a martyr or a man of the people, but he was devoted to his family. I realize that he was not a hero of any cause, but the circumstances of this life under the rule of despots allowed him to prosper and led to his death."

"Don't you think that a violent death is inevitable if you also pursue that life?"

"Yes, I do!" Karime's voice grew more solemn. "But I don't have a choice. The cartel will survive without me, but, for now, we will not survive without it."

Carmella looked at Tony with tears forming in her saddened eyes.

His face reflected her concerns without a word being spoken.

Karime reached across the table, one hand on each of theirs and said, "Tony, you must go home now. We have this under control. Manuel will be free by morning."

"How, and what about Diego?" asked Carmella.

"He is in a secure place. Tony, he will meet you in Boston tomorrow night."

They looked at each other knowing what she was saying, but they did not want to hear details.

"I hope you achieve your goals, Karime, but I believe there is another way!"

"Would you care what methods we were to use if I were a man or an ugly woman?' Karime responded with an overwhelming smile and a gentler handshake.

"I hope we meet again under better circumstances," answered Tony returning her smile. He rose from his chair realizing that there was not any more to say and holding her hands in his, placed a soft kiss on her cheek. "I trust that you're doing what you have to do and I wish you well."

Chapter 74

Jonathan Buckman had passed his father's competency test. He had succeeded in establishing the satellite banks in Massachusetts and Rhode Island that were the basis of their banking enterprise's expansion. His father was proud of his younger son's determination and his ability to overcome regulatory impediments. Jonathan had managed to keep his older brother at bay while he did what was necessary to get the job done.

Jim was not interested in the business and that was fine with Jonathan. The My Lai fiasco was keeping him busy during his final year of active duty. He had caused a stir in the government, but in time the evidence proved too much for the military to hide. As Jim told a colleague, "Eventually you trip over that dirty mound under the rug!"

Lieutenant Calley, the face of My Lai, would be brought to trial for war crimes, but the hierarchy managed to end-run the indictments that would implicate them in the massacre.

Jonathan was to meet with his dad again to discuss the future, his and that of the family business. He was anxious and somewhat stressed. He had big plans for Buckman Enterprises and he needed the family, or more precisely his father, to back them. They decided to meet at the Club for dinner to keep it relaxed and yet businesslike. Jonathan had his own home on the Westport waterfront. Jim senior didn't want to have the family involved in their conversation.

Jonathan arrived early to gather his thoughts and to demonstrate to his father that he was a responsible leader and serious about the future of the family business. Being on-time was a basic rule of the Buckman business philosophy, "Never give the other guy an excuse to disrespect you," was one of his father's mantras. He spotted his father as he came through the lounge area towards the dining room. He noticed his gait was no longer that of the strong leader that he looked up to. His head was not high, his eyes not focused, his posture did not display the full height of a 6 foot 3 inch athletic man. Jonathan sensed that time was taking its toll on the family patriarch.

"Jonathan, have you been waiting long?" he asked as he sat across from his ambitious protégé.

"No, Dad, I just thought I'd spend some time with my thoughts. How are you?"

"I'm fine son. I just got back from my monthly meeting with the boys in D.C. It's becoming a debilitating activity. Tom Masters is promoting an agenda that I believe will decimate our economy and play into the hands of the liberals. I need a drink. What are you nursing there?"

"It's just Chavez on the rocks, but your drink is usually gin and tonic?"

"Well, I need something stronger. Scotch tends to soothe my temperament," he smiled as he signaled the waiter to order his liquid tranquilizer.

"It was that bad? You're usually able to handle that egomaniac. What happened to upset you?"

"Well, you met the 'Bulldog' last month. Remember our discussion about the price per barrel of oil in the Mideast?"

"Yes, but I doubt that he'll succeed in raising the price at the pump by much. The American people won't stand for it. I know you've said it will kill many businesses and deplete the disposable income of the average consumer. Why would he do that? Doesn't he respect your thoughts on such an important matter?"

"Why do you think? He's a greedy man without principles. There's a way to make profit, and sucking the life out of the American economy is not the way! He's afraid that Nixon won't be re-elected and a Democratic President will find a way to stop his plan. Our man Spiro Agnew turned out to be a disaster as vice president. We endorsed him to assure that Nixon didn't step out of line and his replacement, Gerald Ford, is too upright and honest to control."

"What can we do about it? You've said that he's tied tightly to the rulers of the Middle Eastern countries, which is where we get most of our oil. We know that the more crude oil he gets from them the less he has to drill for here," stated Jonathan.

"And if he can raise the price after refining it at his companies' refineries, then it's a double win for him. He can save his American resources while diminishing theirs. Actually, as long as the Mid-Eastern 'fiefdoms' are paid well and their families prosper they'll not worry about the long term effect. In fact the higher the price the less the demand and the longer their limited resources will last," added his Dad.

"So, should we be taking some action to prepare for what seems like the inevitable?" asked Jonathan.

"I'm not sure of what can be done. He isn't confiding in us as to the details of his plan. Rather, I believe he's preparing us for the impact of a devastating storm that is looming on the horizon. He thinks advising us is his only duty as a member of our group. But we're here to discuss our immediate situation. You've done a good job expanding the banking operation and we're now a major player in the Northeast."

"I only did what you asked me to do, but I have ideas that I would like to explore with you about the other family enterprises."

"Such as?" responded Jim as he sipped his scotch.

"Real estate development in the southwest! We need to invest in the cheap land in Texas, Arizona and Nevada. That's where the future is for expansion, but we need to get in before it becomes obvious to everyone."

"Jonathan, real estate is always a risky business. Yes, I know there is big money to be made, but it's a risk - reward situation that could turn on us, especially at such a distant location where we're not knowledgeable about the people or the governments. We've done very well by staying in our own strawberry patch. Do you realize that when you buy land in the southwest that you're only buying the surface? The mineral rights to oil and other valuable resources are not part of the deal unless you pay dearly for them. So don't think that you're going to make money that way. The Bulldog Masters of the world have all that tied up."

"I do realize that, and obviously you've done very well for our family, but I believe that there's an opportunity out there that we shouldn't ignore. I think we should start a new banking operation in that area and use the money to finance our ventures, as we do here in the Northeast."

"Jonathan that's a very dangerous plan. We've been successful doing that because we laid the political groundwork for it here. That takes years. We need to be sure of the players. Without the right government officials appointed by our financially supported politicians, it can't work. You can't legally use the people's savings to support private ventures and you wouldn't take that risk unless you're on firm ground with the politicians and the regulators, and what do you think your brother would do if we were to take a chance with the law?"

"My brother? You're not still thinking of bringing him into the business? He's become a flaming liberal thanks to that bleeding heart girlfriend of his. Don't you realize that he wouldn't be happy with the business as we operate it today?"

"Jim has always been part of my plan for the family business, and now that he's an attorney he can be a valuable asset to the business, and I understand from Sam Polowski that Jim and Sharon are not seeing each other anymore."

"I hadn't heard that. Do you know why?" he responded, acting as if he cared about Jim's troubles.

"He said she's considering the Peace Corps. Maybe it has something to do with that? I suspect your mother knows, but she isn't talking. I did hear her pleading with Jim on the phone to give her a second chance, whatever that means. I'm not going to get involved in his personal life. I'm sure that after what he's been through he can handle the situation. Jim's a bright and able man and I believe that he has toughened up and that he'll add value to our operation."

"Add value? Do you think that he's going to be okay with the improprieties of our existing business practices?" his voice lowered, "I thought you'd given up on him?"

"I never gave up on him. There's a role for Jim in our business, as there's a role for you. You've done a good job. Don't spoil it by defying my wishes. You're both loved and you're both talented and valuable assets to the family enterprises. Is this going to be a problem for you?" Jim's penetrating eyes and stern look were reminiscent of those times that he let his children know when they were stepping over the line.

"I can't lie to you, I'm disappointed, but... I'll deal with it!" answered Jonathan.

"That's good, because we're going to Washington to meet with him on Friday. He'll answer to me directly and I'll try to keep the peace between you, but if it becomes a serious problem we'll all suffer. I don't intend to be a referee. I don't have the energy for that!"

"Has he said that he'll join us?" asked Jonathan in a voice that reflected his frustration.

"No, but why wouldn't he? He's proven himself to be a tough leader in spite of his emotional involvements and political leanings. I'm sure he'll do what's best for the family."

"I hope you're right, Dad. If not we'll be in serious trouble."

"It'll be fine son. Oh, and we'll also meet with Bert Obersham. He has information from his Middle East confidant that may help us devise a strategy to counter Masters' plan. I want you and Jim to assist me in devising and implementing that strategy."

"You know that I'm on board, but Jim has his own agenda."

"Just be tolerant, son. We can't afford to be divided by infighting."

Part Three

The Chaotic 70's

Chapter 75

The decade of the 1970's brought the American public into economic and political confrontations that changed the landscape of the country from one of hope to one of confusion and chaos. The end of the Vietnam War, promised in the election of Richard Nixon in 1968, went on for five more years. The My Lai massacre added to the public's anger and anxiety over the American presence in Southeast Asia. Only Second Lieutenant William Calley, the platoon leader, was indicted and sentenced originally to life, but only served three and half years of house arrest.

On June 17, 1972, six months before the re-election of Nixon, men loyal to him burglarized the Democratic National Committee's headquarters seeking information about their opponent's strategy. The burglary occurred at the *Watergate* complex in Washington, D.C. Nixon denied knowledge of the illegal activity and did his best to cover up the White House Involvement. His cover-up failed when his White House Counsel, John Dean confessed to knowledge of the fiasco and of the cover-up. In his New York Times bestseller published in 2006, Dean called those who currently control the Republican Party as Authoritarians and *Conservatives Without Conscience.*

On August 9, 1974, after a year of investigations, Nixon, under the cloud of an impeachment, became the first President of the United States to resign the office. Gerald Ford, who had replaced Spiro Agnew after Agnew was indicted for inappropriate financial practices, took the reins of office and pardoned Richard Nixon. The country accepted the gesture of loyalty from President Ford wanting to put the drama of Watergate behind them.

The oil embargo of the organization of the Oil Producing Exporting Countries, better known as OPEC, caused a shortage of fuel oil and the price of gasoline to increase from 40 cents a gallon to more than $1.50 a gallon; interest rates rose dramatically and the cost of the Vietnam War put Americans in financial and moral debt. Instead of fighting the war on poverty that Johnson had declared as the goal of his Administration, we fought a war on the impoverished. As lines formed at gas stations with limited supplies of fuel the American people realized their vulnerability to the economic whims of powerful and the wealthy.

The 1970s were also the years of social revelations, as many sought reform and a forum to express discontent. The discontent reached its apex with the massacre at Kent State University in 1970 when the Ohio State National Guard opened fire on unarmed protesting students, killing six students and wounding more than forty in an attempt to quell their constitutional right to protest. Had these events taken place in a foreign country they would have been considered a breach of human rights, and their over-reaction would have been condemned by Americans.

The middle class of the 1970s would never rise above their economic status of the time in real income or achieve their piece of the American Dream. They had reached the pinnacle of their position relative to their share of their country's wealth under compassionate Presidents and would spend the next 30 years in a self-destructive mode. The old cliché attributed to the king of the circus world, P.T. Barnum, that "you can fool some of the people all of the time and all of the people some of the time," became the successful strategy of the very wealthy.

People voted against their self-interest to the benefit of those with wealth and power, whose collective ownership of the American Dream and assets went from 13% in 1973 to 43% during the next 30 years. Religious ideologies became the basis for securing votes blurring the constitutional requisite for separation of church and state. The constitution allowed for the tax free status of all religions with the understanding that they were not to be a force in government.

The election of Jimmy Carter, the former Democratic Governor of Georgia and a Born Again Christian, to the Presidency in 1978, was an attempt to bring back normalcy in the person of a man of undisputed integrity. But the out- of-control economy spawned by the unprecedented increases in the cost of energy, inflation and interest rates during the Nixon/Ford administrations could not be overcome.

Carter's Presidency proved that there was no room for an honest man in the White House without a political agenda that favored the very rich. He was doomed to failure since he didn't cater to either party's ambitions. He was too conservative for his fellow Democrats and too liberal for the Republican opposition. The holding of hostages from the American Embassy in Iran for more than a year cut deeply into his Presidency. After losing eight military men in a rescue attempt, his humanity would not allow him to take further action fearing that it would harm those being held in danger. His hesitation to act militarily was used by his opposition to defeat him.

Chapter 76

It had been nearly ten years since Sharon Polowski left for her assignment in the Peace Corps. That duty took her to a village in Africa whose people had only their pride and their families as assets. She had no idea how she would affect their lives, but she knew she would. Although they lacked most of the resources Americans took for granted, the villagers had a sense of purpose and that purpose was their daily struggle to survive and to take care of their families.

After a year in the wilds of Africa Sharon realized that the instinct to survive was the predominant element of social interaction. Whether rich or poor one would do what was necessary to live and to protect what one had, even it was to the detriment of others. She also realized that instinct was the driving force that led to wars and that it was often fueled by the greed of the very rich and powerful to protect their *entitlements.*

Sharon returned to the United States to a position as Counsel to the Department of Housing and Urban Development. HUD, as it was known, was created to improve cities and the lives of their inhabitants. She believed that there was hope for the working class in the programs that progressive presidents had put into motion.

Jimmy Carter was President and she had confidence in his vision for the future. Her father was elected for his second term and he was determined to help Ronald Reagan reach his goal of the Presidency at the expense of Carter's re-election bid. Sam believed that the governor of California shared his conservative views. Reagan, a former actor, former Democrat and former union president, saw the benefits of the elitist life after serving as spokesman for General Electric, a major player in the military defense contractor world. He had backed Senator Barry Goldwater of Arizona in his bid for the Oval Office and he had his eye on that prize.

Sam hoped that Reagan would reverse the downward trend of the seventies that began under the Nixon/Ford administrations. Once Reagan was nominated, Sam would work with Reagan's campaign and his running mate for Vice President, George H.W. Bush, to get them into the White House. One of the Republican Party's strategists was Dick Cheney, well respected in the inner circles of the Right Wing politics. His five deferments from military duty during the Vietnam War did not diminish his enthusiasm for a patriotic war or for the military/ industrial complex that financially supported the so–called "conservative" movement.

But Sam Polowski would not get the chance to see a Reagan Presidency. On his way to meet with the governor of California his twin engine Cessna crashed in the Sierra Mountains during a storm.

The death of her father was devastating to Sharon who loved him despite their many political differences. She knew him as a man of integrity who always did what he believed to be right without regard for his own wealth. She regretted that her last words with him were within an emotional discussion in her attempt to dissuade him from supporting Reagan. He just became agitated and said, you just don't understand! She realized then that he thought of her as being naïve rather than enlightened. She had always thought that although he often disagreed, he had respect for her opinions.

The Buckman family attended the funeral. It was the first time that young Jim and Sharon met eye to eye since they had parted at the airport for his trip to Vietnam. It was not a time for reconciliations, only for condolences. They exchanged a gentle kiss and a hug and Jim left to catch a flight to Washington, feeling a tug on his heart that couldn't be denied.

Having completed his active duty with the Army's JAG operation, Jim Buckman, gave the family business a try but found the conflicts with his brother were matched by those of his conscience. He decided to run for Congress as a moderate Republican. He still believed in the supposed principles of efficient government and was hoping to bring the Republican Party back to its Abe Lincoln/Teddy Roosevelt/Eisenhower roots.

Lincoln freed the slaves, angering the southern agricultural community that depended on their labor; Teddy Roosevelt tied the American corporations to rules and regulations intended to stop monopolies and profit gouging and General Dwight D. Eisenhower, the heroic Commander of the European forces in World War II, despised war and having witnessed the bravery of American minorities believed in their quest for equal rights. As President he had the American Interstate Highway system built as an element of defense and became America's major job creator.

After his father was released, Diego returned to Boston and pursued a career as an air traffic controller. He was told by his cousin Karime that she had negotiated a deal with Rodriguez and his thugs to represent the cartel in California for Manny's release and for his and Tony's safety. Three months later the Rodriguez gang was met on a road south of Tijuana, Mexico by government troops where they were slaughtered in an ambush. Their demise was in a manner reminiscent of her father, Juan Carlos' final conflict. Their illegal cargo of drugs was confiscated and served as payment for the deed.

The irony was not lost on Diego, nor was the effectiveness of his cousin's leadership. Soon after the incident Karime gave up the leadership of the cartel to Pedro Valdez and was now employed as a professor of sociology at the University of Mexico.

For Tony Benedetto, the decade of the seventies was a time to get grounded. His goal was to grow his newly established engineering firm. He found his niche and he was going to make his mark. He kept in touch with Diego and Jim Buckman. Although Democrats, they both supported Jim's campaign for a seat in Congress. They believed in his determination to center the Republican Party. They accepted Jim's invitation to meet at the Buckman family's Vermont cabin in the woods for the weekend, to help him strategize his campaign.

The Buckman family patriarch was distraught at the economic mess the oil industry had perpetrated on the country. The greed of people like Bulldog Masters had sent the cost of living to new heights and dramatically affected the real estate, banking and automobile industries. The cost of oil at the pump had risen more than 400% under Republican Administrations.

The only good news for the Republican Party was that beginning in 1977 the chaos was now the problem of Democratic President Jimmy Carter, and there was no easy solution to the economic crisis caused by the dramatic increase in the price of oil. It was the autumn of 1979, the third year of his administration, mortgage rates had peaked at 18%, and gasoline cost well over a dollar a gallon. The automobile industry was on its knees, the economy was in shambles and Jimmy Carter had no answer to his inherited plight. And if his plate wasn't full enough he had the fate of 66 hostages taken from the American Embassy in Iran to worry about.

Jimmy Carter had only one term to respond to his predecessor's fiscal incompetence. Being a "Born Again Christian," Carter believed that the solution to the myriad of economic problems he inherited was to sacrifice and for Americans to live lean. He also believed that as President he had to lead by example. He cut White House spending on the traditional frivolities of the office including selling the Presidential yacht, an Eisenhower favorite amenity and dispensing with much of the costly "pomp and circumstance" of the Presidency. He initiated energy-saving policies in his personal life and encouraged Americans to do the same.

When he addressed the American people in a televised fireside chat, sitting in an easy chair in a sweater, to emphasize the need to turn down the thermostat and live frugally, it was labeled by the media as his "malaise speech." Although to Carter it seemed like the best way to emphasis the need to offset the energy crisis caused by the 400% increase in the cost of fuel. Both progressives and conservatives saw it as being too negative and depressing. He soon learned the lesson of political favor, and it had little to do with the attitude of the American people.

Chapter 77

Jim Buckman heard the car coming up the gravel road to his sanctuary in the Vermont hills. He smiled as he saw the dust generated by a little red sports car driven by Tony Benedetto. Diego Martinez waved from the passenger side when he saw Jim on the front porch of the cabin.

"You guys are crazy, driving a sports car up a rutted dirt road into the deep woods of Vermont," was Jim's greeting to his old buddies. "What is this thing? I'd be surprised if you still have an oil pan and a gas tank under there."

"Hey Captain, It's a Mazda RX 7. Isn't it cool? I couldn't afford a Porsche like my rich friends," smiled Tony. "It's got a rotary engine and five speeds. It just came out this year."

"Yeah and no suspension," quipped a rattled Diego. I bumped my head so many times coming up that road that I'm seeing double and two of Tony is one too many."

"Well, I'm glad that you both could make it. I need to make some serious decisions and I need the advice of you two members of the middle class, even if you've shown poor judgment in your means of transportation. How are your families?" Jim asked as they entered the home.

"Keisha is fine, she's a nurse at Massachusetts General Hospital in Boston."

"Great! It seems like yesterday that we were at your wedding in LA. Wasn't she in medical school?"

"Yes, but we don't have the money for her to complete her degree and her scholarships dried up. She got her nursing certificate instead."

"It's a shame that her mother passed away after recovering from that coma. Did you ever find out if she remembered that fateful night?"

"Yes, before she died, we were alone in her hospital room and she said 'Diego, I remembered that you were there, but I forgave you a long time ago. Please be good to Keisha."

"What did you say?"

"I said that I was very sorry and I cried. She died that night."

"She was a special lady my friend and she obviously believed that you were a good man who made a dumb mistake as a kid."

"I just wonder if she always knew and yet she didn't try to discourage Keisha from loving me. Keisha said that she never told her about my arrest or the plea bargain that Joey Consalvo tried to pull off with the DA that would have gotten me at least 10-years in Quentin."

"One thing the three of us should realize after what we've been through on this journey we call life, you can't lose if you don't give up, and if you have good friends!"

"Good thought, Jim, You have good friends and you're not a quitter, so you'll win this thing," declared Tony.

"Thanks Tony. By the way, the last time we spoke you were thinking about getting engaged to that French girl. What's her name, Meghan? Did you take the big step? When's the big day?" asked Jim as he handed them each a Heineken.

"We're looking at some time next year, maybe November. But don't worry. It won't be until after you're elected to Congress. Here's to your success," added Tony as he raised his cold brew in a toast to Jim's political goal.

"Well, I'm happy to hear you're so confident, but then that's what I need to feel if I'm to win that seat."

"You're the right man for the job, Jim! You got it all, good looks, money and brains, but why do you even want to do it?" asked Diego incredulous that a guy who has everything would expose himself to the dirt and slime of politics.

"I'm not sure, but I think I know what's needed to fix the mess that this country is in, and I don't know any other way to get it done."

"That's a good place for us to start. What is it that you think is wrong and how would you fix it?" inquired Tony.

"You may not believe this coming from me, but I believe it's our survival instincts that are out of control and we've made greed the means to an end rather than using common sense to make life more livable for people."

"Whoa, aren't you running as a Republican? You sound like us," Diego noted. "Your Republicans are the ones in power for eight of the last ten years, they made the mess. You need to change Parties, amigo."

"Diego's right! How are you going to go against the political philosophies of those who are making the profits and have the power? Your family will disown you and you won't be able to raise the money you need to compete."

"I'm counting on the people of Connecticut to cut through the politics of stagnation and self-interest and see a renewed Republican party. Like Massachusetts, the Connecticut electorate is not averse to splitting their vote. There are many independents and Democrats who are rational voters and vote for the man, or woman, rather than the party. I can have a bigger impact as a Republican who proposes progressive, common sense programs than I can as just another liberal Democrat. Besides, Democrats have shot themselves in the foot many times for their own selfish reasons. Many of them seem to believe that their specific agendas are more important than winning. Since Johnson they haven't had the guts to implement needed change and we all know that Carter won't survive the re-election."

"We all saw what happened in 1968 and 1972. Those who were anti-war gave away the presidency by protesting against the only party that would stop it, believing the rhetoric of demigods," added Tony. "But do you really think you can win the seat with that platform?"

"I don't know. That's why I've asked my two most cynical friends for advice and direction," quipped Jim as he paused and for a sip of his beer.

"I see where you're coming from, but I doubt that having good intentions will be enough. You know better than most that there are some very powerful people running this country, and your dad is one of them. How will you overcome their efforts to stop you?"

"The same way they gained the power they now covet. I'll make them believe I have something to offer them."

"You're going to lie about your intentions, then how will you get that independent and progressive vote?" asked a confused Tony.

"I don't know that I will go in the 'all or nothing' direction of trying to be a liberal Republican, but I do know how I'll act once in office."

"Wait a minute, Jim, my head is hurting and I don't think it's just because of Tony's toy car. Are you saying that you're going to fool the people into voting for you? I guess you are a true politician!" stated Diego.

"No, I'm not saying that. How I make the Republican Party comfortable is not necessarily the same way I make the electorate comfortable with my candidacy."

"Hmmm, okay, I need another beer," declared Diego.

"Are you sure this place isn't bugged? They've been known to do unscrupulous things to defeat a candidate," suggested Tony sarcastically.

"I think Watergate taught them a lesson. Besides I'm not even a little fish in their pond, as yet. I intend to stay well below the radar for another few months while I get a feel for the race and do some fund-raising."

"Do you think your dad will support your candidacy?" asked Tony.

"I don't know, but I know that my mother will," winked Jim.

"I suppose that you heard that Sharon Polowski has announced her candidacy for her father's seat in the Senate?" asked Tony.

Jim turned, to Tony, a wide-eyed look of disbelief on his face. "No, I didn't know that!"

"That should be interesting," added Diego, as he raised his green bottle of Heineken to his lips, his eyes fixed on Jim.

"I saw her at the funeral, but there were so many people there I didn't get a chance to talk to her. How do you know, Tony?"

"We've communicated over the years. She asked my advice. She wasn't sure that she was strong enough politically to pull it off."

"And you advised her to run for the office?"

"Not exactly, I told her that politics suck and she should only do it if it was in her heart to take the abuse that is inevitable in order to accomplish her goals. It's also my advice to you. For whatever it's worth. And, yes she did ask about you," Tony answered the unspoken question with a smile.

"Yeah, I can imagine, she was probably hoping I was hit by a train!"

"Would that make you feel better for being the jerk that you were to her?" asked Diego, already feeling his second beer. "Sorry, amigo it just slipped out."

"No apology necessary my friend, I agree. I hear she's engaged and very happy. My mother still exchanges letters with her. She deserves to be happy and I was never sure that she would be with me."

"Back to your future, Jim, we can't change the past, but hopefully we can learn from it. What do you need from us? I hope it's not money," laughed Tony.

"I do need your support and advice! Will you both help me organize my campaign in central Connecticut? As a Buckman I'm not exactly viewed as being either ethnic or middle class savvy. I need to know and understand their issues and I need to relate to people in the cities to win that seat."

"You think a couple of carpetbaggers from California and Massachusetts will make you look more attractive to the Connecticut voters. I don't know, Jim," responded Tony

"Tony, I see where Jim's going here. He's not asking us to get the votes, just to find out what he needs to do so he can make them feel that he's the right guy for the job. Is that right?"

"Exactly, Diego, I know that if I entrusted that work to someone in my political inner circle I wouldn't get the answers or direction that I need. They would tell me to promise tax cuts and be pro-life, as they like to call being against a woman's right to control her own body. I don't need the party line ... I know the rhetoric and the bullshit. I need to know what are their true needs and I don't want to make promises that are not realistic. Can you do that for me?"

"We can try. What do you think, Tony?"

"Yes, but we're not politically savvy ourselves. We'll need the help of your professionals so we don't waste time and get you what you really need," answered Tony. "But you do realize that the strength of the Democratic candidate is to get out the Black and Hispanic vote in the cities. You don't have a base there."

"Okay, I agree. In fact it's my point exactly. But how do I do that?"

"Bring your Vietnam record into this. Try to get members of your squad to be by your side during campaign events. It worked for JFK! One thing that the three of us have in common is the war and the Purple Heart. There are many veterans and their families from that ethnic and minority class in the city who will respect you for that service and your tour of duty in Nam. That is where you will be considered one of them!"

"I don't know. I'll think about it. I'm not sure they'd do that. Why would they? It's been more than ten years and we left many good soldiers behind. The memories aren't good and bringing them up for my personal gain doesn't seem right."

"It all depends on whether you believe in yourself and your ability to make changes in Washington that will benefit their lives as well as your constituents' in Connecticut. Isn't it the job of a Congressman to represent the interest of the people? They're supposed to propose and vote on legislation for the benefit of the masses and not just the few," offered Tony. "I think if you sound that message you will do ok."

"Obviously, you've been talking to Sharon. Be careful or you may find yourself running for governor of Massachusetts," quipped Buckman.

"Not likely! I couldn't win an election for dog catcher in Southie," responded Tony. "Besides, Massachusetts likes to elect Republican governors and Democratic legislators. It's some kind of masochistic thing."

"Here's to your future, man!" declared Diego as he raised his brew. "May the better man win, and not forget his friends!"

Part Four

The Trickle Down Years

Chapter 78

The end of the seventies was greeted with relief by those who were tired of the turmoil and the dysfunction of the country's government under Nixon, Agnew, Ford and Carter. The election of 1980 was marked by a controversial challenge by members of President Carter's own party that was spearheaded by Senator Ted Kennedy. It was a challenge that proved fatal to the Democrats and detrimental to the middle class.

Reagan's rhetorical question to the American electorate, "Are you better off now than you were four years ago," echoed throughout the country and signaled the end of a chance at a second term for the Carter presidency. Although devoid of promise, it had the same effect as JFK's, "Ask not what your country can do for you, ask what you can do for your country!" inaugural address.

Carter's failure to secure the release of the Americans held hostage by Iranian radicals hastened his demise. A military action designed to rescue them ended in a sand storm in the desert, as a rescue helicopter crashed into a C-130 cargo plane, killing eight soldiers and wounding many others. It was a sad day for Americans and an embarrassment to Carter.

The Iranian radicals did, however, have a plan. They wanted weapons. They were on the verge of war with Iraq, which at the time was an ally of the United States. Carter was not about to arm the enemy of the United States. The hostages remained until Carter was physically out of the presidency. They were released in accordance with a last-minute deal known as the Algiers Accord signed on January 19, 1981, the day before Reagan's Inauguration, supposedly by the lame-duck Carter administration.

Curiously, the hostages weren't released until the day Ronald Reagan officially took the oath of office. They had been held for 444 days, a fact that some considered as more than a little bit suspicious. Years later it was revealed that the Iranians eventually did, in fact, receive American arms. The sale was done covertly, during the Reagan administration, under a plan devised by Oliver North, a staff member of the National Security Council. It was brought to light in 1986 as the "Iran Contra Affair," a convoluted attempt to have a new class of American hostages being held by Hezbollah, a radical mid-eastern organization, released.

The beneficiaries of the deal were to be the Contras, who were Nicaraguan rebels funded by the CIA to overthrow the communist government of that country. The idea was to sell arms to Iran at a highly inflated price and divert the money from that sale to the Contra rebels in Nicaragua who were fighting an alleged communist regime. Reagan's paranoia about communism paralleled that of Senator Joseph McCarthy, in the early 1950s.

Some believed that the promise of such a deal with Iran was possibly the reason the American Embassy hostages were held captive for more than a year, and were not released until the moment Reagan took office. They believed that here was a deal made covertly to embarrass of the Carter Presidency during the election campaign. Did a candidate for the Presidency of the United States, offer such a deal? If proved to be true, it would be treason!

A Congressional investigation committee asked President Reagan about "the Iran Contra Affair." Initially he told them that he didn't recall any such weapons sale. Eventually the truth was told after he was re-elected in a landslide in 1984, he took responsibility for the action but couldn't remember the details and curiously, was left unchallenged.

Chapter 79

Young Jim Buckman rode the coattails of the congenial Reagan into Congress as a moderate Republican with strong financial backing. Sharon Polowski managed to overcome a well-funded Republican effort, which attempted to deny her goal to fill her father's seat in the Senate as a Democrat from a blue-collar state. She knew that the Senate was the "Good Old Boy" club. She would have been less conspicuous in the House of Representatives, but then as individuals, Congressmen were not as powerful as the 100 Senators, and she needed to get things done! She believed that the so-called "Moral Majority" had captured the heart and soul of the Republican Party and was intent on leading the country into an abyss of arrogance and self-righteousness.

Sharon feared that their moral issues, such as the prohibition of abortion and the strengthening of State's Rights, which had been the basis of discrimination for over a hundred years after Lincoln's "Emancipation Proclamation," would replace the President Johnson's War on Poverty. The Kennedy and Johnson administrations believed in the basic Democratic principles of improving peoples' right to better working conditions and freedom from discrimination. They embraced the American Dream! She believed the country was being diverted into a pattern of apathy, hate and anxiety about the future.

The new Republicans were pushing their self-defined morality over the needs of people to survive, and the distraught masses were buying it. It became obvious to her that they wanted the government out of the business of regulating and taxing big profit corporations and into the business of regulating the behavior of individuals using their new morality packaged coined as "family values."

Newly elected Congressman Jim Buckman first saw her walking down the hall to the Senate chamber for the swearing-in ceremony. He would be doing the same in the House chambers later that morning. It had been nearly ten years since they had last exchanged letters and less than a year since they met briefly at her father's funeral. It was over and he lived with the regret.

She didn't see him at first but felt his eyes on her. She stopped, turned her head, and with some hesitation, smiled back to him, nodding a greeting and then continued on to her appointment to begin her new career as the freshman senator from Michigan. Her step was a little less assertive, her heart a little heavier, her thoughts confused. She had known they would cross paths as legislators in Washington, but she wasn't prepared for this sudden encounter.

Jim returned the smile and the nod then turned towards his original destination. He realized that he had forfeited his chance at being with the woman he loved and thought of how emotionally empty the past years had been. He questioned his wisdom in making the decision to let her go, rationalizing that it was what she wanted, but without her acknowledgement of that conclusion. He had to get his head back into the game. There was work to do and he was determined to do it right. He admired her decision to take the big step into the Senate. She was very capable of the challenge. He smiled as he thought, but was the Senate prepared for her? His plan was more cautious, thinking he had to start at the lower chamber to prove himself as a competent Legislator. The war, and a lost love, had humbled him.

The Inauguration of President Ronald Reagan brought personality back to the office. Not since Kennedy had charisma been so key to the most powerful political position in the world. Although Johnson had managed passage of important legislation, he was not a motivator, unless intimidation counted as motivation. Nixon, Ford and Carter were hardly inspirational and the country needed an upbeat leader to overcome their alleged media label of "malaise" at the presidential level."

Jim Buckman believed that Reagan, a man who had grown up without the benefit of wealth in a dysfunctional family, was a Democrat in his youth; had achieved success and had even headed a union, would appreciate the American working class and adhere to the principles of Lincoln, Teddy Roosevelt and Eisenhower. He believed Reagan to be a moderate Republican behind the facade of a conservative.

Senator Sharon Polowski, the freshman Senator from Michigan, couldn't get past Reagan's support of the out-of-control, anti-communism paranoia of McCarthyism or his alliance with Goldwater, whose stated position on foreign policy was one that the electorate believed would be a hair-trigger response that would lead to nuclear destruction. She wondered how Reagan could turn on his fellow actors while President of the Screen Actors Guild, actually naming names of those he believed to be Communist sympathizers. Their lives and careers were ruined as they were falsely accused by the McCarthy/ Nixon "investigations" of being traitors to their country. She wondered, did he really want the best for the American people? She wasn't convinced that Reagan was a man-of-the-people, but she accepted the invitation to the inaugural ball to be held at the Smithsonian Air and Space Museum, out of respect for her father.

Senator Sam Polowski was a loyal and well-thought-of Republican. Many of his fellow Senators and Congressmen had shown their respect by attending his funeral. She believed that she owed him and his colleagues a showing of mutual respect. Her mother declined the invitation, having been to several such events with Sam. She found such galas to be overcrowded and chaotic.

But Sam loved the atmosphere. He had learned the ways of Washington and enjoyed working the room but still held to his ideals of honesty and forthrightness. He regretted his vote on the control of oil prices, but rationalized that the increases were inevitable given the world situation.

Sharon would attend the ball with her campaign manager and fiancé, Tim Falstaff, the son of a close friend of her father's. Like her, Tim didn't buy into the right wing political philosophy of his father and welcomed the opportunity to work with her. He also wanted to pursue a relationship that he hoped would lead to a lifetime commitment. He had admired Sharon since they were teenagers in high school. He was considered to be cute, but too nerdy by many of the high school girls and not a fun date. But a degree in government from Harvard, and a successful college career in track bolstered his confidence. They didn't date until after her father died. Sharon saw Tim as a soul mate and someone who shared her beliefs. She was comfortable with him. She grew to admire him and respect his thoughtful advice.

Life was good for Tim Falstaff.

Chapter 80

"Why do we have to go to these affairs, Jim? They're so crowded and we never get a chance to spend time with the President. I doubt he'll even remember you were there," declared Nancy Buckman as they dressed for the event. "And the food, if you can call it that, isn't enough to count as a real calorie."

"What did you say? Are you still complaining about the pretzels? I hear they'll have cheese and crackers this time, but you have to be quick to get them," he laughed as he shaved and responded to what he believed to be his wife's complaints, muffled by the sound of running water. "Don't you want to see your son's moment of triumph before the President?"

"I would rather celebrate his moment of triumph over a glass of Chardonnay at a fine Washington restaurant!" responded Nancy as she applied her eyeliner. "But I'm anxious to see Sharon Polowski. She's done what I wish I had the courage to do!"

"And what is that, run for the Senate as a liberal Democrat?" Jim said sarcastically as he slipped on the jacket to his tuxedo.

"Exactly! She has the heart and sense of purpose I wish I had," she said straightening his tie.

"That would have made for an interesting marriage, my dear. Well, at least Jim wised up and left that relationship before it got too serious."

"Oh, did he? Well maybe our son made a big mistake. How many meaningful relationships has he had in the last ten years?" retorted Nancy.

"He's a very busy and serious young man. He doesn't need to be tied down at this stage in his career."

"Yes, you're right dear, he's going to need all of his energy and effort to catch up to that woman," smiled Nancy in response.

"I believe you've become even more liberal over these 40 years of marital bliss," countered Jim with a smirk. "Maybe you should have married that hockey player I rescued you from at Yale. I see him at the Rangers' games. He works the beer concession."

"You're a cruel man, James Buckman. I still love you, but not your politics. Are you ready to go? I don't want to miss any of the excitement," she said as she rolled her eyes and placed a kiss on his cheek.

"Okay, I'm ready but promise me you won't mention how you hated Reagan's movie 'Bedtime for Bonzo' to anyone, especially to the President," he said, feigning a serious look.

"I won't unless you leave me alone to talk to some boring ambassador!" she responded with a mischievous smile.

The Smithsonian Air and Space Museum was a major tourist attraction in Washington D.C. Fronting on Washington's National Mall, it housed the Wright brothers' plane, the Kitty Hawk, a tribute to man's first successful manned fight, and many tributes to man's achievements above the earth, such as the capsule that brought Allan Shepard back to earth after his successful first journey into space and the Apollo 13 moon vehicle that didn't quite make it. This evening the Museum would be the preferred setting for the nation's gala affair, the Presidential Inaugural Ball.

Congressman Jim Buckman decided to bring his chief of staff, Ann Hilman as his date. Ann, fifteen years his senior, was a seasoned veteran of the political wars in Connecticut, and as he would often say, a lot wiser than he. She was recommended by his father to manage his campaign. Jim realized that dad was hoping to keep tabs on him through her, but he was able to control that by only telling her what he wanted his father to know.

He was impressed by her dedication and competence. She was able to overcome the many obstacles facing the candidacy of a rich white boy in a district with more than 50% ethnics and minorities who were struggling to survive. She relied a lot on the efforts of Diego Martinez and Tony Benedetto to better understand the political needs of Blacks, Hispanics, Asians and, although not considered to be a minorities, the Italians and

French. They did their job well, even inspiring her with a passion for middle of the road Republicans. Jim wanted to reward her for her hard work. He didn't have a special woman in his life, and she had never been to such an event.

As a freshman Congressman he knew he would be limited in his ability to sponsor real change. The secret to success in one's early years was to join the causes of those who held the power.

Jim was interested in getting to know the more moderate members of the House, even if they were Democrats. He believed that the right and left wings of both parties were more obsessed with their ideology than with the welfare of the people they were elected to serve. Many ignored the needs of those who hadn't vote for them but were relying on their competence.

Jim Buckman knew first-hand how the system really worked, thanks to his own "family's values." As he stood in line for drinks he heard familiar voices. He turned to see his mother and Father attempting to work their way through the crowd to him.

"I didn't think we would find you in this crowd!" He heard his mother exclaim as they managed to reach him. "This gets worse every year. You'd think people would realize how frustrating an experience it is and stay home and watch it on television."

"Now Nancy, you know you love being here with all of my conservative Republican friends." countered the elder Buckman. "How are you doing, son?" giving him an awkward hug and hand shake simultaneously. "And Ann, how are you? Congratulations on doing such a great job!" he declared as he hugged her and kissed her cheek in a more competent manner.

"Yes, Ann, thank you for your hard work and wise counsel to my normally headstrong son!" Nancy said as she also hugged and kissed her family friend. "Obviously he listened or we wouldn't be here celebrating his success tonight."

"Well, I appreciate the compliments, but Jim is a special guy and it was a pleasure to work with him. He will be a great Congressman," offered Ann Hilman, to her close friends and admirers.

"Okay you two, let's try to enjoy the party," offered Congressman Buckman as he handed Ann her drink."

"What are you each drinking?"

"I doubt they can make a decent Martini, so get me whatever you're having, and what would you like my love?"

"A glass of Chardonnay at Dominic's Restaurant," answered his mother sarcastically.

"She'll have a glass of Chardonnay, son. Maybe it'll mellow her out for the evening."

Jim looked at his mother and with a tight-lipped smile, shook his head slightly, letting her know that he understood the reference to his and Sharon's favorite Washington restaurant. "You're relentless, Mother!"

"I know. It's a trait I passed on to my children," she explained with a mischievous smile.

The night went on as Reagan gave his welcome and thank you speech. Jim saw Sharon had secured a place near the stage and was looking as beautiful as always. She was dressed in a blue gown, her red hair flowing down over her bare shoulders, a glass of red wine in her hand, attentive to the words of her less-than-favorite President. Again, as if on cue, she turned her head, feeling his eyes on her through the crowded audience, and acknowledged him with a smile. Startled by this gift of her sixth sense, he returned the smile and nodded, as he had that morning in the halls of Congress, and raised his drink in a salutary manner that was often a part of their dates in "the good old days." She responded in kind, but returned her attention to the President, with a sigh as she closed her eyes to regain her composure.

Jim found himself glancing in her direction as the speech ended and noticed that the tall good-looking man standing next to her in the crowd was actually with her. He noted, that when he turned to say something to her, he smiled, kissed her briefly and then offered her his arm to lead her to a group on the far side of the museum.

He realized, that this man must be her fiancé, the one that won her heart, the heart he had broken. Holding back his emotion, he silently wished her well and, spotting a colleague, proceeded to where he was standing alone to chat about whatever.

CHAPTER 81

Reagan's first year in office tested both his mental and physical fortitude. He soon found out that being President was not like portraying a character in the movies. Reading prepared speeches with emotion didn't substitute for knowledge of complex issues or for understanding the consequences of actions at the top.

While Reagan was governor of California a college student was shot and killed by National Guardsmen while demonstrating with a group from UCLA Berkley who were seeking the use of a piece of public property for public recreation. They were considered trespassers on the public property. When interviewed Reagan told the reporters, "He shouldn't have been there!" Life was tough without written lines.

He had the most powerful job in the world, and he believed he could talk his way through it. He promised the American people to end the "malaise" of the Carter Presidency, to bring good times and to lower taxes. But as Governor of California he had raised taxes more than anyone before him.

Less than three months into his first term he faced the worst challenge of his Presidency - his survival! A delusional young man named John Hinckley Jr., intending to impress actress Jodie Foster, met him on the street in Washington and fired eight bullets in his direction, hitting him and members of his entourage before being subdued. Over the next two weeks Reagan showed the American people what he lacked in solutions he made up for in courage.

The televised sight of a smiling President Reagan sitting in a wheelchair, clothed in his robe at the hospital, was uplifting to a Nation that needed uplifting. He had the compassion and respect of the people, which proved to be better than a mandate of an election.

The depraved Mr. Hinckley did more to improve the image of Reagan as a leader than his policies or advisers could hope to do. Few Americans realized how close Reagan came to death, but they were awed by his courage under fire and his resilience in recovery. For the first time in his political career, he was able to personify his screen image and the part seemed to come natural.

Congressman James Buckman III appreciated the man that he saw during those trying times and believed he was a good and decent person. He had one worry. Why was his father one of Reagan's biggest financial supporters?

Senator Sharon Polowski had no use for Reagan's politics but was saddened that there were still people out there thinking that the road to fame was through outrageous acts of violence and destruction. The politics of hate was not what America was supposed to be about. Reagan was a good man with what she believed to be misguided beliefs and values. She felt for his wife Nancy and prayed for his recovery and, of course, for his defeat in the next election.

One of Reagan's first acts as President was to end the wage and price controls put into effect by Nixon and supported by Ford and Carter. A primary target of those controls was the increasing price of oil, which had such a negative effect on the economy in the 1970s. Republican leaders believed that price controls exacerbated the problem and were an affront to the free-market system.

However, wage controls catered to the corporate community by preventing any increases that addressed the needs of workers and their families. Having less money for discretionary purchases made the average American less of a consumer and more of a survivor. This proved to be a significant factor in the downturn of the national economy and the slide of the middle class, which began in 1973.

One group that were adversely affected by Reagan's political decisions was the Professional Air Traffic Controllers Organization better known as PATCO. Air traffic Controllers had complained for years about the increased stress of the job and the lack of reasonable compensation. The union, PATCO attempted to work through the political system to address the impacts of increased air traffic resulting deregulation of the industry under President Carter, which caused extensive work days and jeopardized public safety. Its 13,000 members worked diligently to keep airplanes flying safely but the problem was ignored. The union believed that they were making a dangerous system work by not solving a critical problem of understaffing the Towers.

As a last resort PATCO members went on strike on August 3, 1981. Reagan gave them 48 hours to return to their jobs. Only 1300 complied. The rest were fired by Reagan, enforcing the 1947 Taft-Hartley Act's prohibition against federal employee strikes for one of the first times in the Acts' history.

Amongst those affected was Diego Martinez. After three years on the job he was devoted to the union. He believed in its goals and knew firsthand that what they were fighting for was necessary. As a child he had seen the way migrant workers were treated by farmers and the government. But this was a government job that was supposed to ensure the safety of people. Why wouldn't the government want to ensure that safety?

Before the strike the word was that if there was an incident, he had better hope that he wasn't in the tower at the time. The only government assurance was that there would be a scapegoat if there were a tragedy resulting from an exhausted controller who had worked ten to twelve hours a day for seven days and was no longer sufficiently alert to do the job. Shutting down the system was not what they wanted but there were no other choices. It was only a matter of time before this make-a-bad-system-work philosophy would cost lives.

"How could he do this Tony? We work hard and we've tried to reason with our employer, the FAA, for years about the problems in our towers," lamented Diego in a call to Tony Benedetto.

"Diego, my good friend, this is what happens when we have leaders who are trying to show how tough they are rather than how smart they can be. Reagan said he was concerned about the safety of the public if the air controllers didn't return to work, but he didn't seem concerned about safety if the understaffing and overwork conditions weren't addressed. He must have been a hell of a union leader for his fellow actors."

"Yeah, like when he turned on his own members at those McCarthy hearings. He fingered those who disagreed with his narrow minded bullshit as being Communist. It's well known in LA what Reagan is all about. He was a disaster as governor," declared an enraged and depressed Diego. Is this the American way, Tony?"

"I'm afraid it is in this administration. Reagan is at a high point in popularity with his recovery from the assassination attempt. He was feeling his oats and testing his power. Conservative Republicans are dancing in the streets at this action against a major union.

"Well I wish that..."

"Hold it Diego! Don't even say what you're thinking. I know what you're feeling, but this country doesn't need more violence and it doesn't solve any problems."

"Tony, you know how hard I worked to get a job as a professional. Now it's gone because I did what is supposed to be the American way to solve stuff like this, peacefully. Our union leaders told us that a strike is the only way to get an employer to fix the bad situations."

"I know, but PATCO thought the President was on their side since they supported his election over a Democrat. They were suckered by a man who wanted to show his mentors how conservative and tough he was. They should have known that he had a record of turning on anyone who stands in his way. Just ask the members of his former union."

Chapter 82

The news of President Reagan's action against the air traffic controllers reached James Buckman Jr. and his son Jonathan as they listened to the radio on their drive from Dulles International Airport to their monthly meeting with the Washington Action Group.

"Damn it! This guy's worse than Nixon. He's one of these fire, ready, aim characters. He does whatever gets him center stage. I warned Masters about supporting him against George H.W. Bush."

"I don't know, Dad. I think he did what he had to do. You can't let labor control corporations. Look at the Teamsters, the United Auto Workers and the Steel Workers unions. They control the profitability of companies. And since when are you concerned about labor?" asked Jonathan.

"Jonathan, there has to be a balance, and I agree that some unions have stepped over the boundaries of common sense, but he's done serious damage to the economy by crippling air transportation. This isn't something that can be fixed overnight. You need to deal with these things intelligently, not as some macho cowboy."

"You obviously don't like Reagan, but he's doing what needs to be done. I think he's a true conservative!"

"Listen Son, we're not conservatives. We're businessmen, and if you get tied to some ego-based ideology you can be dragged down into an abyss of economic blight. We're living with the result of what Masters and his friends did to the economic balance of the country by his callous support of the oil industry price gouging at our expense. If you destroy the ability of millions of consumers to buy homes and cars you destroy our way of life and also limit our profits, because our profits are made selling houses and cars and financing the so-called American Dream."

"Well, I doubt we'll agree on that issue, but then we have other things to resolve with your Washington friends. I hear that this meeting will be about encouraging Reagan to support tax reform to reduce the burden on people who are the corporate leaders and investors of the nation. You must be on board with that issue?"

"It depends on what the solution is going to be. I'm not for it if it continues to drain the American middle class. It could backfire."

"How could it backfire if we have more money to invest in our operations by paying less taxes?"

"It's not that simple, Son. It will backfire if we take more money out of the consumer's pockets, like we did by increasing the cost of fuel by 400% in the last decade. I'm willing to pay more taxes if I make more money and we can only make money if we have a good economy. If the people can't afford to purchase products from our companies and borrow money from our banks, we lose! Take away their money for the sake of a making a few more dollars for ourselves and we'll all suffer financially in the long run."

"Well, the current tax code would have us paying up to 70% on taxable income this year. It's obvious that we're being over taxed!" offered Jonathan Buckman.

"And how much did we actually pay Jonathan? You know as well as I do that the highest rate, which was 92% under Republican President Eisenhower, was only on the highest increment of the adjusted income. We actually never paid more than an average of 30% of that income in taxes. There are so many loopholes in the tax code, that most corporations paid less than 15% in federal taxes. I'll take the bogus high tax rate over the increased scrutiny that could result if we lower it."

"Actually, last year we paid nothing and got some tax credits on our developments," Jonathan exclaimed with a devilish smile! "But we can't rely on that for the future. What if we have a liberal President? He'll want to close those loopholes and we might be paying that 70%!"

"Well, we're here. Let's hear what they have to say. I was told by Bert Obersham that this is being proposed by our good friend Masters, and that's always a bad sign! Bert is concerned that less revenue for the government will mean less money to spend on government contracts for defense, and he's not happy about that."

"I think that the government will make it up somehow. There are almost 100 million working taxpayers in this country. The government just needs to spread the burden a little more."

"That's' what worries me son! What is that old cliché, 'penny wise and pound foolish?

CHAPTER 83

"Tim, what do you think of Reagan's *Trickle Down economic theory*?" Sharon asked her chief of staff and fiancé about Reagan's plan for rewarding his wealthy benefactors as they discussed the current legislative slate of budget bills over dinner.

"It's ridiculous to think that if you take money from the working class and give it to millionaires and billionaires they'll use it to improve the economy and not invest it overseas; hide it in offshore banks in some secret account or buy another vacation home in the Caribbean. Simple-minded solutions are no solutions at all. But what can we do to stop him? He's riding a wave of popularity right now," responded Tim realizing that it wasn't the answer she had hoped for.

"I don't think it has a chance? How does he convince hard working people to agree to some self-destructive policy that will cost them their means to survive? Who will pay for his gifts to the rich and for his warlike defense budget?" I agree that they'll use it to live like royalty and invest the rest in tax-free shelters in the Caymans, Bermuda and Switzerland.

"I wouldn't sell him short. They say Reagan can sell refrigerators to Eskimos living in igloos."

"Yeah, as long as they're General Electric refrigerators!" Sharon quipped, referencing Reagan's long-term career as the spokesman for GE.

"Good one hon! I left myself open on that one! But he's no fool. He knows in order to win a second term he needs to keep the money guys happy and do their deeds. I understand that he has a degree in economics and believes in the Keynesian theories. Keynesian theory promotes deficit spending and so-called supply side economics."

"Whatever happened to the Republican ideology of fiscal responsibility? They preach smaller government, then spend our money on irrational wars, subsidies for companies that support them and tax breaks for those who already have so many loopholes that the Tax Code is nothing but Swiss cheese."

"Well, our only chance is to nip it in the bud at the House level where Democrats are still in control. If they can defeat, or amend his initiatives we'll have the opportunity to have an impact in the Senate. How about your friend, the one that you pointed out to me at the inaugural, Congressman Buckman? You said that his father is James Buckman the financier. I understand that the Congressman is a moderate. Can he help us with this?"

Sharon stared at Tim as he spoke, but her mind wondered to a different time and a different place. It had been nearly a year since her eyes met Jim's at the Inaugural Ball. She hadn't told Tim the whole story when he had noticed their eye contact, only that they were old friends and who he was in the political spectrum. "I don't think he'd be interested. He has his own agenda and he's voted with Reagan's supporters on nearly every issue this year."

"What about the air traffic controllers? Reagan's use of a rarely imposed anti-strike law in firing more than 11,000 men and women has got to be making the unions in this country angry. Can we encourage them to respond to this budget issue? They've always been on board with our party to assure that the American middle class gets its share of the pie."

"I don't know Tim. I have a good friend who was one of those fired. He's a Mexican-American and a citizen who worked hard to become a controller, and he was fired for doing what he thought was right. Last I heard he couldn't get another union job because the unions are afraid of Reagan and don't want the stigma of hiring any of those strikers. It seems that unions that were once as strong and arrogant as the corporations are trying to stay below the radar. They don't want to give Reagan another chance to grandstand."

"Well, we need to have a strategy to defeat this *trickle down* nonsense or we'll be chasing our tails fighting tax breaks for the rich for the next six years. They'll then use the lack of funds in the Treasury as an excuse to eliminate educational and social programs for the middle class and the disadvantaged. But they'll keep funding the $2,000 toilets in their defense budgets. I'll do a quick covert survey to see if there's the will and the means in Congress to stop this wave of insensitivity before it's too late. But for now let's talk about that wedding date!" exclaimed Tim, a smile broadening on his previously serious face.

"Why? Are you in a hurry, Mr. Falstaff?" Sharon answered with a mischievous smile.

"No, but why wait? Let's not waste time planning a big wedding. A nice quiet, private ceremony in Hawaii would do."

"It's not the right time, Tim. There are too many issues in the way right now. It would take away from our moment if we tried to fit it in between all the controversial things we need to deal with this year. We need to focus on why we're here."

"I know why I'm here Sharon!"

"And why are you here, Tim?" she asked taking his hands gently in hers, her eyes fixed on his.

"For you, Sharon! That's the only reason I'm here!"

Chapter 84

"Gentlemen, we finally have a man in the White House who understands how capitalism works and we need to support his programs. Supply-side economics is the way to get this country out of its doldrums. Reagan can sell it better than anyone and now's the time to get tax cuts into the legislative process," lectured Thomas "Bulldog" Masters to his captive audience.

"Tom, I'm all for protecting and maximizing our profits as businessmen, but if we keep sticking it to middle class families there'll be no middle class and we'll reach the point of no return. I know you don't want to hear this, but the increase in the price of gasoline and heating oil put this country into an economic slide that consumers and workers are still trying to recover from. If we keep going in this direction we'll be taking all of their discretionary income," asserted Buckman.

"Jim, we need to take care of our interest while we have the opportunity to do so. Look, Reagan did a slam dunk on the unions when he fired the air traffic controllers and there wasn't even a whimper from the American public. He's talking about reducing taxes for his supporters who financed him and the public is buying it. Don't underestimate his ability to sell unpopular ideas. His recovery from the assassination attempt made him a hero in the eyes of the people," offered John Carlton, CEO of American Defense Industries, "If we don't take advantage now, then when?"

"If the government doesn't have enough tax revenue to spend on education and infrastructure, we will all suffer. If we take more from the average Joe, there'll be less money for them to spend and pay their bills," countered Buckman. I know we have a base in the religious right, many of whom ironically, are on Social Security and Medicare and worked under unions before retirement, but they are not stupid. They will eventually realize that they have been used.

"Jim, John's right! If we act now, we ride Reagan's coattails and we make it impossible for the Democrats to spend our money on socialistic programs like welfare and education for people who have no interest in being educated," added Donald Peters, III, CEO of Continental Trust Corporation.

"Don, how can we be against education? If we don't have an educated society we fall behind countries who would like to defeat us for economic supremacy. We can't survive as a feudal society. If we want to remain prosperous we need to have a strong middle class as consumers, borrowers and entrepreneurs," continued Buckman.

"Dad, I think they have a point. We can't be sure that a future President, with a favorable Congress, won't take away the advantages that we've worked hard to put in place."

Jim Buckman couldn't believe that his son was countering his argument. He stared across the table and into his eyes attempting by telepathy to tell him to shut up! "Jonathan, this is much more than a chance to take advantage of an opportunity. This kind of action will give the liberals a reason to fight harder and to appeal to the 95% of the public that will learn that their quality of life has been sacrificed for the sake of greed. How much do you think they'll take?"

"They'll take what we give them, Jim. We proved that with the price of oil," declared Masters. "You were against that and it worked out as I expected it would. We just kept increasing their cost until it reached its peak level of pain, and frankly Jim, that was higher than we had anticipated. The American public just needs to be sold on the fact that it is in their interest to allow those who give them jobs to maximize their potential. We as corporate leaders take all the risk and we deserve the rewards for taking those risks."

"You believe that putting the economy into a downspin actually worked? Okay, so we had a Democratic President we could blame, but Carter didn't have a chance to offset the increased cost of energy and pay for the Vietnam War that our Watergate boys extended for five more years than necessary. We need to tread carefully here, gentlemen!" exclaimed Buckman as he looked despairingly at his son.

Bert Obersham, a retired 4 star general; close friend of Jim Buckman's and a Director of Consolidated Aeronautics Corporation came to Buckman's defense, "Jim's right! We need to have some balance in our economic program. If we attempt to reduce taxes to save a few dollars, we risk the wrath of millions of Americans, and that's not a reaction that we want to incur. If we have less money in the treasury we can't afford to manufacture the kind of weaponry that we will need to defend this country, and that will put America at risk."

"Well, gentlemen, I believe that the train has already left the station. I'm told that Reagan is going to attempt to reduce the tax burden for those of us who make this country work down to 28%, but first he will go to 50% from the 70% we now are supposed to pay on the highest increment of earnings. He realizes that if we don't make it, then the country doesn't make it," remarked Masters. "So we either catch that train at its next stop or we'll be on the wrong side of the tracks!"

"You know, as well as I do, that we don't pay anywhere near 70% in taxes. We've worked hard to gain tax credit, subsidies and deduction benefits. Tom, if we follow your line of reasoning we'd better be ready to be hit by that train as we expose our tax-paying records to more public scrutiny! I will not support such an irrational program of self-destruction," declared Buckman as he gathered up his papers. "Let's go Jonathan we have no more business here!"

Bert Obersham stayed to hear the reaction to his best friend's words and his sudden departure. Jonathan Buckman reluctantly packed up his work as he glance at an enraged Masters, and followed his father. He knew that he was only a guest, and he was not ready to defy his instructions. He had already stepped over the line by contradicting his argument, but he believed that they had to be on that train! He also knew that his father was not a quitter and that he must have a plan to derail Masters and the group from supporting Reagan's tax-reduction plan.

As they walked to their car the senior Buckman gave his son a lecture on respect. "Son, if you ever contradict me again in a meeting of any kind, you'll be the sweeping the floors of the banks that we own. Do you understand me?"

Jonathan hadn't heard that tone since he was sixteen when he borrowed his father's Rolls Royce to show off to his girlfriend without having the benefit of either a driver's license or permission. Of course, having to call his dad from the police station only added to the emotional discourse.

"I understand, but I thought you wanted me there to speak my mind?"

"I wanted you there because I'm almost 70 years old and you hope to be my successor and the protector of the family and its businesses. I brought you there to listen and learn not to be another short-sighted nitwit that I have to overcome with logic. Yes, I've worked my entire adult life to give our family all the advantages, but there's a limit to greed. Doing inane and self-destructive acts that attract the attention of the people we depend on to make our profits is unwise and potentially dangerous."

"Okay, I get it! Where are we going? Weren't we having dinner with Bert after the meeting?"

"Yes, and we'll meet him for dinner at the hotel as planned, but we need to talk to your brother first. We may need his help to defeat Reagan's initiative."

Jonathan resisted the urge to react. It was obvious that his father still had more confidence in Jim's intellect and leadership abilities than his. But he's the one who's done the hard work to keep the family enterprises profitable. He wasn't happy and he realized that his father thought of him as reckless and extravagant. He was just trying to assure prosperity for the Buckman family. He didn't believe his father had all of the answers. He was a product of earlier times and reluctant to embrace the hardball solutions available to them. He'd find a way to catch that train!

Congressman Buckman expected his father and brother to be at his legislative office at 6 p.m. He was surprised to see them walk in an hour early. "Hey guys, what happened? Did Masters have laryngitis?" he quipped as he got out of his leather chair and greeted them with a cordial handshake, realizing they wouldn't be there unless they needed something.

"No, but that wouldn't be a bad affliction for him to have. I doubt it would shut him up though," answered his father with more than a little anger in his voice.

"Why? What's he up to now? Hasn't he and his friends done enough damage?"

"That's why we're here, Jim. We may need your help in the legislature to curb his appetite," responded his father.

"Dad thinks that reducing taxes is a bad thing," offered Jonathan. "Masters is pushing for Reagan to reduce the high-end taxes so that those of us who are the employers will have more money to invest. He calls it supply-side-economics."

"I heard that in the chamber. It sounds reasonable, so what's the problem?"

"Well son, I know you think I'm a greedy old man, but I've lived long enough to learn that you can't make money in business if you haven't got customers! If we keep taking their money they'll soon need more and more government help to survive. What people like Masters don't realize is that they, not us, are the largest voting block and when they eventually realize we've been playing with their money and losing it for them in our greedy schemes, they will rebel."

"Whoa, Dad, it sounds like mother has finally gotten through to you!" quipped Jim.

"Yes, I think so, brother! Dad's getting soft in his old age!" added Jonathan.

"I'm not getting soft, and your mother has nothing to do with it. I always want the advantage when I am in competition for the dollar, but I want it for our family. I've seen wealthy people screw up because of insatiable greed. Yes, I know we've played on the edge with some of our investments, but only when it made sense and we believed it was safe to do so. I don't want to pay a dime more than I have to in taxes, but there's a point of no return with this smart-ass, holier than thou politics."

"I'm confused. Didn't you suggest that the way to win the vote of the blue-collar workers, who used to be southern

Democrats, was to play the religion card? You embraced Jerry Falwell's 'Moral Majority' strategy that would encourage God-fearing people to vote against their own interest by electing those opposed to Medicare and Social Security. I remember you boasted about how the southern vote was organized in churches and that the 'waving of the flag' and the 'sight of a cross' would win more votes than the social programs that for many, was their only hope of survival," asked Jim, confused by his father's social rhetoric.

"That was then, when I believed we had gone too far to the left with the Kennedy-Johnson initiatives, but now the pendulum has swung too far to the right. I'm strongly against poorly run and expensive social programs, but if we don't educate our kids and provide 'Joe Blue Collar' with reasonable wages the unions will rise again or those social programs will become an albatross around our necks with more people needing to be on government relief just to survive."

Jonathan was stunned by what he was hearing. All he knew was that he wanted to emulate and eventually exceed his father's success. His goal was to make more money and be even wealthier and more powerful.

Jim was also stunned, but for a different reason. Did he misunderstand his father's motives? He had long since felt his love as a result of what he did to help rescue him in Vietnam. Now he was awestruck by his sense of compassion. Was this the epiphany of a man trying to rectify his past deeds? Maybe he hadn't really understood him. He was always a strategist and, as Bert Obersham had once referred to him, with due reverence and a smile, a "persevering bastard" when he wanted to get something done.

"I don't know what to say. What is it that you want me to do? How can I help? I'm only a freshman Congressman. I'm just above the level of gopher?"

"At this point you only have to keep your eyes and ears open and try to befriend those who are taking up Reagan's cause. You need to stay low-key and under the radar on this issue, for now. I don't yet know how we can stop its progress. I'm hoping that we can determine its vulnerabilities and act to derail the President's plan. What committee assignments do you have?"

"You know that I'm a Reagan supporter, but I'll do what I can because I am indebted to you, for many reasons. I'm on the National Security and Housing and Urban Development Committees."

Jonathan winced at the man-hug that followed. He had assumed that Jim was no longer a threat to his position as the successor to his father's legacy and controller of the family fortune.

"I appreciate that, son. We'll stay in touch weekly, but don't hesitate to contact me if you come up with anything. Bert stayed behind at the meeting with Masters to see what developed. I doubt they'll be too candid with him in the room, knowing our close relationship, but he may have found out some useful information. We're meeting him for dinner tonight. Can you join us?"

"Sorry, Dad, I need to review legislation that another freshman wants me to endorse. Have a good dinner and say hello to Bert for me."

The walk down the halls of Congress was silent but for the echo of their heels on the marble floors. Jonathan hesitated to say what he felt knowing that it would anger his father, but the thoughts that broiled within his head would not allow for restraint, "I understand you're serious about getting Jim involved in this but why didn't you discuss it with me? After all, how we approach this political issue could affect our business, and I'm not sure that we should be out-front in defiance of the President or of your colleagues in Washington."

Buckman senior stopped and looking into Jonathan's eyes said, "Son, as long as I'm the head of this household I make the decisions. When I need your advice I will not hesitate to ask for it, but I'm not going to get involved in your petty self-serving motives and jealousies. You both have a role in the family business. Yours, right now, is more formal that Jim's, but if your emotional baggage becomes a problem and not in the best interest of Buckman Enterprises or adds stress to my life, that will change! Do you understand?"

Jonathan was shocked. He was being dressed down again by his father as if he was a teenager, and he was being chastised in a public building that was the seat of all American laws as if he was being handed the rules that dictated the protocol for his future actions.

Despondent, he turned and continued the walk to their car, not wanting to say what he felt and destroy the future for him as head of the Buckman family's businesses. His father followed, somewhat regretting the showdown but believing it necessary. He had felt Jonathan's animosity for his brother for years and he'd had enough of it!

The twenty minute trip back to the hotel was quiet and solemn as Jonathan drove and his father rested his eyes. He had conceded him the last word, for now!

Bert Obersham was waiting for them at a table in the far corner of the hotel dining room, his facial expression suggesting that he was not the bearer of good news.

"Jim, Jonathan, I see that you're both in an upbeat mood," he commented sarcastically noting their equally less than jubilant demeanor.

"Good evening Bert. I hope you have some good news to round out this fine day," responded Jim as he and Jonathan took their places.

"Afraid not, Jim. After you both left, Masters went into a ten-minute diatribe about loyalty to the Group's objectives and being a team player. He even said that you have become a liability to their cause."

"He did. Well I wouldn't expect any less from that self-serving bastard!"

"He seems to have the backing of the rest of the Group to pursue his, and Reagan's initiatives. They believe they'll never have another opportunity like this when they will control the House and be able to get their programs through to a President who will sign them into law. They know they have a battle in the Senate, but they believe many of the Senate Democrats are fearful after Reagan's landslide win. They won't oppose a President who is considered a strong leader, especially after his recovery from the assassination attempt."

Jonathan looked to his father expecting some acknowledgement of the facts that his most trusted and true friend, Bert Obersham was sharing with them.

"It looks like we have our work cut out for us Bert. Any suggestions?"

Jonathan looked to Bert in disbelief. He had never heard his father's tone to be so despondent. He would always be ready with a plan to counter that of his enemy. James Buckman Jr., retired colonel, war hero, self-made man and master of manipulation in politics, had lost his fastball. He was vulnerable, depressed and a liability not only to the Group, but to Buckman Enterprises.

"Jim, I don't think this is worth the fight. We need to pick our battles and we can only hope they won't be able to win this one. The American electorate isn't totally self-destructive. Do you really think they're going to allow the wealthiest of Americans to pay less so they can pay more and get less services?"

"Yes, I do Bert! They believe that if we, as the wealthiest Americans, have more money we'll invest to provide them with jobs so that they can take care of their families. That's the sales pitch and they'll be convinced, and they will believe it! And there will be jobs, but if we need to build roads or fight wars we won't invest our money, we'll borrow from the oil-rich Mideast countries who already bleed us dry."

"Yes, but jobs are jobs! What difference does it make where or how they originate? The American people who want to work will work. Those who are lazy and want to live on the dole will be where they should be, at the bottom of the pile," remarked Jonathan having been rejuvenated by the weakness he perceived in his mentor.

"Son, what you don't realize is that most of their jobs come from the government's perceived needs for defense, infrastructure and social services, and when there isn't enough tax revenue it has to borrow for those needs in order to pay us to provide them. We make money on the government's spending. We, as Republicans, just don't want to spend it on the social needs of millions of our people! This strategy will create debts from borrowing, which become deficits, which we will dump on the masses with regret and then talk of reducing deficits by eliminating the programs they depend on."

Bert and Jonathan shared a telling glance and a thought. Has he given up on the basic principles that got him the prosperity that he and his family enjoy today?

"Jonathan, why don't you give your dad and me some time to discuss this situation, he'll be up in a while."

Jonathan felt like a kid being asked to leave the room while the adults discussed important business, but then he realized, as he looked into Bert's eyes, that there was concern in his look of compassion for his good friend, and obliged.

"Yes, I have some work to do before I turn in so I'll see you in our room later, Dad," he said clumsily.

Both men took a sip of their after-dinner drinks, then Bert asked, "Okay Jim, what's going on here?"

"What do you mean, Bert? I told you my concerns."

"Jim, we go back more than forty years. I know when you have something on your mind and it isn't just Bulldog Masters or the plight of the average American."

"You were always an insightful character, that's why I've always trusted your opinions and why we've been friends for so long. I am concerned about our way of life, Bert. I am most concerned about my ability to lead my family through the next financial crisis, which I believe is inevitable if we keep going down this road of fiscal irresponsibility."

"What do you mean your ability to lead? You're an excellent leader, and you're only sixty eight years old. Are you giving up?"

"Not voluntarily Bert, but...I have lung cancer. The doctor tells me I might have a year."

"Oh my God, Jim, does Nancy or the boys know?"

"No, and I'm not ready to tell them. I'm concerned that Jonathan doesn't have the maturity or the sensitivity to run the businesses in the best interest of the family and that Jim would not tolerate the way we've operated. Jonathan is easily swayed, as you can see from our discussion today, and he's hostile to any interference by Jim, who is much more grounded and has proven himself to be a better leader."

"But Jim, you have to tell Nancy, and soon. What will she do if something happens and she's not prepared for the consequences, and Jim, she loves you despite your flaws," he finished with a strained smile.

"I know Bert, but what can I do? I'm thinking that I need to sell the businesses or go public, but I'm worried about the scrutiny that either of those choices will incur. I doubt that we'll survive a due diligence process."

"Damn it Jim, I don't know what to say."

"I would turn it all over to you as my successor if you were willing to take on that role? You're the only one I could trust."

"Jim, I'm willing, but not capable. I'm not a businessman. I'm good at being an adviser, a follow-up guy and a loyal friend, but business is not my forte."

"Well, in any case this can't become public or even known by the Group. I'm trying to avert what I believe will be an economic disaster if this administration gets to borrow us into bankruptcy. This President believes in this ridiculous trickle-down effect that results from his equally ridiculous supply-side economics policy. He thinks that it's okay to borrow to fight wars and give tax breaks to our friends and that deficits are fine. It doesn't make common sense. The only way to get money for the type of programs this country needs to get us out of these doldrums is to increase taxes. I won't be here to pick up the pieces when his policies hit the proverbial fan, Bert. I'm worried and believe it or not, afraid for my family's well-being."

Chapter 85

Diego Martinez believed that being an air traffic controller would be his ticket to a future as a middle class American. Keisha had given birth to their first child just days after Reagan's firing of more than 11,000 air traffic controllers and the dissolution of their union. It was nearly a year since he had been in the tower at Logan International Airport and had been without a job for eight months, until he started working as a day laborer for a landscaper on Cape Cod. But today was going to be a good day!

Tony Benedetto and his family were coming to spend some time with him and his family. It was the Labor Day weekend 1982, and Tony was bringing his family of four to enjoy a beautiful summer weekend on the Cape. Tony and his wife Meghan had twins, a boy and a girl just six months after the Martinez family was blessed with their son Manuel.

"Hey Tony, don't worry about bringing diapers. We have a year's supply here," quipped Diego.

There was something magical about the Cape even when it was full of tourists and summer residents. There was a mystical quality to this peninsula of sandy beaches and quaint cottages. The picturesque towns, ocean breezes and beautiful sand dunes transformed many who crossed the bridges leading to the Cape into carefree beach folk. Many seemed to leave their woes and anxieties on the other side of the canal to be retrieved at a later date.

Diego and Keisha lived in a cottage in Truro, a down-cape community. Keisha now worked at a nursing home as a night nurse, which offset some of the uncertainty of Diego's seasonal work. Part of the rent was also paid in kind by Diego's work repairing the roof, replacing a deck, painting and landscaping the cottage grounds. He realized that he was working them out of their home, since when he finished and their lease was up, the landlord would want to rent at a higher price than they could afford, but for now it was their only option.

Tony had called ahead and rented a motorboat to go fishing on Cape Cod Bay. Fishing was not one of his favorite pastimes but he knew Diego would enjoy it and it gave them a chance to drink cold beer and reminisce. He felt that Diego needed to get away from reality for a while. It had been a rough year for the Martinez family.

Meanwhile things were looking up for Tony's engineering business. He had taken over from an older engineer who had nearly bankrupted it by allowing clients to avoid paying. He now had fifteen employees and prospects for some good projects. He tried to get Diego to join him, encouraging him to take courses that would lead to a technical position as a draftsman or a surveyor, but Diego refused, believing he would be a burden to an already overburdened friend.

Tony told him how he had to mortgage his home to buy the small firm and that it was tough to keep it going and collect monies from those who owed him. Besides, Diego held out hope that he would someday be rehired to do the job that he was trained to do and that he had been commended by his superiors for doing so well.

Diego was at the side of the cottage working the barbeque when Tony and his family arrived. He smiled at the Ford wagon as it kicked up dust on the long dirt driveway reminiscent of their adventure in Tony's Mazda RX 7 a couple of years earlier in Vermont.

"Hey amigo, I see you're driving a real car now. What happened to your toy?"

"He traded it in for twin babies, Diego. How is your little guy?" responded Meghan as Tony removed the new additions from their car seats, handing Bobby to her while he attended to Rachelle.

"He's fine. He has his mother's good looks and my even disposition," quipped Diego.

Meghan was an attractive young woman, only five feet tall with auburn hair and a smile that would light up a room. Diego knew when he met her two years ago that Tony had found his soul mate. She was straightforward, easy to talk to and un-fazed by a person's position or status. To her, people were people and façades were easily penetrated. The Martinez's were people without façade and they had an abundance of sincerity and compassion. She loved being with them and knew why Tony and Diego were always there for each other. She firmly believed that Diego's friendship was as important to Tony as Tony's was to Diego.

"Well, let's get you guys settled. I'll put the burgers on the grill. Lunch will be ready in about 15 minutes," advised Diego as Keisha came to the door.

"Meghan, Tony, I'm so glad you could make it. And look at these two, they grow so fast!" declared Keisha as she took Rachelle from Tony's arms.

"Where is little Manny, we haven't seen him for months," asked Meghan

"He's taking his nap, but he'll be awake soon. Come on in. We'll let the amateur Chefs deal with the grill. I'm in the middle of the potato salad," responded Keisha.

"What's going on buddy?" asked Tony as he put his hand on Diego's shoulder.

"Hey, we're surviving, and that's good enough for now. With Keisha working nights and me doing the day labor for this landscaper, it has worked out. One of us is always here to take care of Manny. We can't afford a babysitter, so it's all good."

"Yeah, we had to ask Meghan's mother to take care of the twins when she works at the store. Since my parents retired to Florida it's been difficult on her mother. I think we'll need a nanny soon, but they make almost as much as Meghan does running her small shop. I would like her to stay home but then she has her ambitions too and it isn't right for me to tell her what she must decide for herself. The good news is, I seem to be building a nice client base. If this economy improves my business should be making a good profit in a couple of years."

"It's a good thing you don't work for some company that has a union. The President would find you and destroy your life!"

"I know, Diego, life can be very unfair especially to those who have no power to fight back. I'm not sure about this guy, he seems like a congenial and thoughtful man, but he does things that seem simpleminded. But at least he hasn't invaded any countries yet, and he did lower taxes."

"Yeah right, he lowered it for his wealthy friends from 50% to 28% and got rid of some of our deductions for taxes we pay to the state and towns. My neighbor is an accountant and he told me that we got snookered on this so-called tax cut. We're actually paying more because we have fewer deductions."

"Snookered? I like that word. Is it actually a word?"

"I don't know but it seemed to fit," laughed Diego as he repeated the word. "Snookered, I think it means fooled...or maybe screwed? Like when we were 'volunteered' for the point man position in an Army patrol."

"Maybe both, I'll have to look it up!" smiled Tony in response, taking another drink of his Gansett. "I know I don't have any more money than last year and both of us are working!"

"Hey, what are you two doing? Are the burgers ready?" yelled Keisha from the kitchen window.

"Oops, I hope that Meghan likes well done," said Diego as he looked to the flame-engulfed grill.

"She'll love it. Put plenty of barbeque sauce on it," laughed Tony as he took another swig. "Hey, I've got that boat for tomorrow morning at 5:00 am. We're going to find out why they call this place Cape *Cod,*" declared Tony. "I hope you're an early riser."

"Of course, I wouldn't want to miss feeding the fish their breakfast. I hear that some fishermen have caught sharks out there. I hope they're not hungry for breakfast, too."

"Don't worry. I hear they don't like Mexican, it gives them indigestion."

"No, but they do like Italian!" laughed Diego as he finished his third beer and called to the women, "Come and get it, lovely senoritas."

"Lovely Senoritas, huh, we'd better go out there and have our burgers while they're still recognizable and our men are still coherent," declared Keisha with a knowing smile.

The dew was rising from the forest floor when Tony and Diego drove down the driveway at 4:30 the next morning. It was cloudy but there was a promise of sun by 7am that would burn off the moist vapor.

"I love summer weather, but when it's humid it still makes me think of those unbearable days in Nam," offered Tony as they drove to the town wharf.

"Every day in Nam was unbearable for me, Tony. I was happy to get out of there as long as it wasn't in a body bag, and thanks to you I did."

"You know, I keep telling you that it wasn't just me. The medic, the rescue copter, the whole company managed to get you out, but hey, that was then and we've got to move forward," Tony said noticing the tears welling in Diego's eyes. "How's Carmella and your cousin Karime doing in Mexico?" asked Tony attempting to change the subject.

"They're doing well. Carmella is not as she used to be. Her diabetes is doing a job on her, but she still walks every day. Karime is happy to be out of the cartel, but her brother was captured in a raid on their mountain hideout. She wants to come to the U.S. but the authorities won't give her a visa and she won't do it as an illegal. She would be giving up a good position at the university. They both ask about you in their letters."

"They do? And what do you say?"

"I told them when you and Meghan were married and about the twins. Carmella was very happy, she said you will be a good father."

"Tell Carmella I think of her often and wish her well. She's a very special lady. And Karime?"

"She said that Meghan is a lucky woman. You know, I think she liked you."

"Karime is a beautiful woman and she's right about being lucky, but it's me who's lucky."

They arrived at the wharf as the morning fog was lifting, exposing the glass-like waters of a calm Bay. They were led to a white wooden boat. "Yup, it has seen better days," declared a feisty old man with an unkempt grey and yellow beard and the stub of a stogey between his lips. He gave them a five-minute course on how to operate the boat, which included a three-minute attempt to start its 50-horsepower outboard motor.

They loaded their cooler, their limited fishing gear and bait into the boat while listening to its owner's advice about where the fish were running, "You're more likely to catch stripers, than cod in this here area and, oh yeah, you might see a shark this late in the summer since the waters are damn warm. Just stay away from them and if you catch one, don't bring it into the boat, cut the line," were his final words of wisdom as he pushed them away from the dock. "Be back by 6 or you'll pay for another day."

The morning calm gave way to a slight sea breeze that cleared the waters of its blanket of fog. The amateur fishermen decided to navigate to an area populated by others in pursuit of the big one that wouldn't get away. Diego drove the boat while Tony went about the business of baiting their hooks and preparing them for a day of fun and relaxation.

"Have you been out here before?" he asked Diego.

"No, but it looks like there are plenty of others who think there are fish here," he said pointing to the half dozen vessels that had chosen the area.

"Well, don't get too close. People get upset if someone invades their space," cautioned Tony.

"Okay, we'll anchor here. We're about 300 yards from them. I'm sure it's far enough to keep them happy."

As they settled into the task at hand Diego used his army issued binoculars to view the area. "Only a couple of the boats are fishing. The others, the bigger boats, seem to have people sunbathing on their decks."

"Hey remember we're here to fish old buddy, not to sight-see," responded Tony with a wink, noting the bikini clad sun worshippers on the decks.

They each cast their line to opposite sides of the boat and settled back into their "this is the life" positions. Tony handed Diego a cold one, "Here you go Captain Ahab, cheers!" as they raised their drinks to honor their day of carefree recreation.

"So Diego, how is life treating you?"

"I guess I'm doing okay. I have a great wife, a cute little baby and a roof over our heads. It hasn't turned out as I planned, but it could be worse. How about you? Is engineering what you had hoped it would be?"

"Not exactly, but I too have a great family. Engineering was just a way to get off the bottom. I grew up, like you, seeking respect. I was the first in my family to go to college, but I sometimes wonder if it was worth it. It takes a while to make up for those years of paying for education and not earning money, especially when you still owe money for that education, but I do like being respected as a professional engineer. Before I was college educated and an engineer, people would talk down to me. I could feel their disrespect as if I was not as good as them, just some guinea kid from the city.

"I know what you mean, about the respect thing. When I was a controller people looked up to me. They knew it was a hard job and that it took intelligence. Now I'm thought of as being stupid for not going back to work when Reagan told us to. But how can you do something against thousands of fellow workers and friends?"

"He seems to do things for the political effect. He wants to prove that he's a tough guy, a macho man, like the parts he played in the movies, like the Gipper!" offered Tony.

"Yeah, but no one thought he would do something as crazy as what he did. Our union supported him in his election. He knew air travelers were at risk not having enough controllers in the towers and that people were working long hours and continuous shifts causing fatigue and illness. We were whistle blowers in a system headed for disaster, and he made it seem that we were being selfish. He is not a nice man! I talk to Sharon Polowski once in a while. I asked her if there was anything she could do to get me reinstated. She tried but she said they want to punish us all and that it's a bigger issue than just our union.

She said that it was a message to all unions that their day has passed."

"Funny, I spoke with Jim Buckman the other day and he believes that Reagan is doing a great job. He thinks he's a moderate Republican and that this trickle down bullshit can actually work," commented Tony.

"Well it worked to screw me out of my... whoa!" Diego's fishing line was suddenly yanked. "I got one, I got one Tony!" He yelled as he grabbed hold of his fishing rod with the both hands, dropping his can of brew in the action.

Tony turned to see what was happening. At about fifty yards from the boat the line grew taut and sliced rapidly through the calm waters, away from them. "Hold on amigo, it looks like a big one!" declared Tony.

The fish breeched as Diego tried to reel it in. "What is it, Tony?

"I think it's a striper, I hear they can be tough, give it some slack and sit down or you'll be swimming with him," Tony laughed enjoying the struggle.

Diego did as he was directed as Tony got the net to pull him in when he got closer to the boat.

The battle went on for several minutes. As the fish tired Diego started to ease him towards the boat. Then, without notice, a much larger 'fish' leaped from the waters and took Diego's trophy for its breakfast, along with his hook and dove deep beneath their boat.

"Oh mi Dios, it's a shark!" screamed Diego as he let the rod go.

The reel of the rod hit Tony on the back of the head and he toppled into the water. Diego could see the shark fin as it emerged on the other side of the boat moving away. Tony was not to be seen. Without hesitation, Diego grabbed the fish filet knife and dove into the water. He could see Tony's form about twenty feet from him and he was being dragged, the fish line tangled around his right arm.

Diego didn't notice that one of the boats that were fishing in the distance had seen and heard the commotion and were speeding towards them. Diego swam as fast as he could beneath the waters to reach his buddy. Then all of a sudden Tony's body stopped moving away and started to sink. Diego thought that it was a good thing, he would be able to reach him, but then he noticed the silhouette of the shark in the distance. It had grown tired of dragging its burden and decided to investigate. Diego, in a hyper-adrenalin stage, swam as fast as he could, the knife at the ready in his mouth. But he knew that the shark was going to win this race.

Tony became conscious as his nemesis was with striking distance and gasped for air as he swam to the surface. He expected to feel the jaws of this angry predator but heard a shot instead. Diego surfaced to see a ringing pool of blood around Tony. And the roar of an engine as "The Fishing Fool" passed them, a smiling bearded gentleman on the starboard side of the deck, rifle on hip, gave an informal salute as they coasted by and then maneuvered to haul the great white aboard.

When he reached Tony, Diego saw that he had not been sampled by the eighteen foot predator that had wondered into the Bay.

"I hope you guys don't mind our claiming your friend here!" the sharpshooting stranger yelled as he used a grapple-hook to bring their prize onto the deck.

Tony and Diego just laughed, a very relieved but nervous laugh, and as they treaded water, Diego yelled back, "No, we're having steak tonight, thank you." They didn't hear the under-breath response from their hero of the day as they cruised away. "Dumb ass Dagos, we'll get about a thousand bucks for that white!"

"You're the dumb ass, you should have let the shark eat the guy it would have added weight and gotten a higher price," laughed his partner over the roar of the boat.

They swam the twenty or so yards to their skiff and decided that they had done enough fishing. As they sat exhausted and soaked in the boat guzzling down a beer, they decided that they couldn't go home before lunch, it would be too embarrassing and bringing the boat back too early would be equally unmanly. They decided to spend the afternoon in a sports bar on the Provincetown waterfront, which was only a few miles up the coast.

"Let's dock there, say until four o'clock. The Red Sox are playing the Yankees at one o'clock and I can use a nice fried fisherman's platter."

"Yeah, great idea! We can buy some stripers at a fish market on the dock. We don't want the women to think that we were totally incompetent!" quipped Tony as they both laughed at their unbroken streak of troublesome adventures.

Chapter 86

The Economic Recovery Tax Act, which passed Congress in 1981 didn't do the job the Reagan Administration had said it would. The reduction in the top tax rate from70% to 50% on millionaire's highest increment of earnings reduced revenue. This caused the administration to look to another means for income. In 1982 they introduced the Tax Equity and Fiscal Responsibility Act, which effectively increased taxes for the middle class by eliminating deductions while again reducing taxes for the wealthiest Americans from 50% to a maximum 28%.

In 1983, still not satisfied with the poor results of that strategy, the Reagan administration decided to increase the so called FICA or payroll tax by 25%, which applied primarily to the middle and lower income tax classifications, since there is a limit on the earned income that can be taxed for Social Security.

To add insult to injury, in 1983, as part of a set of Amendments to the Social Security law, the Reagan administration taxed Social Security benefits that are received by retired individuals. This was intended to make up for the "shortfall" created by reducing the taxes paid by the wealthy. Retired seniors were now contributing to the financial well-being of the wealthiest 1%.

To Sharon Polowski, the Republican-controlled Senate was a runaway train of excesses for the richest Americans. Defense spending was putting the country in an indefensible position and tax reductions for the very rich were incentivizing the wrong element of society, those who had already realized the American Dream and now wanted more!

It didn't go without notice that Representative James Buckman III had voted for the Reagan tax plans, but she was not bitter. That was his prerogative and she had heard his more moderate arguments for increasing some deductions and providing tax credits for the middle class tax payer. Although he was unsuccessful, it seemed that he was trying to be a good representative. It was obvious he didn't buy into the total rhetoric of the right wing element of his party.

Sharon hadn't spoken with Jim since her father's funeral and was saddened when she heard of his father's passing. She knew from her communication with his mother that it was imminent. She had an opportunity to know him better during those last days.

Although she disagreed politically with him, she had empathy for his pain and suffering. He had been such a powerful and intimidating figure. When Sharon called to give her condolences, Nancy Buckman told her that she appreciated that he had survived almost a year longer than predicted, but that the last few months were hard on her and the family to see his deterioration.

"He failed badly during the last three months, Sharon, since you saw him last month on your brief visit. He really appreciated seeing you. He said after you left, 'You know I like that woman!' He would never complain about his pain, but he worried about me and our sons. Young Jim would come home and spend the entire weekend, reading and comforting him." Nancy found it hard to speak, as she tried to tell her how she would open the door and see him holding his father's hand and weeping over him as he slept. "They're so much alike and yet so different," she would eventually manage to say through her tears.

Jonathan was less available, especially when Jim was home. He was *busy* running the bank. Nancy knew her husband was aware, but he didn't say anything and always treated Jonathan with expressions of love.

Sharon knew she would have to go to the funeral. Jim had gone to her father's. It would be three months until her wedding to Tim Falstaff. She had some anxiety about seeing Jim. But at thirty six years old it was time for her to move on with her life. Tim and her mother would go with her to Connecticut.

The funeral was a grand procession of dignitaries. The senior Buckman would have been proud to see that those he had supported over the past four decades were showing their appreciation. The ceremony at the local church overflowed and the procession to the military airport involved more than a hundred vehicles. Retired Army Colonel James Buckman Jr. would be interred with military honors at the Arlington National Cemetery later in the day.

Bert Obersham and young Jim gave eulogies, both acknowledging the tough and brilliant man as they had known him. Jim relayed the story of how his father had risked everything to find him when he was captured by the North Vietnamese Army and validated General Obersham's insight into his devotion to his family and his country.

Tony Benedetto and Diego Martinez were there to support their friend. They had driven down to Connecticut early that morning to honor their Army buddy's father, but would get back to their families that evening. They had only met the senior Buckman once, at Jim's swearing in as a freshman Congressman, but they knew of him as a powerful man whose influence was not well received by his son or their friend Sharon.

Sharon had stood in the reception line with her mother and Tim for nearly two hours. She felt the emotion well up in her body as she hugged Nancy Buckman expressing sorrow for her loss. Jim greeted her as he did at her father's funeral, stoically, as she kissed him on the cheek and introduced him to her fiancé. He politely shook Tim's hand and wished them well, being careful not to show emotion. Before she moved on Nancy turned to her and asked if she would be joining them at the National Cemetery in Washington D.C.

Sharon looked at Tim for a response. "I can't make it honey, but you should go," was his unexpected answer.

She looked at Jim, catching a look of surprise in his eyes. "I don't know, but I do have to be in Washington for a committee meeting on Monday afternoon," she heard a voice say and realized that it was her own. She had an apartment in D.C. so packing was not an issue.

"You can fly down with us. They're providing a military plane for us at Bradley Airbase," offered Nancy.

"Mother, Senator Polowski is a very busy woman. We shouldn't impose on her," was Jim's feeble attempt to provide Sharon with an excuse for not accepting the invitation.

Sharon was the daughter that Nancy wished she had and she still had hope.

"No, it's all right. I would need to fly down tomorrow night anyway," again that voice! Where was it coming from? "And I had wanted to discuss a House Bill with you Jim, if you have the time?"

"Mother, you're holding up the line," declared Jonathan as he stood next to Jim not wanting to watch this drama unfold any further.

"Okay Sharon, I'll make time," responded Jim, uncertain as to the subject of the meeting and feeling uncomfortable discussing it.

The flight to Washington's Dulles Airport took only an hour. The military plane was a converted 727 commercial jet with seating typical of that model. Jim, Jonathan and their mother sat together in the first-class section.

"I'm happy that Sharon is able to join us, aren't you, Jim," asked his Mother.

"I don't know, but don't think it's going to affect our relationship. She's getting married in a few months and she doesn't need this game playing."

"What game playing? She's a family friend and one that I cherish. Your father was actually starting to appreciate her in those last months. He often asked about her. Did you know she came to the visit last summer and spent some time with him? They seemed to laugh a lot and she was very caring."

"No, I didn't know. We haven't had much contact for a while," Jim responded, surprised that they would have even have spoken.

"Well there's a lot you don't know, son, and you won't understand until you open up your heart," his mom spoke as she did when he was but a boy, placing a comforting hand on his and looking into his eyes and into his heart.

Jim looked over his shoulder to the rear of the plane where Sharon sat with Connecticut dignitaries who chose to complete the journey with their good friend Colonel Buckman. She was in a conversation with General Obersham. She caught his glance and looked up with a somber smile on her lips and a nod of her head. He smiled back as he had before when his attention was acknowledged by her incredible instincts.

The pomp and circumstance of a military burial was even grander for a ranking officer. As a Colonel, James Buckman Jr. was afforded a horse drawn caisson for his casket, with a rider-less horse following. The flag that covered his casket was appropriate, for he was patriot and a war hero who did his duty and did it effectively and without recognition. The captain of the honor guard presented the triangularly folded flag to Mrs. Buckman, who accepted it without emotion. The sound of taps echoed in the distance as they said their final goodbyes with the sun setting over the canopy of trees. General Bert Obersham brought his hand to a salute to his closest friend and comrade in arms as Jim's casket was lowered into his final resting place, a tear visible in the general's eye as the rifle salute echoed through the cemetery.

A reception was held at the Arlington Country Club so that the many guests from Connecticut and Washington could have dinner and complete their lengthy day in honor of the Colonel. Jonathan introduced Thomas Masters to his mother as a close friend and colleague of his father's. "Your husband was a fine man and a good friend. We will miss him," offered Masters. "But I know that Jonathan will carry on his legacy."

"Thank you for coming, Mr. Masters, and for sharing in this tribute to my husband. I'm sure that Jim would be pleased that his many friends and associates are here to honor him."

Nancy insisted on Sharon sharing their table, arranging for her to be seated next to Jim. Jonathan was seated on Nancy's opposite side, a tactic designed to limit conversation between him and his brother, which was always a good thing to avoid.

The evening continued with casual talk and an occasional laugh, that is often a part of an otherwise solemn funeral process. Most of the laughter resulted from Bert Obersham's many humorous stories about his forty-plus years of serving with, and being a friend of, the deceased guest of honor. He told with vigor how Jim was so adept at speaking French while behind enemy lines in Vichy France that even Bert wondered if he was on our side. He left out the part about them blowing up the family home of a French sympathizing family that gave them cover in order to kill the fourteen German officers who were living there, the day before the Invasion of Normandy. That would have spoiled the humor and the dinner.

"So Jim, are you available for dinner tomorrow?" asked Sharon before dessert was served. "I want to go over the Senate's response to one of your House bills."

Nancy caught the gist of the conversation and could not restrain her smile as she looked away to one of the other guests.

"Well, I'm not sure whether mother is going to need me but..."

Before he could finish his Mother commented, "We're fine, Jim! Jonathan and I are going to have dinner with the general and his wife."

"Then it's settled, you can pick me up at six. Is that all right?" asked Sharon, still not comfortable with her actions.

"I guess its okay. Are you sure that you don't want me to join you, Mother? We can work around it."

"I'm sure!"

"Well, six o'clock then. I have to go now and work on a bill to keep Reagan from selling the White House," she commented facetiously hoping that she hadn't offended any of his supporters too seriously.

Jim had a sleepless night. He had just buried his father and yet all he could think about was his dinner meeting with Sharon. "What is this all about? Is mother behind it, doesn't she realize that Sharon is in love and about to be married? Maybe it's all innocent? We shouldn't be avoiding each other. We're both legislators and mature adults. It's time to get over it. That must be it, she wants to clear the air and be friends again."

Jim spent the morning at his office going over the bills being processed out of committees. He tried to anticipate the concerns of Senator Polowski. He wanted to know if this meeting was about legislative cooperation. Normally he would rely on staff to give him a briefing on issues. He often sought their advice since they were of like mind politically. He didn't have right wingers on his staff. He required a moderate mindset and a pragmatic approach to problems. He tended towards those with a somewhat independent, yet moderate thought process for his staff.

As he studied the language of several tax initiatives he became aware of a pattern. There was a give and take in every bill, the take was often much larger than the give and in the end the Democrats were selling out their constituents for a few crumbs off the table. They had been duly intimidated by the "Great Communicator." Reagan developed a style that would encourage whatever he could get from the Democrat controlled House, and have it seriously modified in the Republican controlled Senate. For those Democrats not sufficiently intimidated by his popularity he would use the traditional political technique of promising defense contracts and special projects for their districts to attain the favorable vote. The only thing unusual about the process was that the concessions made were often short-sighted and not always in their constituents best interest.

At 5:15 pm he took a cab to Sharon's apartment. He had made reservations for 6:00 at the Roof Terrace atop the Kennedy Center, overlooking the Potomac River. He had called her before he left the office so that she would be waiting in the lobby of her building. He had this phobia about knocking on the door of her apartment.

She walked out the building before he reached the lobby door. As usual she looked radiant and confident as a person of her stature and professional credentials should. Jim didn't know it at the time but she had been waiting there since he called, not wanting to "mess up" as she had when they had their last real date in D.C.

"How was your day? You must be exhausted from the week's events. I'm truly sorry for your loss, Jim," commented Sharon as they were driven to the Terrace.

"I know you are, and I sincerely appreciate that. Mother told me about your visit and how you got to know father better.

I wish that I had been a fly on the wall. It must have been an interesting conversation."

"I was traveling through Connecticut and your mother invited me for dinner, but I was surprised and happy that he wanted to chat with me in his library. It wasn't much about politics. It was more about you and the family. He was very anxious about what would happen when he was gone. It was tearful for me, but he made sure it was also very light. He had a great sense of humor. We laughed a lot."

"About what? I've never known him to be that humorous."

"Mostly about you and your childhood escapades and how he had to be stern with his sons because it was tough world out there. How you were always in a mess that he had to bail you out of, and how Jonathan at sixteen tried to impress his girlfriend by taking his Rolls Royce to a drive-in. He said he had to act like a stern father, but that he and your mother didn't want you to know that they thought you were just typical boys and that they enjoyed those humorous moments. We laughed, but he was serious about his fear of not being here to guide you and Jonathan, especially Jonathan, and to take care of your mother. He even likened me to your mother. He said there must be something about Buckman men and bleeding- heart women."

"I realize that he was apprehensive about Jonathan running the family businesses and so does Jonathan, but I don't want to be involved in that drama."

"He knew that too, but was hoping that you would find a way to participate for your mother's sake. He was afraid there would be a serious recession because of Reagan's economic agenda and that the family would lose everything he worked for."

"He came to my office over a year ago with Jonathan to ask me to help him defeat Reagan's economic policy agenda, especially the tax cuts for people like him. I didn't understand then, but I see what Reagan is doing and to tell the truth, I am very disappointed. I think dad was right."

"The Kennedy Center!" announced the cab driver as he pulled to the curb.

"No traffic, we're twenty minutes early. Let's have a drink in the bar," suggested Jim as they made their way to the elevators.

Jim could not believe how comfortable he was with her. He wondered if she felt the same. He also wondered if she was on a mission out of respect for his father and his mother, to bring him back into the hierarchy of the family business.

Their table was ready by the window overlooking the Potomac. The view was of the orange ball of sun setting over the D.C. skyline. They decided to take time for a glass of cabernet and continue their discussion at their table before ordering dinner.

"I'm trying to have some kind of an impact on this runaway train called Reaganomics. Each success makes the Republican Senate bolder. There's now talk of taxing Social Security payments. Most of the people on Social Security are hardly in a position to pay their bills never mind pay more by being taxed for their benefits."

"I hadn't heard that. How can you tax a benefit that is, in effect, payment of an insurance annuity?" It hadn't come to the floor of the House yet.

"There's talk of it being presented as an amendment to the Social Security Act in the next session. It's an attempt to ride the momentum of the *Great Communicator's* popularity. They truly believe they have the American people where they want them, focused on religious issues and not aware enough to understand that they are being raped."

"Well, that might be a little harsh, but I understand where you're coming from, and I see why you and father may have been in agreement on that issue. He expressed similar thoughts about such issues to me that day in my office."

Their discussion was interrupted by the presence of the waiter. They ordered dinner and continued their conversation.

"Do you know that your brother has been conspiring with your father's so-called Washington Action Group to support their self-serving agenda? Your father said that his friend, General Obersham, told him that Jonathan has pledged millions to the party to help assure Reagan's re-election. Your father said he believed that it will finance the downfall of our American way of life. He told me that if Reagan gets re-elected there will be a serious recession by the time he leaves office in 1988. He said that it's because he's spending money that he doesn't have since the taxes of his friends who can afford to pay have been cut in half."

"Why didn't he stop him? Jonathan was a wimp when it came to his fear of dad. He was always afraid that he would strike him out of his will."

"He tried to influence him, but he was too weak to watch over his antics. He said that he reluctantly subordinated his power to him so that the businesses could still operate. He didn't realize how aggressive he would become."

"And what do you think I should do? I don't want any part of that business or of my brother's arrogance. Those business enterprises are doomed because it would take the ingenuity and power of my Father to keep all the dirt under the rug."

"Yes, I figured that out from what he told me. He said that he couldn't sell the enterprises or go public because those actions wouldn't survive the scrutiny of due diligence. He wanted you to take them over and clean them up and then sell them off."

"He told you that?"

"Yes, he called me last month. Neither your mother or Jonathan was to know. He asked me to tell you that, if anything happened to him."

"Why would he do that? Why not tell me himself or have Bert tell me?"

"He said that I was the only one who could influence you."

"He said that, to you? Why did he think that?"

"Because he said..." as she looked him in his confused eyes. "Because he believed that you still loved me... and that I still loved you!" her eyes dropped as they welled up with the words. She had promised herself that she wouldn't show that emotion."

"And, what did you say?" he asked in a low and somber voice, fearing the answer.

"I said that... he was right, I do still love you!"

"But Sharon, you mean as a friend. You're getting married to a fine man in few months." He said the words quietly, although he realized that she had opened the door and he was closing it again.

"And how do you feel, do you want me to marry Tim? ...Do you still love me, Jim?"

Jim paused and took her hand in his. "If I could reverse time, I would never have left you, but how can I justify loving you when I treated you so badly? I forfeited my right to have you love me and I've regretted it every day since."

"Is that a yes?" A weak smile pursed her lips.

"Jim felt lightness in his heart and said, "Yes, I still love you and no, I wish that you were marrying me and not Tim...but what about Tim?"

"I wouldn't be true to him if I still loved you. He realized that there was something wrong that night we saw each other at the Inauguration Ball and has asked me if I'm sure almost every day. We finally discussed it and he wants me to be sure. You're right, he is a very fine man and I don't want to hurt him, but then marrying the wrong person would be a real tragedy for the three of us."

"Are you sure that this is what you want?" asked Jim, still in shock at the events of the evening and that it took his father's intuitive sense to bring them together for life.

"Yes, but are you?"

Jim met her lips across the narrow table as the patrons sitting nearby applauded their renewed and very public expression of love. Their waiter, burdened with the dinner tray, was startled by the applause. He smiled thinking that it was for him, giving a nod in response.

They settled back in their chairs, embarrassed by the attention they had aroused.

"Here's to our life together," declared Jim, his glass of cabernet meeting hers at mid table, the waiter standing stunned beside them, the tray of entrees still held upon his shoulders.

Realizing the importance of the scene he was witnessing as he began serving their dinners the waiter looked to Jim, "This is an occasion to be celebrated with a Champagne toast monsieur?"

Sharon looked to Jim for his confirmation. "Are you proposing, Mr. Buckman?"

"I'm not as prepared as I would want to be, but we've waited long enough, Sharon ...will you marry me?" Jim's expression was one of anticipation, but not necessarily of confidence.

"You are right, Mr. Buckman, we have waited long enough," Sharon paused and looked down without a sign of excitement, then her eyes met his and she declared, "Yes, I'll marry you, Jim!" Sharon's smile countered the effect of her tearful eyes.

This time the applause was led by their waiter as many of the guests of their impromptu party raised their glasses of whatever they were drinking to toast the moment.

That night at Jim's Washington apartment he gave her the ring he had planned to give her ten years earlier on his trip back from Vietnam. "I had hoped this day would happen many years ago, but I let my pride and my ego get in the way of our destiny."

"I believe there's a reason for everything and maybe we weren't ready then to give our love freely. It's beautiful Jim, and since you kept it all these years it tells me that you never really let me go."

Chapter 87

Nancy Buckman was thrilled at the news that her son had finally realized that Sharon was the woman who was destined to share his life. She arranged to give them an intimate engagement party at her home in Westport. She needed to experience some joy in her life after her loss of the only man she ever loved. She invited Mrs. Polowski, the Benedetto's and the Martinez families for a weekend in July.

She knew that Jim and Jonathan were in a strained relationship, but hoped this might help bring them together. Her husband had left her and her two sons equal shares of his estate, including the businesses. This meant that she had one third of the businesses and related properties. She had full ownership of the Westport home and their winter home in Naples, Florida.

Each brother had a one-third share of the business enterprises, which caused Jonathan serious anxiety. If his mother sided with Jim on any issue it would weaken his hold on the business. He would meet with Jim before the party and determine his intentions.

They met at Jonathan's downtown Westport office. "Jim, I know you don't want any part of this business, but that you may feel obligated to the family to participate."

"You're right, brother, but I'm in a bit of a quandary. Dad wanted me to work with you to clean up and develop a less precarious operation. I'm aware of some of the things that he did to grow the business and that he worried about whether that business plan would be viable when he was not here to monitor its effectiveness."

"I know how he felt about my competence, but I've nearly doubled our portfolio and our profits in the last seven years and I'm not about to give up what I've accomplished."

"Dad knew you were competent or he wouldn't have trusted you with the family's future, but he was fearful of the higher level of scrutiny that increased visibility would bring. He was an expert at being covert and of developing strategies to get what he believed he needed. He was anxious about being too arrogant or brash, or of making enemies."

"So he thought I was arrogant and brash! Well he was making enemies with most of his friends before he died. He had Tom Masters and his Washington friends planning his demise. He may have cheated them out of some of their goals, but don't think that they're not thrilled that he's gone!" exclaimed Jonathan out of anger and frustration.

"Are they now your friends, Jonathan? Do you think they give a damn about you? Dad had them pegged from the start and he used them for his purposes until he saw that their success was creating serious problems in the economic balance of this country. Masters is a devious, egotistical and selfish individual. He has no family. He plays the game for the sake of power and control."

Jonathan got out of his chair and from behind his oversized mahogany desk and confronted his brother, fingers pointing, voice cracking, "What do you think, I'm some naïve kid? I know what he's about, and like dad I can use him to our benefit as well! You're not the only one in this family with intelligence. You barely made it through Yale. Do you think that because you're a war hero and a Congressman you're better than me? You've been so badly whipped by that liberal bitch you think we need to save humanity, even in its lowest form...."

Before he spoke the next word Jim rose from his chair and lifted him pinning him against the wall as he did when they were kids. "Listen, you half-witted asshole, this is between you and me, don't play the insult game with me or you'll be seeing how what you call the lowest form of life lives. I don't want your job, but I will not allow you to wreck what Father worked so hard to create." Jim lowered him to the floor and threw him towards the leather sofa.

"Ok war hero, so you're stronger than me, but we're not through. You're going to wish you never did that, I promise you."

Jim looked at the pathetic figure, his tie to the side, clothes ruffled and his red face flushed with anger. "The only promise I have for you, brother, is that if you misstep I'll be all over you and between mother and me, and our two thirds ownership, you'll be working in a teller's cage in the Bronx," Jim grabbed his brief case and started for the door.

"We'll see about that big brother. We'll see about that!"

Jonathan was noticeably missing from the weekend engagement party. Nancy announced that he had been called to Washington on business and sent his regrets. Jim knew that Jonathan would have reason to regret if he was in Washington for the wrong reason. Sharon looked at him with concern having been told the story of their meeting. Her response was succinct but supportive.

"Jim I appreciate that you want to defend my honor, but his attitude is not my concern. He's a very troubled guy and he can only add grief to you and your mother's life. I'll support you if you decide that you need to play a bigger role in your family's business for your mother's sake, but you may have to decide on whether you want to continue your political career."

"I don't know what I want, but I know what I don't want." I don't want to deal with Jonathan's attitude."

After dinner Jim asked his two Army buddies, to join him on the terrace overlooking the pool.

He explained his dilemma. "What do you think guys? What would you do in my place?"

"I'd do him in, Jim. He's trouble and he'll always be trouble," answered Diego. "You should take over while there's still something left to take over."

"That won't end the conflict, and I don't want him controlling my life by antagonizing me or my family," answered Jim. "Tony, you're being unusually quiet. Don't you have any advice for me?"

"I'm confused. You're a Congressman with a job to do, a job you wanted to do. Can you still do that job and be the kind of guy that you wanted to be when you decided to run for office? I don't know, Jim. Why not let him have the business? Let him buy you and your mother out and move on," suggested Tony.

"How do I do that? What if he messes up? He may incriminate the family and my father's memory. Mother would be devastated."

"And what if he messes up while you're involved? How is that better?" responded Tony.

"Tony's right, Jim, your brother's a loose cannon and your father knew that. You told us that your father asked Sharon to influence you into taking over the business, but he was desperate, he knew he was dying. He didn't think it through! You need to do what's good for you and Sharon. Your mom will be okay."

"I guess it comes down to whether or not you're going to run for a second term?" commented Tony. "I don't think that you can do both!"

As he contemplated his future Jim realized his hopes for a moderate Republican response to the country's needs were fading with the right wing takeover of the party. The pendulum had swung too far to the right and he was ashamed of his family's role in the process. The Reagan administration managed to get the House to pass the Amendment to the Social Security Act, to tax the monies paid to the retired elderly who paid into the program with their tax money for more than forty years.

Sharon made a valiant attempt to thwart the passage of the tax on the benefits received by Social Security recipients in her pleading to the Republican controlled Senate:

> "I'm sure that you are all aware that Social Security is the only means for a reasonable quality of life for the millions of retirees who paid into that program. Unfortunately, over the years it has been raided for funds to fight wars and to make up for revenue losses due to tax cuts. We have an obligation and a duty to protect that program and to assure the promise made when the hard working Americans who built this country were told that they would have some basic where-with-all to survive in their retired years. To take money from those who earned its benefits by taxing those benefits

is not only wrong, it's dishonest. This program is, in effect, an insurance policy that working people paid for. It promised to pay, what was effectively, an annuity when one retired. Taxing that earned benefit at any level is not only an abuse of process, it is an abuse of those who believed in that promise! It is up to this body to defeat the attempt to further impact the lives of senior members of our society by defeating this Bill."

Sharon's plea fell on deaf ears, some of which were belonged to her own party who sold out their senior citizens for some other perceived benefit. The Republicans voted as a block, defeating any potential for a display of conscience. Their reasoning was that the Social Security program needed more money, so why not get it from those who benefit by it. They wouldn't acknowledge the fact that it was the tax cuts for the wealthy, the cost of poorly conceived wars, the limit on the income taxed for the funding of the program and the raiding of those funds that were the cause of the shortfall and not the benefits paid to its lawful participants. Sharon wondered whether she would ever make a difference as a United States Senator, but she wasn't about to stop trying.

Chapter 88

The popularity of President Reagan had emboldened his supporters. It seemed he could do no wrong. His detractors labeled him the "Teflon President," since unlike Carter nothing negative seemed to stick to him.

The Washington Action Group or WAG, as James Buckman Jr. had called them, saw Reagan's presence in the Oval Office as an opportunity to push the envelope until it bulged with the excesses that they had pursued for more than twenty years. The loss of Buckman senior was looked upon as a benefit by his colleagues due to his mellowing on issues of financial dominance and self-interest, but Jonathan Buckman assured them he was devoted to their cause and would work to promote their strategies and programs.

The death of his father left Jonathan in, what he believed, to be control of the family's assets, until the confrontation with his brother suggested otherwise. He needed to strike a deal with Bulldog Masters and his associates quickly before his brother could respond. He decided it would be best to meet with Masters privately, knowing that his Father and Brother had the allegiance of Bert Obersham, a member of the Group.

"Jonathan, I'm glad that you called. It's a good idea that we meet like this so we can talk straight and find a way to continue our relationship with the Buckman family," stated Tom Masters, the now unopposed leader of Group.

"Tom, thanks for meeting me on such short notice, but I wanted to make sure that we're on the same page going forward. As you know, my brother James is a much more moderate Republican than my father was. In fact, he is engaged to Senator Sharon Polowski, a very liberal Democrat. I want to make sure that his misguided ideology does not get in the way of our family's business or of the Group's work."

"I can appreciate your concerns. As you know, we were feeling that liberal pressure from your dad. Don't get me wrong, he was a wonderful man and a key figure in our Group. He understood that we need to protect our position of leadership in the political atmosphere of the party, but he seemed to be mellowing the last couple of years."

"Yes, I believe James and my mother had a lot to do with that. They're both more into social causes than my Father or me. That's why it's important for me to act as swiftly as possible to offset their impact on Buckman Enterprises."

"What do you mean? Do you think your Brother will attempt to control the businesses? He would have to leave Congress."

"Six months ago I would have said that there was little chance of that happening, but I'm no longer sure. He has threatened to do that if I don't do things his way. Between him and my mother they own two thirds of the business now that Father has died."

"So what can I do to help you? Who are your directors? Can you stop them there, at least for the near future?"

"That's unlikely since the board of directors consists of the two of them and Bert Obersham, and I doubt that I have any influence with the General."

"I think you're correct in that assumption. Bert was very close to your father and I believe his relationship with your brother is almost as strong since Vietnam. So what's the bottom line, Jonathan? What do you need from my Group?"

Jonathan responded aware of the implication that it was now Masters' Group. "I want to be able to buy them out of the businesses and I need you to help me arrange a loan with Donald Peters and his Continental Trust Corporation, to purchase their shares. Don's in the Group and has the same goals you and I have. I think he might be interested."

"What kind of money are we talking about? As you well know, bankers are tough to deal with right now. They want a lot of protection for the use of their money."

"Buckman Enterprises' consolidated holdings and physical assets are valued at about $140 million. I'm familiar with the banking industry's dilemma in this economic climate, since 50% of our assets are related to our banking business, but I can't finance this buyout with loans from our bank. It wouldn't survive the scrutiny of the State's banking commission."

"I believe you're right, but maybe we can figure something out between us. Let me think it over. I'll talk to Peters and we can meet again next week, here at my office. Is that okay with you?"

"Yes, and I thank you for your interest and your continuing efforts. I'm sure they would rather pursue their life without the burden of the business, and I doubt Jim wants to give up his political aspirations."

Once Jonathan had left the office, Masters placed a call to his good friend Don Peters.

"Don, this is Tom, I have an interesting proposition for you. Can you be in Washington on Thursday?"

"Yes, of course Tom, but won't it wait until our next meeting?"

"Not if we want to *strike while the iron is hot*." A grin came across his face that was perceivable through the tone in his voice.

"All right Tom, I'll be there. Is Thursday evening at 7:00 pm for dinner at the Club okay?"

"I'll see you then. And Don this could be big! Keep it confidential, even from the Group."

"Sounds interesting. I hope it's legal," Peters exclaimed with a chuckle. "You're not going to try to raise the price of oil another 100% are you?

"No, not yet at least. Let's just say I'm considering a final tribute to our fallen leader, Jim Buckman!" the smile on his face grew with the expectation.

Masters had a plan he believed would result in control of Buckman Enterprises. He recognized that the antagonistic relationship between the brothers Buckman exposed them, particularly Jonathan, to be careless in the anticipation of ending their business partnership. He needed to think about this potential windfall.

Don Peters arrived on time for his dinner meeting with Masters. "Tom, how have you been? You seemed excited when we spoke. This must be good!"

"I'm fine, and yes, it could be very good if it is presented properly," said Masters. He told Peters about his impromptu meeting with Jonathan earlier in the week. "This guy is so anxious to get his brother out of his hair that he is ready to be taken."

"Well, from what I've seen of him he's the typical black sheep in a family of achievers. It was obvious that he was trying to upstage his father at our meetings. I'm surprised Jim didn't slap him on the side of the head," smirked Peters. "But how do we benefit? I wouldn't be anxious to lend him my car never mind millions of dollars."

"My plan centers on his ownership of the Buckman banks. He has over 40 branches and they are all doing well. But it is how they got to be so prosperous and expansive that is their weakness."

"What do you mean? You have dirt on their operation?" asked Peters his interest suddenly perked.

"About a year ago I hired a detective who specializes in bank fraud to investigate their banking businesses in anticipation of Buckman's illness being terminal. Although what he found was not unusual in this day of loose regulatory enforcement, it was illegal. A certain percentage of their funds have been lent to offshore development corporations they own under a variety of names. These corporations have more than $100 million invested in real estate projects throughout the east coast, from Maine to Florida."

"That's not surprising. We all have skeletons in our closets. Why would we want to get involved with theirs, especially given Jonathan's lack of business finesse and a brother that's an attorney and a Congressman?" asked a confused Peters.

"Don, that's exactly why this is such a good plan. They have too much at stake to allow for tight scrutiny of their improprieties. Young Jim has political aspirations that I don't believe will be satisfied by his current position and, most important, he's engaged to Senator Sharon Polowski, who has been a real pain in the ass to all of us."

"I'm still not getting it, Tom. Break it down for my banker's mentality. Why would we want to get into a deal that could become our downfall if the federal regulators figure it out?"

"Actually it's pretty simple. We'd lend Jonathan the money to buy out his brother and insist on him putting up his only real asset, one hundred percent of his ownership of Buckman Enterprises. Once the deal is complete we'll leak the regulatory improprieties to the feds and when they act, we'll call his note. He won't be able to pay and we'll foreclose on all of his assets with a promise to the feds to clean up the business. We'll sell the real estate as part of our negotiated deal with the Feds."

"It still sounds dangerous Tom and why would he agree to such a deal?"

"Well, I think you know the answer to that Don. He's desperate! If we can pull this off we'll have two thirds ownership in their assets with only the mother as a partner. We'll offer to buy her out at a significant discount, as a goodwill gesture once the feds step in. Plus we'll own all of their branches, some of which we'll close, but the remaining will become part of an east coast expansion of your Consolidated Trust Corporation, of which I will become a 40% owner," continued Masters.

"Well, I liked it up to that point Tom, but it seems that I'm taking all the risk and then I give away 40% of the gain?" responded Peters. "That's a tough sell to me and it will be impossible to my Board."

"If this is done properly you'll regain all your loan value with the sale of the real estate and still own the banks. You need to convince your Board that this is a good deal without revealing the nature of the real estate ownership. And you need to emphasis the value of the gained banking enterprises, but without revealing the integrity of their operations.

"And what about Jim Buckman and his mother and don't forget Senator Polowski?"

"I'll handle them. I'll convince them we weren't aware of the condition of the assets and because we had such respect for his dad and the family, we didn't do an exhaustive due diligence. Jonathan will become the goat, and given their strained relationship and Jim's propensity to protect his mother, they'll all fade away with the initial buyout being sufficient for Jim and our follow-up buyout adequate to take care of his mother.

I believe he'll look at it as good fortune and he'll be happy to keep him and Sharon a good distance from the action."

"Tom, I think that you're assuming a lot in your plan, but basically, I like it. It needs some refining. Let's both think about it and get back together on Monday."

"That reasonable, but we don't want to wait too long. I don't want Jim to step into the picture as Jonathan tells me he is thinking of doing. I know that if he does he'll attempt to clean up the operation and kill our leverage," cautioned Masters.

"Doesn't he run for re-election in '86?" asked Peters.

"Yes, but if he decides to get involved with the family business he won't run. At least that's what Jonathan tells me. The potential for conflict wouldn't be something he'd want to deal with at this time in his career."

"That makes sense, but I remember his father's description of him. He said that Jim may not be as intellectual as his brother, but like his dad, he's a leader and a fighter. We need to be careful Tom. We can't afford to be naïve in this deal and think there will be no retaliation."

"I know, but the upside is worth the risk we could gain a $140 million of assets for less than 25% of their value and if Jim and his mother have been paid he'll be able to get on with his life without the burden of his brother or the family businesses. It's unlikely that he'll protest."

"I hope your right, Tom, but we need to firm up that upside and diminish the downside, like Jonathan's reaction? But first we need to see their books and to do some due diligence. Can we get ninety days for that effort?

"That won't be a problem. I'll take care of Jonathan. We'll get him on the hook and reel him in with a 'partnership' deal. We'll make him feel he's important. Play to his pride! That will keep him under control. In time he'll think of me as a *father figure*. He'll feel guilty for not disclosing the vulnerabilities that we're forced to defend and he'll believe he owes us for helping him out of the mess. But then again, he might go to jail," offered Masters with a smile.

"Obviously you've given this a lot of thought, Tom, but is it worth the effort? What if we can't rescue the banks?" asked Peters.

"Remember we're only loaning him the money to buy-out young Jim. Once Jim's out we'll make sure that he can't comply with the terms of the loan and then we will pick up the remaining pieces for pennies and restructure them into our operation. I'll call him and tell him we have a serious interest in financing the buyout of his brother and I'll ask him to provide the financial information."

Chapter 89

Faced with a decision to give up his seat in Congress or become deeply involved with the family businesses, Jim Buckman decided it was time to gather his thoughts. Since his brother offered to buy him out of his shares he managed to stall him for weeks before he would make a decision. But he knew he must make that decision soon. He thought of the benefits. He would no longer be concerned about the business and could remain in politics. But there was a downside. His mother would still be exposed to potential liabilities if she participated in any way, even as a director.

"Sharon, how about getting away this week?" It was mid-January 1985. It had been four months since that night at the Roof Terrace. It was just two months after the presidential elections and Jim's successful attempt at his second term in Congress.

Reagan's popularity carried him to a landslide victory. With 97.6% of the Electoral College vote Reagan had a mandate that would prove to be unstoppable in his quest to restructure the American economy for the benefit of the few.

As a United States Senator, Sharon was in the fifth year of a six-year term and wouldn't have to face re-election until 1986. The forefathers, in writing the Constitution, believed that the staggering of the terms for Representatives and Senators in Congress was a way to stimulate continuity of process and to balance the effects of legislative branches and executive power. The four-year term of the President was an integral part of that plan.

"Where would we go? We have the President's State of the Union Address next week. Do you think it would be wise not to be there?" asked Sharon.

"We can watch it on TV. I was thinking about the family retreat in Vermont. I just need some time away from the crowd to make some decisions. It's all your fault, because of your undue influence on me and my father's obvious manipulations, I'm now in the middle of a midlife crisis!" he exclaimed with a smile on his previously stern face.

"Maybe you should go alone, not that I don't want to be with you, but you might need to be isolated from outside influences, especially those that are as powerful as mine," she offered as she got close enough to plant a loving kiss.

"Seriously, after dealing with Jonathan and listening to his ambitions for the businesses I'm worried, but I don't think I'm ready to leave the Congress."

"I don't know what to say, Jim, but this is a decision that you have to make without my influence. I delivered the message your father asked me to, but I'm also torn as to what's right for you. I think it's best for you to think it out alone."

"That place can be very lonely when I'm there with only my thoughts. I need your intuitive wisdom and counsel. Besides, we could ski and drink hot chocolate in front of a roaring fire," pleaded Jim, "and you need a break too."

"I would love to go. But I don't see how it'll help you make a decision that may change your life, and I have several high level meetings next week. Why don't you and Jonathan go and talk this thing out like mature adults and without the animosities of your misspent youths?" offered Sharon in her distinctively sassy way.

"You're right! It'll change both our lives, but do you think I'm the cause of his selfish and devious animosity?"

"No, but I have faith in your ability to resolve the issues that are interfering with the lives of all of us. As long as this chasm exists within your family it will affect all of our lives!"

Chapter 90

Jonathan Buckman's greed and insecurity were intended to be played like a classical concert led by Thomas "Bulldog" Masters. As the plan unfolded, it was apparent that the senior Buckman had created a maze of financial interactions that would take years to uncover. And, much to Master's and Peter's concern, that discovery would take down political operatives, financial institutions and companies.

"Tom, I don't think that this is going to be as easy as we anticipated. If we attempt to pull the plug on this guy we could go down the drain with him. The old man's investments in our companies were routed through his off-shore operations in a way that makes it look like we were a party to the illegal transactions," lamented Peters. "I think we may have underestimated his ingenuity."

"It's apparent from reviewing this material that all of the Washington Action Group members are tainted by the manner in which he either lent or invested money into their operations. The bastard must be grinning down on us. What were our attorneys doing while this was going on?" added Masters.

"Obviously, they were busy making money and I'll bet that not all of it came from us," commented Peters. "Jim knew when to strike. He waited until we were in need of a quick and easy deal for cash and he made it happen."

"Okay, so what do we do now? I still think that Jonathan has made them vulnerable and I doubt that he fully understands the strategies that his father implemented to protect their interests. He's a numbers guy who thinks he has his father's intelligence, but he hasn't got a clue," said Masters. "But his brother's a strategist and an attorney. He might be able to figure it out. We need to act now before he has a chance to understand how his father has tied us all up in a knot that would unravel into questions of conspiracy, money laundering and bribery by the feds."

"But what if the threat of criminal action doesn't scare Jonathan into giving up his shares after we finance the buyout of his brother?" asked a confused Peters.

"Don, the only way we can protect our interest is to gain control of that operation before his stupidity brings us all down!" declared Masters. "Now we know we have no other choice. In fact, we may have to loan Jonathan enough to overpay Jim for his brother's shares to make this plan work. The more money we lend under tight terms the less chance he'll be able to pay it back. Let's bring him in here next week!"

Chapter 91

After sleeping on it Jim Buckman decided to take Sharon's advice and invite Jonathan to join him at the family's retreat in Vermont. Jonathan accepted the offer. He was excited after meeting with Masters and Peters. They proposed to lend him up to $25 million to buy out his brother's shares of the family business, but cautioned him that he should not offer that initially. "Obviously the less you pay the more profit you can make," advised his new best friend, Tom Masters.

The terms of the loan were attractive to Jonathan; quarterly payments of interest-only for five years and then a balloon payment of the balance at the end of the fifth year. Jonathan had confidence in his ability to make money, especially if there was no interference from his brother. He was anxious to meet with Jim and thought the idea of going to the retreat was a good one. He would tolerate his big brother for the time it took to secure his shares.

Jim arrived early in the morning and took some time to think about the impending meeting, hoping it wouldn't become an encounter. He remembered their numerous confrontations when they were teenagers. He smiled when he thought about the night he snuck out of the house to meet a girl from across town. Jonathan went to their dad and said that he couldn't find James, knowing that he had taken his dirt bike cross country to meet her at the lake. He was grounded for a month but Jonathan paid dearly when Jim planted a Playboy magazine in the 12-year-olds underwear drawer. It was found by his mom and he was treated like a sex deviate for months. But the worst of it was that he had to bear the brunt of a detailed "birds and bees" lecture from his dad. It was, of course, the classic sibling rivalry that grew in intensity as they grew physically. Jim's heroic actions in Vietnam only added to the stress of their relationship.

Jonathan drove up in his Cadillac SUV in time for lunch. "How was the drive?" asked Jim as he walked up to his younger brother's car.

"Not bad, there was some construction on 91, but it was fine," answered Jonathan in his most cordial tone. He was not going to spoil the plan by getting into a conflict with Jim. He would show a level of maturity that would take Jim by surprise and, hopefully, win him over.

"Do you still like your steak well done? They've been marinating all morning," asked Jim. As they walked to the cabin, "I used Johnny Walker for the marinade."

"I'm good at medium-rare since I became a risk taker," joked Jonathan. "How's everything going for you and how's Sharon doing?" as Jonathan continued the folksy conversation.

"Everything is going well. Sharon is starting to make headway in converting the Senate to her liberal ways. We don't always vote alike, but I understand the reasons for her decisions. She believes that Reagan is just a spokesman for the wealthy and she thinks she's the last line of defense before the middle class disappears."

Jonathan knew that he had to be careful when discussing his brother's love. "Well, she's obviously a very intelligent woman, but so far Reagan's a popular President and he's doing good things for people like us who have worked hard to build this country.

"Sharon has a different view. She thinks we're in for a serious recession because of his economic policies, but how is the business doing?"

"It's doing well. It can be very frustrating keeping up with the markets and the changes in the economy, but Reagan is spending money on defense and that creates jobs and jobs create profits. That brings me to why we are here."

"Well, Jonathan, you asked if I was willing to sell out my shares of Buckman Enterprises to you and I told you that I had some interest. Since father died having the ownership of a large and complex business has been a potential problem to my political career. I know he wanted both of us to stay with the business, but I have my reservations."

Jonathan was encouraged by Jim's words. "I know you're torn because of his wishes, but you have your own life to live and it might not involve the world of business. I've always been the nerd in the family and I enjoy the business world," he said as he received his steak from Chef James.

"So what do you have for me, brother? How can you buy me and mother out? Where would you get that kind of money and most important, what do you want to drink, beer or wine?" joked Jim to lighten the discussion.

"The steak is perfect! It must be the Johnny Walker. I'll go for a beer. Wine might put me to sleep," said Jonathan. "I've been working on this deal for months knowing you want to make a decision before the next election, having won your second term. I've secured a loan I believe will provide you with a reasonable buyout."

"And what about mother's interest? Does she want to stay in the business?"

"I assume she'll want to stay as a shareholder. I haven't asked, but I doubt I would be able to raise enough money to buy both of you out."

"What kind of a loan have you negotiated and with whom? Are you sure the business operations can survive its impact?" asked Jim.

Jonathan felt the stress beginning at the back of his neck. He knew that Jim had little respect for the Washington Action Group, especially Masters, believing him to be devious and arrogant. He decided to divert Jim's attention by making the initial offer. "Jim, I'm willing to offer you $18 million for your shares so that you will be free to pursue your political career."

"Well it sounds like a good number, but I'll have to see some financial information. Did you bring the books so that we can go over them?"

"I did bring our consolidated financials," Jonathan stated as he opened his briefcase and handed Jim a copy. "As you know, we're a multi-level business involved in real estate, banking and corporate investments. The banking operation has grown steadily over the last five years and it's doing more than $30 million in profits, but it's still expanding. We're currently opening branches in New York, which will absorb some of that profit. Real estate seems to be doing well, but state regulations have held up one of our major projects, the condominiums in Connecticut. Corporate investments are up and down. Dad had us into defense contracts and Reagan is spending heavily in that area."

"It looks like you're already highly leveraged. Are you sure this can work for you? What if the economy tanks for a year or two, like it did in the mid-seventies? How will you service the debt?" asked Jim, displaying the kind of insight that Jonathan feared could kill the deal.

"Jim, I'd pay you the full amount up front. If the business has tough times in the future it will be my problem and I have confidence that I can make this work."

"But what about mother's interest? Her whole life depends on the viability of Buckman Enterprises. Have you even discussed this with her?" asked Jim with concern for the way this negotiation was going. "I don't, as yet, have a feeling for the buyout figure but I'm very concerned about mother's future, and Jonathan, do you have partners involved in this deal?"

Believing that his older brother was talking down to him Jonathan's composure cracked. "Why do you ask? Don't you think I can do this on my own? "I've been running the operation for you and mother's benefit for more than a year!" realizing that he was "losing it" he paused, catching himself before it was too late and apologized. "I'm sorry Jim. I guess I'm just a bit tired from the trip. I share your concern for mother and I'll make sure she'll benefit and prosper."

"It's okay Jonathan. I know you have her best interest at heart. I just worry about the economy and whether the businesses will survive if we get into another recession. It wouldn't be fair to you if I get paid and leave you with all of the responsibility of making it work, and due to unforeseen circumstances, it doesn't work. But let's think about it. I want to study these numbers.

"I appreciate your concern, but I wouldn't take this on if I didn't think I could do it."

"Okay, well let's take a break this evening. I have tickets for a James Taylor concert in Stowe this evening. Remember when the family used to get together on the green to listen to folk music?"

"It sounds like fun. I have to make some calls. Is the house phone operational?

"Yes, it's kept alive in case we have an emergency. I'm going into Town to pick up some groceries for tomorrow. The stores will be closed when we go out later. You can just relax! I'll be a while. There's more beer in the cooler on the back porch. The refrigerator wasn't on when I arrived this morning."

"I'm going to take a walk around. I haven't been here for more than ten years. Everything looks the same but I'm seeing it from a different perspective. It's a beautiful place. Remember when dad would wake up early on a Sunday morning and make pancakes, eggs and bacon? It was usually a borderline disaster that mother had to rescue when she awoke to the smell of smoke from burning eggs and bacon, but it was always good for a laugh."

"Yes, but I also remember that we had to do the clean-up," added Jim. And I hated scraping the burnt eggs off the frying pans."

As he drove into Town, he thought about their discussion and hoped that their father didn't leave a bigger mess for him to cleanup!

After two days of informal negotiations about the potential for a buy-out of his shares Jim became concerned. He suspected, from Jonathan's avoidance of any discussion about his financiers, that Masters had something to do with this deal, and he grew more suspicious with every ambiguous statement his brother made regarding his backers.

Before they parted company, Jim confronted him with a direct question, "Jonathan, before I can even consider this deal I must know who your financial backers are. Is it Masters and his boys?"

Surprised at his brother's directness he responded, "Jim, I signed a confidentiality statement that I wouldn't disclose any information about the financial transaction. If I violate that I won't be able to secure the funds to buy you out."

"I think I know the answer to my question and I'm concerned for both you and mother being involved with those characters. You know father never trusted them? He wouldn't want you to rely on their business integrity and he'd be very upset if you put mother at risk."

"I appreciate that Jim, but I need to know within the next thirty days or I'll lose the opportunity to complete this deal."

"Well, I know how much this means to you so let me think about it. But I strongly advise you to seek other funding and don't worry, I won't disclose my assumptions publicly."

The long drive back home gave them each time to think and reflect on their time together. It had been many years since they actually had a mature conversation and Jim was thankful that they remained civilized. Jonathan, however, was disappointed. He couldn't understand how Jim could think about turning down such a lucrative deal that would both enrich him and allow him to pursue his career.

Jim decided to call Sharon on his newly installed hard-wired mobile phone. The Motorola Executive phone depended new technology which relied on the location of cell-phone towers, and they were few and far between, but he would give it a try. There was no service in the backwoods of Vermont but he hoped he could pick up a signal as he ventured down I-91.

After several attempts he heard her voice. "Hello, Sharon? Can you hear me?" he asked as she responded in kind.

"Jim? Can you hear me? Are you on that damn car phone? I told you that it was a waste of money. Are you okay? You didn't fight like children did you?

"No, we didn't fight. Actually it was the most civilized discussion we've ever had. Maybe he's grown up finally."

"Oh you think he's the one that has grown up? So what happened?"

"Well the good news is that he wants to pay me $18 million for my share of the business."

"And the bad news is?"

"Actually there are two levels of bad news. One, he's not planning to buy mother out of her interest and second; I believe that he's being financed by Masters and his devious colleagues."

"Hmm, that is disappointing, but why does it matter to you?"

The call faded and was then lost as he left the signal range of the last tower. He tried several times to reconnect without success.

Maybe she's right! Why do I care? I know that if he totally screws up I'll have enough money to take care of mother. Eighteen million dollars is a lot of money even after taxes, but with Masters involved, the dirt under the rug might be discovered and exploited. He wouldn't hesitate to ruin dad's reputation if there's some financial gain for him. His mind could not escape these thoughts as he pondered the ramifications of taking the money and leaving Jonathan to deal with the consequences.

His deep thoughts were interrupted by the unfamiliar ring of his new car phone.

"Hello, Jim? Are you there?" Sharon's voice was raised thinking that it would help the communication, but it did provide a pleasant diversion from his thoughts. "Why don't you stop at a gas station and use a real phone?" she joked, half seriously.

"Hold on! I'll pull off the highway so we can talk," answered Jim smiling at her frustration with modern technology.

"Maybe if you stand on the roof and hold the antenna above your head it might work," she said continuing her rant.

"Very funny my dear, just be patient. This is the future of communications. You don't want to be left behind in the dark ages, do you?"

"Hmm, let me think about that," contemplated Sharon. "Do you mean the Reagan years?"

Jim managed to find an area that allowed him to pull over to the side of the road and maintain his phone signal. He explained in detail what he believed the deal to be and why he was concerned.

"I hate to say it but I think that Jonathan is naïve and being used within some sinister plan by Masters' Group or worse, he may be a knowing participant in the plan. The business as a whole is worth a lot more than three times $18 million. But if he attempts to expand too quickly using that value as his leverage it could become devalued quickly. There are already signs of trouble in the savings and loan business."

"I hear you, and you're right there's talk of Senate investigations into poorly regulated bank practices. I was asked my opinion by the Chair of the Senate Finance Committee last week. There's a bank in Nevada and one in California that are under investigation," Sharon paused. "Is this phone line secure, Jim? I think we better wait until you're home to continue this discussion."

"Okay, but that just adds to my concerns. I'll see you in Washington tomorrow night. I'm going to stop by to see mother. She and I need to talk. I'll stay there tonight and call you later. Love you, bye!"

"That's a good idea. Please give her my love and I love you. Bye and be careful driving...and put that damn phone down!" she smiled as she said, "A man and his toys!"

By the time Jim reached his mother's home in Westport, he had decided that there was a better way to free himself from his relationship with the family businesses and protect his mother's interest.

He found his mother in the corner of the library, sitting in her husband's soft leather chair, his favorite place to read when not doing business behind his ominous looking African mahogany desk. She looked up surprised, but broke into a smile as her oldest son peeked in on her.

"James, what a pleasant surprise! I didn't hear you come in. Is everything all right?" she asked as she rose to give him a welcoming hug and kiss.

"Everything's fine, Mother. I was passing through on my way back to Washington and I wanted to see you, and I also thought we could discuss some matters having to do with the family enterprises," he said in an awkward introduction to his primary reason for the visit.

"Well, you're not running off are you? You're staying for dinner aren't you?

"Yes, I would like that. In fact I was hoping to stay tonight unless you have plans to go skiing or bowling," he said in an attempt to be humorous.

"Very funny! I haven't been skiing in over thirty years and I don't remember when the last time your father and I bowled. I think it was before the war," she laughed and then sighed remembering the early days. "I heard from Jonathan that you two were getting together at our retreat in Vermont. How did that go? You boys didn't fight did you?"

"Not at all, but we did discuss some very important issues about our futures," he said as he sat in the chair next to her. "Actually, that's the reason we need to discuss the business. Jonathan wants to buy me out and if I'm to continue in Congress I'll need to do something about my holdings."

"How would he do that? Are we doing that well that he has the means to pay you for your shares?" she asked.

"No, and that's the problem. He intends to borrow the money."

"I'm not up to date on the banking regulations, but I don't think that he can do that from our bank."

"You're right, he can't and he said that he can't tell me where he'll get the financing to do the deal. I suspect that he's dealing with Tom Masters."

"I don't think that's a wise thing to do. Do you? Your father was always suspicious of Tom and the Group since he encouraged the increase in the price of oil in the early seventies. Your father thought it caused high inflation and recession."

"I agree and I told Jonathan that it wouldn't be a good idea to deal with him or his colleagues, but I believe that he thinks that by buying me out he'll have two thirds majority ownership and be free to do as he pleases with the business assets. I know that it was that possibility that worried dad most."

"And what did Jonathan say? He must know they're not the kind of people he can trust.

"All he can see is the opportunity to get me out of his way. He's always been afraid that I'd become active in the operation, as dad wanted me to. And I really don't want to be involved except to protect the family's interest, so I've come up with an idea that I wanted to discuss with you. I'm willing to sell an equal amount of my shares to both you and Jonathan on an installment payment basis. The quarterly payments to be made into a blind trust not to be accessible by me until I am no longer involved in public service."

"How will that affect the operations of the companies? If you sell both of us equal shares obviously we would both own 50% of the businesses on a consolidated basis. Do you think your brother is going to be happy with that arrangement?"

"No, I don't. He'll try to either buy you out or into a minority ownership position, but we would have a clause in the by-laws that would prohibit that action without a two thirds majority vote of the Board of Directors and the Board would continue to consist of you, Jonathan and Bert Obersham, whom I trust explicitly."

"I don't know dear. Why would he agree to those terms if he's trying to gain absolute control?"

"Because he won't have another choice if I won't sell and I join the operation. We know he doesn't want that to happen."

"Didn't you say you would have to give up your political career if you did that?"

"Yes, and I'll do that rather than allow the family business that father built to go into bankruptcy or fall into the hands of Masters."

"And what if Jonathan isn't able to make the payments?"

"Then it will be obvious that there's something wrong with the operation and I'll have to call in the note and recover my shares; hopefully in time to be able to help turn things around."

"Won't you need to recover my shares too? If you have to do that it will be all right with me since you would be doing it to save the business."

"I knew you'd understand. I want to give Jonathan what he's looking for as far as control of the business operations, but with a chain attached that keeps him from going too far off track."

"I just hope it doesn't cause more problems between the two of you. Sibling rivalry is not much fun for a mother to watch. Have you discussed this with Sharon? I'm sure she'll have some sound advice for you."

"Only briefly while I was driving down here. She'll help me work out the details. She's a good lawyer and has some of the same concerns you have about the sibling rivalry issue."

The next morning Jim began the drive to Washington with a good feeling about his plan to outsmart Masters and placate his brother's appetite for control. He needed one more term in the House before he could take the next step in his political career. He would be married soon and have new obligations to deal with, not the least of which was the support of his wife's political ambitions.

Being a moderate Republican was a hard road to follow in the days of right wing political ascension. His father was right when he surmised that if you cater to the churches and their natural biases you can control a large mass of the southern vote. By professing "family values" and criticizing anyone who was not a "Christian" by self-serving standards, the charlatans were able to convince the faithful to tighten their belts while their righteous leaders picked their bones clean.

There were definitely intelligent men and women who felt as he did about the direction of their party, but they'd become outcasts. The financial support came only to those who "believed." But he wasn't going to give up.

His grandfather was a Rough Rider with Teddy Roosevelt in the Spanish-American War of 1898. He remembers the stories of his adventures with Colonel Roosevelt. After reading about the man in school, Teddy became the hero of his youth. His motto was, "walk softly but carry a big stick." He was a pragmatic man who was tough. He would fight with all of his being to win. He was a true leader and yet he cared about the American people and embraced issues like preserving the environment and its wildlife. He was called a progressive and he was a Republican!"

Teddy understood how greed and monopoly could be the downfall of a capitalist economy. Reacting to the greed of Standard Oil's monopolistic agenda he "busted" them and others using his legacy of anti-trust laws. They were laws designed to preserve the true meaning of capitalism, which was based on the "natural laws of supply and demand" without the manipulation of either. He was an enthusiastic supporter of the regulation of railroads having seen what monopolies in the transport of goods and people could do to a society.

Seven decades later, the word "Progressive" was looked upon with scorn by those who claimed to be Republicans. Many of whom made their wealth under rules that gave them a level playing field and protected consumers against devious and corrupt criminals. Having achieved success, as measured by their wealth, they sought ways to undermine the laws and regulations to realize more advantages to satisfy their appetites.

The greed of the unscrupulous and apathy of the government towards enforcing regulations, were conditions encouraged by Presidents Calvin Coolidge and Herbert Hoover in the 1920s, resulting in a free-wheeling American economy and the devastating stock market crash of 1929, the cause of the great depression.

The controls over human temptation to commit self-serving acts were not reestablished until Teddy's distant cousin, Franklin Delano Roosevelt was elected President in 1933. It was four years after the crisis of greed and apathy had consumed the American economy; the heart of the stock market and the spirit and where-with-all of the middle class.

Under the guidance of FDR the regulation of business practices was again recognized as required for a democratic society to truly benefit from capitalism. The government role as the means to build and maintain America's infrastructure and to ensure the integrity of its educational and economic systems was again recognized as its priority.

Chapter 92

The 1980s were difficult times for the Martinez family, but Diego and Keisha managed to buy the little cottage they called home. He earned money as a landscaper and Keisha continued to work in the nursing home at night when Diego was home with their son, little Manny. They often had to work on weekends to make their mortgage payments. The mortgage company lent them the money for 100% loan even though they didn't have enough income to qualify. The loan officer told them that they would probably qualify in two years when their adjustable rate mortgage, which she called an ARM at 10 % would be subject to adjustment.

"In any case real estate values always appreciate and your income will increase by then," were her last words before they signed the 20 page agreement.

The news of the passing of Carmella hit Diego hard. She had raised him and given him the values and work ethic that he relied on to survive. He managed to go to her funeral, but it set him back in his work and his finances. It was good to see his papa again, but he was growing old and seemed to be tired all the time. Diego suspected that he had diabetes, like Carmella, but didn't know it. He wouldn't go to a doctor. He blamed them for his wife's death and his deportation from California.

Tony was in New York on business and couldn't make it to the funeral. He sent a note with a bouquet of white roses with a note telling them that Carmella was a very special lady who meant a lot to him. He promised that they would get together when he returned to Massachusetts.

Manny told his son that the money left to them by his brother, Juan Carlos, was running out and that he would have to sell the hacienda. "I don't need this big house or the ranch. It is too hard to care for. Carmella wanted me to sell it years ago, but it's the only thing we have left," Manny explained to Diego.

"Where would you live and what about Maria? She's been with the family for more than twenty five years? Who would take care of you?" questioned Diego of his ailing father.

"There are apartments in the city, they don't cost a lot of money and I was told I can get a good price for this place. I will be fine! Don't you worry! How are you and Keisha doing? Are you still working as a gardener?" asked Manny with a look of concern.

"I'm a landscaper, not a gardener, Papa. I have my own business. It is good. Keisha works as a nurse and we own our home on Cape Cod. Here's a picture of little Manny. He's almost four years old. He's a lot like you, very stubborn!" he said smiling with his words.

"Ah you think that I'm stubborn you don't remember your mama. She was the stubborn one." Manny smiled at the thought of his life's love and shed a tear thinking of how he missed her. Are you going to be all right, Diego? I'll send you some money after I sell the house."

"No, we're fine. I have work and Keisha is a good nurse and mother. You need to take care of yourself and that means you need to see a doctor! You know that you have the same symptoms as Carmella, and she was on medicine for her diabetes. You can't ignore that disease."

"Well, my mother did everything she was supposed to do and where is she now? I'm not going to stick pins and needles into me. That is no way to live."

"Papa, it is the only way for many people to live. Here, Keisha gave me this testing kit for you. Let's take a sample of your blood. I'll show you how it works."

"I told you, I don't want to be stuck with needles," answered Manny shrugging away from him.

"Here, I'll do it first. Watch how easy it is." Diego stuck his finger and tested his glucose level and was surprised that it was over 120, a number of concern. He then tested his reluctant father and wasn't surprised that it was over 300, a very bad sign. "You need to get on some medication. It may be just a pill for now, but you need to do something. I'll ask Karime for a doctor's name. She knows everyone in this town. I'll see her at the funeral tomorrow morning."

Although the funeral was not as elaborate as Colonel Jim Buckman's at Arlington National Cemetery, it had its own elegance. The procession through the village, on the outskirts of the city, had more than a hundred mourners. Carmella was known as a compassionate and intelligent woman who chose to return to her people after having the benefit of being an American citizen. Her people, outside of her family, didn't know the circumstances that brought her back to them. They did know that she was the mother of their Robin Hood-like benefactor, Juan Carlos, and they still held him in reverence.

The Mass at the Church of the Madonna was filled with teary eyed mourners as Manny told of his mother's caring and love for her family and her people. "Carmella was not a woman who wanted. She was a woman who gave. She was a woman who loved all of you as her family and believed in the good of people. She raised my son Diego when I could not and never asked for help, but gave it freely. She is missed and will be loved forever."

After the funeral the attendees were welcomed to Manny's home for a Mexican feast, as Carmella would call it. The family and close friends brought their special dishes for a potpourri of Mexican cuisine.

Diego found Karime in the garden that was Carmella's pride. He embraced her with a hug and looked into her teary eyes.

Her words displayed her compassion for her grandmother, "She loved this place. She would come here when her world was in chaos and she was fearful of the future. She would pray for you and your papa. This was her sanctuary, her church! I would come by and see her. Her head would be down and her words would whisper your names, pleading to God for both of your well-being."

"I owed her everything, Karime, but I'm afraid I only brought her heartache," responded Diego, his tone subdued and filled with remorse. "She had to come back here because of me after all she had been through to become an American citizen. She was very proud of that accomplishment."

"It was time for her to return. Her sons needed her and she was able to live better here without the hard work, thanks to her errant son, my father. I don't know if she ever knew that it was not Manny's money that gave her that life, but I suspect she did."

"Karime, I'm worried about my papa's health. I'm sure he has diabetes and that it's weakening him. He won't see a doctor and doesn't want any medication. Do you know any doctor that would be good for him to see, maybe someone at the University?"

"I'm no longer at the University, Diego. The United States FBI had me fired because I wouldn't cooperate with them. The Mexican police already have my brother in prison, but he won't talk, even though they have tortured him. They told me that they'll have the Mexican authorities will leave him alone if I disclose the names of the members of the cartel."

Diego listened incredulously to Karime. She had given up a life of crime, but was being forced to let people she cared about be slaughtered. She knew the authorities would prefer to kill them in an ambush, rather than bear the cost of trials and imprisonment. Her words worried him. He suspected she had rejoined them. "Karime, you're not back with the cartel?"

"I'll find a doctor for your papa, Diego. Come, we must go now to join the guests." she said as she walked briskly towards the house. Diego knew the answer and it brought fear into his heart for her.

Chapter 93

The re-election of Reagan proved that charisma overcomes substance in elections. There is a reason that it is called the "popular vote." As a spokesman for the very rich he had the charm; good looks and acting ability to sell anything from GE refrigerators to anti-union sentiment. His feel-good demeanor gave the public a sense of enthusiasm as he followed the guidelines of his backers while diminishing the financial well-being of the working American.

At the end of his first term in 1984, the unemployment Rate was at 7.2% exactly the same as when he took office from Jimmy Carter in 1981. Although it showed no improvement over his first term, it had reached a high point of 10.8% during the second year of that first term in office. The reduction from that peak rate came at the price of an annual budget deficit of over $200 billion, caused primarily by Reagan's spending on defense. Government spending was again the catalyst for the reduction in unemployment and together with the reduction of taxes for the wealthy, was the reason for the runaway deficit.

Reagan's stimulus program consisted of spending billions of dollars for defense projects to keep his financial backers happy. He believed he could spend the Soviets into submission, not acknowledging that they were doing that task quite well without his help. They had spent themselves into virtual bankruptcy by wasting their resources on attempting to prove their military might instead of developing a sound economy. Their experience in their futile war against Afghanistan proved that betting their future on conquest was a bad choice.

To pay for his spending spree he taxed the meager Social Security payments that the elderly relied on to survive, reduced the tax deductions of the middle class American and yet managed to get the very rich a tax rate of only 28% down from 70% for their top increment of earnings. To paraphrase David Stockman, Reagan's Budget Chief, "trickle down" was a Trojan horse designed to bring down the highest tax rates for the wealthiest Americans.

Fortunately for Reagan, his Teflon Presidency ended the year the trickle down economy came home to roost with the near collapse of the poorly regulated banking system and the businesses that they financed. Unfortunately for the middle class American they experienced another drain of their hard earned assets.

In late 1988 the country began its slide into a deep economic recession, the third in a line that included the aftermaths of the Hoover (1929) and Nixon (1973) Republican administrations. It lasted four long years, nearly destroyed the real estate market and eliminated many small banks.

More than 700 savings and loan institutions collapsed after being allowed to speculate in the real estate market in contradiction of traditional regulatory process. Many regulatory activities were either eliminated or weakened with reduced funding to the detriment of the consumer and the American economy.

Reaganomics worked well for the very rich, but left American working men and women worse off for their efforts. Their real income declined as did the value of their primary asset, their home as the earnings of the wealthy rose to unprecedented levels. Reagan did the job he was hired to do by the wealthy elite, and the misinformed American people. Unfortunately the majority of Americans *were not better off t*han when he came into office eight years prior, but they still loved him.

Chapter 94

The Reagan legacy left his successor and former Vice President, George H.W. Bush, with a serious financial mess to clean up, the most damaging of which was having to renege on his "read my lips" promise of no new taxes made during his 1988 presidential campaign. Bush was forced to raise taxes to offset a tripling of the national debt as a result of what he had previously referred to as Reagan's "Voodoo Economic" policies.

The Bush Administration, with Dick Cheney as Secretary of Defense, and James Baker, a longtime Bush protégé, as Secretary of State, realized they needed a distraction to offset their unpopular moves and the economic disaster of the previous conservative administration. They took the opportunity by initiating Operation Desert Storm in response to Iraq's invasion of the oil-rich monarchy of Kuwait. They justified their action as being to protect the oil rich nation of Saudi Arabia, which was being threatened by the Iraqi Army. Iraq had already conquered the Saudi's equally rich neighbor of Kuwait. The United States would now fight as a mercenary army with a promise by the Saudi's to compensate them for their intervention.

For the one to two percent of Americans that benefitted from the politics of the "Great Communicator," the 1980s were great and prosperous years. They spoke of Reagan with sincere reverence for he accomplished more for them than any previous President. For the rest of Americans it was a turning point, in a downward direction. It would take years of painful suffering for those 98% of Americans who bore the burden of a government that was always ready to fight irrational wars and be guided by precarious economics. They would be affected by the actions of the disingenuous that they had elected. And now it would be decades that they would be frustrated in their struggle to improve upon the earning level that they had achieved by 1973.

For second term Senator Sharon Polowski, George H.W. Bush was more of the same. The overwhelming defeat of Geraldine Ferrraro, the first woman and first Italian American to run for the Vice Presidency on a major party's ticket with Walter Mondale in 1984 was debilitating to her spirit. The election of another Republican to the Presidency in 1988 caused her to believe that the American people just didn't get it.

Her husband and friendly opposition, Jim Buckman, realized that he was wrong about Reagan being a moderate, but was convinced that George H.W. Bush was what the party needed to get back on track. Bush had been a loyal Vice president but was a reluctant supporter of the Reagan's economic policies. He would continue attempt to bring his moderate programs forward under this new administration.

After three years of marriage Sharon was pregnant with their first child and was seriously considering not running in the next Senatorial contest. It would be 1992 and Bush would be running for his second term. She had maintained her residence in Michigan and her surname when she married Jim. Both spent much of their time together in Washington D.C. at their Capitol Hill apartment. She didn't look forward to another term as a minority party Senator spending most of her time and energy trying to keep the Republicans from destroying the middle class. Her dreams of helping to re-create the Great Society were fading with every electoral display of American apathy.

"Okay, I know, you told me so, but we did have some prosperity with Reagan," declared Jim in his attempt to lift her spirits.

"And what we have now is, what, our punishment for being ignorant of the basic needs of our society? Jim you're a good man but your politics suck!" responded Sharon with a half-hearted smile. "And you're an eternal optimist, but the only moderates left in your party are those who believe that Social Security is a necessary evil!"

"You have a message that only you can deliver, my dear. Don't give up on it or the bad guys will win. Ferraro didn't give up!" exclaimed Jim.

"No, and look where she is now, on the wrong end of one of the biggest landslides in American political history."

"Well, I have a couple of years to change your mind. In the meantime let's see if we can affect this Presidency from both sides of the aisle," declared Jim in an effort to appease her and justify his politics.

Laura Marie Buckman was born with auburn hair, which seemed to be a compromise between her parents' colors. Jim held his daughter soon after her birth as Sharon slept, exhausted from the hard work of giving birth after twelve hours of labor. As he looked into her eyes he realized the miracle of birth. Here in his arms he held a human being that didn't have a breath less than an hour ago. Their love had produced a real person who would also feel love, joy and of course pain. Her head turned toward him and their eyes met as his thoughts of her being his, brought a tear to his eyes. He whispered to no one in particular, "I must have done something right to deserve you!"

Over the next year Bush attempted to deal with the economic disaster he inherited from his former boss. He found he would have to raise taxes to overcome the Reagan deficit. His action amounted to treason against the right wing's principles and caused a rift between him and his party's conservatives. George H.W. Bush found himself moving closer to the center with his moderate actions including his endorsement of immigration laws that increased the number of aliens allowed to legally enter the country, the signing of the Americans with Disabilities Act and the re-authorization of the Clean Air Act.

Even the downfall of the Soviet Union, which occurred on his watch - not Reagan's, was not enough to gain the support of the conservatives. With his popularity declining from a high of 79% many believed that he chose war, too often the remedy of choice of presidents, to increase his approval ratings.

To Jim Buckman, the President's legislative actions proved that there was hope for a return to the rule of fiscally conservative and socially conscious moderate Republicanism. Although he had reservations about going to war to rescue the Saudi and Kuwait governments from Saddam Hussein's highly touted Iraq forces, he understood the reasoning. We had to protect our oil interest in the mid-east. He appreciated the President's restraint from invading Iraq itself. Being entrenched in a region where tribal wars have dictated the quality of life for thousands of years was not a rational option.

Sharon Polowski Buckman also found George H.W. to be a reasonable man and began to believe in her husband's cause, but fell short of embracing its politics. "I'll have to admit that he has surprised me to date. I thought that Dan Quayle would have more influence on his actions as his Vice President."

"He's his own man, but I don't think that the party is behind him. There's talk of Quayle running against him in 1992 if they see an opening. I'm not sure he can maintain his popularity while unemployment is on the rise and banks are still being closed. It seems that each successive president needs to atone for his predecessors blunders."

"He does have the advantage of not having a high profile Democrat to run against. It looks like Jerry Brown is running again and that governor from Arkansas, Bill Clinton, are his only serious opponents," offered Sharon. "I think I could beat those two."

"And what about Ross Perot? He's leading both parties candidates in the polls. He's more conservative than Bush, he has the money and seems to be saying the words that the public wants to hear."

"He's a fringe candidate and they all fizzle out near the end when the electorate has to get serious and make a decision that will affect their lives," answered Sharon as a cry from the baby's room interrupted their intellectual sparring.

"I'll be right back. She probably wants to express her opinion in this debate."

"I look forward to the day when I'm arguing politics with the two of you," grinned Jim.

"If you have trouble overcoming my logic I doubt you'll fare any better against two well informed, intelligent women, dear," chided Sharon as she left the room.

Jim thought about it and had to admit she was probably right.

Chapter 95

By the late 1980's Tony Benedetto's engineering business had grown exponentially. The real estate boom fueled by easy credit, and a thriving but fragile economy, was creating numerous development projects. To continue growth Tony needed working capital. Three Boston area banks offered him credit lines, each anxious for his business. He had come a long way since his days as a cashier in a supermarket earning money for college. He had seventy five employees and a year's backlog of business.

Unfortunately, his honeymoon with the bank was over in two years as the economy crashed and crushed the real estate market. Hundreds of banks were brought to their knees in late 1988 as Trickle Down economics proved to be a policy of smoke and mirrors. Businesses, small and large were brought down, including law firms, accounting houses and banks - those who should have known better, but were in it for the brief and precarious Reagan windfall.

Tony's bank called him in to discuss his credit line. He was confused since his company was not behind in payments and he had experienced only one negative quarter in eight years. Tony had his in-house accountant Steve Landon accompany him to the bank's headquarters.

"Good morning, gentlemen. My name is Tyler Worthington and I'm a *Work Out officer* with Bayside Bank and Trust. We've reviewed your last quarterly statement and note that your business had an 11% decline in the quarter and we're concerned. It also appears that collection of your receivables has slowed during that period."

"Obviously, that's due to the dramatic slow-down in the economy. You must realize that the whole country is suffering right now. Everyone is feeling the effects," explained Tony.

"Well, that isn't our problem. The bank is not in the business of financing businesses that are in a negative mode. The Board has reviewed your loan's status and has decided that we need our credit line repaid immediately. Since you have all of your accounts with us we realize that you don't have that kind of money on hand so we must demand that you sell your assets or we will be forced to go to court and take them in lieu of payment."

In shock, Tony asked, "What do you mean? You want me to sell my business? I built this from scratch and worked day and night to make it as successful as it is today. I have a reputation and I have employees that are dependent on their jobs. You can't do this."

"Yes we can! Your credit line is a *demand note* and we can call it for any reason. As part of allowing you to continue your operation while you find a buyer, you will have to have a lock box at this bank that will receive all of your accounts receivables or we will be forced to shut you down immediately! Here's the paperwork for you to sign. You're to notify all of your clients that they must send their payments to this P.O Box," stated the young man matter-of-factly as he sat across from Tony.

"How old are you? Have you ever been in business? What is this really about? Is this bank one of those that are in trouble?" demanded Tony his voice rising in tune with his Italian temper.

"Not that it's any of your business, but I'm 28, I have an MBA from Harvard and no I haven't had a business of my own and this bank's business is none of your business," declared the arrogant messenger of bad will.

Tony's accountant grabbed his arm realizing that his temper might propel him over the width of the table that protected his sassy 28-year old antagonist.

"Mr. Worthington I don't understand why this is necessary. We haven't even drawn down our total credit line, and yes, we are being affected by the sudden downturn of the economy, but we selected your bank because it was the most progressive and supposedly business-savvy. Your commercial loan officer, Mr. Donovan, said that this bank was different, that it would be there when we needed it," offered the accountant, Steve Landon.

"Regrettably, Mr. Donovan is no longer with the bank," answered Worthington. "Things have changed and the fact that we are business savvy is the reason we want our money now. We will allow you to continue to operate, but we will collect all of your receivables and you will need the bank's approval to pay any debts, including payrolls, and insurances until we are paid in full. And speaking of the company payroll, Mr. Benedetto, in order to show good faith as President of the company, you will have to reduce your personal earnings by taking a pay cut of 50%, beginning with the next payroll.

"You sons of bitches, do you realize what you're doing?" declared a shocked and angry Tony. "You're destroying the lives of people, and for what, because you mishandled your banking business!"

"Mr. Benedetto, we expect your compliance with these demands and we'll meet with you next Friday at 10:00 am to discuss that compliance," the young man stated, his voice beginning to crack, as he nervously gathered up his papers and proceeded to leave the room. "Here's a list of bank-approved financial workout specialist who will monitor your check book and the company's financial condition until we are paid in full. You need to pick one and let us know whom you have chosen at our next meeting!"

As they left the building Tony asked, "Steve, what are we going to do? Everything I have is tied up in this company? How can they do this? If I take that pay cut I lose my house. What will I tell my wife?"

"I don't know Tony, but we need to get in touch with the company's attorneys. I heard that a number of Boston banks were hurting and possibly merging, but I didn't think that it was this bad," responded Landon. "It has something to do with their real estate portfolios."

"It's November, and they want me to lay off people before the holidays. I'm not going to do it, Steve. There must be something we can do."

"I don't see how you have any alternatives without a viable credit line, and with the bank taking our clients' payments at their "lock box" to pay down their loan. What choice do you have?"

"Something isn't right! No business, even a bank, shouldn't be able to change the rules as they go along to suit their own inadequacies."

"Tony, the banks have the money and he who has the money has the power!"

It took only six months for the bank to sell the assets of Tony's engineering business to one of its prime competitors. The house and cars would go next as the repossessions and auction sales would leave nothing for the Benedetto's. The bank induced recession made finding a job virtually impossible. He was either too experienced or too old at 45, even with a Master's degree in engineering, for the few entry level jobs available in the deep, Reagan induced recession.

As he stood in the unemployment line for the first time in his life, his heart and spirit broken, he knew that he couldn't do that for long. He had sent out numerous résumés and gone on many interviews. It was obvious that he had passed the age of consideration. He had only one option - he needed to find a way to start a new engineering business. He had neither cash nor credit, but as one of his close business acquaintances told him, "You still have your ingenuity, and you've already done it once!" It was two weeks before Christmas 1990 and each day brought him heightened anxiety about his family's future.

He wasn't going to give up. He knew that the unscrupulous can't be allowed to win!

Chapter 96

The banking crisis was felt across the spectrum of the American economy. Speculative investments and curious loans involving savings banks which were supposed to be the most conservative financial institutions, had backfired. Savings banks had been established to serve the traditional financial needs of a community. They were designed to use their customers' individual savings to provide mortgages and personal loans to the people in their own community.

Deregulation had encouraged such banks to push the envelope. Too many had loaned money or invested in projects that looked good until they were brought down by the shaky basis of supply-side economics. This caused the FDIC, the insurers of customers' deposits, to become aggressive and exacerbate the problem.

Jonathan Buckman was confused at 5:01 p.m. on Wednesday, when his business manager Raymond Berkowitz burst into his office with the bad news. "The Feds are in the building, Mr. Buckman, and they've vacated the bank and locked our doors. They want to see...."

Before he could complete his sentence three dark-suited men came through the door gently pushing past him. "Are you Jonathan Buckman, President and CEO of Buckman Bank and Trust?" asked the lead suit, flashing his identification.

Jonathan, stunned, his mouth and eyes wide open, could feel a sudden pain in his chest and a cold sweat overcome him. He finally managed to say, "What is this? Who are you? Raymond, call the police!" he instructed his manager, his voice cracking.

"That won't be necessary, sir. We're from the FDIC and your bank has been determined to be insolvent and undercapitalized. You are to collect your personal possessions, leave all of your bank-related keys and files and vacate the bank immediately," ordered Agent Harold Goetz. "We will be in touch with you within the next 24 hours. We advise you to not leave the area!"

"What do you mean? We're not insolvent. We have assets. You can't do this! I'm not leaving until I speak to our attorneys."

"I'm sorry sir, but you don't have a choice. We're here to protect the depositors' assets, which we have reason to believe are in jeopardy. You can call your attorneys from your home. My associates will escort you there."

The two colleagues of the lead agent went to Jonathan's side and began the process of escorting him out of the bank.

"Am I being arrested? What did I do? What will happen to my customer's funds? They'll panic if they can't access their money," asked Jonathan, trembling, confused and rambling. "Can I call my wife?"

"No sir, you're not being arrested. This is part of an ongoing investigation. We will need to retain Mr. Berkowitz and his staff. I assume that he has access to all of your files and systems. Your customers' funds will be available through a bank that we have arranged to take over and service those assets," responded Agent Goetz.

"What bank? Where are our funds going? I have a right to know." demanded Jonathan.

"You don't need to worry about that sir. A national bank, Continental Trust Corporation has agreed to work with us in this matter."

Jonathan felt faint at hearing those words. "Donald Peters' bank was part of this fiasco. What did he do? He trusted those bastards!" His thoughts raced through his disoriented mind.

His fighting spirit and energy to fight were siphoned off by the words spoken by Agent Goetz. Resigning himself to his immediate fate, his head down and despondent beyond words, he walked to the door escorted on either side by the government enforcement agents. For the first time he wished his father were still alive. He would be able to fix this. What were Jim and his mother going to say?

A number of shiny black government cars were pulling into the bank's parking lot as he walked to his Rolls. They would be diligent and efficient, confiscating all his files, transferring the bank's funds and locking down the building until its disposition was finally determined. "What if they discover the offshore operations and their illegal situations? He could go to jail!" The same lock-down activities were initiated at all of Buckman Bank and Trusts' branch banks.

The agents drove him home, one in his Rolls Royce and the other behind in their government-issued black Ford Victoria. They were instructed to stay with him. Suicide watches were not uncommon under the circumstances.

Part Five

The Payback Years

Chapter 97

Payback came in the form of an economic meltdown in Reagan's last year in office. Trickle –Down economics left the country in shambles with more than 700 banks failing, billions of dollars in deficits and millions losing their jobs. Reagan's Vice President, George H.W. Bush had correctly labeled Reagan's policies when he was his opponent, as VooDoo economics. The answer to Reagan's question in 1988, which he asked eight years earlier in the 1980 campaign against Carter, was that Americans *were not better off* now than they were eight years ago. America was on life-support!

Jim Buckman called his wife in her Senate office. "Sharon, you remember Tony Benedetto, my drill sergeant from Devens."

'Of course I do. He was my confidant while you were in Vietnam. How are the Benedetto's doing? They have twins don't they?"

"Yes they do, but they're not doing very well. He's a victim of the banking crisis and this recession. His bank, which is rumored to be one of those in trouble, has demanded payment of his credit line. They're forcing him to sell his business. He says he'll lose his home and everything he's worked for."

"That's awful! I thought he was doing well. His company was written up in a trade magazine as being very successful. Is there anything we can do to help him?"

"He didn't ask for help. He was just despondent and wanted to talk to a friend. I'm going to call Jonathan to see if his bank can do anything to help him. I'll vouch for a loan, if that will get him started again."

"Is that a wise thing to do in your position, Jim? It could lead to all kinds of questions. Tony had government contracts. You sold off your interest in the family business to avoid such perceptions," cautioned Sharon. "When did this happen?"

"He said it was last month. He thought it could be worked out with the bank, but they only want their money. I know it might cause a problem, but he's a friend. I owe him the courtesy of trying to help him and his family," responded Jim thinking that Tony has always been there when he needed his support. "I'll give Jonathan a call."

The call to his brother's office at the bank's headquarters went unanswered. "Alice, will you try to reach my brother Jonathan. There's no answer at the bank. You have his other numbers, see if you can locate him," Jim instructed his secretary.

After twenty minutes his intercom rang. "I have your brother on line 3."

"Thank you Alice! Hello, Jonathan, where have you been? I haven't heard from you for days."

"Jim, I'm at home. I have to talk to you. When will you be in Connecticut? It's important!"

"What's wrong? Is it mom?"

"No, she's fine, but we all need to talk. I'm afraid it's bad news."

"What kind of bad news? Tell me what's going on Jonathan!"

"The Feds have taken over the bank," Jonathan blurted out, his voice trembling. "I'm sorry, Jim, it looks bad!"

"What do you mean the Feds have taken over the bank? What agency? What did you do?" Jim's anxiety was rising fast.

"The FDIC, they came into the bank yesterday and shut it down. They said it was insolvent! They're doing this all over the country. The President's sons were involved in banks in California and Nevada. You've heard about the Silverado Bank. But we have assets."

"Jonathan, stop!" Jim's heart missed a beat as he thought of ripping into him, but wisely held back. "We need to talk face to face. I'll be there this evening, by about 6 o'clock. I'll see you at your home. Don't talk to anyone until after we've met," commanded Jim, afraid that their words may not be private.

"Alice, get my wife on the phone and tell her I'll meet her for lunch at Fresco's at 1 o'clock. Tell her it's important...and cancel my appointments for the next two days," Jim grabbed his brief case and bolted out the rear door of his office, his heart beating as rapidly as his mind was racing. This was the situation he had feared when he accepted Jonathan's offer to buy him out.

Sharon was waiting at their favorite table when he arrived. "Jim, are you okay? Alice said that it was important to be here."

"Well, I'm okay physically, but my dear brother just dropped a bomb on me!" he said as he leaned over and spoke quietly. "The Feds have shut down the bank!"

"They did what? How could that happen without any warning? What did he do?"

"I'm not sure, but I have to go up there and see what's going on. He said they were FDIC agents and they told him the bank was insolvent."

"Jim that could mean that you lose everything. What will your mother do? And your reputation, oh my God, this is serious!" Sharon exclaimed in an equally quiet voice trying to stay composed.

"Not everything! I still have you and Laura Marie, but I know it could mean the end of our family's wealth. I hope it's not too late to save some of the family's assets. I booked a 2:30 flight to Hartford. I'll call you when I know more. Sorry to 'not eat' and run, but I didn't think it would be wise to meet in either of our offices. I'll grab a sandwich at the airport. Love you!" he kissed her as he rose to leave.

"Love you too Jim. Please call when you get there, and no violence!" she offered with a look that told him to stay calm.

It was 5:48 p.m. when Jim arrived at Jonathan's 22-room oceanfront mansion. He had cautioned him about going easy and staying under the radar. Now everything he owned could be subject to attachments and foreclosure if there's any wrong-doing associated with the bank's failure. The maid led Jim to Jonathan who had sought refuge in his study, his head in his hands, elbows on the desk and his eyes closed, listening to Bach.

He had sent his wife Kathy and two-year old son to her mother's home to give him time and space to think. Before she left she went into a tirade blaming him for this debacle, declaring that she never should have married such a loser. He realized that she wasn't going to be part of any solution.

"Thank you for coming here so quickly, Jim. I'm so sorry that I messed things up for all of us." Jonathan's words came slowly and painfully with somber tones that Jim had never heard uttered from his mouth.

Jim noticed a half-empty bottle of Scotch on the credenza behind him. "Jonathan, we're family and we'll work this thing out together. I'll take some of that medicinal treatment from behind you." Jim knew he must remain calm in order to get Jonathan to tell the whole story. Showing his anger would only cause him to become defensive and possibly deceitful.

"Sure, why not? It might help you think. Unfortunately, it won't help solve our problem." Jonathan reached back and grabbed the Dewar's by the neck and poured them both a double and then proceeded to tell the whole story as he knew it, realizing that his brother was being unusually compassionate. His revelation about the participation of Don Peters' bank got Jim's attention.

"So the bastards got us anyway. Have you spoken with Bert? Was he aware of what was going on?" asked Jim believing that Bert Obersham, a close friend and Director on the Board would not be part of this scam.

"I haven't, but he's called several times. I don't know what to say to him. It would be like talking to dad and that makes me very nervous."

"Well, we need to have that conversation. He may be able to shed some light on the situation, and he has liability as a director. Has the FDIC contacted you since you left the bank?"

"Yes, they called last night at about 7 p.m. to ask questions having to do with that day's investigation of the bank's documents."

"Will they call tonight? I want to listen to the conversation, but I don't want to let them know I'm involved yet," Jim spoke in a whisper.

"That shouldn't be a problem. But what are we going to do? They haven't asked about the off-sho...

Jim put his hand over his brother's mouth and a finger to his own pursed lips in a quiet "sshhh" to signal his silence. He feared the possibility of listening devices in the house and didn't want to disclose any more than they had to.

"Let's go have dinner, my treat," Jim was holding in his anger and anxiety, but he wanted to find a place where it would be difficult for the Feds to bug and listen to their discussion. They decided on a private dining room at Jonathan's club. He needed to ask some very demanding questions, some of which might have incriminating answers.

Chapter 98

The economic chaos of the early 1990s was like a tornado tearing up everything in its path. As the banks went down like pins in a bowling alley, businesses that relied on them collapsed and real estate lost significant value to the foreclosure frenzy. Diego Martinez saw his landscape business decline again as his customers struggled just to pay their mortgages. "I understand Mrs. Carson. Maybe next month, if things get better?" he responded to another cancellation of his monthly landscape appointments. He had a mortgage payment that was three weeks late and his truck needed a transmission. He'd thought these days were behind him. He was no longer a young man and he hoped he would have the security of his home for his family by this time in his life.

Keisha was working seven days a week, but for less pay since the nursing home she worked for went out of business, unable to pay their bills due to late Medicare payments. She was taking care of an elderly lady at the woman's home through an agency that paid half of what she made at the nursing home, but it was all there was.

Young Manny had done well in school, inspired by his parents to take advantage of the opportunities offered by being an American citizen. He would be a freshman in high school next year and he was college material.

Keisha was getting more anxious with every passing day, "Diego what are we going to do? Are we going to lose our home? We don't have the money to pay the mortgage. Can't you get a regular job? The landscape business isn't working."

"I've tried. There are no jobs. Even the restaurants on the Cape are going out of business and no one is building houses. The banks won't finance them and people can't buy houses without mortgages."

"What are we going to do? Can your papa help? He sold his home and he's offered to give you money before?" asked Keisha reluctantly, but out of desperation.

"I don't know. He's not well. He might need money to go into a nursing home soon. I can't take money he might need to survive."

"How about asking Tony for a job? He offered before."

"I spoke with him last week. He's losing his business and he and Meghan are losing their home because he signed personally on all his office leases. They are in worse shape than us."

"Oh my God, is it that bad? What going on? We were doing okay. It happened so quickly. It isn't supposed to be like this. You work hard and do the right things and you're supposed to be able to live a good life. Isn't that the American Dream?"

It was obvious to Diego that life was not going to get any easier. There was no work and no money to be earned...legally. He decided to call his cousin Karime. He just needed enough money to get by for, hopefully, just a few months. She might be able to help. Maybe she'd hire him so that he could make some money. He couldn't let his family go hungry and homeless.

Karime was not happy to hear from him under the circumstances. He called her at her home, but when she realized what he might want, she told him that she would call him later. He knew that she didn't trust her phone and would find a safer location to call from. He gave her the number at a neighbor's home. He told his neighbor that his phone was out of order and he was expecting an important call. The neighbor said he wouldn't be home, but he was welcome to use the phone. Diego had a key since he was helping him renovate his kitchen.

"Diego, I can lend you some money, but you can't be involved in anything here. You have a family and remember what happened to your papa. Do you want to repeat history?"

"I can't just let all this happen. We've worked very hard and it's all going to be lost."

"You know it's not just you. You say that your friend Tony is also losing everything and he's an educated engineer with two children and he had a good business. It is a disease Diego! It's called greed. The rich people got what they wanted from your Reagan. Now they're laughing at the rest of you as you ensure their wealth and pay for their mistakes," exclaimed Karime.

"What can we do? I don't care about politics and I'm not Cesar Chavez, I can't start a revolution," pleaded Diego.

"I don't know, but in America you have a government that can be changed by the people without guns and bloodshed. Things won't change until the people realize that they're being used by those who care nothing about them. They need to elect people who do care!"

"That sounds too idealistic Karime. No one really cares about anyone but themselves!"

"If I were an American citizen I would find people who care and organize those who are being used to stop these bastardos. There are leeches in your country that will suck the last drop of blood from the workers and the poor so that they can have mansions and private jet planes. They think they are princes and kings, but they are parasites. They're no different from the scum here in Mexico."

"I know you're right, but I'm only one person and I'm just trying to have my family survive. The only thing I have is a $50,000 insurance policy, but they don't pay for suicides."

"Diego, don't talk stupid. Your family needs you more than they need money. I'll help you so you don't lose your home or starve, but things need to change. I too have limitations."

"Tell me what to do. I can't take your money for doing nothing. What about you, are you safe?"

"I'm fine and I'll be able to travel there soon with a new identity. I'll be in New York in two weeks. We should meet. Can you get your friend Tony to meet also?"

"I'll ask him. Are you sure you'll be all right in this country? And what about this phone call, can they hear you?"

"No, we're more sophisticated now and we're not into the old ways. We're trying to make changes here. I'll tell you about it when we meet. You'll hear from me as to where and when that'll be. Talk to Tony, but be careful where and how."

"We'll be there and thank you, Karime. I'll find a way to repay you."

"Diego, repayment will be by your actions not your money. We're family and we must be able to rely on family, especially when it's all there is."

Diego decided to call Tony from his neighbor's phone so that his discussion about Karime would not be overheard if they had connected him with her.

Meghan answered, "Hello Diego, how is Keisha and Manny?

"They're fine and how are you and the kids doing? I know things haven't been good for you and we're feeling very sad."

"Thank you, but we'll survive. Tony is the eternal optimist. He says that he started with nothing and now he has his degree, his engineering license and his family, so he is way ahead!" Her voice cracked as she relayed Tony's rationalization. He's not here though. One of his clients called after hearing that he was losing his business and wanted to meet with him. Tony's hoping he has a project that he can work on."

"That would be great! Who is this man?" asked Diego out of curiosity and concern for his amigo.

"He's an older gentleman. He was one of Tony's first clients and has always been loyal to him. I hope that it's something good. Tony tries to be positive on the outside, but I know he's hurting badly. I'm worried Diego. It will be good for you two to get together, maybe go fishing? You both seem to have had such a good day that last time you went fishing on the Bay."

Diego smiled, thinking about what a disaster that last time was and how their pride caused them to keep the details from the women. "Yes, that was an adventure, but I think our fishing days are over. Will you have him call me when he gets home?"

"Yes, of course and give our love to Keisha and Manny."

"I will Meghan, and our love and prayers are with you and your family."

Chapter 99

The Buckman brothers met to discuss the details of Jonathan's activities that led to the visit by the FDIC. It was obvious to Jim that Jonathan's greed and naiveté had played into the hands of Masters and his Washington Action Group. It was time to meet with Bert Obersham. They decided to meet him at a restaurant in Baltimore's airport at 7am to limit the possibility of anyone setting up a listening device to monitor their conversation.

Bert already knew the details from Masters. He had called Bert to warn him of the impending fiasco, but did it as it was happening.

"He told me that there was a mess about to be uncovered by the FDIC and that I should resign as soon as possible and declare that I wasn't aware of the situation. I told him I doubted that anyone would buy that. I asked him how he knew about the FDIC action," explained Bert with a tone that expressed a feeling of betrayal.

"What did Masters say? How did he justify his knowledge of this pre-emptive strike against our family?" asked Jim his temper beginning to show.

"He didn't! He did say that Peters' bank had been asked to assist the Feds in these takeovers. He said that he believed it to be an opportunity to help, but he wasn't clear how taking over our assets would help our bank."

"Do you think they're really trying to be helpful?" asked a naïve Jonathan hoping they were still friends.

"Only if they thought that they could help you lose weight by eating your lunch. Wake up Jonathan these guys set you up and played you like a harp," Bert responded angry and impatient thinking that their father would not only be turning in his grave, he would be trying to climb out of it. Bert said what Jim wanted to say and for that Jim was pleased, but it didn't help the situation. They needed a plan!

"What are your thoughts Bert? Do you have any ideas about what we can do beyond contacting our attorneys and hope that there are no criminal charges?"

"Well, the only thing in our favor is that I don't believe either Masters or the Feds know the details of the offshore investments. Masters is guessing, but your father set up certain triggers that would alert us to any actual penetrations into those operations and none of those triggers have been tripped, as yet."

"How does that help us at this point? The actions that the FDIC has already taken can lead to serious indictments if they find criminal fault."

"My theory is that the feds have a lot on their plate with literally hundreds of banks going down. We need to be cooperative and make it as easy as possible for them to do the minimum that they believe they must do. The offshore funds are much greater than those associated with our onshore banking operations. We need to protect them and we need to neutralize Masters and Peters."

"I'd like to neutralize them," declared Jonathan.

"That won't make anything better, but I can't blame you. They're a despicable group. Your father knew that and he knew how to use them to his benefit. He often said that they were too smart for their own good. We lent Continental Trust $100 million discreetly through a Canadian bank that holds the paper. Although it could expose our operations to greater scrutiny we'll threaten to call that note. It'll probably put them under without recourse if they add to the probe. We'll also agree to a merger with CTC to make them feel more comfortable with our presence. It's important for the Feds to believe that Buckman Bank and Trust is no longer a problem needing their attention."

Jim listened intently and thought that Bert's friendship with his father through battles and business had borne a special fruit. His thought processes had developed by osmosis from his dad, into an ingenious capability to strategize while under fire. He was impressed!

"I like it Bert! But what's our next step?" quizzed Jim.

Before Bert could answer Jonathan intervened, "I don't know. Do you think we can pull it off without getting them angrier? What if they retaliate?"

"Well, do you have a better plan?" responded Bert in a condescending voice.

"Jonathan, I think we need to act quickly to establish this innocent and cooperative tone with the Feds before they stumble onto more interesting information," added Jim.

"I understand. I'm just being cautious, that's all."

"It may be a little late for that!" responded Bert, letting his anger slip out. And we need to keep you out of it, Jim, at this point. And you, Jonathan, have to stay composed. Don't panic. Be business-like. Say as little as possible when asked questions, but be direct. Call me if there's a problem, but be sure the phone you use is secure. Use a pay phone if you have to."

Jonathan left to catch a flight back home, but Jim stayed and got a ride with Bert to his Washington apartment. He wanted time with him to discuss a number of matters.

"Do you think we can pull this off? I'm worried about Jonathan. He was never good at being tough or composed!"

"I share your concern, but we have no choice. We need to watch him closely. Unfortunately you'll have to assume that role, but somewhat covertly. Call me if you suspect a weakening in his resolve."

"How much should we tell mother about our plan?"

"Nothing more than what we would tell the Feds. We don't want her to worry any more than she has already. We can assure her that it will be taken care of and it will eventually be okay, but I would hesitate to offer more. Tell her it's in my hands. I believe that she trusts me not to let the family down."

"There's one more thing Bert. When I called Jonathan, I was about to ask him to arrange a loan for a friend of mine. You remember Tony Benedetto, my old Army sergeant? His faltering bank has called his note on his otherwise successful engineering business. Can we help him out?"

"I don't see how, Jim. We'll all have our actions, especially financial, scrutinized for the near future. We would have to do it from an offshore account, which might leave a trail. I'm sorry, but how much money are we talking about?"

"I don't know how much, but I'll be talking to him soon."

"How's Sharon taking this? You might want to limit her knowledge and potential for involvement in this debacle."

"She's tough, and she's a major source of advice for me. I know she'd want to know all of the facts no matter what the consequence."

"Let's see what happens over the next week or two. We'll need to meet again, probably secretly, to keep our plan on track," recommended Bert as he left Jim off.

Chapter 100

Diego hadn't been back to New York since his initial tenure as a day laborer rooming with derelicts and druggies. This trip would be different, but in some ways he was nearly back to that same financially distraught situation. He was meeting Karime at an Italian restaurant in what is known in the city as "Little Italy." When he was last there, he couldn't afford a glass of wine in a restaurant like this, never mind the food. In fact, he tried unsuccessfully to get a job as a bus boy there once.

He saw his favorite cousin at the far end of the room. He recognized her even though she was wearing glasses, no makeup and her long black hair was pulled back in a bun. She looked like a plain school teacher, but her beauty still showed through, especially when she smiled.

Diego took a seat opposite her without much ceremony, not wanting to attract attention. "I am so pleased that we could meet..." He hesitated to say her name.

"Ms. Montego," she responded, impressed at his indiscretion, putting out her hand. 'Mr. Ramoz," she greeted him in the name that they had agreed upon in their earlier phone conversation. Her almond shaped brown eyes slowly surveyed the room as they began to talk. They had taken precautions to avoid discovery. Her eyes caught the silhouette of a man approaching their table.

Diego turned to see what was causing the sudden anxiety in her facial expression. Was immigration on to her? His eyes focused on the figure as he got closer causing a déjà-vu experience as he flashed back to Rodríguezes bar in LA. "Tony, I'm so glad you could come. I was worried," Karime's eyes brightened as she realized that it was a friend and that there was no danger.

Diego headed off Tony's salutation to Karime by introducing her. "Tony, this is Ms. Montego. She wants to discuss a business proposition I thought you might be interested in. Ms. Montego, this is my good friend Tony Marino.

Tony became immediately aware of the situation and returned the greeting. "It's a pleasure to meet you," as he looked into her mesmerizing eyes.

"You are very kind Tony, Mr. Ramoz has told me good things about you," responded Karime. "He tells me you're looking to improve your situation and you are an engineer."

"Yes, I am. Mr. Ramoz must have told you how I've lost my engineering business and everything I've worked for all of my life? I guess I'm in the majority being a victim of this banking fiasco."

"Yes, and I asked to meet with both of you to discuss how I may help. First let me tell you I have sold all of my interests in my businesses. Unfortunately, there are still some liabilities that are limiting my ability to invest in new ventures, but I wish to do that locally," Karime responded attempting to talk in code, but without being so covert as to undermine their ability to comprehend what she needed to tell them.

They listened intently realizing that this could be something big and possibly well above their capabilities to be helpful. "You must realize that these things that have happened to you are not by accident. They are the result of the manipulations of those who look upon you and people like you as pieces in their game of greed. I want to assist you in changing the direction of that game," she continued realizing that the looks on their faces reflected not only attentiveness, but confusion.

Tony interjected, "But why do you care? How would that benefit you?"

"What happens here affects me and my people. There are over ten million Mexican nationals in this country who were brought here illegally to work for pennies and are now without a country. America is being run by an abusive group of individuals who believe that its benefits were conceived for them and only them. They use our labor and your naiveté to satisfy their need for power and wealth. They've found a formula that works. They make people believe that they are one of them, morally and religiously, while they convince them that sacrifice is good for the soul. The problem is that it is only the poor and struggling people who sacrifice, as they have in many civilizations before, while the leaders live like royalty, making more money in one day than most people make in a year."

"This is true, but what can we do to stop it. They have the means to buy whatever image they want and use whomever they need to get what they want," said Diego. "They find ways to raise prices, and then make excuses to justify lowering workers' wages. They make exorbitant profits on our backs and our lives even more difficult."

"He's right, we're always in a survival mode. I believe it's to keep us from fighting back as they reap the benefits! The rich rationalize and make promises that if we give the big corporations more money from our tax dollars and give the people who run these corporations outrageous compensation somehow we'll benefit from their excesses."

"Yes, they preach to us as about sacrifice as they buy their yachts, big homes and jets. And all we get are their constant lies. All it takes is a few well-orchestrated deceptions and a condescending smile. What did Reagan call it, the trickle-down effect?' Well he got it right, we got trickled down on while his extremely wealthy constituents earned and kept 40 times more than what they made twenty years ago. I don't see how we can make a difference?" offered Diego despairingly.

"I realize your frustration and anger, but are you just going to let them continue to play their vicious games with your lives? There are people in this country who are intelligent enough to get it and who aren't afraid of confronting them, but they need to be organized and to know that they're not alone. I believe that even the apathetic and the weak, once the light is shined upon the abuse, will become part of a movement to remove their greedy claws from America's democracy," continued Karime.

Diego leaned over the table and whispered to her, "Are you talking a revolution?" His eyes widened in fear of what that word means. He had experienced Watts and Vietnam and he wanted no part of that kind of action.

Tony looked at him and then to her. "We've seen war and the pain that it brings. We would be the ones who suffer. We're not going there!" he exclaimed quietly, but firmly.

"No, I'm not talking of violence. I'm proposing a kind of movement that brings together the ninety plus percent of Americans who have like needs, to a cause that has like purpose. The kind of movement that Gandhi, Mandela and King led! One that exposes violence and vicious rhetoric for what it truly is, the means to control the masses."

Diego and Tony sat back in their chairs and looked at each other with relief, but also with disbelief. Their minds raced with the thoughts provoked by her words. Could she be serious? And how could they lead such a movement even one that was peaceful?

Reading their eyes she said, "You're correct in believing we can't do it alone. We can only be the catalyst, but we must be able to inspire others to join with us, yet to not become so angry that they add to the problem by choosing violence. There are millions of people in this country who were brought here to work for low pay and in poor living conditions. They can't vote but they can work with us to bring the message. They're no longer wanted, since that work is now sent to countries like China and India where the elitist pay little. But they are feared by those who profited by their work because of their numbers! I have limited means to buy the seeds, but I need you both, as well as your friends, to sow them into the fertile soil of frustration. Are you willing? You and your families will be taken care of and you'll have legitimate work to earn that money, but you must be dedicated to the cause."

After a long pause Tony spoke first. "I don't know if we're capable of doing what you ask. What do you think?" He asked as he turned toward Diego.

"If Tony, the optimist is worried, then I'm worried! This is a big job and we're not big people. We're not politicians! How can we stand up to people who can do what they want with us? Where's King and Gandhi now, or the Kennedy brothers, and look what they had to go through? Mandela spent 27 years in prison for his beliefs. We could be putting our families in danger! I don't know. I respect you for what you're trying to do, but I don't think we're the right ones to make it happen."

"I remember you talking about your friends, the Congressman and the Senator. I believe that they married even though they're from different political parties?" You said that she was a liberal Democrat and he was a moderate Republican who admired Teddy Roosevelt. They're the kind of people we need to be part of this effort. They can be our voice and, from what you tell me about them, they're good people who would listen to both of you."

"I don't know if they would have interest in this type of action. They are sophisticated and into political solutions. I doubt they would want to lead a peoples' revolution for reform," declared Tony,

"I only ask that you give it serious thought, but I do believe that you are the right ones to sow the seeds and that we can be successful. You know how to get in touch with me. Please call me by this time next week."

"We'll think about it, but it's an overwhelming proposition, to change a society from self-destruction," answered Tony. "We'll be in touch soon."

"Thank you for meeting with us. I hope we can find a way to help," offered Diego as he gave her a kiss on her cheek and they parted company.

Diego had taken the train to New York but Tony drove since he was in Connecticut for a job interview. "We can talk on the ride back. I have my *new* car. It's an old beat up 1980 Buick, but it was all I could find for $500."

"Are you sure it'll make it?" grinned Diego.

"No, that's why I want you along, in case I need you to push it!" laughed Tony, trying to make light of their dilemma.

Chapter 101

Tom Masters and Don Peters anticipated the visit from Bert Obersham. They knew that his loyalty to the Buckman family was unconditional and he would be in their face in short order. Bert decided to wait until the next meeting hoping he might have an ally within the Group. This made Masters and Peters nervous. They had operated their deception outside of the Group and now they needed to be prepared for a possible counter attack from the General.

They knew he wouldn't just be upset on behalf of the Buckmans, but as a Director of Buckman's banking enterprises, they had put him directly in harm's way. Earlier that day Masters had a brief telephone conversation with Bert attempting to convince him that they were brought in by the FDIC and had accepted the offered role believing they could help minimize the damage. Bert wasn't buying it! Master's was worried!

The room was relatively quiet when Bert arrived. He assumed that the 'Group' had been briefed on the issue and they had been told a story that suited the story tellers. Jonathan was noticeably absent.

"Welcome Bert. We're all truly sorry to hear about the current events and hope that we can help you and the Buckman's work your way out of the mess. As I told you on the phone Don Peters' bank is charged by the FDIC with helping to get the bank's funds and portfolios back on track, and..."

"Let's cut out the bullshit, Tom. You pulled a fast one on the Buckmans with Jim's body not yet decomposed in the ground. It's going to cost you and anyone in this room that was part of it."

The members of the Group were startled by his accusations, especially those who had just listened to Masters' version of the events. "I resent your tone and your accusations, Bert," declared Dale Watkins, counsel and host for the Group. "Yes we were aware of the FDIC action but we didn't know the circumstances until Tom just explained them to us before you walked in."

"Well let me clarify the circumstances for all of you!" Bert proceeded to describe his understanding of the events leading up to the FDIC action. He told how Masters and Peters attempted to connive to get Jonathan Buckman's interest and when that failed due to young Jim Buckman's intervention, they came up with the plan that could lead to their control of the businesses through the FDIC action.

He went on to describe, in detail, how the senior Buckman had arranged offshore loans to Peters' Bank and to Master's oil companies as well as too many of the holdings represented in the room. He told how the takeover of the Buckman banking operations by Peters' bank would not only negate those hidden loans but possibly lead to the takeover of the offshore enterprises and their real estate holdings. "Is there anyone in this room who doubts my explanation?" asked the General in his most commanding war-room manner.

The room was silent as he looked around and took note of those who seemed embarrassed and obviously shocked. The embarrassed, with heads down, were most likely the exposed perpetrators and the shocked with eyes wide open and mouths' agape, were most probably the innocent bystanders.

Masters and Peters were visibly shaken.

"This is all nonsense. I can understand why you're upset at the bank's closing by the feds but there's no truth to your accusations. You need to calm down, Bert. We're all friends, and we're here to help you and the Buckmans, believe me!" declared Masters.

"That's the problem Tom. I don't believe you, and I'm putting you on notice that the house of cards will soon fall if the situation is not corrected immediately. I expect to hear from you within 48 hours." He followed a lesson learned from his close friend and mentor Jim Buckman, gathering his brief case, bidding them good evening, and striding out the door as only a General can.

Chapter 102

Tony and Diego had a lot to talk about on their five-hour ride home from New York City. Karime was a very intelligent woman, and she knew what she was talking about when she spoke of political corruption. But were they the right guys for this ambitious undertaking? They decided to call Jim Buckman's Connecticut home when they stopped for gas and water for the steaming radiator at a service station on Route I-95 near Westport. Nancy Buckman answered the phone and when she heard that they were nearby she invited them over for dinner.

"Jim and Sharon are in town and they'll be here with little Laura. I'm sure they would love to see you both," they took it as a good sign and accepted the offer.

"We'd better let the women know we'll be later than we thought," suggested Diego. "They'll think we're having too much fun and Keisha thinks that I'm coming home on the 9 pm express. She was going to pick me up at South Station."

"Good thought. Well, what do you think about Karime's offer? Can we do it? Would you do it?" asked Tony.

"I don't know, but I was thinking, we fought for this country because we had to, but also because we thought it was our duty to protect America. Tony, is this the America that we fought to protect or did we do it to protect the lifestyles of those greedy insincere bastards and is that why so many of our friends died? Maybe this is just more of that battle, you know to keep America great?"

Nancy called Jim and Sharon on their car phone to let them know that their friends from Boston were also on the way. If you lived within 100 miles of Boston to outsiders you were from Boston. Although, they thought it a strange coincidence, they welcomed the opportunity to see them. They were visiting to have a face-to-face discussion with Nancy about the FDIC takeover and Bert's plan to remedy the situation, but they would make time to renew their friendship with Tony and Diego.

Dinner at the Buckmans was always a grand affair. Tony and Diego felt as if they were in a very fine restaurant and enjoyed the ambience and the break from the doldrums of their life's struggles. But they also felt guilty, for a moment, that their families were not with them and they were dining in the world of the wealthy they perceived to be the enemy, but Jim and Sharon were not of that ilk.

After dinner, Nancy took her granddaughter Laura Marie, the star of the dinner table, up to her special room for a nighttime story as the younger generation talked of life.

"Tony, I didn't forget you. Since we last spoke I had contacted my brother to see if he could arrange a loan for you, but I'm afraid that he is in a similar mess." Jim went on to describe the circumstances of the family bank's demise. "I'm afraid we might also lose everything. Jonathan will be here later. Actually, we're here to discuss the situation with mother."

"Oh, Jim we're sorry to hear that. What will you do?" asked Tony, shocked to learn that they were also vulnerable to the whims and reckless behavior of others.

"We'll survive, we still have our elected positions and there's always a law practice," offered Sharon. "But how are you and your families coping?"

"My business has no customers and as you know Tony's is a victim of a bad bank. That's why we were in New York today," responded Diego. "But we'll also survive. We have good families and our wives are supporting our efforts."

"What do you mean is there work for both of you in New York?" asked Sharon.

"Not exactly, do you remember me mentioning my cousin Karime?" We met with her in New York today," answered Diego.

Jim and Sharon looked at each other as they shared the same thought. Karime was involved with a Mexican drug cartel, what were they doing with her?

Diego, noticing their look said, "Tony maybe you'd better explain."

"We know what you're thinking and she's no longer involved with her late father's cartel. She was a college professor for several years until the FBI, in an attempt to pressure her into giving up the cartel members, had her fired hoping to make her desperate enough to give them information. Her brother's already in prison. She was here to offer us a role in her ambitious plan to correct the injustices in this country and in Mexico."

He detailed her ideas for a peaceful revolution to gain the faith of good, hard-working people who she believed, had been used for decades for the benefit of the few. Sharon's interest was piqued when they expressed her thoughts on a King/ Gandhi type movement to organize those of like mind to end the abuse of American democracy and capitalism. Jim knew of what they spoke since his father had played the role of political manipulator for years believing that it was the only way to live a quality life in this competitive world.

"She's willing to take on the enormous task of educating and inspiring Americans who have all too often opted out for a less contentious role? I need to meet this woman!" exclaimed Sharon, enthused by the very thought that such a person existed.

"I'm afraid you may have to go to Mexico to do that Sharon, but I know she has great respect for you and also you, Jim, even though she realizes that you're a Republican," Tony said with a smile remembering how he once yanked his chain as his drill sergeant.

"My cousin is a good and sincere woman. She believes what is happening in the United States is adding to the problems in her country. She loves Mexico, but she would also have loved to be an American citizen. She graduated from Stanford and she has a doctorate from the University of Mexico. She's very bright and I think that she'll find a way to make this happen, but we don't know if we're the right people to lead the way."

"As we were leaving Karime suggested that we seek the help of both of you, but I'm not sure how she means for you to help," added Tony.

"I think I know how she means for us to help. You're right she's a very bright woman. She sees Jim and me as being on two sides of the political spectrum and both of you as men driven by your love of your families and having a pure sincerity. She has it figured out, but the weakness in her plan is her source of money. We know that it had to have its origin in drugs and that will cause a serious problem of credibility at some point," pondered Sharon.

"But it doesn't have to be an issue!" interjected Jim to the surprise of each of them. "It's just like raising money for a candidacy. We need to convince a lot of people to join the cause and contribute their time and money. It's a matter of educating the electorate. And we may have to find a candidate that can create the passion to inspire the masses out of their doldrums."

Diego looked at Tony, his eyes in a quizzical expression, meeting Tony's look of "why not," so you think that it can be done, amigos?

"I only know that something has to be done to stop this slide of the middle class America!" responded Sharon with a feeling of enthusiasm that her experience in politics was rapidly diminishing. "What do you think Jim?"

"It's a very interesting proposition if we can figure a way around the money issues, especially the initial funding, but tell Karime that we are interested in discussing this some more. Sharon and I will find a way to meet her within the next few weeks. We realize that our whereabouts attracts a certain amount of attention, as does, from what you tell us, hers."

"Well, I'm willing to hear more, what about you Diego?" asked Tony.

"I'm not going to be left out. Yes I am 'on board' as the rich guys' say," answered Diego a broad smile on his face. "I don't know how I can help but I'm willing to work with all of you."

"Well, we need to get on the road. We have a more than a three hour ride, if that old Buick makes it," declared Tony.

"You're both welcome to stay. It's getting late and there are plenty of bedrooms in this place," offered Sharon.

"Thank you, but we need to get home to our families. We go with our spirits lifted and knowing that we have good friends in high places," responded Diego.

"I take it that it's your car in the driveway?" asked Jim.

"Yes isn't it a beauty, not quite the lines of a Mercedes but then who needs luxury?"

"Well, Tony, you might not need luxury but you do need a radiator. It's leaking water all over the driveway. Hold on for a minute my old Beemer is in the garage. I'll get the keys."

"You don't have to do that Jim we'll just fill it up and take a couple of gallons of water with us. We'll find a service station that sells that gooey stuff that seals radiators."

"Not at this time you won't. Jim said as he returned to the room. Here take good care of it. It's older than your Buick. It has a full tank of gas. I still drive it occasionally. I keep it in good shape for old time's sake. I'll see if anything can be done with your car, just consider it a loaner until you get back on your feet."

"Thank you Jim, we really appreciate it. I'll get it back to you soon," he said as they man-hugged and he kissed Sharon good night.

"There's a mobile phone on the console. Call me if you have any problems. Just speed dial #10 for my home; #11 for my phone in the other car and #12 for my Washington office. I'll have your car fixed and you can pick it up on your next trip out here."

Diego followed suit adding, "I'm looking forward to working with both of you. Please thank your mother for dinner and thank you both for your encouragement."

"Thanks again Jim. I hope we don't have any more problems."

Jim's 1968 black onyx BMW looked brand new except for the style. It was a thrill for Tony to drive and very comfortable for Diego to sleep in the soft leather seats on the way home. It would soon be considered an antique.

Chapter 103

Jonathan glanced at his brother's BMW as it passed him on the long winding driveway to the house. He didn't see who was driving. Jonathan remarked when he arrived, "Hey brother I think someone just stole your old BMW. I just saw it going down the driveway."

"No, that was a friend of mine borrowing it, you remember Tony Benedetto from Boston, his old car is broken down in the driveway. How are you doing?" asked Jim with concern in his voice.

Sharon greeted her brother-in-law with a hug and a kiss on his cheek. "Hello, Jonathan you missed your niece, she's already in bed, probably asleep by now. Mother will be right down. How's Kathy and little Jonathan doing?

"She's at her mother's but she's not taking things very well. She blames me for everything," answered Jonathan obviously distressed just talking about them.

"I'm sorry to hear that. Hopefully things will work out for both of you. Have you heard any repercussions from Bert's meeting with the Washington Group?" asked Jim.

"Only from Bert, a couple of hours ago, he said they were shocked at his attitude and he left them with their mouths open. He gave them 48 hours to correct the situation that he accused them of creating," explained Jonathan. I'm worried Jim. I don't see how we can change what's happened.

"It all depends how it happened. Did the Feds have information or did your friends lead them there with expectations? Let's go into the library, mother will join us there. We'll call Bert and put him on speaker to discuss this further," added Jim.

Nancy joined her sons and Sharon as Jim completed the call to Bert. "Hello, General. I hear you kicked some butt yesterday!"

"I don't know if I reached anyone's butt, but I did do some kicking. I didn't give them much time to respond. I want them to stew for a while wondering what I was going to do.

"Have you heard back from any of them?" asked Jonathan.

"No, but they have about 38 hours left of their ultimatum. Who's there? Hold on Jim, someone's at the door." They heard his footsteps as he walked across the room, then a loud crashing sound.

"Bert, Bert, are you there? What happened?" The phone went silent, as if it was hung up. Jim hung up his phone and called the Washington police. They immediately dispatched a cruiser to Bert's address.

The call back from the police took only about 20 minutes. "This is Sergeant Upton, Washington PD, I'm sorry sir but General Obersham isn't here. It looks like a robbery. The place was ransacked."

Jonathan's face was flushed, "Oh no, what's going on? What are we going to do?" he was shivering and holding his head.

"How can this be, who are these people? What do they want?" asked Nancy.

"We shouldn't jump to conclusions, we really don't know what happened, but we'll find out. Sharon, I've got to go to Washington in the morning. Can you and Laura Marie stay here with mother? I'll arrange to have police protection on the grounds until I return."

"Do what you have to do. I'll take care of things here, but be careful. Please don't try to be a hero, you have a family!" cautioned Sharon.

"Don't worry, I'm not going to take any chances, but we need to find out what's going on. Jonathan, can you stay here too? They need a man in the house and your family isn't home."

"I'll stay Jim, but don't you think that I should go with you?"

"I think you're needed here, If you don't mind," Jim tried to reinforce his brother's confidence. He knew that they needed to stick together, possibly for the first time in their lives, but he hoped that he wasn't making a mistake relying on him.

Jim lay awake all night thinking about Bert, realizing that the General lived through the chaos and dangers of three wars and yet he might lose his life to protect the Buckman family. He also realized that Bert's the only one who knows the secrets of the offshore enterprise account. Was that the motive for the break-in? Did they kidnap him or...he didn't want to think it...and would they kill him? Bert was tough. His Father had told him stories, during his long illness, of the brave things his closest friend had done to help them survive as subversives behind enemy lines.

He would find the answers and he would also have to learn about those offshore operations! He closed his eyes, and put his arm over Sharon, but his thoughts were of his family's loyal and caring friend and of those whose insatiable greed for more may cost him his life, if they already hadn't. His father was right about the need to be aware of those who would take away their wealth, but maybe he was looking in the wrong direction. He had feared the populace, the poor and the middle class, but was it his peers, his colleagues, the wealthy manipulators of power, who presented the real danger?"

Jim left for the airport at 5:00 am arriving in Washington D.C. on the first flight at into Dulles. He drove immediately to the General's home, a two story brownstone near the Capitol Building. A police car was parked in front of the residence and the front door displayed the yellow caution tape used to identify a crime scene. He approached the officer who was sitting in the vehicle, talking on his radio.

"Officer, I'm Congressman Buckman. I'm a close friend of General Obersham. Is he okay?" he asked as he showed his identification.

"Sorry, sir, I can't discuss the situation, but you can contact my watch commander, Captain Williams. He may be able to answer your questions. He's at the precinct."

Jim drove the six blocks to the police precinct trying to prepare for the worst, but hoping for good news. Maybe the General got out of there. He probably chased the intruder down the street, knowing his macho attitude and inability to accept defeat. He's probably sitting in the Commander's office right now telling him war stories.

Captain Williams was sitting at his desk, his eyes on the ominous pile of papers that would occupy his 10-hour shift. He was a distinguished looking man who appeared to be embracing his sixth decade. He had the appearance of a military man who stayed fit and was serious about his responsibilities. He looked up from his work to greet his announced visitor.

"Good morning, Congressman. I understand that you're a friend of General Obersham."

"Good morning, Captain. Yes, my father and the General had been Army buddies since the World War II. Have you any idea where he is?"

"No, but we know where he isn't! We've checked the bus terminals, train stations and airport videos and there's no indication that he has left Washington, but he's not at his downtown office and, obviously, not at home."

"I was on the phone with him when whatever happened went down. He heard a knock on his door and went to answer it. We heard a loud crashing noise, our phone was on speaker for the benefit of my mother and brother, who were in the room."

"May I ask what was the nature of the conversation?" asked the captain.

"It was just a social call. Why do you ask?" Jim realized that the "nature of the conversation" could be related to the General's disappearance and that it was best not to discuss it with the police.

"Was he calling in distress expecting something bad to happen?" questioned the Captain.

"No, the General is like family. We were just exchanging greetings. Would it be possible to visit his apartment? I may be able to note some indication of what might be missing, if it was a robbery? I've been there many times over the years," Jim explained somewhat clumsily.

"I'm afraid not, Congressman. At least not until we've released it from crime scene status. I'll let you know when that is. You can leave your contact information with the officer at the front desk. Sorry I can't be more helpful, but these things tend to sort themselves out."

"That's fine, Captain. I understand. Please don't hesitate to contact me at any time if anything comes up."

Jim decided he needed to find a way to get into Bert's apartment. He knew Bert's wife was in Florida for the month. He doubted the police would have an all-night surveillance on an empty apartment. He had remembered that Bert had a place where he stored important papers. When he was about 11 years old his father brought him and Jonathan to Washington as a treat during their spring vacation and they had visited the General before taking in the historic sites. During their visit he noticed Bert go into his study and, since the door was slightly open, saw him climb a ladder and remove several books from the top shelf of his bookcase. He came out with a steel, safe-like box. Bert and his father opened the box on the dining room table while the boys enjoyed milk and cookies in the kitchen.

They both became very serious, keeping their voices down as they viewed the contents of that mysterious box. Jim often wondered what was so intriguing about its contents. He now believed that it was probably what the intruders were looking for last night. If whatever it was is still there he had to find it before the police did and, more important, he had to find the General.

Jim waited until evening and parked a block away observing the lone police vehicle that held vigilance near the General's apartment. The vehicle left at 9:10 pm, passing him without acknowledgement. The officer was occupied by his radio conversation. Before he reached the next intersection his blue and red lights went on as a silent warning of his approach, with bleeps of his siren sounding as he came to cross streets.

He didn't know when he would be able to return. This was his chance to search the apartment. He had gone to Bert's downtown civilian office and found a set of keys in his desk. He was hoping that one of them would allow him entry. Leaving his car parked two blocks away he walked briskly down the street to the building. A quick look around as he climbed the outside steps to the brownstone's front door assured him that he was alone on the street.

He fumbled through five individual keys before he could breathe a sigh of relief from success. The door opened to the high ceilinged foyer. It was pitch-dark. He had purchased a small flashlight at the local pharmacy. The darkened corridor leading to the study caused a sudden flashback to the tunnels of Vietnam. Startled for a moment, he went on, slowly opening the door to the Bert's study. He stopped. Hearing a noise coming from the kitchen, he looked over his shoulder towards the direction of the sounds. Listening intensely he saw movement coming towards him. He flashed his light in its direction. There was an immediate response, as he noted reflective green eyes and a meow as the Bert's cat, General Patton, passed beneath his feet.

Jim's heart stopped pounding and he smiled at his vulnerability. As he opened the door to the study he noted that there were books strewn across the room, but not all of them had that fate. Jim pulled a chair from the nearby desk and climbed to reach the top shelves, which were undisturbed.

The twelve-foot ceilings allowed for two extra rows of shelving at the top. It was still out of reach of his six foot height and the two foot reach achieved from the chair. As he focused his memory, he remembered that the General had a ladder he used to access the higher shelves. He looked around from his perch. His light caught the end of a ladder lying on the floor behind a sofa at the far end of the room. Whoever was here gave up before they searched the top row. The quick response of the police must have scared them off. He secured the ladder to its proper configuration with its small wheels on top hooking on to a slotted runner and the bottom wheels positioned at a safe angle so as to provide stable mobility.

He heard the steel box before he saw it, as his fingers pushed aside the books shielding it, scraping them against the metal. Jim struggled to lift it from its secure place and carry it down the ladder to the desk. It had a built-in combination lock and he didn't have a clue how he would open it. He decided that it would be best to complete the task in a safer location.

Feeling relieved at his good fortune he decided to take his bulky prize to his office where he would try to open it.

As he descended the ladder he heard a noise from the rear of the apartment. That damn cat again, he thought as he continued to the rear door of the apartment in darkness. He would go through the basement and out to the courtyard, just in case the stakeout had returned.

To his surprise a figure was there in the shadows and before he could react a clenched fist hit him square in the jaw and he was down. He heard a loud shout of pain as the heavy steel box dropped on his mysterious opponent's foot.

The voice, even as a painful yell was very familiar. "General, is that you?" he asked as he lay on the floor holding his abused jaw.

"Jim, what are you doing here?" was the reply as Bert reached for his arm. "You've got the box. How did you know it was here?"

"Oh my God, it is you. What happened? Where did you go?" Jim was confused and hurting." And where did you get that right hook?"

"I wasn't sure that I still had it, but quickly, come in here," Bert commanded as he led him into a small room that was in the middle of his row house apartment and, as such, had no windows. "It's a long story, but I'm glad you're here." We shouldn't stay very long. I came back for this box. Did your dad tell you about it?"

"No, he didn't, but I guessed its significance remembering seeing you and my father talking over it when Jonathan and I were visiting as children."

"Well, your instincts were right. This is information that we don't want either the authorities or the Washington Group to get their hands on."

"Who was it that broke in? Did you know them?" asked Jim, wondering why they didn't take him or worse, kill him.

"There were two of them. They wore ski masks. I answered the door while you were on the phone and took what I think was a nightstick off the side of the head," Bert showed Jim the bump and bruise off the right side of his forehead. "They must have been here for a while because I woke up as they were going out the rear door and the place was trashed. I got in my car and followed them to Arlington, but lost them in traffic."

"Did you get a license number? What were they driving?" asked Jim.

"It was a black pickup truck, but they were too far ahead of me to read the plate. They seemed to be going towards the Beltway."

"I'm very curious Bert, can you open this box? I need to see what has your friends so worried?"

"I can Jim. But are you prepared to learn more about your dad than you may be ready to absorb?" cautioned Bert his eyes piercing Jim's in the dim light of the windowless room.

"I doubt you can shock me Bert. Please open it."

Chapter 104

It was the second day since Jim had left for Washington. Sharon prepared breakfast for Jonathan, Nancy and her daughter and decided to call Jim's car phone. Although they often took cabs in Washington Jim had a car garaged in Washington. She hadn't heard from him the previous day and was worried. When she picked up the house phone receiver she was surprised to hear Jonathan's voice.

"Yes, I think that he's there in the city now," said Jonathan.

"I just heard a click! Are you alone there?" came the caution from a strange voice with a distinct southern accent.

"Sharon, is that you? I'll call you later," Jonathan and his friend hung up abruptly.

Before he could move, Sharon was at his door. "Who was that Jonathan? And why did you hang up so quickly? What's going on?" demanded Sharon.

"It was just a friend. I was telling him about last night and that Jim was in Washington trying to make sense of it all," declared Jonathan, his words stumbling out of his mouth.

"Jonathan, I hope you're telling me the truth, because if you're not you have breached a trust that you need right now. Your brother is risking everything to straighten this mess out for you and the Buckman family."

"Listen Sharon, I know that and I appreciate it, but he doesn't always know what's best for our family."

Jonathan's words cut into her heart and added to her fears. He was undermining Jim's efforts!

"I think you had better leave. You have no idea what you're doing," declared Sharon. Realizing that there was a chance for a negative reaction given his emotional instability, she noted the location of a heavy ceramic vase within reach of her right hand.

"I'll leave Sharon. I'm sorry if I've disappointed you and Jim, but I can solve this problem without his help!"

The voices awoke his mother who appeared at the bedroom door. "What's going on here? Did we hear from Jim?" asked Nancy as she noted the tension in the room.

"Not yet mother, but Jonathan has to leave for an appointment," explained Sharon.

"Is everything all right? Jonathan can't you stay for breakfast?

"No, I need to get going mother. Someone is waiting for me. I'll have breakfast with them," answered Jonathan knowing that Sharon was not one to counter. "I'll call you later," he said as he kissed his mother on the cheek and picked up his briefcase.

"What was that all about Sharon? You look quite distressed!" Nancy queried.

Believing that she needed to know what was going on and trusting in her strength, Sharon explained the morning's conflict.

"Oh my God, do you think Jonathan had anything to do with what happened to Bert last night?" Nancy said wide-eyed and stunned at the thought.

"I don't know, but I do know that whatever he's doing, it isn't good for the family. He's an emotional mess, but I'm at a loss as to what we can do about it. I need to let Jim know that there is another element at play here."

She made several calls before reaching him at noon on his mobile phone. She explained the morning events and her concerns. "I think he believes he can solve the problem, but he's very distraught, Jim. I'm worried that he's going to do something destructive."

"I share your fears. He doesn't always act rationally even when he isn't distraught. Who do you think he was talking to?"

"I don't know. It wasn't a voice that I recognized, but he spoke with a heavy southern drawl."

"Damn it! I'll bet it was Masters. Jonathan doesn't realize how over-his-head he is dealing with those bastards. They'll chew him up and spit him out!"

"Do you think he would hurt the family for his own sake?"

"What do you think? He believes he's in competition with me and he isn't thinking about the consequences. Well, the good news is that I found Bert, or he found me," Jim relayed the previous day's adventures. I saw what was in that steel box, Sharon. I'll tell you more when I'm home. I don't trust these phones."

"I understand. Laura and I will be in Washington tomorrow. We can talk then. Can you pick us up at Dulles at 6:45 pm? We'll be coming in on the Shuttle?"

"I'll be there. Miss you, and don't worry, we'll work this out."

"I hope so, but can we work it out? Give my love to Bert. I'm so relieved that he's all right."

"I will, and try to keep mother calm. She'll worry more about her sons' conflict than the money!"

Jim was on his way to meeting Bert for lunch at a private club in Arlington. Jonathan's actions that morning would complicate things. It would be a topic for discussion with Bert. Why would he be talking to the man who is obviously trying to steal his family's fortune? Jonathan might be emotional, but he isn't stupid!"

Chapter 105

It was 1:35 in the morning when the red and blue lights of a Connecticut state trooper's vehicle flashed behind them. "Where did he come from?" asked a startled Tony. He knew that he had been speeding at more than 70 miles per hour in a 55 mile per hour zone, but there was no one on the highway and they just wanted to get home.

"Sir, do you know why I stopped you?" asked the big burly black trooper in a stern baritone."

"I assume it was because I was driving slightly over the speed limit, officer?"

"Your license and registration please," his voice, gentle but firm, caused Tony to look up at his intimidating figure.

The trooper took the license and registration then began to laugh in a very subtle manner. "Well, I know you're not Captain James Buckman," he said looking at the BMW's registration and flashing his light on Tony's face. "Sergeant Benedetto you haven't learned to slow down after all these years and you need to update this picture. You're getting a lot uglier in your old age." Tony and Diego looked up as the trooper shined his flashlight on his black face with the big toothy smile.

"Ortiz you son of a bitch, what are you doing out here? We haven't seen you since Jim's re-election in '82'. So you made the troopers. Congratulations, I think," Tony said with a smile glancing over at Diego who was also grinning.

"Making a living off of saps like you, Sarge. How are you doing and look who's riding shotgun" as he shined his light on Tony's passenger, "If it isn't the man who falls out of trees, hey Diego what's happening? You know, Tony, you're getting old too, man. You gotta slow down!" chided Ortiz.

"So are you going to earn your money and give us a ticket or what?" asked Tony, a forced smile on his face as he thought of the days when he was the tough drill sergeant and Ortiz was a green kid from the Bronx, and one of the men who survived the escape from the North Vietnamese with Buckman.

"Hey, I've a better idea. I'm off duty in 20 minutes how about a coffee at the Howard Johnsons in Mystic instead? I haven't seen you Nam rats for years - lets catch up!" he said as he handed Tony back his papers.

"You're on! We'll race you there!" Tony said with a grin and a feeling of relief.

"No racing! I still need this job, but I'll see you there in twenty!" responded Ortiz.

Tony and Diego looked over their shoulders as Ortiz walked back to his cruiser. "He's a big guy but he's lost some weight," remarked Tony. "He used to look like a football lineman, now he's more of a linebacker."

"He's a great guy. Jim talks about him as if he was the strength of that escape squad in Nam. He says that Sergeant Eagle and Ortiz gave him the courage to go on. They were all tough bastards to survive that stuff."

"Yeah, there was no easy ride in Nam! We were all wounded in some way. For most of us it was deep inside where it doesn't always show," reflected Tony.

As Ortiz reached his cruiser a black mustang traveling at well over 90 miles per hour flew by. The trooper jumped into his car and began his pursuit, lights flashing and siren blasting.

"Whoa! What the hell was that? How dumb can you be to put the throttle down as you pass a trooper?" remarked Tony!

"Let's go, he might need help!" added Diego anxious for adventure.

"Okay, but we better be careful. He's probably called for backup and they'll be coming up behind us. We don't want to be their target."

By the time they approached the flashing lights of Ortiz' vehicle no backup had arrived. The Mustang was pulling out of the breakdown lane tires screeching.

"They're really stupid doing that in front of a statey!" exclaimed Diego.

"Oh shit, Ortiz is down! He's in the road. Diego get out and see what you can do for him. I'll go after them. Call on his radio!" instructed Tony his eye on their tail lights. I'm going to call Jim."

Tony reached Jim and told him about meeting Ortiz and that he was down.

"Go get them Sarge. Don't let those bastards get away," ordered Jim upset at the thought of possibly losing another of his squad.

"I'm on it, Captain!" The Beemer was old, but it had a V8 and it was very fast. Jim had it souped-up when he was young and foolish.

Diego reached Ortiz as he was beginning to move. He was moaning in pain; bleeding profusely from his right side.

"Don't move, amigo! It's Diego. I'll call for help. Tony's on their tail," he ripped off his shirt and pressed it against Ortiz's wound, hoping to slow the flow of blood.

'It's bad ain't it? If I don't make it tell my wife and daughter that I was thinking of them. My little girl's in high school."

"You're going to be okay. Did you call for backup?"

"I did, but just before I stopped them. I don't know if..." Ortiz passed out before he could finish.

Diego called the state barracks, and explained the situation leading with "officer down" to get their attention. He told them of Tony's pursuit, describing his car so they wouldn't shoot at him traveling at high speeds. "The shooters are in a late model black Mustang heading east on I-95 just before the Mystic exit"

"We're on it sir, Can you stay with Trooper Ortiz until the medics get there?"

"Yes, but hurry, he's bleeding badly and he's unconscious!"

Tony gained on the mustang over a five mile interval. As he got closer, traveling at 128 miles per hour, he hoped they wouldn't stop. He had no weapons. He slowed to their speed of 92 miles per hour wondering if they were straight out. That must be an underpowered car. They probably stole it, he thought, unless they slowed to take a shot at their pursuer.

The question was soon answered as a shot rang-out and his windshield shattered. He steered to the right side of the road trying to stay directly behind them making another shot more difficult. He noted their plate, a New York number beginning with BRK. Must be Brooklyn, he thought and it ended in what looked like "8899," but the numbers were obscured by dirt and grime.

He saw a gun appear out of the right side of the car. Another shot was fired. He ducked and held the steering wheel straight. The bullet whistled by his head and hit the leather seat back. All he could think of was that Jim was going to be pissed, he cherished his Beemer. When he looked up he saw the flashing lights of a police cruiser coming down the ramp to his right and about a quarter mile in front of them. He then heard the screaming sirens as it was followed by another in tandem.

The shooters saw them too and steered to the left side of the road looking for a place to cross the grass median strip which encompassed a drainage ditch. Tony gunned his high powered engine and headed to the left, towards their escape route to cut them off. He couldn't let them get away. The troopers' vehicles crossed the road in front of the ramp intending to block the I-95 lanes and their escape route. Seeing what was happening one cruiser turned, tires screeching and headed against the traffic towards the dueling cars in the outside breakdown lane.

Tony slowed down as the Mustang veered into his lane trying to drive him of the road, but their momentum caused their car to catch the top of the grassy slope of the ditch. Their momentum caused them to careen down the embankment flipping over several times before they came to a stop against an old oak tree. Within seconds their car burst into flames. Two figures emerged just before the explosion, as the Troopers approached running down the embankment, guns drawn yelling for them to hit the ground. They did, without their weapons that were just trying to escape the inferno.

The second cruiser pulled up to the BMW. "Are you all right sir?" asked the officer riding shotgun.

"Yes, I'm okay, but they shot up my buddy's car."

"Well sir, you're lucky that's all they shot up!"

As they spoke, an ambulance with lights flashing and siren screeching, passed at top speed. Tony was hoping they were in time to save Ortiz. A third cruiser pulled up near where Tony was standing at the side of the road and Diego jumped out. The trooper took off immediately following the ambulance to the hospital.

Tony called Jim on the car phone and gave him the bad news.

"Don't worry about the car. I hope Ortiz is okay. Are you going to the hospital? Call me when you know something."

"I will Jim, at this number?" asked Tony.

"Yes, leave a message if I don't answer."

"How is he?" asked Tony, as he approached Diego, anxious to know if their fellow soldier had survived.

"He was conscious when they put him in the ambulance. Wow, what happened to Jim's beautiful car?" Diego was shocked at the site of the Buckman's shot- up BMW. "He's not going to be happy amigo!"

"I told him about Ortiz. He agreed that I couldn't let those bastards get away, but a bullet hit the radiator and it isn't going anywhere. Officer, can we hitch a ride with you to the hospital? Officer Ortiz is a friend of ours."

"Sure, we need to get a statement from you and from Ortiz, if he's able to talk. Get in!"

Ortiz was conscious long enough before they began operating on him to answer some questions! He told his fellow troopers that he could tell that they were white supremest, skinheads proudly displaying their symbolic bald head and Nazi tattoos. What he didn't know, but was about to find out, was that there was a warrant out for them as suspects in the burning of a Black church in the New Haven area. The attempt by Ortiz to have them get out of the car gave them a motive to add to their racists acts. They shot him twice and attempted their escape, not realizing that the headlights of the fast approaching vehicle in their rear view mirror were those of very persistent friends of the officer.

Diego and Tony waited at the Hospital for the results of the Ortiz's surgery. I'm worried about Ortiz. He was bleeding pretty badly. Why would those guys shoot him like that?

"You know, Tony, some bigotry is not so subtle! People still hate for no reason and too many claim to be religious! Are you religious, Tony?"

"I grew up a Catholic, but I realized at an early age that religion is our primitive need to explain the unexplainable. It's part of our instinct for survival. Religion itself isn't the problem. But it's also the way used to get the masses to follow some dictatorial leader who interprets a religion to suit their purposes, usually to gain wealth or power."

"So you don't believe in God?"

"Actually, I believe in all religions that are based in compassion and love, but I have no use for those based in hypocrisy, hate and the control of others. They think they're special and judge others as being less than they are. Some believe that they gain favor with their God if they put down others. They're not true Christians, Muslims, Jews or Buddhists or true to any other so-called religion. They're bigots pure and simple!"

"Well Tony, I'm sorry I asked. You have strong feelings about religion! I believe in God, but I haven't lived a perfect life. I think I might go to hell! Does that make me dumb, to believe and not do what I need to do to go to heaven?"

"No, not if having that faith works for you in life!" responded Tony. Diego, you believe in the Jesus Christ, right?

"Yes, he's the one who started it all."

"What do you think he would say if he were in this world today? Do you think he would tolerate the injustice? Do you think he would think its okay for the richest country in this country to ignore the 14 million children living in poverty? Do you think he would say its fine to be bigoted and to judge people for not being like them, as many Christians do in this country today? I don't think he would tolerate that hypocrisy! And I don't understand how so many people are sucked into believing that contributing to the obscene tax free wealth of those who claim to be evangelist is fine while they fly in their corporate jets to their numerous mansions. I don't think that Jesus would be happy with their self-serving rhetoric and might remind them of words attributed to him that, "it would be easier to put a camel through the eye of the needle than for a rich man to enter the kingdom of heaven."

"But Tony, what if there is a God... and there is a heaven and a hell. I don't think I can make it to heaven. I have not lived a good life?

"I believe strongly in the man named Jesus and his philosophy on life, but question those who claim to follow him thinking it will gain them wealth and advantage over others and I'm not sure about the heaven and hell thing. But in case you don't make it to heaven, at least you'll be someplace with a good friend," answered Tony with a grin.

"Thanks! That makes me feel much better, amigo!"

"Thinking about death, I wonder if Ortiz will make it?" asked Tony, "He made it through a war and now he's lying in a hospital bed because the country he fought for harbors radical bigots who claim to be Christians, racist Christians calling themselves White Supremest! They believe they're better than others and that America is a White Christian country."

"They're not the only ones who think that, Tony. There are a lot of people who think they're the chosen ones and that others are on this earth to serve them. We Latinos came from civilizations that were highly intelligent, but were subdued by warlike peoples from Spain, some who called themselves bishops. They claimed they were serving their God. But they were there to steal our gold and rape our women and they left us with disease and death!"

"You know that haters join together because they can't make it alone in a civilized society. They're paranoid. They only feel special if they can be above others or, even worse, destroy others. There have been people like that since there have been people."

"My padre used to say it takes all kinds to make the world and most of them are not going to be your friends. I always thought he was too, how you say, cynical? Now I know what he was saying, but I also know that there are good people, like Keisha, you, Jim and Sharon in this world too. I too believe that we can't make it alone, that we have to stick together or the greedy and the haters will take everything and leave us to die poor."

As they finished their conversation, they noticed a doctor walking with a trooper, approaching them from the direction of the operating room.

"Here comes the bad news!" exclaimed Tony.

"How are you gentlemen doing? Your friend is going to be fine. The bullets didn't injure any vital organs, but he's lost a lot of blood. He'll be here for a few days.

"Can we see him? asked Diego.

"He's in recovery but he won't be conscious for several hours. You might want to go home and visit him tomorrow," suggested Dr. Raymond.

Trooper Daniels drove them to the local bus station from where they would take the two hour trip to South Station in Boston. Meghan would pick them up and Tony would take her home to Southie and then drive Diego to the Cape. They were both relieved at Ortiz's prognosis and exhausted. Sleeping on the bus was not a problem.

Chapter 106

The 1990s had started with both confusion and apprehension. The lives of many were adversely affected, but not all suffered. The wealthy became wealthier as the result of the Reagan tax breaks of the 1980s. The crash of trickle down economy in Reagan's last year was a windfall for the so-called "Vulture Capitalist" who used all the loopholes and benefits that their loyal Congressman could provide to make millions of dollars, as millions of people lost their jobs, their homes and their dreams for their children's futures. The national deficit had risen while the rich got richer and the poor and the middle class working American were ignored as being no longer important to society.

Tony saw first-hand how manipulated capitalism worked. The company that bought his bank-damaged firm for the 10 cents on the dollar with a promise of contracting with him for three years reneged on their obligations putting him and his family under the proverbial bus after he signed over several million dollars in contracts. He lost his home, his retirement and his pride. They knew he didn't have the money to fight their outrageous behavior. It was corporate America at its worst.

The American economy was in free fall. A Republican President was in office again. It was time for another war! Our wealthy allies, Kuwait and Saudi Arabia were being attacked by another of our wealthy allies, Iraq. All three had an ample supply of American made weapons. Our help was requested by the Saudis to level the playing field. Iraq had the bigger force and they were the aggressor. It was time for "Shock and Awe" round one. We called it "Desert Storm." Americans were told that their national interest was at stake and that our Middle Eastern friends would compensate us for our efforts. We should have known better as we absorbed another round of increased oil costs.

Ortiz recovered, but was cut from the force, he was told that it was due to budget constraints brought on by the failed Reagan-Bush economy. He was healthy enough to perform at a desk job, but instead was one of the first determined to be expendable when layoffs were imposed. His color had nothing to do with it, they claimed.

Bulldog Masters, was in his 60's, but age didn't dissuade him from his goal of controlling whatever elements of the economy that lay vulnerable to his tactics. Although his plan to gain the Buckman family assets for the benefit of his cause did not go as anticipated, he believed that all was not lost. He was counting on Jonathan Buckman's greed and envy to overcome the obstacles set by his older brother, Bert Obersham and his late father.

His Washington Action Group remained active and cautiously optimistic even though the trickle down American economy began its bank induced slide into oblivion. It was the eighth and final year of the Reagan Administration and the trickle was not even a drip. The hard earned profits of the elite were safe offshore in Bermuda, the Caymans and Switzerland.

A significant amount of their assets were tightly tied to profits in the ever increasing cost of oil. They had benefitted by their shrewd investments in mortgages, which in the first 10 years of activity would generate nearly 60% of its value in interest alone while homeowners monthly payments would pay less than 10% of the principal. The upfront earnings left homeowners with little equity and their properties prime for profits to the bottom feeders of foreclosures. Due to job insecurity the average homeowner lived in their home an average of seven years. As long as the real estate market appreciated in value, mortgages were a good investment for those with money to invest, with foreclosures the safety net after profit-taking a sure bet.

A $400,000 loan would have paid about $360,000 in interest alone at 7.5% in 10 years, while only paying down about $40,000 in principal. Banks could afford to foreclose and put the poor homeowner in the street without the cost of a sympathy card. Unfortunately, when too many banks grant loans that rely on foreclosures the system breaks down. Greed amongst thieves can be as big a problem as greed perpetrated on the working class. The American dream had become subject to the whims of a bank or a mortgage company's fast buck mentality.

Although the demise of many financial institutions from 1988 to 1993 nearly destroyed the American economy, Masters believed that he and his Group were still in the game. They had some cards to play, and one of them had Jonathan Buckman's picture on it.

Jonathan wanted to better his brother Jim. His goal was to prove he was as cunning as his father in creating and protecting the family assets. Masters needed to gain his confidence and find out how vulnerable he and his colleagues within the Group were as a result of the elder Buckman's investment strategies. Did the Colonel really set it up so that any action by the Group to "secure" his family's assets would be offset by self-incrimination? Masters called a special meeting of the Group, inviting Jonathan to discuss his need for assistance.

"Gentlemen, Jonathan Buckman needs our help in overcoming his family's business problems. You are all aware of the federal investigations that are ongoing into the Buckman Enterprises. Jonathan is here to explain his dilemma and, in particular, how his brother Jim has become part of the problem. We owe that much to our late colleague, Jonathan's father," announced Masters.

"Thank you Tom, I do appreciate your offer of assistance. As most of you know, thanks to my father, Buckman Enterprises has played a vital part in the propagation of the Republican Party's political philosophy. The current effort to undermine that work by a Republican administration is curious. The new President seems to have lost control of the Justice Department. Our family has worked diligently over the past 25 years producing significant benefit for all of us. The current scrutiny by the federal government seems to undermine that effort. I'm told they'll soon be looking into offshore operations to determine if their financial activities were legal," explained Jonathan.

Masters interrupted, "Jonathan believes that his brother Jim has information that could benefit their investigation and that General Obersham, who is noticeably absent, may be assisting him in his attempt to derail our Group's philosophical and political efforts. You all recall the General's last appearance here when he, not so subtly, implied that he would be so inclined if we didn't comply with his demands."

"Well, Jonathan, you know how much we admired your father, but Buckman Enterprises is in serious trouble and we believe that your father may have left a trail behind that could cause us harm." explained Don Peters, CEO of the banking conglomerate CTC. "Before we can commit our resources to helping you and your family we need to know more."

"Yes!" added Masters, "Don's right, we believe your brother and General Obersham have information that could clarify that risk, but the General seems to be aiding Jim in his effort to blackmail this Group, and we have no idea why. We need your help in finding out what they think they have against us and what they want. We need you find out whatever damaging information they think they have? Keep in mind that we have offered to help before and your brother stopped us."

'I believe I can find out what you want to know, but first I need to know what you're going to do for me and I want it in writing!" demanded Jonathan his voice beginning to quiver.

Masters looked at Peters who gave him an affirmative nod. "You'll have that by this time tomorrow. We'll see you here then."

"I look forward to meeting with you tomorrow."

Chapter 107

Jim met Sharon and their daughter at Dulles airport at 6:45 p.m. as planned. "How was your flight?" he asked as he kissed two of the most important women in his life.

"It was fine. I saw the news about Ortiz before we left. They interviewed Tony and Diego. I'm afraid your car is a wreck. I'm surprised they didn't get hurt!" exclaimed Sharon as they walked to the baggage claim area.

"Tony called me when he began his pursuit and I told him to do what he had to do," He paraphrased his verbiage about not letting "those bastards get away," in consideration of his young daughter's presence. "It was probably not a wise thing to encourage him, but he would have done it anyway, and the car is insured."

"Did you learn anything more from the General when you met?" asked Sharon curious about his last words of not trusting these phones."

"Yes, I'm afraid so. I made copies. We can discuss it at the apartment." His face grew solemn and his lips tightened as he recalled his meeting with Bert Obersham.

"I'm looking forward to it, but I have work to do. I'm presenting my counter arguments tomorrow against President Bush's desire to send American troops into Kuwait to stop Saddam Hussein's Iraq army from threatening Saudi Arabia."

"That's one position that we agree on. We don't owe the Saudis anything. They've been doubling and tripling our cost of oil over the last 25 years to the point that it's destroying our economy. I attempted to contact the Secretary of Defense, Dick Cheney, but he was out of Town."

"You'd think they'd have learned from the past that we can't be the world's policemen," added Sharon, "Just a few years ago Iraq was our ally and now we're going to fight them and face the weapons we sold them and troops that we trained? The argument then was that they're friends we needed to keep a balance with Iran.

"The turmoil in the mid-east has survived for thousands of years and we aren't going to stop it," added Jim as they drove to their Capitol Hill apartment.

"Have you given any thought to the discussion with Tony and Diego about demonstrating for change?"

"I have, but I don't have any answers. How about you? This is more in your philosophical realm. I represent a family that has been an integral part of the problem for almost 40 years."

"That's true, but you're getting wiser with age," chided Sharon, with a smirk.

Turning towards her, eyebrows raised, he said, "Maybe I'm feeling compassion since we may soon be part of the have-nots. Dad's little steel box is a time bomb set to go off."

Sharon's eyes widened as she realized he was serious, but she was more concerned about a criminal investigation and the consequences to their life. The money didn't mean much to her, but Jim and her family meant everything. "Is it that serious, Jim? What can we do?"

"Truthfully, I don't know, but we may not have the credibility to lead the movement described by our good friends. We need to see how this plays out before we can commit. I may have to pay for the sins of my father."

He had cautioned Sharon not to discuss the contents of the steel box once they were in the privacy of their Washington apartment. He assumed the place would be "bugged." He gave her an overview of the dilemma during the drive home. He showed Sharon copies of the important papers that the General and his father had secured in the steel box, stopping in a shopping center parking lot to answer her questions, their young daughter asleep in the back seat.

It was obvious to her that tax laws and reporting requirements relative to profits and political contributions had been avoided. It was also obvious that his father had made sure that the "fingerprints" of all of the Washington Action Group were clearly visible on one or more of the documents, whether by their signatures on loan documents or by incriminating notes in the margins of each page.

The senior Buckman had set up three secret offshore accounts, the codes and account numbers of which were identified in the original files contained in the steel box, which was still in Bert's possession. He also set up a separate account that Jonathan had access to, if needed for emergencies. That accessible account was to be funded by transfers from one of the three secret accounts. Bert Obersham was the only one entrusted with that responsibility. It was Jim's father's intention to keep Jim clean of that activity since he was an elected official.

"Jim, this is sure to lead to federal indictments, but you're not mentioned in any of these papers and it's obvious that your dad consciously protected you and the family, but left himself exposed. Your family will probably lose everything if the Federal investigation uncovers these documents, but I don't see a trail that leads to you or that would result in any of your family's indictment," advised Sharon.

"No, but Jonathan has managed the family businesses since father's death. He might be vulnerable. As much as he deserves a good kick in the butt I can't let him take the fall for this."

"Do you have a plan for preventing that and what about the loss of millions and the fate of your mother in all of this?"

"Bert and I are working on a plan, but there's no clear answer. We'll survive somehow and mother has other assets, homes she no longer needs and investments not related to this fiasco, but I may have to prove that, if the investigation reaches that stage. So far, it appears that it hasn't. The importance of these documents, according to Bert, is that they contain the codes for each of the offshore accounts set up by my father, and except for that fourth account that Jonathan has access to, they don't have those numbers."

"What can I do to help?" asked Sharon, her world shaken. "You know I don't care about the money. I do care about our reputations and the impact it will have on our lives and our effectiveness in trying to change what's wrong in this predatory society. People will think we're as hypocritical as our right wing counterparts."

"I know and I'm sorry for that, especially given your dedication to that cause. If we use the codes to access those funds or if our association with this tax dodging situation is revealed then my explanation of innocence might not be accepted, then maybe...maybe you'll have to divorce me!"

Shocked at the suggestion, Sharon turned to him, grabbed his face in her hands and kissed him, a tear forming in her eye. "You're not getting off that easy, Jimbo!" she declared attempting to use her wit to soften the moment. "This is our fight and we *will* win it!"

Chapter 108

For more than twenty years Bulldog Masters and his associates had managed to manipulate Congress, and to some extent, the sitting President, to do their bidding. Colonel Jim Buckman had been a useful colleague, but he developed a conscience in the vulnerable state of his terminal illness. He was an excellent leader and motivator, but he had started to worry about his legacy, a condition brought forth by observing his sons' relative behaviors. He believed Jim had inherited his courage and perseverance, and Jonathan his ruthless urge to succeed at all cost. For the senior Buckman it was like he had gotten religion. The Washington Action Group missed his financial contributions, but Masters didn't miss his adversary leadership or commanding persona.

Now they had Jonathan, not a man of creative ideas but the best hope to secure the funds they needed to continue. Masters believed that the Feds had Jonathan and his family on the ropes, but he also believed that if they continued their pursuit they might find that much of the financial where-with-all that backed their Group's loyal candidates came from illegal sources. And they would also find that most of it came from offshore monies that never bore the burden of taxation when earned as profits by the Group's members.

As General Bert Obersham indicated, by his not-so-subtle threat to the Group, the traceability of the sources of wealth were not as discreet as they had believed. He told them they would be wise to use their influence to stop the federal investigation into Buckman Enterprises as soon as possible or they would bear the consequences.

Master's knew they needed to see what the General had that was such an imminent danger to them. But they wanted to use the threat of financial disaster as leverage to manipulate Jonathan into turning over control of that wealth to them before the FDIC and the Justice Department closed in. Time was the enemy! They needed to accelerate their plan. They needed to seal the deal with Jonathan.

He began their promised meeting with Jonathan with an ominous statement, "Jonathan, Don and I have thought this situation through. You know how serious this federal investigation is and that there is a good possibility that you, your brother and possibly your mother may get indicted for your father's actions. Although, we weren't aware of your father's activities we might also be hurt by the investigation and we will have to defend ourselves."

"I'm not sure that I know what you're leading up to Mr. Masters, but I thought you were interested in working with me on this matter? I had nothing to do with dad's financial decisions or, until recently, with your Group's activities," responded Jonathan, his voice cracking. "And I doubt that Jim or mother knew anything about them either. Father was very secretive about his investments."

"We may believe that, son, but the Feds will be looking for a scapegoat and you have been involved with the financial end of the family businesses for years and your brother is an attorney and a veteran Congressman. Do you think that the media won't use that to drive public opinion and put the pressure on the Justice Department to seek indictments?"

"Yes, Jonathan, Tom is right! It would be very dangerous for you to go down that road," added Peters. "In deference to your father, Tom and I have been trying to figure out if there's any way we can help the Buckman family avoid that disaster?"

"But I must warn you that it may already be too late," declared Masters as he sensed the anxiety reflecting from their guest and potential victim.

"I can't let mother take the blame for any of this. I don't really care about Jim. He's a big boy and a war hero, he can fight his own battles," answered Jonathan, despondent and confused.

Masters looked at Peters, not able to hide his smirk. "There's only one way I can think of to get you and your mother out of this."

"Me and my mother, and what about Jim?

"You just said he's a big boy. Let him fight his own way out of this. What did he ever do for you?" answered Peters.

"I don't know, but he is my brother. Yes, he's been a pain in the ass since we were kids, and my father's protégé. The *heir apparent* they used to call him."

"Well then let's make sure your father's wishes are realized, he will be the heir of the Buckman dynasty and he'll find a way to overcome the accusations. Yes, he may have to resign from Congress, but he was never much of an ally to the conservative element of our party and I'm sure he'll do anything to protect your mother. I would, however, advise you to stay on the good side of your brother. Knowing Jim and his bleeding-heart wife, he'll feel compassion and protect you, if we handle this properly."

"And how do you plan to do that? I don't understand. If I set him up to take the fall he'll know it. He's not dumb! Shouldn't we wait to see where the Feds are going with this investigation?"

"Well, that would definitely be too late, and we need to act while we still have a Republican in the White House. This guy Clinton is gaining in the polls and if he gets in we'll only have a short time to clean this mess up. It will be tougher to do if there's a Democrat in the Oval Office. The good news is that there will be a lame duck session from early November until the inauguration of a new President and a new Congress in January. This may provide a window of opportunity for this investigation to disappear, but we need to get you and your mother out of it before then!" Masters leaned forward to emphasize the strength of his convictions to Jonathan. "And that requires an aggressive plan and your cooperation."

"Yes, and we need to pump some money into the President's campaign with only a month left to see if he can overcome the advance of this upstart governor from Arkansas. We'll need to draw on those off-shore resources to do that, Tom," added Peters.

"Won't that be dangerous if those funds are being scrutinized by the Feds?" questioned Jonathan, becoming more confused as the plan unfolded. Jonathan decided not to reveal his access to the emergency fund account.

"Our sources tell us that they're not at that point in the investigation, but the information that the General claims to have may lead them there, and possibly sooner than later. We need to know what it is he has and as we told you before, you're the only one that can find that out for us," declared Peters.

"But what good is it to know what you already suspect if it is inevitable that they will eventually learn that information and start indictments?" questioned Jonathan, his head spinning.

"This is where the ingenuity comes into play. As you know, Don's bank, is one of the banks that has been contracted by the FDIC to purchase the assets of any banking enterprise subject to their investigation. They're already servicing your bank's accounts. The more successful banks will purchase the assets, such as the funds, the customer accounts and properties of the problem banks to prevent a panic on the system. If we negotiate to do that now we may be able to take the issue of the source of monies off the table and keep it at the level of determining the integrity and viability of the banking operation. This would be preferable to any possible criminal indictment. This would be Plan A, the preferable solution."

"Not only that, I'm not a lawyer, but I think that it would be much easier for your brother to beat any indictment, if there is even one, if there is no offshore scenario introduced into the case," interjected Peters. "We want the Feds to think the bank failed due to bad business practices and not find that it was involved with any quasi-criminal activity."

"So my reputation gets ruined as a banker. What do expect me to do claim ignorance, and if your bank purchases the assets now, how will we survive? That money will go to the government, not to our family," asked Jonathan his confusion intensifying.

Masters responded. "I need to work out the details, but in general, you would become an employee of Don's bank with a long term contract that will be very comfortable for you and your family with options for shares to be vested over time. Your mother will receive an exceptional price for her properties. We understand that your family has at least four homes and several commercial properties. She would also keep her present home."

"And what about Jim? What does he get out of this grand plan?" asked Jonathan.

"Well, If Plan A works and there is no indictment, he gets free of the potential impact of Congressional censure and legal action against him as counsel and chief strategist for Buckman Enterprises."

"But he wasn't in that role. You know he gave up that opportunity when I bought out his shares on a long term repayment basis."

"Do you think anyone will believe that he gave up scrutinizing the business activities while you still owed him millions of dollars over time? I doubt it. What do you think Don?"

"Jonathan, I think you need to stay away from explaining that deal if it comes up in the investigation. It would place you in the role as sole administrator of Buckman Enterprises, not a place that you want to be."

"As in the demise of any business, the operation will file for bankruptcy and the assets will be sold to us, to pay the creditors. All of the collateralized debts will be paid first. To the extent his loan is collateralized and not for the benefit of a shareholder, it will receive some compensation. I doubt, however, that the debt owed Jim can meet that test," declared Masters.

"Are you saying he'll get nothing? My brother won't accept that, he's a fighter!" exclaimed Jonathan.

"He won't have a choice. If he doesn't, we'll go to Plan B, which will surely lead to indictments. If Plan A works he'll escape with his reputation mostly intact, but at a cost. He's not a poor man and if there's no indictment he'll continue to practice law and his wife, Sharon has a strong political following in the Democratic Party. Face it, Jonathan we're the only hope for this thing to stay under the radar and possibly go away, but we need to know what cards the General has in his hand and where he can be found."

"I'll think about it. I need to figure out the ramifications to my family and if there's any other way to unravel this mess. I still don't understand why the Feds decided to make this move.

Our books aren't any worse than those of a number of banks in this economy."

"I don't know the answer to that, but I do know that Plan A can only be effective if we implement it immediately. I'm afraid you only have 24 hours to decide. After that we will most likely be using our resources for damage control," asserted Masters.

"I'll call you tomorrow with my answer."

"I suggest that we meet here again, at the same time tomorrow. The phones aren't safe when the Feds are in an investigation mode!" remarked Peters.

"Okay, I'll be here with my answer and I'll see what I can find out about the General's information."

"Remember, stay away from your phones. If you need to make a call use an out-of-the-way public phone and only for short calls and don't mention us by name to anyone," cautioned Masters.

Jonathan left the meeting, his mind trying to sort it all out. What was it that his father told him about how far he trusted them? It had something to do with how far he could kick the 6 foot, 5 inch, 300 pound Masters. But his plan had merit. He would have to think hard on it.

Masters and Peters believed they had hooked their game fish, now all they had to do was be patient and reel him in for a big payday.

"I think it went well. What do you think, Don?" asked Masters, expressing confidence in their performance.

"I agree, but I'm not sure he's going to go with Plan A given his ego and need to better his dad and brother. We really didn't offer him anything that attractive to someone of his character."

"I think we offered him his only choice to the alternative of losing everything."

"Maybe, but if the General has damaging evidence against us and it's revealed we will suffer the consequences. Of course there's a possibility that the FDIC won't ever get there, given the number of banks being processed for failure, and the possible change in administrations," offered Peters.

"Obviously, we need to do whatever it takes to get the information that Obersham has and destroy it!" stated Masters in a sharp and bitter tone.

"And what about Obersham?" questioned Peters. "He's not dumb! He must have made provisions for that possibility, and most likely Jim has copies of any incriminating evidence."

"I'm counting on that evidence being incriminating to them too. They won't risk revealing it if it is. Otherwise we may have to resort to a more aggressive plan."

Peters looked at Masters with concern and anxiety at his words.

Jonathan had left the meeting with some hope, but also with trepidation. He drove to his brother's apartment. The only way he would find out what they wanted to know, including the General's whereabouts, was from Jim. He needed to rely on his brother's compassion and caring for the family in order to secure that information. He was greeted at the door by his sister-in-law with a less than welcoming expression on her face. At forty seven she was still a stunning woman with a commanding presence.

"I didn't think we would see you for a while Jonathan, actually I was hoping we wouldn't," she declared in her usual candid, to the point style.

"Is Jim home? I need to talk to him. It's very important."

"Yes, he's home, and you need to talk to both of us and tell us what you've been up to with your friends!"

Jim came into the living room from the den and was surprised to see his brother in confrontation with his wife. "What's going on? What do you want, Jonathan? I hear you've been up to your usual mischief."

"I know what you're thinking, but it isn't like that. I'm just trying to get information and Masters said he could help us with this federal investigation. I just met with him and Don Peters. I wanted you to know what they told me," Jonathan expressed himself as sincerely as he believed necessary to overcome their suspicions.

"Really? And what did they tell you, Jonathan?" asked a cynical Sharon as they sat down in the living room. "I'm sure it was enlightening."

"Yes, did they tell you how they dropped a dime on your operation hoping to make you squirm and give in to their desire to own Buckman Enterprises?"

"I don't believe that, Jim, it makes no sense. From what I understand dad has them so intertwined with our businesses financial matters that they would be cooked if the Feds find that link."

"That's what they told you? That they're worried about the Feds coming down on them too?" queried Sharon in her lawyerly tone.

"Yes, they're worried about Bert and what he might have in his possession that could hurt them. Doesn't he have some incriminating evidence related to illegal political campaign contributions? And where is he? Can we meet with him?"

"Nice try brother, but you're not going to be privy to any such information, I can only tell you that you don't want to go there! You're in the middle of being conned by one of the best and now, as far as we're concerned, you're on the outside looking in and you'll stay that way until this is sorted out. I would recommend that you stay away from the Group until it is resolved or you will dig a hole so deep that it will take you a lifetime to climb out of it."

"I'm only trying to help. This is my life too, and I have a family to protect. It isn't wise for you to threaten me. I'm not without resources."

"This isn't a threat. This is reality and I would advise you to heed my warning and stand clear until we get this fiasco under control."

"Okay, if that's how you want it. I'll stand clear of you, but I will protect myself and my family. I tried to work with you Jim, but it's obvious that you're not interested in me or my family's welfare. You always were a selfish bastard!" The door slammed behind him.

"You were right, Jim. He's been processed by the boys and he can't be trusted. What do you think he'll do?"

"Whatever he can do to beat me, and survive, including making a deal with the devil! What do you think, Bert? He turned and addressed the figure emerging from the guest bedroom.

Chapter 109

Believing Bert's apartment to be unsafe, given the interest in the steel box, Sharon and Jim thought it best that he stay with them for a while. The visit by Jonathan was not completely unexpected, but it was sooner than anticipated.

"I think that he's being his usual loose cannon self. He can be dangerous to all of us, including himself," offered Bert. "He's obviously already in bed with them, but under what terms? The question is, has he already sold you out or is that contingent on him delivering the goods?"

Sharon was concerned that he might know more than they gave him credit for. "Jonathan isn't wise, but he isn't stupid. I'm sure he thought he could play on Jim's compassion. I think he believed he could convince Jim that he's on our side and he's playing the Group."

"He's not in their league. As I've said before, they'll chew him up and spit him out when it's in their interest to do so," said Jim. "But we may have overreacted. Maybe we should have let him have some slack to find out what he's actually up to?"

"I think we know what he's up to Jim. He slipped when he asked where Bert was. Obviously he isn't interested in Bert's health and well-being. Bert's whereabouts are only of interest to the Group who want to silence him," surmised Sharon.

"Do you think that they're capable of that Bert?" asked Jim concerned about Sharon's remark.

"Jim, your dad and I were in their confidence for over thirty years. They're capable of doing whatever it takes to protect their interest and make more money."

"What do you think will be their next move? They don't have much time to act given the FDIC investigation," asked Sharon, concerned that her brother-in-law may cause greater scrutiny by the Feds or possibly give up the family to Masters and his Group.

"First, I think Jonathan will make a deal with Masters and that they'll be here looking for the incriminating information within 24 hours," declared Bert. "Then, I think we need to get updates on all these accounts without raising suspicion, and third - and don't take this personal - we need to hire a good lawyer, just in case."

It didn't take long for Jonathan to take the next step.

"Hello Don, I just heard from Jonathan. His encounter with his brother didn't go very well and he wants us to put the paperwork together to do Plan A."

"Great, I can go ahead and make contact with Fitzgerald at the FDIC and see if they'll negotiate a deal on the purchase of Buckman Enterprises' assets. We'll leave the worthless corporate shares for Jim to play with. According to Jonathan that's all Jim had as collateral for the buy-out loan when Jonathan bought his stock. I understand he still owes Jim more than $15 million."

"Well, we still need to worry about what incriminating evidence that he and the General have that they can spring on us. This might be a good time to bring others into our plans," suggested Masters.

"Do you mean the rest of our advisory group? I'm not sure they have the guts to follow this through."

"You're right! It's best to keep them on a 'need to know' basis for a while longer. The less they know the less chance for a leak," declared Masters. "I told Jonathan we would meet with him at 6 pm tomorrow and he should have the information with him. If he doesn't, and I doubt that he will, we'll expand our team appropriately."

"That sounds fine. I'll be there."

In anticipation of having unwanted visitors, Jim and Bert moved into a hotel suite in Arlington, Virginia. They hired a security firm to stay at the apartment for the week. Bert engaged Bud Conroy, one of his old Army and CIA colleagues, who had a small but sophisticated D.C. detective agency. Conroy's job was surveillance of Jonathan and security protection for the Buckman family. Within twelve hours Bud's team planted a tracking device on Jonathan's car and bugged his home. Sharon took Laura Marie to her mother's home in Michigan with security added to that location also. Bud personally attended to the duties of bodyguard for Jim and Bert.

"It's just like the good old days Bert, where we don't know where the next incoming round is going to come from."

"Knowing you Bud, you wouldn't want it any other way. You thrive on the mystery of this stuff. I just hope you haven't lost a step in your old age," quipped Bert.

"I may have lost a step, but now I just come up from behind and surprise my prey rather than meet them face to face at the OK Corral!" laughed Bud. Don't worry General, we're a very sophisticated operation and I have my 40 years of intelligence experience to try to remember," Bud continued to attempt to lighten up the situation. "Seriously, I have six operatives working with me on this and they're all former Special Forces personnel. We're connected by a special radio frequency and, of course, well-armed."

"Hopefully that won't be necessary Bud. There's family involved here and we won't know who is who until it may be too late," responded Jim.

"Yes, Bud, It's more important to know what our enemy is doing, at this point, than to destroy them. In fact destroying them would bring on unwanted scrutiny, which we want to avoid at almost all cost except as a last resort," added the General.

"I understand gentlemen, we're not looking to incur any more scrutiny than necessary and you've briefed me on the family connection. Believe me, Jim, I'll do anything for you, the General and your late dad. He was a remarkable man, and the one you would want to cover your back in dangerous circumstances."

"Thank you Bud, Bert has told me some of your war stories. I have complete confidence in your abilities or I wouldn't entrust the safety of my wife and child to you."

The scene at Don Peters' office the next day was tense and anxious as the three potential perpetrators met to seal their deal.

"So Jonathan, what did you find out? Do you have the information we need?" asked Masters, knowing that it was unlikely.

"No, I need more time. I went back to the apartment this morning thinking I could apologize and get some indication of what was going on, but I was met by a football linebacker type who said he was security and that the Buckman's weren't home. I told him that I was his brother; he said "I know" and closed the door. I heard voices inside, not my brother's, so there's more than one of them."

"That's interesting. The information we need must be there. They wouldn't go through all that trouble just to protect the apartment."

"My thoughts exactly, but what can we do about it? We can't shoot up the place and try to find the papers! Maybe you should call Jim. He doesn't like you, but he must realize that you're the only one that can make this go away," suggested Jonathan. "Just be straight with him. He can sense insincerity.

"That's not a bad idea Tom. You and his dad managed to get along in spite of your issues. Talk to him and convince him we can help. Avoid ultimatums except as a last resort. I think Jim's a reasonable guy. Hey, he's still a Republican despite being married to the Senate's big mouth liberal," added Don Peters. "Oh, and Jonathan, I received a favorable response on our idea of purchasing your corporate assets from my FDIC contact."

"That's the key to this mess going away and being able to use the offshore resources for the political campaigns. This Arkansas hick, Bill Clinton is gaining every time they debate. He might carry in a Democratic Congress with him if we don't buoy up the House and Senate Republicans," declared Masters. He was doing what used to drive the Senior Buckman crazy by interjecting divergent goals when he was trying to convince the group of an objective. This time it was a Buckman that Masters needed to convince who didn't really care about the House and Senate races.

"Tom, I think all that will be worked out, but right now we need to help this guy get out from under! Jonathan, Tom is right about the urgency. I need to make this deal with the FDIC before they get any deeper into their dissection of you and the businesses. I've prepared this agreement to allow our purchase of the assets of your corporation from the Feds when they conclude their takeover."

"How quickly will that be and even If I sign how do we know that they won't continue their operation and don't I need mother's and Jim's consent to sign?" asked an anxious Jonathan.

"Well, Jonathan, you need to take a stand and..."

Interrupting another of the less than diplomatic Bulldog's tirades, Don said, "What Tom is saying is that we've done a lot of work on this and you need to trust that we can pull it off or you should find another solution. Buying the corporate assets is the safest way to avoid revealing the sins of the corporation. The assets will be evaluated by the Feds and by us and an agreeable price will be paid. You're the majority shareholder of the corporation at two thirds. You hold Jim's stock and your mother owns the final third. Jim will have a bankrupt corporation's stock as his collateral and your mother will have the same, but as we said before, we will take care of your mother by purchasing property she owns and allowing her to remain in her present home at no cost."

"And what about Jim? How do we appease him?" Jonathan asked.

"We don't have to appease him. He's lucky to not be indicted. He will have to..."

"Tom let's stay with the plan," interrupted Don again, staring at Masters with a look that clearly said shut up let me handle this. "I think we can work out something with Jim. He's a reasonable guy and I'm sure he doesn't want the family to suffer through a federal investigation." We'll make sure he and his family are taken care of and you'll be free of this burden that your dad, in good faith, brought on to the family."

"What about the steel box and its potential to harm all of us, including the Group? I have no knowledge of where it is or what it contains. Is it wise to take that chance?" asked Jonathan.

"We'll make that part of our negotiation with your brother, but not until he's lost all of his other leverage with your signature on this agreement, and our gaining control of those troublesome offshore assets. This agreement would give you a ten year contract as a consultant with CTC for $2.5 million per year, plus stock options for meeting certain performance goals. This would be worth more than your present resources under the current circumstances. It's a very fair agreement," offered Don Peters in his most sincere banker style.

"It sounds good, but what if the feds give up on their due diligence and we are reinstated as an operating bank?"

"They won't! Damn it, Buckman Enterprises is through and you will be too if you don't sign this agreement!" Masters temper was exposed much to Don's chagrin. "And Don, don't you interrupt me! This is real life Mr. Buckman. We're trying to help you, but I have no patience with wimps, you're either on board or you're overboard. I have more important matters to deal with. If you leave here without signing this agreement I will have no more interest in resolving your problems." With that said, he took a page from Jonathan's father's negotiating tactics book and picked up his briefcase and headed for the door. "I'll be at my office, Don. Let me know if we have a deal by 9:00 p.m. If we don't Jonathan, I wish you luck. You're going to need it!"

It was 7:45 pm, Jonathan sat back and wondered, "What just happened?"

"He has a volatile temper. He and your dad used to go at it, arguing over everything from the weather to the price of oil. I think he means what he says and it'll be difficult to get him back into this resolution. Most likely it will be too late, for a number of reasons, if it doesn't happen tonight. As they say, the ball's in your court!" stated Don in his best "good cop" impression.

Jonathan left the meeting believing Don's words, but also worrying that he was being railroaded into signing the family fortune away. He thought, they have the leverage and they're using it to its maximum advantage. Can I trust them? A signed agreement is only good as evidence in a lawsuit and all too often the plaintiff runs out of money before a wealthy defendant. He wished he hadn't pissed off his brother, but then it seemed that whatever path to a resolution he chose Jim would likely be on a different one.

Chapter 110

It was a cool, but sunny afternoon when Keisha left the doctor's office not knowing where to turn. She walked the streets of downtown Boston wondering how she was going to tell Diego the words that followed Dr. Bernstein's apology. "I'm sorry Mrs. Martinez, but the tests indicate that you have diseased kidneys and a weak heart. I'm afraid you're in the process of renal failure and will need dialysis on a regular basis. The condition of your heart might mean that you waited too long for this diagnosis. You should be in the hospital."

She knew that being admitted to the hospital was impossible. Since Diego lost his landscape business, he's been working odd jobs and often they couldn't pay for oil to heat their home or pay the rent on time. Like millions of hard working Americans they hadn't had health insurance for more than two years. What would they do? Ironically she was able to fill in as a temporary part-time health care aid for an agency, but it would barely pay their weekly food bill and had no benefits.

Dr. Bernstein did say that if she waited much longer she could become a candidate for a heart transplant as well as a kidney transplant. That would cost tens of thousands of dollars and a heart transplant would depend on the misfortune of someone who happens to be a match. She believed that she didn't have any feasible options. If she didn't survive, Diego, without a regular job, would have to take care of Manny alone and she would no longer be part of their lives.

She stopped to rest on a bench beside the Swan Pond in the midst of the flowery décor of the Boston Public Garden. She thought of the day she and Diego took little Manny to Boston to ride the Swan Boats on this pond and then to see a Boston Red Sox game. Her tears flowed freely and her lips tightened as she thought of not living to see her son grow up or being there for Diego.

Diego knew she had gone to Boston at the advice of their local doctor. She had been feeling tired and weak for several weeks. She took their old pickup truck making the trip with high anxiety and increasing pain. Diego stayed home to meet Manny at the school bus stop three blocks away. He was worried but hoped it was just a stomach virus or maybe an ulcer that was causing her pain and distress.

The drive home for Keisha was through the blurred vision of tears as she tried to think of how she would deal with the reality of her illness. She had only a $5,000 life insurance policy, hardly enough to have a funeral, not enough to help her family. It was dark as she pulled into the driveway of their little cottage in Yarmouth on Cape Cod. Diego came out on the front porch. He walked towards the truck, squinting to see Keisha behind the wheel. The headlights turned off as she opened the door and stepped down from the truck's cab.

He reached her as she stepped around the truck and gave her a hug. As he pulled back and focused on the look in her eyes, his fears were confirmed. He knew his wife was hurting physically and spiritually. The news would not be good.

"I'm sorry, Diego. I am very sick! I have failed you and Manny. I don't know what we're going to do," she sobbed as she held him tightly to her.

"I'm the one who's sorry, you shouldn't have to go through this. We'll find a way, we'll find a way," he declared as his eyes filled with tears and his heart with anger after hearing her repeat the doctor's warnings. He felt incompetent for not being able to take care of his family and his only true love in this world.

His work with Karime had ended with his frustration trying to raise money from those who had less money than he had. He knew that Karime was also struggling as she attempted to resist the persistent attempts by both the Mexican and American governments to have her give up those who were presently, or in the past, members of her father's cartel. She had left that life many years ago and had worked for the betterment of her people and those of her cousin Diego, but she was not going to do what they wanted. Her brother had served a ten-year sentence for his participation in the cartel, but also refused to cooperate. Diego knew that she was unlikely to have the tens of thousands of dollars that would be needed for his wife's survival, but she was his only hope. He knew what he had to do.

He hoped that even though his good friend Tony was also suffering, he could rely on him for a small loan so that he could go to Mexico to visit Karime. He thought that she still might have access to monies from her father's illicit operations. She would be as reluctant to access them as he was to ask her, but Keisha's life was at stake. He called Tony.

"Diego, why do you think that Karime can help you?" There was a pause then Tony declared, "Tell me you're not going there to get involved with the cartel? I know that you're desperate my friend, but your family needs you to be there for them, especially for your son, if the worst happens. Keisha would not want it any other way."

"Tony, I believe Karime has money hidden away, but doesn't use it because of her moral convictions. She's a good woman. She was born into a bad situation that she managed to escape, and she has been harassed and persecuted for her actions. I wouldn't ask her if it wasn't for Keisha. There's no other way for me to raise that money!"

"I hope you're right, but I'm more afraid of you accepting other options, like your father did, more than 40 years ago. You remember Yogi Berra, the often misspoken New York Yankee catcher of the 1950s and his often quoted remark about something being 'Déjà vu all over again,' well I feel that now for you. I'll get you the money for your trip, but you need to promise me that you won't get involved with the cartel."

"I promise, Tony. I promise, but what would you do if it was Meghan?"

"I don't know what I would do, but then, as you know, I've done a lot of dumb things in my life. Hold on, Meghan is here beside me. She wants to say something to you."

"Diego, I overheard you and I'll stay with Keisha while you're away and take care of Manny." She looked at Tony for his nod of approval and said, "We'll be there in the morning. Here's Tony, and tell Keisha I will pray for her."

"I'll make your flight arrangements and drive you to the airport. Meghan will use your truck while you're away. How long will you need, is five days enough?" asked Tony.

"Thank you both! You are real friends! Five days should be plenty of time. I don't want to be gone too long. I don't know what we would do without you and Meghan," responded Diego, his voice cracking with emotion.

Chapter 111

Jonathan made the call to Peters. "Don, I've reviewed the agreement and, subject to a couple of modifications, I'm ready to sign," he declared with some reluctance, but without a viable alternative.

"You've made a wise decision Jonathan! You won't regret it and I think you'll find that not being the guy at the top, with all the responsibilities, can be a good thing. CTC will be your home from now on and you'll find it to be a very comfortable fit," said an obviously pleased Peters. "Come into the office and we'll work out the details."

"I'll be there with my attorney at 3 pm. It's John Walters. He has an office in your building."

"Fine, I know John. I look forward to seeing both of you this afternoon at three."

John Walters had been Jonathan's personal attorney since he became CEO of Buckman Enterprises when his father became ill. Walter's advice to Jonathan had been to take care of himself and his family. They had gone over the agreement late into the night and decided it just needed some assurances or guarantees, but he was not going to worry about his brother's fate. Walters never did like Jim Buckman since he was embarrassed after losing a multimillion dollar case to him when Jim was practicing law. The case was decided on evidence whose importance Walter's had underestimated. His client sued him.

The meeting with Peters and the Group's counsel, Dale Watkins, was cordial and productive. The contract for Jonathan's services would be for ten-years and $25 million. He would be the Vice President for Commercial Loans nationwide and be vested in 10% of CTC stock in 5 years. His mother would receive $7 million over the five years for her real estate properties. She would continue to own her present home, a concession that Jonathan insisted on. Buckman Enterprises, Inc. would file Chapter 7, dissolving it and all of its debts, except those that were secured by collateral. Jim Buckman would have to make a claim, but he would realize that his only collateral was Jonathan's shares in the corporation, which were to secure his payment for his shares. Selling his shares to Jonathan gave him control of the family businesses and relieved Jim of that conflict as a Congressman.

The offshore operations were not mentioned in the agreement, but they believed that ownership of Buckman Enterprises' assets would give CTC control of those covert accounts. Peters and Masters were pleased. As long as the transaction of acquiring the assets of the Buckman operation was approved by the FDIC, the scrutiny into its practices should cease.

Jim Buckman learned of the anticipated transaction on CNN. "What now Bert? Do we drop a dime and blow this thing up? If we do, what do we gain other than revenge and the possibility of being entangled in the mess of offshore money laundering?" surmised Jim, realizing that his younger brother had indeed won this round.

"Well, we may need to wait until they make a move to use the funds in the transitional account and then see where our leverage takes us. I won't add to that accessible fund and they don't realize that its viability is under my control, as yet. Once they're in an incriminating situation we'll be in a better negotiating position given the information that we have."

"But how will we know when they make that move?" asked Jim.

"Well, Jim, we have what you might call a mole in the Grand Caymans and a good friends in Switzerland and Bermuda. We will know!" Bert said with a slight, uncharacteristic smile.

"Do you think they'll do that sooner or later?"

"We're nearing the end of a tight Presidential race, and their candidate is slipping in the polls. They need funds and they'll be reluctant to use their own. It will be sooner!"

Chapter 112

Diego arrived at Karime's Mexico City apartment in late evening. He had called ahead to tell her he was coming and that he would stay at a hotel. She insisted he stay with her at her small two-bedroom flat. She had regained a position at the university, but was not tenured. He told her about his wife's condition, but not the full reason for his visit.

The neighborhood was not the best, but it was far from the worst. There were several brightly lit cafés along the boulevard and professional offices of doctors and lawyers could be seen on every block. Apartments were located above the businesses in walk-up three-story stucco buildings. Karime's was above that of a Dr. Romero Valdez, an "Internal Medicine Specialist," it said in Spanish. It was after 10 pm but the streets were alive with people.

By the time he reached the second floor she was standing in the open doorway, her arms extended and a warm smile emanating from her still beautifully sculptured face.

"Diego, my American cousin, it is so nice to see you." Without her signature boots she was much shorter than he remembered, but it didn't diminish her stature. She had a presence that impressed all whom she met, including Tony. They often talked of her as if she was a Mexican princess.

"Karime, I'm so happy to see you too. I hope that my visit hasn't imposed on you. I know you're a very busy woman, but you're the only one I can turn to," he said as they hugged and kissed each other's cheeks.

"Come in, you could never be an imposition to me, Diego. How can I help you through this horrible situation with Keisha? The poor woman! She must be in great distress!"

Diego told her the details of his wife's condition and of his need. There was no reason not to be candid. Karime was a very direct person and expected the same of those who were close to her.

"I don't know what to say. It seems that you will need much more than I can provide. Yes, I do have some money left from my life with the cartel, but it is only about $12,000. I don't think that is enough for what has to be done to help Keisha."

"I will pay you back, but you're right. I'm thinking that if her heart could survive a kidney transplant that alone will be at least three times that. The kidney transplant doesn't require the death of the donor and may in itself make her stronger. We need to have a match. I have been tested and I am not one."

"And what about her heart, is it strong enough? There is a doctor below us who is well respected in the transplant field of medicine. Do you think she could come here? He is a very good friend. He also teaches at the University and...he is very fond of me. I'm sure he would examine her as a favor to me, but I doubt he would extend that favor to an operation."

"I don't know if she could make the trip without a healthy kidney. I need to find more money, but I am very grateful for your generous offer."

"We'll figure something out. There's always a way!" stated Karime as she reached for his hand. "Why are you smiling?"

"When you said that, it made me think of Tony. That's what he always says when he is thinking like an engineer trying to solve a problem. 'There is always a way!' He doesn't know when to give up. I guess he's like you in that way."

"I like Tony. He is not a big man, but he has a big heart and you're right. He doesn't give up on his friends."

"And he likes you. We talk about how he admires you for your intelligence and, of course, your beauty. I think if he hadn't met Meghan he would have spent more time in Mexico," offered Diego with a smile.

"Oh, stop it. He's a lucky man to have met her and she's obviously a lucky woman. We would never have made it together. We're too much alike! We're both as stubborn as mules," her smile still dominant.

"Come into the kitchen, I know you must be hungry from your long journey. I made you some enchiladas, unless you're too old to handle that kind of food this late at night."

"No, I think I have a cast iron stomach from Carmella's 'Mexican Feasts.' As a teenager I would come home at three in the morning and finish off the spicy meal that she had prepared expecting me for dinner. I so disappointed that poor woman."

"I think that you turned out fine and so did she. She was very proud of you and your efforts to become a responsible family man. Look, here you are trying to do the best for your family and, of course, for your wife who you love with all your heart."

"Speaking of family, how is your brother doing?" attempting to change the subject that was tugging on that heart.

"Gonzalo, he's fine, I guess. I don't see him very much, but since he was released from prison he has been driving a taxi in the city. You should see him before you leave."

"Has he stayed clear of the cartel? I'm surprised that he's not in Guadalajara. Did he marry?" queried Diego.

"He's not married, but he lives with a woman in the worst part of the city. I think she walks the streets for money, but I've never met her."

"I would like to see him. We have so little family left."

"I'll call him tomorrow and see if he can meet with you. I have to go to work at the university tomorrow until about 4 o'clock. Maybe he can meet you for lunch in this area. You don't want to go into his neighborhood, you might not come back!" she said with a concerned look and a half smile.

She called Gonzalo before she went to work figuring that she would catch him sleeping late from an all-night shift, which he seemed to prefer. She managed to have his girlfriend wake him after telling her that it was an emergency and he would want to talk to her.

"Hello Karime, what emergency? I'm very tired. I just got in at five this morning. What's so important?"

After calming him down she explained the reason for the visit of their cousin and then put Diego on the phone.

"Hello Gonzo, I hope you're not upset at our waking you this early, but I was hoping to see you before I go home."

"I'm sorry to hear about your wife. Yes, I would like to see you. Don't worry about my sleep. I am an angry bear in the morning, but I want to hear about your life in America."

They met at a little café two blocks from Karime's apartment. At first Diego didn't recognize the grey bushy haired and bearded mass of a man limping towards him as he sat at a sidewalk table. He remembered his only male cousin as a big, but fit man with coal black hair and a swagger that was a warning to anyone who dared challenge him. He was only sure that his vision was indeed Gonzalvo when he approached him with his hands open in a welcoming gesture and smiled saying his name, "Diego, you haven't changed but for some gray hairs. America has treated you good?"

"Gonzalvo, I didn't recognize you under all that hair. How are you?"

"I'm fine, but I told you I am a bear in the morning. This is my bear look," he said with a gruff laugh. Karime told me about your wife. Is there anything I can do for you?" he asked as he sat overwhelming the wrought iron café chair.

"Well, not really. But I wanted to see you before I left, unless of course you have about $50,000 dollars that you don't want," Diego quipped.

"No, I'm afraid I have very little money, but I am surviving. The police made sure that I can't be very useful to my friends in the cartel. They broke my legs and the fingers on my writing hand, but I wouldn't tell them what they wanted to know. He leaned forward and whispered, "Don't tell Karime, but my friends still help me with stuff to sell when I need it."

"Isn't that dangerous? Don't they still watch you?"

"Yeah, I get picked up sometimes, but I'm never carrying any drugs or weapons. I sell only to those I know and I tell them where they can find their stuff. I put it someplace and they have to get it themselves. I just take their money. Pretty smart, hey cuz? But how about you? Where are you going to get this money for your wife's operation?"

"I don't know, I was hoping Karime had hidden some of your padre's money and could loan it to me if she didn't need it."

"She did have money like that, but she spent a lot on lawyers trying to get me out of prison. She was afraid I would die there. She got me released last year, but it cost her not only for the lawyers but for the warden and a high-up official, over $100,000. I am so ashamed. I used to take care of her; you know protect her from bad people, but she showed me the love of family that I can never repay."

"Well I'm sure your padre would have wanted her to do that. Don't be ashamed. You would have done that for her."

"That is why I'm ashamed. I don't know that I would have. If I had that money I would have gone to Columbia and joined a bigger and badder cartel," he laughed at his own humor.

"I don't think so. Remember, you were her protector. You would have done the right thing."

"Maybe, but who knows? Did you ever get your pilot's license? I remember you were taking lessons when you worked at that airport as a controller."

"Yes I did, but I haven't kept it up. Flying was too expensive. You had to have so many hours and I couldn't own a plane and renting one cost too much. Why do you ask? Do you want to learn?"

"No, but I know of a way that you can make the money that you need and I can make some too!" Gonzalvo leaned forward again and in a whisper said, "My friends need someone to fly some cargo over the border. We could do it together."

Diego pulled back and looked him in the eye. "Are you crazy? We would both wind up in prison. You would be deported back here, and I would spend my time in Leavenworth, Kansas as a guest of my government."

"Shhhh! That's only if we're caught. Believe me, it's a good plan. They do it every month, but their regular pilot is sick. Well, actually he was shot. After we eat we'll talk in my taxi. It's the only way, Diego!"

The taxi ride outside the city limits took nearly an hour. Gonsalvo talked non-stop about the "only way" that Diego could earn the money to save his wife.

"What are your choices? Do you have any? I know you! You're not going to let Keisha die. This plan will work. You will get the money you need to take care of her, and I'll get to America where I can disappear into the city with enough money to be comfortable."

"I can't take that chance, Gonzalvo. I have a family and a wife that needs me badly."

"This is a big shipment worth over $10 million American on the street. Can you fly a Cessna 175?" asked Gonzalvo. You fought in a war this will be nothing. All we do is fly this stuff over there and leave the plane at a small airport for others to unload. They leave a pickup truck for us at the airport. We drive to wherever we need to go. We get half the money here and the other half will be taped under the seat of the truck."

"You have this all planned out. Have you done this before? And yes, with some instruction, anyone can fly a Cessna 175."

"I did this once last May, but I had to return and it was a smaller shipment - less than $1 million, not enough money in it for me to stay there and live. When I heard of your troubles I called my friends and asked if they had a pilot for this week. They know you and trust you. You're a war hero and they respected your padre. There is $200,000 in this for you and me. You can have 60%, because you need it for your wife. I will be happy with $80,000. I will work for them in New York when I need more money. They're all right with that."

"This is wrong Gonzalvo, it won't work! I'm not a smuggler. We'll get caught and my family will be shamed, my wife will die without the operation and my son will be an outcast."

"Would you do it if the money were sent to you before we even take off? Then if you are right your wife will still have her operation."

"Where would we fly to, just over the border to Texas or Arizona? And where would I send the money? I can't put it in an American bank, and if it went to my home Keisha wouldn't know what to do with it. She would be so ashamed of me and probably send it back."

"Our destination is a secret until we are in the air. They don't want too much information out there too soon. What about your friend, that Italian guy in Boston?"

"No way, he wouldn't want me to be part of this. He warned me not to get involved like that. I promised him I wouldn't. What if he were caught with illegal money? His family would also be destroyed. I couldn't do that to them."

"Then there is only one way! We need to get this thing done right. If we don't we're both screwed!" added Gonzalvo.

Diego looked at his grisly looking relative and thought that he knew him as the macho, not too sharp brother of his bright and beautiful cousin Karime. His years in prison seemed to turn him into a thinker, which could prove extremely dangerous for both of them. He thought, Is he right? Is there no other choice?

"I'll think about it. I'll let you know in the morning. Can you meet me at that café at 8 o'clock?"

"I'll be there, but you know what you must do!" advised Gonsalvo in his strongest tone possible. "It's for your wife!"

Gonsalvo dropped Diego off in front of Karime's apartment building. She was standing at the door to Dr. Valdez's office, obviously anxious and seemingly upset at his lengthy visit with her brother.

"Where have you been? I took the afternoon off from my work to talk to Dr. Valdez about Keisha and you're out partying with my brother?"

"I didn't know you were going to do that. I'm sorry for the inconvenience, but your brother likes to talk," he answered less than candidly knowing she would disapprove of the subject matter.

"Yes, I'm sure he did a lot of talking. My brother is an opportunist. He will use you to make money if he can, and he knows you're vulnerable. Tell me you told him no!"

"I told him no, about what?" responded Diego wondering if she really knew what they spoke about.

"No, about whatever scheme he asked you to participate in. I know he still has contact with the cartel. Don't get involved! They'll use you and let you rot in jail. Your family needs you. Keisha needs you to be there for her."

"How am I going to help her if I can't get the money for the care she needs? We don't have health insurance. It would have cost us more than what we make and now it's too late."

"That's what I'm trying to tell you. Dr. Valdez says he will review her medical records and speak with her doctor. Surgery is much less expensive in Mexico and unfortunately, due to the killings, there are more opportunities to get transplants here. Do you think she can travel?"

"I don't know. What are you saying? I don't understand. How can he help her if we don't have any money?"

"Come in, I want you to meet him," she said as she lead the way into his office.

The meeting with the doctor enlightened Diego as to the possibilities if Keisha was able to make the trip. There were no clear answers and, according to the doctor, even with the requested information and discussions with her doctor he could not be sure of the prognosis until he actually operated. Given the limited information he believed the kidney replacement was the important part of her health care.

"She probably will need to stay several weeks in a health care facility in Mexico to monitor her heart and to get her stronger. The heart condition may be a more difficult situation if it is not just a bypass since a transplant requires a donor with a healthy heart. That's not an easy condition to satisfy. With your permission, I will contact her doctor tomorrow. I know Dr. Bernstein. We see each other at conferences. The last time was in Madrid, in the spring. He's one of the best surgeons in the world. We have referred patients to each other for more than twenty years."

After they left the doctor and retreated to the apartment, Diego said. "I don't understand how I can pay him. And it'll be costly for her to come here to be treated."

"I told you, it can be done in Mexico for much less than in the States. I'll lend you the money for the hospital and the care, and we'll arrange a plan to pay the doctor."

"You're very generous, but I think it's going to take more money than we can pay. Where will we get the rest of it?" I don't have a job!

"Let's wait until the doctor has spoken with Keisha's doctor tomorrow and see what they think about her prospects if she was to come here."

Chapter 113

Two months had passed since Jim and Bert received the news of the imminent CTC purchase of Buckman Enterprises assets when the call from Bert came early on a Friday morning.

"Jim, they made a move from Jonathan's accessible account. My contact in the Caymans told me that our friends transferred over $5 million into a construction company they own in Texas. The construction company deposited it in five separate CTC branch banks."

"What does that mean? How are they going to legally get it into the campaign's coffers?"

"Well, they need to stay under the cap on contributions from individuals. In the past they've been able to overcome that restriction with deceptive financial manipulations."

"I doubt that the President would have any part of that. We might not agree on the issues, but I believe him to be an honest man," responded Jim,

"He probably won't know about it. He's too busy trying to survive the downturn in his campaign. The 'read my lips, no new taxes' fiasco is doing a job on his campaign strategy."

"What's our next move? Do we meet with them or drop a dime to the feds? Sharon and I have reviewed the documents and have some ideas."

"I don't know, but we need to think before we act. There are serious consequences if we make the wrong move."

"I realize that. What about later today? I'm free at 2 pm. Let's meet at the Club.

"That works for me, Jim. See you there at 1400."

The deal to purchase the Buckman assets was completed expeditiously under the prodding of Masters and Peters. As part of that deal Jonathan was given a seat at the Washington Action Group's table. He had insisted on that consideration and looked on it as a major victory. It was another step closer to being "as good as his father." He hoped in time he would exert the same kind of influence and control over the Group as his dad. Masters was getting old and he believed his father's oft-declared evaluation of the man as, "aggressive and obnoxious, but not the brightest bulb in the room," to be true!

Bert was late to arrive for the meeting. "Sorry, I felt someone was following me from my office so I took the long way around the Mall."

"They've got what they wanted, but they're not giving up," declared Jim.

"I'm sure they're still worried about what we have and are waiting for the shoe to drop. They're aware that there's a limited amount in the transitional account and they want it all. They can't access those funds without the codes."

"Obviously it's our only leverage to derail their objectives, but if they were to access the offshore monies they could expose themselves to some serious consequences," commented Jim, his mind working on a solution.

"I'm sure they would use your brother to attempt to secure that access, but he's not a signatory unless I give him that privilege," added Bert. "That's our leverage! Are you ready to expose your brother to potential indictment?"

"I'd like to smack him, but I'm not going to take him down that way. We need to devise a plan that doesn't create that kind of havoc. Knowing Jonathan, if he's exposed he'll take everyone he can with him. How much money are we talking about here?"

"Last count, there was more than $21 million. The interest accumulates daily. Why, what do you have in mind?"

"It seems there's no way those funds are legally accessible for our use. Also they were funded by businesses owned by each of the members of the Group. What was our family's contribution?"

"About $9 million, but your father managed the system. None of the others, including Masters, wanted that exposure and he used their insecurity to increase his control over the Group."

"Here's what I think. Let's clean out those accounts by contributing the monies to a number of charities. It would reduce the potential for a finding of tax fraud and if exposed would not result in negative public opinion. It will take some creative legal and accounting tactics, but the members won't protest even if they can figure it out. They won't want their participation in the political funding scheme to be exposed, and Masters wouldn't be able to stop the process."

"It's an interesting idea Jim! I like it, but it needs more thought. How do we avoid some smartass reporter finding out the true reasons for our generosity?"

"The only way to do that is to contribute relatively small amounts to many charities and space them over a reasonable time period and geographic area. It's not foolproof, but I don't know of any other way to put this behind us without benefitting the Group and exposing you and our family. I'm thinking we do it from the three accounts with less than $100,000 from each bank within any one quarter. If there's exposure, we need a cover story that these funds were set up for that purpose and hope that the banks are secure enough in their covert accounting practices that past activities can't be identified.

"I see where you're coming from. Your father was right when he said that you have his ability to strategize your way out of hell."

"He said that? Well I hope I never have to use that ability in that way!" responded Jim feeling a sense of pride at his father's back-handed compliment.

"I believe he was commenting on your escape from the hell of captivity in Vietnam. He was well aware of your tendency towards decency and your integrity as a man, although it took his illness to realize their value."

"Thank you for that, Bert. I appreciate your comments. I did ask myself, what would he do under these conditions and I think he would approve of our tactics in this situation.

"I agree, Jim, not only due to his ideological epiphany, but also due to his dislike for Masters' heavy handedness."

Chapter 114

Diego stalled Gonzalvo telling him he needed to find out more about how the compensation would work for him. He wasn't ready to buy into the plan. He couldn't wire it ahead or rely on it being there in the getaway truck, when he had already done the deed, and he wasn't going to expose his friend to potential arrest.

"I can only hold them off for a little while. They'll find another pilot if I tell them you're not sure or afraid," cautioned his cousin.

"I'm not afraid, but I'm not comfortable with the payment arrangements. I need another 24 hours to figure it out, but if they have someone else then it is okay too," declared Diego, believing that Gonzalvo would not get as good a deal from another pilot.

"I'll do what I can to get you the time you need, but I know we need to fly in two days at the latest, to meet their commitments."

"I'll tell you my decision tomorrow afternoon by 4 o'clock. I'll meet you here."

"I'll be here, but don't disappoint me...or your wife!"

The meeting with Dr. Valdez lasted more than an hour. He told of his conversation with Dr. Bernstein and that he had some hope that Keisha would be able to travel after a dialysis treatment and that he believed he could help her with the kidney condition.

"We'll need to work quickly to find an appropriate donor. We can test all your relatives here in Mexico, at least those willing to go through the operation and loss of a kidney. We should also have her relatives in the States tested. Do you know them?"

"I know of some, but they're in California and I don't know if they're that close to her. She's an only child and her mother passed away several years ago."

"You'll need her cooperation to find them and to ask if they are willing to save her life. There is no easy way to do this. We all have two kidneys, unless we gave one up already, and we can live with only one. Karime has already been tested and she's not a match. She'll seek out and ask your relatives to find a willing donor that we can test. We'll test you tomorrow morning at 9 o'clock at the hospital."

"Doctor, what will all this testing cost? Karime has told you that we have no insurance and no money," Diego looked towards Karime whose sad eyes told of her concern and caring.

"Yes, Karime has committed to pay for whatever it takes to find this donor, my friend. Your cousin is a very good woman! Her word is all I need. There is one more thing I should tell you. As Karime knows I treated her brother Gonzalvo when he was released from prison and I had my nurse check his file. He is a match!"

Karime looked at the doctor shocked at this disclosure, "Why did you not tell me this before?" she asked, shocked at the revelation.

"I'm sorry, but I was told this just before you arrived today. I asked my nurse to check the records of patients you would know and he was the only match."

"He would never agree to give up a kidney. He's a very selfish man!"

Diego's head was spinning back and forth between the two. "Wait, are you saying that we have a match already and we can spare the time and expense of testing others?"

The doctor and Karime stopped their discussion and turned their attention to Diego. "Yes, I'm saying that, but he would still need to be evaluated as to his health and his willingness to be a donor."

"Diego, you know he's not going to be a willing donor. Of course he would sell his right arm for the right price. Forget that idea. We need to find someone else!" advised Karime.

"How can you be sure unless we ask him? He's asking a favor of me, maybe we can trade."

"What kind of a favor? I told you do not get involved with him or you will live to regret it, if you live at all!"

"I'll leave you two to discuss this. I need to go to the hospital to see my patients. Karime, I think that you should keep an open mind about this. He may be the only possibility."

After the doctor left Karime declared, "That's not a possibility! He doesn't really know my brother. He treated him when he was physically damaged from the abuse he took. He did it because I asked him to and I paid for his care because he's family, but he is not a good person and you are."

"What else can we do? What if we wait and test many people at a cost that could be used for Keisha's surgery and we don't find anyone. Do I watch her die? I can't do that. I just can't!"

"What does he want you to do? Tell me, Diego! What crime does he want you to commit to make you equal to him? Do you think your wife would want that and what about your son, Manny? Who will take care of him if this grand plan fails?"

The night went by slowly as Diego lay awake thinking of all that he heard. Could Gonzalvo be the solution to this terrible situation? What would it take for him to agree? Could he be trusted and would Karime ever forgive him for giving in to Gonzalvo's greed? He needed to make a decision within the next few hours.

Chapter 115

The generosity of the Buckman offshore fund's charitable contributions caught Jonathan and Masters by surprise. By the time they figured out what was going on two quarters of donations had depleted the accounts and had gained little notoriety. They were hesitant to disclose the information to the members of their Group fearing their recognition of the fact that a Buckman had outwitted them.

They knew the members would not take kindly to the fact that their contributions of profits over the years had not resulted in the promised benefits and there was nothing they could do about it. The only public knowledge was of some of the well-known charities acknowledging donations of $50,000 to $80,000 from anonymous donors. Not an unusual occurrence and hardly worthy of much attention.

"How did they pull this off right under our noses?" Masters demanded to know as he addressed his intimate sub-group of Jonathan Buckman, Don Peters and Attorney Dale Watkins. "Are they that smart or are we that dumb?"

Silence pervaded the room as each participant looked to the other hoping someone else would speak up.

Don Peters dared to be first. "Give them credit. It was a very smart move if the intent was to deny us the funds, but I don't see what they gained."

"I'll tell you what they gained. They put the issue of their potential for being indicted, and our leverage, into a deep hole that if dug up would become our graves," answered Watkins.

"No one does that to me! We'll respond! I'm not sure how, but we will respond!" Masters declared, his voice loud and demanding and his nostrils flaring. He had been bested again by a Buckman. But there would be no response. They could only hope that it was over.

Jonathan had mixed emotions, but he wasn't about to show them. This was another nail in Masters' coffin as their leader, and in spite of the financial loss he was in awe of his brother's resolve. He would use it for his own benefit. He decided to act!

"I had assumed that when I turned over my wealth to you, it would be protected. I trusted in your leadership, and now I believe it's time for you to step aside. I'm very disappointed in your ability to lead this Group."

"Oh you are! Well you wimpy bastard, you think you can do better. I saved your ass and you dare talk to me like that!" Masters rose from his chair at the end of the long mahogany conference table and headed for Jonathan's position midway down the side.

Peters and Watkins intercepted him and told him to sit down. They had enough problems to deal with given the depletion of funds that they relied on. They both looked at Jonathan and thought, that's all they need, another smart ass to piss off the Bulldog, although they agreed with his words.

Peters took command as Masters continued to fume. "We can't be tearing each other apart here. We need to face the rest of the members with the bad news. They're very powerful men and they're not going to be happy. This was their money as well as ours. What will we tell them to keep them in the program and how do we explain the actions that we took without their knowledge? This is serious and we need to stick together!"

Jonathan did all he could to keep from smiling. He believed that Masters was doomed and his time was coming.

Chapter 116

Diego explained his dilemma to Gonzalvo, leaving the part about his potential as a match for his wife's kidney transplant until the end. His cousin was almost ecstatic at his agreement to do the flight, but he told him that it was under two conditions.

"Here's the deal! I'll fly this cargo to your little airport in the States but I want all of the money to be paid up front, to me, the whole $200,000, and I'll put it in a bank here in Mexico. I'll pay you 50% or $100,000 when I complete the mission. But you will not be coming with me."

"What is this? Do you take me for a fool? You get all of the money and then go home and I stay here. Are you crazy!" exclaimed Gonzalvo angrily as he was about to come out of his seat to show his little cousin that he was no fool.

"Hold on, I'm not finished. You know why I'm here in Mexico and why I would even consider your offer. It is because of my wife and if she doesn't benefit from my being stupid enough to do this then I'm not interested. If I'm successful I'll return to do another flight next month. I'll be coming back with Keisha so that she can have that kidney transplant. That's why I'm leaving the money here in Mexico, it is for her operation."

"Oh, I see, so you have found a donor. That is good! How did you do it so fast?" asked Gonzalvo smiling at Diego's good fortune.

"Well you know we have been talking to Dr. Valdez. He was your doctor when you got out of prison, right?"

"Yes, he is a very good man and an excellent doctor. Is he going to do the operation? Who is the donor?"

"You, Gonzalvo!"

The smile quickly disappeared from his face. "You're crazy! I need my kidneys! I'm not doing such a stupid thing!"

"That's the most important condition, without it there is no flight, no $100,000 and no United States for you. The doctor says you'll be fine with one kidney. I'll pay you when I return with Keisha in two weeks and you donate that kidney. It's your choice, but I must know today! If you back out for any reason, you get nothing. Do you trust me?"

Gonzalvo was shocked and scared at the thought of giving up a kidney. He knew he had been out-foxed but he wanted that money and to be in the States more than anything, maybe even more than one of his kidneys. "I trust you because if you don't do what you say you will be the one giving up body parts. I will see if the cartel will put the money up front. What if they don't?"

"Then there is no deal! I'll see you here same time tomorrow morning. Time's running out!"

"Does Karime know of your plan? I don't think she will be happy."

"No, but she knows I have a flight home tomorrow night. She doesn't know that our plan involves my flying your friends' plane to the States."

"Won't she wonder why I'm willing to give up my kidney?"

"You need to make her believe that it is to pay forward her generosity to you and that you have changed. Show her you have a heart. It will make her very happy."

"I don't know if she will believe that, but I will try, but she will want me to give up that heart too if she thinks I have one," he joked, but without a smile.

The cartel agreed to pay half of the fee up front, the other when he returned for the second flight, which would also command a fee the size of which depended on the value of the cargo. Diego thought that it was doable since it was Gonzalvo's money that would be delayed. If he was okay with it, they had a deal.

"They will have one of their men fly with you, but he will have to return."

"I don't need a co-pilot and I'm not going to be watching my back for some assassin to attack. I go alone or I don't go."

"They worry that you will take their precious cargo and disappear. They're not interested in hurting you. They need you for the future. They hope you'll continue to do this for them and they respect your father and our family especially Carmella and Karime."

"I don't feel comfortable with someone I don't know."

"They're sending a primo, Raúl Martinez, he is a young man and he is not a bad person. Carmella was his grandfather's sister. You are a legend to him! He volunteered."

"Great, now I'm going to babysit some kid too?"

"No, he's 28 years old and a good mechanic. He's no dummy!"

"What's the weather report?" he asked Gonzalvo on the ride to the field.

"I'm not sure, but we have been in a drought for more than a month. I think you'll be fine! You can fly by instruments, can't you?"

"Sure!" he lied, having failed that test, but it was too late to back out now.

It was dusk when he arrived at the landing strip 30 kilometers south of Mexico City. The beat up Cessna 175 was sitting at the end of what was loosely called a runway. At the other end was a tree line that wasn't going to be forgiving if he didn't gain enough speed to rise above it. The strip was narrow, about 20 meters wide, with some protruding boulders to be avoided along the way. An overcast sky made the prospects of a smooth ride even more doubtful.

"There they are at the south end of the strip," declared Gonzalvo pointing to a green pickup truck barely visible within the tree line, behind the plane. Three men stood beside the truck. Two of them armed with AK-47s, the third a slightly built young man who anxiously awaited his cousin, the war hero!

The departure from Karime was not a smooth one. Diego told her of his convincing Gonzalvo to be the donor. She didn't buy it.

"I know you have sold your soul for this and for that I am very sad. I don't know what you're doing for him, but I understand. Please be careful, your family needs you," and with that she gave him a hug and a kiss on his cheek.

The thoughts of her words would not leave his head. He knew that he had to concentrate on doing what he was being paid for and not on any other consequences. He had rented a safe deposit box in a local bank and put all but $5,000 into it. He would need money to get home from wherever they were sending him. Raúl would be driven back by one of the cartel's American-side members. Before they left the city he mailed a letter to Karime telling her of the money and where to find the key to access it. He put her name as a person that would be allowed access to the box.

He wondered if he would remember all of the intricacies of flying. If he didn't his worries would end very quickly. It's like riding a bicycle. He kept telling himself. It will all come back to him. He just hoped it would come back sooner than later.

The pre-flight checklist was in Spanish but Diego was not intimidated although he was no longer as fluent as he was as a child. "Here Raúl you read this to me, in English, as I go through the list."

Once complete, Diego took a deep breath and pushed the throttle. The plane shook, wobbled and started to move forward, seemingly as reluctant as he was to fly this mission. The sun was setting to his left. The rickety plane picked up speed as it traveled down the rocky runway. He realized that he was carrying a heavy load of illicit cargo and pushed the throttle to its limit as the far end tree-line loomed closer.

"Hold on cuz this is going to be close!" he warned as the nose lifted and the wheels left the ground, trimming the tree tops as they cleared the first hurdle.

Once confident that he had made it he looked over at his passenger whose head was back and mouth agape as he gasped for air. "You can open the envelope, Raúl, and find out where we're going."

Raúl ripped open the envelope and read their instructions. It had only the latitude and longitude of the strip that they were to land on and a distance of 698 nautical miles. The normal range for the 175 with a 42 gallon fuel tank and without a full load is less than 600 nautical miles. He was told that the two fuel tanks were increased to 50 gallons, adding some weight and some added range.

It was going to be a tight flight and at a top speed, loaded, of about 150 mph, it would take nearly five hours to reach their destination. The instructions had a fuel stop that was identified as being west of Monterey, Mexico, with a notation saying that it was only to be used in an emergency. They would stay at about 5,000 feet and keep a visual for other aircraft especially government issue. They had been known to shoot first and ask questions later.

The first hours of flight were uneventful, with clear skies and light winds. The long flight gave Diego a chance to get to know his young cousin. He reminded him of his own youth. He was a young man looking for a way to live in an unfriendly world. He had little formal education, but seemed to be intelligent conversing on many subjects. He knew Diego's history from those who were his padrés peers.

"Did you really get shot out of a tree?" was the first inquiry into his war hero days.

Diego just looked at him and shook his head. "I was the point man in my company and I was checking out an enemy village. I took a round from the village that sent me crashing to the ground. I broke both legs."

"Yes, and your sergeant, that guy Tony saved your ass? I met him when he visited you. I was only 10 years old. Carmella told me he was a special hombre."

"He was and he still is. I would not be here with you today if it wasn't for him. There is nothing better than a good friend, he..."

"Diego, look over there." Raúl interrupted pointing to Diego's left. The blinking lights of a midsize plane were visible in the bright moonlight at about 10,000 feet and at least 2 miles to their west.

Not being familiar with the silhouette of Mexico's Air force he decided to bank away from their flight path to see if they followed. They didn't. Diego shut off his external lights. He would fly blind as long as he could. He could see the city lights of Monterey in the far distance. His fuel was just over a half a tank. He decided that he didn't have an emergency and flew west of the city towards his destination.

Forty minutes past Monterey the clouds came in followed by lightning, the kind of lightning that indicates a major storm in the southwest.

"It looks like we're going to have a wild ride. I don't have enough fuel to get above it."

As he spoke he heard the boom of thunder and saw a blinding flash almost simultaneously indicating that it was close to the plane, which dropped in response.

"This is going to get worse. We need to find a place to land until it passes," declared Diego." See if you can find a field or even a road that isn't being used."

The storm clouds brought intense darkness. There was no full moon to guide them or light their way. They turned on the plane's lights, as another bolt hit the trees below them. The lightning revealed a small road running north and south to their east.

"Over there!" Raúl pointed to his right! "I see a roadway. There are no cars on it.

Multiple burst of lightning lit up the way, but brought high winds that tossed the plane about, making control difficult as it descended. Diego held tight to the wheel and attempted to use his ailerons and rudder to offset the effects of the turbulence. He was not trained for this kind of flying. He was running on instincts...and fear.

"There it is, to the right we can make it!" exclaimed Raúl. "You're going too fast! Slow down!"

The plane's right wing was down, they were at 1200 feet and dropping fast. Diego tried to correct the plane's roll using the ailerons. Another burst of lightning and wind brought the wing up. The road was in front of them, but so was an 18-wheeler moving towards them through the blinding rain.

The driver, not believing his eyes as the blinking lights of the Cessna descended upon him, decided to speed up fearing the impact of whatever it was that was threatening him from above.

The truck passed under the plane as its wheels just touched its roof before it descended and was deflected onto the roadway. As the plane hopped onto the road surface Diego tensed as he tried to control its side to side movement with flaps up and brakes fully depressed. It screeched to a grinding halt, nose dipped towards the ground.

The truck never stopped. They were still in the road and believed that there might be another vehicle threatening them if they didn't get off. There was a flat area at the side of the road, about 50 yards from them.

"We need to get this plane over there." Diego pointed to the flat spot in the distance. "We'll wait out the storm there."

It was more than an hour before the sky cleared. An inspection of the plane indicated it was no worse than it was when they originally took off, which wasn't very good, but it got them this far.

"Let's turn it around to take off downhill. It might save some fuel," suggested Diego.

They were airborne in minutes and headed north to their secret destination in the States. He still wondered if he was doing the right thing. He rationalized that if he didn't do it someone else would.

They passed over the Rio Grande at 3:45 am. They were 15 miles east of Laredo, Texas. They had crossed the border. Diego couldn't help feeling that it was too easy. They would follow Route I-35 north for 14 miles then turn east for 17 miles to the site defined by its coordinates.

"I don't like it Raúl, There should have been some evidence of border patrol in the area we just flew over. This is a big delivery, maybe they know we're coming and are waiting for us at the landing strip?"

"What should we do? We can't go back?

"No, but we can go someplace else and call back our location for a pick up."

"But what if you're wrong and we can't reach them? They'll think we stole their drugs and come after us."

"Well there's our answer. Diego pointed to a caravan of a half-dozen vehicles defined by their rear red lights heading towards their proposed landing area on a secondary road. There's no reason for that many vehicles to be on that road at this time of the morning. They must think we're already there.

They don't know we had a delay in the storm. There must be a mole in the cartel. They were tipped off."

Diego banked the plane left and headed for a more northwesterly landing area. He had less than an eighth of a tank of fuel left.

"We can't use the radio. We need to get to a phone. Let's check out those lights clustered to the left. It looks like a gas station and a diner on that country road."

"You should be good at landing on roadways cousin. Just avoid trucks."

Raúl was right. The landing was uneventful. The gas station was open, but the diner was closed. There was a phone booth in the parking lot.

The attendant came out to see why there was a plane in his gas station. "Are you guys okay? I don't know if I have fuel you can use in your plane."

"We're all right, but I need to use your phone. Can you change a five?"

"Sure, I have a roll of quarters, come on in. I have coffee on. Where are you going?"

"Just to Austin, but we need to contact someone and let them know we'll be late. Where can I refuel? Is here a small airport nearby?"

"There's one about 25 miles northwest of here, but I don't know if there's anyone there. It used to be Charlie Smith's. He did crop dusting, but I think he retired. Do you have enough fuel to get there?"

"Yes, we'll be fine. We'll just rest until sun light. I need to make that call, but thanks again for your help."

The call was made to Gonzalvo. "What do you mean you didn't make it to the drop site?" They'll think you stole their cargo and come after you."

"We didn't steal anything. Did you hear from your people at the site, we saw what looked like an unfriendly caravan going in that direction and we diverted to this place. We were an hour late because of a storm about a half hour past Monterey and had to land on a roadway there."

"Where are you? I'll contact them and see if they can meet you there," responded a calmer Gonzalvo."

"Be careful who you talk to. I think there's someone tipping them off. We can't stay where we are, but we'll be going to an airfield and should be there in about two hours. I'll call you from there. Stay by your phone and talk only to someone you trust."

They took off at dawn. With the sun rising behind them they spotted the small airfield about two miles west of the nearest paved road. An old, poorly maintained Quonset Hut, the type of building often used as a an airplane hangar, had the words "Smith Crop Dusting" in faded red paint written on the top. The field was overgrown, but looked to be usable.

"That looks like the place, but it seems deserted," commented Diego somewhat disappointed, but thinking maybe that's best. "We're running on fumes we have no choice. We need to land and hope we can find a way out of here."

As they circled to land, Raúl using binoculars, noticed an old pickup truck on the far side of the building. "I wonder if there's anyone in that trailer at that end of the field?" he said as his eyes surveyed the property.

"We'll soon find out. Hold on! This field is overgrown and in rough condition," with that warning Diego brought the beat-up Cessna to a three-bounce landing catching the tall grass with its landing gear as they went, slowing them down quicker than expected.

"I think it's better to land on paved roadways, cousin," a jostled Raúl declared.

No one emerged from the trailer home as they stopped about a hundred feet away watching for any sign of life.

"It seems like the place is abandoned. That may be a good thing. Let's go over to the hangar while we still have some fumes left. It would be good if we can hide this poor excuse for an airplane in there. I doubt we'll find a live phone here."

"We can check out that truck too. Maybe it still runs?" added Raúl.

They were able to break open a side door to the hangar. The main lift door was locked and more secure. The interior housed a number of airplane parts, one 55 gallon drum labeled "lubricant" and a second labeled with the painted word "fuel." There was plenty of room for their plane so they opened the wide door and pulled it in using a tow rope found hanging on the wall. The drum labeled fuel was about half full. They would need a pump to siphon it into one of the plane's tanks. The phone on the wall was dead.

"Go check out that truck. We need to get to a phone and let your friends know where there precious cargo is so they don't use us for target practice if they find us."

After about 20 minutes and several trips back and forth between the truck and the hangar to get tools Diego heard the roar and backfiring of the truck's engine. He had managed to start a siphoning system with an old garden hose. He elevated the drum with a chain and pulley that was probably used to pull engines. The siphoning required using his mouth to create the initial suction, causing some fuel being sucked into his throat, which he vomited out by necessity.

"We have about a quarter of a tank of gas in the truck. I had to clean the spark plugs and adjust the rotors to get it started. We have trucks like this in our village. They need a lot of attention to keep them going. They say I am one of the best at doing that," said Raúl proudly. "That's why they sent me, to fix this old plane if it gave us trouble."

"Well, if it gave us trouble at 5,000 feet you would only have time to pray!" laughed Diego.

Once the hangar was secured they drove to the nearest gas station nearly three miles away, to phone Gonzalvo.

He gave him the coordinates of the new drop-off point and told him that they would stay within sight of the location, but would leave the area before either his friends or their pursuers arrived. He would take Raúl to a place where he could be picked up by his people and contact Gonzalvo to let him know that location.

"I did hear from them after I talked to you and they also saw the border patrol approaching and left the area. They're driving a large black Ford van with the words 'Maria's Bakery' in white on the side. They should be there within the hour," responded

Gonzalvo. "And cousin, don't worry, they think that you are a very smart hombre."

"Well, I don't know about smart, but I am desperate and very tired!" answered Diego. "Raúl has done a good job too, make sure they know that."

Raúl, standing beside him, smiled at his words. "Thank you for that and I'm happy that I came. I learned much from you."

"Well, you're a good man and I hope you'll be able to get away from this life while you still have life," responded Diego with a man-hug that surprised his young cousin. Affection between men was not part of Raúl's tough and precarious life.

As Karime read the letter from Diego she could not help but cry as she realized her worst fears. He had crossed the line and would now be a wanted man. Despite her reservations she would follow up on his wishes, access the money and go to the States and bring Keisha to Mexico City, if as he stated in the letter, "I don't survive!"

Karime,

"I will contact you within five days, but if I don't, I hope that you will find it in your heart to follow through with my wishes and see to Keisha's health. I realize that this might not be possible and that would be understandable. Gonzalvo will know my fate!

Love, Diego."

She put the key to the safety deposit box and the access code in a safe place and hoped she would not be the one to use it and that Diego would survive his poor judgment and reckless behavior.

The van appeared as promised. They could see three men as they entered the side door that they left unlocked. They found a good place to watch the site from a vantage point on a rise about a quarter of a mile south. The front lift door was opened and they pulled up as close to the plane as possible and they began to load its cargo into the van.

"Look, over there, Diego!" exclaimed an excited Raúl.

Diego redirected his attention to where he was pointing. At first he saw a cloud of dust then several vehicles moving at high speed down the dirt road, the access to Smith's Crop Dusting landing strip.

Raúl, in the driver's seat of the borrowed truck began flashing its lights and beeping the horn hoping that their elevated position would afford the busy men a warning. One of the men looked up and shielding his eyes pointed to their position. Another looked around and caught sight of the billowing dust trail moving rapidly towards them. They scrambled to complete the reload but decided that they were gaining too quickly. As they pulled away from the building an explosion signaled the end of the Cessna. They joined the dirt road and sped westward, away from the rapidly gaining Border Patrol vehicles.

"We need to get moving!" ordered Diego as they turned to leave their hilltop position. "We'll go to Laredo. You can walk across the bridge to Nuevo Laredo and your friends can pick you up there. Just don't say 'si' if asked if you're an American Citizen," instructed Diego with a wink and a smile.

"I wonder how much of the cargo they lost?" questioned Raúl.

"We did our job, but someone set us up," was Diego's only response.

Diego managed to reach Laredo and see to it that his young cousin made it across the bridge to the sister city of Nuevo Laredo.

He left the truck with its dated plates in the city and took a bus to San Antonio, where he managed to catch a flight to Boston. The $5,000 in cash he took with him came in handy.

While in an overnight layover in Charlotte, North Carolina, he called Gonzalvo for an update on their mission.

"It is not good news amigo. The Border Patrol caught up to our people. There was a shoot-out. They killed two and caught one of our men," lamented Gonzalvo.

"Are the bosses upset with us? They realize that we did our best to complete our end of the mission, don't they?" asked Diego worried that they would become targets for revenge.

"Yes, they do and they're grateful. Raúl made it to a rendezvous and told of your efforts. They know that you did your best and you were right about the mole, but he managed to get back to the states. They want you to do the next mission, if you are willing. It may be a while. They want things to cool down."

"We'll see, but I'm happy that our cousin made it back. He's a good man!" Diego was relieved that his efforts didn't result in more drugs on American streets. He had taken the job by necessity but thought of the impact such actions would have on his fellow Americans and considered sabotaging the mission if he could find a safe way to do it. That was one of the reasons he wanted to go it alone. He felt badly for the two men who died, they might also have been cousins, but they knew what they were risking, just as he did. He also knew that even though the drugs didn't get to the streets he was still a criminal for his part in the fiasco.

Part Six

The Clinton Years

Chapter 117

By 1992 racial, class and income inequality was still in effect and the plight of the middle class was becoming more precarious with each election. Society had yet to notice the "elephant in the room" or admit to its cause and effect. The failure of supply-side economics was rationalized by right-wing radicals as being the result of the lazy poor, the inept middle class and greedy labor unions. If America was a business it would have been more correctly classified as "skimming of the top!"

The "Reagan Trickle" had vaporized before it reached the fifty plus percent of the electorate that had believed in its promise or the balance of those who voted against him knowing it to be a scam. Ironically some senior citizens revered the wealthy for their accomplishments even as they succeeded in draining the equity from their homes and their investments. Despite the failure of their policies they voted for conservatives who aggressively attempted to kill their Social Security and Medicare benefits.

After twelve years of Reagan-Bush it appeared that the "beat would go on" until, to the chagrin of those in power, William Jefferson Clinton, the young governor of Arkansas, came onto the national political scene. George H.W. Bush had succeeded Reagan to the presidency but couldn't overcome the impact of his predecessor's economic short-falls.

Bush's challenger, Bill Clinton wasn't born with a silver spoon in his mouth, but he did have exceptional intellect, and a driving ambition to make a difference. As a youth, he often confronted his alcoholic father to protect his mother. Eventually he went to live with his grandparents in a compassionate household that had no use for hate and bigotry. He was an achiever and he had confidence in his ability to lead. He was a progressive governor and, at 45 years old, he was running for the Presidency of the United States.

Diego's cousin Karime had a strong desire to someday become an American citizen and saw the possibility of Clinton's election as a step in the right direction. She encouraged Diego to raise money for him early in his campaign and to do whatever he could to support his candidacy. As an academic she noticed Clinton when he gained some notoriety at the 1988 Democratic National Convention, which nominated Michael Dukakis as their candidate for the Presidency. Dukakis, considered a liberal Democrat, was the former governor of Massachusetts. He lost to the senior Bush in 1988. Bill Clinton, a young, confident, verbose speaker and rising star in the Democratic Party, gave the opening night address at the convention. Some say it was one of the longest on record.

He was recognized as being intelligent not only for having been a Rhodes Scholar, but for his depth of knowledge and responses to questions during his debates and presentations. The electorate admired his ability to discuss issues during the campaign and not the personalities of his opponent. It gained him the credibility that lead to his nomination as a candidate for the Presidency, a goal that began as a young high school student in Arkansas.

On July 24, 1963, as a 16 year old year-old and member of Boy's Nation, during the organization's visit to the White House, he shook hands with JFK. His fellow students smiled and rolled their eyes when he declared that, "someday I'm going to have his job." Now, nearly 30 years later, he was being compared to his idol and was looked upon as the rock star of the new Democratic Party.

For Sharon Polowski, it was a sign that the majority of Americans were finally realizing that they had to protect their own interest and were rejecting the smoke and mirrors of old. The attacks on the Clinton's character began almost immediately from the righteous right, but for Senator Sharon Polowski Clinton offered hope. Although of different political persuasions she would often discuss her ideas for making American government more compassionate and fair with her husband during the rare occasion of a dinner at home.

"Jim, I'm thinking about presenting a bill in the next session of the Senate that would change the tax code. It's one item that I agree with your party needs to be changed, but I also believe that it needs to eliminate their special treatment and loopholes."

"Well, I'm sure it'll get some attention, but it won't make it through without some consideration of their issues. Every year, since we've been in Congress, there are bills filed to simplify the tax code. Reagan was the only one who succeeded."

"Yes, by reducing taxes for the very rich and adding enough loopholes to give them the potential to avoid taxes altogether. We need real reform, but I'm not opposed to a flat tax for a full range of income."

"Well, we like flat tax talk, but I have a feeling that you're not thinking of it the way me and my colleagues do."

"Well, listen to my proposal. Tell me what you think of it as a moderate Republican. Could you support a simplified code that doesn't tax monies needed for basic survival, such as a no tax status up to $20,000 per person and $40,000 for married couples? The first bracket would be on an adjusted gross income greater than $20,000 of 10 % up to $100,000 and a 2.5% increase for every $100,000 after that with a maximum of 30% after $1 million."

"And what about incentives for home ownership and investments?" queried Jim.

"There would still be some limited deductions, but I like credits. Let's not play math games with deductions, make it simple. However, I do propose some deductions to income, but they would be capped so that they aren't extraordinary incentives for the very wealthy. They should be for the average American. I would limit the mortgage interest deduction to $50,000 and the real estate tax deduction to a maximum of $20,000. Let's stop financing mansions, claimed to be business properties with tax incentives. I'd propose a *tax credit* up to $20,000 per year be allowed for college tuition. I also believe that renters should have some benefits and propose a maximum of a $5,000 deduction for renters."

"Your tough, but I can't say I find it that objectionable...yet! What about investments and capital gains?"

"This is the bone I'm giving you and your buddies, but I want to see an end to this volatile buy-sell epidemic. Capital gains would be taxed at 25% for the first year held and reduced by 2.5% off the rate the second year and 2.5% each year following, to a low of 10% after 7 years. Let's encourage reinvestment in American businesses instead of offshore savings and investment schemes.

"But no exemptions? That won't go well with the electorate!"

"Hold on! I'm going to propose a tax credit, not a deduction, of $2,500 per child up to a maximum of three children, so as not to encourage over population. How's that for a liberal?" Sharon said with raised eyebrows and a smile. "And I propose a credit for health insurance premiums with a maximum of $5,000 in 1992 dollars. With no tax on interest earned from banks up to $20,000, and that profits be considered the same as earned income. So what do you think?"

"I think you'd better do some serious marketing if you expect Congress to absorb that much all at once. Too many of my esteemed colleagues aren't visionaries."

"That's the point my dear. It takes a major renovation of the tax code to be meaningful. Let's get rid of all of the complex language and curious incentives and, most important, the thousands of pages of booby traps and keep it really simple. No hidden loopholes or secret benefits and no tripwires to harass the populace. Let's make it a 200 page code instead of a ten thousand page attorney's dream. I would even agree to have corporations write off equipment purchases in the first year up to $1 million; major improvements in 5 years and property purchases in 10 years."

"Okay, so let's do the math! A family of four with an income of $55,000 a year wouldn't pay any tax since they could be exempt for the first $40,000 by being married and have $5,000 in total tax credits for their two children and, if they own their home, have paid $5,000 in Real Estate tax and $10,000 in mortgage interest. They would have $60,000 against their income of $55,000 and no tax liability? Isn't this number considered the beginning of the middle class level of income, shouldn't they be paying something?"

"I think you'd agree that it would difficult to survive on an adjusted gross income of only $55,000 with two kids in 1992. These people are contributing to the economy and to the wealth of those who pay low wages and make high profits off their efforts. Remember American workers have the highest level of productivity of any industrial nation. The benefactors of their work are the same wealthy individuals who pay a very small portion of that windfall wealth in taxes after they take advantage of all of the loopholes and gifts that your party has given them. They aren't worried about putting food on the table, paying for health care, going bankrupt due to illness or being able to heat their homes or run their cars."

"I would think better of it if they paid some minimum tax, say 5%, to go for Social Security and Medicare exclusively. Those are programs that they most likely will eventually benefit from."

"I'd be okay with that if there was no income limit on that taxation so those programs are properly funded and at a lower rate than they are now!" As it stands now in 1992, only those making up to $55,000 pay into Social Security. I suspect that the rate might be much lower if it applied to everyone at every level as it should! We need to cut out the inequalities of the tax code."

"Obviously, you've put some serious thought into this hon. I don't disagree with the premise, but I don't know if it has legs. When will you present it?"

"When you agree to support it in the House and Clinton wins the Presidency!" she said with a kiss on his forehead. "All of this creative thinking has made me exhausted. Let's go to bed!"

Chapter 118

Sharon got her wish. In November 1992, William Jefferson Clinton, at 46 years old, was elected the 42nd President of the United States. A moderate self-declared "New Democrat," Clinton proved to be conservative on fiscal issues and a pragmatic progressive on social problems. He reformed welfare and raised taxes on the 1.2 % wealthiest while lowering taxes on 98.8% of Americans.

Although there was a limited military action in Serbia as part of a NATO effort to quell the slaughter of people, Clinton ended the era of deficit spending for wars, the funding of irrational defense programs and the blaming of the country's woes on the poor and middle class.

He proved that he was not an isolationist when in 1993, as a result of a thwarted attempt on the life of his predecessor George H.W. Bush by Iraqi zealots he authorized a missile attack on a military target in Baghdad. This limited action showed their regime that there are some things that are not tolerated by Americans and that we will always be non-partisan in our response to such acts.

Unfortunately for the immigrant population, tens of thousands of whom were enticed to work as illegal aliens for low wages by American farmers and businessmen, he supported those politicians who found them to be no longer necessary and he unwittingly agreed to what he believed was a way to gain trade advantages.

Corporate America found the North American Free Trade Agreement or NAFTA, a more effective way to deal with their need and greed for cheap, high profit labor and to elevate its offense against American unions. The Republican Congress, having the Clintons in a defensive mode with their constant attacks and witch hunts, assumed him to be weak and malleable and started on their course for social program reforms, something they couldn't achieve during the twelve previous years of the Reagan-Bush administrations. Speaker of the House Tip O'Neil having successfully defended those programs.

Senator Polowski's tax reform legislation never saw the light of day. It was sent to a study committee where it would surely die a slow and painful death. She found that even her Democratic colleagues didn't like the idea of losing control over tax code incentives. Being able to offer constituents, both rich and poor, a tax benefit of some kind was too much of a political tool to give up.

Chapter 119

Keisha was never told that her surgery and follow-up care in Mexico were the result of her husband's criminal activity. She believed what he told her, that it was a part of the estate of his grandmother that Karime was managing. Karime knew there was no benefit in countering that lie and just didn't discuss it. She was happy that he survived his poor judgment and illicit activities and that she played a part in Keisha overcoming her illness. With a healthy kidney her heart improved and within three months she was able to go home.

Diego had managed to get back to Massachusetts. He used the money from the flight for his family's survival. Although the mission failed, the Cartel also paid the additional $100,000, which he gave, as promised, to Gonzalvo, who had reluctantly given up his kidney for the money and the opportunity to go to America. He accomplished that feat on a similar mission two months later, but without Diego, who had enough adventure, declined future assignments. He left the balance of the money in the safety deposit box in Mexico City realizing that it would be difficult to transport it to the United States without causing curiosity. He would visit frequently and take funds back in small quantities as he needed it to repay Tony and catch up on his debts.

The declaration of amnesty by Bill Clinton in his early years as President for those air traffic controllers fired by Reagan in 1981 was a statement that the U.S. Government's anti-union policies were over, at least during Clinton's administration. Diego was inspired to apply for a position. He had missed the silver bullet and exposure in his debut as a pilot for the cartel and he hoped to regain his status as a controller. With a little help from his friends in Congress he managed to return to the Logan Airport Tower. Life was good again!

Not able to find a job that paid a living wage to a 47 year old engineer, Tony started a new company with virtually no resources, but with clients that wanted to work with him. Within a year he was back to being over-committed and making enough money to support his family. The playing field of life was beginning to level out again with a President whose agenda matched the majority who elected him. The scams and deceit of the righteous right had their day and now it was time to correct the damage.

The Republican tactic to regain the White House during Clinton's administration was to keep the upstart back on his heels and ineffective. They believed that if he failed to improve the condition of middle class he would not be re-elected. They would stall his legislative efforts to improve the lot of the working class as best they could and spend their energy and the tax payers' resources keeping their wealthy contributors happy. The anti-abortion, anti-gay rights and religious dogma would keep the newly chartered "conservative" electorate in line. "Family values" would be their mantra with few realizing that it really meant the "value of wealthy families" portfolios." The harassment of the President and the First Lady by the opposition party during his years in office was unprecedented and gnawing on the American people.

An Arkansas Right Wing billionaire by the name of Richard Mellon Scaife, was said to be the nemesis stoking the anti-Clinton fires. Mr. Scaife was familiar with the act of stoking fires since he was an heir of the Andrew Mellon Banking fortune, which began in America's 19th century lumber and coal industry. As the publisher of the *Pittsburgh Tribune-Review* in 1993 Mr. Scaife stayed the course of financing the persecution of the President and the First Lady despite the facts to the contrary.

Eventually the heavily financed dissemination of information about Mrs. Clinton's investments, prior to her becoming First Lady, became even more heavily financed by American tax payers and sanctioned by Republican Congressional Representatives. The investigations, which were continued by special prosecutor Kenneth Starr, appointed by the Republican controlled Congress to replace the more moderate Robert B. Fiske, became a personal vendetta that began to annoy the public. During the ensuing years several conflicts of interest became apparent between Scaife's money and Ken Starr's employment opportunities, causing Starr to wisely dodge the obvious implications as they became visible.

The White Water Investigations began as a witch hunt of Mrs. Clinton's past investments. The initial actions, which involved a real estate development project in Arkansas, dragged on for years with the Special Prosecutor Starr spending money like it was his duty to do so. After several years of intense scrutiny and tens of millions of taxpayers' dollars wasted, all he had for his efforts were dead ends. But an opportunity would eventually present itself for a dramatic and relentless expansion of the Congressional inquiry to include a totally separate matter involving the President's personal behavior.

The constant harassment didn't deter the President from achieving many of his goals and failed to quell his popularity. Bill Clinton was re-elected to a second term in 1996, much to the chagrin of his opposition, who were to spend more than $43 million of taxpayer's money on superfluous investigations designed to harass him throughout his two administrations.

The opposition, spurred on by then Speaker of the House, Newt Gingrich, whose own personal indiscretions had not yet surfaced, didn't accept defeat easily. The Republican Congress turned up the heat during Clinton's second term.

In 1998 Special Prosecutor Ken Starr, who seemed to have found a full time job doing the bidding of his party, stumbled onto an incident that would give his futile and expensive work new life. It was discovered that President Clinton had an illicit affair with a White House intern. In the past there was a code of silence on these matters for many public figures, including a number of Presidents, both Democrat and Republicans. But for this Congress and their "family values" leaders, a number of whom who would eventually fall to similar dark-side circumstances, it was not going to be.

The Monica Lewinski affair was disclosed by Linda Tripp, a conservative Republican of suspect motivation and support, who had "befriended" and taped phone calls with Ms. Lewinski. This would normally be considered an illegal act without the permission of the person being taped. Tripp deceptively acted as if she were Monica's concerned friend, as she probed a rumor of the impropriety, which was reported by a journalist. She learned that the 21 year old Lewinski had a "crush" on the President and would do anything for him. It was the nature of the "anything" that interested Ms. Tripp and her "holier-than-thou party" led by a soon-to-be-known philanderer, the Speaker of the House. The Speaker, also married, had no qualm about exploiting the talents of one of his own young female government employees. Opportunity overcame hypocrisy as he was the driving force in the impeachment movement against Clinton.

Determined to embarrass the President in a mid-term December lame duck session, the Senate, with a majority of Republicans present voted to impeach Clinton. The action was short lived however, since once the full Senate returned from their Christmas recess they acquitted him of wrong-doing with a vote that included ten moderate Republicans joining the Democrats.

Time would reveal that a number of his leading detractors, including his primary antagonist, the self-righteous Speaker of the House as well as a number of the "devout Christian" crowd proved to be hiding their own sexual affairs and indiscretions while feigning their happy marriages and Christian values. Hypocrisy as well as dishonesty were alive and well in Washington! But then again, most eventually "found Jesus" when they were caught in their indiscretions and lies and in the spirit of "Halleluiah" they were saved!

Clinton left office at the end of his second full term in 2001 with a 65% approval rating, the highest rating of a two term president since FDR. He had succeeded in turning the Reaganomics deficit-ridden economy around by reinstating certain taxes on those whose wealth benefitted greatly by Reagan's efforts. He left office having established an unprecedented financial surplus, and extraordinary job growth by adding 22 million jobs. He did his job despite being under constant attack and attempted humiliation by Republican opposition."

Fiscal responsibility again proved to be the strength of Democratic leadership rather than that of the Republican Conservatives. Although their hate rhetoric was virulent, it lacked the hoped-for effectiveness as Clinton earned a reputation as a highly competent leader. In the end there was no smoking gun found after tens of millions of tax dollars were spent on the White Water investigation, and the American public had had enough of the self-righteous hypocrisy of the persecutors.

Clinton did, however, inadvertently do to the bidding of his loyal opposition by agreeing to the North American Free Trade Agreement. NAFTA, as it was known resulted in the exportation of jobs and not just products. It was so successful and profitable that its principle was expanded and applied into the Asian countries of China and South Korea. It found one of its biggest allies in India where wages were well below the American minimum. In time American manufacturing became the endangered species of the economy and capitalism evolved into manipulation of the markets to maximize profits for the benefit of the haves.

American companies were quite profitable and their shareholders were happy. The American worker became unemployed and underemployed and many slipped into the expanding ranks of the have-nots. Membership in the middle class was being dramatically reduced, thereby reducing numbers and capabilities of the true American consumers and entrepreneurs.

Having wages equivalent to those at the 1973 level in 2000 meant less disposable income. The con that started in the mid-1970s of telling the electorate that they should worry about social issues like prayer in school, a women's right to control her own body, who marries who and who has sex and not kids, was still working on at least 25% of the electorate while causing serious damage to the lives of nearly 99% of them.

The average American began the millennium with a need to rely on foreign sweatshop manufactured goods sold in big box discount stores in order to survive. The more they were affected by their lack of prosperity the more they contributed to the prosperity of those who were victimizing them. They were told they would be better off as long as the very rich were controlling their lives and spending outrages amounts of tax saving dollars on their own exorbitant lifestyles. They were slow to realize that hope for a better life was slipping from their grasp as was their American Dream.

Part Seven

The Son of Bush Years

CHAPTER 120

The end of the Clinton administration opened the door just wide enough for another quasi- conservative Republican to gain the White House. In 2000 George W. Bush, a former popular Governor of Texas and the son of Clinton's predecessor George H. W. Bush, secured the nomination of his party. In a very controversial election against Clinton's Vice President Al Gore, he managed to win the office while losing the nationwide vote of the people by more than 500,000 votes.

The popular vote in favor of Democrat Al Gore was an obvious indication of the American electorate's hesitation to allow the right wingers back into power. Adding insult to injury were the results in the States of Ohio and Florida, both of which had questionable vote counts. Florida, the state with the highest percentage of Social Security and Medicare recipients, had people voting against their self-interest in favor of the political party that would eliminate those crucial programs for the benefit of their wealthier benefactors.

Al Gore, the people's clear choice by more than a half a million votes, was forced to concede the election after several days of waiting for due process in the form of a fair judicial decision by the United States Supreme Court on a recount of the flawed Florida ballots. He wasn't looking for the Court to declare him the winner, just a recount of the suspicious ballots that tipped the scales of the Electoral College in favor of his opponent, just enough for Bush to win the election.

The conservative court, a majority of whose members having been appointed by Reagan and the senior Bush, refused to allow Florida to recount their votes. Adding to the fiasco of injustice was the fact that at the time Florida was governed by George W. Bush's brother Jeb Bush. The insidious decision defied all logic and gave George W. Bush Florida's 25 Electoral College votes and the presidency by five Electoral votes.

The Republican efforts to make it more difficult for the Democratic Party based minorities to register and vote didn't keep enough of them from the polls. But manipulation of the Electoral College system proved to be effective.

It was January, 2001 and George W. Bush, former Governor of Texas, son of George H.W, Bush and, at one time, an owner of the Texas Rangers baseball team was now President of the United States of America. He entered the White House after the Clinton-Gore administration created the first budget surplus in more than 40 years and managed to do it without the chaos of foreign wars and without an economy in recession.

Except for Wall Street's *Dot Com fiasco*, times were good. Day traders had embraced greed. They believed the emergence of the internet to be a way to make the fast buck. Companies were formed as fast as the net was expanding and everyone wanted to be the first in on the next Amazon. Unfortunately, they would have had a better chance at winning the lottery, as many computer geniuses lost their hard earned money trying to catch that wave.

President George W. Bush brought with him the ancient guard of his father's right wing in Karl Rove, Dick Cheney, James Baker and Donald Rumsfeld. Some believed that the younger Bush was just a front man chosen by his father to be the face of an administration controlled by the senior Bush's loyal entourage. They had served both Reagan and Bush senior, but didn't make it to their anticipated second H.W. Bush term. It was obvious that they had unfinished business to do and they intended to see it through. Five hundred thousand American voters, the plurality that voted for Al Gore, didn't like the idea, but they were ignored and overrun by power politics.

For Diego Martinez being allowed back in the tower at Logan International because of Clinton's rescission of Reagan's hiring exclusion was a dream come true. Keisha had regained her health, and his fears about the quality of his cousin's alcohol-and-drug-impacted kidney were never realized. She was able to go back to school, complete her nursing degree and was now working in a Cape Cod hospital. Life under Clinton had improved dramatically.

His son, Manny, was in New York working as an intern with a major stock brokerage firm. He would graduate from the University of Massachusetts in the spring of 2002 and have a position with that prestigious firm, if he wanted it. The Martinez's were proud of their son's achievements. Diego knew that if Clinton hadn't lifted the ban on his employment with the FAA his son would never have had the opportunity to go to college or seek a meaningful career.

Sharon Polowski decided not to run for another Senate term and accepted a position to teach at Yale University. Jim Buckman joined a Connecticut law firm that specialized in defending corporate fraud. Their daughter, Laura Marie was a junior in high school. Life was settling into a normal routine. The contact with Jonathon was virtually non-existent and they both appreciated that.

Jonathan got his wish of overtaking the Bulldog. Masters died of a heart attack while shouting down a colleague. Jonathan believed he could fill the void with those who still had the fire to assert themselves as a behind the scenes political force. He was feeling invincible and he would forge an alliance with his boss, Don Peters for control.

Tony and Meghan Benedetto survived with their engineering business, but knowing that whenever the economy faltered his business would follow. His work depended on permitting projects for clients during times of positive economic development. Trying to overcome their substantial losses of 1980s was a fulltime job in itself. They managed to send their children to college, but the cost was overwhelming. Education was very important to both of them. As children of blue collar parents they knew you needed the advantage of knowledge to even hope to live a good life. Their children, Bobby and Rachelle, were attending separate state universities as sophomores. Being twins attending different schools was important to them. They wanted to be able to have their own identity and not to be known as a twin.

The election of another right wing Republican made all of them uncomfortable. Even Jim Buckman realized there was something wrong with a philosophy that clearly benefitted only those at the top of the pyramid. He gave up on the idea that he could be part of a significant moderate force in a political party that actually cared about people and not their personal wealth and power. The Clinton years proved to him that progressive leadership and fiscal responsibility provided the only path to the American Dream for the millions who sought its benefits.

Before securing the Presidency, George W. Bush was a popular Governor in Texas. He was known as a friend of both the loyal white conservatives based primarily in north Texas and the large Hispanic population living in southern Texas from San Antonio to Laredo. It was hoped that he would utilize that ability to bring people and the country together after an unusual election result that divided the American electorate. He wouldn't have the constant harassment experienced by Clinton since his party no longer had reason to exert that pressure.

His wild and carefree partying days as a college student, his avoidance of the draft by being in the Texas National Guard and his family's involvement in the half trillion dollar Savings and Loan bank meltdown led by the demise of the Silverado Bank, were all considered acceptable faux pas. The allegation that laundered mob money was used to influence lending decisions at 130 banks wasn't important enough to investigate the Bush family involvement. Nor was the alleged Medicare fraud by acquaintances of his investor brothers deemed important enough to besmirch their reputations.

George W. had his problems before becoming the leader of the free world with alleged insider trading of a declining oil drilling company when he sold his stock before it tanked or the deal that he borrowed $600,000 in 1989 to become an owner of the Texas Rangers baseball team that resulted in a sale that made him $15 million in 1998.

But these incidents and relationships which occurred during his father's Presidency were not important enough to warrant the type of investigation that White Water did during the Clinton administration. They weren't worth the $43 million it cost taxpayers to investigate Hillary Clinton when she became the First Lady for a real estate deal in which she lost money more than twenty years prior. The end result of that fiasco proved it to be a frivolous overreach.

The first eight months of the "Son of Bush" Presidency went relatively smoothly. His mentors were settling in and determining their strategy to overturn the Clinton actions that had righted the economy, eliminated the deficit and cost their benefactors a small increase in their tax liabilities. It was the end of summer 2001 and all was well and orderly for the masses.

Diego had his second cup of coffee and was settling into his seat behind the radar screen at Logan Airport's control tower.

"It looks like another beautiful day!" was the comment from his fellow air traffic controller Tom Kelly, who sat to his right. The sky was clear and the runway was orderly.

It was 7:59 am. "This is the Tower American Airlines Flight 11. You are cleared for takeoff," announced Martinez.

"Roger Tower, we acknowledge your transmission," responded the pilot.

"It looks like they'll have a smooth flight to Los Angeles," commented Martinez to no one in particular as he took a sip of his coffee.

Fifteen minutes later United Airlines Flight 175, lined up for takeoff at the end of the runway. They would follow the American Airlines Flight 11 into Los Angeles.

"United Airlines Flight 175 you are cleared for takeoff," directed one of Diego's colleagues.

"Roger Tower, we are on our way," responded the pilot as he revved up his powerful jet engines and began his movement down the runway.

"How's your boy doing in New York?" asked Kelly.

"He's doing great. He's working with a company on the 98th floor of the World trade Center. They really like him. They've offered him a job for when he graduates next year. I think he might take it. Not bad for a kid whose dad grew up in the ghettos of LA."

"You must be proud. I'll bet he has a great view of New York City from that height."

"Yes, he said the view of the river is spectacular! He can see the Statue of Liberty."

At 8:32 am the FAA got a report that American Airlines Flight 11 had been hijacked. Two F-15 fighter jets were dispatched from Otis Air National Guard Base on Cape Cod, less than 20 miles from the Martinez home. Their mission was to intercept that commercial airliner.

The tension in the Tower was overwhelming! It had been years since a plane was hijacked. What was going on?

Fifteen minutes later the Tower heard the news. American Airlines Flight 11 had just hit the North Tower of the World Trade Center in New York City.

"Oh my God, my boy is there!" Diego looked to his fellow controllers. Their shocked faces turned towards his in his moment of fear and emotional turmoil. "It can't be! They just took off from here. They're going to LA. No it can't be!" as the blood began to drain from his face, he gasped for air.

"What's going on?" asked another controller. "United Flight 175 has just veered off course and is also heading for the Towers."

At 9:03 am the United Airlines Flight 175 slammed into the South Tower as the world watched live on television.

They all turned to look at the reports on the television hanging in the corner of the room. "Oh my God what's happening?" came the words of someone as others voiced their disbelief in what they were watching.

Diego watched the North Tower burn and the black smoke envelope the buildings. He yelled to the TV, holding tightly to the back of a chair for support. "Manny, go to the roof, go to the roof they will rescue you. Go to the roof my son!" as he sobbed. He learned later that the doors to the roof were locked and that it was not possible for a rescue helicopter to land in the thick black smoke.

He was on the phone with Keisha when the North Tower began to fall and he heard her ungodly scream as she watched it crumble to the ground taking their only child. Diego's legs that bore the scars of war, could no longer bear the weight of his sorrow. He collapsed, unable to help his family.

The terror wasn't over! American Airlines Flight 77, which had just taken off from Dulles International Airport hit the Pentagon at 9:37 am. Generals and admirals were the target.

At 9:45 am an announcement rang over the control towers speakers, "Washington has ordered all planes within the continental United States to land, we are under attack, and they're using our own planes as weapons."

The passengers in a fourth plane, United Airlines Flight 93 from Newark en route to San Francisco, became aware of the turmoil, but too late to help the flight crew who had been murdered. The flight was taken over by terrorist. Several passengers, who were able to use their cell phones and the plane's air-phone service learned of the tragic events of the day and knew that they would soon be part of the terrorist plot. They were able to tell the world what was happening adding to the accounts of a flight attendant on Flight 11 and a passenger on Flight 175 who had secretly phoned authorities before they crashed into the Towers.

Without hesitation the courageous passengers of Flight 93, with the words "Okay, let's roll," attempted to take control of the plane before it became another weapon of destruction of the terrorists. It was assumed by those tracking the doomed plane that it would be used against the White House. Their plane had reversed direction and was flying southeasterly over Pennsylvania, heading back towards Washington D.C. As the result of the passengers' courageous actions the terrorist never reached their target. Flight 93 crashed nose first at 563 mph, disintegrating upon impact into a field outside the town of Shanksville, Pennsylvania.

President Bush and his security team were in the air on their way to a secret control center to monitor the situation and determine the response. He had been visiting a Florida elementary school when he was told of the terrorists' actions. Protecting the President was a non-partisan action that was necessary to assure the integrity of the government of the United States. George W. Bush, shocked and dismayed as were his fellow Americans, had his finest hours of leadership during this crisis. He acted on his own instincts. He showed a true compassion and pledged to right the wrong done to the country. The attack was an act of war and war was believed to be the only answer to the terrorist atrocity. But who did this horrible act?

On October 7, 2001, the United States, with the backing of the American people, took revenge on the country of Afghanistan, believed to be the refuge and training center of al-Qaeda, the terrorist organization that claimed responsibility for the September 11th attacks. Osama bin Laden, the titular head of the organization, boasted of its success in their Jihad against the world, but in particular against America. Like so many former allies, once supported by the United States in their war against the Soviet Union, the Afghans, Osama bin Laden and their Taliban rulers, were now the enemy.

It was late October on Cape Cod and the once colorful leaves were holding on to the last days of autumn. Diego and Keisha were joined by their community and their friends the Benedettos and the Buckmans, as they held a service for their son at the local Catholic Church. Like most of the families of the nearly 3,000 innocent victims of the 9/11 massacre they didn't have his remains to inter, only the memories of his life to celebrate.

Diego gave the eulogy for his son, gripping the podium for stability. "Our boy Manny was our life. He was what we lived for and he brought us much happiness. We worked hard so he would not be exposed to the dark temptations that are part of too many young people's lives... and he responded with love, caring and appreciation that we all hope will be our reward as parents. Keisha and I spoke with him the night before he faced his death..." he paused, his throat unable to release the words. "He talked about his future and how much he enjoyed being in the big city," his voice cracking. "He said that it was where he wanted to be. Where he needed to be..." he stopped again before completing the sentence, repeating. "...where he needed to be, and now...where he will always be!"

Keisha was comforted by Karime who held her tight as she wept openly at the thoughts of her son's last moments on earth. The tears flowed from all of those listening.

Tony looked at his children, Bobby and Rachelle and then at Meghan, all trying unsuccessfully to withhold their emotions. He wondered how they, as parents, would endure such a loss.

Jim and Sharon, sitting on either side of their daughter, Laura Marie, held her hands tightly as emotions overcame their normally stoic demeanor. The forces of hate had won again and those who suffered for it didn't matter to those who callously sought its undefined benefits.

Chapter 121

Not satisfied with their limited victory over the Taliban in Afghanistan and frustrated in their attempts at finding Osama bin Laden, the Bush White House advisors believed there was an opportunity to complete the task of revenge against Iraq and its cruel leader, another former ally, Saddam Hussein. They needed a premise good enough to convince George W. and the Nation that it was worth the effort.

The allegation that Iraq was also a supporter of al-Qaeda wasn't sound enough since it was known that Hussein didn't trust bin Laden or al-Qaeda and was not a friend. But then there were the allegations of Iraq having "weapons of mass destruction," a hypothesis that was encouraged by Saddam since he wanted his hostile neighbors to believe it so they would not risk attacking his country. Was there ever a stockpile of poison gases or attempts at securing nuclear weapons? Although it was possible, intelligence reports couldn't validate either situation and some believe that President Bush was actually the last in his administration to know the truth.

Contradictory reports, some as misinformation purposely promulgated by high-level government sources, led to the "outing" of Valerie Plame Wilson a CIA official. She was publicly identified as an undercover CIA operative as revenge for her husband, Joe Wilson, a former Republican congressman, not playing along with the charade. His investigation and disclosure to the CIA that Iraq didn't have nuclear materials from Nigeria as claimed by Vice President Dick Cheney, became evidence of the dark side of the administration's policies. By the time the lies and false accusations were disclosed, the United States was deep into another war. The weapons of mass destruction theory proved to be a fabrication to get Congressional approval of the money for war. The justification for sending our young and courageous men and women into harm's way then became the need to remove a vicious dictator, one of many we supplied with lethal weapons when we deemed them to be our friends and allies.

It was March 2003 and the Iraq war, known as the second gulf war, resulted in the relatively efficient disposition of the Iraqi forces. Our overwhelming offensive capabilities were too much for Saddam's U.S.-trained military to defend against.

Saddam was eventually captured, as he crawled out of a hole - an appropriate ending for his regime. His ruthless sons who took delight in torture were killed in an exchange with American military. He was tried by an Iraqi court and sentenced to death by hanging. Unfortunately, the thousand year tribal wars between the Shiite and Sunni tribes, enhanced by the military contributions of insurgents, consumed the efforts of our triumphant occupiers.

"Winning the hearts and minds of the people," was the mantra and "nation building," became the justification for our enduring presence. The trillions of dollars and thousands of lives lost in that venture were of no consequence to the fiscally conservative administration, as the United States fell deeper into debt and sorrow. It was déjà vu all over again!

The wars served their political purpose. The American people were reluctant to change parties in the *middle* of major conflict, and it would soon be obvious that we were *only in the middle* of the Iraq/Afghanistan wars. In November 2004 George W. Bush was re-elected to a second term over John Kerry, a Senator from Massachusetts. The dirty-trick party succeeded in besmirching the Vietnam War record of Kerry alleging that he wasn't the hero that he was portrayed as being by the media. The "Swift Boat Veterans for Truth," a right-wing group, sought payback in response to the antiwar stand Kerry expounded once he returned from Vietnam. As is often the case, lies and innuendo proved to be an effective weapon of those lacking integrity and believing the American people to be gullible.

Chapter 122

A new generation of covert political supporters took control of the Washington Action Group. Jonathan filled the void left by the death of Bulldog Masters. He found an ally in Don Peters, his boss at CTC. Don liked his attitude and his drive and believed that he could manage it to his personal benefit, while keeping Jonathan out front to take the abuse. The oil entity was represented by Masters' business partner Dave Hunter, more of an intellectual than Bulldog, but not a timid man. Except for the retirement of Bert Obersham the rest of the Group, although aging, remained in force.

Jonathan addressed the Group about the coming elections. "We need to decide if we're going to get behind John McCain. His selection of Sara Palin doesn't help. He had plenty of acceptable conservatives to choose from. She'll be a heartbeat away from the Presidency and I don't think she's intellectually prepared!"

"We don't have a choice. Do you want this liberal black guy to get elected? That bitch Hillary would have been bad enough, but who is this guy? What has he done to deserve being President?" added Peters. "He was just a community organizer before he was elected Senator. What is that?"

"The problem is, we don't know if McCain shares our values. He says he's a *maverick*. What does that mean? He's not loyal to our philosophy and he has some liberal tendencies," offered their counsel, Dale Watkins. "He seems to like working with the Democrats, like Ted Kennedy."

"I disagree! McCain is for a sound defense and he has the courage to do what's necessary to protect our freedom," declared John Carlton CEO of American Defense Industries, Inc., one of the veterans of WAG. "This Obama guy can't be trusted to have the courage to send our troops in where they're needed. We need McCain."

"Well, Obama is gaining in the polls. We need something to derail him," suggested Jonathan. "And John's right - without a strong defense initiative our country is at risk... and so is our prosperity!"

"I've had my staff check this Obama character out. He was raised by his mother who lived out of the country in Indonesia for a while. She was a white woman from Kansas who married a black man from Kenya. You know how these mixed marriages are regarded by most Americans. They were illegal in some states until just a few years ago. She lived in Hawaii when he was born," explained Carleton.

"John, how does that help us *derail him*? asked Watkins

"There's a certain percentage of the electorate that is always ready to embrace scandal and bigotry. I believe that we can question his birthright to become President. His mother's world travels and marriage to a Black African gives us the means to make people wonder where he was actually born. Once we light that fire, there are enough of our right-wing media friends out there to keep the flames fanned. They'll just keep repeating it and eventually it will stick with people who want it to," rationalized Carlton. "And it will keep him off balance! All we need to do is put him on the defensive and have him and his campaign staff spend their time and resources responding to our allegations."

"Well it's a start, but we need to pump some money in there too. Then there's this so-called Tea Party that has an agenda that's not necessarily aligned with ours. We need to win their support or at least neutralize it. We must also make sure that the tax breaks Reagan and Bush worked hard to pass stay in place. The only way they will is if we get Congress to cut those social programs like Medicare, Social Security and food stamps," declared Peters. There's only so much money out there!"

"Of course, but most people realize that Social Security is paid for by the people who will hopefully benefit by it, and only the people making less than $55,000 per year pay for it. Our friends have succeeded in keeping that tax off our backs. It's only a matter of time before more realize that they pay an additional 6% in taxes for those benefits than we pay," commented Watkins.

"In any case, if Obama is elected I've been told that the party will keep him looking over his shoulder like they did with Clinton," offered Jonathan. "He won't know which way is up!"

"Yeah, and how did that work out? Clinton raised *our* taxes, managed to have a significant budget surplus overcoming Reagan's deficits and was the most popular President since Reagan and FDR," added Peters.

"Gentlemen, we might have a bigger problem than the election of some Black guy to the White House! Not to be negative, but has anyone looked at what's happening in the banking and housing market? It looks like those high-risk packaged mortgages are starting to come apart. If this economy tanks before the elections Obama might win no matter what we do," suggested Watkins.

Don peters added, "I sold my shares in those speculative products and I suggest you all do the same. It's going to be a real mess. Maybe it would be better if the Democrats win. Then it will be their problem and we can hammer them about their spending during a bad economy. We know that the annual deficits will remain high due to the Iraq and Afghanistan presence. The rebuilding of those countries that we committed to will continue to increase our national debt. There's nothing the next President can do about that. It'll give us the excuse and opportunity to reduce spending on the bleeding hearts programs such as Social Security and Medicare."

"The Democrats already claim that because of these wars and the Bush tax cuts the national debt is heading towards $11 trillion and that it'll continue to rise for several years to pay for the wars and our reconstruction efforts in those countries. We need to deflect that rhetoric and burden onto the Democrats if they win," offered Carlton.

"The public doesn't want to hear about the past, and most won't even understand it or even want to understand it. It's important that we don't let up on Democrats. If they win the election, they inherit the problems. The economy will be theirs to deal with and in about a year the public won't remember who did what and won't care," added Peters.

"What about the billions of dollars in no-bid contracts awarded during the wars to Vice President Cheney's former company Halliburton? They go back to the days of Desert Storm. Won't the Democrats try to make that an issue?" asked Carlton. "We've all benefitted by those no-bid defense contracts."

"They wouldn't dare! Our conservative friends in the Republican Party and the media would counter-accuse them of favoritism and it will confuse the public. Anyway, the average American is apathetic to that kind of "politics as usual," declared Peters. We know that the public, in general, is not interested in facts, but they are easily confused and often aroused by innuendo!

"I'm still worried about the possibility of a meltdown since much of our political contribution money comes from our derivative investments," cautioned Watkins. "We need to get a handle on this now. It could be a real mess!

"We all knew that 'derivatives' were risky but they came with high profit returns. We did what the liberals wanted. We targeted the lower economic class for mortgages and made it easier for them to own homes. Isn't that what they wanted, for everyone to have a piece of the American Dream? It's a high volume market. Our strategy relied on the fact that most of them can't possibly afford these mortgages in the future. We overlooked the documentation of jobs or wages, especially with adjustable interest rates increasing at 2% every two years," responded Peters.

"We've been aggressively writing these risky mortgages just as we do credit card agreements with imminent potential for high interest rates knowing that they will be defaulted. By packaging them with good loans and selling those packages to investors in bundles of two to three thousand we've made some serious profits. The money is made on the high interest loans, the sale of the packages to investors and the eventual foreclosure sales of the defaults," explained Jonathan.

We knew by our own actuary calculations that most people don't live in their homes for more than ten years. We also knew when we wrote these mortgages that if they default they'll still owe most of the original amount that they borrowed, and given the history of significant appreciation of real estate in this country, foreclosures were not only our safety net but our secondary level of profit," added Peters.

"For those of you who haven't been involved in this market, the program was designed by some young geniuses at J.P. Morgan. They devised a method of reducing the risk to both the investors and to the originators. They call it *Credit Default Swaps* or CDS. The idea being that an investor can buy these derivative packages and hedge their bet, so to speak, on their investment. It has the added benefit of no regulatory reporting or scrutiny required," added Watkins.

"It's like selling a box of apples that have a few bad ones, but not visibly bad enough to offset the total value. The problem seems to be that there may be too many boxes with bad apples being sold and not a big enough market for apple pies, and without reporting regulations no one really knows how many bad apple baskets are out there," commented Jonathan.

"The election is in eight weeks and that scenario would not only hurt us financially, but McCain would surely be defeated if it looks like Republicans caused such a mess by looking the other way when they were in power."

"It doesn't help McCain that our national debt is approaching $11 Trillion with billions added every month, but without those wars and the profits that they provide, our defense and oil industries would be suffering," commented Bulldog's protégé, and former partner, Dave Hunter. "I doubt this guy, Obama, has much of a chance, but we have to make sure that his chances aren't enhanced by our actions. We need to turn up the volume on his issues with our friendly media personnel. It's time to increase our sponsorship budget of those programs and remind them why they're making the big money."

"I agree with Dave!" offered Jonathan in a gesture of solidarity. "These conservative media people give us our biggest bang for the dollar and they'll say anything that gets them a paycheck. Let's feed them the rumors, and they'll keep repeating them until they stick. They're like the bullies you had in school. Racism is still alive and well in a good many American minds. These media talkers are experts at stirring that element up and they are relentless. They thrive on ignorance and apathy. They're our kind of people!" offered Jonathan with a grin.

The deprecating humor broke the meetings air of seriousness as they all laughed at Jonathan's categorization of their base constituency.

The Groups' fears were soon realized when the bottom fell out of the lending schemes during the week of September 25, 2008. It became obvious to Treasury Secretary Paulson and President Bush that a major financial player, Bear Stearns, was going under. They were burned by the weight of poorly performing derivatives, including the CDS packages that they had sold to investors with reckless abandon. Their demise would be followed by the exposure of Lehman Brothers. It was soon apparent that other brokerage firms would follow, putting the United States on the verge of an economic depression the likes of which had not been seen since the 1930s.

Foreclosures, which were contrived as the financial industries fail-safe means for making them whole, were overwhelming their ability to function as predicted. Millions of working Americans would lose their homes as the financed properties would flood the markets well below their cost to construct, depleting homeowners of their equity and trapping them in an unforgiving scenario. Thousands of American companies would be forced to lay off their workers at the rate of over 700,000 a month before a new administration could be elected and take over in January 2009. Many companies ceased to exist as the economy was victimized by the fast-buck mentality of the poorly regulated financial industry. Banks failed taking businesses with them.

The industry would say that the mortgages they sold were to satisfy the desires of every, American to achieve the American Dream and that they were bad because of the home-buyers incompetence! They refused to take responsibility. They claimed that it wasn't due to the connivance of banks and finance companies, who had the means to know better, but were too greedy to care.

Forewarned executives bailed out of their companies as the Bush Administration was bailing their businesses out with the multi-billion dollar Troubled Asset Relief Fund, better known as TARP. They cashed in their stock, secured their multi-million dollar bonuses and left on their tax deductible jet planes to a better climate, one in which they would be admired for their ingenuity, tact and achievements in their respective pursuits of *their* American Dream.

Adding to the chagrin of Republican stalwarts was the fact that the Bush military initiatives in Afghanistan and Iraq were beginning to lose their luster as well as their political benefits after years of frustrated efforts to stabilize corrupt governments at the cost of American lives and tax dollars. Those who remembered the reasons for invading those mid-eastern countries in which tribal wars were a way of life, did not recall nation building as being one of them.

The skeptics declared that announcing our departure date from Iraq would be a sign of defeat? They argued that it would increase the enemy's resolve to continue the war. They obviously hadn't learned the lesson of Vietnam or realized that they had only interrupted a thousand year civil/religious war, which would continue as soon as America and its allies got out of the way!

Chapter 123

It took more than seven years, but the Bush-Cheney administration managed to undo much of the progress made during the Clinton years. Just after taking office in February 2001, President Bush told Congress that his Administration had calculated that over the next ten years the American people could expect a $ 5.6 trillion dollar surplus. Although he forgot to thank Clinton for that gift, he used the surplus to persuade Congress to accept his $1.35 trillion annual tax cut for the wealthy. He argued that he wanted to "return the money to the people." His initial Secretary of the Treasury, Paul O'Neil, cautioned that such a tax cut would result in the return of deficits and undermine Social Security.

The Bush tax cuts passed and the anticipated deficit outcome was soon realized. Job growth was minimal, but the wealthy got wealthier by as much as 40% since the final days of the Nixon years in 1973, while middle class earnings remained stagnant and for many millions, were in decline.

The National Debt was at $ 11.3 trillion and was still growing as the Bush-Cheney administration supported the perpetual wars and the rebuilding of countries destroyed by those wars.

The Dow Jones average dropped from over $12,000 to less than $7,000. The Bush tax cuts for the wealthy didn't satisfy the promise made when he gave away the Clinton surplus to the wealthiest Americans. They didn't create jobs or enhance economic prosperity, instead they guaranteed a ballooning deficit and the continued wealth of those who created the debacle.

Unemployment rose from 4.2% to 7.2% after Bush took over the office from Clinton as the Bush economy began its descent and the recession took hold. The impact of the worst recession since the depression of the 1930s had not yet been realized, but it would be in full effect in time for the next President to take the oath of office. Bush, like Reagan, didn't quite make it out-of-town before the bottom fell out of their economic fiascos. Like Reagan, the Bush administration saw their version of voodoo economics crash and burn before their second term in office was completed.

By October 2008, a month before the Presidential election, as a going-away gift to the American banks and brokerage firms, Bush-Cheney and the Congress authorized up to $700 billion for what is known as the "Trouble Asset Relief Program." TARP was designed by Bush's Secretary of the Treasury Paulson to buy the "troubled assets" of failing banks. The Democrats, realizing that the Republicans were attempting to do a quick bail-out of the errant financial institutions without constraints and before the elections, acted just as quickly to amend the final bail-out bill reducing its generosity to $475 billion.

The importance of the bail-out of American banks to Republicans was emphasized when John McCain called for a recess in his presidential campaign efforts against Barack Obama to help get it passed. He left his road campaign to go back to Washington to make sure that the bank bail-out legislation was passed expeditiously. The fact that Congress failed to require any conditions for the Bush-Cheney TARP money, such as assuring that the banks would lend money to businesses so that they could survive and possibly hire the unemployed, proved to add to the crisis.

Without available credit to businesses it would be impossible to create jobs and improve the economy. But because of the Bush-Cheney bail-out, the banks didn't need to make money on loan interest. They would find other ways to profit such as implementing exorbitant fees and fines on the struggling middle class. Their reluctance to lend money would act to further stifle economic growth, which was the plan of the Republican Congress as openly expressed by its Senate minority leader Mitch McConnell.

This latest attack on the financial where-with-all of the American middle class, the true backbone of the United States economy, proved to be brutal. Millions of Americans suffered the loss of their jobs and their homes with its equity and their 401K and Ira retirement investments because too many believed in the American Dream of home ownership and accepted the subversive acts of the shifty and greed obsessed financial institutions and politicians. The perpetrators of the financial chaos made millions of dollars on their unscrupulous acts and, in their cowardliness, blamed the victims for the crisis. But as they say in the world of law enforcement, "if you want to find the guilty party in an unscrupulous financial transaction, just follow the money! It will lead you to the perpetrators, those who benefitted by the action."

Jonathan and his colleagues were shocked at the swift effects of the economic meltdown. How could this happen when the best financial minds in the country had designed this plan for acquiring wealth and power? Once they lost access to the offshore funds they relied on their ingenuity in investing in these precarious schemes to benefit their wealth and power.

It was late October when the Group met to discuss the financial chaos of the economy. "We're in serious trouble my friends!" were the words of their counsel, Dale Watkins. "There can be no creditable explanation for this crisis. Obviously, we're going to have to live with a Democratic administration for at least the next four years!"

"Our only hope to retain some leverage is to align ourselves with this so-called Tea Party. They've won primaries over a number of moderate Republicans and have the tenacity to demand that the government cut spending. That alone will sink the next administration. They're outsiders, but that's their strength. They don't know how a democratic economy really works, nor do they care," declared Peters.

"Can we afford to be dumb about that issue? We all know that history has proven that we need to spend on programs to improve society and get our get people back to work. Investment by the government is vital to overcome recessions and expand the economy. I know that the Tea Party's 'no compromise' philosophy is self-destructive, but I'm afraid, we need their votes to gain back the White House!" advised Dave Hunter.

"I don't know if it's wise given that our financial well-being will also suffer. Yes, we'll still profit by our overseas investments, but what if they're also affected? If the American dollar weakens, it affects the whole world. Can we risk that?" asked Peters.

"Do we have a choice? We need to make sure that if Obama becomes President that he has no victories!" declared Jonathan. "We need to make sure that the message is out there to stop his programs! If we don't demonize him we will suffer, and it will be for the long run! He thinks that we want to work together, but we know that would mean less for us if we spread the wealth with 350 million other Americans! If alternative energy becomes dominant we all lose!

"Let him think that! It will slow him down if he thinks he has a chance of compromising with Congress. He's supposed to be an expert on the Constitution, but he'll soon realize that there would be no Constitution if these characters were there to write it. We would still have the Articles of Confederation, which gave the States and the land owners all of the power!" commented Watkins.

It soon became apparent that the financial chaos had been covered up by the wild and the reckless until it burst at the seams from its very weight. When it was obvious that the Republicans would probably lose the White House they acted quickly to make their benefactors in the financial world whole again. With TARP the Republicans succeeded in giving their investor and banking friends an expeditious, generous and unconditional bail-out. They had reaped the benefit of their lobbying wisdom for seven and a half years of the "Son of Bush" administration and had billions of dollars in profits to show for their efforts. Unfortunately the promised jobs, and the benefits of the trickle-down-effect, were never realized. The crisis anticipated by those hoping to cover up their mistakes and perpetuate their prosperity was, however, realized!

In November, Senator Barack Obama was elected President of the United States. The celebration of his supporters was short lived as it became evident that he had inherited a government mismanagement fiasco of historic proportions. Acting without Republican support, the newly elected administration managed to keep the unemployment rate from exceeding 10% and the "investors" from sacrificing the lives of millions more working Americans not yet subdued by those attempting to eliminate their jobs and take their homes. Many Americans were already suffering from the very incompetence of a government administration that the Republican Party embraced as conservative.

By the time Obama took office in late January 2009 it was too late to save the millions of hard working Americans who had already been flushed by the insidious actions of the wealthy political investors. All the new administration could do was attempt to stop the bleeding, and slow the momentum of job losses and foreclosures. The Republican right-wing fiscal incompetence was consuming the hope and dreams millions of Americans at a record pace. In their arrogance, they demanded that Obama back off and let the "free enterprise system" take its course. Unfortunately the only thing free about the system was its fall. In spite of the crisis, monies managed to flow to the perpetrator's portfolios at a record pace.

The downfall of businesses and real estate provided renewed opportunity for bottom feeders and venture capitalists. They would continue to profit off the pain of millions of American workers and small business owners, a condition not realized since the end of the Reagan administration. Some economist believed that it was not a coincidence that the Hoover, Reagan and Bush Presidencies all ended with a major economic crisis. Fiscal incompetence seemed to be part of the ideology of certain factions of the Republican Party. It was obvious that the Teddy Roosevelt, Eisenhower Republican doctrine of compassionate leadership was no more.

Obama attempted to jump start the economy by encouraging the availability of stimulus monies which were allocated for construction jobs on "shovel-ready" projects. He recognized the vital role that the auto industry played in the American economy and acted to save that it from certain destruction realizing that it would have resulted in the loss of well over a million jobs directly and indirectly. It also provided tax cuts for the middle class and funding to states so that their cities and towns could keep their police, fire and teachers in their jobs. Bail out for the financially devious was sanctioned as necessary while the remaining 99% were said to be not worthy of consideration by the self-serving "free market" disciples. If the American economy tanked there would be a potential for the investors who escaped with their wealth to again 'bottom feed' buying businesses and homes for pennies on the dollar as they did post-Reagan from 1989 to 1991.

Within months of Obama's election Senator Mitch McConnell of Kentucky publicly and proudly declared on the floor of the House of Representatives that the goal of the Republican Party was to ensure that Obama didn't get a second term. They wouldn't lift a finger to help him improve the economy, save jobs, create jobs or save homes. Their answer to the economic chaos they created was to let them all go bankrupt! But "them" were not the banks, the oil companies or the wealthy – "them" were middle class Americans!

They were there to say "no" to any proposal that would improve the economy. They even attempted to undue funding for previously approved programs by threatening to not raise the debt ceiling hoping that most Americans wouldn't realize that it was money for programs they had already passed. Their insidious actions resulted in the historic downgrade of America's credit rating and had the potential of increasing the cost of interest paid for borrowing! And to assure that they could continue to damage the American way of life, there would be a new norm for the passage of legislation. It would take a 60% majority in the Senate instead of the constitutionally required 51% due to the use of the virtual non-speaking filibuster by Republican obstructionists, tactics that would cause our forefathers to roll over in the graves. Majority rule at 51% was the basis of American democracy and the cornerstone of the Constitution that conservatives so often cite as their guiding principle.

In spite of their fiscally incompetent actions they insisted on additional tax cuts and loopholes for the wealthy while declaring an uncompromising desire to reduce the budget deficit of nearly $12 trillion, created by unfunded wars and tax cuts. They refused to admit that they placed that burden on the backs of the American middle class and the disadvantaged and they would make sure that it would continue into the new administration. Their disciples attempted to convince people that the dollar they needed to put food on the table for their families was not as important as the millions of dollars that their elite constituency needed to maintain their exorbitant lifestyles! Their mantra was, "those liberals want to take money from the rich and give it to the poor." The response by those who understood the reason for their demise was, "no we just want our money back!"

Chapter 124

A sound real estate market was the historic basis of American economic growth and it was also the basis for survival of millions dependent on the housing industry for survival and for many, the only means of attaining funds for their retirement other than Social Security.

As the housing market crashed again for the second time in twenty years, Tony Benedetto, one of millions of small businessmen, again fell victim to its fate. The Benedetto's were dependent on designing and permitting their clients' real estate development projects for their economic health. When their clients, who were often local small businessmen, couldn't get funding for expansion or for new projects, or to pay for those they had already begun, their businesses suffered. It was 1989 all over again, but without a sitting Congress that was inclined to solve the problem. Democrats controlled the House of Representatives, but were intimidated by their adversaries. They fell short of their professional duties as elected representatives of the vast majority of Americans.

In order to not foreclose on his business and preserve his company for sale the bank insisted that Tony cut his income in half. The same bank that sold them on choosing them to support their high growth, when they were a highly profitable engineering firm was not interested in their plight. The economy had crashed again as the result of another bank-driven crisis. Derivatives and Credit Default Swaps, which were designed to make big profits for the very wealthy, came with a price to pay. And just twenty years after the payments came due for Reagan's VooDoo economics in 1988, it was time to pay again. With reduced pay the Benedettos could no longer pay their mortgage. The bank sent them a foreclosure notice when they fell two months behind on their home mortgage.

Although he had just taken the oath of office, President Obama wasn't going to allow Americans to go without some help to save their homes. He initiated a loan modification program without the benefit of his loyal opposition in Congress who criticized it as a bail-out and socialism. It was shamefully obvious that only the banks and the rich would be bailed out by the 'conservative' Congress. TARP, the expeditiously approved, pre-election, Bush-Cheney bail-out was fine with them, but any more was deemed socialism and a hand-out by *conservative* politicians.

But for Tony it was too little too late. He didn't qualify since he was self-employed and couldn't show a steady income. And, in fact, he sold the company through the bank to pay the debt, but the multi-million dollar company that purchase it from the bank didn't honor their commitment to Tony leaving him and his family with nothing. There deceit was considered business-as-usual. They would have to move again and their children would need to leave college and try to get jobs in a rapidly declining market.

"I don't understand Tony. Why is this happening again? We're good people. We work hard. We don't take expensive vacations or buy new cars. We've both got college degrees and now we're faced with starting all over again, for the third time in thirty years," asked Meghan, her voice laced with anger and sadness.

"I don't understand any more than you do, but it seems there are those who are doing very well while others are homeless or struggling to survive. But one thing I do know is that whenever we work hard and play by the rules and the economy goes bust, it's always because the big banks and Wall Street financial geniuses have screwed up. I think that eventually people are going to get fed up with these elitists and reckless characters. I just hope that it's a peaceful rebellion," declared Tony. "Violence will never result in positive change. I don't know. Maybe this new guy, Obama will find the answer."

The irony didn't escape the majority of the people who realized that the very "too big to fail" banks and financial management firms that were saved by the government would not show similar compassion for their customers in need and instead acted with insensitivity to foreclose on Americans and their dreams. It was also ironic that many of individuals who were retired and collecting Social Security and on Medicare, were still listening to the righteous right. They didn't want "their money" used to help others. After all, they believed that those affected did it to themselves, didn't they? Not understanding, and not wanting to understand the true causes of the economy's demise made them the focal point of the Republican Party efforts. They could be stimulated by fear and prejudice to secure their votes. They would be welcomed into the club and be called "conservative," but it would be as conservatives of the wealth and power of the elite. They would continue to be the pawns in the game of the "haves versus the have-nots." Many chose to forget how they and their families had benefitted from the government programs, union jobs and quality education that they would now deny others.

Chapter 125

To the Martinez family the collapse of the economy was life changing. Keisha's health care had consumed all the money Diego had secured from his illicit activities in the early nineties. But for much of the next decade, under President Clinton, life was good. It looked promising until 2001 when they lost their son on 9/11. Diego continued to work the Logan Tower until 2007 when Federal budget cuts resulted in the loss of his job.

They were without health insurance and lacked a steady income. They couldn't withstand another year of Diego being unemployed and doing odd jobs. Keisha worked part-time filling in at the local hospital, but it was never quite enough to keep up with their bills.

After years of perseverance Diego's cousin Karime had managed to secure a visa and was teaching at a community college in Sacramento. She was active in the Hispanic community's efforts to gain economic equality and told her cousins Diego and Keisha to come to California and live with her. There were still jobs in the vineyards and on the farms. They didn't pay much, but if they lived with her they'd make it.

She encouraged them telling them that things would be different. The newly elected President, Barack Obama, was sensitive to the needs of people and was supported by both middle-America and poorer minorities. She had worked the Hispanic vote for him when Hillary Clinton was no longer a candidate. She had believed that Hillary would do her best for the American people. Obama seemed to express that same attitude of caring and sensitivity in his book "The Audacity of Hope." They needed to believe that there was still hope for a better life. Their spirit was broken, but not their resolve.

Karime told Diego of a movement for a national strike and possibly a march on Washington in the spring. They would challenge those who had reaped the benefits of the right wing agenda, which were now being recognized as adversely affecting more than 98% of the country.

She was asked to speak to an amphitheater class on theology and politics at her college. She had always been a woman of faith and of little patience with hypocrites. Religion was important to her!

She began, "There are many whose faith in God is their strength and others whose faith is their weakness used by others to keep them from facing the reality of the class struggle. Some religious leaders profess their faith to help others, but some have used their rhetoric to keep people in line. They preach in God's name and try to convince us that they have the right to judge women for their choices, gay men and women for their desire to marry, and immigrants for their language and religion. They preach that America is a Christian nation and has certain values that must be shared by all - not a country founded and built on diversity, religious freedom and an individual's freedom of choice.

She continued, "These self-serving religious interpretations ignore the doctrine of the first true Christian, a man named Jesus who taught tolerance, and showed, by his actions, that those who followed him are not to be in judgment of others. Yes, Jesus may be our savior, but he is not our excuse for bigotry and selfish acts for personal gain. Today, many who live for wealth prefer to ignore his profound anger towards the money changers in the Temple who took advantage of the poor and hard working for the sake of unreasonable profit. They prefer to ignore his views of the wealthy, that 'it would be easier for a camel to pass through the eye of a needle than for a rich man to enter the kingdom of heaven.' They ignore his intolerance to the judgment of others in his acceptance of Mary Magdalene. There is nothing wrong with wealth. It is for many in this country, part of their American Dream. It is how it is achieved and maintained, and at whose expense that is the problem.

The pretenders cite and interpret scripture, written many years after the time of Jesus, scripture that is a preferred mixture of selected stories which were collected and *published* in a book called the Bible more than 300 years after the crucifixion of Jesus. They were stories originally written by the scholars of the day and were compiled to teach civilized behavior to those needing structure in their lives and the desire to live in a lawful society.

There have always been rulers who used organized religion to demand dogmatic responses to their commands in order to exert their power and control. The demand for strict adherence to certain beliefs with the condemnation of others failed in Germany and Spain under fascism and in Russia and China under communism, and in the country of my birth, Mexico, under chaos and corruption. The masses in these countries paid a painful price for the obsessions of a few who sought to rule many by dictating and controlling their beliefs!"

Karime concluded, "History has shown that religion is an element of personal belief, it is how we live our lives as individuals. Except for guiding our conscience, It has no place in government, but as a right to be protected, unless it is based in violence, then it must be restricted! History has also proven that when religious dogma is imposed by a government to control the people and to secure wealth it eventually leads to a dictatorship. And once the frustration of the people reaches the point of no return, in effect a critical mass, it leads to the rebellion of its dominated people! For those of us who believe there is a God, we must reject the idea that those who worship wealth and power, but kneel at an altar for personal gain, represent our beliefs!

We know in our hearts that our personal God does not favor the abuse of the masses by the few. We know in our hearts that religion is not government. We know in our hearts that it is the basis of our personal strength that allows us to govern our own behavior and to serve others. And we know in our hearts that we as individuals must each take back our religions from those who have confiscated and abused their purpose, whether they call themselves Christian, Muslim, Jewish, Hindu or Buddhist, we must insist that it is not theirs to rule by, it is ours to live by."

As Karime completed her presentation a young women in the third row stood and began a slow rhythmic applause. The rhythmic sound expanded, swelling throughout the auditorium until all were on their feet chanting her name. She looked at the enthusiasm of the youth before her and knew that the frustration, with the lies and deviousness of those who seek to control others for their own gain would eventually end. A tear came to her eye and a smile brightened her presence. She realized that there is still hope!

Chapter 126

Diego and Keisha believed in God and had faith in the future, despite their tragic losses and frustrations with bigotry. They had no choice. Faith was all they had left. The bank had foreclosed on, and sold their home in an auction for less than half of what they had into it. They accepted their fate and packed what they had left into their old pickup truck, covering their life's remaining assets with a tarpaulin. It was Monday morning. They were told that they had to vacate their home before noon. They began their journey west on a bright and brisk winter morning, to start a new life in California. The Martinezes were going home to where they had begun their lives more than 60 years earlier.

After selling their furniture and paying their bills they had less than $400 left. They hoped it would be enough for gas for their cross-country venture. They would sleep in their truck, if it wasn't too cold. Without jobs or unemployment benefits they had to apply early for Social Security last year when Diego was only 62. Their monthly check was less than $486, reduced due to early "retirement," but not enough to survive on. Federal law restricted those early-benefit recipients from making more than a few thousand dollars per year before the government would take back $1 for every $2 earned. Why? No one could tell them why, but it amounted to a 50% tax on those who were just trying to survive. It was just another inconsistency in the way the government treated those who couldn't fight back.

Medicare helped pay for Keisha's care and her medicines, but it wasn't quite enough. She insisted they not ask their friends for money. She told Diego, "They've done enough! They have their own problems! We will make it on our own!"

Realizing they didn't have enough money for both food and gas, they took all of their food hoping that it would keep in boxes and placed it in the truck-bed where it would be kept cold in the winter air. It would take them four or five days to reach Karime's home in Sacramento. They looked forward to the warmer weather and a new start.

"If we drive all day, every day, we should make Sacramento by Friday. I hope that this old truck holds out. It has over 230,000 miles on it and the heater still isn't working," commented Diego as they climbed into the cab.

"It'll be fine. I kept these blankets out of our luggage. Don't worry! Just be careful with the gas. No speeding! I figured it out and we should have enough to make it to California," advised Keisha.

"I hope you're right. I don't want to push this thing the last hundred miles," joked Diego, trying to lighten the mood.

"Don't worry, the Social Security check is deposited directly into our bank on Wednesday, that's only two days. We can use our debit card on the road for gas after that if we need it, but I don't think that we have enough money to stay at motels. We better not get lost or we'll use too much gas!" advised Keisha as they began their journey west.

"It'll be okay, my love. I know my way! Things will get better when we get to California. Karime says that I can probably find work in the vineyards," Diego said as he reached for her hand. "We'll be fine!"

"I'll try to find work there, maybe in a nursing home, but only part-time. I'm not as strong as I used to be."

"I think we can make it to Pittsburgh by late tonight. That's the shortest route across the country. We'll get an earlier start from there tomorrow morning. I heard on the radio that we might get some snow on the way."

"Manny always loved the snow!" responded Keisha as she looked away from Diego. Her eyes began to tear as she glanced at the barge being towed slowly through the Cape Cod Canal as they crossed the Sagamore Bridge for the last time.

They reached Pittsburgh at 1:00 am. The anticipated snow was becoming of blizzard proportions. The temperature was 8°F with a wind chill of minus 20°F.

"We're going to need gas and none of the stations seem to be open. We have to find a place to stay," declared Diego.

"But I don't think we have enough money and where will we find a place this late and in this weather," added Keisha.

"There's a sign for a motel at this exit. I'll get off here. Maybe it won't cost too much."

The old pickup managed the snow bound off-ramp onto a city street that appeared to be in an industrial area. The motel, an old rundown truck stop, had a full parking lot of 18-wheelers and a "No Vacancy" sign displayed in flashing neon.

"We'll have to find another place, but the weather is getting worse."

The snow was thick and visibility was diminishing as Diego noticed bright headlights heading directly towards them. It was a snow plow. He spun the wheel to the right to avoid a collision, driving the pickup into a snow bank that was already three feet high.

"He didn't even see us. We could have been killed!" Their truck was firmly into the snow bank, its rear wheels deeply into the snow. "We're stuck, Keisha. I didn't bring a shovel. We'll have to stay here until someone finds us."

"We can't do that, we have no heat and that plow might come back and hit us. Maybe we can find someplace if we walk down towards those lights," suggested Keisha.

"I don't know if we would be any better off out there."

"We don't have a choice, Diego. It's too dangerous here!"

They walked the city block to the lights that were visible through the near blinding blizzard.

"Diego, I can't walk any further. Maybe we can get into this building. It looks abandoned and I see a broken window over there. Maybe we can get in there. At least we'll be out of the wind and the snow."

"Okay, we can try. Anything is better than this, my feet are already frozen."

Chapter 127

It was February 6, 2009. "Karime's phone rang at 7 am. "Hello, this is Sergeant Barrett, Pittsburgh Police Department. Are you Karime Martinez?

"Yes, is there a problem Sergeant?"

Do you know a Diego Martinez from Yarmouth, Massachusetts?"

"Yes, he's my cousin. Why, what's wrong, Was there an accident?"

"No ma'am, we found his pickup truck stuck in a snow bank on a city street. We had a big storm last night and obviously he got stuck, but we have to tow the truck out and thought you might know where he is. Your name and telephone number were on a piece of paper on the seat of the truck."

"I don't know, but he and his wife were on their way here. Maybe the truck broke down, or they had an accident? Did you check the hospitals?" asked Karime becoming concerned that they may be hurt.

"We did, and there was no one of his description. We have his picture and description on his license. It was in the glove compartment. You said, he and his wife? She was with him?"

"Yes, his wife Keisha, are you sure about the hospitals? What about hotels in the area?"

"Please hold on a minute, ma'am?'" the officer turned to another and she could barely hear him ask about a fire...and a medal?

"Ma'am is your cousin Diego a war veteran?"

"Yes, he was in the Vietnam. Why do you ask?"

"Did he have a Purple Heart?"

"Yes, why? Is he alright? Is Keisha alright? Where are they?"

There was a pause then, "I need to call you back? I have to check something out."

"Yes, of course, do you know where they are?"

"We may be able to locate them, ma'am. I'll be back to you later today."

Karime wondered where they could be and if they were okay. Their truck must have broken down in the storm. Maybe they found shelter in the city. Why didn't they call?

They were to be in California by Saturday. She had gotten the extra bedroom ready for them.

The call from Sergeant Barrett came in just before noon.

"Ms. Martinez, I'm afraid we have bad news, I'm very sorry. There was a very bad fire in an old factory here last night and..."

Before he could finish his words he heard her gasp and the phone drop to the floor.

"Ms. Martinez! Ms. Martinez! Are you all right?"

Chapter 128

Tony Benedetto and Jim Buckman got word from Karime in late afternoon. She asked them each to join her there to identify the Martinez's' belongings and complete the paperwork to release what they had left behind. Although a strong woman, the loss was almost too much to bear alone.

"Damn it! It isn't fair. Diego did everything he could to achieve the American Dream and they had nothing but tragedies in their lives, all he ever wanted was respect," declared Tony. He had driven down to Hartford to join Jim in the flight to Pittsburgh. "What a terrible way to die and after all they've been through!" Tony said reflecting on their tumultuous past. "Diego made some bad choices, but were they really choices? I don't know. I think he did what any man would do for his family."

"I spoke with the desk sergeant. I understand it was probably the smoke that killed them. They were burned beyond recognition. I hope they died without the pain," added Jim. "It's been a wild and often painful ride for them and actually to some extent, for all of us, Tony. You and Meghan did the best you could and now you need to start all over again. Can I help?"

"You and Sharon have done enough. You've been great friends to us, as well as to Diego and Keisha. We need to handle this on our own. You know Meghan! She'll have it no other way. We'll survive! But I do think that something has to be done about this country and its destructive attitude towards its people."

"Now you sound like my wife! But believe it or not, I agree with you. I've seen it up close and personal and it isn't pretty. Greed has torn this country apart. I'm ashamed to say my family has been, and continues to be a part of it," Jim spoke over the roar of the jet engines.

"Well, Karime is meeting us at the airport and she wants to talk to us about that very subject. She says she needs our help with an idea to help that situation. She says it's will be a tribute to Diego and Keisha. I don't know what she has on her mind, but she's a brilliant an aggressive woman."

"I just hope she doesn't expect us to start a revolution. You know that my brother Jonathan has assumed my father's role in the politically covert operations of that Washington Action Group. He's now the CFO of CTC, the bank that's the main money feed to the right wingers?

"Yes, I saw it on television. He was involved with that media scandal, backing those nasty bastards who take freedom of speech to new lows."

"Well, I'm ready for some kind of a peaceful revolution. This has gone too far. What does Sharon think?"

"Actually, she does have an idea. She's been talking about it for years," responded Jim. "She believes people, corporations and politicians have to be held accountable, and not rewarded for what she calls their devious deeds or bailed out when they screw up."

"Why am I not surprised? Sharon is like Karime. They believe they can the change the world!" Has she ever thought of running for President? The country needs a woman like her to restore its humanity and common sense!"

"Well she believes that Hillary Clinton is that woman and she's backing her if she runs again. We'll be landing soon. Let's wait until we get back to your home and have time to talk to the women. Karime's flying back with us to arrange a memorial for our friends. I'll let Sharon tell you her plan. She has a better way of explaining it. She'll meet us in Boston. I understand Meghan will too."

"She's making arrangements with the Martinez's' church for a service and with the National Cemetery on the Cape for a military ceremony on Saturday. Diego used to visit there about once a month, it was near his home. He would check on all of the Vietnam vets. He said that it kept him grounded. It reminded him of how close he came to never leaving Nam. We can both relate to that!" offered Tony.

Chapter 129

It was a bright sunny and brisk midwinter day on Cape Cod. The freshly fallen snow glistened on the lawns of the village-like community. It was piled along the streets by the evening efforts of the town's snow ploughs. The friends of the Martinez family gathered to pay their respects and say their goodbyes. The family's pictures were displayed in the vestibule of the little white church that had celebrated the life of their son eight years earlier. Diego and Keisha would be proud that the church was so full that people stood along the walls to be present to pray for them.

Being from Southern California, the Martinez family cherished the winter landscape of the Cape after a fresh snow. An enlarged photograph of the three of them standing in front of their brightly Christmas decorated home after a deep snow, greeted those who entered. It was prominently placed on an easel near the entrance door. Manny was only nine years old. Their cottage in the background added to the nostalgic effect of days past in a postcard-like fashion.

Karime, representing the Martinez family, took the podium. "This is my first visit to this beautiful place that my cousin Diego and his wonderful wife Keisha chose for their home. I now see why they loved it so. It is all they said it was in their letters to me, and I can tell you that you're all of what they loved about it. I can see by your presence it was a mutual love. My cousin was a good and loving man. He had found happiness here with his family. As many of you know he would do anything for Keisha and his son Manny and as a few of you know there were no limits to that effort. Like the man that many of us owe our basic civil rights to, he also had a dream! His dream was to be a good American, to have a loving wife and a family."

She paused, holding back her tears. "He fought in a war to prove he was a good American. He worked hard to prove that he was a good father and husband. He died with the person who meant everything to him. We are now here to celebrate his life and that of his wife. Keisha was a special woman. As a Black woman married to a Hispanic man she faced many challenges. Your presence here shows that she overcame those challenges and brought you into her life with her unconditional love. It is difficult to think of how these beautiful people died," Karime paused again to hold back her tears. "But we must instead think of how they lived. They found love and happiness in their lives and now they are with God and their son Manny looking down upon us as those who cared and loved them."

Captain James Buckman and Sergeant Anthony Benedetto gave homage to their dear friend and Army buddy. Buckman told of how Tony and Diego helped rescue a mutual friend, destroying his prized BMW in the process, and that he was proud of them for their action.

"Diego was a caring man who knew the value of friends. He found his strength in their strength and wanted only to be treated with respect and dignity. Your presence here shows that he did, in fact, achieve that respect."

Tony told of the infamous shot-out-of-a-tree incident in Vietnam and how that set the tone of their relationship of more than forty years. He described their fishing venture on Cape Cod Bay in a humorous way as he looked at Meghan's wide eyed expression at his words of confession.

"And that was the day that we gave up fishing! My amigo, Diego Martinez, was a very special man who hoped to achieve that somewhat elusive American dream. Like many he believed that it was within his grasp, but often found it to be a mirage. Like many Americans he was victimized by the greed and heartlessness of money politics. But in spite of his setbacks he was proud to be an American."

After the service the congregation formed a caravan of nearly a hundred cars following the lead funeral car to the National Cemetery in Bourne, Massachusetts. The remains of Diego and Keisha received the honors deserving of an American war hero and his wife to the adulation and a tearful response of those who missed them.

Chapter 130

Karime and the Buckmans stayed with the Benedettos in their South Boston home. They had a lot to discuss. They believed that they owed it to the Martinez family and the millions off frustrated Americans to bring America back to being a country dedicated to its people and their well-being! Tony and Meghan invited several friends of like-mind to hear Sharon speak. Bob and Rachelle Benedetto and Laura Marie Buckman had flown in for the Martinez funeral and were anxious to hear Sharon.

"Jim asked me to tell you what has been on my mind for several years about the path that our country has followed since the seventies. As you know the past forty years have had us experience a transition that has created a society of the 'Haves and Have-nots.' It's been a time of social arrogance and animosity by too many of our leaders. The Haves, the self-declared privileged class, believe that they alone are entitled to the benefits offered by the American Dream. They've embraced greed as a religion. They've succeeded in controlling and manipulating the so-called free enterprise system with successive political allies so that they were in control of both the workforce and the money. We all know that in the past four decades the American workers real income, which pays for the basics of life, has not reached a one percent increase in value."

She continued, "During that same time the privileged class, which consist of only about four hundred American families, have managed to control the minds, politics and spiritual leanings of those who would follow them. Because of that control they were able to secure an increase in their real income by more than 45% as a reward for their deceptive, and in many cases, devious efforts. This abuse not only has to stop, the trend has to be reversed! Through their power politics they managed to avoid their real tax rate with loopholes and deductions to a level well below that of the average American. Many billionaires pay less than 15% of their aggressively adjusted gross income in federal income tax, while the majority of Americans pay more than 25% to 30%, when you include the withholdings for social security and Medicare. These are dollars that the American working class need for their basic survival, not for luxuries and not to fight wars. They didn't get the precarious benefits or exorbitant bonuses given as rewards to financially reckless companies that were deemed too big to fail."

Jim Buckman added. "Sharon and I realize that not all wealthy people are devious or heartless. Many have used their earned wealth for socially sensitive purposes. The desire for some level of wealth is part of the American Dream. We realize that not all have benefitted due to the politically devious actions which have been part the American experience. Some have a conscience and want to restore a balance to the American experience. They recognize that the more we deplete the middle class the more we reduce their ability to achieve their share of the American Dream. It took my dad a lifetime to realize that there are millions of people who are actually excluded from achieving their dreams."

Jim continued, "As a result they have had their capabilities as consumers and entrepreneurs and innovators severely diminished. Many are unable to contribute to our society the way that previous generations did. They live week to week and can only hope to survive. We recognize that for the struggling poor it is a mistake to present them with no hope of achieving middle class status. The obvious consequence of having no hope is desperation. And desperation breeds rebellion. I think my father recognized this after a life of paranoid obsessions with gaining and protecting our family's wealth at the expense of others."

"Jim, we believe what you're saying, but this is a problem that has survived the efforts of people who are more powerful than any of us. Massachusetts is proud that it has always led the way for liberal causes, but history has shown that we often stand alone," responded the local state representative, Brian O'Neil.

Karime offered her perspective as an observer. "But if you ignore it, then it will continue to grow and eventually consume your country like a cancer! I'm from a country that refused to recognize the value of its people. I believe it is where this country is going because of the arrogance of many in power, especially in Congress, whose integrity is for sale to the highest bidder. Mexico is a dysfunctional country because it has been apathetic, allowing the devious and the criminal element to govern it. It is, as you say Sharon, a country run by the privileged few. The American people have lost much during the past thirty years and this trend will continue as long as you allow the selfish behavior of those few to buy power and control your destiny."

Tony spoke up, "I think we all understand the problem, but as I frequently say, *a problem by definition has a solution otherwise it's a condition that we have to learn to live with!* Diego used to tease me whenever I used that expression, but it's the truth. I believe that this is a problem, because I believe it has a solution. So Sharon, what is your solution?

"My solution is not to rebel or just demonstrate, but to take the perpetrators to task and punish those, corporately, politically and individually. We need to punish those who have conned, swindled and attempted to control our lives with their ill-gotten means to their wealth. As a former member of Congress I've seen how the legislative process is manipulated for the benefit of those few and how the three branches of government don't provide the balance as intended by the Constitution. If they can buy the Executive Branch by buying elections, in time they can control the Judicial by appointments and by being able to fund lies and deception under the 'First Amendment of Free Speech' they can control the legislative branch and the laws."

She continued, the fire in her heart burning, "The so-called Right Wing knows that if they want to be at the top of the pyramid they must have free flowing dollars. They need to assure that their benefactors have the wealth and the inclination to provide those dollars. But there is only so much money to go around. The only way to do that is to take assets from the people who produce the wealth. And they do it by reducing their personal tax obligations; by limiting the regulatory processes that affect their ability to make more money; by cheating the people and most important, by controlling the government. There is nothing truly American in the spirit of their actions. It is fueled by incredible egos and sustained by obsessive greed."

"But we're just little people, we have only the power of our individual vote. How can we make a difference," asked John Highland, a local businessman and a progressive thinker who has been frustrated in his attempts to convince those who buy the rhetoric of the Right. "The Republicans claim that they're for small business yet we have had two serious recessions due to their obsessions with protecting the wealthiest of the wealthy not small businesses. Their successes at de-regulation of financial institutions have taken down thousands of reckless banks and investment firms and the hundreds of thousands of small businesses that relied on them. Those businesses are where more than 700,000 jobs were eliminated each month of the last administrations tenure. Congress is not only unconcerned, we aren't even on their radar screen."

Laura Marie, a professor of History at Yale interjected, "But they can only do that as long as people don't understand what they're actually doing and the consequences of their actions. Apathy and misinformation is what Hitler and Stalin relied on. We know the far Right uses religious rhetoric as a powerful weapon. They cite scripture, as they interpret it, to validate their bigotry and hate. They want people to believe that what they're doing is for a higher good. They want us to blame the victims, the poor and disadvantaged for the dysfunction that they cause in their lives. They hope that fear of change will keep their followers in line."

Bob Benedetto, an accountant with a New York firm declared, "Laura's right! What they've done in the last forty years has stepped across the line and we need to take them to task for their actions. They targeted the middle class and those less fortunate using various bank related scams that promise a piece of the American Dream at high interest credit and a homeownership scheme that was doomed from the start. They offered programs that were designed to maintain their life style while burying their fellow Americans with ever increasing interest rates and fees. They relied on the confiscation of assets by repossession and foreclosure to gain more wealth. Their programs have affected so many that the sheer volume of their deceit is now being exposed for what it is, the fast-buck game of scam-artist in white collars! The company I work for specializes in auditing suspected corporate fraud and it is very busy due to its prevalence.

He added, "The programs that Sharon refers to are the *subprime mortgages* that we hear about in the news. They were freely given to those who were led to believe that they could achieve the American Dream on their substandard earnings. It also involved the easy credit card scams offered to kids at 18 years old that buries them for years and the high interest college loans and outrageous tuitions. Tuitions and fees that have increased many times the inflation rate causing graduates and non-graduates to be subservient to lenders for 10 to 20 years. It includes the cost of health insurance that has more than doubled in the last ten years and the fast buck scam of *'Credit Default Swaps'* that make home loans attractive to investors for the promise of high profits."

"The combination of outrageous examples of greed from the top, have led to financial debacle of epic proportion. These were all designed to profit the already wealthy by sucking the financial life out of millions of individuals, many of whom can barely survive on their low wage jobs. And our Congress, on both sides of the aisle, allowed and encouraged this abuse. There was a time when the Republican Party was for the people and provided a balance in our government. I had hoped to restore that moderate perspective, which was nurtured by Eisenhower and Teddy Roosevelt, but I must admit, I failed."

"But I believe that we can fight back and that we can win," added Sharon, "The Information Highway, as President Clinton called the Internet, gave the world a tool that was envisioned by many to communicate the truth among the people of the world and, to a certain extent, it has. But it has also been used by those who are devious and subversive to deceive people for the sake of their personal wealth. I believe it can be used to punish them for their actions and restore the balance needed for this country to survive! That is the basis of my idea.

I propose we use the capabilities of the internet as an effective way to alert, educate and eventually, litigate our society's way back to a reasonable balance and a better life for the people, the 99% who are the real strength of our economy."

Rachelle Benedetto, a North Carolina Assistant Attorney General added, "It's important that we encourage peaceful demonstrations and actions. Violence only plays into the hands of those who want to diminish the validity of a cause. But Sharon, how do you propose to pursue such an enormous task?

"As I see it, our goal is to gather support and raise funds to pursue this cause as a class action suit against financial institutions and their leaders that participated in these scams and especially those who chose to foreclose on their victims. This will be a civil suit without the benefit of government actions and no fees for litigating services other than expenses. Congress had their chance and chose to allow the fiascos to happen and the bonuses to flow to those who perpetrated these wrongs on our society."

"That sounds good but I'm still not convinced that we can fight big money or survive the obstacle of time delays? They have the means to appeal and delay and they have the majority of the United States Supreme Court on their side," declared State Representative O'Neil. "It's ironic that the arming of Americans under the second Amendment, which was to establish a well-regulated militia when our military was weak may be the biggest threat to having a peaceful solution as people realize that they've been conned. I hope that wisdom will prevail!"

"It is an enormous task, but there are more than 100 million people who have been adversely affected by these absurdities. They are starting to realize they've been conned into a state of apathy and their pockets have been picked. Statistics don't lie! They have been left behind. It's time to reverse the trend!"

Laura Marie suggested,"We'll need volunteers to research and to help litigate the issues. College students are the generation we are fighting for and I believe that they will take up the cause to save democracy and restore hopes of achieving the American Dream."

Rachelle added, "I also believe that there are many good and conscientious attorneys in this country who would be willing to share the burden of legal intervention. Some are young and ambitious and yet others are retired and distinguished in their field. They could form a team that would be organized and managed to meet the anticipated challenges!"

"I like what Sharon is saying. I believe it can work if we are true to the cause," added Karime. "We need to educate the public, especially the apathetic, as to how they've been used. We need to show them how their lives are being ruined for the sake of a few devious bastardos, otherwise America will become as distressed and blighted as Mexico. Believe me, you're well on your way!"

"We might think that Karime's thinking is extreme, but we have seen how elections have been manipulated, uncompromising politicians are telling us what to do and our voting rights are being assaulted by those who want to maintain control over the people. The will of the majority no longer rules and religion is being used to control those who are apathetic, easily led and unwilling to understand the issues," added Sharon.

"I'm afraid they're both right, and I've seen it from both sides," declared Jim. "Congress is subject to the whims and financial where-with-all of a very few individuals, much less than the 1% who are at the top of the earnings scale. I know many members of Congress take office wanting to do the right thing, but they can only do what they think is right for their constituents. But to be elected they need funding. It's the old story about making a deal with the devil. Once they accept the money they are owned by their benefactors. Look how the Supreme Court has made that situation worse."

A voice arose from a corner of the room. Sitting quietly as others expressed their frustrations sat Meghan Benedetto, "I'm not into politics or finance, but what do you expect to gain by all of this?" They're too big, rich and powerful and we're just normal people. How can we win? Tony and I are well educated, but we're struggling because we're just two of tens of millions who have little power. Yes we vote, but how has that worked for us? We've been slammed by the actions of these people because we can't stop them without money and they control most of it. We've seen what banks can do to a small businesses whenever their financial institutions are in trouble. We're not apathetic. We just don't have the means to fight or to sustain a fight and they know it."

"Meghan, we realize that funding is a serious problem, but we also realize that each day more and more people are becoming aware of how they have been deceived. Jim and I have managed to retain some of his family's wealth, which he will be the first to admit much of which may have been ill-gotten. We're willing to prime the pump, so to speak, and fund the initial stages of this effort but we need the help and energy of all of you and those we can recruit and educate to make it happen. As attorneys licensed to practice in federal court we can start the process. That alone will get the attention of the American people and once we have that attention we need to cultivate it and make it more powerful."

"You realize that we'll be attacked at many levels, particularly by the media stooges of the Right Wing. Their jobs and their comfortable means of living gained off our struggles depend on it. Our message must be true, aggressive and relentless. We need to use the news media and the social media to keep it in front of the public. Marketing will be a big part of this effort. We need to wipe the smiles off the faces of the arrogant!" declared Rachelle.

"I'm with you in spirit," responded Tony, "but Meghan's right! What do we expect to gain? What is our goal? We'll need to have legislation passed and raise enough money to offset the challenges. Expenses can become a major obstacle even without attorney fees. Can we really hope to correct the wrongs that have devastated the lives of millions of people? Can we restore the hope of achieving a share of the American Dream to the level we had for our lives in the 1950s and 60s and the hopes we had for our children's future?"

Jim looked to Tony, "Tony, we're not just seeking justice for justice sake we're seeking retribution in the form of the billions of dollars that were scammed from homeowners and credit card holders. This will be a long fight, but in addition to the victims of these scams there are literally millions of witnesses out there, some of whom worked within these programs and many of whom have recognized the wrong doing of their former employers. And those individuals that allowed these scams to happen will also be pursued. Many of them escaped with literally millions of our tax dollars thanks to the Bush-Cheney gift of TARP."

"But can we have justice as long as we have a political party that's based in self-interest and in the denial of the rights of those who rely on their compassion to remedy their plight? Just look at how hard they fought to protect the profits of the health insurance companies, the pharmaceuticals and doctors!" Tony asked. "They would deny literally millions of Americans health insurance, and life itself as well as the basic opportunities to realize their American Dream! Can we successfully defeat the devious politicians and their backers?"

"Yes, we can, by voting them out of office! I believe that as we shed light on the problem that there will be many who'll realize that we need to elect those who are progressive and unselfish and rid our government of those whose narrow vision is not that of a caring American," responded Sharon, "This country was not established to promote and protect self-centered greed! Let's investigate each of them for corruption. Let's find out who benefitted from the financial where-with-all of the billionaires whom they served and send them to jail instead of rewarding them for their selfishness."

The room grew quiet as they contemplated Sharon's words. They looked to each other and thought of the strife and debilitating experiences that life's unfulfilled promises had wrought. They wondered, was the American Dream still possible for those who worked hard and lived a good life. Will apathy and fear win the hearts and minds of the people whose rights this country was formed to protect less than 240 years ago? Is America, as feared by the Founding Fathers, destined to become a third world country ruled by the very rich and the powerful? Will the right to vote become a privilege?

"I hope that Sharon's plan can work. I will work with you and the Hispanic Americans to get it done," declared Karime. "I know my cousins would be with us and they would do whatever they could to help this cause. I vote for them, in favor. I'll give you all that I have and work to make this happen. There are more than ten million of my people here who gave what they could of their labor to build this country and who are to be cast aside because they are no longer needed by the rich and powerful."

"I don't have much to offer. Tony and I have lived a roller coaster life of hopes and dashed dreams. We're educated small business people who have never benefitted by the schemes of the so-called conservatives. It's obvious that they're in office for one purpose and that purpose is to stay in office and gain wealth from the apathy of their constituents. Anyone in business knows that it isn't the tax laws or regulations that cripple us; it's the inconsistency and instability of financial institutions who pledge support and quit on us when they're in trouble. Regulations are needed to level the playing field for small businesses against unscrupulous predators. I'll do what I can to support Sharon's plan," offered Meghan. "But I don't know what it is that I can offer."

"Obviously, I support my wife's ideas. But more important I need to do whatever I can to correct the injustices that my father was instrumental in creating. I'm heartened by the fact that he eventually realized his actions were destroying the very fabric of the country that he loved and served. I don't know if we can win all the battles, but we must be determined to win the war!"

"Jim and I can't do this alone. We expect to be criticized and rebuked for our efforts. They have the means and the media network to purvey lies, create false facts and attempt to ruin reputations. They believe that they have a Constitutional right of free speech to do just that. It's a right that they would deny others, if they could. But the truth has a way of converting those untainted by bigotry and fear. I believe they'll eventually fall to the peoples will"

Sharon continued, "This last election showed that people are awakening to their self-induced plight. The election of a man of color who inspires the people is a good sign. Although, he has the obvious obstacle of the 'Righteous Right' to contend with, I believe that he has the support of those who've tired of the abuse and, in time, he will overcome the obstructionist!"

Karime added, "We need to realize that extremist, on both sides of the aisle, are also the obstacles to a true democracy. *It's impossible to go forward when you are being pulled to the far-right and the far-left! We all have our wants and our ideologies*. They can't all be satisfied! I believe that this President, from reading his book, *The Audacity of Hope*, and noting his actions, is a conciliatory man, but that he'll find little of that from those who believe that compromise is a sign of weakness. They are just bullies who want it their way or no way! Democracy depends on the ability to compromise for the greater good, otherwise you will have the *democracy* of Iran, Syria, Egypt and Mexico! We mustn't forget that a fascist dictator was *elected* to govern Germany and brought the world to war and the demise of millions! Those who'll stop at nothing to represent the elite, believe that *they* are the entitled. They must be voted out of office! They are not our friends!"

"Karime you're right! I find it curious that those who are against women's rights; voting rights, gay rights and health care speak the language of control of others that was the basis of the Communists and Fascists governments who they claim to hate. Yet they insult progressive countries like Australia, Canada, Norway, Denmark, Switzerland and Sweden, humane societies that are based in compassion and govern for the benefit of all of their people. Our right-wing politicians and their backers pocket the wealth of *our* country, and it is *our country*, and label progressives as socialist, as if that's a dirty word, because they want it all for themselves!" declared Sharon.

As he listened Tony's thoughts were of the two people who couldn't be there to speak for themselves and whose lives were impacted by pain and uncertainty from a society that became numb to caring and compassion. They grew up in an underprivileged world, seeking an elusive American Dream. Diego fought for the country he hoped would accept him. They worked hard. They were citizens of an America that promised opportunity and equal rights to pursue their dreams, but were often denied the realization of those dreams.

"Sharon, I'm on board and if we all agree to go forward with this plan let's dedicate our efforts to our friends, Diego and Keisha! Their struggles were not unique! There are literally hundreds of millions of Americans whose lives have been adversely affected by those whose arrogance is only exceeded by their hypocrisy! Many don't have enough money for their daily living expenses, but they have their vote, which are in the numbers that are feared by the privileged. It is the most powerful weapon we have!"

"Are we all in this action?" asked Sharon. The vote was nearly unanimous. The only dissent was Representative O'Neil, who explained that he would be limited in what he could do given his public position.

CHAPTER 131

Six months passed when Jonathan got a call from Don Peters. "Your brother and his wife, that liberal bitch, just filed an action against our bank and a number of others."

"What do you mean they filed an action? Based on what?"

"They've started a class action lawsuit against any financial institution that loaned mortgage money to what they're calling unqualified buyers and any credit institutions that they claim deceived people into high interest loans and credit cards."

"That's crazy! That was standard banking practice. People want money and we provided them with what they wanted. We satisfied a need. They agreed to the terms. It's not our fault that they were too ignorant to read or understand the terms," declared Jonathan. "They can't win! Can they?"

"Well, we can't afford to find out. This is serious. It's already gaining momentum. Your brother outsmarted us on the offshore funds. He's not going to do it to us again! He has to be convinced to stop this action!"

"How do we do that?"

"I'm afraid it's your problem for now, Jonathan. This is a very serious situation. If you can't resolve it, we will!"

The Beginning!

About the Author

Born in Boston to a blue collar family, DeBenedictis worked his way to a Bachelor of Science Degree in Civil Engineering. He began his career as a State environmental regulatory engineer serving a term as President of his employee union. In 1976 he received a Masters Degree in Engineering. Recruited into the private sector by a small local engineering firm, his entrepreneurial spirit was revealed when he took over the struggling company. In less than twelve years he guided it from a fifteen person local firm to a major northeast environmental engineering company with a staff of more than two hundred.

In 1988, his company was recognized by INC. Magazine as one of the 500 fastest growing privately owned companies in the U.S. and by Engineering News Record as the 321st largest engineering firm in the country. In 1989, in the aftermath of more than 700 banks failing as a result of "Trickle Down Economics" he was forced to sell his company to pay a demand note to its troubled credit-line bank, which merged soon after with a larger bank.

Within a year after losing everything to financial predators and without financing, he rebounded to create a new company. In less than two years and in a time of deep recession, he had twenty six employees, many of whom had also been unemployed. His story is not unique. It is shared by millions who believed in the American Dream, only to see it become the bounty of the Privilege Few.

He walked the walk and now he talks the talk about how the past 50 years have impacted the lives of the average American in this fact-based fiction novel. Once touted by a mentor for his resiliency and perseverance, quitting has never been an option!

CPSIA information can be obtained
at www.ICGtesting.com
Printed in the USA
FFOW02n2330040716
25634FF

9 781496 954732